THE SWORD
OF KNOWLEDGE

THE SWORD OF KNOWLEDGE

C.J. CHERRYH
LESLIE FISH
NANCY ASIRE
MERCEDES LACKEY

BAEN

THE SWORD OF KNOWLEDGE

This is a work of fiction. All the characters and events portrayed in this book are fictional, and any resemblance to real people or incidents is purely coincidental.

The Sword of Knowledge has been published in slightly different form as *A Dirge for Sabis,* copyright © 1989, *Wizard Spawn,* copyright © 1989, and *Reap The Whirlwind,* copyright © 1989, by Tau Ceti, Inc.

A Baen Books Original

Baen Publishing Enterprises
P.O. Box 1403
Riverdale, NY 10471

ISBN: 0-671-87645-7

Cover art by Gary Ruddell

First printing, March 1995

Distributed by Simon & Schuster
1230 Avenue of the Americas
New York, NY 10020

Library of Congress Cataloging-in-Publication Data

Cherryh, C. J.
  The Sword of Knowledge / by C.J. Cherryh with
  Mercedes Lackey, Nancy Asire & Leslie Fish.
    p. cm.
  ISBN 0-671-87645-7 : $15.00 ($20.00 Can.)
  I. Title.
  PS3553.H358S9   1995   94-24611
     813'.54--dc20   CIP

Printed in the United States of America

Contents

MEDHYRAS

(tin)

Gol River

PEGYRAS

TORRHYN
(barbaric)

Armu

Irdanu River

Azesu River

PESEDUR

JARRYA
(grain rural)

AZGUNEDES

Zebes

YAZKIR

Cerinde

Amaz

Partha

Sefet

SABIR

Sukkti Ruin
Alise

Baiz

Sabis

Apadis

Pergia

Nomes

MURREK

Antiras

Pesh

Bas

Anbas

Dhesthin

Archipelago
of Sakar

Sia

Esthen

Mez

MORMUZ SEA

ESHA

Tari

Ista

Bay of
Naydres

AnHalas

Strait of
Halas

Asum

Wadi

Sefir

Nadres

Thinos

HALAS

Kirdis

Yula River

1042   From founding
of Sabis

Book One
A Dirge for Sabis

Part I
FIRE

✧ CHAPTER ONE ✧

"Fire ready!" Sulun shouted warning.

"We're safe," and, "Go ahead!" came two muffled voices from the trenches behind him.

In the middle of the dirt courtyard, a careful arm's length from the metal tube posed on its wooden mount, Sulun hitched the hem of his tunic above his knobby knees and inched the glowing end of the lighted reed toward the waxed string fuse.

The flame caught, sputtering a bit, and the fuse began burning toward the hole. Sulun dropped the reed, turned, and ran for the trench. Omis's fire-scarred arms caught him as he tumbled in.

"Shhh!" snapped the burly soldier beside them. His studded leather armor creaked as he peered over the trench's edge. "It's burning, almost there . . ."

The other two stuck their noses out of the trench and watched as the sullen little flame worked its way up the fuse, across the base of the squat iron tube, and into the narrow hole.

Nothing happened.

A snickering came from the windows of the mud brick house that closed the courtyard behind them. The apprentices.

"Don't laugh yet," snapped Omis, looking over his shoulder. "I've seen fire play worse tricks—"

A roar came from the bombard. Smoke and flame belched from its raised mouth, and a rattling something whistled out too fast to see.

" 'Ware 'low!" bayed the soldier, as he always did, as if this were an ordinary catapult.

"Going out to mid-river," Sulun noted, peering after the

whizzing projectile as the crooked smoke trail arched out the ruined garden wall between two eight-story apartment buildings, and across the dike and moored rowboats.

"Kula, Mav and Deese of the Forge, let the seams hold!" Omis was praying.

The little gang of apprentices cheered and whistled from the house behind them. Neighbors on either side shouted and swore, heads came out of apartment windows, and the neighbor next door threw some garbage out his window. Out on the river a sudden waterspout rose, crested, and fell back.

"Within a yard of the buoy!" Zeren the soldier announced, standing up and starting to climb out of the trench.

"Not yet!" Sulun caught him by a booted foot. "We have to inspect the tube first."

Zeren waited, grumbling. Ordinary catapults weren't so temperamental; once fired, they were done. This iron bombarding tube of Sulun's seemed as fractious as a bored palace lady.

But oh, if she could be made to perform reliably . . .

Big Omis reached the bombard tube first. He inspected it anxiously, peering at the welds, poking at the touch hole, and patting the base of the tube to check its heat. "She seems to be holding," he shouted back. "I think that lard-flux weld is just what we needed."

"Will she fire again?" Zeren shouted, scrambling up from the trench at Sulun's heels.

"Should," Omis said.

Sulun, likewise patting the tube to check its heat, cautiously waved toward the house, toward youngsters clustered in the courtyard doorway.

His apprentices came tumbling out like puppies, toting the necessities in a proud little procession: tall, twenty-year-old Doshi hefting the stiff leather tube of round stones; Yanados with the measured bag of firepowder, swaggering enough to show the width of her woman's hips under the man's robe and cape; skinny little Arizun bearing the fuse and the reed and the tamping brush in his arms as if they were sacred symbols in a temple procession.

Omis chortled at the show, but Sulun scarcely looked up.

First he took the brush Arizun offered and worked it cautiously down the tube's barrel, feeling for obstructions. Next he took the new fuse and worked it carefully into the touch hole. Then he pulled out the brush and delicately poured the black firepowder into the tube, at which point everybody else took a respectful step back.

He reinserted the brush, tamped firmly twice, and withdrew it.

Last came the greased leather canister filled with stones. He struggled, lifting the heavy container so as to position it into the muzzle of the bombard tube. Failing to do that, he set it down and prepared to try again.

Omis stepped forward and shoved him grandly aside. "Here," Omis laughed. "That's another job for the blacksmith." Omis picked up the canister in one hand, hauled it up, and shoved it smoothly down the barrel.

"Still, better let me do the tamping," Sulun insisted, taking up the brush again and pulling the tattered ends of his flapping sleeves up to his elbows. "After all this time working with firepowder, I've learned a certain touch for it. . . . Ah, there!" He tamped carefully, withdrew the long brush, and checked the fuse. "Ready, test two!"

Everybody but Sulun ran for cover in the house or the trench.

"Now where's my tinderbox?" Sulun searched among the half-dozen pouches on his belt.

"Here." From the trench, Omis clambered out of his refuge with the little box in hand. "You dropped it when you fell on me."

"Oh. Um. Yes." Sulun scratched repeatedly at the box's scraper, lit the whole tinder compartment, then realized he didn't have the reed ready to hand. Inspired, he shoved the burning tinder at the end of the fuse. It caught.

Fast.

"Fire ready!" Sulun squeaked, scrambling for the trench. Once more he dived in headfirst, and once more the blacksmith caught him.

"You've left your tinderbox up there," Zeren commented, watching the fuse burn. " 'Ware 'low!"

The back door of the house slammed. Yells. Arizun's voice protesting.

The bombard fired with another roaring belch of fire and smoke.

Again the canister whistled off toward the river, leaving a snaking trail of smoke between the buildings, and finally landed, sending up a geyser of muddy water and reed.

"It hit the marking buoy!" Zeren crowed, starting to his feet. Omis jerked him down.

Again the neighbors swore and yelled, "Noisy wizards!" Another load of garbage came flying out the window over the south wall, this one containing parts of a freshly slaughtered chicken.

Once more the engineer, the blacksmith, and the Emperor's soldier inched out of their safety trench and went to inspect the bombard.

"I don't know, I don't know," Omis fussed, brushing his curly black hair out of his eyes. "The seams look all right, but she's hotter this time, I think. . . ."

"Best wait till she cools a little then," said Sulun, fumbling around in the weeds after his dropped tinderbox. "Hmmm. Of course that could be a problem in actual combat. . . ."

"No worse than reloading and rebending a catapult." Zeren waved the objection aside. "We'd have a whole battery of these things, half a dozen at least, the first would be cool again. Definitely faster than catapults, Sulun! And the distance! Given a dozen of these pretty bitches, we could retake the whole north country. . . ." His pale eyes, seeing a vision far beyond the muddy Baiz river, held a look of quiet, infinite longing.

"Don't count your conquests yet," Sulun said, waving for his apprentices and their gear. "We're still not sure this model can withstand repeated fire."

"Good ten-times-hammered iron!" Omis snapped, indignant. "And fluxed with lard in the mix, this time! Those welds could hold an Eshan elephant!"

"But it's not an elephant they have to hold," Sulun muttered, peering down his long nose into the barrel of the tube. "I suspect we're dealing with forces stronger than any beast that walks, any whale that swims or wind that blows—"

"Magic!" Arizun chirped at his elbow, handing him the tamping brush. "*True* sorcery!"

"Natural philosophy," Sulun corrected him, plying the brush. "Sorcery deals with spiritual forces. I deal only with material— Hoi, Omis! It's snagged on something!" He poked it again with the brush.

Omis took the tamp into his hands and tried it, then pulled it out. "Obstruction," he said gloomily. "About halfway down the barrel. And I left my tools back at the big house."

"Let me." Zeren drew his sword in a quick, smooth motion, and poked its satiny grey length down the tube. "Ah, there. Soft . . . Just a second. Ah, there!" He pulled the sword out, held it up, and displayed the blackish lump stuck on the end. "What in the hells is this?"

Sulun rolled his sleeves up above his bony elbows and took a close look at the thing.

"Mmm, some sulfur? Perhaps not mixed smoothly in the grinding?"

He shot a look at his apprentices. Twelve-year-old Arizun looked indignantly innocent. Yanados shrugged and shook her head, denying responsibility. Doshi looked hangdog guilty, but that proved nothing: Doshi always looked guilty when anything went wrong, no matter whose fault it really was.

Sulun studied the mass again. "Huh, no . . . I think it's a piece of charred leather from the canister. Ah, *that* would mean that the stones weren't contained. They spread in a wider pattern. No wonder the buoy went down!"

Omis, busy with the tamping brush, didn't notice. "It goes all the way down now," he announced. "Do we try again?"

"Yes." Sulun straightened up and reached for the bag of firepowder. "We've got to. The whole point is, we've got to be sure this design holds repeated firings."

"Better than the last one, anyway," Zeren muttered, shaking the lump off his sword as he headed for the safety trench. He called back, "That one peeled like an orange at the second blast!"

The apprentices fled. Omis took cover beside Zeren in the trench. This time Sulun took care to have the reed ready, lit it off the tinder, closed the tinderbox, and put it away before he lit the fuse. Once more he shouted warning and ran for the trench. Once more the door banged, everyone ducked, watched, and waited.

Nothing happened.

They waited longer.

Still nothing happened. Smothered chuckles from behind the wall and opened shutters above told that the neighbors were listening. A knot of local boys leaned out the windows of the left-hand apartment building, throwing out catcalls, jeers, and one or two empty jugs.

Still nothing.

"Hex," Zeren whispered. "Dammit, the neighbors—"

"Hex, hell. Hangfire," Sulun whispered. "It hasn't caught yet, that's all, it's just smouldering."

"Hex," Zeren said.

Possibility. If the neighbors got a pool together, they might afford someone potent enough.

Or if their master Shibari's fortunes were truly slipping . . .

Sulun ran his fingers through his wiry bird's-nest of dark hair, bit his lip, then scrambled for the rim of the trench.

Omis grabbed him by the tail of his tunic. "Uh, I wouldn't go out there yet."

Sulun sank back again, unnerved. Hex or not, dealing with a smouldering waxed wick in the touch hole was not a comfortable situation.

And even a little hex could overbalance an already bad situation. With firepowder involved . . .

"Oh, piss on it!" Zeren picked up a stone from the bottom of the trench and threw it toward the iron tube, striking it neatly at the base.

The bombard tube exploded. With the loudest roar yet, the flames and smoke erupted from the mouth and center of the bombard, throwing stones, leather shreds, and splinters of hot iron skyward. Quick thunder echoed off the surrounding walls. Dark orange flame lit the ground and the weeds of the garden court, making new shadows where the sun should have painted light. Thick yellow-white smoke rolled outward, filling the yard with heavy, dry mist that made everyone cough.

The echoes faded, leaving a shocked silence. Even the river birds were struck dumb. Then shutters opened in the haze of sulfur reek and a ragged cheer went up from the neighbors, followed by applause, more catcalls, whistles, and laughter from the apartment buildings. The southside neighbor threw a whole cabbage over the wall.

Sulun and Omis climbed gloomily out of the trench and plodded over to study the damage. Zeren didn't bother to watch them. There was no bombard. There was no firepowder. Therefore there was no danger. The apprentices had figured it:

the house door had opened. Zeren tromped toward it, collared Doshi, clapped some copper coins into his palm, and sent him off to fetch some wine at the tavern on the corner. Arizun, after a moment's look at the disaster, scampered back into the house to get clean cups. Yanados, out in the yard, commented to anyone listening that the cabbage was big enough and clean enough to make part of a consolation supper.

The neighbors, seeing victory, slammed shutters against the stink of smoke and went to gossip.

The bombard tube was ripped open along one side and bent by the force of the explosion. Ragged shards of iron jutted from the gaping tear, and the wooden mount was splintered.

"May as well use this for firewood," Sulun noted, picking up the shattered mount.

"It was the seam," Omis said gloomily. "I've tried everything I can think of, or ever heard of, and nothing holds. Maybe it *was* a hex."

"Hex or firepowder, it'll still blow at the weakest point. It's always the weakest point. It can't *have* a weakest point. We'll fix it. We'll come up with a new design." Sulun gave the twisted metal a kick. "No point wasting all this good iron."

"How do I make a tube without a seam?" Omis grabbed and tugged his woolly hair, staring at the mess. "*How?* Out of solid iron?"

"Doshi's back with the wine," Zeren announced.

Sulun shouldered the firewood, Omis gathered up the ruined bombard—at least the major pieces—and they went inside.

"How do you make a tube without a seam?" Omis was asking for the fourth time, over his third cup of wine. In the dimmed afternoon light his bearded, spark-scarred face looked flushed and boyishly distressed, and he drew admiring looks from Yanados, across the table, that were much out of character with her apprentice boy's disguise. Sulun smothered a wry laugh behind his hand; Omis was not above twenty-five years of age, remarkably *un*-scarred for his trade, and certainly handsome enough under the frequent layer of soot.

Omis was also busily and happily married, another of Shibari's freedmen working mostly at Shibari's house. A shop uptown, a wife, couple of kids in the estate itself—Yanados didn't have a chance there.

Yanados, now . . .

Sulun turned the half-full cup in his hand and studied her over its rim.

In the four years since he'd left old Abanuz's tutelage and applied to Shibari as tutor, philosopher, and sometime (more frequently lately) naval engineer, he'd learned that Yanados's case wasn't unique; a young woman with no family, no dowry, and she had few choices in Sabis—or anywhere else for that matter: prostitution, slavery, thieving, begging . . .

Young men, however, could enter the various guilds as apprentices and work their way up to a respectable trade. And disguise, at least as regarded the public eye, was easy. Take off the clattering jewelry, flounced dresses, filmy veils, headdresses, face-paint; take away the willowy poses, fluttery gestures, and giggles. Put on the simple tunic, hooded cloak, plain sandals of a boy of the trades; lower one's voice, stride straight, bind the breasts if need be, swear a little—and behold, a young man.

How many males one passed on the streets, Sulun wondered, weren't? Who could tell? Who even knew to look?

A master would. A master might exact convenient bargains for keeping her little secret. So might other apprentices. But everyone in Sulun's workshop knew about Yanados, and Sulun took no such bargains, nor did anyone else—not even Zeren. Master Shibari had no idea. Neither did Shibari's other servants and freedmen and retainers—which, given Yanados's not uncomely lines beneath her man's garb, argued that a servant was a servant even to other servants. Odd notion! Sulun wondered if anyone in Sabis these days bothered to look beneath the superficial things, like dress, like manner, like social status.

"If we report another failure to master Shibari," Doshi mourned over a slab of bread and cheese, "he'll probably turn us all out. Reckoning how bad his finances are these days . . ."

"So we won't tell him," Arizun piped up, helping himself to another cup of barely watered wine. "What the nobles don't know won't hurt us."

Sulun grinned. Best of friends, total opposites, that pair. Tall, pale, rawboned Doshi was a farmer's son from the Jarrya grain belt, tinkerer, dreamer by nature, with frustrated hopes of becoming a scholar in the city. The Ancar invasions that had driven his family out of their farm and south to Sabis had likewise given him his chance of apprenticeship—but it had ruined the rest of his farmer kin, and *that* stroke of fate left Doshi permanently guilty of something, anything, everything around him so far as Doshi's thinking went, poor lad.

Now Arizun—small, dark, eternally cheerful Arizun—never felt an instant's remorse for anything that *was* his fault. Arizun had been working a street magician/fortune-telling racket in the Lesser Market when Sulun had first seen him—little scamp pretending to a wizard's talent, petty hexes for a few pennies—hexes the effectiveness of which nobody could prove yea or nay. A little sleight of hand, a lot of glibness, a clearly brilliant, and thanks to someone, even literate street urchin who plainly deserved better circumstances—as Arizun himself had pointed out. Sulun had offered him an apprenticeship, and Arizun had jumped at the offer: no relatives to notify, nothing to pack but the clothes he stood in, no regrets, and not a single glance backward.

So now the boy made an honest living, mixing firepowder and learning chemistry, making tools and learning mechanics, running errands and teasing poor Doshi for his gloom and his bookishness—and Doshi seemed to enjoy the association thoroughly. Fair trade: Doshi helped Arizun with his reading and his math, and Arizun taught Doshi a hundred and one tricks of survival and success in the ways and byways of the city—many of them legal. With any luck, Sulun reckoned, they'd stick together, maybe set up a shop as a partnership when they finished their apprenticeship in Shibari's house.

"The best of weapons, if it doesn't come too late," Zeren was muttering to himself, leaning on Omis's shoulder. "If we'd had it twenty years ago, Azgunedes wouldn't have fallen. Of course I wouldn't be *here*. D'I ever tell you my family were educated folk?"

"Oh, yes," Omis sighed. "Many times."

"We owned two thousand hectares above the southernmost loop of the Azesu." The mercenary had that sad, faraway look in his pale eyes again. "A good villa—smithy, tannery, potter's shop, ever'thing. In a good year, we sent ten wagonloads down to the capital. In a bad year we never needed set foot off our own lands:

we could make everything we wanted. There were tutors taught all the kids on the estate. A respectable library. Even the cook's boy could read." Zeren peered into his winecup. "D'I ever tell you, when I was a boy I wanted to be a philos'pher?"

"*Natural* philosophy?" Sulun pricked up his ears. "Is *that* why you hang around our little studio?"

Zeren shrugged, looked away, and reached for the salad bowl.

"Then why'd you become a soldier?" Doshi asked, all innocence, around a mouthful of bread.

Yanados glared, and must have kicked him. Sulun winced.

Zeren favored Doshi with a fast, angry glance, then looked away again, raking salad onto bread.

"Really, Doshi," Omis said.

"Really what?" Doshi asked, looking from side to side.

Sulun said, under his breath, "Everybody knows what happened to Azgunedes."

"Well, of course," Doshi said, rubbing his leg under the table. "The Armu horde—"

"Doshi," Sulun said.

"The Azesu river," Zeren said quietly, looking out the window. "We saw them coming—could see it from the villa wall, the dust they raised. They came wading across the ford half a day north of us, so many they made the river run mud. One day was all the warning we had. One day to pack everything we could carry, herd in all the cattle we could reach, and move everything down the road—right through the troops coming up from Zebes. And the army commandeered half the cattle, right there on the road. We got to the city with almost nothing, and the general ordered every able-bodied man we had pressed into the army—including me."

"I'm sorry," Doshi whispered, staring at the tabletop.

"Wasn't a bad life," Zeren said. "Oh, the food was terrible and the officers were worse, but at least I could strike back at the Armu. We had some hope we could throw them back, at least turn them, establish a new border—at first we thought that, anyway. I didn't see the fall of Zebes, never found out what happened to my family. It was just fighting and running, grabbing what supplies we could, fighting and running again, all the way into Murrek. Those of us who were left signed up with the Murrekan auxiliaries. . . ."

Yanados cleared her throat and offered a lighter tone, "Didn't know Murrek ever had the money for auxiliaries."

"Murrek didn't have shit." Zeren gave two syllables of a sour laugh and leaned back, easier. "Except for brains. Orders and officers changed every fortnight, and the royal house wasn't much better: assassinations, coups, intrigues under every table—total confusion. The wiser heads in Murrek packed up and ran for the south, even before the hordes took Sefet. I figured it was better to join them. South, all the way to Halas, where I joined the King's Own cavalry regiment." Zeren poured the last of the jug into his cup. "The things I saw, the stories I could tell you about Halas, about the whole south coast, in fact. I must have soldiered for every king and lordling clean across to Mez, right in front of the tide—and it just kept coming. Kingdom after kingdom. Never served in anything could hold it back—till I got to Sabis."

"Well, Sabis won't fold." Yanados tried to sound cheerful. "They've hit us before. We're still here. And you're doing all right second captain of the City Guard—"

"I'm not sure even Sabis can hold out." Zeren sighed, refusing now to be cheered. "Good gods, look around you. Who's on the throne? A nine-year-old child and his aging grandfather. Who rules the court? An army of courtiers and clerks and dotty wizards, the whole court worm-eaten with its own petty intrigues—"

"Zeren, be careful!" Arizun glanced significantly at the windows.

"So who bloody cares?" Zeren growled.

"Nobody but our neighbors," Doshi said.

"Gods know, they probably tell worse on us. Hell with the court. Taxes on everything. All of it to feed an army that's full of outland mercenaries like me! *I* make no claims for any great virtue, but most of them are far worse, and far stupider, than I am. Gods, I've seen them back stab each other for pennies, mutiny, duck out of fighting whenever they can, never stop to think this is the last, the last damn place that's got a chance to hold out! If the cities north of here fall, it goes; and their money won't buy them anything—not the court, not the mercs. Not after that."

"Ah . . . should I go out for more wine?" Arizun asked, neatly snagging the empty jug.

"Hell, yes!" Zeren threw him a silver coin. "Keep the change."

Arizun grabbed the coin and darted out the door.

Silence lingered.

"Well," Yanados said cheerfully, desperately. "Well, half an army's better than none. With the Armu busy tearing up the east, maybe it'll be barbarian against barbarian a while; maybe nobody else will push toward Sabis. Why attack the sheepdog in a field full of sheep?"

"Not just the Armu now." Zeren glowered at the dropping level in his winecup; took another drink. "The last few pushes—the ones that took north Jarrya—"

Doshi winced, and took a drink himself.

"—were from a new tribe, these damn Ancar you've been hearing about. Not Armu. Who, d'you think, pushed the Armu hordes south in the *first* place?"

"We always thought it was the drought," Doshi muttered. "Those bad years in the north, Grandpa always said—"

"Bad weather pushed the Ancar. The Ancar pushed the Armu. The battle of the Gor kicked the Armu eastward then, they came down on the south—but the Ancar still kept coming. They're two hundred leagues south of the Gor already, that's what the scouts say. That's what they're not telling out in the streets—yet. Ancar's hell and away a worse enemy than our grandfathers fought in the Armu wars, and Sabis's hell and away a lot weaker now. Lost the east to the Armu, north's already going. What in hell are we going to do with the Ancar?"

"Oh, come, come," Sulun felt obliged to put in. It was all getting too grim, too desperately grim. "Sabis's got more people now than it did then. A bigger army than it's ever had. You can't say it's weaker."

"Where'd it get those people?" Zeren gave him a sad half-smile and idly brushed bread crumbs off the leather strips of his armor skirt. "Same place it got me. Collapsing borders. Lost provinces. Where's the trade that used to feed the world, with the east torn up by invasions and internal squabbles and border wars? Where's the food coming from now? Jarrya-south. Jarrya-north is gone. And overseas from the south. But where's the sea trade in general, with that rat's nest of pirates raiding everything that comes near Sakar?"

Yanados flinched visibly; drew her arms off the table. "What choice did the fleet have?" she snapped. "When the old navy was

betrayed in that damned Pergian coup, who offered to pay them?
Who offered them a port? Where else could they go?"

Sulun raised an eyebrow. Stranger and stranger things, on this
inauspicious day. Just how, he wondered, did his apprentice
Yanados happen to know so much history—and so much about
the lamentable affairs of Sakar? Yanados never had really said
much about where she had come from when she turned up asking
apprenticeship with Shibari's house tutor-cum-engineer. She had
just given the general impression that her family had been
merchants in Cerinde, or maybe Alise. But what if . . . ?

"Doesn't matter now," Zeren said. "Fleet's gone. What does
matter is that Sakar harbors a legion of pirate ships, and they've
sliced a good piece out of the sea trade, no matter if they're
hunting supplies or just damned well looting. Just ask Sulun
how much your master Shibari's lost this last year on pirated
cargoes."

Yanados fell silent. Shibari was indeed neck deep in clamoring
debts. And that was something none of them liked to think about.

There was profit to be had. Sulun knew, for instance, there
was a big cargo coming in from Ista—*big* cargo, big profit in the
shortages that plagued Sabis.

But even if the ships clung to the south coast all the way up to
the coast of Mez, there was still the risk the Sakar pirates would
raid them.

And if that happened, if Master Shibari lost *that* investment—

"The point is," the soldier went on, "Sabis is poorer and weaker
today than it was when the Armu came down. Fifty years ago the
center of the empire fought off the invading barbarians, but is it
going to be lucky twice?"

"There's still the wizards!" Doshi said.

"There's *their* wizards," Zeren said. "Who're you going to bet
on?"

Worse and worse. A man who worked with firepowder didn't
like to go far down that train of thought. The poets made stories
about wizards who could rain down fire and smoke on their
enemies, but that wasn't real. What was, was your wizards sat
down and ill-wished your enemies and good-wished *your* side,
and *their* wizards sat down and did the same thing only in the
other direction, and if your wizards were more powerful than
their wizards, then everything that could go wrong on their side

went wrong and everything that could go wrong on your side didn't.

If a piece of harness had a flaw, if a wheel could come off, magery could find it—and there was no way to tell when a wheel fell off your cart whether it was bad luck or somebody's bad-wishing; if a spark was remotely possible, for instance, too close to the firepowder. . . .

Sulun gave a little shudder.

Not that he *believed* the neighbors could or would hire anybody . . .

Not that he believed that anybody they could afford was more than Arizun had been; or even, if that Anybody had real magery, that anybody could out-mage master Shibari's house wizard . . .

Which ought to let a man stop worrying and do his work, and not think about things like that. *Natural* philosophy didn't have to compass magery; by its very definition, natural philosophy didn't have to worry about things like that. The wizards did, and because they did, you just did the best you could in the natural world and didn't leave any flaws for the mages to get a foothold in; that was the first and best defense.

Of course, if you worried that hex could hex you right into making a flaw in the first place. . . .

A man could go crazy down *that* track. So a man didn't think about it when he struck a spark from the tinderbox.

" . . . still wizards," Zeren scoffed. "And *they* have wizards." The soldier drained his cup and swept the room with a long, sad glance. "Sulun, my delightful little philosopher friend, Sabis desperately needs one wizard-factor that will give it the advantage over a vast horde of dangerously good foot soldiers. Some wizard-factor like this little toy of yours. Give me a hundred of these, a hundred that can be fired over and over without blowing themselves to the nine hells, and I could turn even the Ancar."

There was a long moment's silence, wherein Omis kept running his fingers through his curls, and saying over and over, "It's the seam. The seam never holds. But how do you make a tube without a seam?"

And Yanados said, "And where do we get enough firepowder for a hundred bombards? Charcoal, that's no problem. Saltpeter in every old dungheap. But sulfur, now . . ."

Doshi pushed his cup across the table. "Omis?" he said timidly. "Maybe like this?"

"Huh?" Omis asked. "Like what?"

"A tube. Imagine this cup deeper, longer, more of a tube. There's no seam in it. Look."

Omis picked up the empty tin cup. "No seam, true. But it's only half a ball shape, hammered out of a flat sheet onto a form. Tin-smithery. You couldn't hammer it much deeper, let alone in a tube-shape. You stretch it. You fold it . . ." He turned the empty cup in his hand, studying its shape and its construction. "Thin metal. Bending metal. Thin enough to hammer around a form is thin enough to burst in the charge. But if it wasn't hammered . . ."

"Where do you find sulfur?" Yanados was wondering. "I know you mine it. But from what sort of land? Mountains? Seashores? Where do they find it?"

"Near certain kinds of hot springs," Sulun said absently, scratching his chin. He had an appointment with Shibari: he had to shave, go back up to the big house with the accounts and *explain* his expenses. Shibari was anxious about mounting expenses and little return from this house Shibari's dwindling resources maintained for Sulun and his disciples and hangers-on in this waterfront neighborhood—a laboratorium, as Sulun had called it in laying out his plans and his diagrams and his financial requirements, in a neighborhood, as Sulun had also put it, more tolerant of the unusual and the noisy. Sulun's stomach was upset.

Yanados: "What kind of hot springs?"

"Hot springs in certain mountains," Sulun said, thinking still about those accounts, "the sort where one also finds black glass."

"Maybe not hammered at all," Omis murmured, turning the cup faster and faster in his hands. "Cast? But you can't get the impurities out without hammering. Got to start with twenty-times-hammered iron, a sheet or a rod or a block . . . Maybe drilled? But what could drill iron?"

"Find your answer soon, friends," Zeren muttered under his breath, "find it soon or not at all."

✧ CHAPTER TWO ✧

The great houses hove up in splendid independence on the heights of Sabis—occupying the hilltops, generally, set to catch the wind in their upper tiers. The block-long apartment buildings that were the lot of the most of Sabis's citizens occupied the low ground of the riverside and the valleys between Sabis's fair hills, territory prone to settling (and unheralded building collapses), prone to stale air and river stench (and the stink of other things, since the city provided sewers to the street, but not to the buildings), lately prone to overcrowding, since the city had become, over fifty years of dwindling provinces, the refuge and the economic hope for the world (the sink of all the sewers of the earth, the late Emperor had said on his deathbed—so the story ran).

There were Houses and there were *Houses*, and Shibari's was, like the family, old, well-suited, and cracking in its walls. It sprawled over a large area of the hill of Muzein, with a splendid view of the river and the poor district of warehouses that had grown up in a utilitarian age more dependent on trade than on a warrior aristocracy.

It overlooked the warehouses, it lived off the warehouses, now that the world went as it did. No more divine right for lords: just the Emperor—on the highest of all hills, outside town—and the Emperor's soldiers, also mostly outside town. Sabis had become increasingly polyglot, the old Sabirn aristocracy increasingly strangers in their own city, in the ascendancy of the nine-year-old son of a provincial-born general and his Sabisan maternal grandfather—who had been a gentleman farmer and an atrocious poet before he became a regent.

So in the modern city, the old House of Shibari survived—in the neighborhood of woodcarvers, a couple of taverns, three slightly seedy apartments, and a wineshop of odd and criminal patronage barely down the street from its vine-covered walls and sheds and its still-magnificent front entry, its plaster pillars incised more with accidents—the bash of a cart here, the knock of a box-edge there, over the centuries—than the graffiti that scored the walls in the poorer areas just slightly downhill from here.

The front doors were still bright; the fish-tailed, twenty-breasted goddess Ioth on the right, and snake-tailed Baiz, pouring the waters of his river from a bottomless jar, on the left. The sea and the rivers indicated an ancient past, a claim on Sabis's long past, when the Sabisi had come in from the sea and conquered the peninsula, when the sea-lords had become the first lords of Sabis, the aristocracy of the aristocracy that arrived later and settled at its skirts.

Of that most ancient past, Shibari was one of the most ancient, perhaps—certainly no one of this nervous age dared speculate—with an ancient claim on imperium, on the throne itself.

But mostly Shibari just struggled, like any house however noble, to pay its war-tax, and struggled with business decisions (because the great Houses traded nowadays; the emperor had confiscated too much of the land in too many previous rebellions, and doled too many holdings out to new favorites, and levied too severe a tax on old wealth for a House to live on past glories.)

And business decisions, Sulun knew, trudging up the cobbled, littered street toward that facade and an unwelcome necessity to confess his results—business decisions were what had to prevail, increasingly.

"Sulun! Sulun!" It was a swarm of youngsters, inside the marble hall, with the sea-goddess frescoes and the bronze figure of a ship prow for a centerpiece—ties to the sea, always, where Shibari's fortunes had begun. And always the children: Omis's three, the cook's two, several slave kids, Shibari's own four—voices pealing off the high ceilings, small feet pattering on the marble . . .

He used to make fireworks, little poppers, paper rolls with just enough firepowder to make a flash—to the annoyance of Shibari's house wizard, whose daughter Memi had been no less a participant in the fireworks.

Memi stood at the back now: a quiet, sullen child.

"Did it work, did it work?" Tamiri asked, clapping her hands. Omis's daughter, who had seen the bombard in its forging, who had, at least to her own estimate, considerably helped Omis work the bellows.

"Mostly," Sulun said. It was terrible enough to face the children. But he had to walk down the hall, shake off his young escort, and walk in on Shibari in his study, accounts in arms, and stand there until Shibari, in a spindly chair at a desk piled high with codices and scrolls, realized he had a visitor.

"Sir," Sulun said, finally, and cleared his throat.

Shibari looked at him most carefully in a troubled way, as if he could read everything in Sulun that he possibly wanted to know today.

"A failure?" Shibari said.

"Not unqualified," Sulun said.

"Not unqualified." Shibari sighed and shook his head.

"Four firings and *accuracy*, sir—"

"Accuracy where? Expensive fire tubes, apt to explosions? Four strikes at the barbarians and an explosion wreaking havoc in our own lines?"

Sulun squared his shoulders. "Still four to one, sir."

Shibari's mouth stayed open.

"That's the way a soldier put it to me, sir," Sulun said.

"Zeren. Zeren's a *mercenary*." Disgust came through: the old-line aristocrat against paid soldiers, against foreigners, against a world quite, quite changed from honest, honorable ways. "Blow up one crew, hire another—I suppose that's very easy in Zeren's accounting. I tell you—"

The door opened. Mygenos insinuated himself through the door. "My lord."

"Come in," Shibari said, and Sulun folded his arms protectively across his account book and regarded Mygenos with a scowl. Memi's father. Mygenos the wizard. Mygenos the very well-fed, sleek, and comfortable wizard. Mygenos never had to beg for funds. Even if a house was in Shibari's financial straits, it *paid* its wizard, and paid two of them if it could afford it—the best wizards it could find.

If he's so damn good, Sulun thought, not for the first time, *why is the house in this mess?*

But of course he didn't say that. He bowed to Master Mygenos.
Mygenos bowed to him with a frown that became a sweet,
unctuous look the instant he turned his face Shibari's way.

"I'm very sorry," Mygenos said smoothly. "I was in the garden."

"Master Mygenos asked to be here," Shibari said. "He's quite
concerned about this for another reason."

"My lord." Another bow in Shibari's direction, a straightening
of the body, and a folding of the arms when he looked Sulun's
way. "I hope you'll understand, Master Sulun, I bear you no
personal ill will, all our differences aside. It's priorities, and I
can't advise my lord to pour more resources down this rat hole,
granted, *granted* you've made minor progress with your
fireworks—"

"*Not* fireworks, Master Mygenos. The salvation of this *house*,
Master Mygenos, *and* the Empire."

"The damnation of this house, Master Sulun! I must be blunt
with you; you are a liability! I am a professional in my trade; I
assure you I understand the principle of risk and reward, and
in that professional capacity I have to advise my lord that the
risk, in your case, is constant! I have a considerable ability,
Master Sulun, I would say a *very* considerable ability. I serve
this house with no help, no relief, and I extend my abilities to
all my lord's enterprises, which encompass an extraordinary
range of territory. I do not mind the sleepless nights and the
magnitude of the burden, but likewise I must advise my lord
when a disproportionate amount of my effort is drawn away
from critical matters, by an enterprise which involves a very
poor return on a very high expense—not only of money, Master
Sulun, but of my energies! In short, you are exhausting me,
Master Sulun. I cannot cover the things that truly affect the
welfare of my lord against all his purposeful enemies, and against
the pirates at sea and the chances of weather. All these things,
I say, *are* my responsibility; but I am being drained by *your
enterprise*, Master Sulun, which, even if successful, is years away
from any useful application. It is a *luxury*, Master Sulun, for a
time less dangerous and less critical to our lord. I protect you
as I can—I cannot avoid protecting, considering the possibility
of *lawsuits* and loss of life and limb which could be ruinous to
this house—"

"I hope your protection of our lord is more effective!"

"I am a wizard, Master Sulun, not a blacksmith! *If* your devices are grossly flawed, I am doing all I can to prevent loss of life and property! If you *will* work with firepowder, you can expect I will concentrate my primary effort on preventing your device working destruction on the city and on this house, and *then* I will worry about your personal safety, and *then* I will worry about your personal pride and the integrity of your abominable instrument! But I prefer not to continue to do so!"

Sulun waved his account book. "I require a minuscule amount of support compared to your budget, Master Wizard, and by *your* counsel, this house would venture nothing, run no risks, and make no profits whatsoever! For centuries, Shibari has stood for explorations and enterprises the monuments of which decorate this house, Master Mygenos, and our master is no less than his illustrious ancestors!"

Argue with the house rhetorician, you fat-bottomed, overpaid son of an ape!

Predictably, Shibari's color came up a bit, his shoulders squared a bit, he took a larger breath and looked a half a hand taller.

But he still looked like a worried man.

"I never implied otherwise!" Mygenos was shouting. "I also know our master is not a fool like some I could name! He's been entirely too generous, and you trade on his good will! I wonder where a good part of this money is going!"

"Enough!" Shibari said. "Enough!"

Sulun folded his arms again and bowed. Mygenos bowed.

"I will support this, three months more," Shibari said. "And then I'll see."

"My lord," Sulun said fervently, with another bow.

"My lord!" Mygenos protested. "I feel I have to talk frankly here about due compensation! I've refused offers of a third again what you pay me! And this tinkerer supports a staff of apprentices, diverts your smithy to his own work, appropriates materials, entertains mercenary soldiers and gods know what *other* hangers-on with funds that I'm sure don't appear with the morning dew!"

"Three months," Shibari said, with that jut of his aristocratic jaw that meant Interview Ended.

"My lord," Sulun said, another time around the courtesies. "Thank you."

"My lord," Mygenos said.

And outside the door, in the marble hall with its goddesses and its bronze ship: "You son of a whore," Mygenos said. "You'll cross me once too often."

Ordinarily a man was afraid of wizardly wrath. A man worried about accidents.

This wizard, on the other hand, was Mygenos.

"Somebody'd better be seeing to this house's welfare," Sulun snapped, nose to nose with him. "You don't look like you've spent many sleepless nights, Mygenos, *or* missed any meals lately!"

He really shouldn't have said that, he thought on the way back to the estate storerooms, searching through his belt and the leaves of his little account book for the list he was sure he had brought somewhere about his person. Damn! If he could keep track of things . . .

But a man only got a few good openings with Mygenos. And wizards, they said, couldn't hex against their own work. He *was* right, he *was* going to succeed, he *was* going to do everything he promised, and the very fact that he didn't break his neck going down the steps, for instance, argued that, like it or not, Mygenos had no power to harm him.

Very complicated thing, magery. A *natural* philosopher was quite glad just to keep the wizards all in balance so that good science worked.

Omis held the burin steady with a block of wood and the pressure of his hand while Doshi worked the leather strap that spun it, back and forth, drilling the bolthole. Sawdust made clouds in the light of sunset streaming through the window.

A simple repair on the worktable this time. The aged legs had gone; too much hammering and sitting on it. Sulun tucked himself up in a chair in a sunny patch, working on his notes and his sketches while the repairs proceeded.

"Here, let me," Zeren said, pushing Doshi aside. With the blacksmith holding the drill steady this time and Zeren's strength pulling, sawdust poured, making a little pile on the dirt floor.

And proliferating in the air. Sulun wiped his nose and sneezed suddenly, convulsively.

"Bless!" said Yanados, worriedly looking up from her grinding and mixing. Not only sawdust smell permeated the room—there was also sulfur.

"Umm," Sulun said, and wiped his nose again. "If that's old Mygenos ill-wishing me, all he can manage is a tickle."

"Don't joke!" Yanados gulped.

"Mygenos *is* the joke," Sulun said. "Poor Memi. The poor child used to be a nice kid." Another pass of his arm across his nose. "She looked like a scared rabbit."

"Old Myggy didn't take it real well," Omis said, "that it was *his* precious daughter dropped the poppers in the cistern."

"Wonderful bang," Yanados said. "Tremendous echoes."

"Water tasted of sulfur for a month," Doshi said.

"Memi's changed," Sulun said. "Gods know what he did or what he said. That son of a bitch. Fortunately Shibari didn't listen to him. One of my better—"

The door banged open. Arizun ran in, gasping for air, stirring up a cloud of sawdust. Light from the window showed him as pale as his olive complexion could get.

"Sulun!" he panted, and stabbed a finger toward the door. "The word just came—down the river. A ship got in! Shibari's ship was lost—pirates got it! The cargo, the ship—*everything!*"

"Gods," Yanados said. "Shibari's creditors—"

"They'll eat him alive," Zeren said.

"His whole household will go up on the block!" Yanados said. "What will that mean for *us?*"

Sulun found himself on his feet. In his mind he saw the ravening creditors running through the house. "They'll strip the laboratory," was the first thing he thought of.

"Nine hells, they'll do worse than that," Zeren said, grabbing his helmet. "They'll seize all the household slaves, too—and gods help the servant who can't prove he's a freeman. I've seen it happen!"

"Oh, gods!" Omis howled, diving for the door. "Vari! The children!"

"And his forge," Yanados exclaimed, scrambling after him. "He can't carry that away and hide it! All his tools—"

"Save what we can," Doshi gasped, hiking up the long skirts of his tunic and following. But Sulun was out the door in front of him.

✧ CHAPTER THREE ✧

Only Arizun remembered to latch the door behind them. Their little party went skittering up the street, right turn at the main avenue, up the hill toward Shibari's house at the best speed they could make. Zeren led the pack for the first few streets, but by the time they reached Shibari's walls, Sulun passed him.

They scrambled to a halt as they sighted the front doors and saw the small but noisy mob gathered there—assorted money-lenders, peddlers' agents, even a cloth merchant or two, all waving pieces of parchment and yelling angrily at the closed wooden doors, while a pair of city guardsmen were glumly hammering on the panels with the butts of their swords.

"Gods," Zeren muttered. "Let me get to the guards, and I can hold off the looting for a while." He turned to face the rest of the interrupted party. "There must be a back door. Take it. Get in, grab everything you can, get out again, and hide until the vultures are gone. And hurry." He turned back toward the crowd at the gate, spread out his cloak so that it flapped behind him like vast red wings, and marched off at his best parade ground strut toward the guardsmen at the gate.

Sulun and Omis traded glances, then turned back and slipped around the corner of the wall. The three apprentices tiptoed after them.

Beyond the corner lay a narrower street, fronted with small shops that backed against Shibari's wall. A dozen shops down, a narrow alley zigzagged between the outer buildings and appeared to end at the wall. Little light reached here, even by day, and in the deepening dusk the whole alley was clotted with shadows, but Sulun's pack knew the way. Down to the wall they ran, quietly as they could, and ducked under the side eaves of the offside shop. A blank wooden door stood there, almost invisible in the dark, featureless save for a knothole close to the top. Sulun reached up, poked two fingers through the hole, and scrabbled for the latchstring beyond it, choking off a curse as he missed. Arizun glanced about to see if any of the neighbors had noticed, but the surrounding buildings were silent. In the desperate quiet they could hear the yattering noise from the front gate, topped off by Zeren's voice bellowing about "—must prevent unlawful disposal of property and any possible bloodshed." The crowd howled furiously in return.

"Hurry!" Omis whispered, dancing from foot to foot.

Sulun's fingers found the latchstring, and pulled. The unseen latch released and the door creaked open. Sulun almost fell through, onto the rising stairs. He felt for the uneven plank steps in the dark and scrambled up them, the others crowding close behind.

The stairs opened out onto the shop's flat roof, beside the peeling wall. A few steps further on, a line of hand- and footholds climbed to the wall's top, some ten cubits higher.

Someone was already up there. A small, curly-headed child in a smudged tunic straddled the top of the wall, feeling for a toehold on the near side.

"Tamiri!" Omis shoved Sulun aside and reached up for the little girl. "Come to Papa, darling."

Tamiri squeaked with joy, dug her toes into the footholds, and scrambled down the wall as nimbly as a monkey. "Daddeee!" she squealed, throwing herself into Omis's burly arms. "Mommy's down there trying to get Mido to climb up, but he won't 'cause he's too scared, and Mommy's got her hands all full of the baby, and there's all the bundles of our clothes and things—"

Sulun was already clambering up the wall, Arizun and Yanados right behind him.

"Vari!" Omis wailed below them. "Help her! Get the children!"

Doshi plucked Tamiri out of the blacksmith's arms. "I'll watch her," he promised. "Go on over. Bring back a rope, and we'll pull up the bundles from here."

"Good thought!" Omis levered himself up the wall after Sulun's party.

At the top of the wide wall, each of them paused in turn to look down into the grounds below. Directly ahead lay the tall hedge that cut off all sight and reach of the kitchen garden from the main formal gardens; under its shelter scurried house slaves and free servants, running for boltholes, trampling the planted onions in their haste. The formal gardens on the other side of the hedge stretched empty and silent save for the drifting noise from the front gate. Further ahead loomed the whitewashed bulk of the house, equally silent and empty, like a fresh corpse awaiting the descent of the blowflies. Brief flickers of firelight from the front windows gave the only hint of life remaining inside.

"But where's Shibari?" Sulun wondered. "Where's his family?"

"Who knows?" Yanados grunted, swinging off the top of the wall onto the hand- and footholds below. "Let's get down and grab what we can."

"Sulun!" wailed a familiar voice directly below, over the sound of a baby squalling. "Come help! And where's Omis?"

They looked down, and saw Vari standing at the foot of the wall, buxom and pretty as ever, but more flustered and disheveled than they'd ever seen her. She was surrounded by lumpy bundles tied up in hastily knotted sheets, clutching the baby, with two-year-old Mido clinging to her skirts like grim death and whining to be picked up. Sulun wondered how on earth she'd managed to get this far with all that, and how she'd expected to get everything over the wall once she reached it.

"Vari!" Omis shouted. "Wait right there, love! I'm coming."

He started climbing down the wall after Yanados. Sulun and Arizun scrambled after him.

At the wall's foot, Omis managed to clutch and kiss Vari for only a moment before she shoved the baby into his arms and ordered him back up. Yanados and Sulun grabbed up bundles. Arizun ran to the gardeners' shed and came back with a small coil of thin rope. Omis carried the baby and the rope's end up the wall, handed them over to Doshi, and scrambled back down while Yanados tied on the first bundle. Vari took up the howling two-year-old and climbed the wall with him. Omis would have followed, but Sulun grabbed his sleeve.

"The equipment!" he panted. "Your tools, mine, everything we don't want the creditors to get—"

"Gods, gods!" Omis groaned, "How do I carry off a forge and an anvil?"

"Take what you can. I have to get—"

"Sulun!" Doshi yelled down from the top of the wall. "Look at the house! The front windows—look!"

They all turned, looked, and froze.

The second-story windows toward the front of the house flickered with far too much firelight for lamps, torches, or braziers. Thickening smoke rolled out of them, followed by a cloud of sparks. The first tips of flames peeped above the window ledges, too widespread, far too many.

"Oh gods, my books!" Sulun ran for the house. "My patron!"

The others pounded after him, dodging fleeing servants, trampling more rows of onions.

At the kitchen door they had to fight their way through a mob of escaping cooks and scullions to get in. Once past the kitchen they split up, Omis running for his forge, Sulun and his apprentices heading for their workshop. The fire hadn't reached this part of the house yet, but the smell of smoke grew heavier in the air. Arizun and Yanados yanked the curtains off the wall brackets and spread them on the floor. Sulun grabbed armloads of books and threw them onto the curtains.

"Books, notes, sketches, models," Yanados panted, tying the first loaded curtain into a bundle. "What else?"

"The tools, the lenses . . ." Sulun looked about him. Damn, no, he couldn't take the lathe: too heavy. So much was too heavy, too big, too cumbersome for three people to carry out, much less over the wall—but much of that was replaceable, even cheaply. Shibari could . . . "Shibari! We have to find him!" Gods, to be patronless in this city was the ninth hell. "Get the bundles out. I'll find Shibari."

Sulun dashed out the door and down the long corridor that led to the Family's part of the house. If he could reach Shibari, help him escape the horde of creditors with the family coffers, the master could set up elsewhere—possibly overseas, more likely up in Jarrya, under another name. The household would be smaller but still intact, still capable of maintaining a small host of craftsmen, and Shibari would be grateful to those loyal servants who had helped him. They could get back to work on the Bombard Project within a few months, with luck.

Beyond the heavy door that marked the end of the servants' quarters, the smoke was ominously thick. Through watering eyes and increased coughing, Sulun searched from room to room. The chambers were empty: no sign of the children, or their tutors or nurses, or Mistress Nanya, or Shibari himself. The clothespresses had been opened and ransacked, but to judge from the clothes scattered about, almost nothing had been taken. Perhaps this meant that Shibari and Nanya had had the sense— for once—to seize only the necessities: a few plain traveling clothes, jewelry, money, easily carried valuables. Maybe they'd already made their escape under the confusion of the fire.

But how could they have fled so fast?

Shibari was famous for doing everything with slow majesty and proper gravity, which always took irritating amounts of time. The man was addicted to Reputation, to the point of spending himself into debt rather than reducing the splendor of his household, which was how he'd backed himself into this wretched position in the first place. Had Mistress Nanya made plans for such an escape when the debts first began to soar? It was possible, but didn't seem like her; as far as any of the servants knew, which was much. Maintaining the household's appearance absorbed all her attention. Possibly one of the upper house servants, the butler or housekeeper or secretary, had made the contingency plans after a passing word from Shibari; the gods knew, the master quite often tossed ideas to his servants and then forgot them himself until presented with their accomplishment later. The problem was, both Shibari and Nanya resented being outthought by their servants, and often resented or rejected out of hand good advice and good projects offered by their underlings.

Sulun hitched his shoulders higher, remembering a few times that had happened to him. The steam powered engine, for example: Shibari had been delighted at the little model, its water-laden globe spitting steam from its four angled jets and spinning merrily on its axle above the brazier, making a grand impression on the dinner guests—but when Sulun later presented him with the list of costs for making a larger version, including a diagram for a small ship powered by the engine, and even some clever suggestions on how the money could be raised, Shibari promptly and sourly lost interest. (Sulun still couldn't understand that. Shibari made most of his money by shipping; why couldn't he see the value of building ships that could outrun any pirate craft, sail straight against the wind, and even drive through storms without the rowers collapsing from exhaustion?) The man's pride thoroughly outweighed his common sense, and in that respect his wife was worse.

So where had they gone so quickly? Not in the sewing room, the herbarium, the bath, the small dining room, the bedrooms, or the study—and the smoke was much thicker here. Sulun could hear the flames crackling now, mostly upstairs in the house servants' rooms, but some seeming closer. The fire must have started down here, in the front of the house, then spread directly upstairs by way of the drapes. How fast was it spreading on the ground floor? How close was it?

Sulun leaned on the study wall for a moment, and felt that it was hot.

On the other side of the wall, he remembered, lay the formal dining room. In it stood the family altar, the ranked busts and portraits of Shibari's ancestors, the canopied great-couch from which the master and his wife dined on such formal occasions as their wedding feast or the first-blessings of their newborn children. Of all the house, that was the room most completely dedicated to family pride.

And the fire was there.

"Oh, great gods!" All the details suddenly snapped into place, and the final picture was monstrous.

Sulun ran for the door, pausing only to feel it, making certain it wasn't hot, that he wouldn't open it to face a sheet of flame, and yanked it wide.

The fire was at the outside wall, a blazing sheet that engulfed the floor-to-ceiling tapestry, climbed the curtains to the window beams, and crawled across the ceiling. By its light, Sulun saw the great-couch, and its occupants.

Shibari lay to the left, his body formally arranged though dressed in ordinary clothes. His bloodless hands were folded neatly on the hilt of a short sword that protruded from his blood-soaked breast. He had, clearly, been dead for at least an hour.

Beside him, as precisely posed as an effigy on a tomb lid, was Nanya. Her hair was impeccably coiffed, as always, and she was dressed in her best formal dining gown and jewelry. Her stiffening hands clasped a small glass bottle.

Around the two of them, likewise dressed in their best, though sprawled in attitudes of natural sleep, lay their four children.

A blackened brazier, deliberately placed against the blazing tapestry, showed how the fire had started.

Coughing furiously against the smoke, throwing silent curses and pleas at every god he could think of, Sulun ran to the couch and gripped Nanya's wrist. No pulse. He sniffed at the glass bottle, then turned away, sickened.

"Gods, not the children too . . ." Sulun poked among the small tumbled bodies, feeling at wrists and jaw hinges. The twin boys were still, lifeless. The pretty elder daughter was warm to the touch, but after a moment Sulun realized that was only because she lay closest to the fire.

The younger daughter was still breathing.

"Teigi . . ." Sulun whispered, dragging her off the couch.

Her body seemed too light. How old was she, anyway? Nine? Despite her small size, she'd always seemed older than that: always sneaking into the workshop, staring fascinated at the engines and workings, poking into the books and actually reading them. . . .

The child's eyes fluttered open. "Mama," she whimpered. "It tastes nasty. I don't want to—"

A shower of sparks brought Sulun's attention back to the fire. It was creeping across the ceiling panels, almost directly above them. The roof could fall in at any moment.

"Out!" Sulun coughed in a sudden gust of smoke. He pulled Teigi onto his shoulder and scrambled for the door.

Behind him, with a roar like Omis's forge, the fire caught the couch canopy.

"Mama!" Teigi shrieked, staring back.

Sulun ran down the corridor, heading for the back of the house and the still-safe exit. Above him he could hear the fire growling. There! The door to the servants' quarters—and some fool had shut it! He tugged furiously at the handle. Gods, the air was like an oven back here.

A sudden rending crash and flare of light filled the corridor behind him. Teigi screamed. Sulun half-turned and saw, horrified, that part of the corridor ceiling had come down, bearing a load of burning rubble with it.

Blinding smoke and a near solid wave of heat rolled toward him. A rain of sparks and small coals peppered his head and shoulders. Teigi howled again, batting at sparks caught in her clothing.

Sulun wrapped both hands around the handle of the heat-jammed door, and pulled like a madman.

With a sullen groan of protest, the door came loose and swung open. Sulun dived through it and ran down the main hallway of the servants' quarters, half blinded with smoke. There, the kitchen, and there, thank all the gods, the kitchen door. He plunged through it, missed the step, fell rolling. Teigi yelped at the impact, and went limp.

Sulun staggered to his feet and stumbled out into the kitchen garden. He could hear shouts and wails, but couldn't see anybody. From the outside front of the house he could hear, above the steady roar of the fire, Zeren's voice bellowing instructions to what seemed to be a quickly organized bucket brigade.

Either the fire or the creditors would be on them soon. Where the hell was the wall?

"Sulun!" A long hand grasped his wrist. Yanados. "This way, and fast. We got everyone over the wall except you. All the books, the notes, the diagrams, some of the tools, some of the models . . . Who's that?"

"Teigi," Sulun coughed. "She's the only one left. Shibari stabbed himself. Nanya poisoned herself and the children, and started the fire. Teigi didn't swallow enough—"

"Gods, we're patronless!"

"Teigi—"

"A child! And female. No property of her own, but she'll be liable for Shibari's debts, being the last of the family. Gods help her if the creditors find her."

"Gods . . ." Sulun echoed. He hadn't thought of that. He was too tired to think of all that. "Hide her. Hide us. The lab by the river."

"Good enough. We can decide what to do tomorrow. Here's the wall." Yanados guided his fumbling hands to the climbing holds. "Can you manage, carrying her?"

"Think so."

He managed. Teigi lay like a grain bag on his shoulder, neither help nor obstruction, her small weight growing heavier with every step. By the time Sulun reached the top of the wall and flopped over it, he was as exhausted as he'd ever been in his life. Multiple hands pulled the child-burden off his shoulder and helped him down onto the shop roof below. He flopped among the piled bags and panted. Arizun wordlessly handed him a wineskin.

From beyond the wall came a vast roaring crash, and a soaring column of flame and sparks.

"There goes the roof," Omis mourned from the wall top. "No saving anything now."

"Let the damned creditors pick through the ashes," Vari sniffed. "Ah, gods, what to do now that we're patronless?"

"We go to the workshop by the river," Yanados reported. "We can all stay there tonight, at least."

Sulun pulled himself to his feet and tottered up to the rest of the party—himself and his apprentices, he noted; Omis and his wife and their children, and Teigi. Vari was crouched over the unconscious child, carefully rubbing her face with a wet cloth.

"How is she?" he asked. "Can she travel?"

"There's no injury I can find," Vari murmured, patting over the girl's head. "I think it's just smoke and fright."

"And a touch of tincture-of-poppy juice," Sulun added gloomily. "Well if need be, Omis can carry her. Doshi can carry your boy, and you take the baby. The rest of us can manage the bundles."

Vari nodded agreement. "We'd best go soon, while everyone's busy with the fire. We don't want to be caught by patrols looking for Shibari's runaway slaves."

"No fear of that," Arizun put in from the top of the wall. "Look: Zeren's got them all busy putting out the fire. I think they might save the back part of the house, our workshop, the forge—"

"And the creditors will seize it all," Omis groaned. "How will I make a living without my forge?"

"And what will we do without the big workshop?" Doshi added. "We couldn't get everything out, had to leave most of the models. Without those, how do we make a good enough impression to get a new patron?"

"Tomorrow," Sulun snapped, impatient with fatigue. "We'll deal with that tomorrow. For now, let's get to the river workshop and get what rest we can. Omis, can you carry Teigi that far?"

Before the blacksmith could answer, the child woke up—and howled. "Mama! Mama, no! Not fire!" She struggled out of Vari's startled grip and crawled blindly across the roof. "Where are you? Where?"

Omis caught her before she'd gone more than a few steps. "Hush, you're safe," he said, swinging her up in his burly arms. "We're on the roof of the house next door. I'm your papa's blacksmith, remember? We're all your papa's people, and you're safe."

"Mama." Teigi sobbed, refusing comfort. "Where's Mama?"

The adults looked at each other, wondering what to say.

"She's dead," little Tamiri cut in brutally. "She was in the house, and it's all burned up."

"Who asked you?" Vari snapped, aiming an outraged swat.

"She did," Tamiri chirped, ducking the swinging hand. "The house is all burned up. You can see it from the top of the wall."

"Let me see! Let me see!" Teigi struggled in Omis's grip.

"You may as well let her look," Vari sighed. "Go ahead, lift her up."

Omis shook his head, but lifted Teigi up where she could see over the wall. Firelight reflected off her face as she watched the flames, the smoke, the fire-brigade working below—and the collapsed, burned-out front of the house. She watched until Omis's arms grew tired, very quiet and still.

"There now," Omis said gently, putting her down. "Your mama and papa are gone, but we'll take care of you. We'll take you to a new house. Do you think you could walk a ways?"

Teigi said nothing, only shook her head.

"Well, that's no trouble. I'll carry you." Omis picked her up again.

"Best cover her with a cloak, too," Arizun pointed out. "In those fancy clothes she doesn't look like a blacksmith's child. We don't want to draw attention."

"Good thought." Vari dug among the clothing bundles for a cloak.

"How fast can we leave?" Sulun asked, eager to be gone. "Let's get out of here before the patrols start searching."

The rest of the group caught the mood, and began picking up various bundles and children.

"The models gone, the forge, the workshop," Doshi muttered, trying to manage Omis's two-year-old and a bundle as well. "How will we make a living?"

"Cheer up," Yanados offered. "It could have been worse."

"Oh? How?"

"Well, what if we'd kept the firepowder in there?"

"Oh."

Doshi cheered up considerably, or at least pretended to, and the small caravan cautiously made its way down the stairs.

✧ CHAPTER FOUR ✧

The little workshop had never been more crowded. Vari marshalled the apprentices to clear and sweep the floors, hunt up and spread a modicum of straw, and finally stretch out the salvaged bedding. Omis tended the children, trying to get a smile or at least a few words out of Teigi. Sulun gloomily inspected the salvage from the house and tried to imagine how to make a living from it.

"It'll be crowded, but there's bedding for all of us," said Vari, inspecting her finished work. "Is there any food in the house?"

"Some bread, I think." Arizun padded off to the cupboard.

Teigi began crying again, very softly.

"Ah, there now, dear . . ." Vari rummaged in one of the opened bundles. "Are those burns paining you? Here, they're not very big. Let me put some salve on them."

The little girl kept crying, not noticing her blisters or Vari's ministrations.

Sulun vividly remembered that last look backward at Shibari and his family, and the flames devouring the canopy of the couch. Gods, yes, that would be pure hell for a child to remember. He sidled closer, and draped a cautious arm around Teigi's shoulders.

"They were already dead," he said quietly. "They died of the poppy-juice tincture, long before the flames reached them. They never felt an instant's pain; it was just like going to sleep."

Teigi sobbed louder. "It tasted nasty. I spat it out." She rubbed a grubby fist across her eyes. "She turned her back, and I spat it out."

"Good thing you did, or you would have died too."

37

"I should have!" Her sudden howl echoed off the walls. "I should have gone with them!"

The others looked up, startled.

"Whatever for?" Doshi asked. "What good would that have done?"

"Honor," Teigi hiccupped.

Arizun made a rude noise. "What sort of honor kills little children? Destroys whole families? Leaves the servants to run or be burned to death? Ha! Honor's a slaughterer, no different from the Armu barbarians—don't they do the same?"

Teigi only shook her head and cried.

"Now hush that silliness," Vari said, slathering on the burn ointment. "I'll tell you what your real honor is, child. You're the last of your family now, the last of Shibari's ancient and honorable blood. That's why the gods spared you, you understand?"

Gods nothing, Sulun grumbled to himself, *I dragged you out of there—and only in hopes of keeping a patron. And, admit it, because I like the little girl. And because I wouldn't leave anyone to a death like that. Gods? Well, if the gods are no more than human greed and human pity, then I suppose Vari could be right.*

Teigi was sobbing a little less, and listening closely.

"Now what you must do," Vari went on, artfully pouring out a spoonful of hemp-seed syrup from her supplies, "is hide your true name until, hmm, the omens are better. Then, when you're old enough to marry, you will refound the family of Shibari. You must live to have children of your own, do you see?"

Sulun raised an eyebrow at the elegance of that argument. Vari held out the spoon and neatly fed its contents to the girl.

Teigi swallowed, then protested, "Papa's creditors . . ."

"She has a nice grip on essentials," Yanados murmured.

"Don't worry, they won't find you." Vari put the spoon and bottle away. "We'll hide you among our own children. Hmmm, we'll have to give you a new name. . . ." She looked around for suggestions.

"Male or female?" asked Yanados. "If we're going to hide her from Shibari's creditors, best to disguise her sex as well."

"Good thought," Omis rumbled. "As a boy, she could pose as an apprentice. Hmm, but I don't suppose, child, you have the muscle to work as a blacksmith. . . ."

"Sulun." Teigi turned tear-wet and disconcertingly bright eyes to him. "I could be his apprentice."

"Wait a minute—" Sulun gulped.

"Of course she could." Vari clapped a firm hand to his shoulder, leaned close, and whispered fiercely in his ear. "Don't discourage her. The child needs some hope to live for, and my silly story won't support hope very long."

"Uh, yes—yes," Sulun stammered, feeling as if the floor were sliding out from under him. "I can always use another apprentice."

Yanados and Arizun smothered explosive snickers. Doshi only looked pained.

"It would look strange if a blacksmith's son were apprenticed to anyone but his father. Er, I'll say you're a cousin of mine." Sulun looked around wildly for inspiration. "What'll we call her—him? What's a good name?"

"Aziya," Teigi piped up. "I used to have a puppy named 'Ziya, but he ran away. . . ." The rest of her tale was smothered in a yawn.

"Hmm, Ziya it is then," Vari soothed. "Come lie down—Ziya."

"Now that we have that matter settled," said Arizun, handing the scant bread around, "what shall we do about making our living, now that our patron's gone?"

Instant silence fell.

Sulun heaved a sigh of fatigue and impatience. "Come, come. Someone must have some ideas. Suggestions?"

Omis shook his head. "Without my forge and anvil, I can't set up a free shop. I'll need to find some other blacksmith who needs a partner, if any such exist in the city."

"We're in much the same kettle," Yanados pointed out. "And I don't know of any natural philosophers who need partners."

"It is a rather specialized field of endeavor," Doshi said dourly.

"If we could get across the straits to Esha, we could set ourselves up a college of magicians," Arizun offered. "Outside the port city, it's a wonderfully backward place. We could dazzle the locals with our knowledge, perhaps even get a position in the king's court—"

"I thought you said you came from Mez," Yanados sneered. "The king of Esha is only a puppet of Sabis, and not a terribly wealthy one; he'd spend no money on luxuries such as us. Besides, with the little we've saved from the house, what do we have to impress a patron?"

"Besides that," Doshi added, "do we have enough money to buy passage for all of us across the straits? Or to feed us afterward?"

For a moment everyone stopped and thought, for the first time that night, specifically about money. The adults promptly checked their belt purses. Arizun also peered into one of the bundles he'd salvaged from the house, and came up with a lame-looking smile.

"Among us all," Sulun concluded, "we have perhaps enough to feed us for a tenday. I think we must forget about crossing the straits."

"There's plenty of employment in the army," Yanados grinned, "Or among the pirates out to sea."

"I rather doubt they'd take a horde of children," Vari sniffed. "What would we do about the children?"

Sulun, who'd been briefly fancying himself as a pirate, came back to earth on that question. What about the children, indeed? For a moment he seriously considered sneaking out of the house before dawn, signing up in the army or going to the docks, leaving his apprentices and friends to manage for themselves. But without his cumbersome books and notes and tools and models, what could he do? He'd make a poor soldier, and a worse sailor, the sort that didn't survive for long. He'd do better begging in the streets of Sabis.

"There's no other way," he said with a sigh. "We simply have to find a new patron, and quickly. Any suggestions?"

There was a long moment's silence.

"Well," Vari finally offered, "Perhaps those very creditors who are hounding after us."

"*What?*" Omis squawked. "Those vultures picking the house bare already?"

"Think!" Vari insisted. "With the house burned, and the money and servants gone, how will the creditors regain their loans? They'll all come up short, and they'll all be greedy for more. Well now, we have skills to sell, don't we? That makes us objects of value that formerly belonged to Shibari, doesn't it?"

Everyone thought that over for a long moment. It was a grim suggestion, but nobody could find fault with it.

"It would have to be a rich creditor," Arizun said slowly, "One who could afford to take on all of us. Otherwise we'd be separated—and then, who knows when we'd get the Bombard Project done?"

Nobody could fault that either.

"How do we know who Shibari's wealthiest creditors were?" Doshi protested. "Only Shibari himself—and maybe his secretary knew. Shibari's dead, and the gods only know where the secretary is."

"Probably halfway across the straits by now." Arizun considered.

"How do we find out?" Yanados asked. "Perhaps the Hall of Records—"

"Any one of us who shows his nose there might be recognized and seized for Shibari's debts," Doshi warned. "Anyone seized would have to prove he wasn't one of the household slaves. How does a servant prove he's not a slave?"

Another long silence followed.

Omis shoved a set of tongs aimlessly back and forth, then smiled suddenly as inspiration came. "I know who could find out for us—walk right into the Hall of Records and ask to see anything, even bully the clerks around if they don't move fast enough."

Everyone caught on at once.

"Zeren!"

Unnoticed, Teigi/Ziya snored gently in Vari's lap.

✧ CHAPTER FIVE ✧

It was a long, crowded, largely sleepless night, and Arizun was stumbling and yawning when Sulun sent him out in the morning. It was another sweaty, hungry, apprehensive hour before Arizun came back with Zeren in tow. The burly captain strolled through the doorway, surveyed the little bivouac in the middle of the workshop, and shook his head.

"You do look a mess," he grinned. "Still, I'm glad to see so many of you got away—and with how much gear?"

"Not enough to complete the Bombard Project without another patron." Sulun cleared off a table and two relatively clean chairs. "That's what we want to talk to you about. Arizun, did you pick up the food and wine?"

"No, he didn't," Zeren cut off the apprentice's reply. "I told him to save his money. You're all coming to my house for breakfast and, hmmm, a bit of a visit."

"And a bath?" Tamiri asked.

"Bath first!" Zeren laughed. "Come along, the lot of you. Pick up that gear and the children; it's not that far a walk."

He was right; being a mere guard captain and not an aristocrat, Zeren lived in a modest house much closer to the river than Shibari's manse. Nonetheless, by the time the little party had moved themselves and their gear there, washed, changed clothes, and eaten, it was close upon noon. Zeren's lone servant, an aged housekeeper, took one look at the invading mob and discreetly vanished. Vari hustled the children off for a nap, leaving Omis, Sulun, and his three regular apprentices alone with Zeren. The others, for all that they'd helped form the plan, were quite content to let Sulun do the talking.

42

Zeren heard him out, then leaned back in his chair and thought awhile.

"The problem is," Zeren said finally, "that getting a list of Shibari's creditors isn't easily done. The creditors would have gone to court, to our own dear Minister of Justice, to get permission to seize the property. The Minister of Justice wouldn't handle such petty business himself; he'd shuffle it off to one of his secretaries, and there are at least a dozen of them. The secretary would pass it on to one of his clerks, and there are hundreds of those. As a mere guard captain, I couldn't approach the Minister; he wouldn't give me an appointment—at least not for months, not without a substantial bribe of money or information to interest him."

"I suppose the possibility of the bombard wouldn't be information enough," Sulun groaned.

"Indeed not. He's not interested in things military anyway, looks down on soldiers, considers himself something of a pacifist." Zeren drained his cup and refilled it with half-watered wine. "Of course, that's a fashionable attitude uphill. Folks there can afford enough guards that they need never take a weapon in hand to defend themselves. They assume everyone can do the same."

"Ye gods!" Sulun tugged at his hair. "Are all the wealthy and powerful so brainless?"

"Damn near." Zeren munched absently on a cucumber slice. "That means I'll have to go from secretary to secretary to learn which one got the appeal from the creditors. Hmmm, just as well that Shibari was a noble; if he'd been a common man with common debts, the writ would have gone straight to some minor clerk, and stayed there. Then I'd have to question my way through all several hundred of them, which could take weeks."

"Weeks?"

"If not months. Then again, such a search would be cheap; as a captain of the city guards, I'd have enough power to bully the clerks into giving me the list without having to pay them anything. As it is, I'll have to work my way through a dozen or so secretaries, which should take no more than a day or two. However, I don't outrank that sort; I'll have to pay some sort of bribe: money, or lucrative information, or the promise of possible money to be gained otherwise by helping me. Now, I'm not wealthy enough to bribe a dozen secretaries, and the gods know how many I'll have to go through before I find the one who has, or had, the list."

Sulun rested his head on his hands, and swore.

"Perhaps just the gratitude, and potential favor of a guard captain would be enough to content them. I wouldn't rely on that alone, though." Zeren leaned forward and fixed Sulun with an intent look. "What sweetening can I offer, what information that would seem valuable to a city courtier, a secretary in the Ministry of Justice? You'll have to tell me. I'm a soldier, and no politician, and I have no idea what that sort would believe."

"Good gods, how would I know?" Sulun groaned. "I'm no courtier, only a philosopher. Petty nobles are as alien to me as they are to you."

"Money and power," Yanados murmured in the taut silence. "They all chase after money and power. How might giving you the list repay some secretary in money and power? Think hard."

"Money and power? Out of the creditors?" Doshi asked, scratching his blond stubble. "Well, any of them has more of either, now, than Shibari does."

"Thieves," Arizun spat, as emphatically as any adult. "Hmmm. Maybe a falling out among thieves? A little thief holding out on a big thief? And the big chief offering a reward . . . Damn, no, that would still require money—which we don't have."

"Still," Sulun considered, "you may have an idea there."

Zeren strolled through the Hall of Records, Division of the Ministry of Justice, with his polished parade armor clashing softly. The loftily impassive look on his face was beginning to slip into grim boredom, despite his best efforts. He'd been through three secretaries so far, was on his way to see the fourth, and already devoutly wished he were out in the clean stink of the streets. At least by now, he had his carefully rehearsed lines as well memorized as any actor in the city could do. He pushed open the fourth ornate door of the day.

"Guard Captain Zeren Roshi's-son, to see His Lordship, Master Secretary Yidar Fiblen's-son." That part he could practically do in his sleep, especially the salute.

"Indeed?" The wizened petty noble behind the wide table had a manner reminiscent of a lizard. It matched his face and hands, if not his overdecorated robe. "Er, do sit down, Captain."

Stage two: getting comfortable already. A good sign. Zeren sat with an unfeigned sigh of relief, and rubbed a little obviously at his knee. "Ah, thank you. Good to get off my feet."

"Some refreshments, Captain?" the master secretary offered, reaching into a closely placed, and well-stocked, wine cabinet.

Wine already? Better and better. This interview might go quickly. "Don't mind if I do." Hmm, well-made goblets, and not a bad vintage. "Thank you much. This is a finer wine than a poor soldier's used to."

"And may I inquire what brings you to my office? No problems with any escaped prisoners, I hope?"

Ah, so that was his worry. Possibly worth looking into later. "Oh no, nothing like that. It's this matter of Shibari's estate, and his creditors. No doubt you heard of what happened last night?"

"Oh, of course. Tragic business—and so unnecessary." Yidar leaned closer, much like a lizard creeping up on a fly. "Were any of the, er, strongboxes recovered?"

Better and better. "That's exactly the problem, Master Secretary." *Now put down the cup and fix the old reptile with an eagle-eyed stare.* "We have reason to believe the fire was indeed deliberately set, but not by Shibari himself." Which indeed it wasn't. Poor Nanya.

"No?" *Ah, see him hesitate, slowly ease back, uncertain.*

"No, indeed." *Very stern now.* "We suspect that the fire was set as a diversion, by one of Shibari's creditors who had entered the house earlier and found what he wanted."

"Good gods." The master secretary plumped back into his seat, thinking that over.

"Yes. I suspect that said creditor either found Shibari and his family already dead or else ..." *Pause ominously.* " ... helped them prematurely into that state—and then searched the house at his leisure."

"W-what—" *How breathlessly eager!* "What do you think he found?"

"Considerably more than enough money and valuables to recover his loan." *Now smile, grimly.* "I suspect he discovered where Shibari's real treasure might be found—and determined to keep it all to himself." *Now wait, watch for his reaction.*

"Good *gods!*" the secretary spluttered. "You don't think I had anything to do with that, do you?"

Better than we'd hoped! But keep calm. "Certainly not. You weren't one of Shibari's creditors—were you?"

"Absolutely not." The secretary smiled with reassured confidence. "I could show you the official listing of Shibari's creditors, if you like."

"Hmm, yes, I would like a copy of the listing, if you please." *Don't seem too grateful for it, not yet.*

"Nothing would be easier." Yidar scribbled briefly on a waxed tablet, then rang a small bell. Almost instantly, a well-trained clerk came in. The master secretary shoved the tablet at him. "Go fetch this document and have it copied, quickly."

The clerk bowed and left. Yidar settled back into his chair. Studying his smile, Zeren would have bet his commission just then that this particular master secretary was skimming sizable sums somewhere out of the Ministry of Justice. Independent debt-recovering, perhaps? Or was it something to do with those missing prisoners he'd mentioned? Worth checking into later.

"Could you tell me, Captain," Yidar leaned forward again, "just how you intend to find . . . the miscreant?"

Now. Drop it now. "I myself was at Shibari's house last night, first making some sort of order out of the crowd of creditors demanding justice and afterward organizing the fire brigade. I had much opportunity, as you can guess, to see just who was present at the front gate when the fire broke out." A grim smile again. "I intend to go visit everyone on this little list of yours and see which ones I recognize on sight—and which one I don't."

"Er, don't?"

"My dear Master Secretary, it must be obvious that whoever was inside setting the fire could not have been outside at the front gate."

"Ah! Process of Elimination!" Yidar seemed terribly proud of using that term. Clearly he'd had some tutoring in proper logic and rhetoric, as befitting a gentleman. "Hmmm, and tell me, once you identify the miscreant, what then will you do with him?"

Oho, see him sniffing the bait! "Why, bind him over for trial, of course." *Now shrug, look unconcerned.* "I leave it to persons more skilled than myself in such matters to extract confessions."

"And to discover the whereabouts of Shibari's treasure?"

Bait taken! "Certainly. It's most important that the debts be settled."

"But you have no idea of the whereabouts, or nature, or total amount of the treasure?"

See the gears engage, as Sulun would put it. "None whatever." *Shrug again.* "But then, that's not my department. My business is to catch the thief—and possible murderer—and hand him over to the Emperor's justice. Let others do the clerical work; I'm a guardsman."

"Yes indeed." Yidar smirked. "And a most dedicated one, too."

See him thinking: what a fool, what a dumb clod of a soldier. May the gods help any of Shibari's creditors who fall into the hands of the Ministry of Justice for the next year or more. This lizard will borrow the Emperor's own torturer if he must, hunting for treasure.

Who would believe that Shibari's only surviving treasure is Sulun? Sulun and Omis, and their cleverness, and what they might yet create to save all of Sabis, and more.

The clerk knocked discreetly at the door, then tiptoed in and handed over a short document with its ink still wet. Yidar took it and studied it, frowning in concentration.

"Let me see the original, for accuracy," he snapped.

The clerk look offended, but handed over another, longer parchment.

The master secretary looked from one to the other, and smiled. "There, you see?" he said, displaying them both to Zeren. "All the names and addresses and amounts are there, as is the complaint. It lacks only the clerk's statement and seal."

Zeren was careful to take the copy without snatching at it. "Hmm, yes. I see I'll have a lot of walking and interviewing to do." Gods, yes, there *were* a lot of them. "Thank you greatly for your help, Master Secretary. I'll remember it."

"Your gratitude is my reward," Yidar almost purred. "You will keep me informed of the progress of your investigation, won't you?"

"I'll certainly let you know when I've caught the wretch," Zeren promised, easing out of his chair. "Now, seeing how many faces I have to go study, I'd best get on with it. Thank you once again for your invaluable help." He clasped arms formally with the master-secretary, (noting that his arms *felt* like lizard-skin, too) rolled up the document, and left as quickly as he could.

A single glimpse back from the corridor showed that Yidar

was studying the document, memorizing the names of Shibari's creditors, already trying to guess which one of them knew the secret of the dead noble's missing wealth.

Zeren hurried down the corridor, out of the Hall of Records, into the clean city air.

✧ CHAPTER SIX ✧

Idleness was too much a burden for any of them. Vari vented her impatience by marshalling a cleaning-party to dust and scrub Zeren's house. The housekeeper beat a hasty retreat to the tiny kitchen garden. Omis got the duty of marshalling the small children, which was exhausting enough to keep him from undue worry. Arizun and Yanados went out to ply Arizun's old trade of fortune-telling; with a little luck, and the credulity of the average Sabisan citizen, they might charm up enough money to purchase a decent dinner. They would certainly pick up an earful of the latest news about Shibari's creditors and the hunt for the missing servants. Doshi took the opportunity to catch up on some sleep—until Omis, worn out with babysitting, woke him up and gave him the job instead. The children, finding out that Doshi was wonderfully teasable, enjoyed him immensely. Teigi, clinging fiercely to her new purpose and identity, practiced—with variable results—disguising herself as a boy. She insisted on being called Ziya now, and a single scuffle with Tamiri convinced the smaller child of two things: the point was not arguable and Ziya was not safe to tease.

Sulun inspected and reinspected the gear saved from Shibari's house, wandered about Zeren's spartan rooms for a time, then went to commiserate with Omis about being skilled craftsmen bereft of their tools.

"But you still have the working model of that steam engine, don't you?" Omis noted. "That's an advantage—a pretty enough toy to impress the superficial sort, useful enough to impress the practical. You can win a patron with that alone. What do I have?"

"Oh come, now, you or Vari must have grabbed some of your

pretty knives and cookware, at least. The masters of the house will be impressed by the one, and his wife or housekeeper by the other. Don't worry." Sulun clapped him on the shoulder. "You're a good craftsman, and it shows plainly."

"I hate patron-hunting. How long before we can get back to the Bombard Project?"

"I suppose that depends on what else our patron will want us to do."

"If he's an ill-tempered sort, we'll never have the time to work on our experiments." Omis pounded one fist on his thigh. "Gods, how wretchedly our business is arranged. There must be a better way than this!"

"There must be," Sulun agreed, lured off into a daydream of some fanciful kingdom where enlightened patrons provided their philosophers and craftsmen with necessities and otherwise left them alone, left them to experiment and study to their heart's content, without interruptions or demands for frivolous work. The gods knew what might be invented then!

The sound of the main door opening interrupted his speculations. Zeren stepped over the threshold, glittering in his parade armor, and halted in something like dismay as the smaller children descended on him with squeals of delight. Tamiri and Mido danced around him like moths, grabbing playfully at his hands, swordbelt, and armor skirt, until Vari came to shoo them away. Sulun choked back a whoop of laughter at the sight of a captain of the City Guard of Sabis brought to a standstill, and very nearly routed, by a small gaggle of children.

Zeren shook his head and took another few steps, recovering his balance. "I'd forgotten what it was like," he muttered, then bellowed, "Buna! Get in here and start supper, with wine. No, bring the wine first." He tugged off his helmet and turned to Sulun. "Gods, I've got to get the taste of parchment dust out of my mouth. Go collect the others; we may as well discuss this over a good comfortable supper."

The housekeeper scurried in, threw Zeren a reproachful look, and hustled off to the kitchen. Sulun collared Doshi and sent him out to find Yanados and Arizun. The others went to help marshal the children and set up for supper.

Zeren dropped into the nearest chair and began removing his formal armor, marveling to himself at how different the house looked, sounded, and felt when it was full of friends and children.

Dinner consisted of wine, sweet and sour breads, boiled white beans with cheese, a large salad, a modest baked fish, and a large roast duck—the duck provided by Arizun, who didn't mention how he'd got it, and Yanados wasn't telling. The pair also brought in a respectable purse of mixed coins and a bigger bag of gossip.

"The old house has been stripped to the walls," Arizun reported around a mouthful of sweet bread. "I even saw charred timbers from the roof being sold for firewood."

Sulun, noticing how Teigi/Ziya winced at that, thought to ask, "Has anyone performed the proper rites for Shibari and his family?"

"Oh, yes. The burial society of the Temple of Inota took care of that. The old master certainly paid them enough in his lifetime to cover the cost of the urns and the prayer service and maintaining the tomb. Nobody had to pay for the cremation, of course, but—Ow!" Arizun rubbed his ankle where Yanados had diplomatically kicked it.

"Yes, we should go to the tomb and pay our respects as soon as we can," Vari said, keeping an eye on Teigi/Ziya's set face.

"We heard that at least two of the creditors are fighting over the house and grounds," Yanados put in. "Some of the house servants have been caught, and the guards are supposed to be searching for the rest."

"Not too hard, I'll wager," Zeren commented over his winecup.

"Without the family records, the law clerks can't tell the slaves from the free servants. It's a wretched mess." Yanados sighed. "We'd best not be seen too much outside, not until we get another patron."

"Or we could all be enslaved," Doshi added.

Teigi/Ziya shivered, but otherwise kept very still.

"Speaking of patrons, Zeren . . ." Sulun hinted.

The burly soldier pushed his plate aside, pulled out a sheet of parchment, and spread it on the table. "The good news," he said, "is that I've tracked down all of Shibari's creditors, even learned which one took the lion's share. He has your forge and tools, and yes, he's rich. Very rich."

The apprentices couldn't keep from cheering, and the children joined in.

"The bad news is, he's Entori of Funay."

Instant silence fell. Omis broke it with a faint groan of, "No, not Entori the Miser!"

"Entori the slave-maker, you mean." Arizun shuddered. "The last debtors who couldn't pay him lost everything but the clothes they stood up in—and then they were sold at slave auction."

"How desperate could our master have been," Vari asked softly, "to risk falling into the hands of Entori the Infamous?"

"The gods know," Sulun murmured. But now he knew why Shibari had fallen on his sword, why his wife had killed herself and their children and burned the house.

Doshi said it for all of them. "Gods, must we put ourselves into the hands of our master's worst enemy? The man Shibari died to escape?"

Zeren leaned back and looked around at the doleful little company. "There are a few other rich men on that list," he said, "but none so rich as Entori. Any of them might be willing to take on either a blacksmith or an engineer, complete with dependents, but none of the others would be inclined to take you both. Entori already has your forge, your lathe, all your large tools and supplies. He may be a wretched man to work for, but he's your best hope. I'm sorry."

There was a longer silence as the others thought that over. It ended in sighs of resignation.

"Ah, well," Sulun made it formal, "I suppose we'd best plan how to persuade him. Any suggestions?"

✧ CHAPTER SEVEN ✧

Entori's house was almost invisible from the street, hidden behind its high wall and skirts of wall-front shops. The front door crouched at the end of a shallow alley between a potter's and a rug merchant's. Small spy-windows flanked the plain doorway, one of them opening when Zeren pounded on the blank, bronze-sheathed door. Omis and Sulun traded worried glances while Zeren bawled out his name and business at the barely visible doorman. What manner of house was this, they wondered, that hid itself from all sight and disguised itself in a screen of the houses and bodies of the poor?

The spy-window snapped shut and the door creaked grudgingly half-open. Zeren, Omis, and Sulun stepped from shade to shadow, into a dim bare corridor scarcely wider than the door, smelling faintly of dust and mold. The doorman, a palsied ancient in a threadbare tunic worn as grey as the rest of him, hurried to close the door behind them. In the deepened gloom, the pale sunlight at the far end of the corridor beckoned like mirage.

Sulun and Omis traded looks again. They hadn't known what to expect of the house of Entori the Infamous: perhaps furnishings of boastful, overwhelming, barbaric splendor; perhaps manacles and whips mounted on the walls, or portraits of all the victims Entori had brought low in his long career. The last thing they could have imagined was this vast, quiet, dusty barrenness.

"Stay here," Zeren barked at the servant. "I know the way." He led the others boldly toward the dim light.

All the way down the corridor they heard no sound but their own footsteps, saw no decorations or lamps or god-shrines of any kind, met no other living thing but a single wayward moth.

53

Sulun felt oddly grateful for the presence of that moth; without it, he might have imagined that he was walking into a tomb.

The room led out into a small courtyard with a square rain-pool in its center. The surrounding walkway, its walls interrupted by closed doors and curtained windows, was covered with slanting tile roofs that aimed toward the pool.

Entori the Miser wasted not even rainwater.

"Is the whole place a silent warehouse?" Omis muttered, under his breath. "How can people live like that?"

At the far side of the rainwater pool, in a narrow bar of sunlight, sat a woman in a plain dark dress, reading a book-sized scroll. She glanced up, frowning slightly, as the trio approached.

Zeren, having no idea who she was, but noting that she didn't strike the usual posture and attitude of a servant, gave her a polite, half-formal salute and repeated the party's names, titles, and business. Omis noticed that she had a most intriguing face: the straight dark hair, almost black eyes, delicate bones, and pointed chin usually associated with the old Sukkti blood; not a young or conventionally pretty woman, certainly, but interesting. Sulun peeked at the book in her hands, and saw that it was a treatise on ancient history by a respectably honest author; it was the most encouraging item he'd seen so far in Entori's house.

"My brother is in his study," the woman said, waving a languid hand toward the mouth of another corridor behind her. "Second door on the right." Her eyes were already straying back to her book.

Sulun glanced back at her as the three resumed march. He hadn't known that Entori had a sister, much less that she was of a scholarly turn of mind. He just might have a possible ally in this place.

The next corridor led into the formal dining hall, a vast and shadowy room filled with enough banners, tapestries, lamps, cabinets of ancestral busts and bits of statuary to have furnished all the rest of the house they'd yet seen. Zeren rolled his eyes at the clutter, searched his way to an ornate door on the right, rapped on it, and announced the party for the third time.

"Enter, enter," snapped a dry, gravelly voice.

Zeren pushed open the door, which did not creak, and led the others into Entori's lair. Sulun and Omis stifled a gasp of surprise at the sheer amount of parchment: countless sheets and scrolls of it, filling and jamming the cubbyhole cabinets that climbed the walls, cluttering the massive table that commanded the center of the room, intermixed with clay tablets, wax tablet-books, weighing scales and weights of assorted sizes, stylus shafts, pens, inkwells, and an abacus or two—enough for the records room of a small tax-office. A large strongbox behind the table completed the illusion, though Sulun guessed that the bulk of Entori's ready money was concealed elsewhere.

The room was lit by thin sunlight through the window behind the table, and by a single bronze oil-lamp set like a wave-washed rock in that parchment sea. The flickering yellow light picked out a circle of account records, a pair of thin hands resting on them, a heavy carved chair, a thick fur robe, the bald head and blinking dark eyes of an indeterminably-aged man who could only be Entori the Miser. The thick white ruff of the fur robe, much too heavy for this weather, gave his thin bald head and narrow hands the unflattering suggestion of a vulture.

"Yes?" His voice added to the impression.

This, Sulun thought, *is he who destroyed our master and all his house.*

Zeren pulled out his own bit of parchment and opened it with a flourish. "You are Entori, Yeshinan's-son, creditor of the late Shibari to the amount of 27,382 silvers?"

Entori blinked. "Yes . . ." He quickly added, "And I did not recover the full amount of the debt."

"But you did recover—" Zeren pretended to check his sheet of parchment again, "one blacksmith's forge and anvil, with sundry related tools, one mechanic's lathe, with sundry related tools, plus several mechanical devices in various stages of completion. Not so?"

"Er, yes . . ." Entori rattled his fingers on the tabletop, clearly dying to see what else was on that list. "But that doesn't begin to cover the debt! Those things are of no use to me, and where can I sell them? And when? And for how much? A pittance, five hundred silvers at best—no, no, they don't begin to cover the amount of the debt."

Omis squirmed, biting back considerable words. Sulun elbowed him still.

Zeren tucked the parchment back in his belt and leaned

forward, smiling. "Still, I think there may be a way to give you some satisfaction," he purred. "You know, we're trying to settle this business as thoroughly as possible for all concerned."

"Satisfaction?" Entori asked, edging further into the lamplight.

"Shibari did leave so many debts unsettled, especially with the house burned and its contents largely destroyed. We're trying to give the creditors as much value as possible, you know—"

"Satisfaction?" Entori nudged.

Spring the trap, Sulun thought, biting his lip.

"As you said, the tools are useless to you." Zeren straightened, snapping out the words like numbers in an account list. "Likewise, Shibari's displaced craftsmen are useless without their tools— like farmers without land, or land without farmers to tend it."

Entori blinked again, registering the truth of the analogy.

"Now, put the craftsman and his tools together, and one might see some profit out of this lamentable business." Zeren leaned closer. "I have it on good authority that these particular craftsmen were working on some most valuable devices when Shibari made his ill-advised sea trade venture. Some of them—" He dropped his voice to a conspiratorial whisper, "—were of . . . interest to the military. They might still be so, if properly developed. Do you take my meaning, good sir?"

Entori took the hint, at least. One hand slid upward to rattle thoughtful fingers on his chin. "And of course," he murmured, "the officer who presented these . . . profitable devices . . . to the right eyes could expect some expression of gratitude from them?"

Zeren smiled like a tradesman closing a deal. "I see that we understand each other."

Entori nodded thoughtfully, and rolled expressionless eyes toward Sulun and Omis. "I assume these are the craftsmen in question?"

"The two masters," Zeren corrected. "There are also their assistants."

Omis crossed fingers for luck behind his back. Technically, the apprentices all belonged to Sulun. Only a long stretch of the imagination could label Vari as a blacksmith's assistant, to say nothing of the children.

Entori's eyes narrowed. "Just how many extra mouths will I be taking into my household?" he asked.

'Will be taking'. . . ? Sulun dared to hope.

"Hardly extra," Zeren snorted. "A grand total of ten—"

"Ten!"

"And a bargain, at the price of their keep." Zeren shrugged with elaborate unconcern. "Of course, if you'd rather not gather the harvest for the price of the seed, I'm sure Shibari's other creditors—"

"Not so fast, not so fast." Entori raised a birdlike hand. "I didn't say I wasn't interested. . . ." He cocked a cold eye at Sulun and Omis. "But of course, I wish to know what value I can expect to receive for taking on this . . . seed money expense."

"But of course." Zeren waved theatrically toward Sulun and Omis, and stepped aside.

At the cue, the two bowed formally. They straightened, whipped two large baskets out from under their cloaks, and opened them together. Sulun pulled out the little bronze steam engine model and placed it on the clearest section of the table. Omis produced a small brass firecup filled with treated charcoal, and slid it under the globe of the engine.

"My design," Sulun intoned, pointing at the assemblage.

"My workmanship," Omis echoed.

The words sounded natural and unforced, as well they should after yesterday's hours of practice. Omis even managed a suitably impressive flourish as he whipped out his flint and steel striker and lit the charcoal.

The distilled wine fumes caught at the first strike, shooting up impressive yellow and blue flames. Omis tossed a really unnecessary cue-glance at Sulun, and stepped back. Now for the distracting patter while waiting for the water to boil. If only he could manage this without fumbling his lines. *Gods, why should I have to play an actor, too?* Sulun complained to himself as he struck an orator's pose and began.

"Know, oh most wise and honored host, that this is but a small version of that which might be." *Pray it so, or ten desperate people might soon be out in the street again.* "As you see this little globe rests, like a wheel, upon an axle whereby it might spin." *And hope the water boils soon!* "Within it lies a small quantity of water, easily replaced."

But how would one replace the water at a steady rate in order to keep the globe spinning? Design problem: deal with it later.

"The fire heats the water, making it boil unto vapor." *Boil soon, dammit!* "This vapor, being closer to that divine state of the spirit than is mere fluid or gross earthly matter, seeks to rise toward heaven."

Seeks to expand, actually, and spirit has nothing to do with it, but this is not time to argue with common misconceptions.

"Yet it must escape this imprisoning globe, and what escape may it find save through these three identically curved little pipes?" *Nudge one of them, encourage the fool toy to spin.* "Thus, escape it does, so fiercely seeking its freedom that in leaping outward toward the free air it doth thrust backward against the door of its former prison."

There, is that a faint wisp of escaping steam? Please? "Even as a sailor, stepping from a small boat to the dock, doth thrust the boat away from him with his lattermost foot . . ."

Yes! Steam at last!

"So this backward thrust presses the pipes away from the direction of the escaping steam, er, vapor . . ." *Move, dammit!* "And as the pipes are firmly affixed to the globe, which in turn rests upon its axle, the globe hath no choice save to . . ."

There it goes!

" . . . spin."

Sure enough, the little globe spun: slowly at first, then faster, whirling merrily in its soft halo of escaping steam.

Entori peered closer, fascinated, his dark eyes very wide and round. *Quick now, before the water ran out or the man's normal suspicion reasserted itself.*

"Consider, milord, a much larger globe spinning thus. Picture it standing upon the deck of a ship. Picture the axle extended over the sides of the vessel, and wheels attached. Picture the wheels rimmed with oars reaching into the water. Consider, oh most wise and far-seeing, how fast and steadily such a ship could go—regardless of the vagaries of winds or fatigue of rowers."

Now hit the conclusion good and hard.

"A ship driven by such an engine would be mistress of the seas, fearing no storm nor dead winds, nor pirates.

"How wealthy would her master be?"

Entori nodded slowly, a smile spreading widely across his face, as the vision took hold. "Tell me," he murmured, "did Shibari commission the building of such a ship?"

"No, milord. He considered it too newfangled and undignified."

Well, that was half the truth anyway. "Also, he would not spare the time required to build it, preferring to gamble on quick profits with existing ships." *That, too, was part of the truth.*

"Shibari was a fool." Entori sat back, folded his hands, and turned his attention back to Zeren. "I agree, Captain, that there are possibilities here. Yes, I'll take in these craftsmen of yours. When we have ships of the sort that will interest the officers of the Imperial Navy, I will certainly inform you."

Zeren gave him a smile and a slight bow. "I have no doubt that there will be other such profitable developments," he purred. "I'll send the craftsmen and their assistants to you before the day is out."

"I'll have rooms prepared," Entori murmured, reaching for a stylus and tablet. "Good day, Captain."

Omis and Sulun suppressed sighs of relief as they turned and followed Zeren out the door. Only when they were out in the corridor did Omis dare to speak.

"We're out of the cookpot, but maybe into the fire. Sulun, it will take months to build a big steam engine, much less mount it on a ship, test it, get it seaworthy. And there are certain design problems. And when will we have time to work on the bombard?"

"We'll manage," Sulun promised. "At least now we'll have the tools, and a roof over our heads."

"I wish," Zeren muttered, "that you'd had a model of the bombard instead. Sabis needs land defense more than fast ships."

The little company arrived, bags and baggage, children and all, shortly after noon. The porter let them in at once, led them down a different set of gloomy corridors and into their new quarters chattering all the way, quite garrulous now that there were none but other Entori house servants to overhear.

"Well, well, well, so you're the new craftsmen of the house! All of you, then? Hah, I didn't think so. Can't quite see the babies hammering iron, eh?"

"Give them time," Omis huffed.

"Oh, yes indeed, yes indeed. Meanwhile, best keep them out of the master's sight, or else put 'em to sweeping floors or some such harmless work, keep 'em looking busy. Master doesn't like to pay for useless mouths. Clever idea, though, claiming four apprentices instead of a wife and three children; he set aside full three rooms for your lot, and as much for goodman Sulun and his. How d'ye like the furnishings, eh?"

Omis and Vari surveyed the first of the three cubicles, and bit their respective tongues.

"Not much cabinet space," Vari dared to comment.

"Eh, well, you can always get more cabinets out of your pay. Don't go borrowing bits of furniture from storage without the mistress's express permission now, tempting as it looks. Always remember Master Entori may run the business, but Mistress Eloti runs the household. 'Tis a fine point in your favor that she likes you."

"Likes us?" Sulun put in. "I didn't know she'd even seen us."

"Oh, she did. She has her ways. Heh-heh! Yes. Master wanted to hire you, right enough, but the expense worried him, so he talked to Mistress about it. When he stopped for breath she put in a word. 'Hire them,' she said. 'Good investment,' she said. Then he went back to talking and rattled on for another good half-hour, and finally concluded by saying he'd go ahead and hire you all. Then it was a question of what to pay you."

"Really?" Sulun said. He hadn't dared bring that up himself; it wasn't seemly for an unemployed craftsman to bargain with a master who was graciously consenting to save him from begging on the street. Zeren hadn't dared to bring up the subject either; it would have seemed out of character, considering his argument for Entori hiring the lot of them in the first place. "And what did they decide?"

"At first Master rattled on and on about the expense of feeding ten new mouths, plus added costs of lamp oil and laundry soap and all like that, and said you should be grateful enough for that and allowance for materials—"

Behind them, Arizun snorted, loudly.

"But then Mistress pointed out that unpaid hirelings tend to steal, and unpaid craftsmen tend to pad their budgets for materials, and that better paid servants tend to keep their mouths shut about their master's business. Master thought about that for a bit, and suggested that two silver pieces a month should buy proper secrecy—"

This time it was Doshi who did the derisive snorting.

"But Mistress pointed out that there's many who would pay far better to keep so valuable a secret as that steam powered ship engine, and she argued for a full gold piece per month. Master ranted and raved a bit, then thought it over, and finally agreed on one gold for each master and eight silvers for each apprentice, which isn't too shabby, especially for so . . . ah . . . economical a household as this one."

Sulun shrugged. No, that wasn't too shabby for this household, and he could make up the differences needed by padding his requests for materials.

The apprentices were already unloading their personal gear in their assigned cubicles, already arguing over who got which bed, which drawer, which clothespress.

"Now, the workshops are down this way."

"This way" led down another corridor, past rooms choked with piles of furniture, parchment, household furnishings, odd tools, clothing, bags of grains, sealed jars of wine, oil and spices, assorted arms and armor, crates and sacks and barrels of unidentifiable goods—loot from unnumbered debt foreclosures. Omis found the sight infinitely depressing, while Sulun took notes.

Then out into a back courtyard near the wall, a courtyard filled with larger spoils, heavy equipment, bigger tools: and to one side of the tangle sat Omis's forge and anvil, and Sulun's lathe. Omis fell upon the anvil with a cry of joy, and hugged it to his muscular chest. Sulun only frowned.

"It'll take days of work to make a proper workshop out of all this mess," he pointed out. "Just clearing space. And where can we put all this other junk? And there's no roof. We'll need to set up a canopy—"

"I'm sure ye've enough apprentices to do it," the porter sniffed. "And there'll be room for storage in the eighth room down the hall, once Master sells that lot—say, another two days."

Sulun and Omis looked at each other. Plainly they'd be given no help settling in or setting up. On the other hand, they'd be left alone to arrange the workshop as they pleased and, incidentally, to explore the other tools and engines in that pile.

"Very good." Sulun put on that polite, politic smile that was becoming easier with practice. "We'll set up the rooms tonight and start on this after breakfast tomorrow. How long until dinner?"

Dinner was at sundown, in the chill formal banquet room lit with a few sullen lamps. The half-seen statuary lining the walls seemed alternately to glower or smirk in the uncertain light. At the high table sat Entori, still wearing his fur-collared robe, and his sister Eloti, to his left, wearing another, equally subdued, dark dress. The entertainment consisted of harp-twanging by a skinny youth who, so Vari whispered for her husband to pass on, spent the rest of the day as a sweeper. A scullery maid doubled as server to the high table.

At the lower table sat Omis and his family, Sulun and his apprentices, the porter, a disturbingly slender cook, another slatternly maid, a sour-faced elderly woman who described herself variously as housekeeper/seamstress/lady's maid, a drowsing ancient dressed in the robes of a third-level mage, and three burly, inexpressive men whose duties were not described but who wore heavy truncheons at their belts. The food was plain, so was the servants' livery, and conversation was subdued.

Noting all the covert glances his party got from the other servants, Sulun could barely wait for the dinner to end, the master and mistress to depart, and the usual after-dinner servants' gathering to begin. There was much he needed to learn here.

He noted that the servants were dawdling over their food.

Dinner seemed interminable, though the master of the house ate fast. Entori gulped at his food like a well-trained but hungry watchdog, with no spattering or notable haste, but with no wasted motion. Mistress Eloti ate with a similar economy, but with less speed. Entori finished well before her, and sat rattling his fingers on his winecup as if debating whether or not to have more wine. Eloti, if anything, slowed down. Entori gave up and had his cup refilled. They finished their last mouthfuls at almost the same moment, and Sulun wondered which of them had timed it that way. Entori stood, obliging the rest of the household (except the harper) to rise too, then swept out the door with his sister on his arm.

"At last," muttered the serving girl, as the rest of the servants sat down again.

"Hush," the old housekeeper snapped. "Wait."

The others gulped their food but kept quiet, watching the door. Sulun's gang traded bewildered glances.

The harper stopped in mid-note and came over to the table, casting a quick look down the corridor as he passed the door.

"They're gone," he said, shoving into an empty seat. "Pass the beans."

"Hell, pass the wine!" rumbled one of the house-guards.

"Amen," mumbled the house wizard, holding out his cup.

The serving girl came over, grinning, and the supper promptly became more lively.

Omis gulped at his refilled cup, and made a face. "Gods! Is this stuff half vinegar, or what?"

The guardsmen laughed. "Entori buys cheap," one of them chuckled. "But don't worry; we've a way to get at the better stuff, once this is gone."

"Hush," snapped the housekeeper again, glaring sidelong at the wizard. "No sense encouraging such things."

"Oh, why not?" Another guardsman laughed. "Let Aobi tell it. Our Terribly Important new friends will find out soon enough, anyway."

"Important?" Vari puzzled in mid-bite.

"Of course," sniffed the housekeeper. "The master hired the whole lot of you at once, and at good money too, after talking privately with a commander of the City Guard. That, from a merchant and moneylender who never parts with a copper bit unless he's weighed it first. We can all make good guesses."

Vari turned a bewildered glance to her husband, who bounced it to Sulun.

"Engine-makers," the wizard hiccupped. "More damned protection for fires—"

"As I was saying," Aobi the guardsman resumed, "the Old Man has barrels and barrels of wine in the cellar, but he hardly touches it himself. Always hoping to trade it for something better, he is. Now the stuff he's had there the longest—and I swear, he has a good lot that's been down there more than four years—might rightfully be expected to have turned sour by this time."

The other servants at the table snickered and grabbed at the wine ewer.

"Now Gipu here—" Aobi nudged the guard next to him, "can tell you about the empty jars he found in one of the storerooms. Enough to hold a barrel's worth of good wine, eh?" He nudged Gipu again, who chuckled mountainously around a mouthful of stew. "Why let the poor things stand about empty, says I. As for the barrel, we refilled it with good wine vinegar, bought with our own pay. Does the Old Man ever tap that barrel, he'll find the wine's turned too sour to drink. Oh, pity. He'll probably sell the vinegar for a better price than we paid."

"Meanwhile," Gipu added, "we get to drink better than this swill. Jug empty yet, Loac?"

The third guard upended the ewer in his cup. "Finished," he announced. "Get the good stuff."

The maid grabbed the jug and ran off giggling.

"So," Aobi purred at Omis, leaning closer, "just what is it that makes your lot so valuable to the Old Man, eh?"

"Ten of you, for such good money," Loac added, favoring Sulun with a thoughtful eye. "A blacksmith, maybe, one could understand. But so many?"

Sulun glanced around, seeing all the servants' eyes on him and Omis's almost desperate look, and realized how close he was to arousing the enmity of his new household. This miserly household thrived on secrets, and he'd best give these people a convincing one. Simply calling himself a Natural Philosopher wouldn't do.

"Engines for ships," he offered in a properly conspiratorial tone. "Ships that can sail against the wind, or outrun pirates. We know how to build them."

The servants traded glances, nodded in understanding, and smiled.

"If you need any help," Aobi offered, "Just ask."

"Forges, fires . . . more damned work," mumbled the wizard. "Where's that wine?"

The maid came back with the ewer full of better-smelling wine, and dumped a generous dollop in Sulun's cup. The other servants promptly clamored for her attention.

Omis took the opportunity to whisper in Vari's ear. She nodded, got up from the table, and began collecting children. "Time the little ones went to bed," she explained to any who might care to listen, then hustled the children and herself safely out and away.

Omis stuck out his cup for a refill, and grimly prepared to make a long night of it.

✧ CHAPTER EIGHT ✧

"Sulun!" a fierce whisper, followed by a heavily shoving hand. "Sulun, get up! The sun's high, and we've much to do."

Sulun opened one eye, closed it again, and groaned.

"Here, drink the winterleaf tea." Omis's calloused hand shoved a steaming mug close to Sulun's nose. "The wife says it good for wine-head. Drink, and get up."

Seeing that there was no help for it, Sulun drank the foul-tasting stuff and managed to roll himself upright. Omis held out a plain robe, and after a moment's hesitation Sulun struggled into it. "Gods," he muttered. "Remind me never to drink more than four cups at one sitting again. How did you survive?"

"There's more of me to saturate than there is of you. Try eating more. Hmm, do you want breakfast?"

"No!" Sulun pulled on the robe, hauled himself to his feet, and stumbled to the pitcher and washbasin in the corner. "Gods, gods . . . was it worth all that wine? I can't remember."

"Oh yes." Omis sat down on the bed Sulun had just quitted. "We learned a great deal indeed. First, the master leaves all the running of the household to his sister, who manages surprisingly well, but is something of a mystery to everyone. Second, the Old Man resents the noble families terribly; it appears that they don't accept him socially, though they're friendly enough with men not nearly so wealthy. The servants think it's because he's such a mean and miserly sort that he can't possibly amuse them; he thinks it's because he's descended from one of the old Sukkti houses, if you please."

"Sukkti?" Sulun puzzled as he dried his face on a threadbare cloth. "I didn't think there were any of the old race left. How many centuries has it been since the conquest?"

"Six at least. Who cares? One doesn't have to be pure Sukkti to have a bit of the old blood, as surely half of Sabis must. I'm just telling you what the servants say the Old Man believes." Omis cracked his knuckles noisily. "But to get on, Entori is the sort who nurses a grudge. He intends to buy that power which he can't win with his personal charm, and for that he needs money—always more money."

"That, we knew," Sulun grumbled, reaching for his comb.

"It doesn't end there. The Old Man cares not overmuch how he makes his money or who he deals with to get it." Omis leaned forward, making the bed webbing creak. "Nor does he care how his servants are treated, so long as the money comes in. Consider, friend Sulun, that galley slaves on his ships tend to die off at a higher rate than usual."

"The steam engine . . ." Sulun frowned, yanking the comb through his woolly tangle of hair.

"Yes, the steam engine for ships. It gets more interesting still. Entori's business has suffered from the loss of the northern trade as well as from the piracy out at sea. Many of his creditors have gone down, leaving him with cartloads of goods that he has trouble selling. He hopes to make up for this by—listen well—supplying the army and navy. You see where this leads?"

Sulun put the comb down and looked about for his sandals. "Does Zeren know this?"

"If he didn't before, he does now." Omis sat back with a satisfied grin. "I sent Arizun scampering off to him with a message, just after the morning report."

"Morning what?" Sulun asked, fumbling his way into his sandals.

"Another little custom of the household. Every morning—early, mind you—all the servants are required to show up in the master's office and give brief, concise reports about their work and the condition of the supplies. All the rest of us went this morning, and we had difficulty enough explaining why you weren't present. You'll have to be there tomorrow, and with something to report."

"Report?" Sulun forced his aching brain into action. "By tomorrow morning? We'll be lucky if we have half the shop set up by then. What, in the name of all the gods together, are we expected to report?"

"We'll have to think of something." Omis pulled himself off the bed and offered a hand to Sulun. "Shall we begin?"

Two hours further into the morning, the task seemed just as formidable, even with the help of all four apprentices and two of the interested house-guards. The storerooms and back courtyard of Entori's house contained an incredible amount of hoarded junk.

There were also a few unsuspected treasures.

"Sulfur," Yanados whispered in Sulun's ear while the guards were busy on the far side of the courtyard. "This room, here— Arizun made the map—by the back wall there are five big grainbags full of sulfur. The dust is so thick on them, I'll wager Entori hasn't seen or thought about them in ten years."

"I'll go see them at lunchtime," Sulun whispered back. "Don't let anyone see that map." Gods, the Bombard Project! He'd almost forgotten it.

Yanados nodded, rolled the parchment quickly, and scurried off. Sulun caught Teigi—no, think of her always as Ziya—watching him, and quickly touched a warning finger to his lips. Ziya looked at her feet, frowned, and trudged off after Yanados.

Them Omis came rolling up, looking harried but somewhat pleased. "I've found most of the tools," he reported, "plus some oddments I never used before. Given a half-noon's time, I think we really can assemble a workable shop."

That struck another memory. "Omis," Sulun asked very quietly, "do you think we can assemble enough money to keep paying the rent on that workshop down by the river?"

Omis thought a moment, cast a quick glance around the yard, and whispered back, "Ask Vari, at lunch."

Sulun grinned agreement and took the tools off to the cleared space around his forge.

Next came Doshi, pausing for a moment in the task of clearing the useless bits of debt plunder out of the courtyard. "Master Sulun," he murmured, keeping his voice as low as the others had, "In one of those storerooms I found some old maps— merchants' work, I think—of the north country: Torrhyn, Jarrya . . . lands long gone to the barbarians. I recognized some of the old hills, the streams. . . ." He shook his head quickly, as if fighting off tears. "Beautiful work. I wonder if I might have time and parchment to copy some of them."

"Certainly," Sulun promised. "We'll discuss it at lunch." Money for good parchment? When they might need every last copper to keep the riverside workshop? But it would keep Doshi happy, and everyone's spirits were unsettled now. . . .

Then came Arizun, toting a basketful of oddities. "Master Sulun," he chirped, not caring if the guardsmen heard him, "we've found some good canvas sheeting, enough to make a sun roof over the forge if Master Entori will allow it. And what in the nine hells are these?" He held out his basket.

Sulun looked in, pawed among the glittering assemblies of metal, and stifled a gasp of recognition. "Valves," he whispered, almost reverently. "Good, solid trapdoor valves. The kind used for piping steam into bathhouses. And a ball-and-socket joint. All made of good brass . . ." A genuine inspiration, breathed of smiling gods, settled gently as a sacred dove on his shoulder. He stood up, smiling. "Yes, I think we have something of value to report tomorrow morning."

Lunch was a simple affair of bread, cheese, dried fruit, and thin beer, eaten out in the courtyard under pretext of not slowing down the work. The guards, chuckling at such unnecessary dedication, went inside to eat where the noon sun wouldn't bother them. Sulun's gang huddled together and spoke in low voices.

"A wretched, dusty place," Vari was grumbling. "Nowhere to dry the laundry save up on the roof, and I fear the mildew will get at it. So little light gets in through those miserable, tiny windows, one can barely see to clean. And the dust! Dust everywhere, especially near those storerooms, where cleaning is just impossible. I said as much to Mistress, when she came up on me in the hallway, and she said there was no help for it and I must do the best I can."

"The Old Man seems to like his house dark and musty," Doshi muttered. "I fear to think how we'd fare if plague came through the city. Plague demons could thrive here."

"Keep out in the sunlight whenever possible," Yanados advised. "We've excuse enough, with the workshop here."

"Speaking of workshops," Sulun cut in, frowning over the figures on his waxed tablet, "we'll earn enough to keep the workshop by the river, but that won't leave us much money else."

"None for the bombard, you mean?" Omis laughed bitterly.

"Easily answered; add to the list of expenses for the steam engine."

"That, at least," Sulun agreed. "How much iron will you need to make another bombard? How much will that cost us?"

"We can always do a bit of work outside," Arizun offered. "I can go back to telling fortunes in the market, and Yanados could always work as a hired sword." He dodged fast as Yanados aimed a swat at him.

"I don't suppose we could spare a few coppers for parchment," Doshi sighed. "Those beautiful maps . . . I wonder how the old country has changed."

"Just take the damned maps," Arizun snorted. "If the Old Man ever remembers and wants them, he'll send one of the servants to get them—and the folk in this house tell each other if they find anything missing, long before they'll tell him. You'll have plenty of time to sneak them back."

"True." Doshi brightened.

"And we have the sulfur now," Sulun went on, noting how the others pricked up their ears and Yanados grinned. "Five full sacks of it, lying unnoticed in Entori's storehouse for enough years to collect a thick furring of dust. I doubt he even knows what it is, let alone what its properties are."

"Rest assured, he'll notice if any of it goes missing," Doshi commented. "From what the servants tell, he keeps a tally of every ounce of straw in a bale."

"But recall the servants' trick with the wine," Sulun reminded him. "Do we replace any sulfur we take with some other yellow powder, and he can be persuaded that the 'mineral salt' has gone bad—soured, like the wine."

Omis guffawed. Vari shushed him, casting nervous glances back at the near doors and windows.

"So we have sulfur," Yanados agreed. "But how shall we purchase charcoal and saltpeter? Can we pad our budget enough to cover that?"

"And flux, for my ironworking?" Omis added. "Most probably, we can ask for it outright. Do we say we need it for making the steam engines, he'll agree to the purchase."

"In any event," Omis considered, "we'll need to show him good progress on the steam engine. We'll not have the shop ready to work for a few days yet. What shall we tell him tomorrow morning?"

"I'll rehearse my speech tonight," Sulun promised, "rather than stay late after dinner again."

Everyone else chuckled at that.

"Another way to cut our actual expenses . . ." Sulun pulled the two brass valves out of his robe and held them up. "Be certain the Old Man doesn't know what these are. Do we ask for time, money, and good brass to make valves for the steam engine, we can apply it to other things—and then use these."

Doshi and Yanados recognized the objects, and laughed agreement. The others looked puzzled. Omis took one of the valves and turned it over and over in his hands, studying its construction. Sulun handed him the ball-and-socket joint as well.

"If you can drill that out and attach a sizable funnel, we'll have a means to keep the steam engine steadily supplied with water."

"Aha!" Omis caught on, peering closer at the brass joint. "If I need to excuse all my ironworking for the bombard, I'll make the funnel for this out of iron. She'll rust, of course, but the Old Man won't know that until later."

"We can do it, then." Doshi actually grinned. "Entori will have his engine-driven ship and Zeren will have his bombard. How long will it take, think you?"

"Oh, that reminds me," Arizun put in, "I took your message to his house. He should give us some answer by tomorrow."

Vari, Sulun noticed, wasn't listening; she was watching Ziya, hitching closer to her, reaching tentatively for a bowed shoulder. Now that he looked, Sulun saw that the child was crying silently, face hidden under the raised hood of her robe. Sulun recalled, with a twinge of remorse, that he'd barely spoken to the child in the past two days.

"Eh, Ziya," he offered, clumsily patting the girl's nearer shoulder, "I hadn't meant to neglect you. What did you wish to say?"

Ziya pulled a deep breath, which caught and then rushed out again bearing a ragged spool of words. "Ohhh, it's all so shameful!"

"Huh?" Sulun couldn't imagine what she meant.

"Shameful!" Ziya gulped again. "All of you plotting lies and tricks to rob your master. Did you serve my father so?"

The others gnawed their lips and looked at each other. Yes, in truth they had played a few such games on Shibari. Not many, not so many as this, but they had done it.

"Not at all," said Vari, sounding utterly sincere. "Your father was a good master, not at all like this one."

Ziya hiccupped, rubbed her nose, and sat up a little straighter. Sulun gave Vari a quick look of guilty gratitude, which she barely acknowledged. He understood. It wasn't the first time, nor would it likely be the last, that they'd used well-meant lies to give the child some hope, some reason not to roll over and die of misery. If ever she learned the truth, would she forgive?

For that matter, Sulun wondered with a shiver, did the gods do the same to men? If so, could mankind ever forgive the gods?"

Then Ziya sniffed and spoke again. "Do bad masters always make their people bad?"

Even Vari couldn't answer that one; she threw Sulun a look of silent appeal. He could feel the weight of everyone else's eyes, and Ziya's question, fall on him.

Well, hang it, couldn't he justify himself in words so simple that a child could understand them?

"No, child. Bad masters only make it difficult for their people to be good."

There. Chew upon that, you gods.

Ziya turned wide, wet eyes up to him. "But not impossible?" she asked.

"No, not impossible. Just . . . difficult."

The child nodded acceptance and went back to munching on her bread and cheese, sorrow passing like a quick summer storm. The others dug into their food, as if determined to finish fast and get back to work.

Sulun pulled up the hood of his robe and glanced suspiciously at the half-clouded sky, wondering why he felt as if he'd just made a pledge before heaven.

✧ CHAPTER NINE ✧

Early next morning Sulun stood in line with the other yawning and bleary-eyed servants, awaiting the audience of accounting with Master Entori. Omis stood behind him, the apprentices in a cluster beyond, after them Vari and the children. They'd all been up long after dinner, rehearsing their lines. Sulun and Omis carried waxed tablets scribbled with lists and figures, Vari would rely on her excellent memory, the apprentices and children would merely look respectful and nod agreement with their elders. The other servants apparently used a similar method, for Sulun noted all three of the house-guards entering the master's office together, just ahead of him.

Given his own gang's agreed tactics, Sulun didn't know whether to hope the guards would stay closeted with Entori for a brief while or a long one. Meanwhile, he pored through his notes one more time.

The guards' interview proved to be a short one, and they came out together looking bored. A good sign, Sulun dared hope. The door remained shut for a few moments more; then the small bell sounded from beyond it, summoning the next in line. Sulun drew a deep breath, pushed on the heavy door, and entered.

Entori sat at his littered table, just as Sulun had seen him first, save that he wore a different dark, heavy robe. He raised his eyes from his pen and freshly marked ledger to acknowledge his latest servant and demanded, simply: "Well?"

Sulun bowed formally, lifted the first of his tablets, and began. "Tools for workshop: nearly assembled save for forge-bellows, estimated at five coppers; double-span tongs, estimated seven coppers; twenty-weight of brazing flux, eight coppers two irons . . ." Sulun carefully made his voice a soothing drone, the reading of the list reminiscent of a prayer-chant.

Entori began fidgeting with his pen, but his eyelids refused to droop.

No, best not to ask for too much new iron today.

Sulun switched to the second tablet. "Now, concerning the first try at a full-sized engine, a small cargo vessel should be used. No sense buying more brass than we need before we've determined the proper ratios and balances . . ."

"I can obtain the loan of a fifty-tonner," Entori cut in.

"Hmmm, so . . . It will not be necessary to take the ship out of service at once, not until we have the engine ready for testing. We need only measure and chart the ship before then, which may be done in a few days. We shall need carpenters to assemble the paddle wheels also. I have here the design, with tentative measurements that can be revised after we've inspected the ship." Sulun handed over another tablet. "We assume that building the engine shall require some five tons of brass, at—"

"Five tons?" Entori sat up, jowls darkening.

"Er, one tenth the weight of the ship, we presume." Sulun managed to keep his voice calm, philosophical, unruffled, despite the sweat gathering on his back. "Sure no more than that, possibly less, but we must be sure—"

"Five *tons!*" Glowering, Entori pulled a short whip up from his lap.

"Master," Sulun bowed low, shivering. "This engine uses forces of great power, and we must take great care to contain them. Better to make the parts too strong than too weak, lest they break—disastrously."

"But five tons?" Entori fingered the thongs of the whip.

"In the event that lesser weight is required, the excess brass will, of course, be applied to the building of the next engine. If Master has any brass already in store, naturally that could be used first."

"Not five tons."

A muffled sneeze sounded nearby.

Entori gave Sulun a sudden, hard look. The two of them were quite alone in the room, and neither of them had sneezed.

"Damned sneaking servants!" Entori sputtered, clambering to his feet. He came fast around the table, giving Sulun barely time to jump out of his way, ran to the door, and threw it wide.

No one stood there but Omis and the rest of the line, looking puzzled, a respectable ten paces away. Entori glared at them. "The lout must sneeze as loud as an elephant," he muttered, settling into his heavy chair.

Sulun said nothing, but thought much. Omis, he knew, did not sneeze as loud as an elephant. Neither had the sneeze come from beyond the door. He could have sworn the sound came from somewhere toward the left wall, where nothing stood but stacks of parchment-laden shelving.

"Enough of this," Entori grumbled, reaching for his pen. "Just leave me your lists there, and get on with work."

Sulun bowed again, set his pile on the least littered corner of the table, and bowed his way out, closing the door behind him.

Omis tossed him an enquiring look as he passed, but all Sulun could give him was a shrug. He paced carefully down the corridor, trying to measure the walls. There had to be a room on the other side of Entori's study, but who would be in there at this time of day? And why? And why so close to the wall that a sneeze might be heard right through it?

An intriguing mystery, that sneeze. What a pity he had really no time to solve it.

Omis with his mercifully short list of requirements, had better luck with the Old Man; Entori curtly gave him leave to use the canvas in stores to make his workshop pavilion, as well as all the charcoal he could find.

The little company was just putting up the canvas when Arizun came scampering up with a short note from Zeren. Sulun read it quickly, stuck it in his robe without comment, and went on with the business at hand.

At lunch hour he warned the others to keep to the courtyard, retraced his way through the house, and headed out the front door. The ancient porter demanded to know why he was leaving, where he was going, for how long, and had the Master been informed? Sulun restrained his annoyance, remembering that the porter really bore him no ill-will and was most probably just following the Old Man's orders.

"I'm off to the coppersmiths' street," Sulun replied pleasantly, "to consult with some smiths there about present prices and qualities of brass. I'll return at the end of the lunch hour, and you can inform the Mistress for me."

"Oh, the Mistress?" the porter cackled. "Aye, I'll tell her and none other, right enough. Heh-heh!"

Sulun shook his head and walked out the door. The whole house appeared to run on petty intrigue. Where did the Mistress fit in?

He did not, of course, go to the market. A few minutes' walk brought him to Zeren's house, where the housekeeper let him in and took him at once to the small dining room. A small meal waited there, and so did Zeren, who had already started on the white wine. He had loosened his working armor, dumped his swordbelt unceremoniously on the floor, and looked distinctly morose.

"Welcome, friend philosopher," he greeted Sulun with a raised cup. "Come, honor my humble table, and we'll trade sad stories. How are you and yours faring in House Entori?"

"Gods!" Sulun dropped into the empty chair and reached for the wine. "It's unbelievable." He gulped down half the cup before he caught himself.

Zeren laughed coldly. "You knew the man was a miser when you went to him. I told you I could do no better for you."

"I know, and rest assured I'm utterly grateful." Sulun set down his cup and dug into the dish of olives. "What I didn't know, couldn't have expected, was how terribly the man's stinginess warps the character of his entire household. One simply can't live there without resorting to theft and intrigue. Oh, let me tell you—"

"In detail," Zeren murmured, pouring himself another cup.

Sulun told, in detail, at length, until the food was gone. Zeren listened quietly, eyes wandering to distances again, until his guest ran out of words.

"So," he said finally, "how long, think you, before you can finish the Bombard Project?"

Sulun stared at him for a moment. "I haven't even mentioned it to him yet. Good gods all, I daren't suggest a new project before the Old Man's seen some profit from this one, and the gods alone know when that will be. Perhaps if you come visit him with more suggestions he'll show interest, but otherwise—"

Zeren heaved a sigh that seemed to come all the way from his boots. "My dearest philosopher friend, I greatly doubt that I could play the same trick twice with Entori the Miser. Quite right, he'll make no new speculation until he's seen profit from this one. Give him his wretched engine soon, I pray you. Soon."

Sulun ran his fingers through his hair. "But there's so much I don't know. I'm only guessing at the proper size for a ship's engine. I've some idea how to keep the steam flow steady, but how can the engine be started and stopped on command? Or reversed? How much fuel will it need? How long to heat enough water? How should it be attached to the ship? How to keep the fire pot from scorching the deck? I should experiment with the model first. . . . Oh, it may take years to learn everything!"

"And the bombard?"

"Friend commander, unless I can steal the money supplies out from under Entori's nose, I have no idea when we can build a workable bombard."

Zeren rubbed his eyes hard, then took a deep breath and sagged back in his chair. Sulun saw that the man's eyes were red. With an oddly slow sense of shock, he realized that Zeren was either very morosely drunk—at noon, on a working day—or else that he was fighting back tears.

"Sulun, my beloved philosopher." His voice was perfectly calm and level. "You have less than a year, perhaps only half that, to bring me a reliable bombard and the skills to make more. After that, nothing will matter. Nothing."

Sulun shivered, and felt obliged to whisper. "Why?"

"Because I've read the latest reports from the frontier patrol officers. Because I know what they foretell, even if the emperor himself can't. Because I've seen this happen before, and before, and before—"

"What?" Sulun snapped, hoping to the gods that Zeren was only drunk.

"Another fall." Zeren fixed him with perfectly sober eyes. "What remains of Jarrya is being overrun. Within less than a moonspan, the Ancar will be at Sabis's northern borders. With what army and supplies Sabis has now, we can last no longer than a year."

"A year?" Sulun set his cup down on the table, very slowly, as if it were made of thin glass instead of good, sturdy bronze. He knew Zeren—his skill and wit and knowledge—too well to doubt this. The unbelievable could happen. Sabis could be invaded.

The queen of cities could burn. He must make himself think about this, try to understand it, believe it.

"No more than a year," Zeren repeated. "Unless the gods open the sky and grant us a miracle. Or unless you give us a weapon that can stop an uncountable invading horde. The bombard. Do you understand?"

"Gods!" Sulun gripped a double handful of his wiry hair and tugged hard enough to hurt. "How? How, when I have to sneak every copper piece past this wretched miser? Tell me how!"

"Steal," said Zeren. "Cheat. Intrigue. Find another patron in secret. I wish to all the heavens and hells that I could do it for you, but none of the nobles, not even the City Guard Commander, will listen to me. Be as ruthless as you must, Sulun, for worse is coming. Worse than you or I or even Entori could ever be. I know. I've seen it. So many times over—"

"Gods, I must . . ." Sulun scrambled away from the table. "Must go back, before I'm missed. I'll find a way. Less than a year, perhaps only half . . . Gods!" He hurried to the door, too distracted for proper farewells, mumbling to himself about sulfur and saltpeter.

Zeren watched him go, then turned to study his almost empty winecup. "Vozai, my patron god," he murmured. "Why are wise men enslaved to fools? Why do the fates of a hundred thousand innocents rest upon one wretched servant? Why do you play such insane games with us?"

The cup didn't answer.

Zeren sighed, and drained it.

"Not enough." Omis sighed, peering again at the figures on the wax tablet. "I can get the iron, tomorrow maybe, but this just isn't enough for the flux and the firepowder ingredients."

"I know, I know," Sulun groaned, tugging absently at his hair. "And before you ask: no, there's no point asking Master Entori to take on the Bombard Project openly. I've tried hinting delicately, tried asking the other servants for advice, and no luck to it anywhere. He's a little man with big fears and big resentments; he hired us to do one project for him, and he won't take risks on anything else. No money for anything more, not until he sees some profits on the engine."

"We could always make haste slowly. I won't have the new

iron for a few days anyway. We could put off getting the flux until next moon, then—"

"No, no time!" Sulun ran his gaze around the room as if looking for omens in the cracked plaster. "The bombard can't wait. We *must* start it as soon as possible. There must be more money, some way—"

"I know of one." Vari leaned over to trim the oil lamp, almost catching her long untied braids in the guttering flame. "The Mistress."

"Eloti?" Sulun sat up, pulling back his ragged sleeves. "How could she help? And why?"

Vari peered out the door, making certain they weren't overheard, before answering. "I've heard she has some money of her own, often funds quiet little projects of her own, without Entori's knowledge. It's a legend among the servants. The difficulty lies in persuading her, and it's said to be worth one's neck to try and fail."

"Worth all our necks anyway," Sulun muttered. Then aloud: "How do I approach her?"

"She takes evening promenades alone in the courtyard, every night. But, Sulun—"

"Every night? Would she be there now?"

"Why, yes. But Sulun, why the haste? This is dangerous!"

"Everything is dangerous now." Sulun stood up, straightened his robe, and made a quick study of his appearance in the mirror. "Third courtyard, you said?"

"Yes." Vari stepped back, watching him. "But are you so sure you can persuade her?"

"Of course." Sulun marched determinedly to the door, and out, and off down the corridor.

Behind him, Omis and Vari stared at each other in dismay.

"What," Omis asked feebly, "has got into the man? Does he realize what he's risking?"

"Something's frightened him," Vari concluded, "Frightened him too much to reveal it to us. And that, love, frightens *me*."

The third courtyard was small and swept clean, containing only a small central fountain and narrow rows of herb beds, circled with a cobbled path. In the lights of the sickle moon the surrounding walls and path and fountain shone dull white, the herb beds and pooled water and shadows dead-black. Eloti in her dark dress was likewise a sketch in faint white and black, passing almost automatically around and around the pool, eyes distant and expression blank.

She could almost be a sleepwalker, Sulun considered, watching from an archway. Best to approach with dignified slowness, let her see him as soon as possible, give her time to travel back from her unguessed mental distance. He waited until her round brought her almost facing him, then stepped out into the open air.

She saw, and stopped, and awaited his approach with no change of expression.

Courage, Sulun reminded himself. "Lady," he began quietly, "may I walk with you?"

"Why do you disturb my evening walk?" she asked calmly, the faintest ghost of a frown creasing the inner edge of one eyebrow.

"I mean no disturbance, Lady Entori. I've come to bring an urgent warning to your ears alone."

"Walk with me, then." The ghost-frown vanished. Eloti resumed her stately pace about the fountain, allowing Sulun to match her stride. "What warning, sir?"

Sulun drew a deep breath. "Within five days, Lady, news will come that the north riverlands have fallen to the barbarians. Sabis will be shaken to its rooftops, trade will be shaken also, and I have no doubt that many of the wealthier families will begin fleeing south across the straits."

Eloti did not so much as slow her steps. "So? And is there any more?"

"Indeed there is." Sulun marveled at her composure. "The Ancar will sweep down the river valley and take Sabis within the year, unless some great change comes to halt them."

Eloti flicked her vision toward the sky, then back to her path. "You are telling me only that the sun will rise tomorrow," she said, "and set, also."

"And set indeed," Sulun murmured, watching her. "Do you care nothing for these things? Would you wish to live in a city while it is sacked by the Ancar?"

Eloti paced on, implacable. "When life becomes insupportable, there is always the quick knife, the quiet poison." An ironic smile touched her lips, ever so faintly. "We all die. What changes?"

"Lady, given the chance, *I* could change this!"

Eloti stopped in midstep. "*You?*" A slight but distinct tone of interest tinged her voice.

"Yes, I could," Sulun gulped. "I know the means to make a weapon that could defeat the Ancar. Given the equipment to make it, the space to test it, I and my friends could make this weapon within . . . um, one moon's time. My Lord your brother, unfortunately, won't hear of this. He wants his ship engines, and will spare no coppers for anything else."

"Ah, so you come to me." Eloti resumed her pacing, a definite smile on her face now. "You want money."

"Yes, Lady," Sulun answered, unashamed. "Enough to pay the rent on our workshop by the river. Enough to buy the flux for Omis's iron. Enough to purchase the saltpeter, sulfur, and charcoal for the powder. Enough for the leather canisters of shot. Not cheap, Lady, I admit—but less costly than the quick knife or the quiet poison, I daresay."

Eloti actually laughed, a low and quiet sound. "You intrigue me, sir, I admit. Yet I've seen that you're honest enough."

"I've no time for anything less, not knowing what I know. I've no wish to endure the fall of the city."

"Nor I, actually." She glanced once at the silver moon. "I've wagered before, the gods know, and for poorer stakes. I shall give you my answer tomorrow."

"Thank you, Lady."

"You may g—Htcha!" she sneezed.

Sulun, already backing away, suddenly remembered where he'd heard that exact sneeze before. He turned and hurried off through the archway, mind rolling with possibilities.

In the morning, after a mercifully brief report of purchases to the master of the house, Sulun chivvied his crew to work with a ferocity that was rare for him. They assembled a small procession of carts and went down to the smeltery to fetch Omis's iron and Sulun's brass, headed home by the emptiest road, and managed to get the whole shipment into the courtyard by lunchtime. Vari was waiting for them there, holding something wrapped in a napkin, looking thoughtful.

"Here." She handed Sulun the bundle. "Mistress came up to me while I was at the scrubbing, handed this to me as quiet as you please, says to bring it to you quietly, and adds that she'll want an accounting later. I haven't dared look. Sulun, what have you gone and done?"

Sulun said nothing until he'd unwrapped the napkin, opened the small drawstring bag he found there, and looked inside. Sunlight caught on the edges of wide gold coins. He stared blankly for a moment, then pulled the bag shut and stuffed it quickly into his robe.

"I've managed to persuade the Mistress," he said, feeling the smile stretch across his face. "How soon can we have those carts ready to go again?"

"An hour! An hour!" Doshi wailed. "Let the poor beasts have their meal—and us, too."

"An hour, then," Sulun agreed, "But no more."

The afternoon passed in purchases of odd minerals and tallows and odd cuts of leather, plus a side trip by Arizun and Yanados to pay the rent on the riverside shop. On all but the latter, Sulun dickered fast and furiously, and kept careful track of the money spent. Not so much as a copper piece went to anything outside the Bombard Project, though Sulun did yield to pressure from Arizun and Doshi and bought some cut-rate sheets of parchment for diagrams. They came dragging the carts home barely in time to unload, no time to wash and dress before supper. They looked a tired and well-worked group at the table, and more than once Sulun caught Mistress Eloti giving him and his crew appraising looks. She must guess, he considered, that they were giving her full value for her money.

After-dinner conversation at the servants' table was unduly full of comments on their industry and devotion to their tasks. Aobi went so far as to growl at them: "Don't work so blazing hard, you lads; you'll make us all look lazy, and the old goat will take it out of our hides."

"It'll go slow after this," Omis predicted, thinking of the days of forging and hammering ahead of him.

"Entirely too slow," Sulun muttered, imaging the gods' hourglass hanging, invisible, over Sabis.

Vari and the apprentices exchanged worried glances, and excused themselves early from the party.

✧ CHAPTER TEN ✧

"Enough of that." Entori cut off Sulun's droning report of items bought and progress made, shuffled through a teetering pile of waxed tablets, pulled one out, and shoved it across the desk. "The fifty-tonner *Yanira* sits at fourth dock south, unloading this morning. Here are the directions." He handed over a scrap of folded and sealed parchment as well. "Here is my note to the captain. Take as many of your . . . scholars as you need, and go make your measurements."

"I beg pardon?" Sulun fumbled, caught off balance by the change of subject.

"The ship you wanted," Entori snapped, impatient. "Go measure it for your engine. It's docked and idle for the day."

"Oh. Yes, of course. Today."

"You have until evening, when she'll be loading again. I trust the time will be sufficient."

"Er, yes, Master. It should be." Sulun ran his eyes once more over the wall behind Entori, wondering where the spy hole was and if it was occupied.

"Then go to it, and don't waste time. Next!" Entori rang the small bell on his desk and turned his attention back to his pile of parchments.

Sulun backed away, bowed, turned, and went out, almost colliding with the three house guards on their way in. He hurried back to the workshop-courtyard, wondering when, if ever, he'd have time to explore the house thoroughly and discover just where the spy hole was hidden. Not that it really mattered; the lady was his ally, for the moment at least.

Omis already had the forge lit and working, with Doshi

pumping the bellows and Ziya shovelling in the woods. "Gods!"
he wailed at the news. "I can't go now! I'm about to start the first
heat, and the forge is nearly ready."

"And no doubt you'll need Doshi and Ziya," Sulun added.
"Don't trouble yourself, then. I'll take the others. Where are they?"

"Back courtyard, hitching up the donkey cart. They've already
heard the news."

"What? How?"

"By being earlier in the morning line than you, lay-a-bed."
Omis grinned without looking up. "Ziya, hand me that first iron
billet."

Sulun shook his head, and went off to fetch his measuring
tapes.

A sea gull creaked and wheeled overhead, throwing its shadow
across the deck. Sulun eyed it warily; he'd been splattered once
already by the pesky birds, much to the amusement of the two
sailors idly guarding the ship.

"Twenty cubits, two spans," Arizun duly reported from the
other end of the tape.

Sulun scribbled the figures on his tablet, and took his foot off
the near end of the tape. "Roll it up," he said, searching down the
column of notes to see if any were left unfilled. None were. "I
believe we've finished."

Arizun and Yanados gave sparse cheers and began stuffing the
tapes and instruments back into their basket. Sulun stuffed the
tablet in his bag beside the others, tried once more to pinch the
pervasive stink of tar and rotting fish out of his nose, and headed
gratefully for the gangplank. The others caught up to him at the
donkey cart.

"It isn't going to work," Yanados whispered in his ear.

Sulun started to turn, then caught himself. The sailors, or
anyone, might be watching. "Why not?" he asked, just as quietly.

"Look at the whole length of the ship. Look at the length of
the boom and the sweep of the tiller. How much space lies
between them?"

Sulun looked, for the first time that day seeing the little ship as
a complete unit. A good, low, wide design, he thought: sleek
enough for speed, but stable in the water. A well-set long boom,
and the tiller's sweep— "Oh." He saw it. "Maybe five cubits," he

said, sighing. "No room for the engine. Very well, the sweep and boom will have to be shortened." But how many cubits? He measured it with his eyes, trying to guess at the right size for the engine.

"Another problem." Yanados pulled out a tablet of her own, showing the basic sketch of the ship mounted with its two side-set paddle wheels. "Were you planning to run the axle straight across the deck?"

Sulun was about to say, "Of course, and why not?" but stopped, reconsidering.

"Yes," Yanados caught the unspoken words. "How would the sailors get past it?"

"So be it!" Sulun flapped his hands in resignation. "The axle and engine should be mounted under the top deck, on that second level, the . . . uh . . ."

"Captain's quarters, crew's quarters, and ship's stores?"

Sulun tugged at his hair, briefly wondering if he saw a few grey threads in it. "It shouldn't take that much room. Hmm, put the supply room behind it, under that last hatchway. A bit inconvenient, but workable."

"True. Now we come to a tougher nut to crack. Sulun, once the engine begins spinning, how can it be stopped quickly? Or made to run backward?"

"Why . . . It can't."

Yanados rolled her eyes skyward. "Then we must devise a way to disengage the engine from the paddle wheels, even turn it around and reengage, and that, speedily. Otherwise, once started, the ship can neither stop nor maneuver."

"Oh." Sulun gave her a sidewise glance. "Forgive me, but I don't believe I've ever so much as set foot on a ship before."

Yanados shrugged and looked away.

Arizun, who'd been impatiently holding the donkey's bridle, asked if they intended to stand there until dinnertime. The other two turned and climbed into the cart quickly, without speaking. Arizun scrambled up beside them, took the reins and fly whip, and chivvied the donkey into a slow but steady walk home.

The other two didn't speak for most of the ride, and Arizun, guessing that something was wrong, didn't prod them for conversation. Halfway past the market, though, Sulun drew out his last unmarked tablet and began sketching a new design.

✧   ✧   ✧

"This isn't what you showed me before." Entori frowned across his table in the dim light. "What are all these complications?"

And how much will they cost? Sulun finished for him. "What I showed you earlier, Master, was a simple illustration of how the engine works. This is the full and complete version, designed to fit the needs of the ship. The finished version is always more complicated than the basic model, just as a painted portrait is more complex than the original sketch. Once we've completed a working model, we can demonstrate for you—"

"Designs! Models!" Entori shouted, his face turning purple. "Do you think I'm a fool to be misled by toys? Waste no more of my money on such playing! Make the engine for the ship, and that right quickly! Do you hear me, servant?"

Sulun only gaped at him.

"Do you hear me?" Entori bellowed.

"Er, of course, Master." It was the only safe thing Sulun could think to say.

"Then get out of my sight, and do it!" Entori lifted the bell's striker as if he might use it on Sulun's head.

Sulun bowed quickly, turned, and fled.

A faint sniff sounded behind the wall, but Entori, grumbling and shuffling parchment sheets, didn't hear it.

"Unbelievable." Omis put down his hammer and wiped his forehead. "You'll make the model anyway?"

"Of course." Sulun sat down on the nearest pile of iron billets and laced his shaky fingers together. "Yanados is carving the ship model right now, and Arizun's measuring out the drawings for the engine parts. We'll simply have to hide what we're doing, and make the usual excuses."

Ziya threw him an unfathomable look, but said nothing.

"Just how complex is the improved design?" Doshi asked.

"With the perpetual feeding assembly, it looks like a hoo-raw's nest," Sulun groaned. "I don't blame him for being perplexed by the drawing, but to think we can proceed without a model for testing . . . How can the man be such a fool? Is he mad?"

"He's probably never dealt with any sort of engine work before." Omis picked up another billet with the long tongs, and shoved it into the glowing heart of the forge. "He's used to haggling and debt collecting with tradesmen and creditors. It never entered his thoughts that metals are less pliable than men; they have no ears to hear threats or promises, no greed to entice, no minds to change. Therefore, smithing can't be hurried, nor engine crafting either."

"Metals have more honor than men," Ziya murmured, dumping more wood into the furnace.

Sulun hadn't the heart to even try answering.

"Enough wood, Ziya," Omis mercifully cut in. "Come here and tend the bellows awhile. That's a good lad. Doshi, put your gloves on and hold these tongs."

Sulun pulled himself to his feet and shambled off to his drawings. Best give Arizun some help finishing them. Time, time, not enough time: two projects to finish, one of them secret and one half secret, and all of Sabis was running out of time.

The bad news came to Sabis with a blare of trumpets in the early morning, a knot of troopers bringing back wagonloads of wounded at the north gate, and a horde of desperate refugees behind them. By noon the word was everywhere: the north had fallen. The riverhead lands were lost, including the last of Jarrya, and where would grain, wool, and mutton come from now? Prices jumped and bucked and jumped again like colts feeling the saddle for the first time.

At noon Arizun ran into the courtyard of Entori's house with a minimal bundle of purchases, a blanched face, and an earful of news. All the others clustered around him to hear it, repeat it, demand details. Yes, the north was gone. No, nobody knew when the Ancar would come down the river valley toward the city. Yes, there were refugees, many now and more coming, all of them desperately poor. Yes, there was talk of another draft in the city to raise troops for the fighting northward. No, nothing had been heard of the northern army except that it was in retreat. Yes, the docks were crowded with panicked Sabisans buying passage across the straits to Esha. No, he had no idea how this would affect Entori's business interests. . . .

It was Vari, looking back to keep track of the baby, who noticed that Sulun wasn't part of the goggling crowd. He was still sitting on the bench were they'd left him, ignoring his half-eaten bread and cheese, looking up at the sky as if hunting for omens. He looked not at all surprised. Vari watched, thought, then paced closer.

"You knew," she said quietly, "You knew it would happen. That's why you've been so strange and furious these past few days. How did you know?"

"From Zeren." Sulun dropped his glance back to the food in his hands, but didn't eat. "He guessed. He told me. We must complete the bombard soon, very soon, or there'll be no city to defend with it. Do you understand?"

Vari nodded, staring at him, then bit her lip and went quietly away to talk to Omis.

Dinner was tense and strange. The master didn't appear, and Eloti put in only a brief appearance. The number at the servants' table seemed smaller too, though it took Sulun a while to realize who was missing.

"Where," he asked the housekeeper, "have our three great watchmen gone?"

There was a moment's silence, and then everyone stated talking at once.

"They've run off, haven't you heard?" said the scullery maid. "What with all the refugees, the big houses fear thieves. There've been criers in the streets asking for trained house guards to come work up the hill, offering much better terms than the old vulture here does. That's where our three louts have gone, I can tell you."

" 'Tis the end of the world," the housekeeper gloomed. "The barbarians could come any day, breach the walls, rape and slaughter us in our beds."

"You've small need to fear that," the porter muttered.

"My spells will protect us," the house wizard mumbled into his cup.

"We'll starve first," the cook grumbled. "No food from the northlands, and there'll be less and less from the river valley as the Ancar come south. Nowhere to buy but from Esha across the water, and their prices are terrible."

"They can hardly feed their own people and us too," Arizun noted. "Best to cross the water, I think, and not stop in Mez, but keep on going."

That started everyone talking about flight, gathering up one's hoarded coppers and taking passage on the next boat. Sulun's party looked at each other and huddled closer, thinking much along the same lines. Sulun shook his head, disgusted at their naiveté.

"Do you think you'll be welcome in Esha?" he commented, mostly to his own people but loudly enough that the rest could hear him. "They've too many refugees already, and most of them starving. In Mez, I'll wager, you can find beggars in the streets and slaves on the block who were once rich folk here in Sabis. Go down the coast to Tari, and you might find the rich folk keeping out of the gutter—but what about poor folk like us? Hah! You'd have to run further than that. And how far will your copper bits take you? You'd do better to go inland, work for the farmers and herdsmen if they'll have you. Or go all the way to the towns at the Bay of Naydres—if you can speak the language, or learn it quickly. You might keep from starving thereby, but don't expect to ever be richer than you are in this house, right now."

He drained his cup and waited, wondering what the reaction would be.

After a moment's silence, the servants went back to discussing passage to Mez. As far as Sulun could tell, the only effect of his words was that some of the servants seriously considered how they would make a living in Esha, a land they'd never seen and knew little about.

Sulun pushed his plate aside, got up, and went out. After a moment's hesitation, the apprentices and Omis and family rose and followed him.

They clustered in Sulun's room, even the children, crowding it unbearably though no one complained. Omis asked first where they could realistically plan to go, if not Mez.

"Could we get as far as Tari?" Arizun asked, guessing that none of them could afford passage to the Naydres Bay cities.

"I doubt it," Doshi answered, consulting a scribbled wax board. "I'm guessing that anyone in the south with so much as a donkey wagon to rent will be charging top prices, with so many refugees on the roads. There are, what, ten of us? Never. Perhaps we should go inland, find a farming town that needs us and our, uh, wares . . ." He shrugged, guessing as well as any of them that their particular wares commanded a poor market.

"Back to where we began when Shibari's house burned," Omis

groaned. "At least now we have our tools, but I'd need a wagon to carry my anvil."

"If you had the anvil, and the rest," Sulun pondered, "could you build another forge?"

"I could, but it would take a good moon and a half—besides paying some potter to fire the bricks. Have we the money for that?"

"If we could reach Sakar, our trade would be welcomed," Yanados put in.

"The problem is reaching Sakar," Arizun pointed out. "We haven't the money to hire a ship."

"South," Vari pronounced. "It's all we can reach. How we'd live after . . . Who knows the most about the southlands?"

Everyone looked at Arizun, who only shrugged. "Why ask me? I was only a baby when we left there. All I know is that my mother had reason to leave."

"Zeren," Sulun murmured, drawing their attention back. "Zeren fought there. He'd know."

"Well, by all the gods, ask him!" Omis snorted. "Ask him tomorrow."

"We will." Sulun straightened up, rubbing kinks out of his back. "Arizun, tomorrow take Yanados and some stout sticks in case of trouble, and carry a letter to Zeren's house. Meanwhile . . ." He looked at Omis. "How soon can we start moving our necessities to the riverside shop?"

✧ CHAPTER ELEVEN ✧

Zeren pondered the question long and hard, letting his gaze wander over the cracks in the ceiling. He looked, Sulun noted, worse than last time. "Nowhere in the south," he finally said. "Nowhere you could reach. Neither could you get safe passage to any of the isles. It's hopeless."

"There must be somewhere!" Sulun insisted. "And no, before you ask, I've not lost hope for the bombard. Given time, I can make it work. If not given time, I ask you, where can I take us to be safe?"

"Us?" Zeren looked at the little gathering clustered in his dining room. "You've never considered going your separate ways?"

"No," said Omis, Sulun, and Vari together.

Vari added, "How would we take care of the children?"

"So it comes to that." Zeren looked at all of them for a long moment. "You may be right, you know. As a family, most especially a family of tradesmen, you could live better than any single man alone—if you could once find a place beyond the reach of the war."

"Where?" Sulun insisted. "Name a place."

Zeren leaned forward, rested his elbows on the table and his chin in his hands. "Behind the lines," he answered. "Could you once get past the army of the Ancar, find a place where they've long since passed, you'd be left alone. Doshi—"

The youth flinched, sat up. "Yes?"

"You know the northlands. Behind the Ancars' lines, what's the land like? What sort of folk live there?"

"Farmers, as I remember." Doshi scratched his arm nervously, unused to being asked for advice. "There were villages, small villas, all over that land before the invaders came. I don't know what's there now."

"I doubt that the Ancar destroyed every village they found," Zeren considered, "or that they found all of them. There's my advice, friends, for whatever good it may do. Go become the blacksmiths and brass smiths of some town behind the Ancars' march—and the further behind, the better. Go up beyond the Gol, if you can, and if you can abide the northern winters. Ah, hell, if Sabis falls, I might even come with you." He poured himself some more wine, seeming in a much better humor.

The others looked at each other, wondering if that was a joke.

Yanados paced back and forth along the worktable, studying the engine model as Sulun assembled it, frowning and muttering to herself until Sulun couldn't ignore her anymore.

"Did you have some complaint?" he asked, setting his tools aside.

"I was thinking . . ." Yanados shuffled from foot to foot. "If such a ship were to meet with pirates, well . . . pirates hire magicians too, you know, to ill-wish their victims."

Sulun shrugged. That made sense, but he couldn't see the relevance.

"Sulun, if a full-sized engine of this sort were ill-wished, what could it do wrong?"

"I don't know," Sulun admitted, peering at his model. "The valves might fail, perhaps. We'll have to make them strong. . . ."

"What else?" Yanados tapped a finger against the tiny boiler tube set over its miniature brazier. "Fire and water, and the fierce pressure-power of steam. Could it . . . explode?"

Sulun dutifully thought about that, thought of the water poured down the funnel, through the trapdoor valve, into the heated brass tube above the brazier, then through the hollowed—and moving—ball-and-socket joint, then into the spinning chamber. What weakness? Where?

The heating tube? Too little water, too little steam, and the jetted chamber wouldn't spin. Too much water would cool the tube, make too little steam, and again the chamber wouldn't spin. Fill the brazier too scantily and you'd have not enough heat; again, no steam, no spinning. Fill it too full, let the flames or even the coals overlap the tube . . .

"The tube might soften, melt, warp," he admitted, "but that would require so much heat, so much wood—"

"Believe me, if it can be done wrong, some fool sailor will do it. It will not be Natural Philosophers who use this engine at sea."

"True, true . . ." Sulun studied the assembly for a long moment, then abruptly smiled. There was indeed one simple way to keep some fool of a sailor from overloading the brazier. He reached for the metal snips.

"What are you doing with the brazier?" Yanados asked, peeping over his shoulder.

"Making it smaller and shorter," Sulun smiled, plying the heavy shears.

Snip, snip, snip—and the brazier's legs were shortened. Snap, snap, snap—and the bowl of the brazier lost its original rim. Sulun carefully tucked the little model back to its place in the assembly. He scratched some notes on a nearby tablet.

"What would that do?" Yanados asked.

"Small brazier, small fire," Sulun explained. "Load the brazier full as you can, the coals still won't reach the tube and melt it. Hmmm, it wouldn't hurt to make the tube thicker, too. . . ." He scribbled more notes.

"Just be certain no fool can work it wrong," said Yanados, padding toward the door.

Not until after she was gone did Sulun think to wonder how she knew so much about the habits and failings of sailors.

The moon wore away her horns, and nothing improved. Morning reports with Entori grew ever more difficult and unpredictable; his shipping interests did marvelously well on the short Sabis-Mez run, carrying refugees south and food north, but elsewhere on the Inland Sea the trade was dangerous and the old man's temper likewise. Always he exhorted Sulun to hurry with the engine.

At least, Sulun told himself after leaving the master's study in a shower of abuse, the engine model was finished. It worked after a fashion; the tiny valves clearly weren't very efficient, but the rotating platform and gears managed well enough. No sense putting it off; he should begin making the full-sized engine for Entori's ship, as he'd promised.

That meant that Omis would have to put aside work on the bombard to cast and shape the brass fittings for the engine.

"Ah, well," Sulun consoled himself as he entered the courtyard, "It shouldn't take more than a day or two. . . ."

He noticed, as he walked past the end of the morning-report line, that one of the maids was missing.

"Ran away," snorted the housekeeper, when asked. "That lazy slut must have had a better offer from some uphill house. Didn't leave word, either; just out the door and gone."

"Went out shopping yesterday," the porter said, "and never came back."

Sulun left them arguing and went off to see Omis, but the permanent unease in the back of his mind grew another degree thicker. It would be wise, he decided, to start moving as much gear as possible to the river workshop. Starting today.

"The heat's awful," Doshi grumbled, slapping the reins irritably across the lagging mules' rumps. "Only fools go hauling loads about at noon."

"Only fools go out without guards at any other time," Arizun snapped, casting a quick look around the almost empty street. "You haven't seen much of the city since the bad times came, have you?"

"Oh, I know there are more thieves and beggars about, but good gods, there are three of us. And we're armed." Doshi tapped his toes on the hatchet hidden under the cart's seat. "And we're not on foot. No need for this."

"Wagoners have been robbed before, and you should keep that closer to hand." Arizun tapped the bulge at his belt under his light cloak. "And three of us wouldn't be enough against a good-sized gang."

"Keep your voices soft," Yanados warned from her perch at the back of the cart. "Don't draw any more attention than we must."

"You've both gone mad with suspicion," Doshi scoffed, in a near whisper. "That or gone silly for the ungodly fun of carrying weapons about. I swear, you're turning barbarous yourselves. Nobody goes armed unless they're looking for trouble—"

"Or expecting it to look for them," Arizun growled. "Keep your eyes on the street, fool."

"Be careful who you call a fool," Doshi muttered, steering the mule team around a corner. "You haven't read half the books—now, what's this mess?"

Several buildings down, the street was half blocked with a tumble of broken furniture and assorted garbage. A man on foot could have passed it, but the mule cart would have considerable trouble.

Arizun saw it, gasped, seized the reins from Doshi, and yanked the mules to a hoof-clattering halt. "Back up!" he hissed. "Back the way we came, fast!"

"What—"

"Damnation!" Yanados yelled, making them both turn and look, as she yanked her hatchet free.

Behind them, perhaps half a dozen ragged bravos—some of them quite young, a few older men—slid out of the doorways to block the street. They carried assorted bludgeons and short knives. They stalked toward the halted cart, smiling grimly, not even bothering to give the traditional stand-and-deliver challenge.

"Back up!" Arizun repeated, shoving the reins at Doshi. Then he scrambled into the back of the cart and fumbled at something under the sacks.

Yanados hissed through her teeth, crouched at the cart's tail, and swung her hatchet in a slow, warning arc. The approaching gang slowed and spread out, still smiling.

Doshi might have argued about backing into a fight, but just then his eye caught motion near the trash pile ahead. Three more club-wielding boys were slinking out of cover, coming toward the mules. Doshi gulped, wasted a precious second fumbling for the hatchet under the seat, and began hauling furiously on the mules' reins. The mules, finally understanding that there was danger ahead, squealed and backed. The toughs ahead moved faster, starting to run.

The six thugs behind the cart stopped where they were, crouched, waiting for the prey to come to them, waited to jump for the tailgate.

Yanados reached out and swung at the nearest, making him hop backward. He recovered and tried to lunge in under her arm, but she caught him backhand on the return stroke. The back of the hatchet head thwacked meatily against his head, dropping him to the ground with a shocked yell and a sudden spurt of bright blood.

The other toughs yelled in outrage, and charged the cart.

Right then, Arizun came up from the cart bed with a short bow in one hand and an arrow in the other. He loaded, snap-aimed, and fired past Yanados, catching one of the boys high in the chest. The boy screeched, dropped his club and knife, stumbled to his knees, and began tugging at the arrow. The others skidded to a stop, unwilling to face arrows. Yanados whooped and swung her hatchet at the nearest, making him dance away.

The thugs ahead of the wagon ran toward the mules, the nearest reaching for the bridles. Doshi, guessing what they meant to do, hauled furiously on the reins, shouting incoherently at the mules. The frightened beasts reared, braying, flailing the air with their hooves, making the attackers scramble out of the way. Doshi used the instant's respite to clutch the reins in one hand and fumble under the seat for the cart-whip with the other.

Arizun aimed and loosed another arrow, this one gouging a path across a half-turned man's ribs and finally lodging itself in his arm. The man howled and jumped away, dropping his knife and club.

The mules dropped back to all fours, and two of the young toughs lunged for their reins. Doshi came up with the whip and lashed out at the nearer, catching him squarely across the face. The thug screamed and stumbled to his knees, pawing at his face, but the other two jumped past him to grab at the mules.

One of the mules reared again, lashing out with its with its hooves and catching one boy with a resounding thump in the belly. The other mule snapped, but missed. The remaining tough grabbed the bridle and hauled the mule's head down, hefted his club, and thwacked the mule about the ears. Doshi snapped out the whip and welted the boy's clubbing arm, making him drop the bludgeon and duck down below the mule's chest, but not shaking him loose. Doshi flailed again with the whip and yelled for help.

Arizun loosed another arrow, puncturing a man's leg. The other two, seeing the odds change drastically, turned and ran. The wounded man limped after them, cursing.

"Back up!" Yanados shouted. "We're clear, Doshi. Back up!"

"I can't!" Doshi yelled, pointing.

Arizun turned around, aimed carefully, and fired. The arrow whizzed past Doshi's ear, through the tangle of reins and harness, and buried itself in the attacker's forearm. The youth screeched and let go of the reins.

Doshi was too frozen to react, but the mules, kicking and braying in outrage, backed up of their own accord. The attacking tough, exposed now, turned and ran.

Arizun, swearing, dropped the bow, clambered back into the seat, grabbed the reins, and pulled the mules further back. A dozen paces and they were at the mouth of the crossing street. Arizun hauled the mules' heads toward the turn, slapped the reins on their rumps, and let them go. The beasts, willing enough, turned and scrambled into the open, empty road.

"No pursuit," Yanados announced from the tail of the cart.

"We'll try again at the second street over," Arizun decided. "It's a good bit wider, no room for traps."

"You had a bow," Doshi squeaked.

"I always do, these days. Lucky thing, eh?"

"You could have shot me!"

"Nonsense, I went right past you. Don't you think I know how to shoot?"

"It's unlawful to carry bows in the public streets!"

"It's unlawful to rob folk, too. Does the law prevent robbers? Hey, pull to the right here; there's our street."

"Is there any blood on me?" Yanados asked, wiping her hatchet clean on some sacking. "And nice shooting, Ari."

Doshi bit his lip and reined the mules toward the turn.

"It might not be that bad everywhere," Sulun considered, remembering his old teacher's endless advice to see a problem from all sides. "This was down toward the river, in a poor section."

"Not that close to the river, not that poor a neighborhood, and in broad light of noon," Yanados glowered, looking up from her long knife and sharpening-stone. "It's that bad, Sulun."

"Very well. We'll have to send out more people with every run to the old workshop. How much do we have there now?"

"Blankets, two changes of clothing, some dried fruit," Vari ticked off on her fingers, her shadow dancing on the yellowed wall behind her. "Sulfur, charcoal, some spare tools (Arizun would know which), some medicinal herbs (not enough), three kitchen knives, four short knives—"

"Not enough," Omis growled. "As soon as I've finished with these cursed brasses, I'll make long knives and arrowheads for the lot of you."

"It might be quicker to go and buy some," Arizun considered. "If enough of us go out together, we should get to the market and back safely."

"We can't spare the money," Sulun pointed out. "We'll just have to make more noon visits to the workshop. You left it closed up tight, I trust?"

"Oh yes," Doshi said, his voice still shaky. "Everything buried, locked, barricaded . . . Do you all intend to carry bows?"

"I can make enough for all of us." Yanados smiled, examining the edge of her knife.

"Was there any sign of tampering about the doors or windows?" Sulun asked.

"A little." Arizun sniffed. "Omis's good iron locks and hinges thwarted them. Hah."

"Well enough. Now supposing we don't have to flee, how much more time before we can get back to work on the bombard?"

"Another tenday, at least," Omis groaned. "All that damned brass, and the gears, and the driving-axle . . . and then the polishing and fitting and assembling . . . Gods, the engine model won't be ready until the end of the month."

Everyone looked at Sulun.

"Gods," he sighed, "What can I tell Zeren?"

Nobody had any suggestions.

"What's that shouting outside?" Ziya piped up, surprising everyone. "Is that robbers?"

Arizun dived for the narrow window, Yanados half a step behind him. "I don't know," he complained. "I can't see a thing from this side. It's toward the front of the house, in the street."

"Go and look then," Sulun ordered them impatiently. "To get on then, Omis, once the engine's complete and we've put it on Entori's damned ship—watch your feet!"

Arizun, Yanados, and Ziya ignored him in their rush for the door. They scurried out into the dim corridor, hugged the wall as they scampered through the darkened courtyard, and clung to the shadows of the main hall as they raced toward the stairs and the front windows. There they pulled up short, seeing two rows of the maids and the porter there ahead of them. Most of the front windows were taken, but the three apprentices managed to wriggle between the maids for a good view.

Shadows leaped in the street, thrown by torches set on top of a huge, box-shaped wagon. Guardsmen stood at the barred rear door of the wagon, and held the heads of the oxen drawing it. Still other guards hurried up the street, driving a knot of complaining men at spearpoint.

As the servants of Entori's darkened house watched, the guardsmen threw open the wagon door and pushed the wailing civilians inside. The door thudded shut, followed by the slam of a heavy bolt. Then came shouts, the clatter of boot heels, and a creaking and rumbling as the wagon rolled off down the shadowed street. The protesting wails of the men locked in the wagon took longest to fade from hearing.

"Why did they take all those men?" Ziya asked of anyone who could answer.

"Press gang," the porter spat. "They're snatching poor folk off the streets to join the army and fight the Ancar."

"We'd best not be seen abroad after dark," Yanados muttered, sliding down from the window. "Still, this might thin out the street robbers."

"Will our walls really keep them out?" Ziya asked.

Nobody answered.

"No sense in delay," Sulun announced, making a last critical inspection of the gear train. "Light the coals and let's pour the water."

"I still don't like the bedding of this axle," Omis muttered, giving the bearings a last squirt of greasenut oil.

"It turns, it turns! Come light the coals."

"All right." Omis poured a few drops of distilled wine spirits on the coals, lit the fumes with flint and steel, and stepped back to watch. The wine spirits burned with a brief blue flame and the coals caught, glowing at the edges first. Omis eyed the copper boiling-tube stretched above the brazier, tapped it to check its heat, then went to the upright funnel at the near end. "Give it another tick of the waterclock, then pour in the water," he decided. "Then, if the valves and tubing can withstand pressure enough to turn the jetwheel, and if the gears don't slip off the paddle wheels' axle, and if the paddle wheels aren't too heavy to turn, this fool thing just might work. Does the old vulture have the paddle wheels constructed yet?"

"Oh, yes." Sulun peered up and down the length of his contraption for the hundredth time, shaking his head over its bizarre shape: the turbine (more like an upright disk than its original globe shape) with its angled escape jets, the copper boiling-tube and brass steam-feed line with their carefully fitted valves and sockets, the short axle with its sturdy gearwheel waiting to engage, the fussy little forest of supports, the bolted-down brazier and the platform they all rested on. It looked utterly eccentric and ridiculous, but he knew it would work. This part of the assembly would, anyway. "He's been nagging me for days about the cost of keeping that expensive gear stored and idle."

"I just hope his carpenters got all the measurements right," Omis worried. "Proper fools we'll look if we get this set on the paddle wheel axle, take it all down to the ship, and the sockets in the deck don't fit."

"Then he can belabor the ship's carpenters, not us. Ah, I think it's warm enough. Pour in the water."

Omis shook his head, lifted the pitcher of water, and poured, carefully, into the upright funnel.

Both men took a few steps back, and waited.

Water gurgled down the funnel, through the first valve, and into the heated copper tube. There was an angry hiss, more gurgling, near-human belches as the steam tried and failed to escape back up the valve, then a faint groan of protest and a puff of steam from the turbine's jets.

Sulun and Omis held their breath and made assorted handsigns for luck. They had made all the parts to triple strength, but still . . .

Slowly, then faster, the turbine moved. It turned, rolled, spun, wreathed in a cloud of dissipating steam like a dimmed sun among roiling clouds. Its attached axle spun with it, and the final gearwheel too.

"It works!" Sulun whooped. "Praise all the gods I ever heard of, it works!"

"And the supports are holding! Look, they're not even shaking! We've done it!"

By the time their combined noise brought the apprentices running in to look, Sulun and Omis were dancing a clumsy version of the Vulgar Hop-Step around a workroom full of warm fog to the tune of the whining, spinning engine. Even Ziya cheered.

"Those sailors will have to cut extra portholes to let out all that steam," Doshi noted, but he was grinning all the same.

"Master, the engine is ready for installation." Sulun did his best to keep his face politely expressionless.

"Excellent." Entori almost smiled, then caught himself. "It took you long enough. Fortunately, the ship is in port at the moment. Do the fitting today, and tell me how well the ship performs. You are excused."

Sulun stifled a sigh, bowed, and went out. There was, he decided, no use expecting any further reaction from the Master.

He supposed he should be grateful for having a whole day to install and test the completed assembly.

"No, no! Great gods, we needed to place the engine first, then the paddle wheels!" Sulun tugged his hair and glared at the sullen ship carpenters. "Now we may have to reset that whole damned axle. Gods! Never mind. Omis, is that platform socket the right size, at least?"

" 'Tis. No trouble there." Omis peered once more at the ironbound hole in the second deck, shrugged, and stood up. "Bring up the muscle-boys, and let's get this thing mounted."

Sulun, still pulling nervously at his hair, stood back and let the assorted crew manhandle the engine's platform into place. Omis did all the directing, complete with howls for careful handling, and the platform settled onto its mounting with a satisfying thud. Omis rotated the platform this way and that, glared for a moment at the huge iron axle cutting across the cabin, frowned at the two iron gears set on it, and finally swung the platform around to meet the right-hand gear.

Sulun squeezed his eyes shut, not wanting to see the expected failure. Surely the axle would turn out to be set too high or too low, or the drive gear from the engine wouldn't meet the gear on the axle, or the gear sizes would be wrong, or the perverse things just wouldn't engage. The house wizard was an unreliable drunk, and who could tell what the ship's wizard was up to? He'd have to go back to Entori and report another delay.

"Deese of the Forge," Omis breathed. "The gears meet perfectly."

Sulun opened his eyes and stared. Sure enough, there stood Omis, smiling as if at his own children, studying the juncture of the two neatly meshed gears.

"So the ship can move forward, at least," Doshi commented at his shoulder. "Now, can it stop and move backward too?"

"No reason it shouldn't," said Omis. He gripped two of the handles at the edge of the platform, and pulled. The platform turned smoothly, pulling the drive gear away from the wheel axle, swung in a neat half-circle, and settled against the opposite axle gear with a smug click. "See? Works fine." Omis grinned. "I'll say this much for Entori's other workmen; they can follow instructions to the last number. And his various wizards aren't all bad."

"Gods be praised." Sulun wiped his forehead with his sleeve. "Now all we need do is light the coals, pour in the water, and see if this engine will actually drive the ship."

"No trouble there." Omis went to the open hatchway in the deck above and bellowed up through it. "Captain, prepare to cast off. We're about to test the engine."

Groans and curses of dismay echoed down with the sunlight, but Omis ignored them and turned away. "Who has the coals?" he bellowed to all and sundry. "And the bucket?"

Ziya waddled up, toting a dipper and a sloshing bucket nearly as big as she was. Behind her Arizun dragged a huge sack of coals. Yanados followed with the bottle of wine spirits and the flint and steel striker. They filled the brazier, poured on the spirits, lit the coals, and stood by with the water in a neat little ceremony that impressed the watching sailors.

"We're cast off," filtered down through the hatchway. "Are you ready?"

"Wait, wait," said Omis, turning the platform until the gears engaged exactly.

"Wait, wait . . ." said Sulun, watching the copper tube above the brazier. "Now. Pour."

Ziya solemnly lifted the ladle, but couldn't quite reach to the top of the funnel. Omis, smiling, took the ladle from her and poured the water himself.

The engine hissed, gurgled, and belched. The sailors took several respectful steps backward. The captain poked his head down through the open hatchway to watch the proceedings. The first plumes of steam curled out of the jets; the turbine muttered, groaned, began to turn.

Sulun chewed his lip nearly raw and crossed his fingers under the concealment of his sleeves. Had they made the boiling-tube thick enough, the turbine sturdy enough, the valves strong enough?

A faint groan came from the main axle, and a heavier gurgling of water from the unseen paddle wheels outside. Slowly, ponderously, the gear and axle and grumbling paddle wheels began to turn.

Mixed yells came from topside. The captain snatched his head back up through the hatchway. A massive thumping, as of heavy oars, sounded rhythmically through the hull.

The captain stuck his head down through the hatchway once more. "We're moving!" he yelled, as if he couldn't believe his eyes. "We're moving!"

Now they could all hear it: the steady thump of the paddles and the sloshing of water moving against the hull. The sailors swapped looks, then cheered. More cheers and yells sounded from topside, along with curses from the steersman and exhortations from the captain. The apprentices hugged each other and danced clumsily around the platform. The rolling turbine shot out steam until the whole engine cabin was fogged and hot. Omis poured another ladleful of water down the funnel and smiled at his sturdily laboring engine much as the gods must have smiled at the new made universe.

Sulun only rubbed his forehead and heaved a profound sigh of relief.

Cheap but colorful banners bearing the name and sigil of Entori's house hung about the dock. A sizable crowd had gathered, and paid criers could be heard to landward summoning still more. Assorted pushcart merchants, taking advantage of the ready audience, peddled their way through the crowd. At the end of the dock, in a small roped-off section, sat chairs and couches for a cluster of Entori's invited guests.

"A good-sized crowd, if not a terribly respectable one," Vari commented from her place by the rail of the ship's top deck. "But as good as our master could manage, I suppose."

"Good enough to spread the word of our success all over the

city," Omis considered, idly patting her hair. "Ah, here comes the old vulture now."

Sure enough: preceded by his porter, with his sister Eloti on his arm, followed by all the rest of his household, everyone dressed well for a change, Entori came strutting down the dock. The crowd stepped aside with no urging, murmuring in surprise; it had been many a long day since Entori the Miser had provided public entertainment for anyone. He paused at the end of the dock to make appropriate greetings and trade bits of conversation with the better class crowd assembled there, then gestured theatrically to the rest of his diminished household. The servants dutifully stopped where they were, taking respectful positions out of the guests' line of sight. Entori with a flourish of his heavy cape, escorted his expressionless sister up the gangplank and onto the ship. A handful of sailors dutifully played a short fanfare on the ship's pacing drum and signal trumpet. Entori took his sister to their waiting chairs on the afterdeck and, with another flourish, sat down.

"Not bad, but I've seen better shows," Arizun whispered to the other apprentices. Sulun shushed him.

The ship's captain, doubtless given the task for his loud if unlovely voice, bellowed a short speech to the audience. Sulun heard a dozen references to Master Entori and not one mention of himself or his crew, but only shrugged. It wasn't fame that interested him now. He peered over the railing as best he could, but couldn't see if Zeren was in the crowd.

Entori raised a hand, the sailors responded with another drumroll, and the rest of the crew cast off lines. The steersman took a grip on the tiller as if expecting to wrestle with it. Sulun could hear the gurgling and belching of the engine below; he wished he were close enough to the hatchway to sneak a quick look down into the engine cabin.

A creaking groan came from the paddle wheels, then a slurging of water as the wheels began to move. The crowd on the deck shouted in amazement. Entori for once beamed from ear to ear. It was not a pretty expression.

The wheels turned faster, bringing the paddles up dripping. Water slid under the keel, and the ship shuddered, then slid away from the dock. The steersman, looking martyred, leaned heavily on the sweep. The crowd on the dock howled in shock, wonder, delight; Entori the Miser had at last put on a real show for them, a marvel such as no one had ever seen before, a bit of history to tell their children and neighbors about. They cheered, stamped, applauded, and threw odd items of clothing and food into the air.

"I think our master will be pleased with his reception," said Doshi, wincing a little at the noise.

"Let's hope he's grateful, too," Sulun muttered, keeping a covert eye on Entori. He knew what today's schedule would be: a leisurely sail across the harbor, a brief circle through the calm sea beyond—enough to test the engine's speed and the ship's maneuverability—then back to the dock for a quick examination of the mounts, valves, gears, and bearings before going home to a victory dinner. Somewhere in that period he must catch Entori in a good mood and entice his permission to work fullspeed and fulltime on the Bombard Project.

Meanwhile, seeing that Entori had begun to relax, order wine, and enjoy the voyage, Sulun thought he and Omis should spend some time watching the operation of the engine. He signalled to the blacksmith and made his way unobtrusively down to the engine deck.

The engine's cabin resembled the steamroom at the public baths, making figures indistinct but carrying sound. Two burly sailors were arguing in the fog while Arizun danced around them, ignored by both, insisting that he would dip the water and load the coals, thank you, but they would have to rotate the platform. Another sailor stood by the porthole, dolefully wagging a palm frond fan, trying to drive out some of the steam.

"Who's oiling the gears?" Sulun shouted, cutting off the argument in mid-yell. "And who's watching the axles for vibration? This is supposed to be a test of the engine, and which of you fools is watching the *engine*?"

The sailors looked guilty. Arizun snickered. Sulun rolled his eyes, flapped his hands in desperation, and got busy with the observations. He made a point of explaining every detail to the sailors at considerable volume, in hope that they'd remember how to do this once the test was over and the ship back to regular work. It occurred to him that he should suggest to the captain that some reliable man be permanently assigned to tend the engine, someone capable of reading the descriptions, understanding the drawings, and making any necessary repairs.

He toyed with the idea of a whole guild of ship-engine tenders while he peered at gears, oiled moving parts, and noted water levels.

Soon enough came the captain's bellowed order to reverse course. Sulun pointed imperiously to the two sailors, then to the handles on the platform. "Pull," he commanded. "No, no, you fools! The other way! That's right. Now wait, wait until the axle stops turning. . . . There. Now pull it the rest of the way."

The sailors pulled, the platform turned, the gears engaged with a minimum of protest, and the big axle began turning the other way. Cheers came from above, mixed with wails of complaint from the steersman. The sailors in the engine cabin studied the spinning axle, gears, and the turbine with growing admiration. Arizun smirked as he dumped on more coals. Sulun, noting everyone's sodden clothes and hair, made a quick recommendation for oiling and waxing the decks and bulkheads, and got out of there.

Back on the main deck, he found reason to be grateful for his steambath. The sun was high, the weather burning hot, and everyone but the sailors was wilting visibly. Entori and his sister sat under a hastily erected awning, sipping cups of chilled wine. The others passed around an ewer of lukewarm beer. Sulun strolled quietly to the railing and watched the captain put the ship through its paces: backing straight, backing and turning, ordering full stop and then forward while timing with a small sandglass how long the changes took. The man seemed to familiarize himself quickly with the uses of the engine. Impressed, Sulun waved him a salute. The captain smiled, nodded acknowledgment, and went back to his tests. Best to talk to him later. Meanwhile, observe Entori and pick a good moment to talk to him.

Yanados stood near, eyes flicking over the working sailors but always coming back to the captain. Sulun edged close to her and quietly told her his idea of specialized engine-tending sailors. She nodded agreement, not taking her eyes off the captain.

"I'll talk to the captain, if you like," she offered. "I know the proper words sailors would use, and he'll listen to me. Best if you deal with our master."

Sulun agreed with the tactic, and eased his way toward Entori, studying his target. The man seemed to be in high good humor, actually smiling for a second or two, no doubt thinking of the profits to be made with such a ship as this. No better time than now. Sulun sidled closer.

"I would say the engine is a success, Master," he began.

"Hmm, yes," Entori agreed, barely glancing at Sulun.

Eloti gave them both an expressionless look, said nothing.

"I have another invention in mind," Sulun plunged, "which may be even more profitable. I could proceed using little more than the supplies we already have, and bring you results within another moon or less."

"Another invention?" Entori peered at him, face falling into that habitual look of suspicion. "What is it?"

Sulun took a deep breath. "A new weapon, one that could utterly rout the Ancar, even regain the lands Sabis has lost. The army would certainly pay well for such a thing, as one may guess. With your permission, Master, I will proceed—"

"Not now." Entori dismissed him with a wave of one hand. "The navy will pay well enough for these ship engines—after I've fitted my own ships with them. You will make more such engines."

"Er, these engines can be readily made, Master—by any good smiths in the city, now that we have the designs. You could hire other smiths to make the engines—far more and faster than my little work gang could do—while I work on the weapon. If you will permit—"

"None of that!" Entori snapped. "I'll not have every rude mechanic in the city knowing the secret of these engines, selling the knowledge to every shipper who asks. No, boy, the secret will remain in my house."

"Certainly, Master," Sulun gulped. "In that event, let us hire more workmen to make the engines—make many of them, and quickly—while I proceed with the weapon, likewise in secret. You'll have two fine devices to sell, and nobody else will—"

"What, more mouths to feed? And at such prices?" Entori purpled. "Your lot is expensive enough."

"But it would take us months to build another engine! The time lost—"

"My next ship sails the day after tomorrow, and will not return to port for two good moons. Take your measurements tomorrow and have the engine ready when she returns. Other than that, I see no call for haste—not enough to require hiring more help."

"The household has lost some servants," Eloti put in, surprising both of them. "For replacements, we could hire skilled mechanics from among these northern refugees. They should come cheaply enough, and grateful for a roof over their heads."

Sulun held his breath, giving Eloti a mute look of gratitude, while Entori thought that over.

"Not now," the miser decided. "Not until my next cargo comes in. Prices have been terrible lately, and too many of my debtors have fled south. Meanwhile, Sir Philosopher, go measure the next ship and work with what you have." He waved to a passing servant. "Hey boy, more wine. Ah, servants are all whores, whining and conniving to scrape up more pennies . . . Pour carefully, you dolt!"

Eloti gave Sulun a sad, resigned smile, and turned away.

Sulun bowed briefly and wandered back to the railing. Gods, he thought, but this was unbelievable. Greed aside, how could Entori not see the importance of the Ancar invasion? Press gangs snatched levies outside his door, and the man would not risk a few silvers to make weapons. Unbelievable.

And how would he break the news to the others?

Sulun tried, quietly and gently as possible, during the long, leisurely afternoon's voyage. The day was hot but pleasant and the ship performed splendidly, but Sulun's work gang could take no pleasure in it.

"Gods," Omis groaned, "back to sneaking and penny-pinching. How will I ever finish the bombard like this? How can we disguise the work under the old vulture's very nose? Could we move everything but the forge to the river workshop, think you? It would take several wagonloads, and the streets so unsafe . . ."

"I don't see that we have any other choice," Sulun commiserated. "The tools, and supplies . . . We'll need to go all together, or perhaps if we can get word to Zeren he can arrange to have patrols passing in the right places and times. Ah, but how would we get messages to him? Arizun alone wouldn't be safe . . . gods, I can't think. We need Yanados's wit. Where is she?"

But Yanados was nowhere to be found, either on the top deck or below with the engine. A discreet search of what areas Sulun and Omis could reach turned up no sign of Yanados—nor, Omis noticed first, the captain either. The two craftsmen considered those facts, looked at each other, and quietly went back to their places on deck.

Yanados eventually reappeared, looking every so faintly smug, just as the ship was turning back for the harbor. The others said nothing, only looked at her, and she returned them a cool stare. Omis shook his head and gazed out toward the approaching port, where the low sunlight danced on the sea. The ship's bell rang twice, passing messages to the crew, and its sweet tone was echoed by the harbor bell announcing the time.

Omis jumped as if he'd been stabbed. "Bells," he whispered. "Gods, I'm a fool. Bells!"

Before Sulun could ask what he meant by that, the blacksmith ran over to the ship's bell and peered up its interior. Next he grabbed the startled signalman and threw questions at him. Was this bell made in the city? Who made it? Where was his shop? The sailor told all he knew, made a quick excuse, and fled. Omis shook his head and went stomping back to the rail.

"Bells," he kept muttering, much to Sulun's and Vari's alarm. "Heavy brass, maybe heavy enough. Lower heat, easy to cast, but how? Sand molds? Where can I learn? Brass! Gods, I'm an idiot."

"Shush," Sulun whispered. "I think the old vulture's looking."

"But how thick, to contain the pressure?" Omis mumbled.

Entori glanced his way, frowning.

"Quiet, Omis!" Varis elbowed him. "Wait 'til we get home."

Omis snorted, but shut up. Entori looked away. The ship chuffed back to its dock, belching coal smoke and steam from its aft sideports, to the welcoming cheers of the remaining audience at the waterside.

"We can do it in one trip," Omis insisted as they sneaked the mule cart out the rear gate. "Just go one street over, let me out at the brassworker's, then come get me on the way home. I'll be perfectly safe, I swear!"

"Very well, very well," Sulun capitulated, closing the gate behind them. "Once again, tell me why it must be brass."

"Because I can't get sufficient heat to melt iron, of course!" Omis snorted. "Make iron flow like water? Cast it like brass? Hah, as easily catch the unicorn. Come climb on the cart, and let's make haste."

"But the force of the explosion—"

"Brass can hold it, be she cast thick enough. I tell you—"

"Get up!" Doshi cut their argument short with a slap of reins on the mules' rumps. The laden cart rolled into the street, armed apprentices watching for danger fore and aft.

"Then what shall we do with all that iron we struggled so to get?" Sulun grumbled, struggling for a comfortable position among the bundles.

"Sell it back for better money now that it's been hammered once. Ah, gods, the time wasted! But we should keep some of it for gears and mounts and axles, damn the old vulture. Hmm, also I could hammer some of it into globes to be flung from the bombard. I've long suspected that those canisters were a problem—"

"Crowds ahead!" Arizun warned. "Great gods, I think they're running to a riot. Let's take the next street over."

"Aye, let's," said Yanados, "but I don't think it's a riot. That lot looks more to be running from a press gang."

Doshi had already turned the mules; now he slapped them into a respectably fast trot, hoping that the sounds of the running mob would cover the noise of the cart's wheels.

"It's a god's sign," Omis observed. "This way leads closer to the brassmakers' street."

The street leading to the workshop was mostly empty—only a few streetside peddlers and a parked covered wagon about— and Sulun's party took little time opening the heavy front door. Arizun noted that at least one attempt had been made to force the latch, but Omis's sturdy iron lock had held well. They brought the cart through the narrow archway and on into the back courtyard, where they set about unloading gear. Arizun went off to lock the door again behind them, and Sulun made a point of listing all the portable goods.

"Travelling clothes, dried rations for two days, our books and tools . . . Damn, it's both too little and too much," he announced. "Too little to supply us for long, too much to carry in one cartload."

"A bigger cart?" Doshi suggested.

"Where? How do we buy one?"

"Sell Omis's extra iron," said Yanados.

"Hmm, that reminds me. Do we all have hatchets, long knives, bows, and sufficient arrows?"

"Also fishhooks and lines, pins, thread, and needles," Vari put in. "And medicines."

Sulun shrugged and made more notes on his waxboard.

Arizun came trotting back into the courtyard, looking a bit pale. "Pardon me, friends," he announced, sounding unusually subdued, "but we have a visitor."

Everyone jumped, and turned to look. Arizun bowed low, with as much of a flourish as he could manage.

Through the archway, dressed in a quietly tasteful gown and carrying a small sunshade, strolled Eloti.

Greetings again, Craftmaster Sulun," she said. "So pleased to find your true workplace at last."

Sulun couldn't think of anything to say, so he bowed low. Eloti smiled politely, and stood waiting.

Ziya broke the awkward silence, toddling forward and making a more elaborate bow. "Good Mistress Eloti," she said, formal as any high-city hostess, "if you would be so kind as to join us for luncheon, we should be delighted to explain everything to your satisfaction."

Eloti raised an eyebrow in respectful surprise.

Sulun, snapped out of his confusion, breathed a quick prayer of thanks to all available gods and snapped orders to the gawking apprentices: fetch table and couches or chairs, get wine and proper food and some good tableware, suitable for a gentlewoman. The others scrambled to obey. Eloti sat down on the nearest bench, fanned herself languidly with a palm-frond fan, and waited to see what would happen. She seemed intrigued, if not downright amused.

The best that Sulun's crowd could produce was a small table (covered with a clean cloak), two chairs (of which Eloti got the better and Sulun the second), some good wine in a plain jug, some coarse but fresh bread, and a bit of cheese, all served in hastily cleaned mortars and mixing bowls. Ziya did the serving, offering the plates and cups in the best high-house style, with all the proper phrases. The other apprentices watched in fascination for a few minutes, then took themselves elsewhere. Ziya poured out the wine, bowed formally again, then excused herself and hurried after the others.

Sulun took the opportunity to marshal his store of facts and arguments, and incidentally raise his estimate of Ziya's intelligence.

He wondered how often the child had observed her mother performing just such duties for Shibari's creditors.

"I regret that the surroundings are less than elegant," Sulun began cautiously, "but we find this location to be useful, quiet, and inexpensive."

"I'm pleased to see you practicing good economy with my funds," Eloti replied, sipping the wine. She raised an eyebrow again in approval of the vintage. "I have also noted the common absence of my mule cart. Might I ask just what tools and other goods you have been transporting?"

Accounting time, Sulun realized. It would not be wise to mislead the lady. "Tools for working on our new project in secret," he admitted. "Everything except Omis's forge."

"Also, I've noticed considerable food, clothing, and household items. Were you expecting to withstand a siege here?"

"It's possible," Sulun hedged.

Eloti tapped a fingernail on her mortar cup. "Is that the only reason?"

"No," Sulun admitted. "If this project fails and the city falls, we hope to escape."

"All of you?" Eloti glanced around at the building that concealed the rest of Sulun's crew. "Your friend the blacksmith, his wife and children also?"

"Yes." Sulun couldn't begin to explain that all of them had become a sort of household, a family, in their own right. "We'll leave no one behind."

"Indeed?" Eloti took another sip of wine. "I find your loyalty strange, but commendable." Her eyes narrowed, skewering Sulun over the edge of her cup. "Could your . . . coterie possibly be expanded to include a patron?"

Sulun gulped. "Do you mean that Entori knows—plans to escape with us?"

"Not my brother. I have tried, many times, to discuss departing Sabis with him. He will not hear of it." Eloti set her cup neatly, precisely, back on the table, and clasped her hands under her chin like any merchant about to do business. "So, I wish to employ you and your students to undertake this new weapon project under my auspices. Is that formal enough?"

Sulun let out his breath in a soundless whistle. "Certainly, Goodlady. I'm honored to have you as our . . . secondary patron."

"Then surely you would not mind storing some of my . . . gear in this workshop." Eloti smiled.

"Not at all, Goodlady." Sulun refrained from asking what gear, or how much. "I do beg you to consider, though, how much equipment we may be able to transport in case of, er, emergency."

Eloti leaned back in her chair, the classic motion of a merchant about to dicker extensively. "I would begin with a larger wagon," she said, "still capable of being drawn by two mules."

Sulun grinned. "It must also be capable of carrying two changes of clothing for each of us, plus our books, tools, sufficient food for at least three days, basic household supplies—and, of course, all of us."

"Of course." Eloti smiled, flicking her fan. "Likewise one larger traveling-chest for myself, and enough sailcloth to cover the load."

"Of course." Sulun reached for his waxboard then frowned. "I confess, I've never had to calculate the carrying capacity of mule wagons."

"Leave that to me," said Eloti, not smiling now. "Of course, I must know how far the wagon is expected to travel, over what roads, and into what sort of country."

Sulun gnawed his lip, seeing where this was aimed. He didn't really have an answer; all of them together hadn't decided. Perhaps another conference was in order. "Doshi, Arizun, all of you," he called to the innocent-looking house, "Get out here. We have . . . travel routes to discuss."

In scant seconds the little crowd came out and ranged themselves on the workbenches, all serious-faced, even the children. Sulun guessed that they'd been listening closely through the doors and windows, and needed no explanations.

"If we run," he said bluntly, "where do we go?"

Doshi surprised him by speaking up first. "To the north," he said with surprising decisiveness. "I've copied all the maps—begging your pardon, Lady—and I know that land. Yes, we'd be hard put to get behind the Ancar lines and I confess I don't know how we'd do that—"

"Zeren might know," Arizun put in. "Going north was his idea first."

"But once past them, we'd be reasonably safe. More, those people up there are poor farmers, not very well educated, and from all accounts the Ancar aren't scholars either. They'd welcome skilled tradesfolk, mechanicals, with our knowledge. We could make ourselves welcome there."

"And how would the Ancar conquerors care for Sabisan refugees in their midst?" Eloti asked.

"We needn't say we come from Sabis," Doshi shrugged.

"We could say we come from Halas," Arizun piped up, in his native element now. "That's the other end of the world, for all the northerners would know. They've never been there, know nothing of its people or customs. We could be as strange as we liked."

"In which case," Eloti pointed out, "they might be afraid to come near us, let alone purchase our wares or work."

"Oh no, that could be an advantage," Arizun insisted, grinning like a monkey. "We could say we were magicians."

"Magicians?" Sulun choked on a mouthful of wine.

"Certainly! Ignorant folk may fear magicians, but they always want their services. I could teach you the basics—"

The others laughed. Eloti smiled widely.

"It's true, it's true!" Arizun insisted. "How do you think I lived, all those years before Sulun apprenticed me? I swear by all the gods I've ever heard of, folk will fee and placate magicians far more than honest philosophers or craftsmen. Folk love mysteries far more than knowledge."

There was a silence for a long moment while everyone thought about that, seeing the grim truth in it.

In that silence they noticed the growing noise outside. From the street came sounds of shouts, trampling feet, noises of smashing wood and pottery, and more—an indescribable growl of no one source, all too well recognized after these long weeks of hard times.

"Oh gods, not another street riot," Sulun groaned, starting to his feet.

"It won't come in here," said Arizun, tugging at his sleeve. "I made sure to lock that door, and it's too thick for them to break down."

"He's right," said Yanados, listening. "If we hear them trying to break in we can go to the upper windows and drop things on them, but there's no danger yet."

"Still, we're stuck here until it passes," Vari worried. "Gods, I hope it doesn't reach to the brassworkers' street."

"Brassworkers' street?" Eloti inquired.

"Omis is there," Sulun explained. "He wants to trade skills with a good brass smith, learn the secrets of large brass casting. It's for our other project."

"Interesting." Eloti fanned herself thoughtfully. "If your project succeeds it may save the city, you've said."

"Yes. But if it fails, we intend to escape with whole skins."

"And," Doshi added, "with enough of our tools and knowledge that we need not live like savages."

"Indeed," Eloti murmured. "Indeed."

Then they heard the familiar iron tramp of guardsmen's booted feet in the street outside, followed by bellowed orders, howls of dismay, sounds of running sandals, and assorted thumpings. "I think the riot is leaving," Eloti observed. "Now should your plan to go north fail, what secondary plans have you?"

Secondary plans? Sulun wondered, looking about him. He hadn't even refined the first one.

But then Yanados spoke up. "The captain of the *Yanira* will take us on board, no fees and no questions, and let us off at any port we ask."

Everyone turned to look at her. Sulun coughed, then asked, "Why is he inclined to be so amazingly generous?"

Yanados bit her lip for a moment. "I . . . made a quiet arrangement, the day we tested the engine. I gave him the design drawings for the engine and paddle wheels, and . . . I told him we could make more, teach others to make more. Such skills would be very useful in . . . some places."

"I . . . see." Sulun no longer had any doubts about Yanados's family or land or origin. Everyone knew about the pirates of Sakar. Ships with Sulun's engines could rule the seas. Any clever captain could add those facts and come to the obvious conclusion. "Yes, we could escape that way."

"Provided," Eloti said, "that the *Yanira* happens to be in port at whatever time we have need of her."

More silence as the conspirators considered that.

Their thoughts were interrupted by a polite but firm knocking at the outer door. Everyone looked at each other.

"I'll go," said Doshi. "None of us looks like a stout warrior, but I think I can pretend to it better than most." He was up and away before anyone could think of a better argument.

"In case of either plan being necessary," Eloti resumed, "we'll require a wagon that can transport ourselves and our goods either out of the city or down to the docks in a single load, yet isn't so vast that it would have trouble at the gates or require more than two mules." She tapped her teeth with her fan. "I think such could be provided, say, by quarter moon."

"So quickly?" Sulun marveled.

"My dear Master Sulun, I have not lived all these years in Entori's house without learning something of the carting business."

At that point they all heard the front door slam shut, and the sound of approaching boots. Everyone froze, wondering which guardsman Doshi had let in, and why.

A moment later the mystery was resolved as Doshi came back, grinning from ear to ear, with Zeren a pace behind him. ""Look what I found on the doorstep!" he announced.

"Zeren, by all the gods!" "Make room for him!" "Where's another bench?" "Do we have more wine?" Everybody chattered at once.

Zeren, a little bemused by all the attention, dropped onto the nearest bench and took off his helmet. "I'm pleased to see you're all safe," he said. "When we cleared out this street and I saw your door, I thought I should send my boys on ahead and see if you were present, and well."

"We are, we are," Sulun fairly dithered, handing Zeren a filled cup. "We've been making plans to complete the Bombard Project. Omis has some ideas about cast brass—he's at the brassworkers' street right now—the riot hasn't reached there, has it?"

"Oh no, it's just down here, near the river. Such troubles are fewer since we started the press gangs . . . though they're worse when they happen at all." He stared past them at Eloti. "And who's this lady?"

Once more Ziya performed the formalities. "This is Goodlady Eloti, sister of Entori, of Entori House. Our new patroness. Madame, this is—"

"Zeren of the Guard," Zeren cut in, impatient with lengthy courtesies. He couldn't seem to take his eyes off Eloti. "Begging your pardon, Lady, but . . . what are you doing down here?"

"Inspecting my investment." Eloti met his stare with a cool smile. She hadn't missed the welcome the others gave him. "We were also discussing means of departing the city, should the invasion reach this far."

"Oh." Zeren glanced at Sulun, his eyes asking: New ally? To be trusted?

"The lady's been pointing out flaws in our existing plans," Sulun explained, then added recklessly, "She's also offered to provide help with anything reasonable."

"I see." Zeren took a careful mouthful of wine, studying Eloti over his cup. "So. What flaws did you find?"

Sulun, caught between them, got the distinct feeling that he'd been assigned the role of either truce negotiator or matchmaker, and that was something new in his experience.

"First, the ship on which we might escape southward or . . . to the islands . . . might not be in port when we need her. Second, if we try to run north, how would we pass the Ancar lines?"

Zeren thought for a long moment, looking from Sulun to Eloti and back. "You'll need a boat in any case," he said at last. "Whether you have to cross the straits, catch up with your ship, or bypass the Ancar lines, you'll need a boat big enough to carry all of you safely. The river's the best place to bypass the Ancar; they're not sailors. When they crossed the Azesu all those years back, they neither bridged nor sailed it. They hunted up and down the river until they found a passable ford for infantry. Same thing when they crossed the Gol a few years later. I doubt that they've changed since. Get a boat, stay on the river as long as you can, and if their arrows can't reach you, you'll be safe."

"How big a boat?" said Eloti, pulling a small waxboard from her sleeves.

Sulun noted that she didn't take her eyes off Zeren either.

By next moon-quarter the wagon arrived. It appeared quietly one day in the stable courtyard, tucked against the wall, half under the stable eaves, looking as if it had always been there. Examining it during lunch, Sulun noted that it was indeed long and wide and sturdy enough to carry all of them, plus their clothes, food, tools, and even Omis's anvil. The flooring was doublebraced, the wheels unusually sturdy, and the whole construction made of good hardwood. A large square of tightly woven, oiled sailcloth was folded up in the footwell below the driver's seat. Sulun reflected that the mistress did indeed know the carting business, and went off to lunch in high good humor.

Back in the working courtyard, he noticed that the stacks of iron ingots were much reduced and their place taken by bags of odd-colored sand. Intrigued, he went looking for Omis, and found him by the rear gate, helping two strangers in workmen's garb muscle in a load of heavy wooden panels. Sulun knew better than to say anything before the men left, but he pounced the minute the gate was shut.

"That?" Omis rubbed his hands gleefully. "That, old friend, is the makings of a sand mold."

"A sand mold?"

"Aye. Our new bombard tube will be cast from good brass, in a mold of wet sand clenched by wooden walls. Heh! Once we've cast her, we can use this trick to make more engine parts for the vulture."

"Hmm. And what shall we use for the casting model? Wax?"

"No, wood." Omis hefted a smoothed round log as big as his leg. "We'll shape this, put it in the casting box, pour the sand around it, wet the sand and pound it nearly solid, then pull out the log to leave its shape in the sand—where we'll pour the brass. Simple, eh? Well, there are some details, but not many. The important thing is, this technique works. I watched the bellmaker do it, from start to finish. I can do it, Sulun. We'll have our new bombard in less than a tenday."

"Er, what did you give him in exchange for the knowledge?"

"The basic design of the steam engine, for which he was sufficiently grateful. So grateful, indeed, that he told me where I might purchase something truly valuable."

"Oh gods, what? And how valuable?"

"A small, portable forge, my friend. I don't intend to be caught without a forge again, not after last time."

"You bought it, of course," Sulun sighed. "How much? And where did you put it?"

"Well, I sold most of the extra iron—the rest went to purchasing the casting sand. Brass casting requires special sand, you know."

"I know. Where is it?"

"Why, right over here in the corner." Omis led the way to a squat metal cylinder half-hidden behind the sandbags. "It's iron, lined with good fireclay. I saw the brass smith using one, and I made certain it could manage small pieces of iron, too. Isn't she pretty?"

"Delightful," Sulun groaned. "How much does it weigh? Can the wagon take it? And how soon can we get it down to the river workshop?"

"Wagon? What wagon?"

"A gift from our patroness. I just found it this morning. Come, and bring your new toy; we may as well learn right now if the wagon can carry it."

"Carry it? Hah." With that, Omis picked up the little forge, straining a bit, and carried it all the way into the stable courtyard. "See?" he puffed, putting it down. "It isn't that heavy."

"Let's see what the wagon says." Sulun dropped the new wagon's tailgate. "Load it," he said.

Surprisingly enough the wagon could and did hold the small forge, with no more than a few creaks of complaint from the floorboards.

"There, you see?" Omis grinned as he wiped sweat off his forehead. "It's light enough to carry, and doesn't take up much room. We'll take it with us when we go."

Sulun started to say that if the bombard could be made quickly enough they wouldn't have to go at all, but then he thought better of it. "Excellent. Leave it in the wagon, then; we'll take it down to the river workshop this very afternoon."

"But I haven't even tested it yet!" Omis howled, offended. "Let me use it for today, at least!"

And nothing would satisfy him but taking the forge out of the wagon, and carrying it all the way back to the courtyard. Further, he wanted to test the sand mold technique by casting the new engine parts therein. Sulun gave up and let him do as he wished. They'd need some finished parts to report to Entori tomorrow morning, anyway.

That evening at dinner the servants' table buzzed with gossip. There had been a big parade down the main avenue—the cook's sister's husband had seen it—of the newly levied troops going out to hold the lines in the north. The scullions were wonderfully optimistic: maybe now there'd be more peace in the city, and prices would fall back to something reasonable. Sulun's crowd said nothing; they knew Zeren's opinion of the levies, their training and armament and skills. He'd had better opinion of the mercenary troops. Still there'd been no further riots, no further advances by the Ancar as far as anyone knew. And there were rumors of further good news.

The Imperial Court, it was said, had received a welcome visitor from the north. Eylas of the presumed lost lands of Medhyras, a former hostage from a noble Medhyran family who had been brought up in the barbarous Ancari court, had escaped his captors and fled south to Sabis, full of information. He knew of the growing rebellion against the invaders in Medhyras and even Pegyras. Given a little time, the Ancar might find themselves with the new Sabisan troops before them and a full-scale rebellion behind them. The Emperor was delighted to hear of this unlooked-for help, and treated the new guest very well. The aristocracy had also been impressed with Prince Eylas's nice manners and appearance, and it seemed that he'd be invited to dine all over high-town soon.

Even Entori seemed to be in a good humor for once, as the servants noted. His comments to his sister, overheard by the serving maids, had revolved around possible improvements of trade now that Prince Eylas had come to town.

"Ridiculous," Yanados muttered into her soup. "Is Entori mad? Nothing's really changed; the Ancar are still there."

"And we still need the bombard," Sulun finished. He wondered what he'd tell Eloti at their brief meeting in the garden courtyard that night. Between reporting on one project to Entori every morning and reporting on the other to Eloti every night he'd soon be running short on sleep.

"Was the wagon satisfactory?" Eloti asked, gazing thoughtfully at the few nightblooming jasmine flowers that remained at this season.

"Excellent, Goodlady. It can carry all our gear—including Omis's new little forge."

"Remarkable." Eloti shook her head. "I suppose the wagon will more than earn its price, even now that escape is no longer necessary."

"Hmm, one would do well not to count the cheeses before the cow is milked." Sulun grinned a little at that phrase, one he'd picked up from Doshi. "Prince Eylas's rebellion is only promised, not guaranteed."

"True. I, of all people, should know how rarely hope ceases flying and actually comes to roost."

Sulun suddenly wondered why Eloti was unmarried. He knew better than to ask. "What do we truly know of this man, anyway? He could be a clever liar, buying his way into the favor of the nobles for his own purposes."

Eloti shrugged. "He seemed knowledgeable enough about the lands near his home. He spoke at some length of the fine cattle of Torrhyn and northern Jarrya, so he's well-traveled at least."

"Well-traveled and well-spoken." Sulun shrugged. "Still not enough to turn the tides of war. I still claim that our bombard offers greater hope."

"I will continue to fund our little enterprise." Eloti smiled faintly. "Will you do the casting here or at the river workshop?"

"At the riverside. It's a cumbersome process, not easily hidden or disguised. Also, if you'll forgive my saying so, Entori House is well-known and ill-loved by too many. I would prefer to do our work in a quieter spot."

"I understand perfectly, but is the river house secure?"

"As safe as stout walls, good locks, and Zeren's watchfulness can make it."

Eloti said nothing for long moments, eyes fixed on the few remaining flowers. "Very good," she murmured at last. "I hope you will not take it amiss if I visit you there on occasion."

"Er, no, certainly not."

"Perhaps I'll come bearing good news. You may go."

"That was all she said," Sulun reported later, in the fitful light of the cubicle's one small lamp. "I can't fathom her intentions, except that she wants us to continue."

"Perhaps she's taken a liking to Zeren," Yanados yawned, shoving a drowsing Arizun off her shoulder.

"*Our* Zeren?" Sulun laughed. "It's not like you to see romance everywhere. What, are you feeling the pull of mating season already?"

"Hardly. But can you think of a better reason?"

"I could imagine dozens, and have no evidence for any of them."

"What was that she said about Jarrya?" Doshi put in, looking up from his precious maps.

"Eh? Why, nothing—except that this Prince Eylas spoke of it." Sulun shook his head. Yanados getting romantic, Doshi getting homesick, Arizun turning mystical, and Ziya fascinated by fire—they were not doing well in Entori House.

"Well then, what is this prince supposed to have said?" Doshi insisted.

"Uhm, something about the fine cattle raised there and in Torrhyn, I think. Nothing of any import or detail. I'm sorry, Doshi. Now, why that odd look?"

"Cattle?" Doshi's frown deepened. "That isn't cattle country, and never has been. The winters are too harsh to keep cattle out-of-doors, and the buildings are all made of stone. . . ."

"I think we've all been awake too long," Sulun hinted, rubbing his back.

"They have to be stone to withstand the winter storms. One can't build very large barns there, not enough to house large herds of cattle. A few milk cows, perhaps, but they're poor beasts by southern standards. Folk there mostly raise sheep."

"Time to sleep, Doshi. We all need our rest."

Yanados took the hint and stood up, dragging Arizun with her. Doshi reluctantly gathered up his maps, but kept worrying at his thought as he shuffled toward the door.

"I don't think this visiting prince ever saw Jarrya. I think he's merrily lying his way through the court. You'd best tell Zeren that when you see him again."

"I will, Doshi. I promise. Now off to bed."

"I think there's no rebellion in the north at all, and we're just as badly off as before, except worse because now the court won't pay as much attention to the northern defenses, and—"

"Good *night*, Doshi."

"We'd best continue our plans to leave," Doshi finished as Sulun closed the door on his heels.

Arizun, perched near a window as lookout for possible mobs, was the only one to hear the soft tap at the door. He quietly slipped the bar and locks to let Eloti in. She drifted silently as a leaf through the passageway, although the noise from the workyard would have covered ordinary footsteps. Once again, Arizun wondered how the lady managed to travel so easily and unnoticed through the dangerous streets, apparently alone, dressed well enough to attract the attention of a thousand desperate thieves. As always, he thought it best not to ask her.

Zeren was already there with the others, stripped of his armor, helping to pour sand and water into the standing mold. He glanced up as the other two came in, and for a moment his eyes met Eloti's. He blinked, nodded politely, quickly, and turned his attention back to what he was doing.

"Enough water!" Omis snapped. "We don't want to wash the sand out again. There, there . . ." He inspected the wet, packed sand in the thick wooden box, poked it here and there with his fingers, grunted satisfaction, and turned to study the mold itself.

Nearly buried in wet sand, the mold didn't look very prepossessing: a heavy wooden tube, no bigger than Omis's leg, sliced lengthwise. Wet sand surrounded and filled it to the top. Omis picked up a short log, fit it neatly inside the tube until it touched the sand, and leaned on it. The sand compressed a bit, and the log stayed in place by itself. Omis nodded thoughtfully, picked up several squared short logs, and poked them endwise into the box, on top of the sand.

"Everyone pound together," he announced, picking up a large maul for himself. "Remember to beat them all equally."

Everyone else sighed, picked up assorted hammers, and converged on the box.

"May I ask the purpose of this exercise?" Eloti asked, dropping gracefully onto a bench.

"We have to pound the sand tight," Arizun explained, taking a light mallet for himself. "We pour it, wet it, pack it, then pray it stays in place when we pull out the mold."

"Fascinating."

"Damned hard work."

"All together," Omis warned, raising his maul. "*Now.*" He struck a good solid blow on the round log. The others followed suit, almost in unison, on the logs surrounding the mold. "And *now.* And *now.*"

Thud. Thud. Thud.

The hammering fell into a smooth rhythm. Water began oozing from the bottom of the box. Inch by inch, the logs drove deeper as the sand compressed. Watching them, Eloti tapped first her foot and then her fingers in rhythm.

Eventually Omis called a halt, pulled out the logs, and

inspected the sand. "Hmm, it should do," he decided. "Pour in more sand."

Everyone put down their hammers, picked up bags and buckets, and carefully poured. When the sand level reached the top of the mold, Omis called for the water. The wetted sand sank hardly at all. Omis poked again, studied the sand for a moment, then took up the logs and hammers once more.

It was, Sulun decided, nearly as hypnotic as the droning prayers in the temples on a great holy day. Pound, pound, pound all together, half a dozen arms swinging as one, and the sodden thudding rhythmic as a temple bell. Pound, pound, pound. If concentration, devotion, and perfection made the best defense against magic, not even the greatest wizard in Sabis could touch them this day. Pound, pound, pound. Now if only his well-worked muscles didn't tire and cramp and pain him enough to break his concentration . . . Pound, pound, pound.

The voice sneaked up on him, interweaving so smoothly with the hammer-rhythm that he didn't notice it as anything separate from himself, not until one corner of his mind noted that he'd never heard the words of the song before.

"*Low* lie the *stars* over *Tos*lagen's *mem*ory,
High hang the *flowers* from the *trees* of her *tomb*."

And was it strange or not that everyone else swayed and swung with the quiet song? Everyone hammering smoothly, rapt as corybantic dancers: pound, pound, pound . . .

" '*Care*,' sing the *birds* in the *boughs* of the *cyp*resses,
'*Care*, love and *care*, win you *free* of your *doom*.' "

Just those few lines, over and over, keeping the rhythm, drawing the arms, the mallets, to swing and pound, pound, pound endlessly, hold the mind tight on the simple action, no stray thought, no deviation, steady as a perfect engine . . .

"Halt!" Omis yelled, shaking his head. "We're down."

Everyone dropped their assorted hammers, rubbed their arms, and shook their heads as if coming out of a dream. Indeed, Sulun noticed, the level of the sand was down—and packed as tight as fine clay.

Magic! Sulun turned to look at the one person who could have provided that song, the only one not hammering.

Eloti sat waving her fan gently, that faint smile lingering on her face.

"Goodlady." Sulun bowed to her. "I had no idea you could sing so well."

"A largely useless skill." She shrugged. "Save on rare occasions."

"Magic!" Arizun breathed. "That was a—a protective spell, or I've never seen one."

"You've never seen one, then," Zeren snorted, rubbing his arm. " 'Twas a work spell, and a rather good one." He grinned a brief salute at Eloti.

Eloti gave an eloquent shrug, punctuated with her fan. "It merely seemed appropriate," she said. "I assure you, I've never been a wizard's apprentice."

The others laughed approvingly, trying to imagine the quiet lady of Entori House as a scampering apprentice running errands for some crotchety wizard. Impossible, indeed.

"Back to the mold," Omis insisted. "Plug the top of the log; this will be the last layer."

The rest duly took up bags and buckets again, and went back to the careful pouring of sand and water, the last layer that would fill the box to the top.

"Gods grant," Omis muttered, easing the wooden plug into the top of the bombard shape, "we can get the pouring done today."

Sulun nodded agreement, but kept only the minimum of his attention on the mold. His eyes kept straying to Eloti, calmly fanning herself while she watched the proceedings, and his head filled with wild speculation where all the facts slid into place with a click as neat as the closing of a latch.

Eloti had sorcerous talent. His mistress was, in common parlance, a witch.

No wonder Entori House could survive the malice of Entori's clients, and with no better protection than the drunken house wizard. No wonder this house, outrageously vulnerable to the ill-will of the neighbors, at least, hadn't been disturbed by thieves nor plagued with accidents, even in these bad days. No wonder the lady came and went as she chose, unbothered by cutpurses or worse, virtually unseen. No wonder she remained unmarried. Who would have a she-wizard to wife, save for another wizard who wished to breed talented sons—and family-proud Entori would never let his sister marry below what he considered her proper class.

Yet she could read, and knew how and where to listen, and learned readily. Perhaps she had cozened secrets out of the house wizard, leaving him to forget her in his cups. Perhaps she had learned everything from books and observation alone. In secret, in whatever fashion, she had learned—and practiced. Eloti was the true protector of Entori House, and now of Sulun and his unknowing friends.

Accident. Fate. Pound, pound, pound . . .

"Enough," said Omis. "Pull out."

The others drew away their logs and mallets, and stepped back to let Omis inspect the mold. The tight-packed sand covered the wooden form almost completely, leaving only the bare disk of the plug's top visible. Omis nodded and breathed a long sigh.

"All right," he said. "Now we take out the mold form."

Only Sulun noticed that Eloti began humming softly, a different tune this time, in rhythm with the languid beat of her fan.

Omis tugged carefully, delicately, at the plug. After a second's resistance it pulled free of the wooden tube, free of the sand, displacing hardly a single grain. Omis sighed again in relief, fitted the jaws of narrow tongs around one of the tube halves, and pulled gently, ever so gently. The wooden half-tube slid quietly out of its bedding, leaving the deep, perfect half circular hole in the packed sand behind it. Omis set the piece aside and reached for the last one with the tongs, careful, utterly careful, whispering prayers to assorted relevant gods.

Eloti's humming purred softly in the air like the sound of drowsy bees in sunlight.

The last piece of the mold slid out smoothly, leaving its shape perfectly molded in the packed sand.

"Perfect!" Omis whispered, tiptoeing away from the mold as if too loud a noise would shatter it.

"Perfect . . ." Sulun echoed, daring a sidelong glance at his mistress.

Eloti sat unchanged, calmly fanning herself, a faint smile resting on her otherwise impassive face.

"Begin the melt," said Omis, very quietly. "And no noise."

The others turned to the forge, gently picking up tools and billets of brass.

Sulun guessed he wouldn't be needed for this part; there was something more important to do. He went into the house, rummaged through the supplies, and came back with some watered wine and light bread. Very quietly, he took them to Eloti.

"Best to refresh yourself, Mistress," he said, noncommittally. "This will be long and tedious work."

Eloti looked at him for a moment, then thanked him formally and took the food.

Sulun hurried back to the group working at the forge and busied himself with odd tasks: tossing in more charcoal as the fire rose, working the bellows when Zeren's arms tired, helping to pitch brass into the heating crucible, wetting down Omis's gloves between pokings and stirrings. Often he glanced at Eloti, noting that she kept her eyes on the undisturbed mold and could be heard softly humming to herself. Despite the heat of the forge, he shivered.

At close to sundown the brass was ready, flowing like milk, glowing like the sinking sun. Omis ran two thick iron bars through the rows of rings on either side of the crucible, took the end of one bar, and they all lifted together. Carefully, carefully, they walked their glowing burden away from the forge and up to the lip of the mold.

"Gently now, gently," Omis fairly chanted, "Set the forward bar, hold it steady, steady . . . Zeren, lift with me. Lift, lift . . ."

Eloti's humming grew ever so slightly louder.

Slowly the crucible tilted, its spout descending over the deep circular hole in the packed sand. The molten brass touched the edge, slipped into the spout, seemed to pause for an instant, then spilled gracefully into the mold. For a moment everyone saw the glowing stream pooling, with scarcely a splash, at the bottom of the long circular hole. Then clouds of steam boiled up to fog the vision, driven up from the wet sand.

"Keep pouring!" Omis snapped. "Don't change position. Close your eyes if it gets too bad. There, there . . ."

Coughing and blinking in the stifling fog, Sulun watched the shining surface of the molten brass rise in the mold. Upward it crept as the crucible slowly emptied, up to the top of the central column of sand and then over it, up to the surface of the sand mold. There it stopped, a gleaming disk in the sand, while the last drops trickled from the almost upended crucible.

"Perfect!" Omis laughed in relief. "Exactly enough. Gods, I

was afraid we'd have too much, have to ease this bucket back down and empty it in a drain ditch. All together now, lift that other rod and pull back. Good, good . . ."

Step by step, with only a little less care than on their advance, they pulled the cooling crucible away from the mold and set it down. The ground steamed where it touched. Everyone else stepped back, and Omis pulled the carrying rods free.

"How long till it cools solid?" Zeren asked, wiping his forehead.

"Tomorrow sometime." Omis pulled off his gloves and tossed them aside. "I'd leave it a full day, just to be safe. So, we'll come back the morning after next to break out the mold and start on the smoothing. I suppose we can spend tomorrow working on another ship's engine for the old—er, the Master." He darted an embarrassed smile at Eloti.

"Should we not celebrate our success?" she almost purred. "I believe a small thank-offering to the gods would be in order."

"A good libation should do," Zeren grinned, starting toward the house. "I brought a few jugs of a very decent wine with me."

"If we wish it heated, we could mull it in yonder crucible." Eloti smiled.

Omis roared with delighted laughter. "Gods, yes! How fitting!"

Fitting indeed, Sulun thought, following Zeren into the house to fetch the cups.

The gears, the hated gears . . . Sulun dourly polished another of the little iron monsters, reflecting that he was beginning to hate the very thought of steam engines and ships. Bits and parts of another engine nearly completed, Entori nagging him to hurry, the bombard waiting like a treasure that could be touched only in few, precious, stolen moments: half a moon like this. *And the news from the north no better.* All Sabis might fall before they managed to finish the bombard. *Damn Entori, damn his engines, damn these interminable gears!*

Seeing no further burrs or irregularities, Sulun dropped the hated gear in a box with its companions and glanced automatically at the sunlight above the roof. *Good gods, nearly dinnertime.* The others had gone inside, leaving him here with his wretched little task, and he couldn't blame them. He rubbed his eyes, back, fingers, and stalked off to his minuscule room. Just enough time to wash his hands and face for dinner, no time or reason to change his clothes; let the old vulture see that he'd worked like a galley slave all day. He washed fast, towelled off faster, and stalked toward the dining hall still damp.

It was the silence he noticed first: the servants eating so very quietly, heads down, trying not to be noticed. Scarcely a head lifted as he shuffled into his place on the bench at the servants' table.

But one of the heads raised was Arizun's. "Keep your head down," he whispered fiercely in Sulun's ear. "Look who's visiting Master at the upper table."

Sulun duly hunched over his plate and glanced sidewise at the Master's table—from which, he now noticed, came sounds of unusually lively conversation.

There sat Entori and his sister, as always: Eloti looking politely attentive, Entori for once animated and almost jovial. Facing them, backs to the servants' table, sat two newcomers. Guests, Sulun realized, probably business acquaintances, hardly friends, knowing Entori. Reason enough for the servants not to want attention drawn to themselves. But why was Arizun so agitated? And why was Vari shooting frightened looks at him across the bread dish? In fact, why was everyone in his work gang looking so frightened? He studied the two newcomers more closely.

Both men were fat and well-dressed, though the leftmost was decked with more jewelry and embroidery—clearly the master. He was, at the moment, almost demanding of Entori, "But gods curse it, man, I'm offering you twenty percent of my cargoes for a full year! I'm not asking for the secret of their manufacture, only for the engines themselves. Just two good engines, fit for hundred-tonners, in exchange for twenty per hundred: Where will you find a better bargain?"

Aha, Entori's little show on the docks with the *Yanira* had borne fruit, and doubtless he was haggling over the price.

Sure enough, Entori replied, "I don't expect a better bargain. It's quite an excellent bargain. It's also quite impossible. The engine is a most complex and delicate bit of work; it takes time to make one, time to mount it properly. That first one took my craftsmen two moons to build, and the second will hardly take less. As soon as my own ships are fitted, of course, I'll be free to discuss fitting others', but you must understand the delay—"

"But then, within two moons you'll have a second ship fitted out. Surely then you could set your men to making one engine—just one—for a single ship of mine. Afterward they could make another for you, then another for me."

"The time involved . . ."

Gods, he's bartering off our services! If Entori yielded, sent the whole pack of them to some other house to make an engine elsewhere, they'd never be able to slip away to the riverside laboratorium and finish the bombard. Sulun found himself praying that Entori's miserliness would endure through dinner.

"It might be possible," he heard Eloti say, "to measure the gentleman's ship, build the engine here, then send it to him when finished."

There was a moment's silence as both men considered that, followed by more haggling over time, prices, who would pay for what.

Sulun wilted with relief. Bless Eloti's cleverness, they wouldn't have to leave the house and work for some unknown master.

Yanados, seeing his expression, nudged him with an elbow. "We're not safe yet, Sulun. Look who else is at the table."

Puzzled, Sulun peered around his shoulder at the other guest, who had said nothing audible so far. The man was fat, sleek-looking, in elegantly cut brown robes with subdued but rich embroidery, and when he turned to reach for the bowl of cut fruit, showing his profile—

Oh gods, it's Mygenos!

Sulun ducked his head down fast, praying to every god he could remember that everyone else in his work gang kept their faces averted too. His hands shook as he reached for the sour wine.

"Right," whispered Yanados. "We've all been keeping our heads down, and don't think the other servants haven't noticed. We'll have to explain later."

"Has he recognized—"

"Not yet, I don't think. None of us."

"If he sees Ziya . . ."

"She saw him first, ducked behind Vari. Gods, if only we could get out of here . . ."

Sulun ran a long look down the table. Vari sat with her back to Entori's guest, Ziya and Tamiri huddled beside her. Ziya—thank gods they'd thought to chop her hair all those moons ago—looked

very much like a small boy, a very silent and pale little boy. Omis—
Deese be blessed, hadn't come to dinner in his working clothes—
was hunched down so far that his beard was almost dragging in his
soup. Doshi, who normally drank very little, kept his face hidden
behind his winecup, though Sulun guessed it was long empty.
Arizun, taking no chances, had both his back turned and his face
bowed over his plate. Yanados, now that there was no more need
to speak with Sulun, cleverly made a play of trying to steal kisses
from the scullery maid; the maid, smiling cynically, played along.

Their gambits appeared to work. Mygenos hadn't bothered to
look over his shoulder at the servants, or hadn't seen more than
drab clothes and bowed backs. Gods, if they could only get out
of here, quickly and quietly . . .

But it was the custom in Entori House that the servants didn't
leave the room until the Master either ordered them out or left
himself. Entori had never bothered to dismiss the servants from
dinner, and showed no sign of doing so now. Neither did he seem
inclined to depart, clearly enjoying the game at the high table.

The game, and the dinner, dragged on for ages. The food at
the servants' table disappeared, the housekeeper frowned, the
maids scowled, the porter muttered, the skinny harper/sweeper
mumbled weak curses in his cup, and Sulun's gang kept silent
and sweated. The house mage finally snapped at one of the maids
to bring more wine, and the woman thankfully hopped up from
her place to comply. Sulun toyed with the thoughts on sending
the children away, one by one, supposedly on errands to the
kitchen, possibly carrying empty dishes away.

He froze as he heard Mygenos's voice, raised for the first time
that evening.

"Bear in mind, my Lord, the difficulty of supplying magical
protection for a device of whose construction we know nothing."
The man's voice was more unctuous than ever. Out of all Shibari's
doomed house, he'd clearly done the best for himself. "Surely
such costs must be considered when estimating the price."

There was another brief silence, then more haggling. Sulun
felt sweat crawling down his back, even as he realized that both
Mygenos and his new master were clearly hoping to get more
than just a ship engine or two; they hoped to learn the design and
construction of the device, in hopes of manufacturing their own—
and that fact was not lost upon Entori.

"The engines made in this house are competently protected by our own wizard, I assure you," Entori said. "Elizan, come here."

Gods! Sulun squirmed. *Don't draw attention to us!*

"Damn," muttered the old house wizard, clambering out of his seat. "Didn' even get my drink . . . Coming, Master."

Get Ziya out, somehow. Sulun glanced at the child, seeing her keep her pale face on her empty plate.

The old house wizard doddered up to the high table, executing a clumsy bow to Entori and his guests. Sulun hoped fervently that he didn't breathe too close to Mygenos and let the man know just how drunk he was. Still, Elizan had clearly played this game before.

"My Lords," he intoned, sounding merely stuffy, "despite the infirmities of age, my powers remain undimmed and indefatigable as ever in ages past. Yea, I have guarded Entori House from ill these thirty long years and more, and pray to do so for as many more. Behold, no ill befalls this house, not its goods, not its enterprises, nor any under its roof, as all may see and report. Yea—"

"Arizun," Sulun whispered under the cover of the fusty oration, "tell Vari: Send Ziya out with some empty dishes, tell her to run to her room and hide. Pass it on."

Arizun nodded quick acknowledgment, leaned closer to Doshi, and duly passed the message on.

"Our ships do not fail at sea, save to the malice of pirates, of course, whose attacks cannot be adequately predicted, nor does our house fall prey to robbers and riots of the streets. Our goods do not rot overmuch, nor are they consumed by vermin." Elizan could certainly provide a good speech, given cause. "Our house remains unvisited by plague, fire, earthquake, flood—"

"Yes, yes, all very well," Mygenos interrupted, winning a frown from his new master and a scowl from Entori. "But this is a novelty we speak of, a thing untried and unheard of before now. Can you deal effectively with such novelties, my good colleague?"

Quick as a cat, he set together two wineglasses—fine crystal, Sulun noticed—and carefully balanced a third on top of them. Smiling almost gleefully, he carefully filled the topmost glass to the brim.

"A small test, good colleague, of dealing with novelty." Mygenos pointed to the filled glass. "Let us contest. Do you attempt to keep this glass in place, and I will enchant it to overturn."

"On my tablecloth?" rumbled Entori.

"Waste good wine?" gasped the house wizard.

"Ah, let them proceed," Eloti murmured. "At worst, the laundress will have a bit of work."

"Hmm, well enough," Entori subsided. "Proceed."

His guest exchanged a glance with Mygenos, and smirked.

Vari whispered urgently in Ziya's ear. Ziya nodded once, picked up a handful of empty dishes, and slid noiselessly out of her seat.

Good, Sulun thought. *Now, while Myggy's busy. Go!*

A bit flustered, Elizan frowned at the balanced glasses. He licked his lips, clasped his hands, stared at the balanced glasses, and visibly concentrated.

Ziya, head down, carrying the pile of dishes, padded softly across the flagstoned floor toward the doorway.

Mygenos leaned back in his chair, stared at the balanced glasses through narrowed eyes, and concentrated.

Sulun, even with his eyes fixed on Ziya's retreating back, felt the slow rise of heat behind him. It was just as he'd always felt it in Shibari's house, when Mygenos was at work. Only an unexplained surge of heat, nothing more, but he'd learned to recognize it as the mark of Mygenos's power. Magery. Wizard work. The force apart from Natural Philosophy and alien to it, the force of gathered will working across the orderly patterns of the Laws of Matter. At that moment he hated it.

And he felt no answering surge from Entori's house wizard.

Gods, what would it mean if that old drunkard lost this duel, if Entori was pushed back on his haggling over the engines? Loss of money, loss of pride—inevitable loss of temper, and where would that outrage go save to spend itself on his servants? No doubt the first fury would drop on poor drunken old Elizan, but the second bolt would land upon Sulun and his colleagues. What form would it take?

What if this kept them from escaping the house, from getting to the riverside laboratorium, from finishing the bombard?

The fate of Sabis, resting on a balanced wineglass!

The wineglass jiggled, softly ringing.

Then, very faintly, he heard the drifting of a quiet song. A familiar song, one heard scant days ago, down by the river. With it came an equally familiar sense of calm, like a memory of bees buzzing sleepily in sunlight.

"Low lie the stars over Toslagen's memory . . ."

The crystal-ringing stopped.

Ziya, unnoticed, padded quietly out the doorway and into the shadowed corridor. Once safe in the shadows she began to run.

At the high table no one moved. Five figures peered, motionless, at the pyramid of wineglasses. The two wizards sweated, frowned, stared, their contesting wills almost palpable in the stillness.

Eloti, unnoticed, sat with her fingers steepled and pressed lightly against her lips, apparently just a rapt observer.

Sulun dared to raise his head and watch, feeling those balanced and battling forces: the beating heat like the wind from Omis's forge, the gently buzzing song that came from no mouth—and nothing noticeable from old Elizan.

Incredible, Sulun marveled. *He's her stalking-horse, and no one knows it!*

Mygenos clenched his fists, gritted his teeth, and the heat rose. Almost visible, darting tongues of hot power surged again and again at the balanced glass. The glass held, calmly immovable.

The old house wizard swayed on his feet, clearly growing distressed. With or without power, he was making effort—and the effort was draining him. Even to Sulun's eyes it was plain that the old tippler couldn't continue this much longer. In another few ticks of the waterclock he'd collapse, and what then?

Eloti flicked her eyes sideways at the old man, then back to the glass.

Almost casually, the silent song rose higher. It soared to a clear, ringing note—then to a falcon's screech of rage and triumph.

The glass tipped over—

—straight into Mygenos's lap.

The wizard yelped and scrambled out of his chair, leaving the wineglass to fall to the floor. Miraculously, it didn't break. Entori and his guest shouted wordlessly in surprise. Elizan gave a whoof of relief and leaned heavily against the table.

Eloti broke out laughing, an amazing sound, like the ring of unbroken crystal.

The hot cloud of tension around the high table dissipated like smoke before a rising gale. Mygenos cursed generously as he wiped his wine-stained robe, ignoring the furious look his master gave him.

"Ah, yes, I think our protections are adequate," Entori smirked, actually tugging a coin out of his belt purse and handing it to the old house wizard. "Thank you, Elizan. You may go."

"Pray, dismiss the rest of the servants too," Eloti smoothly cut in, raking a brief glance over the faces at the lower table. "Best let them get to their tasks while we discuss business in privacy."

"Oh, aye." Entori clapped his hands peremptorily, scarcely looking at the other servants. "You may go. Now, concerning the date of delivery . . ."

Sulun stood up fast, the others barely a second behind him, and headed for the door as quickly as he could manage without actually running. Vari already had the other children in tow, with Omis hurrying at their heels, and the other servants pattered after them.

Sulun had some idea of running off to their rooms to search for Ziya when the porter clapped a hand to his shoulder.

"Come down to the kitchen," the elderly servant hissed. "Ye simply must tell us who yonder guests are, and what's the trouble with 'em."

Sulun complied, tossing a last desperate glance to Omis and Vari. Yes, somebody had to satisfy the household's curiosity, and it seemed he'd been chosen. At least Ziya was safe, they were all safe from Mygenos's knowing eyes. The kitchen then, and more pilfered wine and interminable gossip. Small sacrifice for their salvation. He padded dutifully down the hall to the kitchen, grateful to see the rest of his little mob hurry off to their rooms.

There was still a fire burning in the kitchen, though no pots hung over it now. There stood the cook, who had managed to escape sitting in at the miserable dinner, handing a small pastry to a girl-child huddled on a stool beside the fire.

Girl? Who? Sulun plodded to the fireside at the porter's urging, barely noticing the cup of cider thrust into his hand, wondering where the girl had come from and who she was. Then the child raised her head and looked at him.

"Sulun?" she squeaked, the ghost of an old smile flickering over her face. "Sulun, you're *here*?"

It was Memi. Mygenos's daughter. She remembered him. *Oh, gods!*

All Sulun could think to do was plaster a sickly smile on his face and press a warning finger to his lips. "Hush, Memi," he whispered, grabbing for words. "Don't tell anyone I'm here. You know how people would laugh, hearing that Shibari's old philosopher now works for Entori the Miser."

"Aha," grinned the porter, guessing at the supposed disgrace. "So that's it, eh? 'Brought low, brought low, let none of me old friends know.' Heh-heh!"

"Aww . . ." Memi's face screwed into a grimace of pity. "I won't tell anyone, I promise."

For however long you can, Sulun groaned inwardly. "Thank you much, Memi. But tell me, how have you fared since you left Shibari's house?"

The child's noncommittal shrug told Sulun all he needed to know. Mygenos's fortunes might have improved, but Memi's life was no better. She might remember her old friend Sulun kindly, but eventually her father's sternness would press her too far: To save herself punishment or win herself some pathetic gain, she would let the secret out.

Eventually Mygenos would know who Entori's engineer was. Between old malice and new rivalry, the wizard wouldn't hesitate to ill-wish Sulun and his work.

And he knew Sulun worked with the firepowder.

Sulun sat down beside the fire, drank the cider, gossiped gently with the pathetically grateful child and with the momentarily kind servants, knowing his time had grown drastically short. Soon enough Mygenos would send for his daughter and depart. Soon enough Memi would reveal the secret. Soon enough Mygenos would set his vengeful little disasters in motion.

It was time to get out.

Four more days before they could get to the riverside workshop again: four days of making turbine parts, supports, molds for the steam valves—and hating every miserable hour of it. Four days of sweating over Memi's discovery, wondering when she'd tell and what Mygenos would do then. Four days of wretched work that felt like idleness without its rest.

Four days of bad news: there were more retreats, more losses in the north. The Ancar were moving steadily down the east side of the Baiz river valley, rolling over the Sabirn lines like a flood.

The Imperial House issued no news, but street gossip ran high. Refugees from the upper valley added to it, and none of their news was good. The traffic to Esha increased steadily.

"Perhaps Mygenos's new master will join the panic," Sulun suggested as he helped break down the box of the sand mold. "If he runs south, Myggy just may find it prudent to go with him. After that, he'll have other things to worry about than his old rival from Shibari House."

"Hope high," Omis grunted pulling away the last board. "Ah, that sand was pounded well."

The packed, now dry sand still stood firm as dried clay. Not a grain had moved during the four days of cooling down.

"Break it," said Omis, taking up a heavy sledge.

The rest of the work gang set upon the sand with mallets and chisels, cutting it away from the buried treasure. A familiar rapping on the front door interrupted them.

"Zeren, no doubt," said Eloti, rising gracefully from her seat on the bench. "Go on with the work; I'll let him in."

Ziya was the only one to watch her go, struck by the sight of the mistress of a respectable house going to open doors like a porter. The others kept on hammering, cutting, freeing the cast tube from the mold.

A moment later, Zeren strolled in with Eloti on his arm—just in time to hear Omis's shout of triumph and warning as the last of the sand fell away. They stopped to watch, Zeren unconsciously making a luck sign with his free hand.

The exposed tube didn't look very prepossessing: rough and pebbly, covered with glassy, fused sand, its interior still choked. Nonetheless, Omis cradled it in his arms, beaming, as if it were one of his own children.

"Beautiful," he breathed. "Not a flaw in the casting. Perfect."

"It doesn't look like much," Ziya sniffed, disappointed.

"Well, of course not, boy," Omis laughed. "It still has to be cleaned out, smoothed, polished, and the fuse hole drilled. We'll start that right now. Ah, good morning, Zeren. How is it you always manage to get here when something important's afoot?"

"No mystery," Zeren smiled, graciously lowering Eloti to her seat. "I come by every morning and see if anyone's about. I've told my guards I have a valuable informant here, which isn't a lie. The news is good, then?"

"Good now, better later. Set up the drill, boys."

While the apprentices scampered to comply, Sulun went to fetch food and drink. Zeren and Eloti were chatting when he brought the food out.

"Never mind the fool wizard," Zeren was saying. "He and his master must have better things to occupy them now. The Ancar have been halted above Lutegh."

"Halted?" Sulun crowed, setting out the cups and bowls. "Thank the gods! If they stay put only half a moon, we'll have the bombard tested and ready. . . ." He paused to cross his fingers, hoping that this model, this time, would work.

"Aye, cross your fingers," Zeren smiled sourly. "It isn't our oh-so-invincible troops that have checked them; it's the river. The Dawnstream branch of the Baiz is wide, fast, and deep there, and the Ancar are no sailors. They've only turned east awhile, looking for an easy way across the river. Expect they'll find it soon enough, and then turn south again."

"Surely our troops on the south bank can stop them?"

"Perhaps," Zeren shrugged. "They've had the wit to take every boat and barge from the north bank, burn every bridge, fortify every known ford clean up into the Cerinde West hills—the generals showed that much sense."

"Still," Eloti considered, "the Ancar have taken that hill country, I believe."

"It's crawling with them," Zeren sighed. "If the main horde of the Ancar can't cross any further west, they'll simply go up into the hills, cross where the Dawnstream thins out into its tributary streams, join their Cerinde West cousins, and come marching back down the south bank. A few months, at best." He glanced apologetically at Sulun. "We have less time than I thought, old friend. How long to finish your new bombard?"

"Gods . . ." Sulun tugged his hair, watching the work gang setting the drill bit into the blocked tube's muzzle. "Give us three days, just three uninterrupted days to drill it out, make the powder, test it. . . . How long then, you tell me, to attract enough interest at court that we can have a dozen work gangs, busy night and day, making bombards and powder and shot?"

Zeren shrugged again. "Do I use every contact I have, call in every favor, I could get interested parties to watch you fire the bombard—successfully—at the Sworddance Field within perhaps three days. After that, at best, you might have orders and assistants from the Imperial House itself the next day—or minor interest from the lesser Ministers in half a moon."

"After that . . ." Sulun calculated, allowing for the ignorance of strange craftsmen who wouldn't begin to understand the principles of the bombard. "A dozen workshops could make a dozen bombards, with powder and shot and sufficient knowledge to use them, in perhaps another half moon at best."

"So, if the Ancar can be held off for as long as one moon, Sabis might live." Zeren leaned back to look at the cloudless sky. "There be the gods' dicing floor, right over our heads."

"But we need those three days to finish the bombard, first." Sulun turned to Eloti, wild-eyed with a desperate hope. "Mistress, what if we were to disappear from Entori's house, just for three days, all of us? What would he do then?"

Eloti thought a moment, then shook her head. "He too has favors he can call in," she sighed. "He'd have his clients hunting the city for you, offering rewards far greater than any he's paid you. Too many neighbors know you come here, too many tradesmen, street loiterers, the gods know who else. I . . . couldn't protect you from everyone. Someone would talk."

Sulun groaned and looked back toward the busy group in the courtyard. "Then we still have to steal out here only when we can—perhaps one day in every five."

"Half a moon, then, just to finish this one bombard." Zeren glowered at the innocent-looking sky. "And another moon beyond that, to save our city. If I thought the gods would listen, I would beggar myself making offerings at every temple in Sabis. Gods, give us just that much time."

Out in the courtyard, Omis's drill began to whine through the packed sand in the bombard's muzzle, clearing out the bore.

Eloti, too, looked at the sky, then back at the ground, finally out toward the river. "I had almost forgot. Sulun, while your friends are thus engaged, come with me to the river."

"The river?" Sulun and Zeren gulped together, nonplussed at the change of subject.

"One reaches it through your back gate, not so?" Eloti stood, gathering her skirts and parasol.

"Er, oh, yes." Sulun hastened to lead the way through the courtyard, around the busy crew at the drill, to the back wall and its stout gate. "Uhm, the keys should be . . . Yes, here on the hook. I haven't opened this fool thing in years. Pray the hinges are . . . Yes."

The long-unoiled hinges screeched in protest, momentarily startling the apprentices, though Omis's concentration never wavered. The back gate grumbled open, revealing the thick-weeded bank of the river. The water here was oily and thick with garbage, and the wind off the river blew the stink into their faces.

"Ugh," muttered Sulun, pinching his nose. "It wasn't so bad inside. Let's go back."

"It's endurable." Eloti marched resolutely through the high weeds to the edge of the water. "There," she said, pointing.

Sulun looked, seeing only the wreck of what looked to be a sizable old barge tied up to ancient stakes driven into the mud. "What's there?" he asked.

Eloti smiled that faint, secret smile. "Look closer," she said. "It is not a wreck."

Sulun picked his way closer, hearing Zeren a few paces behind. The thing looked wretched enough, weathered grey hull spotted sickly green with patches of mold, deck covered with scatterings of rotted wood and dead weeds. The tie ropes looked frayed, but were thick enough to hold it steady. Still, he hated to set foot on those loose and undoubtedly rotten boards.

"Pull the top boards and weeds away," Eloti commanded, voice ever so slightly impatient.

Sulun obediently bent down and tugged away the topmost boards, brushed off some of the dead weeds.

Weeds? A lot of them, he noticed now, were artfully bound straw. The rotted boards were light, thin, and dry. No rusted nails threatened his hands. The assorted trash looked . . . fake.

Under it, the deck was clean and sound.

He stepped onto it, suspicion and wonder rising, and looked closer.

The hull and thwarts were solid too, showing little real sign of wear. The seams were caulked tight, no board was warped. The weathered grey color, he saw now, was deliberately toned paint. The mold patches were painted too.

"Camouflage," he whispered, impressed, hearing Zeren whistle in respectful amazement. "No, she's not a wreck at all."

"Below decks you'll find a mast and boom, sails, oars, and an awning," said Eloti. "I would suggest moving some of your provisions on board before we leave today."

Sulun straightened up to stare at her. Zeren, chuckling, replaced the disguising boards and weeds.

"In the event that we fail . . ." Eloti shrugged eloquently. "This can carry all of us, and everything, even the wagon and mules."

"Yes," Sulun agreed, not taking his eyes off his amazing Mistress. "Yes."

Zeren sat down on the deck and looked out over the water. "Win or lose," he muttered, "surer victory or better retreat than I've ever had before."

"That," said Eloti striding nearer to him, "is exactly what I intended."

Zeren laughed shortly. "Ah, Lady, if only some kindly god had given the defense of Sabis to you! To you, and not to those fools up on the hill." He shook his head at the madness and wonder of it.

In the courtyard, Omis stopped the drill and ordered the apprentices to change the drill bit for a heavy wire smoothing brush.

Part II
FLIGHT

✧ CHAPTER ONE ✧

Because a child dropped a book . . .

Memi, toting a pile of scrolls across her father's study, dropped one of them on the floor. She tried to grab it, and succeeded in losing the whole pile.

Mygenos, busy with a long list of instructions from his master, was jarred out of concentration by the sound. He jumped out of his chair, caught the erring child by the arm, and smacked her soundly on the face.

Memi, flinching away from him, blindly planted a foot on one of the unrolled scrolls, leaving a smudgy footprint.

Mygenos, his temper provoked and a target ready, yanked off his belt and began flogging the girl in earnest. The girl's struggles trampled more books, fueling Mygenos's ire to a good high blaze. He whipped her halfway across the room, finally pinning her against the wall, whipping wherever he could reach.

The child's screeches brought no help, no easing of the blows, and in desperation she scrambled for any words that would stop the pain.

"Papa, stop it! Stop it, and I'll tell!"

Mygenos, thinking only that she meant to complain to his master, laughed shortly and hit harder.

"I'll tell where Sulun is!"

Sulun? Surprised, Mygenos stopped in mid-blow. He'd scarcely even thought of the man since Shibari died.

Taking the halt in the flogging for interest, Memi tried further. "I know where Sulun is. I saw him. Just days ago. I saw."

"Where?" Mygenos demanded, twisting her arm.

"At the big house. The one where you took me, last moon-quarter. He was in the kitchen there." Memi sniffled, remembering Sulun had always been good to her. She might not have to tell Papa everything. Maybe Sulun would be safe.

"Why didn't you tell me before?" Mygenos gave her arm another yank.

"Ow! Ow! I wasn't sure. He looked different. And you've *told* me not to speak 'til spoken to . . ."

But Mygenos had stopped listening. "Big house, last moon-quarter . . . Gods, Entori!"

Almost absently, he let go of Memi's arm. The girl lost no time scuttling away from him and out the door. Mygenos hardly noticed, letting the belt swing lax in his hand. He chuckled slowly. "Entori's house, firepowder. Unknown qualities. And his wizard's an old stick, set in his ways . . . No defense. Well, well, well."

Laughing aloud, Mygenos went back to his writing table and shoved the assorted wax tablets aside. Oh yes, he'd have a new plan of attack to give his new master. At a guess, Entori would capitulate before the moon reached full again.

Mygenos reached for his meditation gem and set to work.

Because the city's draftees were hastily trained . . .

The sentry sat shivering on the bank of the Dawnstream, wishing its namesake weren't yet three hours away, wishing he were back in the familiar lands nearer the Baiz, wishing he were south in warm—if hungry—Sabis. Gods, but half a moon's training, mostly fumbling with too-big equipment while armored louts yelled at him, wasn't enough to make an invincible warrior out of a shoemaker. He'd told them and told them he'd do better making boots for the army, that years of bending over lapstone and awl had done nothing to improve his eyesight—which had been none too good at distances, ever, which was why he'd been apprenticed to a shoemaker in the first place—but none of them listened to him.

So here he sat, cold and wet and miserable, on the banks of a strange river in lands he'd never seen before, watching for some sign of invading Ancar. As if he'd recognize an Ancar if he saw one; they couldn't really be tall as trees, pale as fish bellies, dressed in scale-plate armor all over, now could they? And how was he to spot them, anyway? With his shortsighted shoemaker's eyes, he'd be lucky if he could see much beyond the ford itself: and the moon covered with clouds, as usual, and no fires or torches allowed where the Ancar might spot them and pick off troops with their fabled long bows. How was he supposed to see anything, anyway?

Oh, he could hear all right—the faint endless muttering from the entrenched camp behind him, the eternal rumbling of the water, nothing else for hours and hours, just like last night and the night before. Nothing new.

He hoped the other sentries were better at this than he was. They weren't.

None of them heard, beneath the sound of the river, the faint splashing downstream where the water was just over waist-deep for the taller Ancari. None of them saw, in the pitch dark under the cloud-covered moon, the dark-dressed troops struggling quietly through the water.

The attack came before the first dawnlight.

The former shoemaker never heard the arrow that killed him.

Because an old miser was proud and suspicious . . .

First, the coals on the hearth went out during the night, and the cook-fire was devilishly hard to start in the morning. Then the water crock slipped out of the scullery maid's hands, shattered, and splashed half of the kitchen. Then the cook sliced her thumb on a peeling knife. Then the pot boiled over.

It grew worse from there. Roaches got into the larder, followed by mice. Nails pulled out of the walls, dumping tapestries on the floor, which knocked bits of statuary off their pedestals, which inevitably broke. Inkwells spilled, always across important parchments, quill points broke and styli slipped on waxboards to mar whole columns of figures. Mildew grew on the walls and shelves, proliferated in the laundry. Bed webbing frayed and snapped. Old chairs collapsed when sat upon. Everything that could go wrong did.

Beyond doubt, the House of Entori was under a curse.

Morning reports lasted almost until noon, and mostly consisted of lists of small disasters. Entori spent an hour locked away behind his study door, screaming threats and insults at the house wizard. Omis and Sulun, last in line, could hear the shouts through the door, and winced in sympathy for the old drunkard. They weren't at all surprised to see, when the door finally opened, a tattered and terrified Elizan come stumbling out at the best pace he could manage—followed by a thrown inkwell. The old man held a jingling purse in his hand as if it were a large poisonous spider, and as he left he hurried down the corridor toward the front door.

"Going to fetch some professional help, no doubt," Omis guessed, watching him go. "Hope it comes soon. I don't dare light up my forge while the curse is running unchecked."

"We'd best go in together to explain that," Sulun considered. "Oh gods, I just thought: if it's this bad here, what's happening down at the river house?"

"The firepowder," Omis whispered, going pale.

"We won't know until we get down there, which we'd best do soon."

"Make some excuse to go there."

The bell rang peremptorily, and they walked in together.

"No, of course you can't work your forge until the other wizards get here," Entori snapped, looking more than ever like a ruffled vulture. "I don't suppose your other tools will be safe, either. Gods, nothing's safe but what's watched every moment. Nobody can work like this."

"We could test how far the curse extends," Sulun offered. "We'll get out to market—we need some supplies—and see what befalls us once we're away from the house."

"Nonsense! No one leaves the house today, not until the new wizards come." Entori poked among his scattered parchments and waxboards, mumbling something they couldn't quite catch, something about desertion. He paused and glared up at them. "Once they arrive, I'll need you to instruct them on the proper workings of your tools so the protections can be arranged. Ugh, more damned outsiders knowing my business . . . Gods' curses, it can't be helped."

"But meanwhile," Omis wheedled, "perhaps we could investigate, go out and ask in the right places, discover who it is that put the curse on your house—"

"I know who it is!" Entori slapped his hands on the pile of parchments, making another stylus fall off on the floor. "It's that damned Valishni and his doubly damned wizard, the one who wanted my steam engine. Who else? If he can't have it, he'll see to it that I can't use it. Son of an ape, I'll get him. . . ."

Mygenos! Omis and Sulun looked at each other, shivering with dread.

"Oh, get out of here," Entori snarled. "Go keep watch on your tools and apprentices, see that nothing else breaks or disappears. I'll have you summoned when the new wizards come. Go on, leave."

The engineers did, shaking their heads, not daring to speak until they were out the door and a good way down the corridor.

"Memi told," Omis growled. "Myggy knows we're here. Gods, the curse must center on our tools!"

"Don't blame the child," Sulun insisted. "The gods only know how he got it out of her. The old vulture's right about getting new wizards to protect our gear. Hmm, wait. We should talk to the Mistress about this."

"Best find her speedily, then."

The search took not long at all; Eloti was waiting for them in the back courtyard, expressionless as always.

"Mistress, the curse comes from Mygenos, of Valishni's house," Sulun told her without preamble. "He knew us when we worked for Shibari, and hated us cordially. We need to know if the curse centers upon us, our tools, or only on Entori's house."

"But how——" Omis threw him a wide-eyed look, only now realizing that Eloti was, despite her earlier comment, the true mage of Entori House.

Eloti gave him a cold, imperious stare. Sulun met it levelly. She shrugged capitulation. "It centers somewhere in the house," she admitted. "I went out this morning, and it did not follow me. Nor do I think, for all your . . . acquaintance's malice, that it centers on you." She met Sulun's eyes again. "I myself put protection upon you and your people, and your workshop by the river. As you've seen, I have somewhat more power than your Mygenos."

"Thank you," said Sulun, vastly relieved. "But . . . that leaves our tools and gear, here in the house."

"My forge," Omis groaned. "Everything here."

"One cannot do everything," said Eloti. "I'm sorry."

"Mistress, I'm grateful for what you've done already," Sulun vowed. "If we can get to the riverside house, we could work unhindered. Entori's hired wizards can guard this place."

"But we can't leave!" Omis groaned. "Not until the new wizards come. He wants us to show them the workings of our tools, and the engine, so they can apply protections."

"A pity," sighed Eloti. "But for that, you would have a perfect excuse to absent yourself from the house and go work at the riverside shop. I could go myself, except he specifically bade me stay too—and, knowing him, he might call on me at any moment."

"Then we're all rooted here, idle, for the day," Sulun said gloomily.

"A single day." Eloti smiled. "I doubt that our projects will suffer much for losing a single day."

✧ CHAPTER TWO ✧

It took three days.

The two new wizards arrived, ushered in by a much crestfallen Elizan, before lunchtime on the first day. They spent the rest of the morning and afternoon inspecting the house, muttering, making notes to themselves and generally giving an impression of serious study. Entori, stamping along two steps behind them, was not much impressed. They did manage, by dint of much muttering and chanting, to clear the curse out of the kitchen and larder so that some sort of dinner was possible that night.

The second day, much to Sulun's and Omis's relief, the visiting wizards inspected the courtyard workshop. Everyone took pains to describe their tools and the workings thereof, and Arizun took particular joy in describing the details of the steam engine's construction—much to Entori's ill-suppressed fury. After much work and two false starts, they managed to disenchant the tools to the point where Omis dared to start up his forge. Between the wizards' prolonged well-wishing and the engineers' care, a few more engine parts were cast and cut assembled without incident—but by then it was close upon dinnertime.

"Two days wasted," Omis complained over the poorly cooked evening meal. "Two days! By now I could have had the bombard smoothed and drilled and ready for its first test. Gods, if we can only get out tomorrow . . ."

"Hope the old vulture's stopped peering over our shoulders by then," Sulun commiserated. "Hope he's turned his attention somewhere else, or at least that Mygenos has. Most likely, though, Entori will want us to make up for lost time on the damned engine."

"And this one's taking longer because we have to make the valves ourselves. Gods' curses! I feel like a turtle trying to outrun a fox."

"With luck, we can get to the laboratorium tomorrow." Sulun wondered if they could expect any luck at all, now that they had Myggy snapping at their heels. No doubt his master would come sniffing around Entori house soon enough, hoping the old miser's ill luck would make him more amenable to a deal. When he found Entori still unwilling, he'd have Mygenos increase the pressure: more trouble, more delays, more work for Entori's hired wizards, more of his attention focused on his engine building, less chance for Sulun and his company to slip away. "We have to get out of here," Sulun muttered to no one in particular.

And on the third day, disaster came home.

The guards opening the city gates at dawn were first to see the dust rising on the road. After that came the first messengers on lathered horses, with the first retreating troops hard on their heels. The news went up to Imperial House first, but it reached the marketplaces less than an hour later.

The Ancar had crossed the Dawnstream by night, smashed the garrisons one after the other, rolled the Sabirn army all the way back down the south shore to the Baiz itself.

Lutegh had fallen.

The Ancar were less than five days' march from Sabis.

Panic hit the city.

Vari heard the signal tap on the rear gate, scrambled up on the small pyramid of barrels, and tossed the rope ladder over the other side. It creaked alarmingly as Arizun, then Sulun, and finally Omis climbed up it. They tumbled, panting, down the barrels as Vari pulled back the ladder and listened briefly for sounds of anyone following.

"How are the children?" was the first thing Omis asked.

"Well enough," Vari whispered. "They think its a fine adventure, all except Ziya, who's turned quiet and morose again. Get inside, quickly."

They hurried through the darkened courtyard past barricades of more barrels and crates, into the silent corridor and off to Omis's room, carefully barring the doors behind them.

Yanados and Doshi, clanking softly with belt-strung weapons, half rose as the others came in. "Are you well?" Yanados asked first. "Sulun, your arm—"

"Only a shallow cut." Sulun tried to smile. "I got it ducking behind some timbers when a gang of mercenaries went by."

Vari shook her head and set to cleaning and bandaging the scratch.

"How has it gone here?" Arizun asked. "Any more rioters trying to break in?"

"Not tonight, not so far." Doshi shrugged, making his hatchet clank against the wall. "The old man has the place barricaded with damn near everything from the storerooms, swearing the house will stand until the very mountains fall. Then again, if the door does go down, there's hardly anyone in the house who could stop then."

"Entori still hasn't hired more bully-boys, then?" Omis winced as Vari pulled the bandage tight. "With all these damned troopers-for-pay hanging about in the streets, one would think . . ."

"Even Entori wouldn't trust that lot," Omis snorted. "Gods, how right Zeren was. We saw enough of them lolling about the streets, drinking the wineshops dry, looting wherever they fancied, and bashing anyone who complained. As if the starving refugees weren't enough . . ."

"What happened to their officers?" Doshi hissed between his teeth. "Why in the nine hells aren't they outside, defending the city as they were hired to do?"

"Too many of the regular army officers were killed during the overrunning of the Dawnstream." Arizun leaned his head back against the wall, as if infinitely tired. "The mercenary troops won't obey anyone but their own commanders, who claim that they no longer had anyone to report to. Now their commanders won't take orders from anyone 'not properly authorized,' so they say."

"Which means no one who doesn't come from high up in the court, with gold ready to hand," Omis finished. "Nobody in the court has done that yet."

"Gods," Vari muttered, packing her remaining healing simples into a bag. "Why not? What's wrong with the high court?"

"Utter confusion." Sulun winced, and not from his minor wound. He hesitated to tell the worst of the news, wondering how the others would take it. "There seems to be . . . some manner of faction fight going on at the moment. Some gang of fools wants to send envoys to the Ancar, make terms with them. There have been . . . disappearances, mysterious sudden deaths, messages gone awry . . . No one's sure of anything. No one knows how bad it is, truly."

"Why hasn't the old Emperor done something?" Vari insisted.

Sulun heaved a profound sigh, feeling Omis's eyes on him, knowing he'd have to say it. "He hasn't appeared publicly. There are rumors that he's . . . ill, perhaps very ill."

"Maybe dying?" Yanados guessed.

Sulun only shrugged. The others looked at each other.

"And . . ." Doshi hesitated. "The rest of the city?"

"Thievings, riots, everyone running," Arizun recited wearily. "The city guards are trying to round up everyone they can, hauling folk off to the army court—not for trial, but to be pressed into service for defense of the city. You can imagine how much success they're having, especially with the mercenaries."

"Pitched battles in the streets?" Yanados murmured. "Have you heard anything of Zeren?"

"Battles, yes; Zeren, no." Omis shook his head. "He's most likely in the thick of the mess, and we stayed away from such whenever we could."

"We may never see him again—" Vari sobbed, then caught herself.

"He'll survive, if anyone can," Omis tried to reassure her. It didn't work, but everyone pretended it did.

"Well, so." Yanados tried to smile. "Did you make it to the river house?"

"Not even near to it," said Arizun. "Where there weren't rioters or mercenaries or press gangs, there were fires. We couldn't get through unseen, had to turn back."

"More fires?" Doshi went pale in the dim lamplight.

"*More* fires?" Omis jerked his head up. "Has anyone tried to—"

"Not here," Vari assured him quickly. "Just . . . down the street."

"How far down the street?"

"Three houses down. But you know how far that is, and it was put out soon, just a diversion, I think, while the rioters broke into the other side of the house to steal things."

"Good gods, fire!" Omis pressed his hands to his eyes. "They'll come here soon enough."

"Maybe not," Sulun tried. "By tomorrow, someone at court may settle the squabbling up there, restore order." But he couldn't believe it.

"Sulun," Omis reminded, dropping his hands on his lap, "what about Myggy's curse on this house?"

Sulun opened his mouth, shut it again, thought fast. "I think he'll have other things on his mind now, too much to bother with renewing his ill-wishing on us."

"But can you be sure of that?"

Sulun didn't say anything.

"We have to get out." Yanados finally said the words, firmly enough that no one would argue. "This very night, out. We'll go first to the river house, then down to the port."

"Why the port?" Sulun raised his head, frowning.

"Because . . ." Yanados let out a long breath. "Because that's where we'll find the *Yanira*. Her captain will take us . . . to Sakar."

Everyone stared at her dropping the veil over her secret at last. It was Doshi who had the desperation, or lack of tact, to say the words.

"He's . . . You're a Sakaran? One of the pirates?"

Yanados blinked, but otherwise didn't falter. "Yes. My father was a most successful pirate. He also knew enough of the ways of pirates that he didn't want his daughter married to one. He could have quietly bought me a respectable marriage to some respectable mainlander, but I didn't want that, and he . . . cared for me enough to listen. I had skills, wanted to use them, persuaded him that I could make my way on the mainland. He gave me the . . . supplies I needed and got me passage to Sabis."

"Where you disguised yourself as a boy and apprenticed yourself to old Abanuz," Sulun cut in, seeing the puzzle fall together.

"Yes." Yanados tossed him a fleeting smile. "I still kept some contact with my father's people, though. Imagine my joy at finding that one of them now works the *Yanira*."

"So you took him aside for a brief chat, and explained to him how useful our steam engines—and we—would be to Sakar."

Yanados shrugged eloquently, not taking her eyes off Sulun. "If—when Sabis falls to the Ancar, who will be left that could defy them?" she said.

"Gods," Sulun breathed, sagging under the weight of the vision.

Sakar, the multi-island fortress in the middle of the world's heart, the Mormuz Sea: the only land safe from the land-devouring northern hordes, one place where civilization could survive, the one kingdom that could restore the sea trade—or attack any seaports the Ancar held. *Irony of the gods! Civilization preserved, even restored, by a kingdom of pirates!* "Why not?" Sulun found himself laughing. "The 'honest' folk of Sabis have served us poorly; perhaps pirates would do better."

"Two small stumbling blocks," said Arizun, stopping the laughter. "One: is the *Yanira* in port now?"

"I don't know," Yanados admitted, "But if she isn't tonight, tomorrow at latest—her captain's a far bigger fool than I believe. With everyone who can afford passage rushing across the straits, anyone with so much as a reed rowboat is growing rich on the ferrying trade. You can wager, the *Yanira's* captain wouldn't miss such opportunity."

"Surely not," Sulun laughed, a little light-headed. It occurred to him that such a captain, in Entori's employ at least part of the time, would be in an excellent position to know when and where valuable cargoes sailed—and to sell such knowledge to his Sakaran friends. "Heh! No wonder Entori's lost so many ships to the pirates." *And Shibari too?* a sudden thought sobered him. Had the loss that ruined his former patron been likewise arranged? If so then the failure of the Bombard Project, the very fall of Sabis, might be laid at the feet of Sakar.

"Two," Arizun went on implacably, "what makes you think we can get to the port?"

Yanados stared at him. "Why ever not?"

"Have you seen it lately?" Arizun glanced at Sulun and Omis. Omis looked away.

Once more, Sulun felt everyone's eyes on him and wondered how he'd ever got himself into this. "We got a quick look, from several streets away," he began. "It was . . . totally mad. Even at night, people crowding the docks, howling like mad things, fighting for a place on board a ship, any ship. Sailors had to beat them back to get room to unload, and then the City Guard had to beat them away from the unloaded grain!" Sulun shivered.

"There were people fighting everywhere, falling into the water," Omis added. "The ships were overloaded, small boats worse. We saw one turn over. . . ."

"The poor folk were begging for rides across the river," Arizun took up the tale. "Just to get west of the city, into the swamps, on rafts made of barrels and scrap-wood, some even swimming. I don't know how many drowned."

"How," Sulun finished, "would you get to the *Yanira* in the midst of that?"

Yanados thought a while, then shook her head. "I suppose it won't get any better, not with the Ancar coming, not tomorrow, not the day after. And how long could we hide out in the riverside workshop?"

"Maybe two days before the food ran out," said Omis. "We might fish on the river, could we get to clear water."

"Upstream," said Doshi. "If we stay on the river, travel only at night, we can get past the Ancar lines soon enough."

No one answered him, but everyone gave a soft, resigned sigh. That simply, it was decided.

"When?" was all Sulun asked.

"Give us some time to rest," Vari insisted. "A few hours, at least. And the streets should be emptier after midnight."

There was a general mumble of agreement. Nobody wanted to risk those perilous streets just yet. A few more questions determined that everything usable was already at the river house, or else already packed. They had only to take up their bundles and go.

Sulun was about to suggest that everyone find bed space and get some sleep while they could when they heard the first noise at the front door: the loud crack of a stone hitting the wood, and the echoes sounding through the house.

Everyone jumped, looked at each other, listened.

Another stone, heavier, and then the sound of voices and fists and feet, that low, growling, tearing sound they'd come to know too well. Cries and thudding footfalls sounded elsewhere in the house, and Entori's voice shouting in outrage and fear.

"The door?" Vari whispered, barely audible over the growing noise.

"Not long if they keep that up," Sulun decided, climbing to his feet. "We go. Now."

It took no measurable time for all of them to take up bundles, check their assorted weapons, blow out the lamp, and peer out into the corridor. Down at the front end they saw a servant run past, apparently headed for the kitchen. Omis and Vari darted into the next room, came out bare seconds later holding the two smaller children, Tamiri running silently ahead of them.

Sulun pointed to the back courtyard, and they ran—down the dark corridor, dodging around bales and barrels, pausing for long sweaty seconds to unlock doors and get through them, out at last into the sweltering night air and the open sky.

"The wagon," Sulun whispered. "Where did you—"

"By the corner of the stable," Yanados hissed back. "There . . ."

They skidded to a tangled halt, seeing the wagon standing, mules already in harness, before the back gate. The tailgate was open and waiting, nothing in the wagon bed but a single large oak chest.

Someone was sitting at the driver's box, a woman in a dark dress. She turned and smiled politely at them.

"Eloti!" Omis gulped. "Er, excuse me, Mistress. Is Master Entori . . . ?"

"He will not come, not even now. Climb aboard quickly," Eloti said, as calmly as if she were discussing a jaunt to the market. "That front door won't hold forever."

"Yes," Sulun agreed. "Everyone, get aboard. Omis, can you get the gate open fast?"

The others complied, with considerable speed and surprisingly little noise. Sulun climbed into the driver's box and took the mules' reins. They seemed restive, but still controllable. He took up the whip, just to be sure.

"Mistress," he asked, watching Omis manhandle the gate, "what weapons do you carry tonight?"

"Only my dagger." Eloti shrugged eloquently. "Gently reared ladies are not taught the uses of the bow or sword."

"Best climb in back then, with Vari and the children. Omis, climb on!"

Omis came running, leaving the gate to swing open on blessedly silent darkness behind him. He vaulted into the driver's box just as Eloti stepped neatly into the wagon box and sat down on the chest. Sulun glanced back and saw that the others were either huddled down among the baggage or else crouched along the sides and back of the wagon, bows and axes ready in their hands.

Behind them came a cracking and splintering sound as the front door of Entori House gave way.

Sulun shook the reins and cracked the whip over the mules' backs.

Willing and eager, for once, the mules leaped for the gate. Sulun hauled hard on the right reins to make the turn into the back alley, grateful that he'd practiced this maneuver a few times before. The wagon wheels growled and rumbled on the packed earth.

"Gods, the noise!" Omis hissed. "In the streets, they'll hear us coming."

"Move fast," Yanados volunteered. "Move fast and shoot arrows early."

Behind her, a child's voice rose softly in a keening wail of grief; Ziya, feeling old wounds reopened. Vari murmured attempts at comfort, but had no effect.

"Don't cry; shoot!" Arizun snapped, pressing another bow into her hands.

Ziya took the bow, nocked an arrow, and fell silent.

The wagon rumbled out into the street—and into a thin crowd all running to the right, toward the street where Entori House fronted. Sulun reined the mules to the left, and lashed wildly about him with the whip. Omis whipped up a heavy bow and let fly into the street, catching the tail of somebody's cloak. At least one of the crowd thumped into the mules, fell, went under their hooves—but managed to roll away from the wheels. Sulun whispered a brief prayer of thanks for that as the scrambling mules began gathering speed. Oncoming looters jumped aside, not ready to attack fast-moving animals and a well-armed crowd on a heavy wagon. Yanados turned and shot a few arrows to the rear to discourage anyone from following. The arrows skittered off walls and pavement, but no one followed.

In a moment, the wagon was thundering down an empty street, dark save for moonlight and an occasional lamplight glow behind shuttered windows.

"Straight three streets, then right," Omis panted. "Pray the fires have died down near the river turnoff. . . ."

"I know," Sulun panted. "Get ready for more mobs. Gods, keep us from the troops!"

At the third street, they saw torches—too many torches, in the hands of too many men—coming toward them from the left. Sulun hauled the mules to the right, hearing shouts behind him.

Someone in that mob had a bow too, for an arrow thunked into the tailgate. Yanados and Arizun fired back together, and Sulun lashed the mules into a gallop. The mob fell behind and the wagon went careening up the street.

Two cross streets up, a handful of silent men made a dash for the wagon. Sulun hit one across the face with the whip, Omis backhanded another with his axe, and a third fell to the now panicky mules. This time Sulun *did* feel the heavy thump of a body going under the wagon wheels, and struggled not to be sick, not now, not here. The other robbers, whoever they were, disappeared back into the shadows.

A straight road then, and no other sound but the rumbling of the wheels and the clattering hooves of the mules.

But there were fires ahead. Sulun could see the fire glow in the sky above the roofs to the right, smell the smoke heavy and fresh on the air, mixed with the smell of spilled wine.

"Third vintners' street," Omis identified it. "Be sure the troops are looting there. Turn left, next chance, then right again."

"Narrow street," Sulun remembered. "If it's blocked . . ."

"Wasn't, earlier," was all Omis could offer.

They swung left. There was another crowd here, but running away from them. Sulun guessed they expected the rioting mercenaries to come this way, and hauled to the right again as soon as a street showed itself.

There was a fire at the end of the street. A house on the left corner was blazing furiously, its roof fallen in but walls still standing. The smoke smelled of scorched wool.

"A weaver's," Sulun guessed. "How will we get the mules past it?"

The animals were already slowing down, tossing wild-eyed heads, unwilling to get close to the fire. Sulun pulled them to the right, scraping as close to the buildings as he dared, lashing furiously at the beasts and thanking any gods who could hear him that this street was wide enough; they could get past the fire if only the mules didn't panic completely.

From behind him, Eloti rested her hands on Sulun's shoulders, leaned forward, and screeched a stream of ear-searing abuse at the mules. Sulun gulped in amazement; there were a few obscenities in that litany that he'd never heard before. Where had Entori's properly reared sister learned them?

The mules, encouraged by a familiar voice, lurched ahead—past the burning house, scraping the off wheels against walls, floundering past running figures laden with bundles and baskets, out and away onto the next street. Their flanks were dark with sweat, and foam spattered from their bridles.

"Give them some rest," Eloti said, stepping back into the wagon bed. "Otherwise they'll never last to the river."

Sulun nodded agreement and let the mules slow of their own accord, down to a lumbering trot for the moment at least. So, Eloti knew much of ships, wagons, and mules; there was much he would like to ask her, if they ever had the opportunity.

Twice more they turned, avoiding any sign of light or motion ahead, away from burning torches, burning houses, even lamplight. Light meant crowds: mobs, rioting mercenaries, even the city guard—none were safe to meet tonight.

Once, looking back up the rising slope of the city, they saw a whole block of buildings on fire.

"Gods," Omis groaned, "Zeren's house is up there!"

"Pray he's not in it," Sulun muttered, whipping the mules to a faster trot. "Most likely he won't be, not tonight."

But it was pain to think of Zeren out in this night of fire and ruin, fighting thieves and rioting mercenaries in a dying city, and nowhere left to go. He might stay to the last, falling in the final defense of the city—and Sabis would fall, was doomed, the weapon that might have saved her lying half-finished in the house by the river, ruined by Fate's connivance and human stupidity and malice. Sulun coughed ashes and prayed that his friend would trust instinct, run while he could, escape one more time—to Esha, or the islands, or somewhere the endless hordes from the north couldn't reach—not to give up and die with the city.

"The river!" Omis gasped. "Smell the air."

Gods, yes: the wind had shifted, and the familiar stink came rolling, welcome for once, up the darkened street. Sulun hauled left, one more time.

Oh gods, there was a small street-brawl in the way—a crowd of bravos smashing into the wineshop. No way to get past it.

"Arrows," Omis grunted, picking up his bow.

Sulun lashed the mules into a dead run, hoping that speed and surprise would serve them one more time.

The outermost of the crowd turned their heads, noticing the

noise, just as the first arrows flew. Screeches of pain and shock followed, drawing the attention of the rest of the looters. Half of them scattered as the mule-drawn wagon thundered down on them, but half didn't. Too many of the crowd were wine-soaked mean, hot on the chase of plunder, and armed. Maybe a dozen of them jumped out into the street, waving assorted bludgeons and a few hatchets.

"The mules!" Sulun shouted warning, laying about wildly with his whip.

The apprentices in the wagon fired off another volley of arrows—all of which hit, hardly room to miss—and maybe four of the bravos lurched aside, cursing or screaming but preoccupied with wounds.

In the next second, the mules ran full-tilt into the crowd, braying wildly. Omis dropped his bow into the driver's box and pulled up his axe, ducking low under Sulun's flailing whip. Two more of the crowd went down under the mules, but the rest converged on the beasts, grabbing at the bridles. The mules reared, squealing, hooves finding enough targets to keep hands away from their reins, but their forward momentum was gone. The crowd closed in.

Yanados, Arizun, and Doshi fired steadily and fast, arrows thinning down the mob, but now the club-swinging crowd was up to the wagon, pawing for purchase. Omis swung a ferocious half-arc with his axe, and the nearest of the looters went sprawling backward among his cronies, face redly smashed. The apprentices dropped their bows, pulled out hatchets, and began chopping at the oncoming fists. The mules brayed wildly as assorted hands finally caught their bridles. Eloti, quick as a cat, stabbed her little dagger squarely into the arm of a man trying to climb the wheel, and Vari finished him with a stout chop from a kitchen cleaver.

"Too many, too many," Sulun muttered to himself, slashing the whip across three howling faces at once. Maybe only a half a dozen attackers now, but enough; they'd be on the wagon soon. Better a press gang than this . . . "The Guard!" he bellowed at the top of his lungs. "Hai, the City Guard!" Maybe that would confuse the mob for a moment long enough for him to whip those three away from the mules. "Hai, the Guard!"

Omis, not knowing what Sulun meant, thought there were actual Guards in sight. "Zeren!" he shouted, hoping to let the

Guards know who their friends were. "Hai, Captain Zeren! Here!"

Further off, somebody swore. A door banged open.

The crowd wasn't confused, and the lead three held on to the mules. One of them pulled out a knife and tried to duck toward the wagon, hoping to hamstring one of the animals. Sulun flailed at him with the whip, but only succeeded in slowing the man down. Omis spotted the attacker and leaned out over the driver's box, hoping to swing the axe at him. Behind them, Doshi yelped and toppled as a well-aimed barrel stave caught him on the leg. The stave carrier started up over the tailgate, then ducked as Yanados flew at him, hatchet raised.

Sulun didn't see the first man go down, only saw the off mule rear up, its head suddenly freed. The second man half-turned, just in time to catch a long blade across the throat. He coughed and dropped, and Sulun got a clear look at the sword and the man holding it.

"Zeren!" he shouted, just as Omis swung at the bravo crouched by the mules' flanks. "Did I conjure you up?"

Omis's axe thudded meatily into the third man's shoulder, dropping him to the stones.

"Yes, I suppose you did," said Zeren, quite calmly, as he trotted toward the continuing struggle at the wagon bed. With equal calm he raised his shield and ran his sword into the side of the looter climbing the nearside rear wheel.

The two louts near the tailgate, seeing the odds change so drastically, jumped away from the wagon and ran into the dark street. What was left of the crowd scattered in the other direction, or dived into hiding in the wrecked wineshop. Sulun dropped the whip and wrestled with the reins, pulling to keep the wide-eyed beasts from plunging on down the street. Zeren wiped his sword on his thigh, sheathed it, turned back, and took the reins of the nearer mule.

"Inside," he said, dragging the unwilling animal toward the open doorway of the workshop. "Hurry, or they'll come back."

Omis hopped down from the seat, ran to take the other mule's bridle, and helped pull the animal toward the gate and through it.

"Zeren?" gulped Yanados, looking over her shoulder. "Where did he come from?"

"Ask later," snapped Arizun, hopping down from the wagon.

"Close the doors first." He pulled the heavy panels closed and shoved the bolt home, then ran after the others into the courtyard.

"Not too bad," Vari clucked, examining Doshi's leg. "Bruise: no break. Soak it in hot water . . . ah, will we have time for that?"

"Not now," said Eloti. "On the boat."

"Boat?" Sulun puzzled. "Oh. Yes, the boat. Do we have everything packed? Put it on the boat, by all means!"

The others, much to Sulun's surprise, did exactly that. In a moment he was alone with Eloti and the mules.

The beasts stood panting, heads down and ears sagging, ribs heaving like bellows and steam rising from their sweat-darkened hides. They looked as if they couldn't move another cubit, and Sulun didn't blame them.

"What will become of these poor beasts?" he wondered aloud.

"Why, we're taking them with us, of course," Eloti snapped, getting down from the wagon. "On the boat you'll find good straw, some tethering ropes and halters, a few days' feed, and some nosebags. I recommend that we get the mules and wagon on board as soon as they're fit to move again."

"The wagon, too?" Sulun tried to imagine sailing this whole menagerie down the river.

"There is no other way to take everything."

"Very well. It's worth the bother." Eloti went to the mules' heads, took their reins, and patted their foamy muzzles. "We'll need it once we leave the river. The north is said to be rough country, and I can't imagine the Ancar keeping the roads in good repair."

"North . . . No hope for reaching the port and the *Yanira*, then?"

"None whatever."

Sulun nodded weary acceptance. "How do we get the mules on the boat?" he asked.

When the last of the gear had been stowed aboard, the apprentices set the planks in a short bridge from the bank to the boat deck. Omis and Eloti took the weary mules by their bridles and led them onto the creaking platform. The beasts were nervous of their footing and moved cautiously, but between Eloti's cooed urgings and Sulun's encouragement from behind with the whip, the team and wagon crawled onto the waiting boat. The moment the rear wheels rolled off the planks, the apprentices made haste to pull the boards up again. Vari hustled to the lines to untie them, but Yanados bade her wait until the mules were safely unhitched and tied in place.

As Omis and Eloti tied the mules, there was a moment of idleness for the others, time enough to look down the river toward the port. Everyone looked, and no one said anything.

Between multiple torchlights and what appeared to be a warehouse fire, the scene at the port was visible in full and ugly detail: overloaded ships crawling away from the docks, loading ships listing visibly under the weight of desperate refugees scrambling aboard, still others waiting for room to reach the docks and take on cargo, smaller boats and even homemade rafts darkening the water as they ferried frantic Sabisans across the river. Too often, ships and tiny ferry craft collided, throwing shrieking passengers into the firelit water. From here, the constant howl of countless frantic voices formed a single, eerie wail of horror and misery.

Zeren's face was a shadowed mask of grim sorrow in the dim red light. "I should be there," he said quietly.

"Nonsense," Sulun snapped, pulling at the tie ropes. "What more could you do there? The city's doomed, and you know it. Come with us, and no more such talk."

"Run again?" Zeren glared into the wind from downriver. "I've been running all my life, it seems."

"This is an age of running," said Eloti, coming up to the huddle of apprentices. "You louts, come help me put up the mast and sail."

Yanados stood up, turned a last longing glance toward the hopeless port, and came to direct the setting of the mast. The others, subdued, followed her.

"I'm no sailor." Zeren sat down on the deck and turned his brooding gaze toward the dark water. "What use will I be to you now?"

"We won't be sailing long," Sulun reminded him. "Once we're safely past the Ancar lines, we'll go inland and north. 'Twas your idea, remember? We'll need an experienced guard in that country."

"And if I'm all you have?" Zeren shook his head in almost reverent wonder. "This is mad, you know."

"Less mad than staying in Sabis to die."

"True."

Zeren heaved himself to his feet and went to help with the sail.

The captain of the *Yanira* cursed in a steady, weary monotone as he steered through the crowded inlet and beat toward open sea. Gods, this was true hell on the water, worse than any pirate raid he'd ever seen. So damned many ships, small boats, unbelievable little junk-rafts, thick as fleas on the water and getting in each others' way: he'd rammed a few of the smaller ones on every trip, and this was his third straits crossing since dawn. Ye gods, the bodies in the water, bumping off the prow even this close to the sea—some of them no doubt his own doing, for he'd had to throw a good dozen off the *Yanira* for crowding too close and fouling the gear. If it weren't for that incredible engine below deck, he couldn't have done this well.

Even so, he swore this was his last run tonight. No more of this madness, no matter how good the pickings—and the Sabisans were spending their coin now as if it would be worthless in a few days, which indeed it might well be. Already there was so much gold, silver, copper, and bartered goods in the hold that he doubted he'd have room for another cargo of grain. He could leave for Sakar tonight, and his crew and himself would be rich men all their days. . . .

Once again he let his eyes range over the crowd huddled on the top deck, looking—uselessly, he already knew—for Yanados and her valuable friends. She hadn't come today or yesterday, and he doubted she'd come tomorrow. How could she reach him through that howling chaos on the docks, anyway? Would she not, more likely, have taken the first available ship? If she reached Mez on some other ship, would she not wait there to get word to him, knowing how often he put in at that port? Surely there were better ways of discharging his debt than by returning to Sabis.

No, the captain decided, feeling the wind of the free ocean ruffle his hair, *I'll come back. I'll keep coming back until the Ancar arrive and all hope fails.*

The crowd groaned in relief and quieted as the fresh sea-wind told them they were safely out of Sabis. *Besides*, the captain considered, *We're growing rich beyond dreams on this run.*

And there was always the ship itself: the marvelous dragonship that spouted smoke and ran against the wind, the swift and maneuverable wonder with its secret brass and steam heart. There was none like it anywhere in the world. Once Sabis died, she would run for Sakar, sell the knowledge of her wonders to the shipmasters there, become the mother of such a fleet as all the ages had never seen. An end for Sabis, but a new beginning for Sakar.

The captain smiled as he headed into the oncoming waves and stamped a signal for more speed to the engine room below him, fully aware that he rode at the beginning of a legend. The gods knew, future ages might make of him a semi-divine hero, little less than the gods themselves.

Not bad for a former cabin boy.

Too bad for Yanados. But then again, from what he knew of her, she would most probably do well for herself in any pass, whether or not she ever came back to Sakar.

❖ CHAPTER THREE ❖

Dawn pearled the mist while Eloti's boat was still on the delta. Yanados frowned at the sky, worriedly studied the east bank of the Baiz, and finally snapped an order to steer into the reeds of the muddy west bank. The others, sluggish with fatigue and the night's desperation, stumbled to obey.

One of the mules set up a petulant braying, and Eloti hastened to distract it with food. "We'll have to rake out this straw and replace it with reeds," she commented, noting the fresh dung piles. "The tools are in the aft locker."

Nobody hastened to take her advice. Sulun grinned wearily, snapped off a passing reed, and cut it into equal length straws, one of them notched.

At length Yanados called a halt, ordered the sails taken down and the anchor dropped.

"Here?" Zeren asked her quietly. "The fog will lift sometime today."

"No matter." Yanados smothered a huge yawn. "The Ancar are still above us, and all boats are busy south."

"Still, if we're seen from the east bank—"

"We can always move deeper into this mass of reeds and channels. In any event, we're safe now. Let's get some sleep while we can, Zeren."

Vari insisted on taking the first watch, but everyone else agreed that sleep right now was a most excellent idea.

After some brief arguing, and more cutting of reeds, everyone settled more or less comfortably on the flat deck and dropped into welcome sleep. Sulun's last sight, before he rolled over and let the silence come, was of Vari sitting alert and upright near the bow, watching the land about them with a short bow and nocked arrow in her hands.

Waking was slow and lazy, to steamy heat and a clouded-brass sky, the buzzing of pesky insects and quiet voices conversing. Sulun yawned, raised his head from the piled rushes, and looked about him.

The characteristic river fogs of early summer rose high around the boat, cutting visibility to a dozen yards or less. Doshi was mournfully shovelling out used straw and rushes, and replacing it with fresh-cut reeds. The mules munched contentedly on piled hay and reed tops, tails busily switching flies. Omis, Vari, and their two elder children were ranked along the sides of the boat near the bow, dangling fishing lines in the water; baskets partly filled with mixed fish revealed their luck. The baby gurgled happily in a lined basket nearby, playing with a heron feather. Arizun, Yanados, and Ziya were nowhere to be seen, but a narrow trampled track through the rushes suggested where they might have gone. Zeren and Eloti sat at the stern, talking quietly.

Boat, rushes, slow water, and hot mist were all that could be seen or heard of the world. The solitude and peace were unbelievable.

Sulun sat up and rubbed kinks out of his back, wondering what he should do next. There seemed to be no reason for activity; food, water, warmth, and safety were here in abundance, and the war might as well have been on the far side of the moon. For the first time in more moons than he could remember, Sulun had no pressing duties. He felt as light-headed as a pearl diver coming up from too long in the depths.

"What time is it?" he asked Doshi, simply for need of something to say.

"Midafternoon." The youth shrugged. "The fog won't lift today. Nothing much to do but rest, fish, hunt ducks—and shovel up after these damned mules."

Sulun nodded acknowledgment more than understanding, and went to sit beside Omis. After a moment the blacksmith looked up, smiled, and handed Sulun a newly made reed fishing pole. The string, Sulun noted, was some of the heavier thread that Vari had squirreled away moons ago, and the hook was one of the lot Omis had cast from brass scraps a few days before. He looked about for some bait, and Omis obligingly handed him a fat caterpillar from a small basketful. Sulun shrugged, stuck the caterpillar on the hook, and dropped it overside. *Why not fish?* he thought, bemused. *One quarter hour's walk downstream a city is dying, but that no longer has anything to do with me.*

As if it were a god's sign of approval, the line promptly tugged with a snagged fish. Sulun smiled to himself, gave the line the proper jerk to set the hook, and began hauling in his prize.

Ziya, Arizun, and Yanados came back a little before sundown, carrying a good bag of ducks, grebes, and a single, good-sized goose. Vari made a fire in a large pot set on a flat stone on the deck, and a good assortment of filleted fish toasted on a grill above it. The birds and the other fish were carefully skinned, gutted, patted with salt, and set to dry in the smoky air above the cookfire.

Dinner was slow and leisurely, as pleasant a feast as any Sulun could remember, though the conversation afterward turned to serious matters.

"Should we smother that fire once it's dark?" Omis asked, wiping grease off his mouth. "Or can't it be seen from the east bank?"

"No one will see a potful of coals," Vari said. "And we'll need some heat when the night chill comes."

"We shouldn't sleep then, but sail on," Yanados recommended. "Now, should we turn a ways down one of the other forks and hide here in this lovely delta for a few days more? Or should we press on northward as soon as we can?"

"How much food do we have stored?" Zeren countered. "There seems to be plenty here. The gods know when we'll get more, once we draw close to the Ancar holdings."

"Hmm . . ." Vari surveyed the day's catch. "Another day like this, and we'll have enough to last us half a moon, do we eat lightly."

"Then I'm for staying another day at least."

"But consider," Eloti added, "that soon enough the delta will be filling with refugees from the city, also hunting food. The gods know when the Ancar will come, but I doubt they'll wait long."

"Upriver, up the Dawnstream as I recall . . ." Doshi furrowed his brow, searching for old memories. "We'll find fewer reed beds and less mist, even in this weather. The river's wide, but we'll have to go hastily to escape the Ancar."

"They're no sailors," Yanados sneered, spitting a bone into the water.

"But they've long-reaching bows," Zeren reminded her. "We'll want to pass them by in darkness, quietly as may be."

"How will we keep the mules quiet?" Doshi asked, throwing a nervous glance toward the drowsing beasts.

"Put nosebags full of grain on their heads." Eloti smiled. "A mule would rather eat than bray, so long as he's not hurt."

"The hard part will be passing Lutegh," Zeren considered. "We'll have to plan our passage carefully to come by there in the dark."

"We've a long stretch yet between here and there," Eloti said. "Even after we leave the delta, there'll be reeds and mists aplenty. Time enough for planning when we reach the Mother Stone on the west bank. Lutegh will then be half a day's sail upstream."

The others stared at her in surprise. "You know these waters, then?" Arizun piped up. "You've sailed here before?"

"Oh, yes, many times." Eloti nibbled delicately at a fish fillet. "Still, I would recommend leaving this delightful spot before the wine gives out. The water's unwholesome to drink unless well boiled, and there's a shortage of firewood hereabouts."

The others looked at each other, shrugged, and resumed eating. Without discussion, they understood that Lady Eloti would tell them more when she chose to, and no sooner.

They spent a second day on the delta, catching more fish and birds, smoking the meat over dried reed fires. The third day brought the distant sound of drums through the mist, though from what direction no one could properly tell. They took the sound for an omen, set the sails at evening, and drove upriver on the night wind from the sea.

Once the boat was under way, Yanados became master. She held the sweep, ordered sail adjustments, suggested load shiftings, and the others hastened to obey. Zeren remarked on the phenomenon of shifting command as he, Sulun, and Omis sat huddled around the firepot warming their hands and some herbal tea.

"Not so surprising," Sulun replied. "Omis and I often took turns being master of the shop, depending upon what work was done and who had most experience and knowledge therewith. Likewise, Yanados knows sailing better than any of us; therefore, when the ship sails, she commands."

"And when the ship is still? Who commands then?"

Sulun scratched at his scruffy growth of beard. He'd neglected to shave lately, saving the soap for more pressing needs. Should he continue to let it grow? "The question hasn't really come up," he said. "I suppose Vari rules on matters of food, which are not to be belittled. In knowledge of the river, the Lady appears to have the last word." He glanced to the little shelter of blankets hung from the wagon that Eloti and Vari had set up as a sleeping place for themselves and the children. "On matters of warfare, I suppose you'd be the authority, Zeren."

"On matters of craftsmanship, we've nothing to do." Omis nudged Sulun with an elbow and a wry grin. "Still, our mannerly apprentices treat us as if we still had some wisdom to impart."

"Wait till we're on land and can set up our tools again," Sulun said, smiling back. "Then our apprentices' obedience will be more than mere courtesy. How is the bombard, by the way?"

"The inside needs more polishing, never mind the outside." Omis shrugged. "And we've yet to drill the fuse hole. And where could we test it?"

"Doubtless we'll find some empty land, where the Ancar have passed."

"Unbelievable," Zeren muttered, casting a long glance over the boat and its inhabitants. "Such excellent logic, such a sensible method of rule. Yet no army has ever run thus, nor city, nor kingdom, nor empire. What manner of world would it be, did they so?"

"A more efficient one, at any rate," said Eloti, padding silently up to the fire. "I think the coals could do with some more dried reeds. Friend Zeren, is the tea ready?"

"I think so." Zeren dipped a cup of the infusion for Eloti, and one for himself. He seemed to have forgotten that the other two existed.

Omis and Sulun looked at each other, smiled, and doled out cups for themselves.

✧   ✧   ✧

The boat worked steadily upriver, and dawn found her safely hidden in another bed of reeds.

The crew slept until late afternoon, waking to find the sky dangerously cool and clear. They scanned the visible western bank nervously while they fished and smoked their catches over the dried reed fire, but no sign of humanity appeared. Still, everyone remained subdued and quiet, even the mules. They ate dinner early, intending to sail on again after dark.

"The Ancar must be on the east bank now," Zeren noted, around a mouthful of smoked goose. "We'll have to be careful. How much grain is left for the mules?"

"Another dozen nosebags apiece," murmured Eloti. "Enough to keep them quiet when need be. Still, they grow restless for lack of exercise."

"Once past Lutegh—" Zeren stopped, then shrugged.

No one else said anything. It was not wise, it was tempting the gods, to make any plans before encountering Lutegh. They finished dinner quickly, bedded the children below with the supplies and gear, and set sail as soon as darkness came.

Near dawn, Eloti sighted the Mother Stone: a great solitary pier of rock nudging out into the river from the west bank. Someone, long in the mists of the past, had carved a huge likeness of a woman's face at the top, and two enormous boulders somewhat lower made good representations of breasts.

"There's a reed bank right beyond her," Eloti added. "We can pull in there for a day. I believe there's still a small channel wide enough to accommodate us."

Yanados nodded, but swore as she hauled on the tiller. Crosscurrents were thick here, and treacherous, and the sea wind was no longer strong or reliable.

It was full daylight when the boat was finally ensconced in the little channel, surrounded by reeds and cattails, masked in the rising mist.

One of the mules brayed petulantly, and everyone jumped half out of their skins. Eloti, quick as a cat, leaped to the mule's head and pinched its nostrils, stifling the noise and neatly avoiding an indignant kick with a forehoof. Doshi helped her tie on the nosebags with their bribe of grain and dried peas, while the others listened for any sign of discovery.

Zeren considered a moment, then tapped Arizun and Yanados on the shoulders. "Bring your bows," he whispered. "We'd best go see if anyone's about who might have heard the brute."

A few moments later, the silent trio slipped overboard—legs bare, tunics kilted up above the knee, bows in hand, and quivers filled with arrows—and waded quietly off into the reeds. The others crouched down along the gunwales, assorted weapons in hand, wondering what on earth they'd do if their best steersman, soldier, and archer never came back.

Zeren led the way through the reeds until the ground firmed underfoot and the Mother Stone loomed ahead. He studied the land about him as far as the mist would allow, looked closely at the ancient monument, then signalled the others forward.

Yanados caught his look immediately. "Up there?" she whispered, pointing toward the ancient goddess's head.

Zeren nodded, and slung his bow on his back. Yanados did likewise, and stepped after him. Arizun nocked an arrow and crouched at the foot of the stone, below the track the others climbed, to make sure they weren't followed or disturbed.

The climb was long, but not difficult until the end, where Zeren and Yanados were obliged to climb around to the back of the Mother's head to find foothold in her rough stone hair. Her crown, though, was surprisingly level and smooth, as if generations of pious (or impious) picknickers had worn a comfortable platform there. Zeren and Yanados turned carefully to all sides, peering for signs of life below.

To the landward side, the mist thinned below them, showing unbroken meadow gone rough with neglect. No cattle grazed there now, only a flock of deer and another of wild goats off in the distance. The weed-grown land might have been abandoned for ages instead of mere months.

"Kula of the Wild Things reclaims land quickly," Zeren noted, unamused. "I'll wager those fields haven't been grazed, let alone farmed, since last autumn. The country folk knew the Ancar were coming, long before Lutegh fell—long before we knew, in the city."

"It could be they simply knew the war would come," Yanados said with a shrug, "and they chose to draw their cattle inland, away from the gracious attentions of any army coming along the river."

"Hmm. Think you the landsmen still thrive, back out of sight of the river?"

"Most probably, but they'll suffer soundly enough when the Ancar come down the west bank—which they'll do, sooner or later."

"Oh, aye." Zeren turned back to the river and the lands beyond it.

Below them the mist rose, pearling in the fresh sunlight, masking the water. From this height, it looked like a shining carpet that stretched almost to the edge of sight. Beyond it rose only the blue silhouettes of distant hills.

Through it came smells of smoke, dung, food cooking: faint sounds of clanking metal and wood being chopped, occasional voices: sullen glowing of orange lights amid the pearly grey, countless numbers of them, just across the river.

"Vozai," Zeren breathed, "it's a major Ancar camp! Countless thousands of them . . ."

Yanados wriggled closer to him on the rock. "Should we try to sneak past them while the mist holds?"

"No. Never trust to mist, not once the sun's up; it could burn off at any time."

"We might get past them first."

"We don't know how many there are. They could line the bank for the next several miles." Zeren shivered in the burning sunlight. "So many of them, always so unbelievably many, stripping the land like locusts as they go. Thank the gods you've never seen an Ancar horde coming toward you! No, our chances are better if we stay put."

"Speak of sleeping in the lion's den," Yanados muttered. "Well, best go tell the others. We'll do no hunting this day."

"Nor cooking, either," Zeren agreed. "Let's go."

Sulun woke suddenly to low sunlight, a clear blue sky shining between the reedtops, and a huge, undefinable sound filling the air. A quick glance showed the others awake, crouched silently under the gunwales, a few clearly praying, the rest just listening. He crawled to Ziya, who was nearest.

"What is it?" he whispered, gesturing vaguely toward the sound.

It seemed to come from the river, or beyond: rumbling, clanking, grinding, somewhat like the noise of a looting mob back in the city, but more vast and slow.

"Ancar. On the march," Ziya whispered back, flicking a strange-eyed look at him. "Be quiet till they're gone."

"Gods." Sulun shivered, reached for his blanket, and drew it up around him. "How many?"

"Don't know. Zeren said a whole army. Hush."

Sulun hushed, trying to think of how great an army would make a noise like that, how long it would take them to pass. The mist, he saw, had burned away in the full daylight. If he wanted, he might crawl through the reeds and take a peek, actually see the enemy on the march, see the plague of this age that had ruined Sabis and was on its way to destroy his city. Surely they wouldn't see him peering through reeds on the opposite side of the wide river; he could watch to his heart's content.

Sulun decided he didn't want to look. Leave the ravaging hordes as a symbol, a shadow, something—pray the gods—he would never have to deal with directly. Look not upon the basilisk. He huddled down in his blanket, prepared to wait out the day.

Even the mules kept their heads down, and munched their reeds quietly.

The sound went on until dark, when it changed to more rattling and shouting: noises of camp being set up for the night. All day marching, and the horde had not yet passed.

Sulun's little tribe huddled in their blankets under the wagon, all but Eloti, who went about fetching drinkable water for the mules, currying them with sacking, and throwing down fresh reeds, just as if the enemy weren't dining in the uncounted thousands just across the water. Dinner was smoked fish, waybread, and wine cut with chilled herb tea. Everyone ate slowly, putting off the inevitable—and necessary—departure.

At length, Eloti pointed out, "We can't wait too long before leaving. We must get past Lutegh before dawn."

Everyone shivered, but nobody argued with her logic.

They waited less than an hour after dark for dinner to settle—and, hopefully, the unseen enemy to sleep—before setting out.

This time they raised no sail. Everyone took an oar, though they began with poles to slide the boat out of its safe niche in the reeds. The treacherously clear sky at least gave them good starlight for reckoning, though they clung to the shore and the banks of reeds to at least disguise their silhouette.

On the far bank, campfires glimmered like malevolent yellow stars—countless thousands of them. One look sufficed. The refugees shivered, looked no more, and bent to the oars.

The mules, muzzles occupied with well-filled nosebags, stamped and grumbled quietly. The noise was slight, but it made the rowers wince.

Omis and Zeren, matched on the two foremost oars, bent their backs with the stoic concentration of workmen at a long, hard task. Vari and Eloti, next, hauled with distinctly different styles: Vari's angular and fierce, puffing for breath to every upstroke, Eloti swaying quietly, smoothly, her gloved hands seeming to grip casually, as if this too were just another passing amusement. Arizun and Ziya, on the third pair, lifted and hauled doggedly in tight-lipped determination to do their share. Doshi and Sulun tacitly worked out a rowing cycle that gave them an acceptable weight on the oars with the best economy of motion. Yanados crouched at the sweep, holding it with her weight, hollow eyes peering at the dark water ahead.

"Stroke . . . stroke . . . stroke . . ." she half-whispered, until everyone's rhythm matched.

The black water growled and gurgled under the hull. The boat moved slowly upstream.

In the muttering darkness the rhythmic labor grew hypnotic. Sulun found himself sinking into an oar-paced reverie, thoughts rolling in stately cadences like the phrases of a holy-day chant. *Who else escaped from Sabis?* he wondered. *Where will they settle? What will they do?* Mez, in the end, would benefit. The refugees who fled there were not all unskilled and penniless; the craftsmen and merchants and even the clerks would put their trades to good use. No doubt many would leave the city, work their way south and east through Esha, set up in the lesser cities and even backwater towns where they'd find less rivalry for their skills and wares. Soon enough the lands of the southern shore would find themselves gemmed with cities of wealth, knowledge, and trade. Give them a generation or two undisturbed, which the Ancar, having taken all the north and east, just might be content to do . . .

And what of the poorer refugees who fled across the Baiz into the swamps of the delta? Surely they couldn't all stay there, hiding in the reeds, living on fish and water birds. Soon enough they'd march west, into the wild lands of marsh and forest, to find some means of living among the thick foliage and wild beasts. Perhaps they'd become hunters, trappers, woodcutters—trading occasionally, resentfully, with the new masters of their old city. Or perhaps they'd go far enough west, into the unknown lands, to find someplace fit to build another city. Give them time, give them time . . .

And we go north, the thought circled to conclusion. *Behind the Ancar lines, into half-wild lands, to found our own little colony. What can we build there that will endure?*

He couldn't imagine it now; his mind was growing dulled with fatigue. Only the resolution remained: find a safe place to settle, some place where a blacksmith and a gaggle of engineers could make their living as they were, doing what they had always done.

Sulun shivered as a touch of wind ruffled his hair, then nudged the hood of his robe off his head.

"Down anchor," Yanados announced quietly. "Up oars and set them."

It took Sulun a few seconds to understand the words, then act on them. Oars rattled on wood as they were drawn in. The anchor splashed down into the inky water.

"Noise!" Doshi gulped. "Too loud. Yanados—"

"We're past them," Yanados panted, leaning on the sweep. "Look."

Sure enough, the far bank of the river was dark and silent. They had finally outsailed the last fringes of the marching Ancar horde.

"Hush," Zeren warned, quietly as he could while still being heard. "They must have guards on the road, messengers, post houses. . . ."

"We'll be quiet," Yanados agreed, tying down the sweep and climbing to her feet. "Better rest, though, and use this wind. Up sails."

"They might be seen."

"Not likely, not at this distance, in such dark. Put up sail."

Sluggishly, the others moved to comply. In less than a quarter-hour the boat was moving again, slowly but steadily upstream. Everyone sagged on the deck, rubbing cramped arms and backs. The mules munched placidly. Weary eyes raked the water, the shores, found only blackness. Eventually Vari got up, fetched a thin wineskin out of supplies, and passed it around. Yanados inspected the sail, reset a few lines, then came back and sat down at the tiller.

"How long?" Sulun panted, amazed at the number of cramps and aches he hadn't noticed until he stopped rowing.

"The wind? Who can tell?" Yanados shrugged. "We'll have to row again in an hour, anyway. Wind alone won't take us past Lutegh in time."

Sulun groaned, thinking of the long night ahead. Best make sure the children were safely asleep and the mules bribed to silence with enough grain.

They were rowing with the wind when the first lights came into sight. Yanados, eyes ahead, saw them first.

"Approaching Lutegh," she almost whispered to Sulun and Doshi. "Keep silence. Pass it on."

Sulun, slow-witted with fatigue, duly passed the message on before its implications sank in.

Lutegh: east, on the fork of the Dawnstream, fallen to the Ancar. And they would turn there, come into the Dawnstream almost under Lutegh's walls. How could they not be seen and noted? How could the Ancar not order some captive boatman to set out after them? It was impossible, suicidal. They should make for the west bank, land, take out the mules and wagon and go overland from here—

Through a countryside crawling with Ancar troops.

Sulun said nothing, only pulled harder on his oar.

Yanados huddled at the tiller, flicking her eyes across the water ahead, the ominous glimmers of light on the distant east shore, and the sails. Keep the sails up? They were dull grey colored, not terribly visible in the dark, would add to their speed—and the boat needed speed now, speed and power to make the turn into the Dawnstream against the gods only knew what crosscurrents. According to all she'd ever heard, the Dawnstream's mouth was wide and deep. Wide enough that a boat this size couldn't be seen by torchlight from the bank? Deep enough that the major current would run low, leaving the surface placid enough to skim quickly? And how much of the night was left? Would the mists rise at dawn, or would the air and sky stay treacherously clear? If mist came, how would she find it anyway, in all this darkness?

No help for it; she would have to steer closer to the east shore, go within sight of Lutegh.

Yanados gritted her teeth and leaned on the tiller, pulling to starboard.

More pinpoints of orange light appeared, shimmering through the night haze, on the east bank. So many of them, no visible end to them ahead. White stars dead above, evil orange stars to the right, nothing else visible in the gurgling darkness. And now there came sounds: somewhere a dog barking, distant creaking of wood, sloshing of water around moored ships' hulls or the piers of once busy docks.

Yanados pulled the tiller straight again; they were close enough. The others didn't look up, only rowed.

And then the wind shifted.

Yanados looked up in alarm as the sailcloth flapped noisily. She swore, tied down the tiller, and ran for the mast. The damp knots seemed determined to stick, but she yanked them out and dragged the sail down. She bundled and tied the heavy cloth, alternately angry and grateful that the others had stuck to their rowing.

Gods, what was the wind doing? Gusts from the south, the northeast smelling different, contending . . . Yanados smothered a laugh as she understood. The Dawnstream brought its own wind down its wide channel, the land's wind running headlong into the last breath up from the sea.

She had her guide at last; steering straight into that grass-scented wind would take them up the Dawnstream, past Lutegh.

But they would have to do it by oars alone.

Yanados went back to the tiller, cast a long glance over the dim lights of the east bank, and steered toward the cool northeastern wind. Stroke by stroke, the malevolent yellow lights crawled by: no end to them, fatigue a growing enemy, and the current heavier now, turbulent, making the rowers fight for headway. They must be right on top of the confluence, the junction of waters and winds, where the rivers met and struggled briefly. Yes, there: the shore lights seemed to angle away in the darkness. Once past this jumble of flowing forces, they'd be safely into the Dawnstream. But, gods, the battle went inch by inch!

"Stroke . . . stroke . . . stroke . . ." Yanados heard herself chanting. *Baiz, Lord of rivers, let us go!* she prayed furiously, knowing that Baiz had never been a patron god of herself or her people, and why should he listen? *Mav of warriors, help us. Ioth of my kindred, help us. Kula of the wild things . . .*

A soft singing flowed across the deck, barely audible, sweet and level and hypnotic in its surging rhythm.

For an instant Yanados thought of mermaids, sirens, river wights who enchanted sailors. Then she recognized the song, and the voice.

"*Low* lie the *stars* over *Tos*lagen's *memo*ry,
High hang the *flowers* from the *trees* of her *tomb . . .*"

Ah, Eloti's magecraft again. That simple chant had worked small wonders twice before; it certainly could do no harm now. Accept its help; steer well.

Yanados rocked gently at the tiller, matching time with the soft repetitive song, watching the water and feeling the wind, letting all sense of time fall away.

The distant orange light-points flowed by.

An angled block of darkness cut off the pattern of stars ahead. For a moment Yanados stared at it, wondering what it signified. Then she guessed what it was, and shoved hard on the tiller with a muffled curse.

The spell-struck rowers pulled on the oars without change, and Yanados hadn't the time to warn them. She pushed harder.

The boat swerved to port, bucking in the cross-chop of the water, turned and pulled sideways along that looming block of deeper darkness so suddenly huge—no, not big, but close. Down and down its length, so close that Yanados could hear the water smacking its side: a faintly hollow booming. Yes, another hull: a ship, sitting lightless and cargoless out on the water—and what that might mean was best not to think. So damned close!

And there, there, the end of the dark patch, the ship's stern, less than ten yards away. Gods, they had been close. Pull away now, quietly away.

Yanados looked up, saw the silhouette of a man at the stern blocking the stars. Facing them, or facing the bow of the ship? No way to tell—save that he didn't move, didn't cry out, showed no sign of having seen them.

" '*Care*', sing the *birds* in the *boughs* of the *Cy*presses,
'*Care*, love and *care*, win you *free* of your *doom*.' "

The damned song—what if he heard it?

No, wait: what if he *had* heard it, heard and been ensorcelled, urged to a dreamy and intent regard for his work—which was watching the deck of the ship? Or perhaps he simply thought that a small boat, laden with passengers and mules and wagon (could he see them in this darkness?), with a mildly singing woman aboard, could surely be up to no harm, only going about its lawful business?

Shoulders hunched, waiting for the cry of notice and alarm, Yanados steered out and away from the darkened ship, steered on until the rising grumble of the water warned that she was drawing near the west bank, perhaps straight at the fork. She hauled the tiller back, turning into the Dawnstream's wind again, back against the oncoming current. Still no sound from the now invisible ship. Still the rowers pulled.

But their rowing was ragged now, breaths audible with labored panting. Eloti's singing was fainter. Fatigue, the other enemy, was winning.

For a long, despairing moment Yanados thought of putting the anchor down, letting them rest an hour before striking on up the Dawnstream, praying the darkness would hold while they idled just across the water from Lutegh's walls. How much of the night was left? Was the sky already paling, just the slightest tinge, above the city? Was that the first breath of dawn that raised the wind in her hair?

Wind—

Once more Yanados quick-tied the sweep and darted for the sails. She'd have to do this alone, no one to help her, and the resetting again soon, and the gods knew how many tacks after that. Swearing quietly, she hauled and reset the lines, tugged the boom over and tied it fast—damned, gods-beshat, back-breaking work to do alone, but she could manage.

The sails filled, swelled awkwardly sideways, ridiculously angled but workable. The boat creaked, groaned, grumbled—but began to pull away from shore. Back toward deeper water, back toward the frowning walls and treacherous lights of Lutegh, but nonetheless upstream.

Yanados leaned against the creaking mast, panting with effort and relief. "Up oars," she gasped to the faltering team of rowers. "Up oars and set them. Rest."

Eloti stopped singing, and gratefully sagged over her oar. One by one, the others fell out of the spell and followed suit. Yanados staggered down the line of the deck, helping the over-exhausted haul in their oars, finding Ziya and Arizun slumped at their stations, already asleep. She pulled the oars in for them, stumbled back to her place at the tiller, and sat down to wait.

Tack and tack, she thought, watching the sails strain. *Zig and zag, one yard sideways for every yard forward, against wind and current, but we move, we move . . . How long until dawn?*

Gods, the eastern sky was no longer black but definitely indigo. Another hour, and the boat would be visible. Another hour, and they'd be almost under Lutegh's docks. Half an hour, then, and she'd have to reset the sails, cross back to the west, hope these short tacks would keep them moving fast enough to get out of anyone's sight.

And if they were seen, would anyone raise the alarm?

If alarm were raised, how long would it take the Ancar to find a boat and a capable steersman and set out on the water?

If the Ancar pursued, would they overhaul, get to within bowshot range? Would any Luteghi boatmen serve their master that well?

And gods' piss, why were the stars ahead blanking out so soon? The sky was still dark. . . .

Yanados blinked twice, shook her head, then smothered a whoop of hysterical laughter.

Of course! Of course! The wind is turning warm!

Dark as unwashed raw wool, just rising now from the surface of the water, came the first of the morning mist. In less than an hour, it would be thick as curdled cream and taller than the mast. Oh, it was going to be a lovely, hot, steamy, foggy day!

Crooning snatches of gratitude-prayers to all the water gods she could think of, Yanados tied down the tiller and crawled over sleeping bodies toward the mast.

Doshi woke to miserable, wet heat, hot mist thick enough to choke him, aches in his arms and back and shoulders that made him wonder if he'd been run over by an ironmonger's cart. It took two tries to roll over and exchange one set of wretched cramps for another. He struggled for sleep, felt it slip away, and resigned himself to being awake in this pitiable condition.

The boat rocked slightly to a heavier than usual wavelet. Doshi turned the gear of thought by one slow cog, and realized that the boat was moving. Moving: not anchored. And where?

He pulled gritty eyes open, and found he was looking straight at Arizun's knees. It was not, he decided, a cheering sight. By slow and torturous degrees Doshi turned his head and looked the other way.

A huddle of robes sat crouched by the tiller, cloak hood draping a face he barely recognized. Yanados, as he'd never seen her: lips dry and cracked, cheeks hollowed and grey-pale with something beyond exhaustion, eyes dull-gleaming as in fever but set in bruise-dark lids that gave the eerie impression of tunnels . . .

"Have you been up all night?" was the first thing Doshi thought to say.

Yanados blinked at him, took intolerably long considering the simple question, and finally nodded, jerkily, once.

"Gods." Doshi started to get up, thought better of it, compromised by getting to his hands and knees and crawling slowly toward her. His own memories came back slowly. "Lutegh . . . Have we passed it?"

Again Yanados fumbled with the thought for impossibly long before answering. She shrugged.

"Gods," Doshi muttered again, looking around him in the steaming mist. A fat blob of sun hung three hands up from the horizon. Then he noted the odd set of the sails, the slap of the water beating slantwise against the hull, the smell of the slow but steady wind. . . .

And he remembered that smell, that wind.

"We're on the Dawnstream. We have to be past Lutegh! Oh gods, Yani, put in to shore. This fog will hide us."

Yanados frowned vaguely, trying to think about that.

Doshi looked again at the water, the sails, the surface ruffling of the wind. "Which way are we going now?" he asked, very slowly and carefully.

Yanados squinted at the sail, and finally answered. "North. Mm, northeast. North shore."

"Ah, good. Wonderful. We'll just keep going until we reach the bank. We'll put in there. Indeed, I'll do it." He sat down beside her and draped one arm over the tiller's sweep. "You go lie down, Yani."

"Down?" Yanados blinked at him.

"Lie down. Sleep. I'll handle it now."

"Mm." Yanados dutifully dragged herself free of the tiller, crawled a yard or so across the deck, then stopped and simply lay down where she was.

Doshi gripped the tiller and stared straight ahead, waiting for some sign of the riverbank to show through the mist. After a time it occurred to him that unless the others woke soon, he'd have to drop the anchor and take down the sails all by himself. He groaned at the thought.

And what if, a sudden worry gnawed, there was no cover on the north bank? What if some part of the Ancar horde was there, waiting for them? What if the fog lifted, leaving them naked to any and all eyes?

Doshi glanced at Yanados, saw her lying motionless as a corpse. No help there. Sulun was nearest in reach, one leg sprawled out toward the stern, foot within jabbing distance. Doshi stretched a cramped leg toward him, trying to reach that foot. Even a kick would do, so long as it was silent—the gods knew who might be close enough in this fog to overhear a whisper.

Then his eye caught something in the mist ahead. Doshi gulped, pulled his leg back, looked about for some way to stop the boat, saw the anchor within reach.

As he picked up the anchor the shapes drew close enough for him to recognize, and he almost whooped with relief.

Reeds.

Near noon the mist thinned, and within an hour it lifted. By then the sturdy little riverboat was safely nestled in the reed bed and all her crew, except Yanados, were awake. All of them were stiff, sore, grateful for the early summer heat, and unwilling to move.

It was Zeren who insisted that someone go out among the reeds and look at the shore, see where they were and how close the Ancar might be. No one volunteered, as he'd half expected, so Zeren took bow and quiver and set off on the task himself.

Vari then announced that the children, at least, be fed, and snagged Sulun's help in digging up supplies and handing them out.

Eloti insisted that the same courtesy be extended to the mules, as well as throwing out their used reed-straw and providing more.

This time everyone drew lots for the unwelcome duty, and Arizun got the short straw. Ziya volunteered to cut the fresh reeds, but Arizun still muttered miserably about the work he had.

Two hours later Zeren returned, muddy to the waist, but grinning widely. He also carried three plump wild ducks.

"Take the mules off and let them graze on solid ground for a change," he said, tossing his catch onto the boat. "We're safe."

"Safe?" Sulun gawked. "I can't believe it. This close to Lutegh? On the north shore? Where the Ancar have already conquered?"

"They don't seem much interested in holding empty land." Zeren grimaced. "Here, go through the reeds and see for yourself."

Sulun slipped out of the boat, picked his way cautiously from tussock to tussock until the reeds thinned, and then peeked through.

Before him lay a wide stretch of placid water. Beyond that was another reed-fringed shore, and beyond that stretched wild meadows and patches of scrubby forest. There was no sign of man, as far as the eye could reach.

Sulun clambered back to the boat, dunking his sandals twice. "They came and passed," he marveled. "There's no one out there at all."

"No doubt they were in a hurry to reach Lutegh," Eloti sniffed, "and Sabis afterward."

"They don't pay much attention to lands they've already conquered," Doshi murmured, thinking of the north.

The others said nothing, but began setting out the boards to make a landing ramp. Not only the mules yearned to set foot on solid land for an hour, or more.

Yanados didn't waken until the next dawn, and then she was ravenous. Fortunately, the larder had been replenished by the hunting and fishing parties. Breakfast for everyone was ample and, for once, served on solid ground.

"If it's safe, we should go on by daylight," Yanados opined around a mouthful of grilled trout. "The wind and current are against us; we'll have to row or tack. Best do that while we can see where we're going."

"In fact," Arizun added, glowering at the mules, "why not put into shore, leave the boat, and go on with the wagon? If the land's empty—"

"We don't know how empty," Doshi cautioned. "We're not even sure yet just where we are."

"I have a suspicion, though, " Eloti put in. "By all means, let's sail on today—and keep an eye on the south bank."

Everyone else looked at Doshi, who shrugged. He didn't know this part of the country well, and Eloti seemed to. By all means, let her be the guide.

They set off an hour later, tacking across the slow but steady water, seeing no one across the empty leagues of the shore.

✦ CHAPTER FOUR ✦

Close on sunset, they saw the first towers of an approaching city. The others wanted to put into the reeds at once, but Eloti smiled eagerly, took hold of the mast, and stood up for a better view.

"No reeds tonight," she announced, smiling. "We'll spend the night in those ruins."

"Ruins?" Zeren questioned. "A whole city? The Ancar would hardly leave it without some garrison, however small."

"Not if they never came near it, and I doubt they would, since the Sabisan troops would have given it a wide berth, as always."

"Eh? How wide? And why? A city, ruined or not—"

"It is the City of Ghosts. Itoma. Sukkti ruins."

"Oh." Zeren didn't say anything more. Even he had heard, during his years in Sabis, of the famous haunted ruins of Itoma.

"They say it's full of plagues, pitfalls, hideous mummies, walls that fall on you without warning, and plenty of angry ghosts to push them," Omis recalled. "No safe place to take the children."

Eloti laughed. "The last tenants indeed placed a number of pitfalls, and centuries of weather have done nothing to improve the buildings, but there are safe sections, if one knows where to find them."

Sulun gave her a measuring look. "You've been here often?" he asked. "You know your way about the ruins?"

"Oh, yes. My mother's side of the family came from there, originally. Unlike my brother, I never thought the old blood a taint or a social disadvantage."

Eloti peered toward the silhouetted towers on the south shore. "Indeed, there's much advantage in not fearing old Sukkti ghosts, bothering to visit one's old home city, exploring the ruins during long summer days. . . ." She sighed, then sat back down in the boat. "Steer there. You'll find that the third stone dock is quite usable."

The sun was slinking among the massive ruins when they pulled up to the third of a series of stone quays, reaching a good distance out into the river. On the upriver side were steps going down to the water, and even a few massive bronze tie rings still bolted to the stone. Yanados made fast the boat, but no one save Eloti was eager to go ashore. A broad, stone-paved avenue ran beside the river at the foot of the docks, and directly across it from their anchorage loomed a huge flat-roofed temple. The architecture looked wrong to everyone raised among Sabis's domes and arches.

Eloti marched up the water stairs, down the dock, and straight toward the temple.

"Wait!" Sulun yelled, floundering after her. "Wait until I can fetch a lamp, at least! Lady—"

"Just bring lamp oil," she chirped back at him, not breaking stride. "There are lamps enough within."

Sulun shook his head, scrabbled among the supplies for oil, tinder, and striker. He remembered to grab some string too, just in case Eloti's promised lamp needed a new wick. Then he ran up the stars and down the dock after her retreating form, and no one in the boat elected to go with him.

Sulun caught up to Eloti on the wide temple stairs, and they paced through the open dark doorway together.

"Hmm, plain slab lintels, and close-set columns to support them," Sulun noted, trying not to look at the darkness beyond the doorway. "Were these folk ignorant of the arch, then?"

"They learned it in later days, but this temple is very old." Eloti disappeared into the shadows, leaving Sulun to follow as best he could. "Ah, here. Just as I remembered. The lamp oil, please."

Sulun dutifully handed over the jug of oil, then the striker and tinder. Eloti didn't ask for a wick. He saw sparks strike, then the tinder's glow, finally a clear flame that grew large enough to show the immediate surroundings—and he gaped at what he saw.

Ranged around the walls, starting near the doors and reaching as far back as the light revealed, were great square-carved statues of every beast, bird, and fish known to man. Between their paws, or fins or talons, rested oil lamps carved from the same stone, and before these were carved depressions that must have been offering bowls. A litter of dried stalks showed that the common offering was flowers or grain. One third of the way in from the walls stood rows of columns, supporting the long stone beams that made up the ceiling. Between them lay a mosaic-tiled path depicting flowers, fruits, and leaves, more species of plants than he could recognize, forming a bright pathway down the wide central aisle. Eloti meandered down the length of the temple, filling and lighting occasional lamps—at the feet of a lion, a fish, an eagle, a bull, a stag—and gradually the shape at the far end of the central aisle emerged in the light.

Foremost stood a wide stone altar, carved and tiled with images of garlands. Behind that was another stone lamp, by far the largest Sulun had ever seen, and behind that a statue easily twelve cubits tall. Despite the rigidly formal archaic pose and unfamiliar attributes carved on her robes, she was unmistakable: Kula, in her Fruitful Mother aspect, crowned with grain and starflowers. Even in the ancient, simplified carving style, her characteristic smile was familiar.

Eloti sighed faintly and poured only a bit of oil into that huge lamp, lit it, genuflected, and stepped back. Sulun thought it wise to imitate the gesture. "So," he whispered, trying to sound respectful, "the Sukkti knew Kula also?"

"Indeed, and under that very name." Eloti sniffed. "The Sabirns took up her worship with no great changes, once they settled these lands and learned they would have to farm for a living. I believe they had worshipped only water, war, and weather gods before then."

"Incredible. How many other deities, think you, were originally Sukkti?"

"Quite a number of them: any that had to do with farming, herding, or manufacturing. Quite often they kept the old names and rites intact."

"And . . . ." Sulun felt a wild idea sprouting. "The priesthoods also?"

"The priesthoods also," Eloti smiled. "Especially those which were exclusively female."

"Family tradition!" Sulun almost laughed, staring at her.

"In my case, an exclusively female tradition." Eloti gestured another salute to the smiling statue.

"Did your brother ever know?"

"He didn't care to know."

"I see." Sulun looked up at the statue, studying it for some sign or omen, reading nothing but the encouraging smile. "Are there any other . . . little secrets of the priesthood that were passed on as tradition in the female line?"

"A few," Eloti chuckled. "Some small magics . . ."

"Toslagen!"

"A distant ancestress, reputed to be a mighty sorceress."

"Mighty enough that even her memorial chant has power?"

"More precisely, she was a poetess who discovered the uses, principles, and techniques of hypnotic chant."

"I see."

"Other things . . ." Eloti glanced around the dimly lit temple. "I know the location of certain discreet chambers where we may be assured of safe rest. There is also a temple garden— long since run wild, of course, but still quite lush—where we can safely pasture the mules for the night. No, no hidden ancient treasure, I'm afraid; that was taken away long ago and put to prudent use. The women of my family have always learned certain trades and possessed their own wealth, usually quite unknown to the men."

"Family tradition!" Sulun laughed, then took a second look at Eloti. "An excellent tradition. And . . . you are the last of the line?"

Eloti bowed her head. "Unless, at my age, I can win a husband and produce a daughter, yes, the tradition ends with me."

"That would be a great pity, Goodlady." Sulun thought of the glances he'd observed between Eloti and Zeren, and prudently held his tongue. Best let that grow without comment. Best change the subject, too. "But how did these buildings remain intact, unmolested so long? How did Itoma earn its fearsome reputation?"

"Deliberate policy," said Eloti, turning to inspect the shadowed space behind the statue. "Itoma was a long time falling, and its people had perhaps a bit more prudence than those of Sabis. When the coastal towns fell to the Sabirns, and the river trade was cut off, Itoma could no longer support a large populace. The people departed for the countryside and other river towns, carefully spreading stories about curses and evil wizardry and ghosts and the like."

"That wouldn't have sufficed without some evidence," Sulun noted. "One of the best antidotes I know to superstition is greed for loot."

"Oh yes," Eloti laughed. "There was evidence enough. The outlying areas of the city were abandoned first, and the remaining people—seeing they no longer had the numbers to withstand a siege—built artful traps all throughout the empty neighborhoods."

"No doubt enhanced with gruesome carvings, paintings, and other stage trappings," Sulun added, remembering stories he'd heard. "Is there truly a palace filled with mummies?"

"There is. It was a prince's mansion, actually; the fellow was famed for squandering money on his lavish tastes, much to his own ruin. Later, defenders of Itoma thought it clever to raid the old necropolis and place the remains in odd places all over the former spendthrift's house and grounds. I'm told that the first Sabirn scouts were artfully led there, and then treated to a most dramatic exhibition."

Sulun remembered the famous story of the Palace of the Dead, and laughed heartily. "The Sabirn tale may have been embroidered a bit, but by all accounts those poor explorers were scared out of their wits."

"I should tell you the Sukkti version of that tale some time," Eloti grinned back. "In any event, the city was emptied by poverty rather than war—which is why you'll find the buildings thoroughly stripped of portable valuables, but otherwise intact. Legend protected it long after the inhabitants had gone."

"Preserved it through the rise and fall of the conquerors," Sulun mused. "What power legends have, and rumors of magic . . ."

Right there, a marvelous idea unfolded before Sulun's eyes: a completion so near perfection that he glanced up at the statue of the goddess to wonder if she had inspired it.

"We should go back and tell the others to come in," Eloti suggested. "Otherwise they'll think we've been eaten by the ghosts. Does that smile signify something particular?"

"Yes. Yes, it does." Sulun pulled his grin down to polite dimensions. "Do you think that the Ancar would have heard of the Lost and Haunted City of Itoma by now?"

"Most likely, if they've spent any time at all in the northlands. The tales spread everywhere in reach of Sabis."

"And . . . was Deese of the Forge originally a Sukkti god?"

"He was that. Hmm, do you see an advantage in being Sukkti, now that Sabis has fallen?"

"Sukkti magicians, more precisely—from the Lost City of Itoma, come out of hiding now that the rule of Sabis is gone."

"Ah . . ." Eloti smiled as the idea took hold, smiled more widely than Sulun had ever seen her do before, until their delighted-idiot grins matched. They burst out laughing at the same time.

Omis and Zeren, come searching cautiously after them, heard the gales of laughter roll out of the temple and were heartened enough to come in and see what the joke was.

They learned soon enough, and they laughed too.

✧ CHAPTER FIVE ✧

Thanig was a small town hidden in a fold of the Jarrya hills: small in size, smaller in fame. It served the needs of surrounding farmers and herders with simple goods, most of them locally made, the rest imported once a year from Athoa, the nearest larger Jarryan town. Aside from pack merchants and tax collectors, no one had much reason to remember its name. Neither did travelers, other than the occasional tax clerk or peddler, visit it from one year to another. Since the Ancar invasion, some ten years back, even those visitors had grown few.

Therefore it was a matter of no little excitement and concern when the townspeople first observed the column of dust, and then the strange entourage causing it, approaching by the main—and indeed the town's only—road.

The townsfolk reacted swiftly: mothers hauled children indoors, craftsmen carried display tables of their wares back into their shops, older children chased family livestock safely out of the street, householders pulled doors and window shutters closed and peeped out through the cracks. Only the innkeeper left his door open, and even he took care to hastily hide his better bottles. That done, everyone watched the strangers approach.

The spectacle was indeed something to see, remember to tell one's grandchildren about. In the lead marched two big men in long iron-colored robes and hooded cloaks, carrying iron-shod staves bound with green branches. At the rear came four similar figures, slighter in stature. Between them rolled a huge wagon, covered with iron-colored sailcloth, driven by a tall man in the same dark vestments as the others while beside him sat an imposing woman garbed in green and crowned with a garland. The wagon was painted with stylized designs that suggested ancient letters, garlanded with leaves and flowers, hung with iron chains and brass bells, and drawn by a pair of large iron-colored mules. The mules' harness was hung with brass bells and luck charms of polished brass and iron, and jingled with their every step. The dark-robed figures were chanting softly, in what the more experienced townsfolk recognized as quaintly accented Sabirn, a hymn to Deese of the Forge—with proper reference to his Lady, Kula of the Wood. The procession marched into and through the village, not glancing to left or right, heading for the long building toward the far end of town whose chimney belched smoke and sparks even at this hour of day.

"Goin' to the forge, they be," the town potter noted, much to everyone's agreement. "Pilgrims might be, but priestish sure as rain."

And, right enough, the strangers drew to a precise halt at the doorway of the town's smithy. With the precision of courtly dancers, the two men in the lead stepped back to hold the mules' bridles, the four at the rear rearranged themselves at the wagon's back and sides, and one of them stepped forward to knock formally on the doorpost.

"Blessings to all within," he intoned, in only slightly accented Jarryan. "Blessings to forge and fire, roofbeam and hearthstone, in the name of Deese of the Forge."

Dunosh, the town blacksmith, carefully set down the horseshoe he'd been shaping, while his apprentices scurried for cover. "Uh, blessings to you, also," was all he could think to say. He tucked his trusty middleweight hammer into his belt, just to be safe, and edged toward the outlandish strangers at his door. "What would ye be wanting here?"

"Food and shelter for two days, and trade also," the stranger recited as if he'd practiced it a long time. "In exchange for your assistance, brother-in-trade, we'll gladly share our knowledge with you."

Dunosh blinked, taking all that in. Too much, too strange: best deal with one problem at a time. "Ah, the inn be back down t'street, six doors down on t'left. The beer be good, and the shepherd pie likewise, but touch not the stew . . . And warn 'em well t'air out the bedding." He guessed he was babbling like a fool, but better that than to seem unfriendly—especially since he had no idea what to say to the fellow's other requests.

But the speaker smiled wide and thanked him profusely, ending with an elaborate blessing in the name of the Forge Lord. "And more," the man finished, with a conspiratorial wink, "would you like a useful bit of magic to help your work?"

"Magic?" Dunosh lifted his head like a bird dog scenting game. In his trade there was so much that could go wrong, any helpful charm would be welcome. "Eh, a spell against splashing, p'raps?"

"Better." The speaker grinned and waved one of the larger men forward. The fellow had to stoop to get in the door, and he rolled up his sleeves as he came, revealing arms as thick-muscled as an ox's leg and streaked with the identifying scars of a smith. Dunosh stepped back respectfully.

The big stranger went to the forge, mumbled something over it, took up the tongs, and studied the horseshoe between their jaws. He waved his other hand over the darkening iron, mumbled something that included the name of Deese several times, then pointed to Dunosh and said something straight and clear in Sabirn.

"Er, what'd he say?" Dunosh asked of the first speaker.

The man leaned closer and whispered in his ear: "He said: 'Temper with cold oil instead of water.' "

"Ey, I should do that . . . and that's all?"

"That's all. The rest's already been spoken."

" 'Temper with cold oil' . . ."

Dunosh was still thinking that over when the strangers rolled out of his dooryard and back down the street towards the inn. Cold oil? Where could he get that hereabouts? Butter? Far too costly. Seed oil? The same. Meat fat? Now that was possible. Rendered sheep fat was cheap enough. Cold? The town boasted no icehouse, but the inn's cold cellar might do. Best go ask at once; he wanted to try that spell quickly, while the strangers were still in town.

Besides, if he followed them to the inn, who could tell what other secrets and charms he might learn?

Dunosh barked an order to his apprentices to bank the fire, and hurried off after the strangers.

By late afternoon, everyone who could leave work had gathered in or around the inn, trying to look casual while ogling the strangers. The innkeeper and his serving maids, of course, had the best excuse to chat with the odd visitors and entice information from them. The strangers proved amenable to enticement, quite glad to chat with the smiling innkeeper and his buxom serving maids, past platters of tough beef, fat pork, and underspiced mutton.

Oh yes, the strangers were devotees of Deese of the Forge—see the pretty amulet pendants: stylized iron hammers inlaid with brass flames—and yes, they were on a pilgrimage to the fabled River Gol and some ancient monuments on its banks. Yes, they knew smithcraft, and engineering, and many other bits of magic besides. Why yes, they'd be happy to talk about some of it. Headaches and joint pains? Invoke Kula three times, and drink a cup of willow bark tea. Cattle plagued with worms? Dry their feed in the first light of the morning sun, bless in the names of Deese and Kula, and feed the cattle lots of raw garlic. How to improve a lady's looks? Hmm . . . Invoke Kula thrice and wash with soap, every day. How to make that marvelous ointment? Invoke Deese's aid, boil fat in water soaked through wood ashes, skim off the result, and pat it into cakes.

And who were these accommodating, fascinating strangers? Ah, that was more fascinating still.

"We are the ancient Sukkti folk," explained one of them—quite young, to judge from the voice. "The lords of Sabis suppressed our worship everywhere, save in the Lost City of Itoma. There we hid, and practiced our craft, and waited. Now, with Sabis overthrown, we dare emerge again into the light of day and visit the ancient sites of our elder worship."

After that revelation, the landlord brought fresh jugs of beer without anyone's asking.

"Ey, but now the Ancar be come," said the nearer serving maid gloomily. " 'Tis new masters now, and worse than the last, if any."

"Ah well, they know nothing of us," said another visitor, a tall skinny one with curly, wild hair. "And surely they know nothing of our magic. Let us just keep this as our little secret, shall we?"

Everyone in the inn hastily agreed. The gods knew, they had secrets enough to keep from the new crop of masters. In exchange they were happy to tell all they knew of the roads, towns, and lands to the north—though precious few of them had ever traveled far from town.

The strangers were in the midst of discussing the best place to set up shop for a day or two and sell some of their metalwares when another, less welcome, racket came from outside.

The townspeople froze, recognizing the sounds.

There were multiple hoofbeats, creakings and groanings of ill-made wagonwheels, shouts and curses in a totally unfamiliar tongue—and all coming toward the inn.

The serving maids hopped off their assorted perches and ran for the kitchen. Several of the smaller and frailer patrons followed them. The innkeeper whisked his better jugs out of sight and shoved his money box into a hideyhole in the floor.

The strangers looked at each other, pulled their cloaks and hoods closer about them, and began humming a quiet, oddly soothing, holy song.

The newcomers came tramping through the doorway, slamming the already open door all the way back to the wall, and tromped loudly up to the inn's serving counter. There were half a dozen of them, dressed in coarse homespun wool and roughly cured leather, hung with assorted bits of horn and plate for armor, and fairly dripping with weapons: daggers, short swords, long swords, bludgeons, horn-tipped longbows and quivers grain-sheaf thick with arrows. Their hair, beards, and even moustaches were braided, and the braids were strung with odd trinkets intended as jewelry. They wore identical scowls, as if they'd practiced the look, and they glared about the interior of the inn as if expecting an armed host and a pitched battle. Despite their carefully cultivated beards, they were surprisingly young; not one of them could have been over twenty.

The Deese priests made no move, only chanted softly and stared as if they'd never seen Ancar warriors before.

The apparent leader of the small invasion force, seeming a bit surprised to find his host so thoroughly outnumbered by civilians, looked around again, bristled and scowled even more fiercely, stamped up to the serving counter, and slammed his fist on it, making the jugs and cups rattle.

"Bur!" he announced. "Dimme bur!"

The innkeeper blinked, gaped, and asked, "Huh?" No one could have mistaken his meaning.

The rest of his troop crowded closer to him, either for better defense against the motionless customers or to better intimidate the innkeeper. The leader grabbed the front of the innkeeper's apron and tried to yank him forward, but succeeded only in pulling the apron off. He threw it to the floor, peevish at his failure.

"*Bur!*" he yelled again. "Von ol ugat!"

"Huh?" said the landlord again.

The squad leader stamped in frustration. He could slaughter everyone in sight if he chose, but he couldn't make himself understood; it was an embarrassing situation for a proper conqueror. He took a deep breath and tried again. "Bur," he said, miming a cup in the empty air and then drinking from it. "Hu noe, *Bur.*"

"I think he means, he wants beer," one of the Deese priests said quietly.

"Ah!" said the landlord, and reached for a mug.

The young Ancar turned, automatically striking a fierce pose and look, to see who had spoken.

Almost as one, the Deese priests pressed their hands together and solemnly bowed. They went on with their quiet hypnotic chanting.

The Ancar youth looked them up and down, scratched his head, shrugged, and turned back to the counter. The landlord pushed a large mug of beer at him. He whooped in satisfaction, grabbed the mug, and emptied it in one long pull. His cohorts looked expectantly at him. He grinned and nodded. In a moment, they were all crowding the counter, yelling for mugs.

The landlord sighed and handed out the foamy cups, clearly not expecting to be paid for this.

In the corner, the Deese priests continued to chant quietly.

Halfway through his third cup, the young Ancar squad leader hit on another thought. He snagged the landlord, shouted unintelligibly in his face, and hand-mimed something bigger, then pointed at his mug. The landlord shook his head, bewildered. The youth went through the pantomime again, yelling louder.

"I think he wants a whole barrel," said one of the Deese priests again.

The Ancar warriors didn't seem to hear, but the landlord caught it. "A whole barrel?" he groaned. "Gods, you know they won't pay for it. . . ."

Nonetheless, he went to the end of the counter and rolled a sloshing barrel into sight.

The Ancar troops fell on it with whoops of delight, and began rolling it toward the front door.

"My pay," the landlord tried, chasing after the yelping squad with his hands held out in the unmistakable gesture.

The last Ancar out the door only laughed, tugged one ear, shook his head, and trotted after the others.

The landlord sighed, watching them go. Everyone else in the room quietly relaxed.

One of the Deese priests got up and peeped out the door after the retreating noise of the Ancar troop. "They've got an oxcart," he noted. "They're loading it on, next to lots of other loot. I think . . . yes, they're leaving."

"Thank the gods for small mercies," groaned the landlord. "At least it was only a barrel of cheap beer."

"Could've been much worse," the Deese priest agreed. "They're going off down the southwest road."

"Oh, my sheep!" one of the locals wailed. "I graze 'em near the road these days!" He snatched up his cap and ran out the door.

"Keep to the back trails!" the landlord called after him.

The other priests of Deese stopped that soft chanting of theirs, and stood up. One of the two biggest came quietly over to the landlord, pulling something small out of his robe.

"I think we'd best leave now," he said quietly, "before those louts tell anyone that there's a small gang of pilgrims available for robbing. Er, could you change this?"

On his calloused palm he held out a small coin, no bigger than his fingernail, but winking unmistakably golden in the candlelight.

The landlord gaped. "Gods, no! I've not seen . . . er, such a coin in years." he glanced about worriedly, watching for unwelcome ears. "Lords of heaven, I've not seen even much silver from year's end to year's end. Have ye no other coin?"

"Unfortunately, no." The priest leaned closer and spoke lower. "Give me what coin you can lay hands on, and a keg of the best wine you have, and we'll call the deal fair."

"Er, a whole keg . . . ?"

"And two sacks of grain for our mules. Keep the rest as, hmm, compensation for your lost beer."

"Ah, ay, that'll do," the landlord agreed. "And, er, not a word to any Ancar louts about seeing the lot of you, eh?"

"Not a word to the Ancar about anything." The Deese priest smiled. "A word to a wise ear: best if your folk learned to understand the Ancar tongue as soon as might be—but never let the Ancar know it."

"Aye," the landlord grinned, showing gapped teeth. "A good word 'tis. Shall I carry out the keg for ye?"

"Best I do it—hidden under the cloak," the priest smiled back.

A moment later the party of Deese pilgrims departed the inn, two carrying grainbags and one toting a keg under his cloak. The innkeeper and his customers watched them go, already framing the tales they'd tell their assorted kin that evening. Two sets of strangers in one day: quite enough excitement for a town this size.

"Strange that those barbarian lads didn't start laying about with their irons," the blacksmith noted. "Mayhap they're settling down a bit."

"More like, the chanting o' those priests had a bit to do with it," the landlord considered. "It sounded most sleepy-like, did you note."

"Why, so it did," the blacksmith considered. "Hmm, a good magic, that, if they be going northward."

"Aye," The blacksmith nodded soberly. "They'll need all their magic there, right enough. Ancar thick as fleas . . ."

"Oh, great doings there!" the innkeeper laughed. "Ancar warriors against Sukkti wizards: yon's a fight I'd love to see— from a safe ways back."

The blacksmith nodded dreamily, thinking about that. From such beginnings were legends born; with any luck, he'd have tales to win him drinks for his whole life long.

Once out of the tavern, the dark-robed pilgrims headed for the stables at the best speed they could make under their burdens.

"The mules . . . ?" the tall thin one panted.

"Safe," retorted the big man with the keg. "Vari sat on the wagon playing with the whip until the stableboys went away. Then she rehitched the mules and took the whole lot around behind the stable. Those Ancar pups couldn't have seen them."

"Pups! If those are the puppies, Zeren, what are the wolves like?"

"Bad enough, but all gone south where the fighting is. Those were bored brats, not fit for the front lines. We'll doubtless meet more, probably house guards of older officers, petty chiefs and the like, who've settled down to enjoy the spoils. Here . . . mind your feet! Let's load these quickly."

The grain and wine went into the wagon, where Vari and Tamiri tied them down with respectable speed.

"Are we moving on again?" Tamiri wanted to know. "I wanted to sleep in a bed. It's been so long, Mama. . . ."

"I know, dearest, but it isn't safe here. Back inside, now." Vari shooed the grumbling girl back into the body of the wagon, and held the end flaps open. "Inside, fast. There won't be much room, but—"

The others scrambled in without ceremony, climbing onto whatever seats they could manage. Doshi, the last one in, retied the flaps tightly. Zeren and Sulun went to the mules, took off their now empty nosebags, led the reluctant animals out from behind the shed, then climbed up on the driver's box and flicked out the whip. The mules plodded sullenly out onto the road.

"North, but for how long?" Sulun asked, encouraging the mules with a few hints of the whip. "The sun's low."

"Just out of sight of the village, then into the first woods near the river." Zeren reached under his cloak and tugged his sword to a handier position. "We haven't time to do better. Hmm, and I don't think it will rain tonight. Bad, bad . . . We'd best take precautions."

"And hide the fire, too." Sulun hitched his shoulders in a sigh. "Well, so that was the enemy. Can they do anything besides fight and steal?"

"Not that I've seen. Gods, that was close, in there. I expected they'd start laying about swords, drive everyone out, steal what they wanted and set fire to the rest."

"Eloti's magic seems to be improving with practice."

"Yes . . ." Zeren set his eyes on the narrow road ahead, and said nothing further for a long while.

Choma's Chargers had grown up behind the lines, never been in on the sack of any of the large cities, only heard secondhand about the Sack of Sabis, and considered themselves most ill-used by Fate. Their older brothers and cousins, they very well knew, were busy down in the fabled southlands fighting heroic battles, collecting fabulous loot, making Great chiefs and small kings of themselves—and here were they, Choma's company, good as any warriors in all the tribes, stuck patrolling the roads in these dirt-poor backwater lands. Wasted, they were: and all because old chief Borath had taken a bad wound in the campaigns ten years ago, and had chosen to settle here and let the rest of the war go on without him. Oh yes, he'd sent troops south with the main army, but Choma and Ruek and Lumaj and their friends had been too young to go with them. Now, by Vona's Lightning Mace, it was too late; the greatest war in history had passed them by. It was the chief complaint of their lives, and they complained about it often—especially when there was, as now, enough beer to keep their voices lubricated.

As always, it was Lumaj who pointed out the necessity of keeping the ancient warrior skills sharp lest they be lost. He explained solemnly, past a few belches, that practice—even with no better foe than a bunch of dumb dirt-farmers—was a duty to themselves and their ancestors. Better to chase sheep than chase nothing: they must patrol the district regularly, as if it meant something.

Ruek added, as usual, that there were a few benefits to such circuit riding—such as this pretty good beer and that well-roasted sheep, and the occasional local wenches.

"Women? Where?" one of the Thona brothers complained. "We've hardly seen any in two days."

"There weren't even any barmaids at that tavern," their cousin Dak agreed. "Gods, you can't compare this goat-snatching to the sack of a real city. Uncle Framm will most likely come home with a dozen mule loads of gold and jewels and . . . and all kinds of loot." He took another long pull of beer, trying to imagine the loot from a fabulous city like Sabis.

"Half a moon of riding round these hills, and we haven't seen so much as one gold coin," the other Thona brother added. "Pah, not even a handful of silver."

"I'll wager those priests had some gold," Choma considered, chasing an elusive flea in his leggings. "Lots of silver, anyway. They wore good cloth, and had plenty on their table. Aye, they were rich enough."

"Priests?" Lomaj hiccuped. "What priests?"

"You remember: the ones at that tavern. They were sitting in the corner, singing some chant or other, remember?"

"Oh yes, those strange-looking ones." Ruek slapped his knee. "They didn't come from anywhere around here. I've never seen robes like that before."

"They must have come from the south," Choma considered. "Hey, maybe they're spies from one of the river towns, maybe Sabis itself. We should go and, uh, question the lot of 'em."

"What, now?" Dak groaned. "In the dark? We don't even know where they are."

"No, not now, of course," Choma snorted, conjuring up rough plans. "Tomorrow we go back to that town, pound on a few farmers, and ask 'em where the priests are."

"What if they don't know?" Dak yawned. "What if they've gone?"

"Then we track 'em." Choma put on his best glower and stared at everyone in turn. "Do you think we can't track a bunch of fat priests?"

"Don't waste time trying to get any story out of the farmers," Ruek laughed. "None of 'em understand us, anyway."

Choma glared at him, wishing he knew how to Strike Terror With His Glance, as his grandfather was said to do. "So it'll be a proper hunt," he growled, "an exercise in tracking. Gods know, we need the practice."

The others groaned, but had no real counterargument to that.

The farmers' road meandered about the feet of hills where thin patches of woodland grew. Zeren automatically noted the signs of infrequent logging, the many birds and occasional deer. Doshi, eyes bright with childhood memories, pointed out the names and uses of the various plants and animals.

"Oh, look: Constable Jays!" he noted, as a flock of crested blue birds took to the air above them, screeching protest about the invasion of their territory. "They cry like that when anyone comes near their trees. Ah, and that's a holm oak: no better wood for long fires—"

"There'll be no long fires until we find a safe place to settle," Sulun grumbled in the wagon bed behind him. "That will be a good ways north, yet."

"How shall we know a good place when we see it?" Eloti asked. "The towns we've met so far are most unpromising."

"All we've gained," Vari added, "are some small coins and a few supplies. What should we expect in the north?"

Sulun ran his fingers through his hair and tugged his curls abstractedly. He'd thought of little else since they left the river and started overland. "We'll want a town or large villa, big enough to have need of us. It will have to be close to the old mines near the Gol. . . ." He peered again at Doshi's maps, which were never out of reach these days. "And it must be long enough conquered by the Ancar that they've settled down to trade and farming, not just looting at random, as those louts back there were doing."

"Well into Torrhyn, then," Eloti considered, craning her neck to look at the map. "Perhaps on the far side of the Gol, where the Ancar have lived for two generations at least."

"I pray not." Sulun shivered in the sunlight as the wagon pulled out onto another long stretch of sheep meadow. "We don't speak the language, and I'd rather not approach the Ancar close enough to learn it."

"Somewhere along the Gol, then, or a little south of it." Eloti peered out at the long, rolling plains ahead. "How many days, think you?"

"Who can tell?" Sulun shook his head. "So many more farming towns to try, so much time in each to gather news . . . A moon, perhaps, to reach the river, the gods alone know how much time to scout the land along it. Or perhaps we'll have a sudden windfall of luck, and find what we need in the very next town."

"Not the next," Doshi put in. "There are nothing but tiny farm villages for the next forty leagues, nothing bigger this far from the river. Expect no such luck until we pass into Torrhyn."

"Can we dare seek the larger towns then?"

The discussion dissolved into a low-level, three-way argument, an intellectual game to pass the traveling time. Zeren listened with only half an ear, keeping most of his attention on the empty land around them. Poor pasturage, this, little to attract anyone. No wonder the land was so empty, the road so narrow and little used.

Behind them, the Constable Jays rose up screeching.

Zeren thought for a moment, nodded grimly, then said quietly to the others, "Ready your bows. We're being followed."

Half a moon or half a dozen towns ago, they might have questioned, argued, otherwise wasted time, but not anymore.

Sulun pulled his bow and quiver up from the bottom of the driver's seat. Tamiri and the smaller children burrowed down between sacks of clothing and food. Omis and Vari rolled the bottom of the wagon's roof cloth up a handspan from the sideboards and tied it in place. Everyone else slung on quivers, wriggled down below the sideboards of the wagon, and nocked arrows to their bowstrings.

The mules plodded on, unknowing. No one watching would have seen any notable change about the wagon, only perhaps noticed that the sound of conversation had dropped off.

No attack came, no sign of followers, though keen eyes raked the open ground that widened, moment by moment, between the wagon and the last stand of trees. "Nobody . . . no sign . . ." the news was whispered back up to the driver's box. Zeren considered that carefully.

"They don't want to charge across open ground," he guessed. "They'll stay out of sight until they can get closer. Maybe in the next patch of woods."

"What if we stay in open fields?" Sulun asked, just as quietly.

"Hmm, then they'll have to wait until dark. They probably mean to attack late at night, anyway."

"We can't drive on all night. Shall we camp in the open?"

Zeren peered down the winding road ahead, calculating chances. "No. We'll need the cover of trees. Go as long as you can, then camp in the woods . . . and set traps." He turned and called softly into the wagon, "Eloti, can you bespell a party of unknowns?"

"Not well," she answered. "If I don't know who they are, I must at least know where they are."

"Where they are . . ." Sulun considered. "Could you, then, set a spell on a section of ground, so as to take effect when, hmm, our guests cross it?"

"Hah, I hadn't thought of that." The lady, Sulun noticed, sounded much more animated these days; she seemed to take on more eagerness for life with every league that grew between her and Sabis. "Yes, a sort of reversed house-blessing. Stationary . . . A trap spell, in effect. Yes, I can do it, but it will cost me some little time. I can't just cast it on the ground as we pass."

"Could you cast it in a circle around our campsite this evening?"

There was a long moment's silence, then a laugh. "Certainly. I can do it while we cook dinner."

Zeren smiled slowly. "Magic traps and common traps: aye, I think we'll live through this night."

By dusk, the Thona brothers were grumbling: they'd wasted a whole day following those pilgrims back north, never had a good chance to jump them, and hadn't collected any more food, beer, women, or other goods. Lumaj insisted that one day's march was no hardship for real warriors, especially since the reward at the end would be much better than they could get out of the dirt-poor farming towns to the south, but his argument lacked a certain enthusiasm. Dak and Ruek were mostly silent, but occasionally speculated about how much food, beer, and other wealth those pilgrims must be carrying; the mules and wagon alone would be worth the effort, and they could have some fun with the pilgrims, too. Choma silently noted the morale of his troops, and made attack plans.

"We stay here till they've crossed the ridge," he announced, "then we hurry up to the ridge line and watch where they go."

"Hurry? With these damned oxen?" Dak grumbled, but not loudly.

"We'll make 'em hurry." Choma glowered and smacked a fist into his other hand. "The spies go into woods, or cross another ridge, and we catch up again. We follow out of sight until they stop."

"We can't charge a mule wagon on foot," Ruek pointed out. "Nor with oxen, either."

Choma casually clouted his head. "Not by daylight, you stupid turd. We wait till they've stopped for the night, set up camp, gone to sleep. Then we take 'em."

"Oh, right," Dak grinned, showing gaps in his teeth.

"That'll be hours," one of the Thona boys gloomed.

"What, can't you hold your water that long?" Choma gave everyone his best glare. Nobody answered it.

"They're over the ridge," Lumaj announced. "Gimme the whip for these damn beasts."

The whip flailed. The pained oxen broke into a trot. The laden cart rumbled out of the cover of trees and into the open pastureland.

❖   ❖   ❖

"Oh Mama, why do *I* have to feed Mido and the baby?" Tamiri complained. "They're so dumb, they're spilling it all."

"'M not dumb," Mido grumbled, smearing stew across his nose.

"You have to, because everybody else is busy setting the traps." Vari studied the fire a moment, then chucked in some more wood—two good-sized logs that would burn half the night and leave a respectable bed of coals without much care or attention. "Now keep quiet, all of you, while I help Ziya with the mules."

Tamiri sighed and rolled her eyes heavenward, silently calling the gods to witness what she had to put up with. Mido shovelled more stew into his mouth. The baby grumbled, but accepted mouthfuls of the savory mess with not much bad grace.

Vari got up and went to the far side of the fire, where the mules were tethered. Ziya had filled their nosebags with a good mix of dried peas and grain, and was busy hauling a second bucket of water up from the small stream a dozen yards off. The mules hadn't been curried yet, and dried sweat tufted their grey coats. Vari took the curry-comb and brush from under the driver's seat of the nearby wagon, and started work on the nearer mule.

Ziya set down the water bucket, checked to see if the mules were still emptying the nosebags, and went to the wagon for a long weed-cutting knife. "Will we sleep first?" she asked Vari as she passed.

"Most likely, dear." Vari didn't miss a stroke with the comb as she answered. "Remember to keep your bow covered by the blankets."

"I know." Ziya went off to cut some fresh greens for the mules, somber-faced, and with no wasted motion.

Vari was just finishing with the second mule when Eloti came out of the wood, Zeren close behind. She looked flushed, tired, but smug; had Vari not known better, she would have guessed that Zeren and Eloti had been off making love in the bushes.

"Is the trap spell set?" Vari asked, setting the brush and curry-comb aside and reaching for the hoof pick.

"Set and ready, twenty-five paces out," Eloti smiled. "Here, I'll do that; the mules know me."

"Oh, tush, I'll manage." Vari lifted an uncomplaining mule's hoof to prove her claim to expertise. "After all these weeks, I've gotten a knack for it. You go get some dinner, and rest."

"She's right." Zeren tugged gently at Eloti's sleeve. "You've worked harder than any of us. Rest for the first watch."

"Very well." Eloti let herself be led away to the fire. "And you?"

"I'll take first watch, just in case our guests are the impatient sort."

"And if they're not?"

"Heh! I assure you, I've had years' practice at waking quickly to fight."

Vari watched them stroll off to the fire, and chuckled to herself between the mules' hooves.

"How much longer?" Ruek whispered, surreptitiously scratching a flea bite.

"Awhile yet," Choma growled. "Their fire's still at flame, not coals."

"So?" the elder Thona brother grumbled, easing away from a troublesome rock that poked his belly.

"That means they're still awake," Lumaj loftily explained. "Flames means new wood, fresh put on the fire, see? That means someone's still awake to've put it there."

"Oh."

"Also means someone's awake enough to need light, firelight to see by. Get it?" the younger Thona smirked. "Fire goes down t'coals, they can't see us."

"Uh, then we can't see them, neither."

"We'll have our eyes used to the dark," Dak volunteered, unsnagging a twig from one of his braids. "Besides, they'll be asleep."

"Just a matter of waiting," Ruek sighed, rolling over on his back. "Wake me when it's time."

"Don't sleep too sound," Choma grumbled, swatting him. "Another hour, maybe two, then we go in."

Slowly the fire sank down to coals. The mules, freed of their nosebags, slurped the buckets half-empty and turned their interest to the piled weeds. Very little sound came from the wagon, or the humans stretched out around the fire, or those whom the mules could smell in the woods beyond. There was no sound or scent of any preying beast larger than a fox anywhere in the small stretch of forest, and no snakes nearby.

Reassured, the mules munched their way through the herbage, then put their heads down and drowsed.

" 'S time," Choma grunted, booting and elbowing his troops into action.

"Which way?" Ruek grumbled, rolling over. "Can't see the fire . . ."

"Straight ahead, and quietly!" Choma got to his feet with elaborate care, setting an example for the others, and inched forward through the dark brush. Too bad, he considered, that they hadn't had time to scout these woods beforehand, let alone divide the company and send half around to the other side of the spies' camp. Now they'd have to do it all in one short charge: messy, no real strategy, and some chance that a few of the outlanders might escape into the woods. Still, they'd catch some; certainly they'd get the wagon and the mules and any goods laid out in the camp. But quietly now, quietly, sneak up all the way to the campsite. Thank the gods, his boys at least knew how to move quietly in the dark.

They'd gone maybe twenty paces toward the fire when they came across what felt like a bank of mist: cold, thick dampness hanging in the air and confusing the senses. But they couldn't *see* any mist.

Dak swore softly. Lumaj shushed him, and they moved on.

One of the Thona brothers put his foot wrong on a tree root and fell, clumping and clattering, right into a thornbush. His squawk of pain seemed loud as thunder in the thick dark.

"Shh!" Lumaj whispered fiercely.

Next instant, he put his foot on something that wriggled, hissed, and sank outraged fangs into his leggings. Lumaj fell backward, howling, "Snake! Snakebite!"

"Vona's balls!" Choma drew his sword and plunged forward, swearing. No hope of a good silent sneak-up now; best to charge ahead, screeching war cries, and hope that the prey would be too confused to know what was happening. "Charge!" he bellowed, followed by a good imitation of his grandfather's favorite war whoop.

The others came yelling and rattling after him, all but Lumaj, who was still rolling around in the bushes clutching his leg and screaming about snakes.

Running through the dark forest turned out to be much more difficult than sneaking through it: overhanging branches snagged at hair and helmets, lower boughs swatted at faces and impeded hand and foot, unseen roots and rocks tripped running feet with what seemed to be calculated malice, and the wild beasts proved numerous and troublesome.

The elder Thona got a spider down the back of his neck, which made him stop to dance and squirm and jab at it with his sword until he got a nasty cut on his back. Dak put a foot squarely into a badger hole, with the badger still in it, getting not only a badly turned ankle but a good fierce bite in the foot. The younger Thona stepped on something squashy and wiggly, which made him both jump and skid—smack into a tree, which thwacked his helmet down over his eyes and snagged him unmercifully by the beard. Ruek hit a hanging wasps' nest, which made him run faster, howl louder, and pay even less attention to where he was going. Choma ran right into what he thought was a rabbit—until it proved in the time-honored fashion that it was a skunk.

Screeching, howling, rattling and clattering mightily—and stinking to high heaven—Choma's Chargers came clanging through the woods toward where they'd last seen the campfire: out of the big trees, and into the low brush.

Then Ruek's foot hit the first trip-cord. He went sprawling flat—into a thornbush—and a big deadfall of a tree fell neatly on top of him. Choma, just a few steps behind him, ran into the tree and fell across it, adding to the volume of Ruek's howls. Somewhere nearby, brass carriage bells tinkled madly.

Off near the campsite, someone shouted authoritatively in an unknown tongue, possibly Sabirn.

Traps! Choma had time to think, as he pulled himself off the log. *They set up trip-cords, alarms—*

Then a trio of small, tumbling flames came whirring through the air toward him. They hit just ahead and to either side, with a sound like smashing pottery.

Then Vona's own fire lit the earth.

Flames exploded from the ground, searing the eyes, lighting up the woods like midday sun, accompanied by a roar like small thunder and clouds of heavy white smoke that stank nearly as bad as the skunk.

Ruek screamed once, impossibly shrill, then went silent. Choma fell backward, clawing at his flare-blinded eyes. Around him, the others screeched in shocked terror, turned to run, fell against unseen trees.

That same foreign voice snapped out another order, and then the arrows came: a rain to match that wizards' thunder and lightning.

The Thona brothers howled and died together, pinned to trees and earth. Dak went stumbling off blindly through the trees, trying to pluck the arrows out of his arm, side, and leg; a second volley of arrows caught him amid a snare of bushes, and he fell into a waiting cloud of wasps. Choma, crawling away through brush and jabbing tree roots, heard Dak screeching for a long time.

They really were wizards, They really were . . . Choma thought inanely as he crawled through the darkness. Somewhere out there Lumaj was still alive—if he hadn't died of snakebite. Sometime the sun had to rise, the light had to come—if his eyes were capable of seeing it. Somehow the two of them could get to the oxcart, wash and bind their wounds, come looking for other survivors— or at least ride back to Borath's holding for help. Oh gods, Borath's holding was at least five days' ride away.

Choma crawled on, listening for some sign of Lumaj, until he collapsed in exhaustion on the edge of the wood.

The team of oxen, tethered less than twenty yards off, blinked in mild surprise at the bizarre sight, and then went back to their grazing.

In the morning Zeren took Sulun, Doshi, Ziya, and Arizun out to search for sign of the attackers. They all carried bows at the ready, save for Arizun who held an amulet and chanted protective countercharms against their own trap spell.

The first thing they found was an armored body pinned under a deadfall, head and hands hideously burned.

"Your firepot must have hit right on top of him," Zeren deduced, studying the burn marks around the corpse.

Sulun turned quickly, thrust his head into a tangle of bushes, and retched hard and fast.

The others looked a while longer at the corpse, Doshi and Arizun paling and shaken, Zeren and Ziya impassive and thoughtful.

In a moment Sulun rejoined them, looking not far from dead himself. "I didn't know it would do that," he muttered to himself. "Before all the gods, I swear, I didn't know. . . ."

"There should be more this way," said Zeren, turning off to his right. "We saw one of them go down here." Almost absently, he plucked the harness bells off their station on a branch and stuffed them into his belt pouch. "Right. There."

The others looked where he pointed, and saw the body of another Ancar lying in a patch of brush. Arrows studded him like the quills of a hedgehog, and every exposed inch of his skin was swollen with wasp stings. Sulun closed his eyes; Arizun and Doshi looked away. Only Ziya and Zeren gazed calmly at the body.

"Best collect our arrows," said Zeren, reaching through the brush to pull them free.

"Gods," Doshi moaned, "can't you leave them there?"

"No, we'll need them." Zeren tugged at a stubborn arrow wedged through the sodden leather armor. "Besides, if any of his friends survived they may come looking. Much can be learned from an arrow; best to keep them ignorant."

They found two more arrow-bristled bodies back beyond the burned corpse, and scrape marks on the ground where a fifth Ancar had dragged himself away.

"No blood," Zeren noted. "That one might yet survive. We'd best collect our traps and be gone soon. We should leave right after breakfast."

But nobody wanted breakfast.

They broke camp and left within the hour, pushing the mules to a steady trot, otherwise quiet and subdued. Clouds sped over the sun, and light, steady rain fell as they crossed the next stretch of meadow and mounted the next hill.

Doshi, sitting next to Sulun on the driver's seat, spread his cloak to protect the map he studied. "Another town, perhaps eight leagues west of this track," he noted. "We could reach it before night. Should we go there?"

"No," said Sulun, huddled small under his cloak.

"Just as well." Doshi folded the map and peered at the raingreyed land ahead. "Let's leave these lands soon as might be. They're . . . ugly."

"Your old home," Sulun murmured, surprised.

"No longer." Doshi shivered. "It's all changed, nothing like what I remember. I don't want to see any more of it."

"Nor I," Sulun admitted.

"We'll be safe in Torrhyn. Safer than here, anyway. Torrhyni dialect isn't much different from Jarryan, and we've heard enough of that to understand it. There were some small cities near the old sulfur mines, should still be there, even with the mines shut down. I don't imagine the Ancar having any use for sulfur . . . but they might have kept after the black glass, mined enough for that. They'd probably use it for pretty jewelry, or surgeon's knives. Find black glass and we find the sulfur. We can settle close enough to the mines—"

"We don't need the sulfur," Sulun snapped. "All we need is a sizable town."

"But—but we need the sulfur to make the firepowder—"

"No more firepowder! Never again!" Sulun slapped the reins fiercely on the startled mules' rumps, whipping them to a faster trot. "Gods, you saw what it did, back there. . . ." He drew a deep breath, and shuddered.

Doshi half-turned, suddenly aware of the listening silence in the wagon behind him. All the others, they were waiting for him to answer. Doshi shrugged off the awareness, and looked back at Sulun.

"You saw the other bodies too, didn't you?" he said. "Forested with arrows, and one of them swollen all over with wasp stings— were they any prettier? Were those deaths any better?"

"Not . . ." Sulun rubbed one hand across his forehead. "Not the same."

"No." Doshi gnawed his lip and made himself remember. "I think they were slower."

"Oh, gods!"

"I can't remember when I last saw a . . . a good death, Sulun. Not even back in Sabis: hunger, disease, drowning, death in burning buildings or riots—"

"Stop it!" Sulun almost dropped the reins, shaking so hard.

Doshi took a long, slow breath. "What I mean to say is that the only 'good' death I can imagine is a quick one: fast, painless—

like a high priest knocking down a sacrificial goat. If you must kill, do it fast. It doesn't matter how the body looks afterward—not to the dead, anyway; that's only a trouble to the living. Firepowder kills faster than arrows."

"Uglier . . ." Sulun whispered, head bowed over the reins.

"So, leave that to trouble that Ancar warrior's friends. Perhaps they'll be encouraged to leave us alone."

From the wagon bed behind them came a quiet sigh. Doshi glanced that way, thinking it was Zeren. Instead he saw Ziya peering at him, face revealing nothing, as always.

Beside him, Sulun huddled over the reins and wept quietly, tears merging with the steady rain on his face.

Doshi sighed and unrolled the map once more. "The nearest sulfur mines, if we keep our present course, should be near the old villa of Ashkell. That's on the northern slope of the Torrhyn hills, near a tributary of the southeast fork of the Gol. Nothing's been heard of it since the old war, more than fifty years ago. The gods know what it's like now, but there was once a prosperous mining town there."

The rain continued on, all that day and into the next.

Part III
CANDLELIGHT

✧ CHAPTER ONE ✧

Wotheng Woshka's-son, Baron of Ashkell, woke to unwelcome sunlight and a twinging hangover. He pulled the sheepskin blanket up over his head, rolled against his wife Gynallea's soft buttocks, and crept back toward sleep.

Gynallea gave him a kick, and grunted: " 'S morning."

"Don' care." Wotheng burrowed deeper into the goose-feather pillows.

"It's morning. Get *up*." Gynallea back-kicked him again. "Work to do."

"No work yet," Wotheng insisted, pulling a pillow over his head. "Yawth hasn't knocked yet."

"Yawth came earlier, knocked, and said something about newcomers. We should go see."

Wotheng counterfeited a creditable snore.

Gynallea sighed, took a deep breath, tightened her belly muscles, and let loose a trumpeting fart.

Under the blankets, Wotheng got the worst of it. He choked, wheezed, and erupted out of the blankets, roaring, "Gods jam your arse with a pine tree, woman! Aaagh, that was cruel."

"That was last night's beer." Gynallea crawled out of the tumbled blankets like a venerable sow from the best wallowing hole. "Tell me no sad tales of hangover, lovey; I drank as much as you."

"Well, who asked you to sit up so late?" Wotheng grumbled as he lugged himself out of bed, idly scratching his bare hide.

"You did, remember?" Gynallea plodded to the nearest carved chair, where her undershift lay. "You wanted my good wit with numbers when those poor North Hill farmers came whining about why they'd have to delay their taxes."

"Ah, right . . ." Wotheng studied his wife's broad buttocks as she tugged the shift over her head. Fart upon headache or no, he hadn't much to complain about; a good clever wife with such a fine, buxom shape was better than most men could claim. And no doubt, the headache would improve after a mug of Gynallea's bitter bark tea . . . plus half a dozen fried sausages and some hotcakes and a handful of coddled eggs, and some bread with jelly, and . . . "Ah, what were those farmers whining about, anyway? Do you remember?"

"Oh, yes." Gynallea batted her tangled brown locks with a pig-bristle brush. " 'Twas that Folweel again."

"Oh. Gods, not again." Wotheng knuckled the last of sleep out of his eyes. "What did he do, set a curse of fire on the poor fools' cowsheds?"

"Sheepsheds. We agreed to take part of the taxes in rough-roasted mutton, remember?"

"Gods. Ah, p'raps your cooks can turn it into sausage fit for siege food." Wotheng hunted the bedposts for his clothes. The underbreeches and small shift smelled suspiciously overused. He tossed them in the corner reserved for ripe laundry, went to the clothespress, and hunted for fresh smallclothes. "Vona blast that pesky wizard. We have to do something about him before we all turn poor, but what, hey?"

Gynallea shrugged into a clean enough outer skirt and glanced about for her stockings. "Sneak into his holding and poison his food stores? Set *his* thatch mysteriously afire? Dig a deep pit and lure him into it? *I* don't know, lovey. My kindred raised no wizards."

"Nor did mine." Wotheng sat down to pull on his stockings and overbreeches. "Don't I wish it so, my sweet moo-cow. Don't I wish I knew *any* wizard who could steal into Folweel's hold without half a dozen curses bringing bricks down on his head. Four good men died trying that. Four, remember. I'd not ask anyone to be the fifth. Give me some better plans, sweet cow, for I'm all shat out of them."

"Do I find any, lovey, and I'll tell you. Let's to breakfast and see what Yawth's news is."

"Aye, aye. And I suppose I should go look at that old ruin Busho was whining about. . . ." Wotheng paused, one foot half into its shoe, hearing faint noise at the door. "Yawth, stop dithering about the door and come in!"

The door swung open and a gangling servant half-fell in. "As ye wish, m'lord," he dithered. "Begging yer pardon, but there's much to tell of, hap'nin' downstairs."

"Then tell it," Wotheng snapped, putting on his other shoe.

"Why, sir, there's these strangers come to the gate early this morning: all robed in fine grey cloth, with a big wagon and two great mules all hung with chains and bells and charms and what-not made of right good iron and brass what twinkled like gold. Most rich folks they must be, nigh a dozen of 'em, all bearin' wands an chantin' the praises of Deese of the Forge in most outlandish High Speech. . . ."

" 'Deese of the Forge'?" Gynallea turned around, forgetting her half-laced bodice, which flopped down to her hips. "Who might that be?"

"They say . . ." Yawth's dark eyes grew wide and round in his long face. "That be the ancient Sukkti name for Clong, the blacksmith's god. Oh, that's put Biddon and his shop all in a dither! They be talkin' with him now, swappin' forge wit like brothers in the same trade. 'Tis a sight to see, I grant—"

"Sukkti?" Gynallea gaped. "What are these folk, to be toying with old magic names? Do they claim to be dealing with ghosts of the Elder Folk, then?"

"Er, no, Mistress. They claim . . . they say they *are* the Elder Folk. They say they hid out in the Lost City of Itoma, far away south, until the last of their old conquerors were overthrown. Now, beggin' yer pardon, they say that with Sabis fallen, they've come out of hidin' and wish to visit their old holy grounds again. That's what they say, Mistress."

"Gods!" roared Wotheng, making Yawth jump. "Not more plaguey wizards!"

Gynallea waved him silent with a quick gesture. "Sukkti? And wizards? And what have they been about since they got here?"

"As I said, Mistress: they came this morning when the villa's gates opened, and went straightway to Biddon's shop. They greeted him in the name of Deese of the Forge, and then fell to shoptalk. They've done naught else as I know, and they be there now, if ye'd care to come see."

"Indeed we will," Gynallea smiled, tapping plump fingers on her chin. "Leave them be; we'll come presently."

"After breakfast," Wotheng put in. "Go bid cook have our plates and cups ready—and I want bitter bark tea, hear?"

"Oh, aye, Master. I hear ye right well."

"Then be about it!"

"Aye, sir. Aye, goin' now." Yawth bowed clumsily, two or three times, and hurried out the door.

Gynallea closed it after him, then turned to her husband with a broad smile. "Sukkti wizards, no less? And serving Deese of the Forge?"

"More damned wizards," Wotheng snorted, hauling on the last of his clothes. "Flocking in like crows to the corpse. Gods, we'll all be eating turnips and wearing straw. Vona, what have I done to deserve—"

"Hush, lovey, and think. A fresh breed of wizards, knowing the Elder Folk's magic, and serving a forge god. Now tell me, from what god or spirit does Folweel get his powers?"

"Yotha the fire, of all the nasty-tempered devils, though I swear 'tis a good question who serves whom. Those wicked predictions of fire that always come true—you know well it's that damned wizard's doing, whether he takes power from Yotha to do it, or sends Yotha to run the errands himself."

"Forge and fire, lovey. Think: do you see a possible rivalry there?"

Wotheng looked up, recognizing that purring tone in his wife's voice. "Ah, you have a plan, my sweet moo-cow?"

"Ah, lovey, lovey, in all your mother's fine books, did you never come across the wise fable of fighting fire with fire?"

Wotheng slowly mirrored her smile. "Or, set a wizard to fight a wizard? Heh! whichever wins, we'll be no worse off than before."

"Possibly better, lovey. Let us go visit these new wizards, shall we?"

"Right after breakfast, sweet cow. Right after breakfast."

Biddon, the villa's blacksmith, peered so close to the anvil that occasional sparks struck his nose. Gods, yes, this stranger knew his business well; if the scars on his massive arms hadn't told tale enough, the man's obvious skill with the hammer was proof. Biddon hung on the magician-smith's every word, wishing these folk were more understandable or that he knew more of the old High Speech.

"Five times," the stranger was saying. "Hammer five times, at least, and (incomprehensible) with a bigger bellows between. This (unintelligible) iron needs plenty. Fold like this—see?—each (impossible) time. Don't bother shaping it until the last hammering. (Unguessable) sheep-fat in the flux . . ."

Biddon nodded eagerly, straining to understand and remember. He could see the axehead taking shape under the blows, its edges showing a grain as fine as oak wood. Gods, no, he'd never seen anything like that. How well would it cut? How sharp an edge could it take? How long would it last? He couldn't wait to find out. There, now: another toasting in the hard-blown coals . . .

"Ah, it's ready," said the stranger, hefting the glowing axehead in his fine set of tongs. "Where's the (incomprehensible) trough?"

"Oh, here. Here." Biddon shoved forward the stone tempering trough with its unaccustomed load of chilled hog fat. "Be it cold enough?"

"(Unintelligible) enough," said the wizard-smith. He dropped the glowing axehead into the trough and stepped back quickly.

Clouds of vaporized grease, reeking of burned bacon, filled the shop like holy incense. Everyone coughed madly and made jokes about roast pork that were barely heard through the lively sizzling.

Another, more familiar, voice coughed also.

Biddon flinched, then peered through the dissipating clouds.

Sure enough, as if the smoke had conjured him, there stood Lord Wotheng himself. Worse, Lady Gynallea stood beside him.

Biddon whispered a quick prayer to all his family gods, bowed low, and began making excuses.

"Oh, hush," Gynallea waved him off. "Tell us what this visitor is working upon so marvelously."

Biddon gulped in relief. "Why, he was but showin' me a better way to make this axehead, my'lady. And a fine piece of work it be, too. Soon as it's cooled and fitted to the handle, ye'll surely see how nice it does."

"We'll leave that work to your hands," Wotheng grinned. "Meanwhile, let not our guests think we're poor in hospitality. Come up to the big house, visitor, and share a cup or two with us. Eh, do you folk speak Torrhyni?"

Another, more slender, stranger stepped forward and bowed low. "We speak it a little, good sir," he said, with an accent that hinted of time spent in Jarrya. "And we thank you much for your invitation. Pray give us some time to wash, and we'll visit you directly."

Wotheng and his lady exchanged looks and smiles. "Soon, then," the lady purred. The pair turned and marched graciously out of the blacksmith's shop, not glancing back.

Biddon wiped sweat and grease off his forehead. "Oh, that were a bit of luck, there. Master and Mistress both be pleased with ye. 'Twere the axehead done it, I'll wager. Eh, I keep the wash trough outside there. . . ."

The wizard-smith murmured untranslated thanks and went outside. The younger wizard ran his eyes admiringly over Biddon's anvil, then leaned closer and asked conspiratorially, "What's the Master's name? And his lady? And, er, what sort of folk are they?"

Biddon was grateful enough to answer at some length.

Doshi caught up with the others at the wash trough, where they'd been idling a while to wait for him.

"The wagon's safe," Sulun murmured in his ear as they both bent over the trough. "Only you, me, Zeren, and Eloti are going in; the rest are watching the gear and the mules. What did you learn?"

"Quite an earful." Doshi splashed water noisily on his face. "Our host, Wotheng, is the son of a clever old Ancar soldier named Woshka. The old man came through here a generation ago, recognized good sheep country when he saw it, and was tired of soldiering anyway. Besides, I suspect he knew he'd get little of the loot of the richer lands once the big commanders were done with them. Perhaps the deciding factor was the buxom daughter of the then master of this villa—which wasn't called Ashkell then, by the way. That happened after Ashkell town proper was sacked and burned, leaving this as the largest surviving settlement."

"Get on with this, Doshi."

"Ah, right. Well, the old lord volunteered to stay behind and keep the roads open when the rest of the Ancar horde moved on. He persuaded the last owner of the villa that a few trained Ancar men-at-arms would be good protection from bandits, then married the squire's daughter and settled down to protect, tax, and manage the land. By all accounts, he did a fairly good job of it, and his Torrhyn-Sabirn wife took care of the rest. Wotheng was their only surviving son, though there are a couple daughters married off here and there."

"How does he handle his . . . subjects?"

"Well, Wotheng has enough practical intelligence and muscle to maintain his authority without having to fall back on his Ancar connections—in fact, he's barely spoken or written to them in all these years. This place is wonderfully isolated from the rest of the Ancar horde."

"Written? He can read and write?"

"Oh, yes; we're not dealing with a fool here. Papa saw to it that Wotheng knew how to manage and protect the land, had a good eye for petty politics and healthy sheep. Mama, who was something of a cultured lady, saw to it that Master Wotheng learned as much reading, writing, and civilized knowledge as the house library provided."

"House library? How good is it?"

"How should a blacksmith know that? He's never seen it."

"Hmm, if only we can get a look at it . . . But go on, Doshi. Is this the sort of fellow we can impress with our 'wizard' act?"

"I don't think so. His mother gave him enough sophistication to take all notion of magic and religion with a healthy grain of salt. He got a good, basic levelheadedness from both parents. He pays his respects to the gods, their priests, and any magician of proven ability, but he's not the sort to be pulled about by a bit of showmanship and some simple tricks. We'll have to be careful with him, Sulun."

"Understood. What other relatives must we worry about?"

"The sisters were married off to his father's old soldiers, and all have sizable farms of their own—far enough away to have no border arguments with Wotheng—and they're barely seen here except for weddings, funerals, harvest festivals, and the like. They won't be a problem, I think."

"What about the Mistress of the household?"

"Ah, she's quite a match for him; daughter of the second richest farm-holder in the valley, quite as well educated as Wotheng's mother—who may have arranged the marriage. In any case, Wotheng's parents managed to live long and die peacefully. He has a clutch of children, all grown and married now, likewise scattered of to various farmsteads."

"That's all, then? No wily courtiers milking power behind the throne?"

"No, just house servants, tenants, and a few men-at-arms who double as shepherds and huntsmen. This is . . . very much the country villa it always was."

"Ah. And the mines?"

"What mines?" Doshi innocently dried his face on his undersleeves, noting that Ashkell lacked knowledge of such niceties as towels.

"Do*sheee!* The sulfur mines!" Sulun tugged furiously at his dangling curls and new beard. "Or black glass mines, as they're probably called now. Don't tell me you forgot!"

"Oh, no." Doshi grinned. "It's just that the blacksmith never heard of them."

"Oh, gods, just ten leagues away by the map, and he's never—"

"It seems that the mines originally belonged to quite another family, no connection at all with the villa. The old invasion did for them, quite thoroughly; on, no, not wrecked, just abandoned and almost totally forgotten."

"How in the name of all gods can everyone forget about a sulfur mine?"

"By not needing, knowing, or caring about it. Sulun, remember that both the villa folk and the Ancar cared mostly about farming and sheep. The former villa holders cared nothing for the mines, and Wotheng's father knew nothing of them. A good iron, gold, copper, or silver mine would have held everyone's interest, but sulfur? And black glass? Even in their heyday, the mines always made their profit on the trade with the south. When the invasion stopped that, well, no trade means no profit, and no profit meant that the mines were abandoned."

"I see. But they're still there? I mean, the entrances and shafts and all?"

"I heard nothing about anyone filling in any old mine entrances. Why should these shepherds and farmers bother, pray tell?"

"Ah, very good, then." Sulun rubbed his cheeks briskly and considered the best lines of approach. "Gods, was it so few moons ago that we played this game with Entori?"

"We've all learned much since then."

"Indeed. Let's go in."

"Sweet cow, the floor's swept clean enough," Wotheng protested, easing back in the big chair.

"Should have been scrubbed. It still stinks in here. Ah, give me that, Noba; some fresh herbs in this pot, and put it on the fire to boil. There . . ." Gynallea rubbed her hands on her apron and raked her glance around the hall. It could have been better, but it looked well enough in the light through the narrow windows: floor swept, hanging banners reasonably clean, a small table (with a clean cover-cloth, thank the gods) and some comfortable chairs near the fire, a pretty jug of good beer waiting, and the sweet-smelling tea heating in the fireplace. Yes, good enough. She tugged thoughtfully at the kerchief covering her hair. Leave it on or take it off? Look more the housewife or the grand lady? Appear simple and kindly, or imposing? "Hmm, these newcomers went first to Biddon and dazzled his eyes with their skill. That smells of serious craftsfolk, concerned with trade. Best we appear as simple farmer folk, lovey. Lull them, see if they try to take advantage. We can always show our wit and authority later." She patted straying hair back under the kerchief.

"Hmm, just as you say, moo-cow. Hey, Yawth, are they come yet?"

"Just now, Master." The servant bobbed his head eagerly. "They be waitin' at the door."

"Send them in." Wotheng heaved a mountainous sigh. He hated politicking before lunch, but a chance such as this didn't come along every day. Besides, the herb tea had dispelled his headache, and he felt fit enough to take on half the earth at full charge.

The door creaked open and the little company of Deese priests, four of them, came padding down the length of the hall. They looked a bit intimidated by the size of the place, and yes, they'd dressed in good robes and washed well. Aha, they wanted something from him. Wotheng smiled benignly as Yawth made the stuttering introductions. Vona, what strange, foreign-sounding names they had!

"Welcome to the villa of Ashkell," Gynallea purred. "Come sit, and join us in a cup of beer."

The little quartet obediently sat and took cups. Gynallea poured.

" 'Tis humble stuff," Wotheng opened, "made of our poor local barley, but 'tis kindly to the tongue." *If not to the head, next morning.* "Have you come far, then?"

"Far, yes. From Itoma, south," said the biggest, in a bizarre southern accent. "This beer is very good." He drained his cup and reached for the jug in honest appreciation.

Wotheng smiled again. "And what brings a company of pilgrims to these poor lands? We've little here to draw worship or custom." *See if that discourages them.*

" 'Tis a long story, Master," said the slender youth with a Jarryan twang to his words. "As you know, we Sukkti held the southern lands before the coming of the Sabirns. As they marched north, we lost all save Itoma—where our mightiest wizards held fast. . . ."

Wotheng nodded as he listened. He'd long known, from his mother's histories, that the Elder Folk were only the first settlers of the south, not creatures of another order. They'd had a reputation for great magic, but had lost their land anyway—except for the Lost City of Itoma. "I'd always thought that city was a fable, stuff of dreams and fireside tales," he prodded.

"Oh no, sir," the lad enthused. "It stands on a stream of the great river, made of fine grey fieldstone and pale sandstone; in good sunlight, it gleams like silver and gold. The roofs are mostly flat, and held up with many columns. . . ."

Wotheng noted, as the youth went on, the numerous details that only a builder, mechanic, or architect would notice. Clearly, these folk had seen a city of unusual buildings somewhere to the south. Just as clearly, they were well-trained craftsmen—and not just in smithing. Wotheng caught his wife's eye, saw her appreciative nod and smile. "Then how come you to leave so fair a place?" he prodded gently.

"Why, sir, we wished to see those ancient shrines that were so long barred to us by Sabis. Now that their crown has fallen, we dared venture out from Itoma's safety to see what had become of the land and people."

Wotheng flicked another glance at his wife. This didn't quite make sense; something was missing. "How came you safe past the fighting?" he temporized.

"The war came not nigh Itoma," the big one answered. "It passed us by, and we came north behind it."

Wotheng shrugged and looked to his wife.

"A long, hard journey it must have been," she tried.

"Oh, yes," the youth replied. "We made our way by selling small magics and forge work. Would you care to see some of our wares?"

Wotheng noted the tallest of the four giving the lad a small nudge with his elbow. Aha, the manner of merchants hoping to make a sale—and taking care not to advertise too quickly. Craftsmen, merchants, and wizards: better and better. "Oh aye, but let's not be hasty when there's a good jug yet to finish. But say, what brings you forge folk to our humble villa? We've little trade here, and I've never heard of any holy ground hereabouts."

The youth chewed his lip and looked imploringly at the tall, thin pilgrim, who leaned forward and took up the tale.

"In truth, m'lord, there is an ancient shrine some ten leagues west of here," he said, in the same heavy southland accent as the first man. " 'Tis the place where black glass is found, which has sacred uses for such as we. Do you know the place?"

Wotheng stared blankly. Ten leagues west: that was steep foothill land, stony and thin of soil, no good for farming, poor pasturage even for sheep. He'd used it occasionally for running sheep a month or two of the year, and no more. None of his relatives or tenants would take it. There were a few ruins there, but nothing of value in them. "Ey, yes I do. That's where a small town stood, back before my father came here. 'Tis my land— poor for farming, but you might graze some sheep there. I know of no shrine."

The tall stranger didn't seem disappointed. "The shrine is a . . . formation of the rocks, and mostly valued for the black glass. If it lies on your land, might we have your permission to visit there?"

Wotheng glanced at his wife again.

"Why, surely," Gynallea smiled. "We'll happily send a guide with you. Do you wish to stay awhile there, we can give you some food and drink to take—poor stuff, but filling. But of what use is the shrine, and the black glass?"

"We would make the black glass into tools and amulets," the tall one replied readily. "When cut properly, black glass takes a fine edge—suitable for small cook-knives and surgeons' blades. Also it makes fair jewels, not so costly that common folk could not afford it, yet handsome enough that quality folk would not take scorn to wear it. Also, it can be made into meditation gems, useful for small magics."

Wotheng and Gynallea looked at each other and grinned. So, these pilgrim-smith-merchants hoped to set up trade, did they? Very good. But now to the serious question.

"Small magics?" Wotheng straightened in his chair. "What sort of magics, sir? We have hedge wizards and granny witches enough, the gods know. What manner of magic do you folk do?"

The tall pilgrim shifted a bit, looking almost embarrassed. "Well, simple well-wishing, of course, and some healing and crop-blessing—Kula the Mother being the consort of Deese—but mostly we deal with forge work, trade craft, mechanical work, that sort of thing."

"Forge work?" Gynallea leaned nearer. "Do you then call, er, Deese to your forge fire to aid your work?"

"Er, yes, something like that. Mostly we call him to encourage excellence of work, protection, inspiration, and so on." The pilgrim glanced at his fellows, giving them a quick smile. "With his help, we do produce work of fine quality—and most difficult to ill-wish or damage."

Gynallea and Wotheng exchanged triumphant looks.

"Protection?" Gynallea almost purred. "Deese, then, gives you control—er, and safety, of fire?"

"Eh? Oh, yes m'lady. We take good care to do that."

Wotheng's smile stretched wide. "How marvelous. Could you show us a bit of your magic? We have so few amusements here. . . ."

The man shrugged, almost resignedly, and reached into his robe. "In fact, I have a small spell here," he murmured, bringing out a tiny packet of folded parchment. He got up and went to the fire, waving his other hand in a circle above the packet and chanting softly in a strange tongue. To Wotheng, listening carefully, it sounded as if the pilgrim were saying: "Pie are square, pie are square, Deese make this work right, pie are square . . ."

He tossed the packet into the fire, and raised both hands in an invocatory gesture.

Behind them, Gynallea thought she heard one of the pilgrims humming softly.

The packet exploded in a poof of smoke and a shower of sparks. Simultaneously, the teapot began whistling.

The fire flared bright and high for a moment, shot through with colored flames: red, blue, green, and purple. Then it sank back to normal, not spreading, nothing changed. The teapot whistled on, throwing clouds of fragrant smoke out into the hall.

The pilgrim turned, smiling—half apologetically, it seemed—toward his hosts and comrades. He inclined his head in a brief bow, which appeared to be aimed at the smallest of his company, the one who hadn't yet spoken.

"Excellent!" cried Wotheng, clapping his hands. "Safe control of fire! And so colorful, so marvelous. Oh yes, you'll find much call for your skills here, Sir Wizard. Ah, say, where had you folk planned to spend the night? Our house is a humble thing, but we can easily fit your company under our roof."

"Well, we had hoped to go look at the shrine while the weather is good."

"Splendid, good fellow. I'll send guides to escort you—and do you need mounts for your friends? But do be back in time for dinner; you'll find the food good, if plain, and the portions generous."

The pilgrims accepted the help with mixed eagerness, but seemed quite willing to start at once and be back for dinner. A brief exchange of pleasantries—and another yell to Yawth to go fetch Tinnod from his sheep and collect some horses—and the little company departed for their pilgrimage.

As the noise and crowd faded, Wotheng and Gynallea exchanged broad and silent grins. Wotheng poured out the last of the beer for himself, and his wife took a cup of the tea from the fire.

"Lovey," she stated firmly while spooning honey into her fragrant cup, "We *must* persuade them to stay."

"I'll see to it. Do you think they can deal with Folweel?"

"They if anyone. Encourage them to buy that western pasture and settle here. Tell them tonight about the merchant caravans to the north, speak of the good prices they could get for their goods, the cheapness of food and cloth and other staples hereabouts—"

"Sell that land? Why not rent it to them? Why should I give it up?"

"Lovey, lovey, that land is all but worthless and those folk are valuable. They may shy away from being tenants, being at a master's beck and call, after being freeholders so long in their own city—oh, we must ask them more about the Lost City, when there's time. The land may not draw them strongly—you've seen it, and 'tisn't attractive—so we must lure them with a bargain no one but a fool would refuse. Sell it to them, and cheaply. Give it to them outright, if you must—but however 'tis done, keep them here."

"Aye, aye . . ." Wotheng considered. "Their goods alone, never mind their magic, could add much to the wealth hereabouts. Do I tell them I—heh! and I alone—can get their goods transported and sold north, at good price, and do they take up the bargain, we might gain more for such simples than we do for our wool. Hmm, perhaps I should make that part of the price for the land."

"Dangle what lures you can, lovey, but get them to stay."

An hour before noon the odd little company arrived at the site of the old mine. Tinnod, a wizened tenant shepherd, rode on a borrowed donkey beside Doshi on a shaggy pony, grumbling about weather and rents and bad luck with sheep. Doshi pretended to listen raptly while running his eyes over the surrounding land. Omis and Zeren, on scrawny horses kindly loaned from Wotheng's stables, rode next in line, murmuring quietly to themselves. Everyone else rode in the wagon, Sulun driving and Eloti beside him.

"What did you make of our host?" Eloti asked. "I suspect there is more to him, and his wife, than they showed us."

"To all accounts they're no fools," Sulun considered. "They were intrigued by our, er, magic, but not frightened of it. They do seem pleased with us, possibly for the promise of goods to trade, and I think it would not be difficult to get their permission to settle here."

"Indeed, they seemed pleased to have us . . . hmmm, and if this is the land you asked about, I think I know why."

The barely visible dirt road led between low hills to a steep one, with some few ruined buildings climbing its slope. A sullen stream meandered down from higher hills beyond, promising drinking water but little else. The soil was thin, poor, showing tan and bald between clumps of coarse grass and brush. As the slope rose the soil thinned further, showing outcroppings of lichened rock like bones emerging through the sunken hide of a corpse.

"Not a pretty place," Sulun agreed. "No good for farming, as our host said. Neither do I see much graze for sheep. To a man mainly concerned with those activities, such land would surely seem worthless. If the mines are still here, not blocked nor worked out, it would be worth the effort to persuade Lord Wotheng to sell."

"Remember to look reluctant when you ask him." Eloti smiled. "Or would you prefer that I undertake the negotiations?"

"Lady, no one of us could do it better. Hmm, but where, now, is that mine?"

Ahead, Doshi turned his pony toward the ruins. His eyes flicked back and forth between the stony hill and the unrolled map in his hand. Tinnod rode reluctantly after him, voicing disquiet about the unnerving ruins and the possibility of ghosts, even in broad daylight.

"I think that's it," said Sulun. "Let's see how close we can get the wagon."

The road actually improved as they approached the ruins, showing traces of ancient paving suitable to heavy loads. Its course led past roofless shells of old houses, up to the largest ruin at the high end of the former town. Here the stream had been diverted, through still intact stone-lined ditches and pipes, to pass under the remains of a millhouse attached to the chief building. The road ended there, but still there was no sign of a mine opening. The old building was as big as a good-sized barn, with a doorway more than wide enough to accommodate the mules and wagon. Despite Tinnod's warnings, the convoy passed inside.

The central part of the roof had come down, leaving a pile of rubble in the middle of the wide, cobblestoned floor. To either side, though, the stone walls of large workrooms had kept enough roofing to hold out the weather.

Sulun halted the wagon at the edge of the central rubble pile, set the brake, and tied it. Eloti got out and went to the wagon bed to fetch tethers and nosebags for the mules. Doshi, Omis, and Zeren dismounted and tied their animals' reins to assorted stones and fallen beams. Tinnod stayed on his donkey and shivered in the dusty sunlight.

The company gathered around Sulun, who cast a warning glance toward Tinnod, who didn't notice. "These ruins don't look very promising," he began, "but there may be much of value *buried* hereabout. Have we lamps? Torches? Good. Let's search, then. No less than two together."

"I be stayin' right here," Tinnod announced stoutly. "Gods know what all might lurk in old corners."

"Right you are." Sulun smiled. "Stay you here to guard the beasts, the wagon, the womenfolk, and the children, and we'll—"

"Women?" Tinnod perked up. "And children too?"

"Why, of course." Eloti pulled down the hood of her cloak, revealing her notably feminine face, set in a punctiliously proper look. "Did you think the priests of Deese and Kula were forbidden to marry?"

"Eh, no, I hadn't thought that, ma'am." Tinnod blushed, tugging his forelock. "Whatever ye need, ma'am, I be glad to help."

"Fine." Eloti smiled sweetly. "Come out, children, but mind how you play."

Vari, grinning, hustled the children out of the wagon, followed by the rest of the apprentices. Tamiri and her brother promptly toddled off in all directions, delighted at the chance to stretch their legs and explore.

"Don't let them wander too far, now," Vari rumbled at their guide.

Tinnod, looking slightly poleaxed, got off his donkey, hobbled it quickly, and hurried after the children.

"That should keep him occupied," Eloti murmured to Sulun. "Take your lamps and go seek."

Sulun, grinning, broke out the lamps and lit them. "Watch the flames," he warned quietly. "If they suddenly spurt, or change color, get back into open air."

The others nodded understanding, formed teams, and parceled out the lamps. Sulun found himself teamed with Omis and Arizun. Seeing the others make for the side rooms, he led the way around the rubble pile to the back wall.

Sure enough, behind a fall of timber and masonry, there stood another doorway. Beyond lay only a vast darkness and a musty smell.

Sulun thrust the lamp within, watched as it burned tranquilly, then hitched up his shoulders and led the way inside.

Two steps past the doorway, and they saw that they were in a tunnel. The walls were roughly hewn from the dark hill-stone, but the floor was sanded smooth, save for the faint ruts of cartwheels. In a few more steps they found the remains of a cart:

large, square-built, stout, but with one axle broken and the front wheels collapsed.

It was piled to the top with butter-yellow sulfur.

Omis and Arizun poked fingers into the heap of yellow gravel, their eyes met, and they smiled. "Enough here alone to keep us in firepowder for a year," Sulun marveled. "But let's go on."

At the end of the tunnel the walls fell away on deeper darkness, with the faintest draft of a breeze flowing from somewhere unseen.

"Must have cut ventilation shafts," Omis murmured, then stopped as he noted the faint echoing of his voice.

Sulun, keeping his eyes on the smoothed floor and his lamp held high, took the first steps into the echoing dark. He heard Omis and Arizun gasp behind him, stopped, and looked up.

He stood in a hall of columns, stretching as far as the light spread and doubtless far beyond. The roof was higher than his arms could reach, rough-cut as the walls and columns.

Roof, columns, and floor were sulfur-yellow, with occasional streaks of obsidian black.

Sulun carefully lowered his lamp, keeping the flame away from the butter-colored stone. "We've found it," he said, amazed that his voice was so calm. "I'll wager, if we follow the wheel tracks we'll find another cart, plenty of discarded miners' tools, and a wall of sulfur thicker than anyone can guess."

"And here," Omis whispered, "an unsuspected fortress, hidden in the earth."

"Earth Goddess temple," Arizun added. "We should make images of Kula and Deese to place by the entrance. . . ."

"We should go back to the others before we're missed," Sulun decided, "and before our talkative guide—who no doubt reports to Wotheng—guesses that we've found something of interest."

"In which case, he will doubtless raise his price." Arizun grinned and turned back to the tunnel. "Let's go, then—and plan our tale to Wotheng."

On the journey back to Ashkell villa, Omis and Arizun rode ahead with Doshi and their guide, while Sulun conferred with the others in the wagon.

"Even the outer building could be fortified," Zeren noted, "which is nothing to ignore in times, hmm, and places, like these."

"Those side rooms were shops," Yanados added. "One of them houses a mill that once turned by that stream. The stones are intact, though much of the wooden gear needs replacing—"

"Omis's ironwork would do better," Vari cut in. "We'll have to ask our host about sources of iron."

"—and we'd have to replace the paddle wheel, but once we have the mill running—"

"We could fix the house with stones from the others," Ziya piped up, surprising everyone. "Make the whole house out of stone, so it won't burn."

"Yes, good thought," Eloti answered quickly. "But where would we put the forge and the larger tools?"

"That big central room, once the roof's on—or even before," said Yanados. "We could use the other side rooms for kitchens and sleeping cubicles."

"Hmm, only with much work," Vari grumbled. "I think we'll need to add more rooms, sooner or later. And a kitchen garden. Hmm, and a surrounding wall."

"Should we bother trying to raise sheep on the surrounding land?" Zeren asked. "We'll need some animals for food, in case of . . . hmmm, siege, famine, other disasters."

"Goats, more likely," Vari sniffed. "They give less wool, but more milk. A few pigs, some poultry . . ."

"How would we feed them? How much of this grudging land must we plant and coax into yielding?"

"Just a little for the birds, I think. Goats can feed themselves well on almost anything, and a few pigs could made do with slops from the kitchen, and perhaps a bit of grain."

"Is it decided, then?" Eloti asked. "Are we determined to settle here?"

Sulun looked at everyone in turn. "Do any oppose the thought?" he asked.

No one did.

"So be it, then." Eloti smiled, a little grimly. "If we bargain well, we may get the land cheaply. Restoring the buildings, however, will be more of a task than we can manage ourselves— and it will cost dearly." She patted the thick oak chest she sat on. "I suspect that our Sukkti treasure will be largely used before we're done."

"Wherever we can manage for ourselves, Lady—" Sulun began.

"No, no regrets, my friend. If we succeed, I'll count it as well spent." Eloti's smile changed to something slightly more wicked. "Now, shall we discuss tactics for bargaining with Wotheng this evening?"

Dinner that evening was a whole roast suckling pig stuffed with apples, boiled green beans with bacon, thick wedges of sheep-milk cheese, roasted grain sweetened with berries, sweet pears pickled in honey, fresh rye bread with new butter, cider, perry, beer, and berry cordial. Everyone in the household, with the exception of the two outer guards, ate at the same huge trestle table. Sulun, remembering his days in Entori House, noted that the only division between the masters' and servants' sections were the bowls of salt, pepper, nutmeg, and vinegar formally arranged in the middle of the table. The servants, he noted, were well and warmly dressed—if in much plainer cloth than Wotheng and his wife—and all seemed healthy and well fed. They also talked freely, laughed loudly, and showed no particular fear of the personages at the high end of the table.

I've known worse masters, Sulun thought, stuffing himself with a clear conscience. The food was well cooked, if a trifle short on spices, and the assorted drinks were superb.

After the dishes were emptied and cleared, Wotheng dismissed the lower table diners with a brief hand clap. Sulun noticed that a few of the servants chose to stay, and that this was not remarked upon.

Wotheng called for more jugs of beer and cordial, and for his pipe: a tiny wooden bowl with an attached hollow stem, filled with some resinous chopped leaf which he lit with a spill of burning wood from the fire. The apprentices watched, wide-eyed, as Wotheng calmly inhaled the aromatic smoke and seemed to enjoy the taste. Sulun guessed that the leaf was some manner of medicinal incense, and the pipe arrangement was certainly more efficient than a Sabisan-style incense burner.

"So, my friends," Wotheng began comfortably, pipe in one hand and full cup in the other, "did you find your shrine today?"

"Ah, yes," Sulun agreed with a mournful sigh. "It's in most wretched condition: all the images gone, the building all a wreck, half buried in rubble. Simply restoring would take, oh, moons and moons."

"Ah, but it *could* be repaired?"

"Oh yes, and the priest house as well, but . . ." Sulun rolled his eyes. "Good gods, the work! The expense! We wondered most seriously if 'twould be worth the trouble, or if we should just continue north to the next shrine."

"Ah, how sad." Gynallea cast a quick look round the cluster of guests. All of them looked mournful. Yes, they might truly consider moving on. "But how can you be certain that the next shrine will be any better? The gods know, all the lands north of here suffered far worse in the wars."

"True, true." Sulun shrugged expansively. "But what can we do?"

"Ah, well." Wotheng waved expansively. "The rent there would be very cheap—oof!" He threw a quick glare at his wife, and rubbed his ankle.

"Rent?" Sulun rolled his eyes piously. "Ah, 'tis hopeless, then. By our most ancient tradition, the land dedicated to the god must belong to the god—of whom we priests are but servants. We were hoping to purchase the land outright, but seeing how much work must be done there, well, the expense . . ."

"Now, now, it need not be so costly as all that." Gynallea seized Sulun's nearer hand and patted it warmly. "Much of our custom hereabouts is done by barter. I'm sure that we could arrange a fair trade for the *purchase* price—" she glared at her husband "—of the land. Your smithy work, for example. Perhaps you might purchase title to the land in exchange for, say, forging goodly blades for our household guard, or some such work, in perpetuity. 'Twould be easy enough, for folk of your skill."

Sulun was about to say yes, enthusiastically, when his memory snagged on the words "in perpetuity." While he was thinking that over, Omis spoke up.

"Ah, good Lady, how could we serve your own blacksmith so? Biddon is a fine workman, and an honest fellow. How, then, should we take his custom away from him? 'Twould be a poor service to a fellow smith."

Wotheng and Gynallea blinked over that, momentarily set back.

Eloti seized the moment to speak up. "Good hosts, 'tis true we have more of smithcraft than poor Biddon does. But how, then, if we were to repay your kindness by teaching the fellow our skills? Then you would have a smith upon your villa who could work iron as well as we, and you'd not have to journey ten leagues every time a horse threw a shoe."

"Oh, aye," Wotheng muttered. "Well for Biddon and his household, and we'd make some little gain thereby, but to purchase a whole stretch of land . . . And how much, said you, that you wished?"

There was momentary confusion while Doshi produced the pertinent map and unrolled it on the table. Wotheng raised his bushy eyebrows and peered closer.

"I've never seen a chart so fair," he commented. "What, be there towns, cities, all that hereabouts, and I never heard thereof?"

"This is a copy of a much older map," Doshi explained, surreptitiously scattering a pinch of salt over certain items on the chart. "This is how the land lay before the great invasions. Many towns and villas you see marked herein be long gone, cast to the winds of fate and war. I suppose there are many new towns now, built in the years since, that this map's makers never knew."

"A well-made copy of that chart could help make up the price of the land," Gynallea purred.

"We are always willing to share learning," Eloti smiled sweetly, "for that too is part of our trade."

"Hmm . . ." Wotheng traded significant glances with his wife. Both of them could read, write, and work figures; hardly anyone else within twenty leagues could do so, which had proved a constant inconvenience. Here, now, an idea caught fire and blazed.

"Well, now, there's a bit more of a fair price," said Gynallea. "Would you make a school, also, and teach whomever we sent you, that would be worth as much as, hmm, the price of a small field."

"Here it is," Doshi cut in, pointing to the map. "This hill, and the ruins upon it, and the field below where the two lesser hills come nigh the stream. That's all the land we need or ask."

Wotheng grinned behind his pipe. That was a piddling acreage, in such poor land as that. "Ey, yes, I'd agree that a school and a goodly map would almost be worth the purchase price, even for so much land as that." He smiled at his wife's anxious look. "Cast in also a simple agreement, and I think we may call the bargain fair."

"Agreement?" Sulun worried. "Concerning what matter, m'lord?"

"Why, just that if you folk should choose to sell your wares beyond Ashkell and its holdings, you shall bring the same to me to sell for you." Wotheng winked at Gynallea, grinning. "I know the roads, aye, and the towns north, and the times when the merchants' caravans come by, and the usual prices as well. Let me arrange the selling for you, friends, and you'll profit more handsomely than ever you could by yourselves."

He held his breath, marshalling further arguments: the danger of bandits, the usefulness of his men-at-arms, his knowledge of the other lordlings to the north.

"Yes!" said Sulun, eager to close the bargain and be done. This Wotheng would make a better patron than any he'd had before. "Certainly, m'lord."

Wotheng beamed.

"Ah, but at what commission?" Eloti purred. "We should agree, before putting seal to any parchment, what part per hundred of the sales shall be yours, and what part ours."

Wotheng narrowed his eyes, but still smiled. Aha, these smith's women were quite as clever at bargaining as his Gynallea. Priests or no, these folk were good merchants, and could make his holdings prosperous. "Well, seeing that we shall share the labor—you of making, myself of peddling—should we not share the profits equally? Say, half and half?"

The others looked at each other. Eloti only smiled and leaned closer, and settled in for a good half-hour's dickering—sure of her element as a bird in the air.

Wotheng closed the bedchamber door while his wife put down the candle. Then they fell upon the creaking bed, grabbed each other, and rolled back and forth, giggling like mischievous children. The hysteria stopped only when Wotheng jabbed himself on Gynallea's brooch, and pulled away swearing.

"Gold in hand, lovey," Gynallea chuckled, sitting up to unfasten her clothes. "One way and another, gold in hand!"

"Umm, yes," Wotheng grinned, sucking his poked palm. "Gods, but they've good wit—and they're rich. Rich! Sweet moo-cow, we're going to be rich!"

"Hah, don't milk the cow before she's bred," Gynallea snickered, pinching his near buttock.

"Let me get out of these clothes and we'll celebrate," Wotheng snorted, tugging at pesky ties and buckles.

"Hee-hee! And you thought the bargaining was done when they signed the parchment and you gave them the deed to the land. Ho, ho!"

"Ah, my cow, you know I always sit about after a good trade, free with the jug, just in case other dealings might be offered. . . . Vona's balls! Woman, can you get this knot undone?"

"Here, turn toward the light. Yes, but whose thought was it to ask them what repairs they'd need to make, what supplies and workmen needed, eh? Eh?"

"So, you got in the first word. I'd have said it soon enough. Ho, they'll have the old mill going, will they? But only for grinding ore? Hah! Do we suffer a siege, or the new mill take storm damage again, we'll have another mill to use at need."

"And where else would they purchase timber, and raw iron? Where else to get the workmen, tiles, mortar, seed, and breeding stock they want? To and fro, the trade shall go—with us and our children to profit, both ways. Yes, lovey, this has been a golden evening."

"Golden, yes." Wotheng rubbed his hands together, smiling from ear to ear. "Show it to me again, dear love."

Gynallea opened her hand with a flourish, letting the candlelight fall on the gleaming gold coin centered in her palm. "A full ounce, I'll wager." She smiled. "Did you ever see the like?"

"Never, sweet cow. Who would have thought a band of pilgrims had such coin about them? And surely that can't be the only one."

"Surely there's more to come; years' worth, with the bargain we sealed. And all this, for our pledge of goods and workmen for barely half a year! Happy enough they were to get it, too. I'll vow, the poor things have no idea of prices hereabouts."

"Hmph, they'll learn soon enough when it comes to selling their goods. Still, once I begin selling in the north—and perhaps in the southlands, soon enough—they'll be content with the bargain. Come, blow the candle out, sweet cow. Let's to pounding the mattress."

Gynallea set the coin down carefully beside the candle, and blew out the flame.

In the creaking darkness, before plunging seriously into the task at hand, Wotheng thought to ask, "Oh, did you say aught to them about Folweel?"

"Mmm, in a manner of speaking, while you were poking up the fire."

"What manner of speaking, cow?"

"Why, lovey, I simply mentioned that other small priests and hedge witches might grow jealous of their prosperity and favor, and if any such did so, they should come complain to me. That was plain enough."

"Oh, aye . . . I suppose that suffices as warning. Move your thigh over."

Gynallea giggled. The bed creaked.

✧ CHAPTER TWO ✧

The burly, grey-haired man sat in the sunlight at the window seat of his study-room, drinking a cup of bark tea laced with spirits of wine and examining a waxed tablet scribbled with figures. The figures were not reassuring. The sunlight picked out a frayed thread in the gold embroidery on his red outer robe. A rough spot in the silver inlay of his brass cup snagged at his lip. Fair weather or not, this promised to be a thoroughly wretched day.

A discreet knocking sounded from the carved panels of the study's door. The man frowned, got up and went to his parchment-littered heavy oak table, adjusted his orange under-robe to show the embroidery to good advantage, and snapped, "Come in!"

A subdued maid in a plain grey dress opened the door, ushered in the visitor, and silently closed the door behind him. The newcomer, somewhat younger, shorter, and less burly than his host, wore a yellow under-robe and an orange outer one, both bearing somewhat less embroidery than the older man sported. His smile was wide, cheerful, and practiced.

"Greetings, Brother Folweel," he chirped, eyes flicking to the waxed tablet lying close at his superior's elbow. "I assume you've read yesterday's tally?"

"Greetings, Brother Jimantam. Pray sit." Folweel pointed to another carved oak chair. "Yes, I've read it," he said in Murrekeen, in case the maid was eavesdropping. "Most unpromising."

Jimantam settled carefully into the indicated chair, his smile sliding away. "Attendance often falls off at this time of year," he offered, in the same tongue. "So much for the faithful to do: first harvest, second planting, shearing . . ."

"Attendance at services was quite good last summer." Folweel interlaced his fingers and tapped his thumbs together. "The temple was packed last year for the Midsummer ceremony. Yesterday there was overmuch room at the same service. Could it be that our herd is being distracted by . . . worldly concerns?"

"It does happen." Jimantam shrugged. He peered at the parchments on the table, hoping to see one in particular. "Still, the temple income is undiminished. The tally at equinox was most, er, generous."

"The tally at equinox was three moons ago!" Folweel slammed his palm on the stack of parchments. "Its figures displayed the expected increase from the temple's own livestock—at lambing time. The only sizable income we've seen since came from northern sales of wool after shearing. Of course the temple flocks and crops are doing well; we've land and servants enough for that. The problem, dear Brother, is that funds from outside the temple have fallen away. That is the precise problem I wish to discuss with you. Just why is there poorer attendance and fewer donations, pray tell?"

Jimantam shrugged again. "Some time has passed since the last miracle. People forget, they grow distracted. . . ."

"We promised—and delivered—the usual miracle of the flame at the solstice ceremony. It didn't draw enough. The crowd was middle-sized at best, and the donations were small. Why, sir?"

"Well, this is coin-poor land; most trade is done by barter. If the folk simply don't have much coin on hand—"

"Coin? After first harvest and shearing? Oh, come."

"The trade caravans to the north—"

"Went out on time, came back in good time, and should have harvested the usual sufficiency of silver. Besides, even donations in goods have fallen off. Explain me that."

Jimantam spread his hands placatingly. "Worldly distractions," he murmured. "There was the usual plague of fleas, for example."

"I heard something of that," Folweel sneered. "The flea infestation was unusually mild this year—and not because of overmuch purchase of our ointment. Why, think you, was that?"

Jimantam rolled his eyes. "Perhaps some hedge wizard or granny witch has also discovered the secret of making soap, or the virtues of fleabane and garlic. Such knowledge is easy to come by, and another wizard might sell it more cheaply."

"Aha." Folweel leaned closer, eyes narrowing. "If so, then what other wizard would that be?"

Jimantam shook his head, accepting the inevitable. "This new batch of wizards off to the west," he conceded. "They have the appeal of novelty, though that should wear off soon enough."

"Yes, these new wizards." Folweel leaned back in his chair. "The Deese priests, worshippers of a blacksmith's god. They have not confined themselves to making horseshoes and praying over anvils, have they?"

"Who can tell, Brother? I know they've been selling pretty amulets of iron and brass and black glass bits, but that seems harmless enough."

"Harmless? When some of said amulets are sold specifically for protection against fire?"

Jimantam pursed his lips, said nothing.

"I have heard disturbing reports." Folweel picked up a sheet of parchment and frowned at it. "There are many of these priests; they have wealth enough that they've hired much of the local labor to build—or rebuild, as they claim—a good-sized shrine and priest house out in the old ruins. They have skills with metal work that entice a goodly amount of the local trade, and have produced enough goods beyond that to send north for sale. They have much favor with our old friend Wotheng. They have, if you please, set up a school in Ashkell villa where they teach reading, writing, figuring, healing craft, and—think on this—mechanical skills. They teach this to any who will sit and listen, and with Wotheng's help and approval. Do you not see a difficulty there, Brother?"

Jimantam sighed. "We have a rival for the people's affections. Some effort will be required to sway them back again. Another prediction of fire, perhaps?"

"Too soon," Folweel snapped. "And you've utterly missed the danger of that—-that school!"

"What danger?" Jimantam was genuinely puzzled. "Our own temple college teaches skills of far greater virtue: magecraft, priestcraft, estate management, merchantry—"

"For our own!" Folweel resisted the urge to tug at his impressive beard. "We teach our own initiates, and grant a bit of harmless hedge magic to our servants. These—these interlopers teach any who care to listen! Can you not see the difference, and the danger?"

"Er, we take those of more quality, better inclined to learning. . . ."

Folweel sighed, remembering that he must be patient with this Brother; the man was very, very good at wringing excellent profit from the temple lands and donations. If he knew nothing of true magic, or wider applications of policy, that only kept him from overmuch ambition. One should explain as much as Jimantam needed to know.

"Dear Brother," Folweel said, very calmly, "these folk offer to teach anyone: nobles, scribes, craftsfolk, farmers, or even servants. They teach skills readily useful to anyone, as even the dullest peasant may see. If all the folk have such skills, why need they come to us for service in such things?"

Now Jimantam began to see it. He frowned, counting off on his fingers. "Reading, writing, figuring . . . But they never did come to us for that. The folk always go to scribes for such. We have no competition there."

"Not there, no: but magecraft, and healing simples, and mechanics?"

"Magecraft . . ." Jimantam scratched his chin. "We've had no trouble from the local granny witches, priests of other gods, that sort. Would these be any greater rivals?"

"They very well might be. We have no idea what their magical abilities are." That wasn't the main point, but no profit in telling Jimantam so; it might give him ideas. "Their healing simples and such spells, for example: what if they teach everyone to make and use soap, fleabane, and so on? Who will buy from us, if every shepherd's wife can make plenty?"

"I begin to see the problem, Brother." Jimantam's lips tightened. "This school must be . . . examined."

"And the cult itself," Folweel added. "We must discover what they know."

"It should be easy enough to place . . . students in the school. As to the cult, I don't know."

"That task I think I shall assign to Patrobe. Send him to see me as soon as convenient."

"Gladly, Brother Folweel." Jimantam stood, guessing that he was dismissed and eager to be about his new task, delighted to learn that the shortage of the temple's income was not to be laid at his door. "May the blessings of Yotha be upon you, forever and evermore."

"Yotha bless." Folweel waved him off, not even bothering to watch the man leave.

His eyes strayed to the image of Yotha standing against the inner wall between two bookcases. "Fire God," Folweel grumbled, in his native Halasan. If anyone overheard, they'd think he was praying or practicing magic. So be it; of recent years he'd come to think aloud at the image, for lack of more trustworthy ears. "You're very good as a sword, but this problem calls for a stiletto. Rival wizards, several of them, and well-educated by all accounts: was it pure accident they came here too? Or did they recognize a good milking herd when they saw it?"

The image made no answer, only stared broodingly at the lamp that burned perpetually in its hands.

Folweel got up and went to the bookcase, searching among the scrolls penned years ago, back in Anhalas, which no one else in this barbarous country could read. "Mechanics," he muttered, "Medicine, Natural Philosophy. Dangerous, my most useful companion. Not merely of themselves, though that's bad enough. Teach such things, and to the very peasants we need? Monstrous! Suicidal! Are these folk utter fools, or are they keeping the greater knowledge for themselves? The latter, most like. Still, don't they realize the danger? Let common folk learn too much of the workings of the world, and they grow confident. When peasants have faith in themselves, they lose faith in gods and wizards. Where are we then, eh?"

Yotha silently contemplated his cupped flame, giving no reply.

Folweel finally located the scroll he wanted, a large medical text. "So, so . . . Much one can learn as a doctor's apprentice in Anhalas: much of chemistry, at least, and the mechanics thereof. Mysteries of the still-room, indeed. What power hides in strong wine, triply distilled, eh? A fluid that burns, and without even a wick."

He flicked a finger playfully through the flame in Yotha's cup, making the shadows dance across the image's face, as if the fire god smiled.

"We've done very well with that one simple trick." Folweel turned the scroll, looking for one section in particular. "Magic alone has power—well-wish or ill-wish, talent and training provide it. Natural philosophy grants knowledge that leads to power . . ." He tapped his finger on the scroll. ". . . such as our useful, most mysterious fire-fluid. But put the two together, my lad—as my old master used to say—and the results are magnified. Heh! I doubt he ever imagined I'd use that knowledge for more than medicine. But then, I doubt he ever thought that Halas could fall. Hard times, these. One must harden one's spirit to match them, use what tricks one can, take on whatever allies may be useful . . . Ah, here we are."

The section revealed in the open scroll dealt with herbs and extracts that affected the mind. Strong drink was listed first, but Folweel passed over it quickly. Opium was next, but he skipped that also; its source plant did not grow in these climes, nor was it available through local trade. The third was belladonna, the description of its properties and uses followed by a list of its herbal sources. Many such plants grew in the north. Folweel ran his finger down the list, and smiled as he read.

The bell in the pigeon tower of Wotheng's house rang twice, then rattled to indignant silence. In the second courtyard, which held the house herb garden, a dozen children and adults of all sizes looked up, startled. Waxed boards skittered off laps as children started to scramble to their feet. Eloti tapped sternly on her slate tablet, and the students hastily picked up their gear.

"Depart in an orderly fashion," she commanded, "and don't forget the song."

The class dutifully lined up and traipsed out of the courtyard, singing in a dozen different keys: "Ayo is for apple, Bith is for barn . . ."

Eloti let her face slip into a smile, watching them go.

The crunch of approaching footsteps on the antique gravel path made her turn. Gynallea, dressed in her usual apron and headcloth, approached with a load of scrolls under one arm and settled beside Eloti on the stone bench.

"I've found some more texts," she said, displaying the collection of scrolls. "One mathematics, two histories, one compendium of medicinal plants, two poetries, and a geography—quite outdated, of course, but still useful. How long, think you, before this lot can read them?"

"This lot? Half a year, at least." Eloti picked up the geography first. "The second class, though, might start on some of these in another moon."

"How have you arranged it? Beginners in the first half of the morning, literates in the second half?"

"Just so. By year's end, I might have my whole day filled with different grades of scholars."

"And by next year, then, will you have scholars advanced enough to enter the House of Deese as apprentices?"

Eloti smiled, seeing where this led. "That would depend upon how prosperous the House of Deese becomes. We can feed, house, and clothe only so many, at present."

"Don't worry about that, dear." Gynallea grinned, patting her knee. "Those little toys you sent north fetched a goodly price. By next year, you'll have fine trade. Surely you can take in another by then."

"Aha." Eloti set the scrolls aside. "Biddon has been plaguing you, too, hasn't he?"

"My dear, what could you expect? He wants to learn more skills, all but worships the ground where you tread, has sworn he's willing to become a lowly apprentice again if you'll but take him in."

"He'll have to master reading, writing, and figuring first. Of course, he does his best at that—he's in the second class already." Eloti shrugged. Biddon had no head for figures and letters, but his pure determination had carried him acceptably far already. "By next year . . . well, perhaps. Certainly by the year after, if all continues as it has done."

"Ah, very good." Gynallea sat back, scratching her belly. "Now, how goes the building at the shrine?"

"Most remarkably," Eloti admitted. "The roof is on, the mill repaired, and the wall goes well. We need do some of the work ourselves on the plumbing, but that can wait until the forge is finished. Oh yes, Omis said to tell Lord Wotheng that we'll need another two hundredweight of firebrick and three hundredweight of clay. The, hmm, 'ladle' will need to be more stout than he'd first thought."

Gynallea shook her head in wonder. "So much brick, clay, charcoal . . . iron and brass I can understand, but the rest is a mystery to me."

"I think I can reveal that mystery to the uninitiated." Eloti laughed. "Only baked clay and firebrick, so far as I know, can withstand the heat of melting iron. The charcoal—oh, I just thought! Lady, don't let the woodcutters and charcoal burners chop down the whole forest, or there'll soon be none left. Make them plant a hundred seed for every tree they cut."

"Oh posh, daughter, we've been doing that for donkey's years. Did you never wonder why the wood on that north hill looks as neat as an orchard?"

"Ah, orchards of oaks?"

"Certainly. Even standing, they're of use; the acorns make coarse flour, or excellent pig feed. Didn't you know?"

"Ah, Lady, I'm always delighted to learn something new."

"There, dear, you may call me Gynna—at least when there are no men about."

Eloti laughed in genuine delight.

They might have spoken more, but Yawth came trotting into the garden to announce the arrival of the second class. Gynallea sighed and got up. "Back to work for both of us, daughter," she sighed. "When this class is over, come find me in the still-room. There are some arcana of equipage design I wish to ask you about."

"Hmm, that would be Sulun's field of knowledge more than mine, but I'll be glad to come. At noon, then?"

Gynallea nodded and walked away. Eloti turned to watch the incoming class, and noted that it was larger than it had been yesterday. She counted noses, discovering one extra; it belonged to a bland-faced young man dressed as a scribe, whom she hadn't seen before. Perhaps he'd kept away until now, believing his skills were adequate, for he appeared quite well fed and well clothed. He had, she noted, brought his own waxed tablets and stylus with him.

"Your name, sir?" she asked.

"Duppa, a scribe," he answered readily, smiling as if he did it often. "I live to the north, near Yedda Stream, by Topa's lane—"

"Very good, sir," Eloti interrupted him, noting the curious looks from the rest of her class. "Take your place, and we shall proceed with exercises in mathematics."

The man dutifully sat and readied his tablets. Eloti turned away to hunt among her original basket of scrolls for the day's text, and also to hide her confusion. Magical training had made her sensitive to the presence and "feel" of other living bodies and minds; she was used to feeling the life-warmth and eager concentration of her students, and normally gave it no thought. This man was different. He seemed strangely blank, not there, a disturbing hole in the air where his body was visible, as if he were no more than a moving puppet. If he hadn't cast a shadow, she might have thought he was a very well constructed thought-sending.

Shielded, she guessed. The man was magically shielded, and so intensely that not even the "heat" of his life-force escaped. Was this pure accident, an unintended construction of the man's own mind? Or had it been done deliberately, placed on him by a competent and talented wizard? If deliberate, why? Why should a common scribe need such shields? Unless, of course, he was no common scribe? *Some local hedge wizard, studying his competition?* she wondered. *Best ask Gynallea about him.*

That decided, she took up the scroll and proceeded with the lesson.

The new forge was beautiful, clean, and cold: a virgin, waiting to be initiated into the delights of her natural fire. Omis walked around her once again, eyes measuring her splendid dimensions and features, itching to fill and light her properly. There, that enormous bellows made of two whole oxhides, waiting to be geared into the driveshaft from the mill. With such a pump, in such a furnace, he could refine purest iron out of raw, red earth in a day's work or less. There, the great pulleys and chain hoist braced into the new ceiling. Once the huge ladle was finished, he could melt and pour iron by the hundredweight as easily as if it were wax in a cup. There, Sulun's precious lathe and the new grinding wheels, likewise waiting to be hitched to the mill's driving shaft. Gods, what he could make with those. He'd made little but toys since they'd settled here—farming tools, buckles, sockets for wooden wheels, even pins and needles—good quality, but such puny common things, small items readily made in the sturdy little portable forge from Sabis, on his old and admittedly worn anvil. But with tools like these, once they were ready . . .

Omis shook his head and turned away. *Patience, patience,* he reminded himself. *All goes well, better than we could have dreamed just a year ago.*

Indeed, a year ago he could never have imagined working in such a manufactory as this. Possibly there was nothing near like it in all the world. What irony to see it here, in this forgotten country estate, when Sabis and all her glory lay in ruins. . . .

Omis turned away from the forge, went to a freshly oiled cabinet under the new workbench, opened it, and tugged out the cloth-wrapped shape within. He lifted the object to the bench, laid it down, and pulled up a stool.

The bombard's outside was still pebble-rough and unfinished, but the interior gleamed like a mirror. She was seamless, flawless, as perfect as human skill could make her, needing only a few finishing touches. Omis didn't ask himself why he felt obliged to work on her whenever he thought of Sabis; her original purpose was long lost, fallen with the city.

Still, the Bombard Project led him on, led all of them still, had led them like a god's sign to settle here in the vestibule of a sulfur mine. Why sulfur, save for firepowder? Why firepowder, save for the bombard? Why the bombard? No answer—yet the pursuit of that idea had brought them here, to safety, protection, promised wealth, even the respect of the local people and the friendship of the local lord. Even a workshop such as this.

Omis cast a glance at the nearer of the two figures carved beside the door. "Deese, thou knowest," he said.

Then he took up a narrow circular brush and a pot of pumice paste, and began polishing the recently drilled fuse hole at the base of the bombard. After this would come the building of its carriage.

He barely heard the footsteps approaching behind him, managed to ignore them until Zeren spoke, almost in his ear.

"Where's Sulun? We have a problem."

Yanados perched on a finished section of the wall, supposedly watching the small flock of goats that foraged contentedly downslope. Under the hood of her cloak, no one could tell at this distance that she was actually watching the work crew busy on the unfinished part of the wall. Biddon sat beside her, clenching his corded hands with the effort not to point. Sulun, Zeren, and Doshi came padding up behind her, climbed the broad stile to the walkway, and peered toward the work gang. Zeren clapped a hand on the blacksmith's shoulder.

"Which one is he?" he asked.

"That'n, sir." Biddon pointed, just briefly. "Yonder thickset fellow in the brown leggin's and yellow shirt. The one up on the stones, layin' mortar. I've seen him before, a'right, comin' to my shop for stone chisels, braggin' to wear me ear off. He's head stonemason of Yotha's temple, and what business, sirs, would he have here?"

"You all know more than I do," Sulun puzzled. "Who is Yotha, and why shouldn't his temple's chief stonemason come to work here?"

"Yotha, according to our friend Biddon, is an ill-tempered fire god," said Yanados, still watching. "His priests came and settled here some eight years back, built a temple some six leagues north, and have been doing well for themselves ever since. As to your second question, the chief stonemason of Yotha's temple is ordinarily paid quite well enough that he'd have no need to come work common labor on our walls. Do you see nothing suspicious there?"

"I see a mystery, and I wish you all would explain it."

"We seem to have some rivals," Zeren sighed. "Yotha's temple was the biggest and wealthiest in Ashkell Vale, before we came."

"What, simple jealousy?" Sulun asked. "How would that explain their mason working here?"

"More nor *simple* jealousy!" Biddon laughed. "See you all these folk workin' on your priest house, these many moons? Ye've *paid* 'em for their hire, day by day, not bought their service outright by the year. You folk pay well, too—in good copper and useful spells, not to mention yonder school at Ashkell House. And ye're none so haughty as Yotha's folk, nor has your Deese done harm to any. Need I tell you, then, how many folk would rather come to you than to Yotha's house?"

"We've drawn away many of Yotha's worshippers, you mean? And his priests don't like it?"

"Neither like it nor accept it philosophically, I imagine," said Doshi. "So their chief mason has shown up here: for spying, spreading disaffection, spoiling the work, or what?"

"Spying, certainly," Yanados guessed. "We may as well assume the rest, too. Now, what shall we do about it?"

"First off, I would have Arizun inspect that section of the wall," Zeren put in. "See if it's made as well as the rest, or if some charm has been set into the mortar."

"Good thought," said Doshi, turning to go back down the stile steps. "I'll fetch him."

"Now wait," Sulun complained, feeling a bit left out. "What harm can a man do, setting mortar on a wall? What harm can his spying do, for that matter? Why not leave him where he is, lest these—these priests of Yotha send another spy who we don't know?"

Zeren laughed. "Sulun, my wonderfully innocent old friend, think; we've seen whole houses ill-wished, and from a distance. Why not a wall? Or the whole house, starting from the wall? That's the harm our insidious mason there can do."

Sulun thought about that, about the curse placed on Entori House, about the possible effects of such a curse in a house full of hot iron, firepowder, heavy tools—and a cellar full of sulfur. He shuddered.

"Very well, get rid of him. What will happen when his friends learn of his failure, I don't know."

"They'll know we're no fools," said Yanados. "That alone might make them behave better."

"High hopes," Zeren muttered. "More like, they'll just take another tactic. We must be watchful."

"Which is the man?" Arizun asked, climbing up behind them. "Where has he been working?"

Biddon gleefully pointed out the suspect, and the stretch of wall, adding: "There's more I could watch out for you, Masters, did I but live here. Would I not make a good initiate of Deese?"

"Soon, soon," Yanados promised, patting his shoulder. "Once Eloti says you're ready . . . Hey, the lunch bell!"

Sure enough, the iron bell so recently hung in its niche over the front was ringing the announcement for the midday meal. All the workmen on the wall cheered happily, put down their tools, settled the last stones they'd been working on, and sat down to eat. The brown-legged spy made haste to join them.

"Doshi's idea," said Arizun. "That'll give me time enough to go look at the wall." He strode off quietly, dark robe blending with the stone of the walls.

Sulun looked around at his companions and wrung his hands in dismay. "Aren't we worrying overmuch?" he asked. "Now that we've come to a good place, I had hoped we'll stop expecting enemies everywhere."

"Were we so free of foes back in Sabis?" Yanados asked, trying not to sound bitter.

Sulun just shook his head and walked away. *Is there no peace,* he wondered, *to be found anywhere?*

Arizun strolled along the new section of wall, running one hand along the stones, keeping an eye turned toward the gang of workmen busy with their meal downslope. Did the brown-legged mason glance this way a little too often? Was he seated so to keep an eye on the wall? One couldn't walk too slowly, then, or seem too interested.

Arizun felt it first as a subtle heat, something like warmth clinging to the shadowed stone, right in the mortared seam between two blocks. He paused to shake an imaginary stone out of his shoe, casually leaning on the wall for support, one hand pressed to the mortar. Yes, the spell was there, probably anchored in a mage sign scribbled into the mortar under the block. He could almost picture the sign, the feeling was so clear. Yes, picture it: no more or less than a script initial in some foreign alphabet, an elaborate letter Y—no doubt for Yotha, very simple and direct. Well, well. Probe further, but quickly; the man might notice. Arizun closed his eyes and dropped for a moment, deeper into the Meditative State that Eloti had taught him to attain and feel with such facility.

Oh, yes: a simple and direct curse, set in the wall, meant to spread through the entire house, partly vitalized already. No doubt it would increase this very night, once the brown-legged spy got home to his friends. Ah, clever.

Arizun ground his teeth in cold, rising fury. He pulled his shoe back on, straightened up, and strolled on down the wall for a few paces more, down to where the completed wall rose over his head and concealed him from the work gang beyond. There he stopped, leaned against the dark stones, reached into his second belt pouch, and drew out a faceted crystal lens. The essentials, as lady Eloti had told him often enough, were quite simple: concentration, visualization, will, focus, purpose. He had will enough; easy for this rage to power it. The crystal would help concentration and focus. Visualization came easily too. Purpose . . . Arizun smiled wickedly. A simple deflection, change of target, would be so utterly fitting—and was much easier than neutralizing the curse altogether. Yes, just a proper deflection to a new target: he had sufficient talent and power to do that by himself. Eloti would be so pleased when he would tell her.

Arizun stared into the crystal, concentrating.

A second ringing of the iron bell signalled the workmen back to their task. They tossed away crumbs, recorked jugs, climbed to their feet, and went back to the waiting stones, derrick, and wall. The senior of the work gang poked at the trough of mortar, shrugged, added a little water, and stirred it in. The rest of the crew shoved another stone down its track of roller logs to the wooden crane and began tying it on. A mason in brown leggings and a yellow shirt trotted around to the back of the wall, up a makeshift wooden stepladder to the top of the present course of stones, and prepared to guide the new block into place.

On the way up, his foot slipped and nearly sent him tumbling off the ladder. He swore, climbing the rest of the way with more care, too busy thinking of his task ahead to question the minor accident.

"Up!" bellowed the senior workman, and the rest of the crew hauled on the crane's tail ropes. The tail sank, the wooden fulcrum groaned as weight came on the ropes, and the tied block began to rise. "Up, up," chanted the gang's senior.

"Now right, right," shouted the man on the wall, as the block rose level with his breastbone. He reached for the trailing guide rope, missed it, leaned further out—slipped and fell flat in the spread mortar.

The work gang below laughed heartily, but didn't let the ropes slacken.

The brown-legged, mortar-daubed man grabbed for the guide rope, and this time caught it. Instead of pulling slowly, he yanked on it in exasperation.

The guide rope snapped taut, catching on one of the support ropes at the near corner of the block. The support rope, dragging along with the guide, pulled free.

The block shuddered for a second, then slid loose of the remaining guides and fell forward.

It tumbled straight into the brown-legged man, carrying him off the wall, and fell on top of him.

The work gang on the derrick fell flat as their ropes suddenly slackened. They all heard the short screech from behind the wall, and the grisly thud. Some cursed, some groaned, some wailed with horror. The bravest got up and ran for the wall at once; the more timorous followed slowly. Up the wooden scaffolding they ran, across the lower course of stones, through the spread mortar to the inner side of the wall—and paused there a long moment, surveying the damage.

It was impressive.

Arizun took good care to arrive after the others, to sound and look surprised. Doshi and Zeren gave him thoughtful looks as he elbowed through the crowd, but they said nothing. Biddon the blacksmith saw him coming and stepped hastily out of his path, throwing him a white-eyed look, like a frightened horse. Yanados gave him a sardonic smile and a hint of an ironic salute. Arizun ignored her, pushed to the front of the crowd, and looked.

The man was still alive, breathing in thin wheezes, fingers scrabbling aimlessly at the edge of the stone. From the waist down, his body was hidden under the tumbled block. The stone appeared to lie level on the ground, perhaps even a bit sunken into it. Blood seeped from under its edges.

"Like a berry under a brick," mumbled one of the workmen watching. A small gang of the more muscular in the crowd was trying to dig under the edges of the block and tie on ropes from the crane. None of them looked at the man under the stone, nor, for all their haste, did they seem very willing to lift the block and reveal what lay beneath it.

"Can't last the hour," one of the nearby watchers mumbled.

"Soon, soon . . ." chanted another, his tone reminiscent of prayer.

The ropes were worked under the corners, looped, tied on, drawn taut. "It's tied!" snapped the head of the work gang, keeping his eyes on the knots. "Haul it!"

On the other side of the wall, the rest of the work gang heaved at the crane's tail ropes. The derrick creaked, and the stone began to rise. Sunlight spread beneath the rising stone. The crowd groaned softly, all together.

The man under the block continued whining thinly, noticing nothing.

The gang on the crane lifted the stone until it reached its niche on the wall, then lowered it. The block slipped neatly into place, perfectly aligned, though no one drew the rope to guide it there. A film of blood on its underside stained the top of the mortar.

Arizun turned away quickly. He'd taken two steps toward the house when a hand caught his shoulder. He glanced up, and saw Sulun glaring down at him.

"No, stay and watch," Sulun whispered fiercely, in Sabirn. "That was your doing; you look at it."

"It couldn't be helped!" Arizun hissed back in the same tongue. "All I could do was deflect the curse, discharge it back on him who set it. Otherwise it would have sprung on us."

"No other choice? Nothing else you could have done?"

"No! I couldn't just wipe it away; I don't have that power, and I didn't dare wait for Eloti to come back and help me. All I could do was deflect it, send it back. Gods, I didn't know it would do *that*. . . ."

Sulun dropped his hand and turned away. "Bad beginning," he muttered.

Then he saw the workmen watching him, trying not to look at the body on the ground being bundled into a stretcher improvised of cloaks. He could read their faces clearly enough, see why no one had dropped the ropes off the settled block, guess why no one now was working the crane. Time to say something. Sulun gritted his teeth, pulled his robe around him, and marched up the scaffolding to the top of the unfinished stretch of wall.

"Carelessness," he intoned, "exacts a heavy price. Carelessness can slaughter more than armies. Carelessness is our enemy here— and we dare not drop our guard against it, not for a moment, not out of anger or impatience or distraction. Not ever." One quarter of his mind coolly approved the balanced shape of the speech; another cringed at its grotesque irrelevance. "You see now what harm even a moment's carelessness can do. Be warned, then. Learn the lesson well. Let us never have to learn it again."

The workmen below him nodded solemnly, accepting the words.

Sulun tried to find words to send them back to work, but couldn't think of any. The sound of the crane's ropes slapping the wood made him think of corpses hanging on gallows. No, no more of this, not today.

"Bear that poor man to his home," he said, struggling to get the words clear. "The rest of you, secure the crane, the stones and the tools, and take the remainder of the day—at full pay—to ponder this matter. Er, dismissed." He strode hastily off the stone and down the scaffolding, trying not to hear the amazed murmurs of the crowd as he passed, and headed for the new house. Somewhere among all the food stocks there had to be some strong berry wine, and he needed a few cups of that.

Behind him, the work gang rumbled in amazement.

"Did ye hear that?" said the senior workman. "All of half the day off, and at full pay!"

"What generous folk they be," agreed the nearest. "And wise, too. His talk of carelessness be good sense."

"Aye," noted his neighbor. "Have ye seen, this is the first sore accident since the building work began? The first life or limb lost, in all these moons."

"And that on a new fellow, first day here, who didn't know the workings," another added. " 'S'truth, I think he was a stranger here."

" 'Tis sure, I don't know him," commented one of the men at the stretcher. "Does anyone here know where his house lies?"

"I do," rumbled Biddon, coming up on them. " 'Tis far off north, by the caravan road. Yotha House, and none other."

The workmen stared at him, then at each other, then nodded knowingly.

An hour later, two riders on mules set out from Deese House. Before dusk they reached Ashkell villa, meeting Eloti on the way and taking her back with them. Gynallea invited them in and set dinner for them at the upper end of the table, calmly as if she'd been expecting them. Wotheng, after his usual custom, asked no questions and discouraged all talk until the meal was finished and the dessert drinks brought out.

"You did say, m'lord," Sulun began, "that if any local wizards tried to harm us, we should bring our complaint to you."

Wotheng glanced sidelong at his wife, then shrugged. "Aye, so we did. What wizards have troubled you folk, and in what way?"

Sulun looked hopefully at Zeren, not certain that he could carry off this little plan. The big soldier launched into the story as smoothly as if he were giving a standard military report.

"Shortly after noon today there was an accident at the

construction site on the new Deese House outer wall. A stone slipped from its cradle, crushing a workman. Upon inspection, the wall was found to have been temporarily ill-wished. The injured workman was found to have been a resident of Yotha's estate. Apparently he was attempting to set a curse on the walls when our own protective spells deflected it, causing it to discharge upon the sender."

Wotheng looked calm, mildly interested; his eyelids barely fluttered at the name of Yotha. Still, Eloti noted it.

"We wish to know," Sulun took up the complaint, "just who these people are, why they tried to ill-wish our house, and whether we may expect more of this."

Wotheng puffed at his pipe, harrumphed a few times, glanced again at his wife. "Well, Yotha's some imported fire god," he began. "Came from off to the east somewhere, no place we ever heard of. These priests of his, now, they've some sorcerous powers they claim he gives 'em; came here about eight years ago and set up to the north, maybe five leagues up along the caravan road. They say that Yotha came first, and the priests were only following where he led. What I know is that fires were seen running along the hilltops—running in lines and curlicues, dancing, like. Didn't harm any but stretches of turf; stampeded some sheep, scared some folk out of their wits, and everyone came hollering to me about it."

Wotheng tapped out his empty pipe, refilled and relit it before going on.

"Next day it was, I clearly recall, these priests of Yotha showed themselves in the village. Very fierce and solemn, they were. Proud, too, as if they held themselves too high to speak to the common run of folk. Came asking to see 'the lord of this place,' which was myself, saying they knew the 'source and nature' of the fires. To be sure, I gave 'em audience."

"It was Yotha, they said," Gynallea sneered, pouring herself another berry cordial. "Their triple-damned fire god."

"Oh, aye. They said they'd been following their god's trail for moons, and now they'd found him here. They said they could entice him into a shrine, keep him appeased, keep him from doing mischief, but 'twere best if they did it quickly. Best, in truth, if they could find some empty building already standing— like the old burned mansion up by the north road. Yotha'd be drawn to that, they said, since fire had 'already frolicked there.' "

"And what of all the poor folk living there?" Gynallea added. "Hah, never mind! Go they must, so the priests could set their god trap there."

"Now what was I to do?" Wotheng shrugged. "Here's the people all afrenzy over these fires, here's these priests saying they can put an end to it, and here's only a few poor folk in the way." He sighed and tapped out his pipe.

"What became of the poor folk who were moved out of the mansion?" Eloti asked.

"Oh, many of them weren't moved out at all—just became builders, then servants, at Yotha House. The rest, well, I granted them some sheep and some help building cottages elsewhere. Tricky juggling with land rights that was, too."

"So Yotha's priests took the house, and its lands, I presume," Eloti considered. "And the mysterious fires stopped?"

"Not entirely, no." Wotheng reached for his cup. "Now they danced all over the altar at his ceremonies there. Folk came from leagues about to attend. At other times the fires would scamper out on the bare hilltops and dance a while, and the priests would go out and chant at them a while, and they'd stop. Then the priests took to saying where fire would strike next—this one's house, that one's barn . . ." Wotheng half-turned, frowned at his fireplace and the innocent flames therein. "Folk took to paying good prices to the priests to discourage Yotha's games. See you where that led?"

Zeren, Eloti, and Sulun nodded slowly. "So, Yotha's priesthood soon became rich," Eloti finished. "Now that we've come, they fear a rival for people's attention—and money."

Wotheng smiled sourly. "Be not surprised, friends, if Yotha's fire comes running up to your gates some evening soon."

"We'll not be surprised at all," Zeren growled. "Is the god truly there, think you, or is it only the priests' sorcery?"

"Who can tell?" Gynallea gulped her cup empty. "I have noticed, though, that the god behaves in such fashion as to make his priests powerful and rich—more like some captive demon doing a wizard's bidding than a proper god."

"These running fires," Sulun put in, "how do they behave? Is there anything notable about their appearance that differs from ordinary fire?"

"Oh, yes." Gynallea laughed. "They burn only at night, save in Yotha House, and they run in trails all along the ground: over grass, over bare earth, over stone, even up the walls of houses to pounce upon the roof. I've seen it myself. You remember, lovey, when Poddil's cottage burned?"

"You saw this fire run across stone?"

"That I did. A most amazing sight, it was, too. I could see the fires dancing high and bright when they crossed dry grass or wood, creeping low and ghastly blue when they crawled over stone, but crawl they did: all the way to Poddil's house, up the wall and into the thatch, where they burned high and fierce."

"Wait," Sulun insisted. "Blue, did you say? When they didn't have dry grass or wood to eat, the flames were low and . . . *blue*?"

"Aye, a most ghastly color for flame."

"I . . . see." Sulun leaned back in his chair, thinking hard.

"Tell me," Eloti cut into the silence. "If you'd had such ill luck with priests and sorcerers come to settle here, why did you accept us so kindly when first we came?"

Wotheng gave her a long look, then a smile. "Because, good lady, when first you folk came hence, we saw that you went straight to the common folk—to our blacksmith, in fact—and freely gave of your skills, in exchange for no more than knowledge. Also, you offered to sell your goods to any who would buy."

"We behaved like merchants, you mean." Eloti grinned.

"Aye, dear," said Gynallea. "You claimed to be priests, but behaved like goodly merchants. Yotha's sort claimed to be priests also, but behaved more like fearsome wizards. See you the difference?"

"Also," Zeren added, fixing Wotheng with a knowing eye, "perhaps we seemed good enough wizards to drive out Yotha's folk, should it come to that."

Wotheng shrugged again, but he blushed a little.

"Well, who else?" Gynallea said stoutly. "You're skilled at such things. You can deal with Yotha and his priests far better than we."

"Perhaps we can," Sulun murmured, rousing a bit. "Perhaps indeed we can. Eloti, how long before you can return to Deese House? We'll need you to lay further protections there."

"Surely you couldn't return tonight," Gynallea protested. "All those long leagues in the dark . . ."

"No, we'll stay until after school tomorrow, and leave at noon," said Eloti. "I doubt Yotha's priests will attempt any . . . visitations of their god tonight."

"The evening still being young," said Sulun, "might I ask if your ladyship has a still-room in the house that I might observe?"

"Why, yes," Gynallea answered, surprised at the change of subject. "I showed it to Goodlady Eloti just this afternoon."

"Hmm. And would you perchance have a distillery there, and possibly some cordial that didn't come out quite right which you could spare?"

"Certainly, good priest. Ah, you have some plans already, then?"

"Perhaps."

Gort and Hobb sat a long time in the donkeycart, arguing, then finally tossing lots to see which of them would go up to the gate of Yotha House to announce the bad news. Gort lost the toss, and tiptoed, trembling, up to the bellpull. Soon enough, a yellow-robed servant opened the door and peered out.

"S-sir Priest," Gort stammered, respectfully wringing his hat in his hands, "w-we've a fellow here as belongs to yer house, what was killed today at stoneworking. Will ye not come take him inside?"

"Bide a moment," said the servant, whipping back inside.

A few minutes later he came back, accompanied by an older, stouter priest in an embroidered orange robe. The senior priest went to the donkeycart, studied the pathetic bundle inside, then signed to the servant. The junior fellow hurried back to the house, leaving Gort and Hobb alone with the corpse and the priest.

"How did this man come to die?" the priest intoned.

"B-beggin' yer pardon, sir, he were careless at the liftin' and the stone slipped its halter and fell on him." Gort got it all out in a rush.

"And where did this happen?"

"Er, why, at the wall-makin', on the new estate to the southwest."

"New estate?" The priest smiled blandly. "What new estate?"

Gort threw Hobb a desperate look. Hobb gulped twice, then took up the tale. "Why, the old house by the ruint village, what Lord Wotheng deeded t'his friends, sir. The place bein' in sad repair, they called for workmen t' mend the walls. Sure, and that must be how this feller come t' be there."

"I see. And how did you come to bring his body here?"

"Er, well, he weren't from 'round our village, sir, but a few folk said they'd seen him here, so we thought he might be one of yer servants. Please, sir, do take him in! It's five long leagues back t' the village again, and in the dark, and all. . . ."

"Yes, we shall take him in."

The servant had returned with three similarly robed companions. The priest snapped his fingers, directed them to the back of the donkeycart, and pointed silently to the sacking-wrapped corpse. The servants lugged the body out of the cart. The priest fumbled among his robes, looking for a coin to give the drivers, but Gort had already snapped up the whip and slapped the donkey to motion. The cart rumbled in a tight circle, then back down the road. The priest watched them go for a moment, then followed the servants inside.

Gynallea's distilling equipment was simple: a glazed, narrow-necked pot corked with boiled wood, a crudely seamed copper tube twisting out of the top, and a simple catch-jar at its lower end. The pot sat on a three-legged iron ring above a small brazier full of glowing coals. The cordial which had gone into the pot less than an hour before was berry purple, but the liquid dripping from the end of the tube was colorless as water though it smelled sharp and strong.

"Wine distilled to winter wine," Sulun recited, watching the drops fall. "Winter wine distilled to cordial, cordial distilled to this. It would require much wine to begin with, or perhaps even strong beer. Does the House of Yotha purchase much wine or beer? Or does its land grow much of berries or barley?"

"Aye to both," murmured Gynallea, fascinated. " 'Tis a joke hereabouts, how much the god and his servants drink. But think you they're not just drinking it?"

"We'll know in a moment. 'Twas an experiment my old master Abanuz once showed me. The result would burn hot enough, and steady as an oil lamp, to work small bits of glass or metal. I remembered that the flame burned a most notable blue. . . . Ah, I think that should do. Take away the brazier, before the leftover syrup burns. Thank you."

"Blue fire? Like oil?" Gynallea asked, shoving the brazier out from under the still-pot. "An oil that could burn without a wick? On bare stone?"

"Not an oil: spirits of cordial. Wait . . ." Sulun took a brush and carefully painted a trail of the clear liquid across a wide stone dish. He took a taper from an overhead shelf, held its wick in the coals until it caught, then touched the small flame to one end of the liquid trail.

The liquid caught fire, flared, lighted down its whole length, and burned for several seconds. The flames were blue, barely tipped with yellow.

"Yotha's fire! That's it, certain as day!" Gynallea crowed. "That's what I saw, only ever so much more of it, climbing the wall of poor Poddy's house."

"And the smell?" Sulun persisted, holding the catchbowl under her nose. "Was there a smell like this one?"

Gynallea sniffed long and hard, wrinkling her nose. "I can't recall truly, but I'll swear I've smelled that before—and in Yotha House, during one of the ceremonies where he came to the altar. I thought it but another incense, such as priests use."

"Then I think we've learned the mystery of Yotha House." Sulun frowned as he poured the liquid into a vial. "Spirits of cordial, burning fluid, more volatile than oil: wicked stuff to be playing at. Especially wicked to mix with magic. Do they dare use magic at all with such stuff lying about? Hmm, they must have protective spells all about Yotha House, against just such happenstance."

"I see it well," Gynallea growled bitterly. "They preach against some poor fellow by day, then by night come and splash trails of these spirits though his fields, up to his house or barn. 'Twould need but a spark at one end of the trail to send fire racing to the other. Gods, what a wicked business!"

"And we've threatened it." Sulun corked the vial and stuffed it in his belt pouch. "We'd best put fresh well-wishing circles all about our house, and that right soon. We'd also best finish that stout stone wall as soon as might be, and sheathe the gates with brass."

"Friend Sulun." Gynallea laid a hand on his arm. "Think you that your folk can defeat Yotha's wizards?"

Sulun gave a long sigh. "It's possible," he said. "But I wish it might not come to that."

✧ CHAPTER THREE ✧

Folweel was sitting at the table in his study when Patrobe entered. He waved the tall burly man to a seat without waiting on the usual formalities.

"You saw Hegg's body?" he asked without preamble.

"I did, Brother." Patrobe clasped his hands and settled into his chair with the smooth calm of a professional soldier or courtier. "We may assume it happened as those louts said: the stone slipped its harness and fell on him."

"He was ordered to anchor a curse into the mortar of the wall," Folweel explained bluntly. "The curse was deflected back at him, and that right quickly."

Patrobe held up two thick fingers. "Either his work was quickly detected and countered, or the wall was already well-wished. Hegg was skilled enough, trained enough, he should have detected a protective spell already set."

"Then there are three possibilities: first, the protective was subtly enough set that an under-priest could not detect it; second, the protective was set not on the uncompleted wall but on the entire house and grounds—"

"Damned difficult, to all accounts," Patrobe cut in. "So much area—"

"Third, the wall was not protected at all, but one or more of the Deese wizards discovered Hegg's work and counterspelled it."

"Quick work of them."

"Aye." Folweel steepled his fingers. "In any event, we are not dealing with amateurs."

Silence stretched while Patrobe considered that. "Subtlety,

then. If they expect magical counterattacks, perhaps they'll not expect, say, a simple visit of Yotha's displeasure?"

Folweel smiled thinly. "Will tomorrow's weather be dry?" he asked.

The ritual in Yotha House began and proceeded much as usual. The flame on the altar leaped up from blue roots when Yotha's name was invoked, and burned there tranquilly during the hymns and the offerings. The tray full of collected coins passed through the flames harmlessly, as usual. A slightly substandard fleece (after being covertly sprinkled behind the altar) caught fire and went up in a spectacular blaze when it was offered to the flame, making the giver almost faint where he stood, but there were no other incidents.

Then came a brief memorial listing of the recently dead, which happened to include the name of Hegg Gebbi's-son.

The column of flame on the altar flared, leaped, danced, and finally shot an arm of fire to the southwest corner of the altar.

The congregation moaned, cringed, and stared. The high priest chanted furiously for a long moment, and the flames finally retreated to their original size and shape. Folweel prayed loudly for understanding, then faced the flame for a long moment. When he turned to face the crowd, his face was quite calm, stern, and composed.

"Thus saith the Lord Yotha, Master of Fire," he intoned. "The god is displeased at the death of his good servant. He holdeth certain of the living responsible for the good man's death, and shall not refrain from chastising them with his wrath."

The crowd groaned, knowing what that meant, and cast suspicious looks at their neighbors.

The high priest swung straightway into his sermon, as if it had been inspired by the omen of the fire: a long diatribe against sins of pride, avarice, undervaluing of the gods, disloyalty, and abandonment of the path of virtue. No names were mentioned, but the congregation made its own guesses.

The noon bell rang, and Eloti stopped in mid-phrase. "Today's lesson is ended," she announced, rolling up the scroll in her lap. "Write one panel's worth of commentary to bring to class tomorrow. Gentlefolk, you are dismissed."

The little class of mixed adults, children, and adolescents duly closed and stacked their tablets, tucked away their styli, and prepared to leave.

Eloti watched them sidelong while tucking scrolls into her basket. That fellow Duppa was still shielded thoroughly, still as bland as an apple, still utterly self-effacing at study. He was probably a spy from Yotha House. What to do about him, though? He'd certainly made no attempts at subtle spellcasting, spreading disaffection among the other students, or prying about the villa. He came, he studied, he went away, leaving as little mark of his presence as possible. Was he merely spying upon her lessons here at Ashkell Villa, or was he biding his time until some proper moment to strike? *No way to tell, not yet.* Eloti took up her basket, wrapped her cloak around her, and strolled toward the main gate, dismissing the problem in favor of the task immediately ahead. The ten-league ride would take longer than the actual spellcasting, but it was unlikely she would finish before the usual dinnertime.

"Eloti, wait a bit." Gynallea caught her at the gate, plucked her sleeve, and drew her aside to an untenanted corner of the courtyard. "Cook's girl went to Yotha's service this morning—on my orders, don't worry—and came back just now with a tale you'd best carry."

"What news?" Eloti lowered her voice and glanced once around the yard.

"Yotha has taken public notice of you and your friends, daughter. His flame spurted up when the dead spy's name was spoken, and the priests say 'tis because he wants vengeance for the man's death. Best watch for fires at Deese House tonight, my dear. Tell your friends that."

Eloti's lips thinned as she thought that over. "Dear Gynna, might I borrow the use of a faster horse, and perhaps a pair of your guards, for the ride home today?"

"Vari, I'll need your help." Sulun leaned in the door of the nursery, startling the children. "Tami, dearest, can you take care of the little ones for an hour or so?"

" 'Course I can," the little girl boasted. "Mama, are you going to make magic too?"

"Certainly not, dear. I've no gift for it at all. Stay here, now."

Vari tugged on her cloak and followed Sulun out into the main hall. Even with the cook fires started, the big barnlike room could be chilly without the forge lit. "For that matter, Sulun, why are you still here? I thought everyone but those guards Eloti brought would be out helping her cast the spell."

"Like you, I've no talent for it." Sulun crossed to the water pipe near the millroom, shoved a bucket under its spout, and turned the stopcock open. "Fill the other bucket and follow me. Ah, damn, we should have thought to buy more buckets. Well, no matter. If my guess be correct, we'll have to wet down only a single section of the wall."

"Wet down the wall?" Vari gave him a sidelong look as she shoved her bucket under the flowing spout. "That won't hasten the setting of the mortar."

"No, but it may prevent a certain nasty trick which I expect. Oof! There must be an easier way to carry these things. . . ."

They dragged the sloshing buckets across the courtyard, up to the half-completed stretch of wall. In the long rays of the setting sun they could make out Eloti, standing a little ahead of the others, down by the gate. Occasional gusts of wind brought snatches of her song up to the wall. Arizun and Ziya stood just behind her, holding a fuming censer and a shielded candle, respectively. All the rest stood in a small knot further back, chanting along with Eloti. The frowns of concentration on their faces were visible even from here.

"Good, good," Sulun murmured, passing to the end of the unfinished section. "With luck, they'll be back at the house before dark. Hmm, now Yotha's wizards won't know exactly where the accident took place, only that it was somewhere along this section. We'll have to wet down the whole thing. Damn. Ah, well . . ." He emptied his bucket over the last of the fresh-laid stones.

"I confess I've no idea what we're doing," said Vari, dutifully emptying her bucket on the stone beside Sulun's. "Do you mean to wet down this whole stretch? Gods, that's a dozen trips to the water, at least. Let's get Omis or Zeren to help us, or maybe those guards lounging about near the gate."

"Alas, we can't. The guards need watch for anyone sneaking close with kegs about them, and the others are needed to help Eloti's work." Sulun turned back toward the house for more water.

"I don't see what help they can be," Vari grumbled, following him. "Omis has no more gift for magic than I do, and I don't imagine Zeren has much more."

"No, but they can concentrate upon an image, and a magician can channel the force of that concentration for his—or her—use. Eloti explained it to me, more than once. I still can't see it. Neither can I seem to concentrate very long upon an image in my mind without playing with it, tinkering with it, which is not what a magician needs." Sulun shoved his bucket under the spout again. "I was designed by the gods to be a Natural Philosopher, a mechanic, not a magician. Let the others help Eloti; I do what I can with my own skills."

"Wetting down walls?" Vari shook her head, but loaded her bucket again.

In the thick brush by the stream Patrobe crouched in his dark brown cloak and held the pack donkey's halter rope. Waiting here in the rising chill of dusk was not his favorite duty; to be truthful, he would rather have been scouting and peering upstream with his under-priests. Still, if those two were, by some chance, seen and caught by the Deese wizards it would be far less a calamity for Yotha House than if he were taken. Patrobe pulled his cloak tighter around him and contented himself with imagining the end of this night's work.

A soft rustle among the bushes interrupted his reverie, announcing that Gidd and Billot had returned. Sure enough, a moment later their dark-clad forms wriggled into view and slid down beside him near the stream.

"Well?" Patrobe asked quietly.

Billot recovered his voice first, while Gidd sucked on a wineskin. "Pah, dusty work," he panted. "We got within bowshot of the walls."

"No more than that?"

"They've guards out, Master; one by the front gate, one by the low part of the wall."

"And themselves are out walking the grounds," Gidd added. "I think they be spellcasting on the land. It felt that way."

"So? Did you note any manifestations?"

" 'Deed we did," Billot confirmed. "Beyond the foot of the hill 'twas suddenly cold and wet, like a wall of mist—but there was no mist."

"Aye," Gidd put in. "We moved slow and careful, repeating the charm, but even so, we stuck our boots in mud and rabbit holes more often than not, and snagged on thornbushes, and met clouds of gnats. The very land is spell-protected, sure enough."

"Yes . . ." Patrobe interlaced his fingers and thought a while. "We must proceed very carefully, my children. Wait until full dark, then go forth with the greatest care. Move slowly as you must, knowing we have all the night, and caution will serve you far better than speed. Use the charmed strings to guide your way back when you lay Yotha's trail; perchance they'll give you some protection against the land spell."

"What of the guards, Master?" Billot whined. "We'll not get close without they see us."

"Listen carefully: start wide apart, crawl as close as you dare. Gidd, you approach the gate, but come not so close as to be seen; lay your trail and come back, then light the fire. Billot, hear me well; wait until the first fire comes up toward the gate, and the guard at the wall goes to look at it. Then hurry you to the wall, fast as you safely can. Start the trail there, then retreat to where you'll be well hidden before lighting it. Mind the guard does not see you. Do you understand me well?"

"We do, Master," they said, almost in unison.

"Good." Patrobe got up and went to the donkey. A few quick tugs untied its pack, freeing two small kegs. He handed a keg each to his henchmen. "Be sure your tapers and flints are well tied in your pouches," he warned, "and keep repeating the charm until you're safely away.

"And be sure to make the trails thick and wide; let them not be so thin as to break or falter."

"No, Master," the men promised, already easing away into the brush.

Patrobe glanced up at the darkening sky, sat down and pulled his cloak about him again. At best, it would be a long wait.

The guards drowsed at their posts, barely sustained by warming-jugs filled with coals and smaller jugs of beer. They glanced toward each other often, catching no more than a glimpse of silhouette or flicker of shuttered candle-lamp, wishing they hadn't been stationed so far apart. An hour ago one of the Deese priests had called down from the wall, kindly asking if they needed blankets, and that was the last they'd heard of another human presence. It was full dark now, and silent everywhere, and if not too chilly still not comfortably warm. Despite the promised pay— in silver, no less—there had to be better work than staying awake all night, waiting for an attack by wizards. Oh, this was a grim and wearing business, it was.

On the wall above, Zeren paced his circuit from the gate to the junction of wall and cliff face and back again. That cliff face bothered him; sometime in the future, they would have to wall off or sheer away all other possible slopes to the hilltop, lest some enemy get above them to throw down rocks, fire or scaling ropes on the house below. Not a problem tonight, though: he strongly doubted that anyone would attempt those steep, crumbling slopes in the dark.

At the gate top, he saw Yanados approaching. Her bow was in her hand, but her arrows still sat in the quiver. She seemed not at all tired, quite ready to walk her rounds until dawn if need be. He smiled, waving to her.

"What of the night, Captain?" She grinned, approaching. "I've heard nothing but the goats arguing in the barn."

"No more have I, but the night's far from old." Zeren turned to look down at the guard below. "Wotheng's fellows seem to know their business. I imagine we'll have some warning."

"You're sure Yotha's lads will come tonight, then? I'd hate to have to do this for the next moon or so."

"Who can predict? Still, I think they'll move tonight. Their god has a reputation for quick temper and quick action."

They leaned on the parapet, gazing out at the darkened land, hearing only the night sounds of wild creatures about their business.

"Have we changed much?" Yanados asked quietly.

"Aye." Zeren shrugged, making his cloak rustle. "We've needed to."

"And for the worse, as Sulun thinks?"

"Worse? No. Sulun broods too much over this little war."

"Ah, well, he was shaped by the gods for the scholars' tower and the laboratorium, not for such work as this."

"Third hell, were any of us born for such—hey, look there!"

A light glimmered, far out in the dark: flame flickering, but blue as no flame should be.

The gate guard shouted and climbed to his feet. So did his

companion by the unfinished wall. Zeren swore, pulled out his sword, and hammered its butt on the iron gateway bell.

The flame came running toward them up the hill, crawling like a bright snake, flowing like water, straight toward the gate. Now the tips of the blue flames gleamed yellow, like spines on a dragon's back.

Running footsteps echoed in the courtyard below. Sulun's voice, mixed with Omis's, demanding to know where the enemy was.

"Blue fire, running uphill toward the gate," Zeren shouted down at them. "Come up and look."

"Is it within Eloti's wards?" Sulun shouted as he scrambled up the stile to the walkway.

"Well within," Yanados pointed. "Stronger magic than hers, think you?"

Below them, the line of fire snaked up the road, making straightaway for the front gate. The guardsman there yelped and jumped to one side. His companion came running, had the sense or training to make certain his partner was unharmed, then stopped and stared at the oncoming flames. "Yotha begone, Yotha begone," he muttered, wagging his fingers in elaborate signs that had no effect whatever.

"Not magic at all," Sulun announced, watching it. "Common chemistry, not unlike our firepowder. But how could they have spread it so close . . . Wait."

Less than thirty yards from the gate the flame-trail stopped. It rose to a snapping tower of fire and danced there, lighting up the ground all around it, as if taunting the defenders of the house. One of the guardsmen covered his eyes, but after a moment dared to peep through his fingers. "What made it stop?" asked a quiet little voice at Sulun's elbow.

He looked down, startled, to see Ziya staring at the column of fire. *Gods, this is especially cruel to her,* he thought, suddenly furious. "It ran out of fuel," he said, hearing a ring of contempt in his voice. "See there, where its tail is shrinking? That's where the fluid that feeds it has burned away. The rest will die soon enough." He leaned over the parapet and shouted at the fire column. "Shrink and die, you worthless conjurer's trick! Dry up and shrivel!"

The guards gaped up at him.

Sure enough, the fire-trail sank down and died. The column of flames grew no taller, whipped and darted for a moment in the light wind, then began to shrink. Within moments it sank to a ring of dying blue flames, then winked out. The sudden return of darkness made everyone blink and rub their eyes. After a moment, the guards sent a ragged cheer.

"Did you make it stop?" Ziya asked.

"No, child," Sulun admitted, shivering as his anger passed. "I only guessed when it would stop of itself."

"It wasn't magic at all, was it?"

"No, not at all. Ask Eloti; magic can only well-wish or ill-wish. All the rest is elaborate tricks—like that one."

Zeren strode up, interrupting him. "Is that it, do you think? Have they done their attack for tonight?"

"Should be . . ." Sulun rubbed his forehead, trying to calculate with too many unknown factors. "They can't have much fire-fluid at any one time: too hard to make, needs too much wine for its source. . . . Besides, who could come sneaking up to our walls with whole barrels full, especially unseen? And yet . . ."

"How much fluid is needed, to make that much fire?"

"Gods, I'm not sure. A kegful, at least."

"A stalking man might carry a single keg, but no more."

"True, true. They may be finished for the night. Yet, I was so sure they'd attack the wall, where the block fell."

"Hah, so that's why you set the other guard there?" Zeren leaned over the parapet and called down to the huddled guards. "You lads, did you see anyone come sneaking close to the new part of the wall?"

"No, sir," one of the guards retorted stoutly. "I been there all night, and seen none."

Zeren froze where he was, teeth showing in a sudden, unlovely smile. "All night—except for just now!"

"What, sir?"

Zeren turned his head just enough to growl at Sulun. "Diversion! Get to that wall and see who's about it right now. Hey, Yanados, go with him! You lad, hurry back to your post and tell me if you see, hear, smell, or feel anything strange. Sulun, what did you say that stuff smelled like?"

But Sulun was already running for the unfinished section of wall. Yanados pounded after him, yanking an arrow out of her quiver. She almost bumped into Sulun as he skidded to a halt, sniffing fiercely, by the gap.

"Gods, it might be, but I can't be sure," he muttered, stalking forward slowly. "Keep watch; they might still be about. Where's that guard?"

"Ey, Masters," the guard called plaintively from somewhere ahead of them. "I don't know if it means aught, but I'd swear I could smell temple incense somewhere close."

Sulun looked where the voice sounded. "Gods, the scaffolding!" he yelped. "It's wood! We soaked it down but that might not be—Water! Yanados, come help me get water!"

He ran back toward the main building, cloak flapping. Yanados paused only to shove her bow and arrow back into the quiver before running after him. Vari met them at the door with two buckets and a large kettle, all sloshing full.

"You guessed, bless you," Sulun panted, picking up one of the buckets.

Yanados grabbed the other. Vari took up the kettle, and they all hurried back to the wall.

"The scaffolding," Sulun was panting as they climbed up onto the stone. "Wet it down, and the ground below it. Water, more water—Gods!"

"Here it comes again!" screeched the guard, pointing.

They could all see it: a narrow river of fire running up the hillside toward them. So fast it came, so wickedly fast.

Sulun swung his bucket in a narrow arc, splashing it contents all over the damp planks of the scaffold. "Get the ground!" he shouted. "The ground below! Hurry!"

Yanados and Vari unloaded their water at the same time, down the braces of the scaffold and onto the ground below.

The fire raced for them at windspeed, and again the guard leapt, howling out of the way.

"More water!" Sulun shouted, dragging the others down from the wall. "If we can dilute it enough . . . Hurry!"

Vari and Yanados duly followed him, casting only brief glances back over their shoulders at the oncoming train of fire.

Zeren watched from the gate, cursing in a dozen different tongues, as the flame snake ran toward the wall. It wasn't going to stop a few yards off this time; the clever pig's son who'd led it here had reached all the way to the wooden scaffolding, at least. Damn, that would burn like a torch if Sulun couldn't wet it enough. He pulled out his bow and nocked an arrow to the string, knowing it was futile. The sneak thief responsible would be far out of sight now, if he had any sense.

The fire-trail darted among the scatter of waiting stones and ran up to the wall, straight for the scaffolding.

And there it stopped, hissing and spouting fireballs, just out of reach of the waiting wood. Flames leapt, spat, crawled in all directions like a baffled flood halted by an invisible dam, seeking some way around it.

"Vozai, the water's stopped it!" Zeren laughed. "It can't reach—"

The cheer froze in his throat as he saw something else by the light of the frustrated flame.

A child stood on the wall, just beyond the scaffolding, almost within reach of the fire. It was Ziya, wearing a look that better belonged on a soldier in battle, and she was shaking her fist at the flames.

"Get down from there!" Zeren managed to yell. "The steam—"

And then Sulun scrambled up on the stones, lugging a bucket. He stepped past Ziya with barely a glance spared, and threw the water out over the scaffold.

The flames hissed, half-obscured in clouds of steam, and sank down to sullen blue niblets.

Yanados came up next, stared briefly, then emptied her bucket over the wall. Vari, barely a step behind, did likewise; then she swung the empty kettle on her arm, grabbed up Ziya, and hauled her down from the stones.

Zeren let out a breath he hadn't realized he was holding. "Is it safe, then?" he called.

"Retreating," Sulun shouted back. "I think we've beaten it."

"Hail Deese and all his servants!" the guard crowed, daring to inch out of hiding. "Hail the Lord of the Forge, who has mastery over fire! Yotha has no power against him, nor his house, nor his servants! A very child can drive him away!"

"Oh, hush," Yanados snapped irritably. " 'Twas water did it."

"Knowledge did it," Sulun amended. "We all did it."

"Oh, yes, sir!" the guard laughed, unwilling to be cheated of his story. "Deese's wisdom, and all his wise servants: none can compare with them!"

"Oh, hell," Sulun groaned, realizing just how wet his robes were, and how cold the night. "Let's to bed, and sleep while we can."

✧ CHAPTER FOUR ✧

By next evening, word was out all over Ashkell Vale; the wizard-priests of Deese had fought off the flames of Yotha, routed his balefires utterly, thrust him off from their walls, and defied him while he slunk away. Workmen at Deese patted the steam-blanched scaffolding for good luck as they labored—quickly, and ever so carefully—to complete the wall. Servants at Ashkell Villa made all manner of excuses, climbed into all manner of unlikely peeping spots, to look at the Wizardess Eloti while she taught her students. Enrollment in the beginners' class tripled.

Attendance at the rites of Yotha dwindled, though the fire displays thereat were spectacular enough to keep gossip running. The god was unquiet, as the priests said, because of wrongs done to him and his.

Gamblers, professional and amateur, argued lengthily over the odds that Yotha would attack again, or Deese retaliate. Alehouse conversationalists speculated merrily on what form the stroke or counterstroke would take.

Consequently, when a whole moon-quarter passed with no action taken on either side, people grew less gleeful and more fearful over the imminent battle. Gynallea noted that students at Eloti's school pressed close enough to hear her every word, yet kept distant enough to avoid any ill fate that might strike her. Wotheng, passing by Deese House while inspecting flocks pastured nearby, noted that the workmen were finishing the wall with amazing speed, as if they were eager to complete their work, collect their pay, and hurry out of reach before the next blow fell.

The respective priesthoods, quite aware of the situation, kept their own council while they brooded upon these matters.

❖   ❖   ❖

"This can't last," Zeren insisted, over the light noon meal. "Yotha's temple isn't used to losing money. The priests will take that as damage, no matter what we do, and they'll find a way to strike us."

"Our protections should hold." Sulun poked at a half-eaten bun on his plate. "They can't ill-wish us, or burn us out, or scare us with their trickery. Besides preaching against us, which hardly weighs heavy with the folk here, what harm can they do?"

"I wouldn't know, not being privy to the councils of Yotha's priests, but we can expect they'll do something as devastating as they can manage. We must take some action, something to scare them into accepting their losses and leaving us alone."

"What would you have us do? March against them with fire and sword? As I'm a true philosopher, I'll not strike first against any man!"

Zeren sighed, remembering all the times he'd had similar arguments with assorted commanders in the southlands. "What I'm trying to tell you, my philosopher friend, is that Yotha's priests believe you've already struck first—by reducing their income, killing their poor harmless observer, and making a laughingstock of their god. They plot what they consider just revenge, and we'd best forestall it while we can."

Sulun tugged at his hair, disheveling it further. "We did nothing to harm their trade, that spy was far from harmless, and their 'god' attacked us. Anyone can see that."

"Anyone who chooses to, which Yotha's priests do not. This is not a case being argued in some pure and unbiased court of justice; this is more in the nature of a border war—and believe me, Sulun, I understand such things. We must take some action."

"Gods' blight! What would you have me do?"

Zeren leaned back in his creaking-new chair and looked at Omis. "The new bombard is overdue for testing, is she not?"

Omis stared at him, horrified. "You—you don't mean to attack Yotha's temple with her, do you? Great gods, we don't even know where it lies! And untested—"

"No, no." Zeren laughed. "Among other considerations, I doubt if our friend Wotheng would take kindly to a new military power at his doorstep. What I have in mind is a simple public display,

something interesting, to amaze and delight our friends and . . .
warn off our enemies."

Omis sat up, eyes narrowing a bit. "Just what," he asked, "do
you have in mind?"

On the next afternoon, Doshi passed among the workmen at
the nearly complete wall and warned them to keep away from
the northern field for the next hour, for the priests of Deese
would be testing a new magical device there. The work gang
swore, one and all, that they had no intention of going anywhere
near the northern field—indeed, had no reason whatever to go
near that field, that not even goats bothered grazing in that barren
field—which was quite true, especially since Arizun and Yanados
had carefully herded the beasts elsewhere. Doshi expressed his
delight at that news, and went back to the house. The work gang
climbed the scaffolding and clustered on the new wall, straining
to see the mysterious test.

Everyone saw the two largest and most muscular of Deese's
wizard-priests lugging a strange object up the stile steps and onto
the northern wall. The magical device appeared to be a thick,
brass-colored tube, set in a sturdy wooden mount, treated with
great reverence. The priests set it carefully on top of the wall,
turned it slightly here and there, raised and lowered the tube in
its cradle until it was placed to their satisfaction.

Next, up onto the wall came two smaller wizards, one carrying
a leather sack as if it contained powdered gold, the other bearing
a heavy canister of what looked to be well-greased, stiffened
leather. The more sharp-eyed witnesses noted that the canister
was as big around as the inside of the brass-colored tube, and
guessed that the one was meant to go inside the other.

Next came two very young priests, plainly apprentices. One
bore an odd assortment of tools: long-handled round brushes
and dashers as if for a butter churn. The other carried thin tapers
or waxed-stiff cords in one hand and a tinderbox in the other.

After them, dressed in fine robes and carrying a meditation
gem of black glass, came the Wizardess Eloti. Her face was stern
and composed, she moved with slow and measured tread, and
none could doubt the importance of her presence there.

As the workmen watched, the priests opened the sack and
shovelled carefully measured handfuls of some mysterious black

powder into the tube. They used the dasherlike tool to tamp the powder firmly in the bottom of the tube, then eased the greased canister down after it. The smaller of the apprentices delicately maneuvered one of the oiled cords into a small hole at the back of the tube, working it in as far as it would go.

The wizardess rapped out a quick order, and all the other priests made a ring about the strange device and joined hands. The lady began to chant, and the others followed suit. The workmen couldn't quite hear the words, but none of them doubted that the chant was a powerful protective charm.

"Why be they doin' that, now?" Gort asked his companion. "I thought they'd bespelled all the house and grounds, even beyond the wall. Could yonder thing be especially dangersome, or would it need extra charms now that it be all put together?" His usual work was manning and repairing the derrick, and he had some skill at mechanics, as he was always quick to point out.

"Perhaps 'tis because it sits *upon* the wall," Hobb considered. His family had endured a long squabble over precise borders of sheep pastures, and he took careful note of physical boundaries. "Might be, their protection is set on the wall, and all below it, and all within it—but not on what rests *above* it. I hear spells can be particular that way."

"Like land deeds," Gort started to say, but stopped as his attention was drawn back to the wizards. The spellcasting was apparently finished, for the wizard-priests dropped hands, broke up their circle, and moved several paces away from the mounted tube. One of the priests struck a light from the tinderbox, set it to the projecting tip of the waxed cord, then hastened away to join the others. Everyone held their breath and watched as the flame sizzled redly up the cord and into the tube.

Thunder roared! Lightning flashed! Tiny storm clouds rose above the jerking tube, and a whizzing like enormous hailstones filled the air.

Out in the north field, a gout of earth leaped skyward and fountained in all directions.

The work gang cowered on the wall, jabbing quick lucky signs in the air and gulping bits of safety charms. But the priests of Deese gave a great cheer, ran closer to peer at the ravaged field and point to where the fountain had erupted. Others ran to the thunder tube and inspected it, patting it over and peering down its mouth as if it were a fretful baby. One of them took the long-handled brush and poked it down the tube, worked back and forth a while, then removed it and peered into the tube again.

"Perfect!" everyone heard the burly priest announce. "Not a sign of strain."

"She landed right within the flour circle," another shouted, peering out at the field.

Other priests whooped and hugged each other, and danced clumsy circles on top of the wall.

"Do it again," the burly wizard-priest insisted. "Another three times, at least, to be certain."

The apprentices ran back down the steps, to return shortly with more waxed cords and canisters.

"What, again?" gulped the head of the work gang, peeping out from between his fingers. "Do they mean to plow the whole field with thunder and lightning?"

"Nay, look." Gort pointed to the field, where a small apprentice ran out and scattered flour in a circle. "I think they be testin' his aim, like an archer with a new bow."

"Be that a thunder bow, then?" the gang chief marveled. "Gods defend, I'd hate to be struck with such an arrow!"

"I doubt not," Hobb considered, scratching his chin, "that Yotha himself would not care for it, either."

"Oho," said the chief, turning to look at his neighbors. "And do you note, he be aimed not a little in the way of Yotha's temple?"

"Aha," his audience answered knowingly.

By nighttime the tale had reached the villa, and by the next day it had spread all the length of Ashkell Vale.

"This is where the fist of Deese struck, Master," Yawth said, pointing.

"I have eyes." Wotheng stood up in his stirrups for a better view. "A most impressive hole in the ground. Yes, well worth the ride, Yawth. See that the messenger is thanked properly."

"Aye, m'lord. There be other holes yonder. . . ."

Wotheng shook his head, still peering at the nearer hole. "One to study be enough for him with wit," he murmured. "They can aim this thing, you say?"

"Ay, Master. They were out measuring and all. . . ."

Wotheng, preoccupied, didn't look up. "So great a hole and

such a distance. Could it do thus to earth, what might it do to walls? Or to oncoming ranks of men?"

"Ey, sir," Yawth shuddered. "I wouldn't care to think."

"I daresay our most gentle and civilized friends wouldn't, either." Wotheng raised his head, lips pulling back from his teeth in a startlingly cruel smile. "They've the means, but not the will. No heads for warcraft. But if that might be changed . . ."

Yawth, knowing he was out of his depth, said nothing.

"A way can be found," Wotheng murmured. "A way to change their will, make more than one of them think like warriors. Aye, and then the northern lords might find my land less tempting."

He reined his horse around and spurred back toward home, Yawth following silently.

High Priest Folweel stood looking out the window of his study, saying nothing, his stiff back eloquent with outrage. Behind him Jimantam and Patrobe argued in furious half-whispers.

"—but your usual procedure failed! The rebound thereof has cost us badly in donations, not to mention the loss of faith among our herd."

"Well, what action have *you* taken? I haven't seen our herd giving more donations on your account."

"My account? I'm but the groundskeeper! I've delivered enough Blood of Yotha to fire half the vale; 'tis for you to put it to proper use. The Deese wizards have only the one thunder tube—"

Jimantam stopped there and bit his lip, as if he'd caught himself in an obscenity. He glanced to see if the high priest had heard.

Folweel had. He turned from the window and stalked back to his colleagues. "Enough recriminations, please; they gain us nothing. 'Tis clear that we deal with a knowledgeable enemy— and, now, a dangerous one. Have you learned further about this thunder tube?"

Both priests looked at the floor and shook their heads.

Folweel sighed exasperation. " 'Tis also clear we must engage more subtle tools, and right quickly. Beginning tomorrow, start prophesying that the works of these new wizards are dangerous, treacherous, harmful to the innocent. Also, warn the faithful that the very construction of this thunder tube is an outrage to the gods and a threat most undeserved by Yotha and his herd. Say, 'By what right do servants of Deese of the Forge steal the prerogatives of the storm gods?" Stress the impiety first, the undeserved threat to Yotha's herd second."

"Ah, Brother," Jimantam dared to interject, "a thousand pardons, but will not the weaker among the faithful assume that such warnings are simple jealousy?"

"Let them think what they will, but plant that warning well in their ears."

Patrobe noticed the hidden pattern in the instructions. "Brother, do you . . . expect . . . some disaster connected with the works of Deese's wizards?"

"Some subtle evil," Folweel admitted. "Brother Jimantam, pray fetch Brother Oralro for me. Then go fetch me an accounting from stores concerning the following herbs." He plucked a tablet from his worktable and handed it to the priest, who wilted a trifle as he realized he was being dismissed.

The other two waited until he'd gone before resuming the discussion.

"Excellent for accounting, but no head for strategy, that one." Patrobe remarked toward the closed door.

"He serves his function, which has kept us from poverty." Folweel leaned closer and lowered his voice. "Still no spies established in Deese House?"

"No such fortune," Patrobe admitted. "They're a very closed lot, and the laborers at their wall aren't much better. The work will be finished soon, in any event, and the workmen dispersed, so there's no profit making further attempts among them. Bassip the Wagoner says they've even ordered less beer."

"Hmm . . . And Brother Duppa?"

"He reports regularly, that lessons proceed apace in mathematics, geography, history, and literature." Patrobe snorted, dismissing such prosaic subjects. "He says the lessons on mechanics, chemistry, and medicine are so simple and basic in nature that no one could mistake them for any arcane lore. At this rate, says he, they might consider him for acceptance in their order within a year, if at all. I doubt we can wait that long."

"We cannot." Folweel smacked the table in frustration. "Tell me the moment Duppa reports teachings of magic, or any art which the simple might construe as magic or impiety. . . . Hmm, bid him suborn one of the other students into asking questions on such subjects. Any answer the sorceress gives might be useful.

Particularly, ask about Sukkti beliefs—but be sure to use the local word for them, to avoid suspicion. We may get something there."

"How great an excuse do we need?" Patrobe asked, pondering degrees of offense that common folk might accept.

"Enough to merit a small plague," said the high priest, glancing to the space on his table where the list of supplies had lately rested.

Patrobe raised an eyebrow. "Dangerous, Brother, to so risk our only well-placed agent."

"Place another," Folweel snapped. "Put him in the beginners' class—and make certain he be subtle, quick fingered, and deft. Also send for Bassip."

Patrobe raised his other eyebrow, but said nothing.

✧ CHAPTER FIVE ✧

The trouble began near the close of day, when the work gang were weary and hungry enough to think longingly of home and supper. The oldest of the lot, who'd been complaining of bellyache since lunchtime, succumbed first. He clutched his stomach, gasped, then howled. The workmen at the mortar trough ran to him just as he fell over. The gang on the crane and block had the training, or presence of mind, to finish lowering and setting the block before coming to see what the trouble was.

By then, some few of them had belly pains also.

When the uproar reached Sulun's ears, the problem had spread to more than half of the work gang. Arizun rushed into the laboratorium to report widespread sickness, pains, chills, numbness of extremities, delirium, and terrifying visions striking down the work gang.

Sulun slapped off the drive gear engagement of the lathe and jumped up from his bench. "Yotha!" he spat. "It has to be. Find Eloti and Vari, quick."

"They're already out in the courtyard, unless Vari's back in the storeroom hunting remedies."

"Thank the gods for that, at least," Sulun muttered, running for the courtyard.

The sight that met him was ugly: dozens of men rolling and shivering on the ground, others huddled against the wall, groaning through chattering teeth. Doshi and Yanados were just lighting a scrap-wood fire in the center of the courtyard as Ziya came running with a sloshing kettle of water and a packet of willow bark tea. Omis and Zeren followed, bearing as many blankets, rugs, and wraps as they could find. Vari and Eloti stood near the

283

center of the crowd, peering frantically through a basketful of medical texts.

"Gods," Sulun groaned, seeing the sheer number of the afflicted. "Chills and fever—and the sun is going down." No one needed to tell him that the evenings could be chilly now that First Harvest was past. He snagged Omis on the way to hand out blankets. "Is the forge still lighted?"

"The forge? Yes, I was working on some tool-heads. But why—"

"The heat, man! That open fire won't be enough, nor those blankets for so many. Get the worst afflicted inside, close the shutters and curtains, and pump up the fire in the forge."

"Gods, of course!" Omis dropped the blankets and ran to Zeren to explain.

Sulun descended on Eloti and Vari, yanked out one of their scrolls, and hunted through it, dismayed to learn that he didn't recognize half the terms therein. "Is it a curse or not?" he asked, thumbing through the scroll for some hint of an answer.

"No ill-wish: it's too specific," Eloti snapped back. "It's either plague or poisoning, and we've found no mention of any plague that attacks like this."

"Besides," Vari added, "we've taken good care to keep the work camp clean. Those belly cramps speak strongly of bad food or bad water."

"But we drink of that stream ourselves," Sulun protested, "and none of us fell sick for it."

"Besides," Vari barely smiled, "this lot don't drink water when they've a regular ration of beer."

"Could it be their beer, then? How would Yotha's priests get at it?"

Eloti glanced up, face unreadable. "You think it's those priests' doing, then?"

"Of course it is! Zeren warned me . . ." Sulun ground a fist into his forehead. "Ah, gods, he warned they would strike, and I took no care to think how they might do it. I'm ten times a fool!"

"No, no," Vari soothed, patting his arm. "You're just too honest to think like such rogues. Now, how shall we examine their beer, if indeed they've left any?"

"The barrels." Eloti snapped her fingers and turned to look out the gate. "They keep their rations all in one shed out there, one of the ruins they haven't yet pulled down for building stone.

Even the leavings at the barrel bottoms would contain any poison from the beer. Ask one of the less afflicted where they keep their rations."

"What if it wasn't the beer? The bread, perhaps, or the cheese, or—"

"Bring a dozen goats," said Eloti, already striding toward the work gang chief, who was still in the cramps and shivering stage.

Yes, the gang chief remembered where the stores were kept—in the basement of what must once have been a wine shop, which still possessed a stout door. Yes, all food and drink for the workmen was kept there, and no one was allowed—or able, given how easily he'd be seen—to go plunder the same until proper lunchtime.

Sulun ran for the stables, shouting at Yanados to fetch out half a dozen goats from their shed. A few minutes later the big wagon came rumbling out of the stables, Sulun driving the mules in a manner that discouraged argument; Doshi, Vari, and Arizun riding in the wagon bed behind him.

"Be they abandoning us, think ye?" Gort asked, between rattling teeth.

"And leaving their friends, too?" Hobb shook his head, which made it hurt worse. "No, off upon vengeance or healing, say I."

"We'll see soon enough. Ah, gods, is that fire well lighted? Me for sitting thereabouts, do I have to crawl."

Half an hour later the mule wagon came thundering back, echoing the impact of every paving stone through the near-empty barrels in its bed. There, too, thumped sacks of bread, cheese, sausage, and apples: all the stores of the looted basement.

Sulun reined the mules to a hoof-skidding stop, jumped off the wagon, and ran to the nearest workman, which happened to be Gort. "Man," he asked, looking straight and guiltlessly into the bloodshot eyes, "tell me: what did you eat and drink this noon?"

"B-beer," Gort chattered, "and bread. Sausage. An apple . . ."

"Good, good," Sulun patted his shoulder and went to the next man. "And you?"

"Same," Hobb shivered, "except I had ch-cheese instead of the apples."

"Not cheese, not apples," Sulun muttered, hurrying to the next coherent man he could find. "How shall we make goats eat sausage?"

Hobb turned to his partner and grinned as best he could. "Y-you thought they'd be l-leaving us," he jeered.

"W-was only askin'," Gort muttered, holding shaking hands to the fire.

"Pardon me, pardon me," Omis muttered as he shouldered past them, carrying a struggling, howling derrick hauler in his arms as surely and gently as if it had been one of his own children.

Hobb peered after him through the open front doors of Deese House. "Th-they be layin' 'em down on rugs by the f-forge," he noted. "And the f-fire be blazing'. Fetchin' 'em closer t-to the gods's m-magic, I expect."

"Or just g-gettin' 'em warmer," Gort muttered. "Oh, here, s-sir priest. Could we have one of th-those blankets?"

Sulun ran past, shouting. "Yanados, only two goats! Just the bread and the beer!"

"G-goats?" Hobb asked, clutching the blanket that one of the junior priests hurriedly tossed him. "Bread and b-beer?"

Gort only shook his head and reached for the other half of the blanket.

Vari came running up to the fire with a handful of shrivelled rootlets in one hand. She elbowed her way to the kettle of simmering water and threw the roots into it. "Eloti!" she shouted across the fire. "Nabian root! Nabian root! It opens the veins."

"Good," Eloti called back. "How many cups do we have?"

Yanados dragged two squealing goats to a hitching rail by the south wall and tied them there. The goats promptly started chewing on their tie ropes. She slapped their muzzles and yelled for Sulun to bring the bread and beer to her, since she couldn't leave the goats.

Omis came back out into the courtyard, looked around briefly, and went for another seriously afflicted victim.

Sulun came half-running across the courtyard, a sack of bread loaves in one hand and a sloshing pitcher in the other. He ducked and dodged past groaning and raving bodies, ran to Yanados, set down his burden, and grabbed the nearest goat. "Hold it fast," he said. "How do I get its mouth open?"

Doshi, starting back for more blankets from the pile, halted suddenly with a perfectly horrified look spreading across his face. "Wotheng!" he gasped. "If they struck at our provisions, they might have struck his, too!" He changed course and ran to Sulun.

Near the forge, Zeren tackled and threw down the same raving man for the third time. "Must be a better way," he muttered. Then his eye fell on a coil of rope near the door. He hurried to it, cut a yard's length from the end, thought a bit, and cut more. Trailing odd ends of rope, he went back to his charges and began tying them up. "Shut up," he explained to those who protested. "I'm trying to drive the devils out of you."

Sulun, busy pouring beer dregs down the throat of a most unwilling goat, listened to Doshi's warning without looking up. "Gods," he moaned, "it's all too possible. Take that shaggy brute Wotheng sold us—he's the fastest we have, I think—and ride straightaway to the villa. Warn them about the bread and beer, tell them we don't yet know which it is. Bring help if you can. Ask Gynallea if she knows any remedies for this sort of thing. Oh, hurry! The sun's going down!"

Doshi ran for the stables.

It was two hours after dark, and all of Yotha House was quiet and unlit save for the eternal flame on the temple altar and the high priest's study. Folweel was awake, if not overly busy. The scroll on his lap held only part of his attention; his gaze kept straying to the south window, and the smile that flickered over his face was not pleasant.

The distant sound of the gate bell ringing made him sit up so quickly that the scroll slid off his lap. He picked it up hastily, shoved it on the littered table, stood up, and smoothed down his robes. "Back so soon?" he murmured, waiting for the inevitable knock on the door.

The knock came soon enough, but the figure which entered at Folweel's summons wasn't whom he'd expected.

"Pibb?" he snapped, with no preamble. "What in all the hells are *you* doing here?"

"Beggin' yer pardon, Father." Pibb bowed low, vainly trying to wipe his hands clean on his greasy leggings. "I was in the kitchen nook, gettin' a warm pint to sleep on, when her ladyship came poundin' in, yellin' for Cook. She wanted accountin' of all the bread and beer stores, and when they was brought in, and when used and all, and if anyone took sick from 'em."

"What? Lady Gynallea? Said *what*?" Folweel took two steps

backward. "He couldn't have mistaken—And was anyone in Ashkell House sick?"

"None but old Nusher, and he's had the snuffles and wheezes for days, but her ladyship wanted all the bread and beer looked at anyway. 'Test 'em on the smallest pig,' says she. And then she wants some newmade sausage and a cup of hot cider for his lordship, and quick, says she, because he be ridin' out soon, and—"

"Wotheng, riding out tonight? Here?"

"That took me a bit of askin', Father, but—"

"Where?"

"Ey, ey, to Deese House, Father. They said 'twas either the bread or beer was poisoned there, and all the workmen sick, and they be tryin' to figure who'd done it, and they sent a messenger— one of the under-priests, I think it were, but I couldn't be sure— to warn Ashkell Villa lest it might have come there, too. His lordship was downright furious, he was: roarin' and bellowin' and haulin' his big boots on—"

"Oh, gods." Folweel slumped into the nearest chair. "How did they guess, and so soon?"

"I sneaked away when no one was lookin', guessin' ye'd want to know, and nobody saw me take leave, neither. I got a donkey from stables and came here straightaway, but 'tis my guess his lordship took his fastest horses—"

"Horses? More than one?"

"Oh, aye, Father. He took a handful of men with him, too. They went poundin' and clatterin' off down the west road, and none of 'em saw me go, so I came right here. 'Tis my guess they'll be better than halfway there by now. I wager they'll spend the night out of house. Should I go back, Father, lest I be missed?"

"Oh, yes. Back. Here, and be careful." Folweel absently pulled a silver coin from his belt pouch and handed it to the kitchen boy, who stuffed it happily in his neck bag. "Take a pot of coals to keep you warm on the ride back, and remember to thank Yotha for his kindness."

"Aye, aye, thank ye, Father." The youth scuffed backward to the door, bowing repeatedly, and showed himself out.

"They knew . . ." Folweel muttered to himself, not watching the closing door. "They've told Wotheng, and he's riding there. . . ."

Suddenly another thought occurred to him, and he jumped to

his feet. "Gods!" he shouted, lunging for the bell pull. "Dizzag, get up here!"

Repeated clangings brought a dishevelled under-priest to the door. "You wish, Father?" the man panted, eyes wide in bewilderment.

"Dizzag, take a fast horse and ride toward Deese House by the quickest route. At all cost, avoid Wotheng's party on the westward road! Find Patrobe, he'll be somewhere out in the fields near the walls, north of the road. Tell him *not* to loose the fire, you hear? My orders! Something's happened, and the fire must not be loosed. Bring him back here, bring them all back at once. Now go, and hurry!"

Dizzag bowed quickly, and fled. The door slammed behind him.

Folweel went to the south window and peered into the darkness beyond. "Gods," he groaned, "it may already be too late. As good as a signed confession. Gods, how did they guess so fast?"

He stayed at the window, watching, hope growing slowly as the night remained unbroken and black, wondering how long it would take for Dizzag's message to reach Patrobe and his men. Across fields, through sheep pastures, in the dark—or would Dizzag have the sense to take a shuttered lantern? How long? One hour? Two? He peered toward the distant nubbin on the starwashed horizon that was the hill of Deese House, hoping frantically that Patrobe would, with his usual exquisite care, take his time, enough time. . . .

A pinprick of wavering blue and yellow light winked against the blackness.

Folweel slammed his hand on the windowsill and swore in three languages.

The half dozen riders had settled into a long, loping canter that ate up the miles without overtiring the horses. Wotheng cursed perfunctorily now and again, seeing it was expected of him, but his guardsmen saved their breath. They made good time, and the bouncing light of their lanterns on the road revealed landmarks that promised their goal was scant moments away.

Wotheng, riding in the center and free to look elsewhere than the road before him, noticed it first: a flare of blue-yellow light on a nearby hilltop. He shouted warning to the others, who reined

in so quickly that they narrowly avoided running into each others'
horses. They all turned to look, and froze where they sat.

A broad line of yellow-tipped blue fire snaked down the hill,
across the shallow dip below, and up the next slope. At the crest
it divided, two fire tracks running parallel, then swooping away
from each other, then turning back until they met and merged
again. The single line of flame turned back into the middle of its
previous pattern and weaved back and forth in a complex dance,
for all the world as if it were a reed pen writing a letter.

The guards gasped, swore, mumbled obscure charms and
gestured others. Wotheng cursed, partly at them. He might indeed
have expected Yotha's priests to try spreading panic among his
men. Best stop that, right now.

"Damned wizards!" he bellowed, rising in his stirrups. "What
do you think you're doing, burning up pastureland? Do you kill
any of my tenants' sheep, and I'll have you hanged!"

His men gaped at him in awe and amazement.

Pleased by the reaction, Wotheng swore further and more
colorfully.

"Sir," one of the more levelheaded interrupted him. "He—it's
not moving, and the road's clear. Should we go on?"

"Hell's cesspools, yes! Since we've got such good light, let's
make good time." He spurred his horse forward, obliging his
men to get out of the way or ride with him. They kicked their
horses forward, none willing to be last on the road.

The firelit hill fell behind them; the road snaked through a
shallow valley and began to climb again. At this hill's top they
could see the lights and hear the noise from Deese House.
Wotheng pushed his tiring horse faster, up the rough-cobbled
road and through the open gate in the wall.

He halted in the courtyard and stared, amazed.

A small horde of groaning men huddled under blankets and
rugs around a roughset fire. Robed priests of Deese moved among
them, giving them drink from assorted cups. Beyond the open
temple doors, more men lay lightly bound and wrapped in rugs,
moaning and raving, sweating in the heat from Deese's hard-
blazing forge.

Tethered near the south wall were two goats, one of them
backed away as far as its rope allowed, looking wide-eyed and
frightened. Its companion appeared to have gone stark mad. The

beast was bleating, leaping, stumbling, reeling, and dancing, eyes rolling wildly in its head, flecks of foam on its jaw.

Close by stood Sulun, grimly watching the mad goat dance.

"By Vona's iron balls," Wotheng gasped. "Are you trying to magic the poison off into the goat?"

Sulun laughed, startled, and realized it was the first good laugh he'd had since noon. "No, Lord Wotheng, that's the beast I made eat the bread. The other got the beer, and it's well and sound, as you can see."

"Ah, that's good to know." Wotheng swung out of the saddle and went to tie up his horse as far from the raving goat as the hitching rail allowed. "In such case, draw me some beer and tell me what's transpired."

Sulun led his eminent guest into the house, stepping carefully around the rolling bodies of the worst afflicted, through the first door on the left, and into the common dining room. Wotheng's guards crowded in behind him, and they all settled at the end of the table nearest the neglected fireplace. Sulun did the fetching and serving, and lit up the fire.

"We'll have to drink from the jug, I'm afraid," he said handing over an earthen bottle of better than average ale. "All the cups are in use outside. Did Doshi come back with you?"

"No, his horse was too tired for the return gallop—and so was he." Wotheng snagged the jug as it passed around the table end. "So the bread was poisoned, eh? I think we may guess who caused that. How was it done?"

"We're not sure. Zeren says the bread smells a bit odd, something he encountered once before, but he can't remember just what the poison was—except that it's something that can happen naturally in certain kinds of flour. That's why I wanted Doshi; his folk were farmers, and he might recognize it."

"Well, so might I. Bring me a bit of it."

Sulun went to fetch one of the offending loaves. Wotheng's men looked at him, at each other, and at the jug.

"Sir," one of them ventured, "can you be sure it's poison, as he says? Not magic? We know that was Yotha's fire, back on the hill."

"Trust a wizard to know his own business." Wotheng took a pull of beer, then generously handed it around again. "We'll know soon enough once I've my hands on that bread."

Sulun returned, holding the heel end of a loaf almost at arms length. "If only we knew what it was, we might find a remedy for it," he said, handing the bread to Wotheng. "At present we can do little."

Wotheng broke the bread, studied it, sniffed at it. "Coarse rye bread . . . some smell of mould . . . Hmmm."

He leaned closer to the fire, studying the color of the inner surface, then took an experimental bite. His men gasped and jumped away. Sulun started forward, then saw that Wotheng wasn't chewing. The Lord of Ashkell frowned fiercely and spat the mouthful of bread into the fire.

"Pfaww," he grumbled, wiping his tongue on his sleeve. "That's no more nor less than black rye mould! Uchh, filthy stuff. Kills horses. Aye, your folk have fevers and mad visions, do they? And belly pains? Hands and feet gone cold and numb? That's the black rye mould for you. How did that get in my good mill's bread? I'll have Feggle's hide sliced if he's ground bad flour. . . ."

"The remedy!" Sulun cried. "What's the remedy?"

"Ey, the wife would know better than I. No, let me think. Jall, wasn't it two years gone that my good hunting horse came down with that? Do ye remember what the wife gave it?"

The near-left man pulled his lip, straining his memory. "I think 'twas raw beans, m'lord. Raw beans and . . . heh! Beer!"

"Those we have!" Sulun hopped to his feet and hurried out the door. They could hear him shouting to Eloti and Vari as he ran to the courtyard.

"Unmannerly of 'im," Jall huffed, "running off without a word of leave."

"Perhaps, but a good commander's instinct." Wotheng reached languidly for the almost empty jug. "You'll note, he didn't say a word about Yotha's fire. I wonder if he even saw it, being so busy caring for his men."

It was a small but grim delegation that rode out of the gates of Deese House next morning, for now they rode on the Lord of Ashkell's business, which was to determine the source of the mould-contaminated bread. From the gate itself they could all see the blackened mark burned into the next hilltop, and Wotheng swore blisteringly as he recognized it.

"All the gods assembled, that's the sigil of Vona!" he roared.

"There, the lead letter of his name, within the shape of his sky hammer. How dare those Yotha dogs use it?"

He looked back fiercely to see if anyone was smiling. No one was, but his eye caught something else, something odd.

Up on the wall, sitting on top of that odd device which must be the gossip-famed Storm Tube, was a child of perhaps ten years old. The child (Boy? Girl? No telling, in those clothes) was glaring at the fire-etched mark on the hill and rhythmically patting the brass tube. *Cursing Yotha, doubtless,* Wotheng thought as he rode on down the slope. *But I'd hate to have such an expression turned toward me.*

Behind him in the rumbling mule wagon, Sulun and Eloti were quietly arguing over possible remedies. Eloti was insisting that her collection of scrolls didn't tell enough, both rye and ergot poisoning not being common in the southlands where most medical treatises had been written, and she needed to talk to Gynallea. Sulun complained that this whole expedition might be dangerous, and she was too valuable for them to risk.

"And you're not?" Eloti retorted. "Who do you think our leader is, Sulun? Where would we all be, how would we live, without you?"

Sulun gaped at her, lost for words, ideas, or thought.

In the wagon bed behind him, Zeren chuckled. "Welcome to your new post, Commander," he said, clapping Sulun on the shoulder. "Never expected this, eh?"

Sulun only shook his head.

"Besides," Eloti smiled, "we have Zeren and Lord Wotheng and all his guards to protect us. Where would we be safer—or better needed?"

Sulun gave up the argument and turned his mind elsewhere. "The bread," he muttered. "Trace the whole track of the bread, every step. Who brought it to us? Where was it baked? Whence came the flour, and who carried it? Where it was ground, Wotheng's already told us. Where the grain was grown, he can discover also. Somewhere between the field and the workmen's stores the mould got into it, but the most likely places lie between the mill and the bakery."

"Both of which are owned by our good Lord Wotheng," Zeren added. "Don't think he's pleased with that thought."

"Indeed." Eloti considered. "Gods help those guilty when Wotheng—or his lady—lay hands on them."

What slaughters have we spawned, just being here? Sulun wondered, but did not say aloud.

"No, sirs! Never!" Feggle braced his back against the top millstone as if defending a falsely accused child. "I been top miller here these fifteen years now. Do ye think I don't know my own business? Do ye think I can't see nor smell bad grain? B'gods, m'lord, letting bad grain pass would damage my reputation and more; why, the evil would stick to my stones and poison every load to come through thereafter. Now do ye think I'd let my stones be dirtied so?" He patted the smooth, clean-cut boulder affectionately.

Wotheng and Sulun looked at each other, tacitly admitting the miller's point. Sulun thought a moment and tried another tack.

"Goodman, when was the last time you ground coarse rye flour?"

"Ey, let me think a bit. . . ." Feggle rubbed his heavy chin, then went to a shelf on the nearby wall and pulled down a cord strung with tally sticks. "So, so . . . This be the last month's tally, every rod a day. This notch be one bag of barley, and that mark on t'other side be Dawp's mark—see? Now further down . . . here's four notches for wheat, with Cackle's mark." He ran expert fingers over the differing notches.

"Amazing," Sulun remarked, studying the tally sticks. "If ever you'd like to come to the new school and learn to put such marks on parchment . . ."

"Nay, I've no time for such, and these tallies suit me well enough. I'll send my boy, though." Feggle stroked rapidly through the rods, not even looking at them. Abruptly, his fingers halted. "There, m'lord." He shoved the stick forward, displaying the notches and mark. "There're five sacks of rye, and from Pibben's farm. They were the last of rye I've done. Pibben 'twas, but I know his grain's good; his grain's always been good, and I'd surely've noticed if 'twasn't."

"Pibben . . ." Wotheng's eyes narrowed in thought as he studied the tally stick. "Tell me, did he bring the grain himself or have it sent?"

"Why, he brought it himself, m'lord. He always does that."

"But did he take it away himself?" Sulun asked. "Did he wait here while you ground it and carry it off afterward?"

"Gods, no!" Feggle laughed, waving his thick hands. "Grinding takes a bit of time, it does, and there be so many wants grinding after first harvest, how should I do it all at once? No, m'lords, they bring it and leave it in the store-barn here, with their marks on the sacks, and I grinds it when I can. I barrels it after—or bags, if it be small enough—and puts it in t'other store-barn, and then the farmers come fetch it and pay me and take it home, or more likely they go straightaway to Tygg and sell t'him, and he sends his man to fetch it and pay me for the grinding."

"Tygg?" Sulun asked.

"Our baker," said Wotheng. "Would you remember, Feggle, if Pibben came and fetched his own rye or if Tygg's man came for it?"

Feggle ran his thumb over the tally stick again. "All this shows—see yonder cut in the middle?—'tis that the grinding was paid. But I know well enough Pibben sold it; his wife's a wonder at spinning and weaving, but she doesn't bake at all, no sir. He sold yonder rye to Tygg, be sure."

"I'll send a man to Pibben's just to *be* sure," Wotheng promised. "Now would your pretty stick tell us just when the rye was bought and carried away?"

Feggle shook his heavy jowls. "Nay, only when 'twas brought in, but I'll swear, m'lord, I don't keep grain overlong, lest it spoil. Yonder rye flour would've been ground within two days, no more, and gone no less'n a day later." He counted the sticks on the sting, then counted further on his fingers. "It would've gone to Tygg's no more nor three days ago, and no less than two."

Wotheng and Sulun exchanged another look.

"Back to the villa, then, and to Tygg's," said Wotheng. "Let's see if his tallying is as good."

"And we'll pick up Eloti," Sulun added. "I'll guess she's learned much from Gynallea's medicine texts."

" . . . these herbals to open the veins, the beer to flush the poisons out, and the raw bean mash to counter the effects of the poison." Gynallea wrapped up the bundle of packets and handed it to Eloti. "How are the workmen doing?"

"When we left they were resting quietly. What simples we had did them some good." Eloti hefted the bundle, face abstracted. "This won't be the end of it, I suspect."

"No," Gynallea sighed. "You will have to settle with High Priest Folweel, in some permanent fashion, and that soon. Have you any plans?"

"Several, none of them sure." Eloti took a small polished disc of obsidian from her belt pouch and weighed it thoughtfully in her hand. "In any case, we must get into Yotha House and confront that man."

"Daughter, even my Wotheng must walk soft there! Be utterly careful of words with the high priest."

"It's not words I have in mind, dearest Gynna."

"A wizard's duel, then? At the very center of Yotha's power? Is that wise?"

"Not a duel, not there," Eloti admitted, sliding the disc back into her pouch. "We are, as you've doubtless guessed, not precisely nor entirely wizards."

"Ah, some help from your mechanical knowledge will be needed, then?" Gynallea smiled knowingly. "Choose your ground with care, my dear. Have many alternative tactics in waiting, and let everyone know their part well."

"That, unfortunately, is the problem. Sulun wants no such battle; he'll not attack."

Gynallea pursed her lip. "Commendable, but . . . difficult. Plan elaborate defenses, then. And . . . try to shape, in advance, the attack your enemy will make."

Eloti grinned humorlessly. "That," she said, "is the difficult part."

Tygg the Baker looked and spoke much like his counterpart at the mill. "Of course I inspected the flour, m'lord!" he huffed, absently patting his nearest oven. "I always inspect it myself when it arrives, if not before I buy. Great gods assembled, d'ye think I'd pay good silver for bad flour?"

"You inspected Pibben's rye, then, at the mill?" Wotheng asked. "When was that?"

"Nay, not at the mill," Tygg admitted, clenching his broad fists in his coarse bleached apron. "I've bought from Pibben these many years, and never had complaint. I looked at the barrelful when it came here, and 'twas good then, as always 'tis."

He ambled down the crowded bakery hall to a side room, which he opened with a heavy iron key. Within lay shelves of stacked tablets, a writing table and chair, and a large money chest bolted to the floor. He poked through the tablets, pulled one out, and shoved it in front of the questioners. "There, yon's the mark for Pibben, and this for rye, and this for the amount. If 'twere bad, I'd have marked it other."

Sulun, hoping to find a literate accounting, was disappointed to see more tally marks cut in the wax. "Do you recall," he asked, "when the flour arrived? Or when it was baked? Or where you sold it?"

"Oh, aye." The baker pointed his thick finger at further marks on the tablet. "See here: that means it came two days agone. I couldn't say when 'twas baked or sold, but it must've been right soon after. I—I bought it to bake for your work gang, m'lord wizard. . . ." Tygg wilted a little. "They like the rye bread, they do, and the price is . . . well, quite fair, sir."

"Buy cheap and sell dear, I know." Wotheng grinned, making his moustache bristle. "I've no complaint with honest profit."

"Nor I," said Sulun, seeing where this led. In truth, grain prices here were astonishingly low compared to what he remembered in Sabis. "I only ask, did you send any other bread to my work gang these four or five days past?"

"Oh, no, m'lord wizard." Tygg waved his big hands in denial. "I bake and send to them but once a seven-night. My wagon man'd be too busy else for my other work. I send all around the vale, y'know, m'lord."

"So this was the load that was . . . tainted, and no other?" Eloti asked, stepping forward.

"M'lady, I'll swear on a dozen gods the flour was good!" Tygg wailed, almost tiptoeing a step back from her. "I looked when I bought it, and 'twas clean!"

"And how long between the time you bought it, and inspected it, and when you baked it?" Sulun asked, looking for the sequence, the timing.

"No more nor a day, I'll swear." Tygg rubbed his sweating forehead, then automatically wiped his hand on his apron. "I bought the flour 'specially because 'twas time to bake for the work gang again. One can't be late with food for that lot, y'know."

"I know." Eloti smiled, considering the uproar a gang of hungry workmen would make if their bread didn't arrive. "You bake for them once a seven-night, then, and send it out how soon after?"

"Wh-why, soon's 'tis out of the oven. It must go soon, d'ye see, for it's got to last seven days, and for all that rye bread stales but slow, in seven days 'twill be a bit stiff, so the sooner 'tis delivered, the better." The baker shrugged eloquently.

"Sir Baker," Eloti purred, well knowing the answer, "is there any means by which the ergot could have entered the bread after it was baked?"

Tygg struggled mightily with his fear and conscience, finally had to admit, "Nay, couldna," in a defeated voice. "If it struck then, 'twould only dot the crust with black spots, easily seen and cut off."

"So the ergot entered the flour sometime between the hour when you inspected it and when you baked it?"

"Aye," Tygg almost whispered, "while 'twas here, in my storeroom . . ." Then he brightened, seeing a possibility. " 'Twas there almost a day. Anyone could have come in and traded it for bad flour while I wasn't looking."

"But wouldn't you have noticed the change when you went to bake it?" Wotheng cut in. "Surely you'd have seen, or smelled, if something were wrong when you went to measure it out."

"But—but—" Tygg bounced on his wide feet in agitation. "I confess, I didn't bake that load! I've so much to bake, y'know, m'lord, I can't do all at once. 'Twas only common rye bread, if all be told, and I'd the more dainty breads an cakes to do, as I can't trust to 'prentices, y'know." He waved a dusty hand toward the bake shop, where easily half a dozen assistants were measuring flour, rolling dough, and tending the ovens. "I left the rye bread baking to . . . gods, who was it? Ey, 'twere Meep and Higgle!" he stomped to the door and bellowed, "Meep! Higgle! Get your lumbering feet in here, and be quick!"

A fat boy and a stout woman jumped as if they'd been stabbed, pulled their hands out of huge basins of flour, and came hurrying in.

"Aye, Master, what's the matter?" the woman asked, shifting from foot to foot as if her arches pained her.

"I'm hurrying with the barley bread," the boy whined. "Gods' truth, I'm hurrying, Master Tygg, it's just that—"

"Never mind you that," Tygg snapped. "Which of you baked the rye bread that went out yesterday morn?"

The two baker's assistants looked at each other, Meep woeful, Higgle smirking. " 'Twere *he* done it." Higgle pointed triumphantly to the cringing fat youth. "I lost the toss, so's *I* had to haul the wood and light it off and sweep out the oven and tend the fire and such—while *he* made the bread."

"Aw, Master," Meep whined. "I ain't never made rye bread before. The loaves looked right when they came out t'oven, crusts dark like *she* said. How's I t'know they weren't right?"

Tygg heaved a mountainous sigh—of relief? Exasperation? "And what was wrong with them?" he asked.

Meep's jaw dropped, flapped a bit, quivered. "I—I don't know, Master. Did I make the dough too heavy? Not baked long enough? Ye *said* t'leave 'em a bit moist, as they was t'last awhile. . . ."

Tygg was trying to say something, probably explosive, but Eloti touched his arm and he jigged away in silence. "Listen, boy," she crooned hypnotically at the young lout, "you know who we are, do you not?"

"Y-yes, m'lady. Ye're one of the new wizards as serve Deese." His plump cheeks quivered as he tried to edge away, but Eloti caught his face neatly between her hands.

"Think, boy," she murmured, fixing his eyes with her own. "Remember well, from the beginning. When did you come to work that day?"

"T-two hours afore dawn, like always," Meep whimpered, staring.

"Where you first in the shop?"

"I came in . . . after Higgle. She'd the key."

"And what next?"

"She said t'make the rye bread, and I said—"

"Never mind what was said. What did you *do*?"

"I—we argued, and then we tossed a copper, and she lost . . . so she went t'get the firewood and I went t'get the rye flour, and—"

"How did you know which was the rye flour?"

" 'Twas in the barrel Master Tygg showed me the day afore, the one with the half-moon scratched in the wax."

Eloti shot a quick glance at Sulun, who nodded. "You went to get the flour," she said. "So you opened the barrel?"

"Nay, m'lady. 'Twas already open."

"You mean, the lid was loosened or the lid was off?"

" 'Twas off. I thought Higgle'd been there first. I took up the scoop and filled the big measure—"

"I'll fetch't," said Tygg, hurrying off.

"And did you notice anything different about the flour?" Eloti went on.

"N-no m'lady. How would I? I'd never made the rye bread afore." Meep wrung his hands in unconscious imitation of his master.

"So you took up the measure full of flour. What did you then?"

"I brought it back t' the shop room and poured it into yonder big mixin' pot, and put in the sweetenin' and the leavenin' and then the butter and eggs, and last the milk, and then I stirred it with the big paddle, and then I let it sit and rise."

Tygg came back in, holding a measure cup the size of a half barrel. "This be the big measure, m'lady," he said, then halted as he saw the odd interrogation wasn't finished.

"And what did you do while the bread rose?" Eloti asked.

"Ate some buns. They were left over from the day afore, would've gone t'waste, else . . ."

"*And* crackin' jokes at me, while I warmed up th' oven," Higgle added.

"And then what did you?" Eloti bored on.

"W-went back t'see how it'd risen, and it had."

"And did you notice, then, anything strange about the dough? Did it look right? Smell right? What?"

"Nay, it looked right enough—risen right well, good and high. It smelled sour, but rye bread always does, far as I know."

"So what did you next?"

"I patted it in loaves."

"You didn't punch it down and leave it to rise again?" Tygg fumed. "Ye lazy lout, I should clout yer head!"

"Hush," Sulun restrained him. "Let's hear the rest, first."

"And what then?" Eloti insisted.

"I put the loaves in the oven, and bade Higgle watch 'em."

"That he did," Higgle volunteered. "Left me t'watch, and went off t'stuff his face on more sugar buns."

"And were you alone in the shop all this time?" Eloti asked.

"Oh nay, m'lady. Swarp and Dirrot and Buj and Master Tygg came in a bit after us, and they was workin'."

"Aye," Tygg muttered. "I should've seen him nippin' the leftover buns. . . ."

"But did anyone go to the storeroom before you?" Eloti insisted.

"Nay, we was first there, afore the others came in."

"That's true," Higgle agreed. "We come earliest."

"Then what became of the dough left in the big mixing pot?" Eloti asked.

Meep looked blank. "I don't *know*, m'lady," he blubbered.

"I cleaned that out." Higgle wrinkled her nose. " 'Tis the job for whoever's tending the fire. I lost the toss, as we said."

Where did you wash it?" Eloti asked, releasing Meep and turning to Higgle. "And what did you do with the washings?"

"I washed it in the backyard," said Higgle, righteously holding her ground. "I threw the washings in the slops bucket, for t'take t'Mistress Tygg's pig, after."

"Ay, gods!" Tygg slapped a hand to his forehead. "So *that's* what ailed the pig yester'en!"

"You didn't eat any of the dough yourself?" Eloti insisted.

"Nay, m'lady," said Higgle, wrinkling her nose again. "Why eat sour old dough, when I could have leftover cakes later?" Abruptly she blushed, and looked sidelong at Tygg, who rolled his eyes heavenward and muttered about greedy apprentices eating up his profits.

"So," said Eloti, turning back to Tygg. "Meep says he used one large measure of rye flour. If that's the measure, there must still be more flour left in the barrel. May we see it, please?"

Without a word, Tygg led them to the storeroom at the other end of the bakeshop. The room was stone, windowless, with only one other door that led—as Sulun confirmed with a swift look—out to the back alley where the wagons were unloaded. The doors were stout, tight, and well barred. There was no sign of rats, though a plump cat patrolled there, and the floor was quite acceptably clean.

Tygg pointed to a barrel in the near right corner, one marked with a simple half-moon cut into a splash of wax. "That be the one," he said, keeping his distance.

Sulun and Eloti approached the barrel cautiously, as if it might bite. Wotheng stayed back by the door, watching both of them and the baker. Eloti lifted off the barrel lid and peered in.

"Is it customary," she asked, "for your rye flour to be so grey in color?"

Tygg jumped as if stung, and ran to the barrel. "No, by all the gods," he said, staring into its half-filled depths. " 'Tis supposed t'be faintest hint of brown, no more." He reached in, pulled up a pinch of the flour, spread it on his palm, and looked closely. "I'd be sure in better light," he whispered, "but I think I see fine flecks of black in this. He sniffed cautiously at the thin spread of flour. "It doesn't smell bad, though."

"Let us test further." Eloti scooped out a handful of the flour and walked back toward the shop room. "Please fetch me a small bowl and a bit of sweetening and milk."

Tygg practically fell over his feet, running to comply with her wishes.

It took but a moment to mix the ingredients in the right proportions. Tygg asked if she wanted oil, leavening, and eggs too, but Eloti assured him it wasn't necessary.

"If this is indeed the mould I think it is," she explained, pouring out the mixture on a small plate, "then water and food is all it needs. Now let us put this in a warm place for . . . how long does it usually take for rye bread to rise, Master Tygg? Half an hour? Good. Let us take our ease for so long."

Tygg obligingly brought bench seats, cups of his own beer, and a dish of his best sweet rolls, and did his best not to look at the suspect mixture in the bowl near the oven. His staff worked furiously at their business, not daring to look lest Tygg's eye and wrath fall on them.

Wotheng drank his beer in leisurely fashion, wiped off his moustache, and calmly asked. "Goodman, who was present in your shop between the time you first opened the barrel of flour and the time it was baked?"

Tygg paused, half-turned to watch his underbakers, his eyes unfocused with the effort of memory. "Hmm, ah, everyone here, of course—all my help. Also the wagoner who brought it. Many of the villa folk came in and out to buy . . . Ah, gods, I can't remember how many came and went!"

Eloti gave Wotheng a brief nod of respect, then asked. "How many of your customers came into this room, let alone the storeroom?"

"Ey, why, none." Tygg looked relieved for a moment, then sobered as he guessed the implications. "I swear, I'd never believe any of my lot would poison their own bread!"

"I find that hard to believe, also," said Sulun. "How many of them went into the storeroom that day?"

"Gods, I can't recall!" Tygg rubbed his sweating jowls in distress. "All of them, I don't doubt, for I had them all at work mixing and baking. I do try, m'lord, t' make 'em knowledgeable at all stages of baking."

"But then . . ." Wotheng sat up, moustache bristling. "None of them could be sure that another 'prentice wouldn't walk in on them while they were putting the mould in the four. Most risky work, that."

"Oh, aye!" Tygg grinned from ear to ear, seeing hope that his household was no longer suspect. "They were runnin' in and out all the day, save for lunchtime . . ." A beatific smile spread across his sweating face. "I recall, m'lord, the barrels came from the mill just afore lunch. I tapped and 'spected 'em, paid the wagoner, and then all o' we sat down to eat together. They were all there, m'lord; none left the table afore I did. Not one of 'em got to be long alone in the storeroom: not one, sir!"

The other three exchanged glances. "How long," Eloti inquired, "would it take to empty . . ." She thought a moment, trying to remember the ratio of dark flecks to pale flour in the barrel " . . . say, a pint of mould into the flour, and stir it well enough that it wouldn't be noticed when measured out?"

The baker stopped and thought about that. He closed his eyes, measured invisible volumes with his hands, made pouring and stirring motions, then sighed. "To pour, almost no time. To stir so well . . . a good minute or two. Not long, I grant. Still, at any moment others might have come in and see the miscreant at work." He gasped suddenly. "But wait! M'lord, m'lady, think: how would he stir the flour well, save with his hands and by reaching well into the barrel? How should he do that without daubing his arms clean up to the shoulder with flour? I'd have noticed anyone floured so far up the arms! By the gods, m'lord, I would; y'know I pride myself upon having my bake shop so clean."

"Good wit, Tygg," Wotheng approved. "Just to be sure, I would like to ask each of your lot—separately and quietly, you understand—if they noted anyone come out of the storeroom with flour up to the shoulders."

"Do so, m'lord." Tygg grinned. "Yet I think if any had seen such, they'd have told me. As ye've heard and seen, my 'prentices do rival with each other a bit—aye, and carry tales, too, hopin' for an inch more of favor."

"And sweet buns." Wotheng smiled with him. "I'll ask, anyway, but I do believe you're correct, Master Baker."

"Unless, of course," Eloti interjected, "the miscreant stirred the flour with a paddle or stick."

"Paddle? Stick?" Tygg glowered. "Not in my storeroom. I keep the paddles out here where they be needed, near every moment. Anyone seen goin' into the stores with such would surely be noted, and 'marked upon. Besides, where would the poisoner have carried a pint measure of black mould, goin' into the stores, and it not be noted?"

"The mould might have been hidden in a bag under the clothes," Sulun considered, "but you're right about the stirring. Where could anyone have hidden even a stick that was long and stout enough to quickly mix a pint of mould into a barrel of flour?"

Wotheng frowned and rattled his fingertips on his knees, and Sulun could guess the man's thought. Either the faithful old baker was lying, which seemed very unlikely, or the poisonous mould had somehow magicked itself into the barrel. *Reconstruct the sequence*, was all he could think of.

"Try hard to remember, good Tygg," he said. "When was the first moment you saw the barrel?"

"Ey? Why, when it came off Bassip's wagon, Sir Wizard."

"What, he brought it to your door himself?" Sulun couldn't imagine any one man shifting that huge barrel alone.

"Ah, I see what ye mean. Nay, sir, I first clapped eyes on it when 'twas *on* the wagon, when the carter came knockin' at the door. I helped him roll it into stores myself. Oh, and I'll take oath, the lid was on it firm and tight then, and sealed with good wax, as Feggle always does it."

"And then you opened the lid?" Wotheng took up the thread.

"Aye sir, right then: opened and looked, and found it clean, on my oath."

"And did you pay the wagoner right then?" Eloti asked, eyes narrowing. "Had you the money in hand when you brought the barrel in?"

"Eye, not so. I went to my officium to fetch it. Then I came back and paid him and he left, and I called my lot off to lunch, and there's an end to it, for surely no one could have come into

stores while I were out fetchin' the money without the wagoner
would have seen 'em."

"True, true," murmured Eloti. "And are you certain you closed
and barred the storeroom's outer door after the wagoner left,
before you went to eat?"

"Aye, for certain, good lady. Don't I know well enough that
rats and thieves get in when doors swing open?"

"Hmm. So after lunch everyone went back to work and the
apprentices came in and out, and at day's end you locked up fast,
I trust?"

"Oh, aye, be certain."

"And you're also certain no one could have come in again before
Meep and Higgle yesterday morning?"

Again the baker struggled with his conscience, and again his
conscience won. "Aye, m'lady. No door nor window forced,
nothing touched. Nor none other thing. Look you all." He pointed
to the doorsill, which had been recently swept clean. " 'Tis an old
baker's trick I had of my father. Every night afore leavin', I sprinkle
a bit of flour about the doors and under the windows. Every
morning I sweeps it up to keep the rats away. If any thief, nay nor
anyone, came in durin' the night, by whatever means, they'd've
left tracks in the flour and on the floor beyond. No way to hide it,
save by sweepin' up all the flour. Either way, I'd have noted *that*
when I came in by morning."

"Marvelous!" Sulun admitted. "I must teach that trick to my
people."

"Aye, would ye that?" Tygg beamed, flattered.

"So, to go on," Eloti murmured. "Meep and Higgle came in,
Meep made the rye bread while Higgle tended the fire, then the
loaves were packed and sent off by your wagoner. And no one
else touched the dough?"

"As ye've heard." Tygg shrugged. "I swear, I cannot understand
it."

"Yet someone did despoil the flour, as you can see." Eloti
pointed to the warm bowl of rough dough.

They looked. They could all see that it had risen slightly, by
itself, with no yeast added.

Tygg grabbed the offending bowl with a curse, and threw it
into the fire. " 'Twas magicked there, good folk," he pleaded, "I'll
swear, it had to be!"

"Fear nothing." Eloti smiled gently, patting his thick arm. "I'm sure it wasn't you nor any of your people who tainted the flour."

"Deese and Kula know it," said the baker, fervently clasping his hands.

On the way back to their mule wagon, Sulun chewed the problem over. "I swear," he admitted, "I don't know where to search next. If Feggle and Tygg are honest, and—" He threw a quick look to Wotheng. "—I'm quite sure they are, then the poisoning happened in Tygg's shop, yet no one there could have done it."

"I should go back and question the kitchen drudges singly," Wotheng remembered, stopping where he was.

"Not necessary," said Eloti. "None of them did it."

"Eh?" Wotheng gaped at her. "How do you know?"

"Consider." Eloti ticked off on her fingers. "The flour arrived just before lunch. The kitchen help wouldn't have gone to fetch more flour, do more measuring, mixing, or kneading, just before lunch; no, they'd have been finishing their tasks, not starting new ones. Any of them doing otherwise would have been noticed, and reported to Tygg, by his rivalrous fellows. So would anyone, after lunch, who took a stick or paddle into the storeroom—or who came out of it with flour high up on his arms. No one broke into the bakery during the night, or Tygg would have seen it in his flour-trap on the floor. Meep and Higgle tossed a coin to see who would bake and who fire the oven, so there was no predicting in advance which of them would go to the stores and get to the rye flour. They might have conspired together to taint the flour, but I doubt it, from the lack of love between them. By the time the other apprentices came in, it was too late; the flour was already mixed to dough, if not in the oven."

"But if none of the apprentices—" Wotheng huffed. "I can't believe Tygg would—"

"Surely not Tygg. But who was the one person left alone with the open barrel of flour while Tygg went to the officium to count and fetch the money?"

Wotheng had the presence of mind to whisper it. "Bassip the Wagoner!"

"If, as Tygg says, he also delivered the bread, then I've seen him coming and going at Deese House." Eloti sniffed grimly.

"He could easily hide a pint measure bag under his cloak, and he would know where the rye bread was bound."

"But," Sulun remembered, "how would he stir it in? Tygg would have noticed flour on the man's arms."

"He drives an oxcart, remember? And he always carries with him his *long-handled* driver's whip."

Zeren was no longer guarding the mule wagon when the others came up, but that wasn't necessary. Half of Wotheng's guards were watching, a few copying the motions, as he showed them one of his favorite moves.

" . . . so you drop low—low as you can—as you step forward, getting under his shield. Lift your own shield, so, to block any downward chop and also to block his sight of what you're doing. Then come *up* with the sword at the exposed body. Up, you see? If the other fellow doesn't counter early, there's almost no defense against it; I've rarely seen it fail."

Wotheng raised his bushy eyebrows and turned to the companions. "How very many skills your folk have. Think you yonder large priest might be persuaded to come give his lessons more regularly?"

"I'm sure of it," Sulun agreed. "But at the moment, what shall we do about our poisoner?"

"We'll lay hands on him shortly, that I assure you." Wotheng's smile didn't reach his eyes, which were as chill as Sulun had ever seen them. "The wife doesn't bake either, having much else to do. We've our bread delivered at about this hour every morning. Ho, fellow!" he called to the nearest guard, interrupting the sword lesson. "Has Bassip the Wagoner came yet with the bread?"

"Why, yessir," gawped the nearer guard. "Has yer lordship been learning magecraft, then? Bassip's only just come his round, bein' at the tailor's shop last, and I think he be at the kitchen right now."

"Come along, then," said Wotheng between his teeth. "I've much to say to that man, and I intend he shouldn't wiggle away before I've said it."

"Er, Lord Wotheng," Sulun put in, looking pale. "If you intend to put the man to—to torture, I beg our leave to retire."

"Pshaw, not now." Wotheng almost laughed. "Torture's no good for wrangling the truth from any man, I learned well enough from my father. Cause pain enough, and the pained will say whatever he thinks the questioner wants to hear. No, 'tis clever questions—and p'raps a well-timed lie or two—will get the story. But that's a tedious business, and no sense to trouble you with it. Pray, go dine with my wife while I front this wagoner. I'll speak to you soon enough."

He strolled off, whistling between his teeth, with his guardsmen shambling after. Sulun, Eloti, and Zeren looked at each other.

"Doshi's inside," Zeren told them. "He and his horse are rested well enough, he can ride whenever we want. Where do we go next?"

"To lunch, as our host said." Sulun shrugged. "I think the investigation is out of our hands now, and if we've had little rest, we may as well have food."

"Besides," Eloti added, half to herself, "I've much to discuss with Gynallea—such as what, precisely, we must do about these pesky Yotha priests."

Wotheng laid his plans with some care, pausing to make a few quiet arrangements before strolling into the back of the kitchen where Bassip the Wagoner lounged against the doorpost and chatted with the cook.

"Ah, the good wagoner!" Wotheng chirped, coming up on the burly ox driver as if by accident. "What luck! Pray lend me your whip a moment."

He snatched that item out of the startled wagoner's belt and carried it back into the kitchen, whistling merrily as he uncoiled the whip's tail from its usual resting place about the handle. Bassip, both curious just what Wotheng intended and unwilling to let his primary tool get out of his sight, trotted after his lord into the kitchen. Behind him, two guardsmen quietly eased through the kitchen door, closed and barred it after themselves, and followed.

Wotheng went to a long wooden table, pulled a heavy cleaving knife off a rack above it, and—before Bassip's horrified eyes—chopped the body of the whip cleanly off the handle.

"Ah, don't fret so," Wotheng soothed the man's wailing outrage. "I'll give you a far better one soon enough." He reached for a plate that lay nearby, set the chopped whip handle upright on it, and began unbraiding the leather straps that bound the handle's core. "I confess, I've always yearned to know what lies under all this leather. Is it bone, horn, or wood? Aha, 'tis whittled bone. From an ox's thigh, perhaps? Ah, and what's this pale stuff?"

Patches and streaks of off-white powder appeared on the unbraided leather and the bone beneath, lying in little pockets where the straps had overlapped and a quick wiping hadn't reached them.

Still whistling tunelessly, Wotheng took a small paring knife and began scraping the whitish powder off the leather and bone, into the dish.

Bassip chewed his lip, mumbled something about seeing if his oxen had enough water, and began to back away.

The guards standing silently behind him clamped restraining hands on his arms.

Wotheng scraped all the available powder into the dish, cast the remains of the ruined whip aside, took a few drops of water from a nearby kettle on the tip of his knife, and mixed the thin powder and water into a flat dough.

"This odd powder on your whip stock interests me." He smiled at the now trembling Bassip. "How came it there, eh? And what is it? I daresay, I've a way to learn. Ey, cook, pray fetch me a squab from the dovecote."

The cook scurried off. Wotheng continued to roll the thimbleful of dough about the plate until it dried and compacted into small pills. The cook came back with a young pigeon hooting mournfully in a tiny cage, set it on the table, bowed quickly, and withdrew to watch.

"I've always had a fancy for stuffed squab," Wotheng commented as he seized the bird handily by the neck, pried its beak open, and began shoving the pills of dough down its throat. "But how does the bird care for the stuffing, I wonder? These creatures are greedy enough for wholesome bread, I've seen. Let us see how this fellow enjoys his, hah, 'drover's meal.'"

Bassip's knees quivered and almost dropped him to the floor. The guards obligingly held him up.

Wotheng finished feeding the bird the last of the dough, tossed the dish in a wash basin, sat down at the bench, and called for a cup of beer, which the cook hurried to fetch. The guards said nothing, only watched impassively. Bassip, sweating now as if he stood next to a furnace, couldn't seem to pull his eyes away from the bird.

"Have you ever noticed," Wotheng remarked cheerily around his beer, "that the smaller a creature may be, the faster it seems to live? Butterflies live but a season. Yet what they lack in time they appear to replace in speed. A bird, for example, eats and sleeps and sings and plays enough in a day that, were he a man, would satisfy for a seven-night. His food seems to pass through him, depositing its virtue, in scant moments. A bite of oilcake at dawn shows its sheen on his feathers by breakfast time. I'll wager this little fellow will show the good of his bread crumb feeding here within the half hour, if not sooner."

Bassip just once tried to pull away from the guards and run. Their grip loosened not a hair's width.

"Oh come, fellow, let's have no impatience," Wotheng purred. "Your oxen, being large and slow-living beasts, will surely wait. Pray, humor me? I've a fancy to learn just how much flour goes out the baker's door on the clothes and tackle of the baker's wagoner—even unto the handle of his whip. Now, by the gods, what ails that bird?"

The young pigeon was showing definite signs of distress, flapping its clipped wings, tossing its head over it back, squawking in short and high-pitched bursts.

"Why, I'd swear from looking," Wotheng commented, "that the poor creature was ill. Yet it was quite well before it ate that flour, wouldn't you say?"

Bassip moaned and sagged in his captors' grip. The squab fell on its side, kicking, as if in sympathy.

Wotheng set down his cup, stretched, and got to his feet. "Well, Bassip," he said. "Who paid you to mix the black mould into Tygg's rye flour?"

High Priest Folweel sat calm and composed before his guests, as if he received the Lord of Ashkell and a delegation of alien priests every day. Not a hair of his long beard was out of place, not a fold of his gold-embroidered red robe was wrinkled, not a single be-ringed finger trembled. Sulun stared, fascinated, at the enemy he'd never before met. However the man's thoughts inclined, he was neither foolish nor easily frightened. A learned intelligence operated behind those opaque black eyes, and a formidable will.

And the house was a well-staffed fortress, and they sat at its very heart.

"Not the least intriguing event in this case," Wotheng was saying, as calmly undisturbed as his host, "was the appearance of the Yotha fire on the hill facing Deese House. I noted, as I rode past it, that it formed the shape of the sigil of Vona." His voice hardened. "My family's patron god."

Wotheng paused a moment to let that sink in. Folweel raised an eyebrow, but said nothing.

"I wish to know," Wotheng continued tightly, "why you priests burned Vona's sigil into the turf on my land."

"Excuse me, Lord Wotheng," Folweel purred. "It was Yotha who—"

"Bull's piss! I saw it myself!" Wotheng smacked an impatient hand on the littered table. "Don't call me ignorant, Sir Priest; that fire was fueled with nothing but distilled spirits of wine. My good wife can make it in her still-room, and I've seen it before. 'Twas you priests who set and lit that fire, sir—on my land and in the sigil of my family's god—and I wish to know why."

Folweel barely blinked at the revelation. He only smiled, shrugged, and spread apologetic hands. "Ah, I see you understand our little secret. Yes, the knowledge of fire elixir is a, hmm, trade secret among the priests of Yotha, most commonly used to feed the god's altar fire—and sometimes to send messages."

"Messages! What manner of missive was *that*, pray tell?"

"Understand, m'lord." Folweel was not to be hurried. Neither, in this dark castle, was he intimidated. "Our priesthood is to perceive and interpret the will of the god. Thought, alas, is not readily visible to the common folk; therefore we use the little trick of the fire to make visible the god's word to men. One might say, we provide the ink for the quill of the god's writing."

"I do not appreciate script which scorches my grazing land, sir. Had you a message for me, a simple letter would have done."

"This is well known, sir, but last night's message was not for you."

"Oh? For whom, then?" Wotheng asked, guessing well what the answer was.

"Why, for the rest of our guests, here." Folweel nodded politely toward Sulun's huddled quartet. "Having no other contact with the House of Deese, and no time to create any, we sent the message by the swiftest and most visible means. My regrets concerning the brief stretch of grass that was scorched, but the missive was urgent and could not wait."

"What message?" Sulun asked. *As if I couldn't guess.*

"Why, simply this." Folweel spread his hands again. " 'Tis written in ancient tomes that the Sukkti wizards were often . . . careless . . . with their art—"

"Careless!" Zeren snorted. Sulun restrained him with a quick touch on the arm.

"In this case," Folweel said, flicking an eye toward Eloti, then away, "you folk have been most profligate with your knowledge. You have given out spells, and knowledge thereof, to any who asked—taking little care for these folks' magical ability or moral condition. Who knows to what ill uses such unfettered knowledge might be put? We received from the god the message that the Lord of Storms was displeased by such carelessness—most particularly your, hmm, stealing his thunder, as it were, in your new magical device—and that his displeasure might soon be made manifest. That is the warning we tried to send."

Folweel bowed politely, and waited.

The reaction was not long in coming. " 'Stealing thunder?' " Sulun yelped.

"The spells we've sold are damned harmless, even beneficial!" Zeren growled.

"Do you claim my folk are unfit to learn common figures and letters, sir?" barked Wotheng. Eloti said nothing, only rubbed her shoe thoughtfully at the edge of the nearest carpet.

"Peace, peace," the high priest intoned, raising his hand as if in blessing. "I but report what the god revealed. Surely you know that Yotha has some divine agreement with Vona; elsewise, why do so many fires start from lightning strikes, despite the presence of rain?"

"Clever," Zeren snorted.

"We received the god's warning that Vona was displeased with the carelessness of Deese House, and we sent on the warning as clearly as we could. Had we but sent a letter by common messenger . . ." Folweel paused to smile blandly at each of Sulun's people in turn, "would you have believed it?"

"No," Doshi admitted, then plucked up his courage to add, "for that matter, why should we believe it now?"

"Why, then, that is your privilege." The high priest rolled his eyes heavenward. "We but reveal the word of the god. Men, in their willfulness, may refuse to believe, but we have done our part."

"At the expense of my grazing land," growled Wotheng.

"A narrow strip, no wider than your hand, easily regrown: hardly damage worth complaint, Lord Wotheng."

"And the fires that danced along the hills, when first you folk came here?" Wotheng's eyes narrowed. "You claimed you were following the god's trail."

"And so we were." Folweel remained bland as ever. "The god did point out his track to us, and where he wished his temple built. We lit the track to show people where he had passed and where he alighted. Again, we but illustrated the god's work."

"And what of the folk who were moved out of the old manse where you wanted the temple built?"

"Not we, Lord Wotheng, but Yotha himself. Had he not sported there long before ever we came here?" The high priest shrugged eloquently. "As for the folk living there, we did offer to take them into Yotha's household. Many chose to do so, as you recall. Others did not, which was entirely their will."

"And not to be wondered at, considering the famed capriciousness of your god, Sir Priest."

"The god does as he wills; we can only interpret his will."

"Yet you cannot deny," said Wotheng, slamming his fist down on the table, "that it was your fire that burned Poddil's cottage!"

Why just that one case? Sulun wondered. *No witnesses to the others?*

"But I can, Lord Wotheng." Folweel clasped his hands calmly. "We knew from the god that Poddil's cottage *would* burn. We sent him warning, several times by word of mouth, and finally by the running fire. The first warnings he ignored, the latter came too late; his chimney had already caught fire when the running fire reached him."

"Chimney?" Wotheng bristled his moustache. "My wife *saw* your fire run to Poddil's cottage, climb right up his wall and into the thatch of his roof. Are you calling my wife a liar, sir?"

Aha, reliable witness. Sulun thought, drawing no comfort from it.

"Certainly not," Folweel smiled politely. "I only say, that, when a warning flame runs up a wall to point to a chimney, and the chimney is also on fire and throws sparks down into the thatch, 'tis very easy to be mistaken concerning exactly which fire set the house alight. You must recall, Lord Wotheng, that witnesses saw sparks shooting out of that chimney and also saw afterward that it had fallen and was burned. The man should never have built his chimney of mere clay-daubed wattle, no matter how thick the clay. Had he not been warned of that before?"

"Poddil's chimney did indeed catch fire once before," Wotheng said slowly, "but without burning the whole house."

"Yet it could have done so, then." The high priest shook his head. "That, too, was warning. Poddil simply would not heed warnings."

"Do you attempt to tell me that Poddil's cottage simply *happened* to catch fire at the moment that your . . . *warning* . . . reached him?"

"Not at all." Folweel shook his head sadly. "In truth, his chimney caught fire a little *before* our warning reached him. We came too late, for which we pray forgiveness; we are but mortal."

"Unbelievable," Zeren muttered.

Don't provoke him! Sulun winced. *We want to get out of here alive!*

"And the fire you loosed at Deese House last night?" Wotheng rumbled. "Was that a 'late' warning, too?"

"How should it be?" Folweel raised his eyebrows, looking most honestly surprised. "Vona has not yet expressed his displeasure at Deese house, has he? Therefore, I trust our warning has reached its goal well before time."

"By all the gods!" Doshi burst out. "Do you try to tell us that you haven't heard about the poisoning of our workmen yesterday?"

"Poisoning? Workmen?" The high priest looked perfectly surprised. "Why, what's this? I've had no word on it."

"I see." Wotheng leaned back in his chair. "Then you wouldn't know that the poisoner has been seized, and has confessed?"

"You are the first to bring me this news, Lord Wotheng." Folweel bowed slightly. "I congratulate you on the speed of your justice."

"Then let me also be first to tell you that the man claimed he was paid to poison the workmen's bread—paid by one of your priests, sir." Wotheng pulled a small scroll from his belt pouch and tossed it on the table. "This is the man's confession, as I heard from his own lips."

Folweel coolly took up the scroll, opened and read it. No more than a righteous frown showed on his composed face. "Indeed a serious matter," he murmured. "This fellow—Bassip? A baker's wagoner?—claims much. Can you be certain he speaks the truth in any of this?"

"I saw with my own eyes the proof that he did the poisoning." Wotheng tapped his fingers quietly on his belt. "I heard with my own ears his confession that Twoz, under-priest of Yotha, paid him to do it and gave him the poison. I wrote with my own hands what he said, as you may read."

The high priest smiled, most gently. "Surely you know, Lord Wotheng, that a man found guilty of a serious crime will often try to shift or divide blame by accusing another. Likewise, one put to . . . serious question . . . in such a case will say whatever he thinks his questioners want to hear."

Wotheng flushed a dull red. He didn't care to have his own reasoning thrown back at him. "There is still the little question of the poison and the money. Bassip told me where in his house he'd hidden the money he got for this task; we searched and found it there. How came he by the money, pray?"

"Who can say? It might have been a long-saved treasure, or the result of robbery, or some windfall prize he did not care to report at tax time." Folweel raised a knowing eyebrow. "He could well have mentioned his secret hoard purely to convince you of the truth of his story."

"And the poison, Sir Priest? There was over a pint of it to poison that barrel of flour. Where came he by that?"

"He could have had that from any patch of mould-tainted rye, field grown or wild seeded. A wagoner who deals with bakers, millers, and farmers would have much opportunity to recognize such." Folweel flicked a long nail at the relevant line of Bassip's confession. "Who can guess his true reasoning for this? Perhaps the man has some grudge against the baker, or this under-priest, or someone who works on the new walls at Deese House. Perhaps, knowing that the houses of Deese and Yotha are, hmm, not speaking to each other, he hoped to raise ill will between us. Who can say?"

For a moment none of the others spoke. Eloti only shook her head in admiration for the well-woven words.

"*We* didn't start any such dissension between our houses," Sulun put in, a bit warmly. "By all the gods, we didn't even know you existed until one of your people tried to put a curse on our new walls. The first blow, sir, was yours."

"I, sir?" The high priest looked genuinely grieved. "All I know of that affair is that the crushed corpse of a man, whom one of the under-priests identified as one of our worshippers, was brought to Yotha House one night. The workmen who brought him said he'd been the victim of some magic gone awry. We buried him with proper rites, and that was an end to it. If indeed there was some ill magic done, then who suffered from it if not our poor worshipper—and, by his loss, us?"

"The man was your chief stonemason!" Sulun snapped. "He put the focus of a curse onto our walls while he worked there!"

"My dear sir!" Folweel raised his hands beseechingly. "We have not had much stoneworking done about the temple estate for many moons; if any of our masons wished to take some temporary work elsewhere, we certainly would not prevent them. As to his ill-wishing your uncompleted walls, who can say why he did so? Perhaps he hoped to gain himself more work thereby. Not all of our herd are free from the sin of greed, despite our best efforts."

"Amazing," Zeren murmured again.

Wotheng ignored him, keeping his steady stare on the priest. "And yet, sir, you loosed Yotha's fire against Deese House on the very evening of that . . . accident. The fire very nearly consumed the workmen's scaffolding. Why, Sir Priest, did you that?"

"Ah, the fire again." Folweel smiled and shook his head. "As I have already said, the god speaks of divine displeasure at the dangerous carelessness of the Sukkti wizardry, of which our stonemason died. As for the scaffolding, well, the under-priests who sent the fire may be forgiven if they were upset by their servant's death and, in their distraction, perhaps let the fire run too close to the scaffolding where the man died." He shrugged eloquently. "In any case, as I've heard, the scaffolding was not burned and no harm was done."

"Except to a bit of grass." Wotheng tapped his fingers on his belt, over and over. "Would one of those under-priests who loosed the fire that night have been this fellow Twoz, perhaps?"

The high priest frowned long in thought. "That may well have been, lord Wotheng. I shall investigate this matter."

"I should like to investigate it myself, also. Pray bring this Twoz fellow to me; I wish to question him."

"That I shall gladly do, m'lord, as soon as he returns from the north." Folweel smiled benignly. "Twoz is one of the under-priests who went north with our last trade caravan, nearly a fortnight ago. Thus he could hardly have hired Bassip to poison your miller's flour two days ago, which is why I suspect Bassip's confession on this point."

"He might, of course, have begun the plot before he left."

"Quite possibly. We shall certainly question Twoz most carefully upon his return—and, of course, send him to you as well."

"Of course." Wotheng tapped and tapped his fingers. "And do you swear, Sir Priest, on your own altar to Yotha, that you have no malice, and have done no ill-wishing, to Deese House or any thereof?"

"Certainly I will swear so." The high priest looked utterly sincere. "Our sole complaint against Deese's priesthood is, as I've said, their dangerous carelessness with magical knowledge and application."

"If that's so," Wotheng smiled tightly, "then this Bassip fellow has done your house as much harm as Deese House, what with making either the false accusations against your under-priest or else entering in a private conspiracy with him. True?"

"Quite true, m'lord."

"Why, then, I shall hand him over to your examination and judgment." Wotheng pulled himself up from the chair. "You have his confession there, and my guards have him in your courtyard. I'll also send you written account of my investigation of the poisoning, and how his guilt was discovered, if you wish."

"I shall be happy to receive them, Lord Wotheng," said Folweel, quite calmly.

"Until this Twoz returns then, I'll leave the matter in your hands. Good day, Sir Priest. Come along, good folk."

Sulun and the others had no choice but to rise, bow minimally in politeness, and follow Wotheng to the door.

At the threshold Wotheng turned. "Only one more thing, Sir Priest."

"Yes, Lord Wotheng?"

"Don't burn so much as another handspan of my land. Is that clear?"

"Yes, Lord Wotheng."

The Lord of Ashkell tramped out, letting the door swing shut behind him.

They were well past the temple's lands before anyone spoke. Zeren leaned over the edge of the wagon to catch Wotheng's attention, and asked in as quiet a voice as he could, "Lord Wotheng, why don't you just take your men-at-arms and clean that snake's nest out? I'll be happy to help."

Wotheng laughed sourly. "There speaks a soldier, right enough. Lad, I'd have done so long before this if I could—and if I hadn't thought ahead a bit. Think you: enough folk would be glad to see the last of Yotha, perhaps happy enough to join a campaign to drive them out like wolves, aye, and even accept the combat losses.

"But think a bit further down the road. In a year's time, or two, or thereabouts, the next of my lot to have any argument with me would get to thinking, 'Wotheng waited for no sure proof of crime before he turned on Yotha's priests, so what will he do to us?' Soon enough they'd find reason to grieve for Yotha's lot, and more reason to fear me. One makes secret enemies that way, my boy, great numbers of 'em. That I can't afford. No, I need proof clear and bald for all folk to see before I send swords against Yotha—or anyone. Do y'see that?"

"I . . . see." Zeren chewed his lip a little. "However, if someone else were to make an end of Yotha's priesthood . . ."

"Then I'd have to sit in judgment on the case. Be careful, lad."

"Understood." Zeren sighed. "I'm a soldier, as you said, and no ruler. These games are a bit beyond me."

"Well, let me suggest—seeing as someone has, most definitely, tried to harm your folk—that you borrow a few of my guardsmen to watch your house and walls and workmen's camp for you. I'll hire them out cheap; all I ask is that you teach them some of the tricks you've learned in your soldiering. Like you the deal?"

"Yes." Zeren grinned. "It's a pleasure doing business with you, m'lord."

"Aye, that's what the wife says." Wotheng spurred his horse forward a few paces to hear the conversation going on in the front of the wagon.

Doshi was cursing bitterly over the whole visit. "Snake-tongued, wily monster, turning our own words back on us. Carelessness! Oh, bull's balls! He sat there and accused *us* of dangerous magic, that—that—"

"Clever old bastard," Sulun supplied. "At least he won't be setting fires so freely again."

"But what else will he do? He has so damned much power! You know that Bassip was his hireling, and could still run around poisoning people. Do we have to watch every drop of water, every crumb of food, for the rest of our lives? What if—"

"I doubt Bassip the Wagoner will do any more poisoning," said Sulun. "To keep protesting his innocence, Folweel will have to punish the man—and none too lightly. In fact . . . seeing that Bassip's clearly guilty, no longer useful, and has some damaging tales to tell about who hired him, I suspect that the poisoner hasn't many days left to live."

"Oh." Doshi thought that over, and was silent.

"I see you understand me," Wotheng put in, startling them both. "So we're all rid of a poisoner, and Folweel won't be so free with his fires hereafter, and I rather think that this fellow Twoz won't be showing his nose in Ashkell again."

"I understand, Lord Wotheng, and I thank you," Sulun concurred. "I only worry about Folweel's next move against us."

"He might have the sense to make none." Wotheng sighed. "Well, if not, then I suspect he'll not move soon or anywhere near so boldly. I'm lending you some of my guards until next harvest comes in. No, don't thank me yet; you'll have only that long to outguess the next move from Yotha House. I trust your own house will be secure by then."

"As much as we can make it, m'lord."

"Yotha will have his own harvest to get in," Eloti recalled. "And if his donations have fallen slack of late, his priests will have to concern themselves heavily with their farming if they want to be warm and well fed this winter."

"Let's hope so," Sulun muttered.

"And if they have time left over for mischief," Wotheng added, "let's hope 'tis not much."

"Perhaps they'll have other concerns as well." Eloti smiled wickedly. "In case of any complaint, Lord Wotheng, remember that one of Yotha's admitted household *did* do a bit of ill-wishing on a bit of our property first."

"Oho?" Wotheng raised a shaggy eyebrow. "And could anyone do a little bit of ill-wishing right back? Even through Yotha House's famous magical defenses?"

"Certainly. One might cast a small curse upon a small part of Yotha House from the inside—especially while the high priest was too busy in a duel of wits to notice." Eloti smiled, smiled, like a cat with a whole bowl of cream.

"What sort of 'small' curse?" Wotheng asked quietly.

"Harmless but nagging irritations: scrolls that roll off desks and hide under heavy cabinets, inkpots that overturn, quill points that break, errors that tend to creep into the household accounts—that sort of thing."

Wotheng snorted, then whuffled, then laughed until he rocked in the saddle. "Small annoyances! Little irritations!" he whooped. "Oh, I have to tell the wife that one! A small curse . . . Aye, Vona, the slippery wizard deserves it."

Sulun chewed that over a while, giving Eloti a long look. "Falling inkpots," he murmured. "I remember that. So it was you, behind the wall of Entori's study?"

"Oh yes." Eloti smiled distantly into the wind. "My brother was a fool in so many ways. I had to keep track of his doings, or the house would have been ruined long ago."

"Lady Eloti, I'm most grateful you chose to come with us!"

"I'm grateful you gave me the opportunity."

Getting over the wall was the easy part. Yotha House stood amid an overgrown former orchard which hid both the approach and part of the side walls. There were fallen tree limbs aplenty, and the stone itself was weathered full of finger- and toeholds, and Arizun had his rope and grapnel in case those failed. Clearly the wizard-priests of Yotha never considered that any thief would dare try to climb into the god's house, or else they actually wanted hidden entrances for themselves.

Ziya and Arizun lay on top of the weathered wall, studied the hated house, and planned strategy.

"We could set it on fire," said Ziya. "Serve 'em right."

Arizun winced. "Not that easy," he argued. "Besides, they play with fire themselves. Don't you think they'd have precautions against it turning on them?"

"It'd be so *right*." Ziya hated to let the idea go.

"Maybe we could poison them right back," Arizun offered, looking half-heartedly about for the house's water supply. He cast a glance back into the orchard, where their horse was safely tied and presumably too busy eating to make any noise.

"We didn't bring any poison with us," Ziya grumbled. "We should've thought of that."

"I don't think Deese House has got any, and there wasn't time to look; not if we wanted to sneak out quick." Arizun's eye fell on something odd, something wrong-shaped, hanging in one of the trees. He looked more carefully, recognized it, and smiled to his ears. "Heyyy, I've got a better idea. Have we got a big bag?"

"The sack we brought lunch in." Ziya squirmed around to see what Arizun was looking at. "What is it?"

"Look there, that tree where I'm pointing, about halfway up. You see that thing?"

Ziya did. Her eye grew big and round, and she smothered a whoop of laughter. "Oooh, how'll we get it?"

"Some smoke, and then the bag." Arizun squirmed back down off the wall. "Come on. This'll take time and we've got to hurry."

Ziya wriggled after him, and they ran back through the old orchard stifling giggles.

Arizun proved to be right; it took a good half-hour's careful work to build a smoky fire of just the right size, keep it from being seen while they steered the smoke upward, and then shinny up the tree with the hastily emptied bag. Arizun did most of the latter work while Ziya kept lookout, and none of it was easy. Still, he came down grinning, mussed but unscathed, holding the reloaded bag at arm's length with the neck tied tight.

"Ick! Keep it away from me!" Ziya wrinkled her nose as she scattered and killed the fire.

"That was the easy part," Arizun warned her solemnly. "Now we've got to get this over the wall, sneak it into the house, and find a good place to open it—and all that without anyone seeing or hearing us."

"We'll be real quiet," Ziya promised. "And I bet I know just where to let it loose."

They reclimbed the wall, scouted the grounds below with elaborate care, and finally sneaked down Arizun's rope to the thick-shrubbed garden.

"Why do they grow all this stuff in their kitchen garden?" Ziya whispered while they paused under a large and stinky bush. "None of it's fit to eat."

"Maybe they're poison plants. Don't touch any with your bare skin."

"Won't. Look: there's the kitchen midden, so the kitchen's got to be right there."

"The kitchen'll have people in it."

"Maybe not. Let's sneak up to the window and look."

Another ten minutes' exquisitely careful stalking brought them up to an open ground floor window. They listened for long moments before daring to raise their heads and peek in.

Inside, a solitary kitchen maid raked ashes out of the cold fireplace and shovelled them into a bucket. There was no sign of anyone else about.

The underage conspirators ducked down below the window and conferred.

"She'll go out in a minute to empty the bucket," Ziya whispered. "That's when we do it. And we shut the window after, so *they* don't get out."

"Right." Arizun carefully untied the mouth of the bag, holding it shut only with his hand. "You watch, and tell me the minute she goes."

The wait wasn't long. The kitchen maid filled her bucket, set down the hand-shovel, and lugged her burden toward the rear door—with her back turned to the window.

"Now?" Ziya emphasized the signal with a light kick.

Arizun stood up, yanked the mouth of the bag wide open, and hurled its contents through the window.

The cubit-long wasps' nest sailed far through the air, hit a table, bounced, and rolled under a bench. The wakened wasps came spilling out, disoriented and furious.

Arizun snatched the support pole out of the window, barely taking time to see that Ziya's head was out of the way, and let the sash fall into place.

The two of them ran like rabbits back through the garden to the dangling rope and up the wall, unseen by anyone, thanks more to luck than caution. They reeled in the rope, squirmed back among the concealing branches, and peered over the wall to watch the fun.

It wasn't long in coming. The maid, her bucket emptied, turned back to the kitchen and opened the rear door.

She took one step through it, froze on the threshold, then jumped back and slammed it shut. The children nearly smothered themselves keeping quiet as they watched the maid drop the bucket, dance furiously while swatting at her hair, and finally run off through the kitchen midden squalling a dozen different names or curses.

"She'll tell somebody," Ziya grumbled quietly. "They'll come smoke the wasps out before they really spread."

"Maybe not," Arizun whispered. "Look through the windows."

For all its size, the house had been built in peaceful times. It was not designed to withstand any assault, and its walls were pierced by numerous large windows to let in air and light. Through two of them the children could see a fat and well-dressed under-priest, apparently wanting a snack or drink between meals, strolling toward the kitchen. They didn't see him reach the door and open it, but they did see the result.

A screech echoed across the kitchen garden, and doubtless through the lower corridors of Yotha House. The pudgy under-priest fled back past the windows *much* faster than he'd come, swatting the air around him with flapping sleeves. What seemed to be a small cloud followed him down the corridor. The under-priest flapped and squawked through a door, shut it behind him, and then discovered that he hadn't shut out all the wasps. He danced around the unlit room, knocking over small tables and chairs, then ran out still another door and was lost to view.

The wasps left back in the corridor buzzed and swirled for a moment, briefly visible in a bar of sunlight, then began scouting the rest of the ground floor. Their progress could be traced by the screeches and thuds and slammings of doors down the length of Yotha House.

On the wall, Ziya pressed both hands over her mouth and nearly choked with the effort of keeping quiet.

Arizun tugged at her sleeve. "Let's go," he whispered. "That's all we'll get to see, and we've got to get home before we're missed."

Ziya nodded red-faced assent, and they climbed back down the wall. The howls of alarm could be heard behind them as they raced through the orchard, but the two didn't let themselves go ahead and laugh until they were on the horse and well away from the lands of the temple of Yotha. Then, of course, they giggled and whooped and howled until they nearly fell off.

Fortunately, the horse was kind-tempered and patient.

In his study, Folweel rested his elbows on the table and sagged with exhaustion and relief. Gods, that had been a close thing! How in the nine hells had those damned Deese wizards guessed so quickly that the workmen had been poisoned rather than bewitched? How had they discovered the source and nature of the poison so fast and accurately? Damn them, and damn that fat fool Wotheng's unpredictable pride, and damn his clever wife who'd discovered the nature of Yotha's Flame. Now he couldn't dare loose the fire again, not on any land Wotheng claimed. As to other means, he'd have to be very, very careful. Putting the rye mould in the workmen's bread ration had seemed subtle enough, but clearly these Sukkti folk were accustomed to subtlety. Damn! What did that leave?

Magic? Folweel shuddered. Besides himself, the only truly competent magician in Yotha House was Oralro, and one had to be careful in handling him. Unlike the rest of them, Oralro truly *did* believe in Yotha; he wouldn't perform without convincing himself, usually by hours of meditation and prayer, that Yotha really and truly did want it done. Once decided, of course, the man was almost unstoppable; between himself and Oralro, they could cast a hefty curse. But then, who could guess how many wizards Deese House had, or how strong they were, or how trained?

For a moment Folweel seriously considered taking the Deese wizards' warning, backing away from the conflict, letting Yotha House survive on its lands and produce and what little donations the local herd would provide hereafter.

No, that way led to poverty by slow degrees; come a bad harvest or a poor year's trading in the north, and Yotha's priesthood would be no better off than the local farmers or merchants. That was no fit ending for Folweel Gilno's-son, late of Anhalas, thank you.

So, retrench and go to the secondary plan. Keep heads down, only preach warnings, keep a good ear as close to the Deese wizards as possible, and wait for the right opportunity. Sooner or later, gods willing, a chance would come. Folweel flicked a glance toward a certain drawer in a wall cabinet, behind which a hidden compartment nestled. What lay there he would use well and subtly, when the time came. Best pen another note to Duppa, warning him to be totally discreet. Bad enough they'd lost the use of Bassip; damn, but now they'd have to find him guilty and condemn him, the fool. Also, best warn the trade caravan to come home one under-priest the less, and make good excuse for the absence—good enough to satisfy Lord Wotheng, anyway. Let the Deese wizards suspect what they would, that fat son of an Ancar barbarian still ruled here, and any clever son of Anhalas could outwit such a creature while the sun still rose—so long as one catered to his barbarian pride and temper. Patience, patience: get on with the letters. Folweel sighed and reached for his quill pen.

He missed, and the shaved quill went rolling across the table. Folweel grabbed for it, and knocked awry a stack of tablets. The tablets slid across the desk, one of them bumping into the inkpot. The inkpot overturned, spilling a black lake across a stack of documents.

The high priest roared a pungent Halasian oath and shoved back his chair. The chair caught on an irregularity in the rug, and tipped over, dropping Folweel unceremoniously to the floor. He landed badly, whacking his elbow, and his arm went numb down to the fingers. He grabbed the table to lever himself erect, bumped into the tottering stack of tablets, and knocked them across the table in all directions. The inkpot fell to the floor and rolled, spilling more ink across the rug.

Folweel swore and stamped. His foot hit a fallen stylus, which rolled, nearly dropping him to the floor again. He scrambled away from the table and its small disaster, intending to reach the bell pull and call the servants to clean the mess. He made two steps across the floor before the rug skidded on the polished boards and slipped out from under him. Down he went again, instinctively grabbing for the nearest support, which happened to be a chair. He hit it wrong, and the chair fell over with him, its seat back catching him a painful whack on the collarbone.

A curse! Folweel realized, as he shook pain streaks from his vision and contemplated the floor under his chin. *They sneaked a curse past our house defenses! Must have done it just now, right here . . .*

But how in the nine hells could they have done it? They'd all been talking, arguing, concentrating on trying to catch him in some slip, some contradiction or admission. Nobody could do magic in that frame of mind, but all of them had—

Wait, not all of them.

That woman! Their teacher at Wotheng's: she just sat, said nothing. . . .

Folweel pulled himself up to all fours and crawled, carefully, very carefully, across the floor to the wall. He leaned on it as he got to his feet with infinite caution and reached for the bell pull, inwardly seething at how neatly he'd been tricked. Oh yes, he'd heard that the Sukkti wizards taught magic to their women too, but who could believe they'd trust a witch with something so subtle and difficult? She'd done it somehow, sitting there so politely quiet while the men argued, never giving a sign of sorcery at work. She'd done it then, while he was busy juggling Wotheng and the Deese priests: set a curse, right in this room, probably centering it right there at his worktable. How? How had she done it? He'd need Oralro's help to find out. Swearing, Folweel yanked on the bell pull.

It tore loose from its moorings and dropped on top of him like a dusty snake.

"Oralro!" Folweel howled, forgetting that no one could hear very far through that thick officium door. "Oralro! Yotha's flaming balls, somebody fetch Oralro!"

Nobody answered, but he could hear thumpings and shoutings from downstairs. Could that be the racket of hauling in Bassip, and him knowing or guessing what was intended for him? Or, worse, could the curse have spread beyond this room already? Folweel made his way to the door and pulled it open.

In through the open door came the wasps.

Two days later, word was brought to Lord Wotheng that underpriest Twoz had died of plague in the north; and that Bassip the Carter had indeed been found guilty of poisoning his employer's flour, and condemned to death by Yotha's Flame.

Wotheng shivered, and shut the informing parchment away.

✧ CHAPTER SIX ✧

The walls of Deese House were finished by second harvest, freeing the work gang for labor in the fields. Harvest was better than average, which the Ashkell folk attributed to the beneficent magic of the new wizards, and in a sense that was true; scythes kept their edges longer, crops fumigated with "magical" herbs were less plagued by moulds and insects, people and livestock suffered fewer ailments thanks to washing ointments and herbal baths provided by Deese's consort Kula.

Attendance at Yotha's temple services dwindled steadily, although the House of Deese provided no public ceremonies to replace them. Still, requests and donations came steadily to Deese House, and enrollment in the Wizardess Eloti's school continued to increase. Biddon the blacksmith built a shrine to Deese within the villa's walls, and local folk made offerings there every day, of which Biddon took only a small share before giving the rest to Eloti to carry back to Deese House. The priesthood of Deese, after giving the matter long thought and much discussion over several dinners, agreed to cast a man-sized statue of the god—and, another of Kula—for the shrine. Omis proposed casting the statue in iron, swearing that with the new furnace and bellows he could actually melt iron to liquid. Sulun complained such heat was too dangerous. The argument was still going strong at harvest time.

No further actions were taken by the priesthood of Yotha, save the oft-repeated warnings in the sermons that magic could be dangerous, the "wizards of Deese" were too careless with it, that the gods were displeased by such carelessness and would eventually make their displeasure felt.

Wotheng counted his trade coins and his produce taxes, and smiled at his new prosperity. Gynallea totted up the household accounts and bought new winter clothes for everyone in Ashkell House. Even the weather was good—sunny days, light winds, rain frequent but light and usually well after sunset. No bandits raided from the woods, no cattle went missing, even squabbles between neighbors were few and slight.

Altogether, it looked to be a very good year.

"Too good," Zeren worried, peering down at the moonlight on the diverted millstream. "Forgive my gloom, Eloti, but I've learned never to trust too much in good luck."

Eloti hitched closer to him, tugging her cloak about her, for the wind up here on the wall could be chilly after dark. "Think, then: what direction could trouble take? What should we watch for, and guard against?"

"Gods, anything." Zeren shrugged, sliding an arm around Eloti's shoulders. "Some seasonal plague we're not accustomed to, mould in the food stores despite our care, anything going wrong with this iron-casting Omis is so determined upon . . . and Yotha's priests may not be done with us, remember. Or our good friend Wotheng may worry that we've grown powerful enough to undermine his rule, unlikely though that is. . . ."

"Gynallea's a good friend to me. I'd know soon enough if her husband's mood changed."

"And I worry about the children. Ziya spends too much time playing with the bombard: raising and lowering the muzzle, turning it, sighting it, even cleaning it. Tamiri runs in and out of the workshop too much, and her little brother tags along; they may be seriously hurt, fooling with the tools, one of these days. . . ."

"Zeren, my love, I think you've been so long at war that you've forgotten how to enjoy peace." Eloti interlaced her fingers with his. "Or do you regret asking to marry me?"

"No!" Zeren pulled her close, as if fearful someone would snatch her away. "I'll never regret it! Set the date sooner, if you doubt me."

"No, spring is the proper time, and solstice is best for publicly announcing the intent. I'll wait to do it properly, for I've no doubts of you."

Zeren rested his cheek against her forehead. "Thank you for

that, I . . . suppose I'm only being the nervous bridegroom, and with too much soldiering to remember. I imagine threats to us, to you, around every corner. And must you go every day to the villa? When can we bring the school here? That's so long a ride, and anything could happen—"

"Oh, hush." Eloti silenced him with a finger across his lip. "We'll bring the school here in winter, once the snow makes riding difficult. As for the ride to Ashkell, don't you always send two of your best trained guards with me? Besides, for policy's sake, not to mention friendship, I prefer to see Gynallea whenever possible."

"Wotheng's guards . . ." Zeren looked down at the millstream and brooded again. "I've gone through all of them by now, teaching them everything I can think of. Gods, it's strange; I've fought the Armu and the Ancar all my life it seems, and here I am teaching the sons of settled-down Ancar soldiers how to fight."

"I doubt if they think of themselves as Ancar twice a year. They call themselves Ashkell Vale folk, if asked, and sometimes remember that Ashkell Vale sits in the lands of Torrhyn. The years of peace seem to have mellowed them."

"That and more. They've never faced an enemy worse than a handful of sheep thieves. I can teach them, drill them, 'til they do the proper moves in their sleep—yet I've no idea how they'd fare in battle. These aren't warriors; they're sheep wardens in armor."

"Let's be grateful for that, love, and pray none of them—or us—need ever be more."

Zeren heaved a sigh that seemed to come all the way from his boots. "And what shall I be, then? A warrior in priest robes? Perhaps I'll end my days as door warden to the House of Deese. The gods know, I'm poorer at metal-working and mechanics than the least of the apprentices!"

"Ah, so that's it." Eloti snuggled into his arm. "There are worse fates, love. Look: here you are, come through Kula knows how many wars, with a whole skin, and now a wedding before you. You could live out your days at far worse tasks than being . . . land warden of Deese House."

"Land warden . . . ?"

"Who else? Doshi knows a bit about farming, but we'll be raising goats and small gardens here. Who else knows anything of that? Did you not begin as a landholder's son?"

"So I did . . ." Zeren frowned with the effort of remembering those long-gone days. At length he laughed. "I recall too, when I was a landholder's son, I wanted to be a natural philosopher!"

"Then here's your wish, granted at last." Eloti smiled. "You've come far to get it."

"Gods, almost clear around the midworld sea!" Zeren hugged her, laughing softly. "And across nearly twenty years. The gods took their own time answering my prayers."

"They often do," said Eloti, grinning to herself. "And if you've no pressing duties tomorrow, come reassure yourself by riding with me to Ashkell Villa. Sit by while I teach, and you'll hear as much natural philosophy as your ears can bear."

"My ears," he said, kissing her, "could bear . . . your voice . . . forever."

After that, their lips were too busy for talk.

High Priest Folweel burned the candle late, grimly reading over reports. He'd saved the ones dealing with Deese House for last, wanting to chew them over in uninterrupted privacy. It had become his chief pleasure of these past few moons: studying, planning, measuring crumbs of opportunity, storing bits of useful knowledge, imagining their ultimate effect. Most often, recently, he slid into sleep cherishing a vision of Deese House wrapped in blue and yellow flames. His fingers rubbed hungrily on the parchment as he pored over Duppa's last missive, a meticulously detailed recital of the latest lessons taught at the Wizardess Eloti's school in Ashkell Villa: geometry, mechanics, drawing of mechanical devices . . .

Wait, that might be something.

Folweel interlaced his fingers and meditated upon the usefulness of drawing. Drawing of tools, drawing of devices, drawing of . . .

Yes!

Folweel sat up straight, smiling like a wolf as he set a few more plotted details in place. At length he got up and went to the bell pull. He paused there a moment, grimacing as he remembered how long it had taken both Oralro and himself to find and remove the focus of the Deese priests curse (a chip of black glass, shoved under the edge of a rug, no more), and resolutely rang the outside bell. Unconsciously he scratched at the scars of long-healed wasp stings as he waited. The soft-footed servitor came soon and quietly to the door.

"Send Duppa and Quazzil to me," Folweel said, still faintly smiling to himself.

"Father," the house servant almost whispered, "I believe they have retired."

"Fetch them anyway. This word they will want to hear."

The man bowed, turned, and padded away. Folweel shut the door behind him and stalked to his cabinet, chuckling to himself at the appropriateness of this new-wrought tactic. Time indeed to use his long-hidden weapon.

How very fitting it would be, to strike down Deese House through the very witch who had dared place a curse inside the House of Yotha.

Losh, the wheelwright's son, had his hand up again. An enthusiastic boy, that: fit to travel, hopefully, to one of the great universities someday—provided any still existed now. Eloti nodded recognition to the boy, wishing she could provide better for his educational future.

"Mistress," Losh said, waving his sketch of a gear train, "if it's all right to draw pictyoors of mechanical parts, is it all right to draw other things too?"

"All right?" Eloti blinked, puzzled by the silly question. "Of course it is. You will have to draw *pictures* of many things in order to understand them properly."

"Even trees? And sheep? And . . . other things?"

Losh's neighbor, Duppa, gave him a discreet elbow in the ribs.

"And . . . people too?" Losh finished, beginning to blush.

Eloti thought she understood. She smiled knowingly. "Losh, if you wish to draw pictures of naked women for your amusement, that is a private matter between you and the woman concerned."

The class, nearly a score of them by now, erupted in a storm of laughter. Losh, blushing red as a beet, scrunched down in his clothes as if trying to disappear into the earth.

"In truth," Eloti continued as the laughter sank to a breachable level, "those of you who intend to study medicine must study detailed drawings of the human body, including all its muscles, bones, veins, and internal organs. I assure you, you will see enough

The Sword of Knowledge

pictures of the human body to become heartily tired of them before you finish your course of study. Since medicine will be the next class, any who wish to see evidence of this may attend. Now, your assignment in this class for tomorrow is, using the *pictures* you already have, to make a model—in clay and sticks, or whatever else you may have ready to hand—of a 'gear train.' You may go now. The class in medicine will assemble here at the next bell."

The class shuffled to its assorted feet and scattered, most students heading out of the main hall for a few minutes of leg-stretching in the courtyard. Eloti rolled and set aside certain scrolls, and hunted in her carry basket for others.

Duppa strolled out to the well, where a slight man in nondescript dark clothing had just hauled up a dripping bucket and was tugging a horn cup free of his belt.

"May I have some?" Duppa asked politely.

The other nodded and handed over the cup. "Losh takes the bait," he murmured, very quietly.

"Follow him, watch well for chances," Duppa whispered. Then he drank from the horn, handed it back, nodded politely, and walked away.

The jeweler's wife watched, fascinated, as the blue fire shot up on the altar. The yellow tips of the flames reflected in her wide eyes and gilded her faintly quivering jowls. She loved fires, was utterly entranced by them, and was fiercely loyal to Yotha. She paid well for private audiences and prophecies.

In return, Yotha granted her clear messages. His fire sketched letters, sigils, and simple images across the altar, plain as the writing of a quill pen. She never doubted his advice, which was always accurate.

And that takes no small doing, Folweel considered, recalling reams of observers' reports that he studied before telling the woman what she needed to hear. *Still, so loyal and generous and . . . useful a worshipper deserves the best.*

A line of blue flame ran out of the great fire bowl and ran to the far left of the altar. From there it scurried rightward, writing recognizable letters in square northern script. The jeweler's wife gasped as she recognized them.

"L . . . O . . . S . . . H. Losh! My son's name!"

"Indeed?" Folweel placed a comforting hand on her shoulder, and watched the flames finish their message.

After the letters, the fire skipped into a neat circle crossed with a vertical bar, an ancient and ominous symbol of negation.

"Death sign," the woman moaned. "Oh, gods, is my son doomed to die?"

"Peace, peace," Folweel soothed. "Remember, goodwife Nima, the sign may also be interpreted to mean only 'fatal danger.' "

While he spoke, the fire sketched one last sign—the outline of an anvil in a circle—and stopped there. The completed message burned tranquilly on the altar, plain to read.

"Anvil? What means that?" Nima couldn't pull her eyes away from the fire even long enough to glance beseechingly at the high priest. "Will my son be killed by an *anvil*?"

"I think not," Folweel murmured smoothly. "Note that the anvil is encircled, which adds much to its meaning. Not an anvil so much as one who uses it. Has your son anything to do with blacksmiths, Goody Nima?"

"No, nothing whatever . . ."

Folweel waited, letting her make the connection herself.

"Except . . . Oh gods, he goes to that school the Deese woman teaches! Could that be the danger? You've warned your herd so often that those folk are dangerously careless and profligate with magic—and my son *will* insist on going to them, learning their magic, no matter what I say to him. Oh gods, there's been no controlling him since he came of age, and he simply won't obey me, and his father thinks there's no harm in it, no matter how often I warn him it's dangerous. Gods, gods, oh beloved Yotha, is Losh going to do something dangerous with the magic they teach there? Is that it?"

The line of blue fire, its fuel exhausted, sank and died away as if on cue. The timing was perfect.

"I think your question has just been answered, Goody Nima." Long practice kept the triumph out of Folweel's solemn voice. "Say nothing of this to anyone, for you know how ill Yotha and his warnings stand in the favor of the faithless mob. Nonetheless, I should watch your son carefully, were I you. See what he does, where he goes, what he has learned, and what he does with it. Perhaps vigilance can avert the danger."

"Yes. Gods, yes," said the jeweler's wife, her heavy jaw set. She fumbled in her purse for more coin, determined to show her gratitude for the warning—and the welcome advice.

No, Folweel smiled to himself. *The danger will not be averted if I have anything to do therewith.*

He bowed to the altar, to Yotha's flame and Yotha's image, with more sincerity than he'd felt in many a long moon.

"Having finished with diseases and injuries of sheep, we proceed to the study of diseases and injuries of men, their causes and cures." Eloti unrolled and hung from a lamp hook on the wall an elaborate drawing of human anatomy. It was a splendid illustration, done in several different colored inks, copied over nearly a moon from a smaller version in her best medical text. The assembled students gasped in awe, and a few of them gagged. "Be not dismayed by its complexity, for we shall learn the parts one at a time. Also, you will soon note similarities to the bodies of those animals which we have already studied."

"We're nothing like dumb animals," one of the older students grumbled.

"No?" Eloti arched an eyebrow at the woman, the daughter of a prosperous freeholder and perhaps a bit set in older ways of thought. "When injured, do we not bleed the same as they? Do our bones not break much as theirs, nor our bellies not gripe like theirs at bad food? Do we not sicken and die of disease or pests, like them? Therefore, let us learn what we can from such similarities."

"But we have speech and thought and spirit," the woman mumbled, covering her retreat. "That makes us different."

"Even so." Eloti took that in stride. "Let us begin, then, with those differences which are readily apparent in the body. Here." She pointed her long staff at the detailed drawing of the head. "You will note the brain: the seat of wisdom, home of speech and thought and spirit, master of the body. Observe that it is much larger and more detailed than that of a sheep, cow, or horse, as compared to the size of the body. Here is the true difference between man and beast most clearly visible. You will note how the nerves descend from the brain through the spine, and from there to every limb and organ. . . ."

The students duly bent over their tablets and drew rough copies of the human nervous system.

Duppa glanced at Losh's meticulous drawing, and smiled.

It was easy work for one with Quazzil's skills to follow Losh through the villa to his parents' shop and house, only a little less easy to find a secure and comfortable listening post in the alley behind the house. An old and fruitful chestnut tree grew there, its boughs wide enough to afford a secure rest and its foliage still thick enough at this season to conceal a listener. Best of all, from one well-concealed branch Quazzil could hear clearly through the upper and lower rear windows as well as watch the house and yard below. He folded and set his dark cloak for a mattress, stretched out on the branch, and observed.

First came warm and dutiful greetings exchanged between the father and older sibs. Then came a dutiful and less warm greeting between the boy and his mother. Next, hurried footsteps as the mother hustled the son into the back of the house, where Quazzil could hear more clearly. After than came a long, nagging interrogation with increasingly irritable answers. Finally the son's temper snapped.

"For the gods' sake, Mother!" he shouted. "It's nothing but Natural Philosophy! She hasn't taught us a bit of magic, only stuff like mathematics and medicine and mechanics. It's harmless and useful, and nothing to be afraid of. In fact, I have to go make a model of a gear train as my assignment for tomorrow, so I can't stay here and argue with you anymore. I've got to go off and get some clay and sticks to make the model, so good *day*, Mother. I'll be back in time for dinner."

The rear door slammed and the boy could be seen stamping his way across the alley.

Smiling, Quazzil slid out of the tree and followed the boy, at a safe distance, down the alley.

Behind them, Nima's voice echoed out the door: "What in the nine hells is a 'geer trane'?"

Patrobe smiled openly as Folweel read over the report from Quazzil, knowing the high priest would find the news as useful as he could wish. Sure enough, by the time he finished reading the scrap of paper, Folweel was grinning from ear to ear.

"So," the high priest purred, leaning back in his carved chair, "Losh has a sweetheart, the daughter of a poor farmer, of whom the mother does not approve."

"His father doesn't care," Patrobe pointed out. "He wouldn't disapprove of the match."

"Which no doubt makes our dear Nima all the more irate." Folweel tapped a finger on the report. "So if the girl falls . . . ill, shall we say, Nima would do all in her power to insist her boy had nothing to do with it."

"Which means she would strive to erase any link between the boy's studies and the girl's bewitchment."

"Therefore, the link must be forged beyond any doubt. The boy has made sketches of her, and he copied on good parchment that drawing from school. The drawings *must* be found together, and with some definite smear or mar across the anatomy drawing."

"How fortunate," Patrobe grinned, "that Lady Eloti pointed out that particular body part first. Otherwise we might have had to wait long, or damage some other portion of the wench."

"Read good Duppa's hand in that." Folweel smiled. "He knows the other students well enough by now to plant the right suggestions in the right ears."

"Most clever, Brother Folweel. But even so, Nima will try to hide that evidence."

"As I said, it will be found—and announced to all the vale—by another party. Losh will appear guilty. Nima will struggle, with all her considerable will, to shift the blame elsewhere."

"And we can guess where."

"Precisely." Folweel smiled as if happy with all the world as he took up fresh parchment and ink. "This goes to Quazzil, as soon as possible."

"And Duppa?"

"Another for him, less urgent. He is only to continue observing, and to drop the proper words in the proper ears at the proper time."

As a small tenant farmer's eldest daughter, Irga had duties that made her waken early. Papa would rise at dawn to take the sheep out to pasture, usually with her brother's help. Brother Wenn would build up the fire and pack lunch for them. Mama would rise later, clean house and wash clothes, make preparations for dinner, tend the household garden, and mend or sew or knit clothing for the winter. Irga had the unloved work of cleaning out the sheep barn, after which she would help Mama about the house. No one could face such a task on an empty stomach, especially not in the cold morning, so Irga would first brew a small pot of herb tea to fortify herself for the wretched work.

On this particular morning, as Irga fumbled her way down from her bed in the loft, she thought she saw someone leaving through the door. She paused to blink sleep from her eyes, guessed she had only seen the tail end of her brother leaving late, and went to put her tea on the fire. The water warmed to boiling while she washed her face and struggled into her clothes.

Perhaps she'd thrown in a bit too much of the last herbs, Irga thought as she drank the brew, for it tasted strong and a trifle bitter this morning. Perhaps she could gather some blackberry leaves to put in the new mix, if there were any good ones left so late in the year, and if she could get away from chores long enough to seek them.

And perhaps, if she went berrying late enough in the day, she could meet Losh a good way from the house and Mama's too inquisitive eyes.

Well, best get the other chores done first. Making a face, Irga pulled on her shawl and went out to face the dismal prospect of a barn full of sheep droppings.

The fouled straw stank, and the cart was heavy, and the reeking load steamed in the cold—and the cold seemed harsher than the clear bright weather would account for. Irga shoved the steaming cart to the compost heap, tilted and pulled it, letting the reeking load tumble out and spread on the pile. Gods, how it steamed in this shadowed corner of the barn wall. So thick, it seemed to form shapes of mist.

And then it did form a shape. A grey, shifting form—something like a bat and something like a monstrous toad—arched up over the manure pile. At its heart, too low for any natural face, formed vague eyes, a squat beastlike snout, a gaping mouth.

Irga let go the cart and scrambled away, shaking with cold to her bone marrow. She bumped into the barn wall behind her.

The wall moved. Only a slight shivering, maybe a squirming, but the wall *moved*. Irga whirled to stare at it, and saw that the rough texture of the field stones was changing, shivering, crawling, forming patterns like . . . like faces, evil faces, all snarling and leering at her.

Devilry! Witchcraft! Irga thought, scrambling away from the barn, the compost heap, the forgotten cart. She turned to run back to the house.

The ground under her feet undulated, rippled like water on a pond.

No, not the earth too! Irga staggered, fell, landed on the hard ground, and felt it wriggle as though a thousand worms fought a war just under its surface. She whimpered in terror, feeling her belly cramp. Her vision smeared, but there was no release from the horror in that, for now she could hear sounds—whisperings full of malice, just under the noise of the wind in the grass.

Gods, is the whole farm cursed? "Mama!" Irga screamed. "Mama, devils! Where are you? Mama!" *What if the curse has already caught her?* "Mama!"

But no, there, hurrying out of the cottage with a shawl just flung over her nightgown, there came Mama running toward her.

"Irga! What's wrong? What's happened?"

The words came distorted through the evil voices in the air, on the ground, but they sounded amazed more than alarmed. More, Mama ran surefooted over earth that rolled like the sea. How could that be? How could it be that Mama couldn't see the horror unfolding all around them?

Only if the curse weren't on the farm, or the barn, not anything else. Only if the witchery had fallen on Irga alone.

"Oh, Mama, I'm bewitched!" Irga struggled forward, reaching for her mother. "Help me! Send for the wizards! I've been bewitched!"

Wotheng sneaked a quick pull from his beer mug as the last supplicant—a tenant asking permission to cut estate wood for the winter—plodded out of the hearing room. With luck, he'd have time to finish the cup before the next petition or complaint came in. Truth to tell, he'd had far more petitions than complaints this year: let me borrow more scythes, m'lord; let me hire more for harvesting, m'lord; let me expand my orchard, m'lord; and so on. Sure signs of a good year—along with the fine sales of wool and other items in the north. Vona grant it would go on this way.

No, there came the knock on the door; no time to finish the cup.

"Come in," Wotheng called.

A woman traipsed in, middling young, well fed and well clothed, somewhat prim-faced. Wotheng tried to place her: that freeholder's daughter, but damned if he could remember her name. "Yes, mistress?" There, polite and neutral enough.

"M'lord." The woman held out a grubby handful of small parchment sheets. "One of my fellow students dropped these. I don't know who it was." Her tone implied that she could guess, though. She also glanced back toward the door as if looking for someone beyond it.

Wotheng took the sheets and looked at them, puzzled frown deepening. Two of them were not bad representations of a young girl's face, quite a pretty girl, even recognizable: Irda? Irga? The daughter of one of the tenants, that fellow who'd been plagued with sheep lice last year, but hadn't that trouble gone away recently?

The third sheet showed a carefully drawn outline of a human body, and within the outline a pattern disturbing and strange. It took Wotheng a moment to recognize it for a diagram of certain human organs: there the spine, clear enough, and that must be the brain, and those lines coming out to all directions must be the nerves. Strange stuff: must be from Eloti's class on medicine. But why had the woman brought it to him rather than to Eloti?

And what meant that damned clumsy smear across the top of it, obscuring much of the carefully drawn brain?

"This is schoolwork," he said. "Why not take it to the schoolmistress?"

The woman fidgeted, glanced toward the door again. "Well, m'lord, that's what I wanted to ask y'about. Is't right to be doing such things if one isn't yet a proper master of the trade? I mean, that's making an image of a real person, m'lord, which I think isn't right, and here, y'see, it's been rolled together with that . . . picture of a body, and a body's hidden parts—and look how that's marred. It seems, well, *wrong* somehow. Mistress Eloti seems to think nothing of that, so I doubt me that she'd worry o'ermuch on it, so I come to ask you, m'lord, if this be proper work for a student."

"I see." Wotheng kept his expression distant, showing nothing, as he peered at the drawings. It could all mean nothing, of course; some fool boy making pictures of his light of love, happening to roll them together with a doctor's drawing with the ink smeared or some such. Most likely, that's all it was: pure accident, no intent whatever. If there was intent, it could be no more than a boy's silly attempt at a love charm: addle this girl's wits toward her swain. In either case, as he'd seen cause to believe, it took more than a picture and a bit of will to make magic.

But if the magical power *were* there, and the intent, and the image . . .

"Is it true, m'lord, as I've heard, that there be some law against making pictures of living folk?" The woman laced her fingers together and squirmed a bit. "There wouldn't be any, ah, trouble at law for Lo—for whoever drew them, would there?"

Oho! Wotheng glowered at the woman. "Goody, you'd best tell me who drew these pictures."

She didn't turn pale; she blushed, and squirmed further. "I . . . I think it was Losh, the jeweler's son. It looks like his way of drawing. Besides, everyone knows he's silly over that chit Irga, and I'm sure that's her picture. The gods only know why he's so mad for her, she being just some poor shepherd's girl and not educated at all nor with any wits for it either, but he *would* go running after her like a fool, though his mother could tell him there be much better prospects at the villa and all . . ."

"Enough, thank you." Wotheng could place the woman now: Pado, Hass's daughter. Rumor said she'd been hoping for a match that would tie her family to the jeweler's, but nothing had come of it. "Isn't Losh a bit young for you, Pado? Wouldn't you do better to seek another match?"

Pado blushed bright crimson. "Why-why of course he is, m'lord," she stammered. "I wouldn't have him if he were the last man in the vale!"

But you'd gladly make him sorry for refusing you. Wotheng set the three grubby parchments down on his table. "I'll see to this later," he said. "I thank you for fetching them to me. Now go send in the next petitioner."

Flustered, not sure if she wanted to complain further or escape with some shreds of her composure, the woman got up and hurried off to the door. She paused on the threshold for a moment, but couldn't think of anything fitting to say. The door thudded to behind her.

Wotheng took a hasty gulp of beer and waited for the next guest. With luck, he'd finish with this lot before noon and could talk to Gynallea before he caught up to Eloti. Of course the Sukkti wizardess couldn't have known about that old obscure Torrhynan law—few of even the local folk did—but still, she should have been more careful about possible mischief among her students. He could silence Pado easily enough, make certain no more would be said of the matter; Gynallea would help with that. A few words in private to Eloti should account for the rest. After all, drawing or no drawing, no harm had been done.

There was a noise outside the door, thudding of footsteps, yelps and growls of complaint, a voice shrilling urgency.

Gods, what now? "Come in!" Wotheng bellowed.

The door flew open and a farmwife, hastily dressed in dishevelled clothes and reeking of hard-ridden mule, almost fell into the room.

"Lord Wotheng," she panted. "I pray you, fetch a good wizard quick, oh quick! My daughter Irga, she's been 'witched!"

Behind her, in the corridor, Wotheng could see Pado watching. A malicious smile spread across her face from ear to ear.

"Vona's clanging shit!" Wotheng groaned.

There'd be no silencing the wretched business now.

Gynallea first heard the news when her husband, looking thoroughly out of his depth, hauled a weeping and wailing tenant shepherd's wife into the still-room to talk to her. Gynallea poured some brandy into the woman, took Wotheng aside, and got the rest of the story from him. Next she dispatched some discreet house servants in a light cart to go fetch the afflicted girl and bring her to Ashkell House by the back doors. She also sent a rider on a fast horse to take the news to Deese House. Then she went quietly down to the hall where Eloti held her school and waited for the class to finish and depart.

Zeren happened to be present at the time, and after Gynallea's quiet explanation of the problem he refused to leave Eloti for so much as a minute.

The afflicted girl and her mother, and the delegation from Deese House, arrived at the villa almost together, and the whole howling problem wound up in the little-used guest rooms on the top floor. By dinnertime—a discreetly quiet meal, held in Wotheng's library—they had collected enough facts to discuss the situation calmly.

"It's poison again," said Gynallea, around a healthy mouthful of mutton. "I'm sure it is. The girl's eye centers were open so wide they looked all black, and her skin was flushed and hot. I'd swear 'twas delirium from a fever, save there's no other sign of sickness and no one else in the family has it. No, 'tis poison, sure as snow."

"But what kind?" Eloti nibbled indifferently on a wing of roast duck. "I don't know of any that leaves such tracks, never mind what the antidote may be."

"Is there nothing you can do for her, then?" Sulun asked, crumbling his bread small.

"We gave her willow bark tea, also beans and herb tea to wash the blood; there's nothing else we can think of, save to keep her warm and quiet."

"She was resting when we left her," Gynallea added. "At least she's no longer so frantic, and her eyes look a trifle better. Whatever it was, it hasn't killed her yet and doesn't seem likely to."

Eloti relaxed a trifle. "With any favor of the gods, the wretched stuff will pass from her in a day or so—unless she gets more of whatever it was."

"That's one of the reasons I wanted her brought here." Gynallea grinned. "No one will sneak poison into *my* kitchen, thank you. Hmm, and once she's calm, we must ask the girl what she ate or drank before the fit came on."

"If it's poisoning again, I think we may guess who did it," Zeren growled, attacking his slab of meat as if his eating knife were a short sword. "They might be clever enough to leave no poisoned food or drink lying about to be found, not after last time."

"Still, it's worth searching the house," Sulun considered. "But how long before we know what to search for?"

"Too long," Wotheng rumbled, refilling his cup. "You're sure, sweet cow, that it's poison—and not magic?"

"Utterly sure!" Gynallea snapped. "What magic would make the girl's eyes change like that? Or give her fever without griped guts and phlegmed lungs?"

"No curse is so specific," Eloti added. "One well-wishes or ill-wishes a person or an object or a space of land. Had the girl been cursed, everything she touched or approached would have . . . gone wrong. She would have fallen into that manure pile, banged her elbow on that barn wall, stubbed her toe and stumbled on that ground—and doubtless torn her dress in the bargain. Furthermore, everyone who touched her would also have stumbled, dropped things, and so forth, for as long as she was in contact with them."

"And what if . . ." Wotheng studied the depths of his cup. "What if somebody placed a curse specifically on one part of the girl's body—say, her . . . brain?"

Eloti stared at him, eyebrows rising. "I doubt if it could be done at all," she said slowly. "I've never seen nor heard of any wizard who could narrow the range of a curse on a living person so tightly as that. The skill, ability, knowledge, and concentration required for that . . . Well, no. No one I've ever met nor heard of, ever, could do it."

"We haven't met everyone in Yotha House," Zeren snarled, "nor observed any of them at magical work. They've had time enough to plot a work like this."

"Besides," Eloti added quickly, "a curse placed on a person's brain would affect the entire organ—and the symptoms would be utterly different. The girl would not be able to see, speak, or walk at all. Most likely, she would be rendered idiot—or dead. No, Lord Wotheng, we are not dealing with a curse here."

"What on earth gave you that idea, anyway?" Sulun asked. "Cursing a specific organ is rather a bizarre notion."

Wotheng sighed, reached into his belt pouch, and pulled out the grubby sheets of parchment. "What else," he said, "should one make of these?"

The other four bent over the sheets, studying them.

"That's a rather poor copy of one of my anatomy diagrams," said Eloti. "Rather dirty, too. These are clearly portraits of Irga, done by a talented but totally untrained beginner."

"What connection do you see among them?" Sulun asked, turning a puzzled eye on Wotheng.

"They were found together, and brought to me by one of your lady's students."

"Oh, ho," murmured Gynallea. "Oh, *ho*. Which student was that?"

" 'Twas Pado," Wotheng sighed. "She said Losh made the drawings."

"Pado? That spiteful little sow?" Gynallea snorted. "I'd not put it beyond her to make the drawings herself, then tell that tale, purely to make trouble between Losh and the girl he plainly prefers."

"Losh?" Eloti wrinkled her brow in puzzlement. "He's in my class on medicine, yes. The anatomy drawing could well be his. Indeed he asked me but a day ago if there were any reason not to . . . draw pictures of people."

"So he drew some pictures of his sweetheart," Sulun puzzled. "What's the trouble with that?"

"More than you think," Wotheng admitted, "seeing that the drawings were rolled together—put in contact, d'ye see—and there's a distinct smear across the brain in this one."

The others looked at each other as that sank in.

"It means nothing whatever," Eloti said firmly. "Items put in contact have no power outside their own natures, none whatever—not unless the deliberate, concentrated will of a trained wizard is aimed at them—no more than logs piled together will catch fire of themselves."

"And . . ." Wotheng shuffled on his chair, but kept his eyes on Eloti " . . . if the deliberate will were applied?"

"You can't be accusing—" Zeren started.

Eloti tapped his hand, silencing him. "I've seen no sign whatever of magical ability in Losh," she said. "Neither has he had any such training, so far as I can see. Finally, if he loves the girl, he would certainly not harm her."

"Could it be done by accident?" Wotheng insisted. "Say, he tried to put some sort of love charm on her, something that would . . . 'turn her head,' and got it wrong?"

Eloti actually laughed. "No, no impossible. Magic doesn't *work* that way. One can well-wish or ill-wish, and nothing more. All love spells are frauds, as I have reason to know." A flicker of some old anger darted through her eyes; passed away quickly. "And last, curse or blessing, magic done wrong simply doesn't work; one wastes one's power, nothing more. It is like—to return to that pile of logs again—trying to strike sparks in a tinderbox, and the tinder doesn't catch. One may tire out one's hands trying, but nothing else is accomplished."

Wotheng looked as grim as they'd yet seen him. "I have . . . only your word for that, m'lady, much as I wish to trust it. And I *did* see friend Sulun, here, make magic with the fire in my dining hearth, the first night we met."

"That was a simple trick with firepowder!" Sulun retorted. "A chemist's trick—just like Yotha's fire fluid."

"And the words you spoke then?"

Sulun blushed. "A bit of showman's trickery, I admit. On our travels, we've found that folk prefer their worldly marvels with a bit of show. Besides," he added with a shrug, "Deese had been good to us, and it never hurts to give him a bit of gratitude."

Wotheng chuckled briefly. "No wonder you guessed that Yotha's fire was likewise a showman's trick. One actor recognizes another, eh?"

"So it is." Sulun grinned lopsidedly. "We have real skills and goods to sell, but folk prefer to call such marvels magic. We've been, hmm, obliged to oblige them."

"Do you claim, then," Wotheng asked, very carefully, "that you have no magical powers among you?"

"No," said Eloti. "There are two of us—myself and Arizun—who have the ability, and the training. Neither of us, I assure you, had either the power or the wish to do what was done to that poor girl upstairs."

"Then who did?" Wotheng leaned back in his chair. "Before you ask: no, Pado spent all yesterday and the day before here in Ashkell, for she stays with her aunt during the days when you have your classes. Other days, she stays with her family, off at the other end of the vale from Irga's house—better than half a day's journey, at best. I had my men go speak to her relatives and whatever servants they could find. Further, Pado has never been to Irga's house, would have had to ask the way there, and no one I could find recalls her ever so much as asking. And if this is indeed a case of poisoning, where would Pado find a poison that no one else in the vale knows aught of?"

"Maybe from our friends at Yotha House," said Zeren. "They've been outside the vale."

"Ah, but so have you." Wotheng grinned. "Stop spluttering, man; I only say it's possible. None of you has any reason . . . hmm, none that I know of, to harm the girl."

"None of us even knew her before this," Eloti pointed out. "She was never one of my students here."

"Nor did she ever come to Deese House," Sulun added. "I doubt if any of us ever laid eyes on her, or heard of her, before today."

"Just so." Wotheng raked his eyes around the room. "I've never heard that any of Yotha's people had aught to do with the girl, either. None of her family were worshippers, nor often went to the ceremonies in Yotha House."

"Then this might have nothing to do with our . . . religious rivalry," Sulun offered. "It could be pure accident."

Wotheng interlaced his fingers and rested his chin on them. "That, I think, we'll learn soon enough.

"How so?"

"If nothing further comes of this incident, if Irga recovers and goes about as before, if nothing changes between her and Losh, if Yotha House does nothing to involve itself in the clamor to follow, then we may believe it was an accident. Now—"

"Clamor to follow?" Zeren caught that immediately. "What clamor? What do you expect here, Lord Wotheng?"

Wotheng hunched his shoulders and looked honestly apologetic. "I expect that Pado has yattered the tale all over the villa by now, saying that Losh magicked Irga with spells he learned at school. I also expect that Losh's mother, who opposed her son's courtship of Irga, will be doing her best to claim her son innocent of wrongdoing. I hope those two will come to blows in front of half of the villa, over the accusation. 'Twould be a disaster were they to join forces."

"Disaster? Why? Two women nattering that one boy did *not* accidentally bewitch his sweetheart—"

"I don't think you quite understand," Gynallea cut in, glancing daggers at her husband. "Lady Eloti *did* say, before her whole class, that there was no harm whatever in drawing pictures of living persons. I heard gossip of that in the kitchen, before this happened. Wager well, there'll be more such gossip now."

"Pictures?" Sulun caught that. "Whatever is wrong with *pictures*, for the love of the gods?"

Wotheng sighed, avoiding his wife's eyes. "Only that it is old Torrhyn law that pictures of living persons are forbidden, lest they be used for cursing."

"What?" said Sulun, Zeren, and Eloti together.

" 'Tis true." Wotheng looked from one to the other. "An old law, and one I've never enforced. I'd not enforce it now, given choice. Still, this has happened: a picture was made of a living person, and then that person fell mysteriously ill. Do you see what may happen? This the perfect answer, should those two fool women join forces over Losh: blame his teacher."

"And through her, the school—and all of Deese House," Zeren fumed. "Now I *know* Yotha's priests did this!"

"What proof, lad?" Wotheng asked mildly. "Give me proof no man can ever doubt, give me what aid you can, and I'll go clean out that snakes' nest. Without such, I needs must take care."

"Gods!" Zeren slammed a fist into his palm.

"Lord Wotheng," said Eloti, "surely this law can be abolished on grounds of its illogic. Should a wizard choose to curse someone, a picture is unnecessary. A thread from the victim's garment, his footprint, knowledge of where his house lies, even a glimpse of his face seen once and remembered—any of these will do as well, or better than, a picture. Forbidding such images is senseless."

"Much like the sword law in Sabis." Zeren laughed sourly. "The city made a law forbidding common subjects to own or carry swords, blithely thinking this would end bloodshed in its streets. Robbers and bravos shed blood enough with knives, bludgeons, and common tools. For that matter, robbers could get swords anyway, law or no law. And they faced a citizenry disarmed."

"Sabis?" Wotheng arched a bushy eyebrow at him. "You've lived there?"

Sulun and Eloti held their breath. Zeren merely shrugged. "Among many others. I'm a soldier, as you know; I've been a hired sword halfway round the Midworld Sea. Many bizarre things I've seen, too—including cities full of wizards and images of the living, and no great harm done thereby."

Wotheng shrugged. "A good argument. Remember it, if this miserable business does come to a trial."

"Why not simply abolish the damned law, then?"

" 'Tis a bit late for that." Wotheng looked to his wife. "Sweet cow, you'd best explain it."

Gynallea snorted and rolled her eyes heavenward. "Politics, my dears, all politics. Had we known this might happen, my lovey would surely have abolished the fool law right then. Now, what with an actual case, he dare not. 'Twould look to all folk as if 'twere done solely to protect favorites. D'ye see?"

"I think so," Sulun murmured. He looked sidelong at Wotheng. "You . . . can't afford to have your subjects in the vale too resentful, can you?"

Wotheng didn't precisely shrink in his chair, but he looked older and wearier than he had a moment before. "You've guessed, lad. Your friend Zeren can tell you how few men-at-arms I have, and how trained."

"Not many," Zeren agreed, "But well-trained enough to handle a mob of disgruntled shepherds, if not to storm Yotha house. You don't expect a revolt over this business, do you?"

"Pshaw, no." Wotheng laughed. " 'Tisn't that I fear; 'tis the neighbors."

"Neighbors?" Eloti asked. "What neighbors, and what of them?"

"Good lady, I'm but a small lordling compared to others." Wotheng's eyes strayed to the fire. "Vona knows, there are other sons of war captains—aye, and some present war captains as well, fresh from taking the river cities—who have far more land, wealth, men-at-arms, and gear for them than do I. There are lords to the north, up where the trade caravans go, who might cast a coveting eye on my lands did they think the vale worth taking."

"With the wealth you've brought us," Gynallea said gloomily, "it just might be worth the taking now."

"Oh, they'll not give me trouble without cause." Wotheng shrugged. "They'll be needing some excuse. 'Come, me loyal boys, let's go rob another Ancar fellow of his land' isn't enough reason, and the troops would not marshal for that. But then, 'Come, me boys, Wotheng's own people rumble against him; let's go relieve them of a bad lord and put a better in his place'—now, that might get some fellows to assemble with sword in hand and hopes of good loot. If I can't keep on looking poor, and I can't raise a sizable armed host, I look a tempting target, tempting enough that any excuse will do. D'you see where my trouble lies?"

"Gods . . ." Zeren breathed, sagging in his chair. "How many could we levy? How soon?"

"Not enough," Wotheng said shortly. "The vale has few folk,

being poor land, and most of those are needed for tending the sheep. Sheep are easily lost, strayed, stolen."

"And we thought we were safe . . ." Sulun muttered.

"Tell me," said Eloti. "How would it serve to discourage such greed if it were known that you consort with powerful wizards?"

Wotheng gave her a long, unfathomable look. " 'Twould have to be proven publicly, Lady Eloti: something strong enough, and witnessed well enough, that the . . . neighbors would think it not worth their while to come troubling me."

"There was Yotha, before we came."

"Aye, and now there is Deese." Wotheng glanced into the fire again. "You've brought health, wealth, and wisdom—but that may be more bait to the greedy than cause for restraint."

There was another long silence while Sulun, Eloti, and Zeren looked at each other, considering how they might have already endangered their patron.

"What can we do?" Zeren finally asked.

"I don't know," Wotheng admitted, "but it must be something that shows strength as well as your other virtues. Think on it, my friends. Pray Deese sends you a revelatory dream."

By next morning, everyone in the vale had heard the news.

The first evidence of this was Losh himself reeling, ashen-faced, through the door of Ashkell House and demanding to know where Irga was. Gynallea got to him first, and fairly dragged him off to face Wotheng. The Lord of Ashkell only pulled out the damning pieces of parchment and shoved them under the boy's nose.

"Did you draw these?" he demanded.

"Yes, I did! Oh, I did!" Losh wailed, beating his hands together. "I swear I didn't know it would do her any harm!"

"Then you did not attempt the use of magic to . . . affect the girl's mind?" Wotheng kept his voice stern, but a smile lurked under his moustache.

"Attempt? No, never! I don't *know* anything about magic, and I'd never do anything like that to Irga. Oh, where is she? I have to see her!"

"In a moment, lad. First look closely at this drawing, and tell me: did you deliberately draw that smear there?"

"Smear?" Losh looked closer, frowning in puzzlement. "No,

that's not my doing. It's messed my schoolwork. It must have happened after I lost it."

"Ah. And where did you lose these drawings?"

"Somewhere at home, I think. When I looked in my schoolbag at class yesterday, they weren't there. Please, please, may I see Irga?"

"Hmm, of course, lad. Come this way."

Wotheng led the dithering boy up to the tower room, then watched the reunion with a thoughtful eye. Irga was indeed much better this morning, only a little pale and weak, and looked ethereally beautiful. Losh practically fell all over her, sobbing apologies and protestations of love and more, most of it incoherent. Irga, understanding none of it, only wanted him to hold her. Wotheng shut the door and tiptoed away, wondering how soon those two would marry. He hoped this wouldn't curtail the boy's schoolwork; from what he'd seen and heard, Losh was quite a bright young fellow when not silly with love.

Certainly there'd been no sorcery, intentional or not, on Losh's part.

Wotheng went back to his morning audiences, thinking much on the incident.

After that, the news came thick and fast, usually brought in by the morning's petitioners. A guard reported that Nima the jeweler's wife had assaulted Pado the landholder's daughter with a market basket in the middle of the villa market square; the resulting knockdown, hair-tearing brawl had overturned a pushcart and spilled several weights of fish into the street, with a total cost of two silvers and seven coppers in damage. The vintner's wagon boy reported that the high priest of Yotha had delivered a furious sermon about the dangerous carelessness of Deese's wizards, claiming—without mentioning names—that this had already led to the bewitchment of an innocent girl, and that worse would follow if such wickedness was not stopped. Biddon the blacksmith, trembling with outrage, came to report that persons unknown had thrown cow manure all over the shrine to Deese and scribbled "nasty words and wild accusations" on the stones.

Wotheng treated each of these separate tales with calm, tolerance, and quiet common sense, sending their tellers away with some satisfaction. To himself, he tallied and weighed and made his own plans.

Finally, another guard came in to report that a small but growing and noisy mob had gathered outside the gates of Ashkell House, shouting accusations, demanding to be let in, threatening the Lady Eloti and her students.

"Aha," said Wotheng, getting to his feet. "Tell the rest of the guards to quiet the crowd. I'll be there directly. Oh, and dispatch a messenger on a fast horse to take word of this to Deese House."

The guard saluted fast, and departed faster.

Wotheng paused a moment, fixing his eyes on the sigil of Vona painted on the near doorpost.

"Lord Vona, make this work well, and I promise you a whole ox on your next feast day," he said quietly.

Then he strode off to deal with the mob at the gate.

"Good Brother Oralro," Folweel enticed, "you know it cannot be done any other way; those Sukkti wizards are an affront to Yotha and a danger to the public morality. Already our herd of the faithful has shrunk notably." He stopped himself just in time to keep from saying: *and the donations likewise*. Let Oralro think of that for himself.

The plump Second Priest of Yotha paced back and forth across the abused rug. "I'm not sure, Brother Folweel," he muttered. "I'm not sure. Certainly this obscene magicking of a young virgin must be punished, and certainly the law is plain. Why, then, may we not openly give our support to Goody Nima's charge against the wizards? Why must we let that good and faithful woman stand alone in her hour of need?"

"Because the fickle crowd has withdrawn from us," Folweel intoned, trying not to tap his fingers with impatience. Oralro might be a splendid wizard, but he was incapable of seeing, let alone handling, matters of politics. "They regard us with suspicion and even contempt."

"Never!" snorted Oralro, pausing in mid-stride.

" 'Tis true, Brother. And worse: that fool Wotheng is likewise swayed by the pretty magics of these newcomers. Do we appear publicly in support of Goodwife Nima, Wotheng will assume we speak only out of jealousy, not righteousness."

"Yet if we speak with righteousness, we shall be heard and answered by Him whose hearing matters." Oralro thrust out his jaw, and prominent lower lip, in solid defiance. "I say, we shall be reticent only in this, Brother; we shall say nothing if not asked, but if asked, we shall answer fully."

Folweel sighed acquiescence. He had the agreement of all the others on this present bit of strategy, and this was as much agreement from Oralro as he was likely to get.

Still, best make some contingency plans in case some questioner did get to Oralro and asked him questions he was all too liable to answer.

"What is your complaint?" Wotheng roared at the sullen crowd. Goody Nima, he noted, was in the forefront of the lot, looking harassed but purposeful. "What brings you to clamor at my door in such unseemly fashion?"

"Vile wizardry!" howled an anonymous voice.

"Let us come in and clean out that nest of vipers!" yelled another, carefully distant from the first crier.

"Lord Wotheng, you have harbored serpents under your roof!" screeched a third. Clumsy, that one: "harboring serpents" was a phrase often used in sermons at Yotha's temple. Someone might notice, and make good guesses.

"Words full of wind," Wotheng snorted. "I doubt that any of you has a true charge of crime to bring me. What harm has been done, what crime committed? Have any of you a true and plain accusation?"

"I do!" Nima darted forward, waving a rolled parchment in her hand. "*I* have a charge of crime committed by that witch who teaches wizardry right inside your walls."

Wotheng waved the near guards aside and let the woman come to him with her scroll. He opened it in front of the expectant crowd and read the crabbed writing. Oh yes, the woman had been careful and thorough.

"I charge the wizardess Eloti," Nima announced to the crowd, straight from the words on the scroll, which she'd no doubt memorized. "I charge her with the crime of encouraging others to break the law against vile and harmful magic, to wit: the forbidden making of images of living persons, so as to allow the working of curses and similar evil magecraft. I further claim that such harm has in fact been done through such means—by an accidental agent—to one of your lordship's tenants." She paused, panting, triumphant at having got through the whole speech without a slip.

The crowd cheered raucously.

Wotheng raised an eyebrow, noting how quickly and neatly Nima had passed over Losh's involvement in the "vile and harmful magic." It was clear enough what direction her argument would take.

"Very well." Wotheng rolled up the parchment and shoved it in his belt purse. "Accusation of crime has been duly brought forward. I will sit in hearing on this case tomorrow, in the great hall, at second bell."

The crowd cheered wildly, with something of that undertone often heard at dogfights.

You'll have your show, Wotheng promised, casting his eyes over the now jolly mob. At the crowd's edge he saw Sulun, just riding up, looking bewildered and horrified at the scene. The man must have been on his way back here, to arrive so quickly. Too late, anyway. *The game is set and moving, my poor friend.* Wotheng stepped back in the doorway to avoid meeting Sulun's eyes. *No choice now but to play to the finish.*

Half the vale, it seemed, came crowding into the main courtyard of Ashkell House for the trial. The baker did a fine business selling smallcakes to the crowd, and the brewer would have done better if Gynallea hadn't bluntly ordered him to stop; clear heads, she explained, would be needed for this business.

Sulun, from his seat on a bench at Wotheng's left, looked about in dismay. Here, ranked behind the accused, sat Eloti's friends and household; ranged behind them, in merry disorder, were students from her school, plus their friends and some of their families. They munched smallcakes, chattered with each other, compared notes, and cheered when Eloti came out and sat in the Accused's chair—more of an arena cheering section than an audience at a trial.

Losh was not among them; he sat, looking miserable, close to his tight-lipped mother in the Accusers' seats, several rows of benches to the right of Lord Wotheng's tall chair, the official Judgment Seat.

The rest of the crowd sat or stood piled in rough ranks before the three official zones, held back by a line of Wotheng's household guards. Some of them wore ribbons or bits of cloth in Deese's familiar colors: iron grey and brass yellow. A few others, arranged closer to the Accusers' side, wore scraps of orange and red.

"This is a game to them," Sulun groaned quietly. "An amusement! Nobody sways an arena crowd with sweet reason. What shall we do?"

"Hush." Vari patted his arm. "We can amuse folk better than that lot."

Wotheng stood up, pulling his best cloak around him, and intoned a brief prayer to assorted gods. The crowd stayed respectfully silent until he sat down, glanced at a parchment list on the table before him, and summoned the first Accuser.

Nima stood, rustling in her starched best finery, and repeated—almost word for word—what she'd said the day before at Wotheng's gate. She would have sat down then, but Wotheng stopped her and insisted she tell her whole tale, as a witness, right then. Somewhat flustered, she related how she'd heard from the housemaid just the morning before how Pado—she flashed a veiled look at the landholder's smirking daughter—had been telling everyone that Losh had gone and bewitched Irga.

" . . . So I went to see her and asked what she meant by such, and we argued somewhat." The whole crowd snickered at that, which made Nima blush furiously but didn't stop her recital. "She told me how she'd found Losh's . . . school drawings . . . and brought them to your lordship, and how she saw . . ." a brief sniff. " . . . Irga's mother come report her daughter's bewitchment. So I went to talk to Losh, and . . ." Nima paused for a deep breath, then said the rest in a rush. "He hadn't known anything about it. He was terribly upset, he was; ran right out of the house, for all I called him to wait. So then I didn't know what to do, so I talked to, er, some neighbors, and they told me to write up a Bill of Accusation, m'lord, and bring it to you, which I did." She fell silent and looked around her, as if for support.

"I notice that you didn't come alone to bring your petition," Wotheng commented. "Why was that?"

"Er, well . . ." Nima glanced about her again. "I was fearful of witchcraft, m'lord, so I asked some, er, friends and neighbors to come with me. For protection, you'll know."

"Protection?" Wotheng's expression was bland, mildly curious. "Against whom? And why?"

"Why, against that Deese witch that corrupted my son!" Nima

shrilled, voice cracking as she pointed to Eloti. "He said she'd told him it was all right to draw pictures, spreading evil magic about . . . Who knows what else she could do? I wasn't safe— none of us are safe—with that sort running about, doing whatever magic they please!"

She paused, gulping for air.

Eloti raised an elegant eyebrow, turned to the crowd, and spread her hands wide. "I'd never even met her before," she murmured, just audible in the moment's near silence.

"Has the Accused any questions to ask of this witness?" said Wotheng.

"Just one." Eloti turned back to face Nima, who squirmed under her gaze. "Goodwife Nima, before you wrote your Bill of Accusation, while you were still asking neighbors for advice, did you not also ask advice of your personal priest?"

The crowd rumbled knowingly.

Nima paled. "I-I suppose so, among so many others . . ." she admitted.

Eloti leaned back in her chair and made a polite gesture of dismissal.

"You may sit down," said Wotheng. "Let the witness named Pado step forth and tell her tale."

Pado clasped her hands primly as she told of finding the three drawings, guessing whose they were, being disturbed by them, and taking them to Lord Wotheng.

"As for telling folk about what I saw and heard of Irga's mother," she finished, "well, why shouldn't I? I *knew* Losh had done wrong."

"What?" said Wotheng, looking most innocently confused. "You mean, in not marrying you?"

Now it was Pado's turn to blush furiously. "That was last year!" she snapped. "No, I meant in making drawings. That's forbidden by law, you know, no matter what Mistress Eloti said."

Wotheng turned to Eloti asked if she had any questions for this witness.

Again, Eloti had only one. "Precisely where and how did you find these three drawings?" she asked, a carrying note in her voice.

"Why . . ." Pado blinked, confused. "In truth, *I* didn't find them. One of the other students did. That clerk, Dubba? Duppa? He gave me them, said he'd found them in the courtyard, and did I know whose they were. I thought I did, so I took them."

"Lord Wotheng," said Eloti, turning toward the Judgment Seat, "I request that we summon the clerk Duppa and ask how he came by those drawings."

The crowd rumbled again; knowing laughter and speculation.

"Quite a good idea." Wotheng got to his feet, rang a handbell, and announced to all and sundry, "Clerk Duppa, stand forth."

Nobody stood up.

The crowd rumbled louder.

Sulun, glancing over the small sea of faces, noticed a shuffling movement toward the rear, by the wall. Who was that? A scattering of figures, robed and hooded in nondescript dark cloth, faces muffled and shadowed: who could they be?

Yotha's priests, I'll wager!

Wotheng made the summons twice more, with no result except more noise of speculation from the audience. "Does anyone here know the whereabouts of Clerk Duppa?" he shouted.

"Try Yotha House!" shouted a brawny youth, one of Biddon's apprentices.

The crowd roared agreement, with some dissent.

Wotheng gave an odd, grim smile. "Be there anyone here from Yotha House?" he asked loudly.

At the back of the crowd there was a brief argument; someone grabbed at someone else's sleeve, which was roughly tugged free. A portly man cried, "Here!" and jostled his way to the front of the throng. "I am Oralro," he announced, "Second Priest of Yotha. I know of no clerk Duppa in Yotha House."

The assemblage muttered and hitched away from him.

"We shall make search for this Duppa," said Wotheng. "Meanwhile, let Ilna, mother of Irga, stand forth."

Irga's mother stood up among the rightside benches and duly gave her stark and pathetic account.

On the leftward benches, Yanados and Doshi conferred in whispers.

"That's done it. That's brought Yotha into it," said Yanados. "Now we'll start getting at the truth."

"Maybe good guesses, but nothing proved," Doshi said gloomily. "You can wager they blotted out their tracks. I'd say this Duppa is probably at the bottom of some well by now."

Ilna finished her tale, recounting how she'd taken her afflicted daughter to a neighbor wife and then come to ask help of Lord Wotheng. "The rest you know," she said, clasping her hands.

Wotheng scratched his chin and asked if the Accused had any questions.

"I do," said Eloti. "Goodwife, did you ask your daughter what she had eaten or drunk before this fit came upon her?"

The assemblage fell silent, surprised by that.

Ilna was clearly surprised too. "Why—why, no. I thought nothin' of that, but only of gettin' her safe. Why?"

"And did it occur to you, at any time, that there might be any other cause than magic for your daughter's fit?"

The crowd muttered, chewing that over.

"Nay, m'lady," Ilna answered. "She said she was bewitched. What else could it be?"

"Poison," said Eloti.

The whole audience gasped, then broke into raucous argument.

Wotheng clanged his bell until the noise stopped, looking oddly satisfied.

"But who'd want t'poison my daughter?" Ilna cried. "What harm'd she ever done t'any?"

The crowd rumbled again, tossing up names like flotsam on an unquiet sea. Pado and Nima looked daggers at each other. Losh put his head in his hands. Only Oralro, standing with arms defiantly crossed in the forefront of the throng, seemed untroubled.

"Huh, he knows *he* didn't do it," Zeren muttered at Sulun's elbow. "Could be he doesn't know who did. I'll wager the high priest doesn't tell him everything."

"Goodwife!" Wotheng thundered, loud enough to make everyone shut up and listen. "Know you if this mysteriously missing clerk Duppa ever showed an . . . interest in your daughter? Ever spoke to her? Admired her from a distance? Showed any anger toward her? Anything?"

Ilna only spread her hands and shook her head in bewilderment. Not that it mattered; the uproar from the crowd would have drowned any spoken answer.

"What's he doing?" Omis whispered to Zeren. "Is he trying to accuse this Duppa in his absence?"

"I'm not sure," Zeren admitted, rubbing his eyes. He'd spent

The Sword of Knowledge

the night sitting, armed and armored, in front of Eloti's door; he
hadn't slept much or well, and that gave no edge to his wit.
"Howsoever, he's opened an interesting line of thought. Did
Duppa steal the drawings, magic the girl, then try to hide it by
passing on the drawings to Pado?"

"Not likely, you know."

"True, but this mob will wonder about it."

Wotheng quelled the chattering horde again, and summoned
forth Losh.

"Damned little we'll get out of him," Arizun muttered.

True enough, Losh had little of substance to add to the trail.
Yes, he'd made the drawings, seeing that his teacher had told
him there was no harm in it. The one sketch was for his class on
medicine, the other two, well, simply to have pictures of Irga to
look at when he couldn't be with her.

The crowd snickered. Goody Nima looked grim. Pado glared
daggers at the lad.

And no, Losh went on, he hadn't tried to bewitch Irga through
the drawings. Why should he, knowing she loved him as much as
he loved her? How could he, when he'd never in his life studied
magical arts? Besides, he'd never do anything that could possibly
harm her, since Irga was the dearest, sweetest, loveliest, and so
on. No one could have doubted his weepy, hand-wringing
sincerity.

This time the chuckles from the audience were fewer,
accompanied by sighs from the younger set and indeed from
anyone who remembered the silly giddiness of first love. Only
Nima and Pado looked as if they'd bitten sour apples.

"Why," Wotheng asked, "did you place those three drawings
together?"

"I didn't intend to!" Losh wailed. "I just stuffed them in my
schoolbag, along with everything else."

"And how came that dark smudge to be smeared across the
anatomy drawing?"

"I've no idea! *I* didn't put it there. Why should I? It's spoiled
my schoolwork."

"Hmm," said Wotheng, significantly. "Has the Accused any
questions?"

Eloti did. "Goodman Losh, when and where were the drawings
lost?"

Losh had to stop and think about that. "I . . . saw they were gone just the day after I made them. I opened my schoolbag at class, and they weren't there. I thought I must have lost them at home, since that's where I saw them last."

"How, then, did they come to be found at school?"

"I don't know. Maybe they fell out on my way into the hall, but I don't see how, since I don't recall that I opened the bag."

"Could anyone have light-fingered them out of your schoolbag, at home or on the way to class, or even after you'd arrived?"

Losh scratched his chin and looked blank. "Well, I suppose so. But why?"

"Why indeed?" said Eloti, leaning back as if she didn't expect to be answered.

The crowd speculated in a low grumble.

Smiling tightly, Wotheng called Irga to stand forth and give her story.

Irga stood up in a halo of sunlight, still a trifle pale, dressed in the prettiest gown her mother could find for her. Her dark red hair was braided loosely down her back, and her eyes looked dark and huge in her drawn face. The whole assembly sighed rapturously at the sight of her.

"She's so pretty, they'll believe anything she says," Ziya whispered.

"Let's hope she doesn't say anything against Eloti," Arizun muttered back.

Irga seemed at a loss for what to say. Wotheng urged her to begin with when, where, and under what circumstances Losh had drawn her pictures.

Irga made a few false starts, blushed slightly, and admitted it had been late afternoon of four days ago, and she was out berry-picking when Losh met her. She didn't mention, though it was obvious, that the meeting had been arranged. Yes, they talked a bit about Losh's schoolwork, besides this and that. Yes, Losh had said he wanted to draw pictures of her, and yes, she'd consented. No, she didn't feel any danger or distress while he'd done so—only love.

This time the crowd sighed and crooned instead of snickering.

Irga blushed again and went on. Losh had left her at about sundown. She'd gone home for supper. Nothing had happened that night. In the morning she'd wakened as usual, built up the fire and put the kettle on, dressed, and went to rake out the barn. It was while she was dumping the manure cart that the fit struck her.

She paused there, shivering. Wotheng gently urged her to continue.

Irga did, describing in chilly detail the horrors she'd seen and felt.

The listening throng groaned in sympathy.

"Bad tactics," Zeren growled. "They'll be wanting blood now, and it just might be ours."

"That would hardly suit Wotheng's purposes," Vari whispered back.

"Then why is he allowing all this . . . detail to her story?"

"I don't know, but the man's no fool. He has something in mind that will be served hereby."

Irga told how she'd cried for help, thinking the whole farm was bewitched, but when her mother came running to her showing no such distress she'd guessed that the curse lay only on herself. After that she remembered little save for her mother bundling her off in the donkey cart to the neighbor's farm, hours of huddling under blankets and seeing horrors crawl the walls, then being brought to Ashkell House and tended by Lady Gynallea, after which the curse slowly wore off. Yes, she was well now. No, she was certain that Losh couldn't have done that harm to her. Yes, Lady Eloti had helped care for her and had been very kind to her. No, she didn't think the Lady Eloti had done anything to bewitch her.

"Lass, whom do you think might have bewitched you?" Wotheng asked.

"I don't *know*," Irga insisted. "I didna' think I had any enemy so cruel."

"Try Pado!" one of the students in the audience yelled.

"Or Losh's mother!" called another.

The crowd roared with unkind laughter. Pado and Nima shrunk in their seats. Wotheng rang for silence, then asked if the Accused had any questions.

"Yes," said Eloti. "Irga, did you at any time think that there might be any other cause for your distress besides magic?"

"Nay," Irga admitted, "but then, I was no' thinkin' well at all."

The audience laughed gently in sympathy.

"Now think carefully," said Eloti. "Between the time you woke and the time the fit came on you, did you have anything to eat or drink—anything not taken by anyone else in your household?"

"Why . . ." Irga thought on that for a long moment. "Just a cup of herb tea, as I always do."

A quiet ripple of gasps went through the crowd.

"Aha!" Eloti pounced. "And was that herb tea in any way different, on that morning?"

"Aye," Irga nodded, remembering. "A trifle bitter, now do I think."

The assemblage rumbled angrily.

"And is there any of that herb tea left in your house?" Eloti asked, leaning forward.

"Nay, that was the last in the jar."

The crowd sighed disappointment.

Eloti paused to think for a long moment before speaking again. "Tell me, Irga: how is your house locked up at night?"

The audience rippled with new excitement as Irga considered the question.

"Why, we but put up the door bar, with the latchstring out on chance that Papa may have to get up and tend the sheep, and aye, he might be too sleepy then to remember to put out the string by himself. I do recall a time—"

"Then anyone could have crept into the house while you slept?"

"Aye . . . they could."

The crowd was chattering loudly now, trading guesses on whom the supposed night creeper might have been. The name of Duppa kept coming up.

Eloti, eyes bright and fierce, plunged into the next question. "Have you or any of your family ever gone to the ceremonies at Yotha's temple?"

The throng hushed, all ears. Oralro flushed with anger.

"Aye, once. We all went to see the flames dance at midsummer rites."

"And were there many people there? Did many of the priests and under-priests and assistants have chance to lay eyes on you?"

The crowd howled understanding, making the connection.

"I resent that question!" Oralro shouted furiously. "That has no bearing on the crime under consideration, which is image-making. This is foul slander, m'lord! Yonder witch is trying to disguise her own guilt by flinging manure—"

"Quiet!" Wotheng roared, clanging his bell. "Witness Irga need not reply to that question. Has the Accused anything further to ask?"

"Only this: Irga, have other swains come courting you, and been turned away?"

"Aye, many." Irga blushed fetchingly again. "The lads always hoot and holler at me when I come to town for marketing."

"Any in particular? Any who have been especially . . . insistent?"

"Too many to remember," Irga admitted.

The crowd laughed knowingly.

Eloti shrugged. "I have no further questions, m'lord."

"Then—" Wotheng started.

Right there the tower bell clanged for the hour of noon, startling the listening throng.

"Then let us halt these proceedings for lunch, and reassemble at next bell," said Wotheng, rising from his seat.

The assembly cheered, and disassembled. Those who had been sitting got up to stretch and rub their cramped rumps. Those who had been standing sought dry and comfortable seats. The baker went back to selling his wares at a good rate, and the brewer—under Gynallea's watchful eye—sold pint crocks of small beer.

Assorted political factions gathered to exchange views and share lunch. Sulun's party, guessing that they'd not be dining with their judge today, sat in a rough circle at their benches, surrounded by Eloti's students. They had little chance to discuss the case among themselves, since the faction of scholars insisted on plying them with good wishes, questions, and suggestions—a few of which were useful.

On the other side of the court, Losh avoided his mother's frantic clutchings at his sleeve, and went to talk to Irga; in a moment they were holding hands and murmuring at each other as if they were all alone in the world. The passing crowd had the decency not to interrupt them.

Pado glanced once at Nima, shrugged apologetically, and went off to dine with her family.

Nima glared furiously at Losh and Irga, stared sourly at Pado's retreating back, then picked her way through the crowd to the nearest visible priest of Yotha, who happened to be Oralro.

At the back of the crowd, draped in his nondescript muffling cloak, Folweel made some fast notes on a waxed board and conferred quietly with Patrobe.

" 'Tisn't going well," Patrobe was muttering. "They've suggested a fine case against Duppa."

"Did you get him safely away?" Folweel whispered without looking up.

"Aye, Brother. He must be halfway down to Gol-port by now. But what shall we do now? There'll be no muzzling Oralro, not after that witch's questioning."

"If we can't silence him, we use him. We'll go to our second plan once the Questioning of the Accused begins." He glanced up, noted Oralro pushing toward him with Nima in tow, and smiled. "And here come our two best tools for that. Step away, Brother."

"Oh, Father, may I speak with you?" Nima gushed, drawing a few startled eyes.

"Certainly, Daughter," Folweel soothed, setting a comforting arm around the flustered woman's shoulders. "Come, let us go outside and away from the ears of the ungodly. Er, Brother Oralro, do keep an eye on that witch and her friends, lest they plot mischief."

With that, he swept Nima outside the court to put a few words in her ear. They stayed there for perhaps half the noon hour, after which Nima came back alone, smiling grimly. Folweel strolled quietly into the court a moment later, and went to find Oralro.

The tower bell rang again, the crowd reassembled, and Wotheng formally took his seat. "Let the Accused stand forth," he announced.

The throng fell so silent that distant bird cries could be heard from beyond the walls.

Eloti stood up, hands clasped loosely before her. "I have little to tell of events," she said, "but much of facts. Yes, Losh is one of my students—and an excellent student at that. He should, in time, go to some great university."

On the far bench, Losh blushed and squeezed Irga's hand tighter. She gave him an admiring look. Nima glowered at both of them.

"Yes, I use pictures as teaching devices—indeed, it would be almost impossible to teach medicine and mechanics without them. Yes, I have said to my entire class, including Losh, that there is no harm in making pictures of living persons—and indeed, there is none."

Both Nima and Oralro, back to their former places, opened their mouths to protest. Eloti went on, giving them no time for it.

"It has been said that drawn or graven images can be used as substitutes for actual persons in operations of magic—and yes, *this is true*."

The whole crowd gasped, including the Deese faction.

"But then, anything can be so used. The mere sight or memory of a person can be used to make him, or her, target for a curse— or a blessing. Should we then blind everyone's eyes, or blot out everyone's memory?" Eloti turned to face the assembly. "Pictures are necessary tools, and no tool is evil in itself. Objects have no will, no power, no purpose of their own, save what people give to them. Good and evil, help and harm, reside in the will and action of the user, not in the thing used."

"Blasphemy!" snapped Oralro. "Objects have power that—"

"Silence!" Wotheng retorted. "Wait until the Accused has finished speaking."

"Magic," said Eloti, "requires a most special and concerted use of will and knowledge. It requires great concentration, long study, much practice, and great knowledge of Natural Philosophy. To be quite honest, I have met no one in the vale—" she flicked a glance toward Oralro "—save in the various temples and shrines, who has the knowledge and skill needed to even begin the study, let alone the practice, of magic. No, not even among my students."

She turned an apologetic glance toward Losh, who blushed further.

"Certainly I have not taught magic to any, neither have I found any who are capable of practicing magic without such a course of study. Therefore I have told my students, when asked, that indeed there is no harm in making images—since none of them could use such images for anything but ordinary learning." Eloti cast a narrow-eyed look around the assembly. "Therefore, also, I conclude that Irga's affliction was *not* caused by anything done in my school. As you have heard, there is reason to believe that either the drawings were stolen by someone else—someone trained and capable of working magic—who then used them, for his own reasons, to ill-wish the girl—"

The crowd racketed with speculation on whom that might be. Oralro purpled with indignation.

"—or, more likely, that someone deliberately poisoned Irga and then made effort to give the impression of witchcraft, even unto casting suspicion upon Losh."

Nima squirmed on her bench, suddenly undecided. The dull-robed figure beside her patted her arm and bent close to whisper in her ear. Her face tightened again. Losh paled and gritted his teeth. Irga clenched her hand in his. Pado pursed her lips and looked vaguely elsewhere. Oralro stamped from foot to foot in steaming frustration. The rest of the throng muttered angrily.

"No," Eloti continued, "I did not know there was any law against making images of living persons, not until I was accused."

Wotheng rolled his eyes skyward. Technically, he supposed, his first questions to Eloti might in fact be called accusations. It wasn't a lie.

"Nonetheless, I maintain that this law should be more honored in the breach than in the observance, seeing that it is useless—as useless as forbidding bows in order to prevent poaching. If the law must be enforced, then let its punishment be altered to better suit the nature of the crime—such as paying a fine of, say, one flower or pinch of grain to be placed on the nearest altar of Kula, along with a prayer that one's work will not be misused."

The student faction broke out in a cheer at the elegance of her solution. They could see in it the beginning of a pretty, romantic custom. Two old grannies who regularly tended the villa's shrine of Kula cheered likewise, thinking of the free bread they might collect from such a tradition. Wotheng smiled and rubbed his beard. Gynallea laughed outright. Eloti sat down amid the growing applause.

Wotheng quelled the noise with his bell. "Do any wish to question the Accused?" he announced.

"Me! Me!" Oralro and Nima yelled simultaneously.

Wotheng clanged his bell for order. "Let the Accuser speak first," he said.

Nima shot to her feet. "Stories!" she snapped. "Pretty tales! No shred of proof to any of this! We've only your word for it—

and maybe your friends'—that your advice was harmless. You've admitted yourself that anyone *could* have stolen the drawings and used them to bewitch the girl. Who can tell but that was what you intended?"

The crowd rustled with surprise.

"Who can say," Nima plowed on, "that it wasn't yourself who stole the drawings and magicked them? 'Twould be a clever way to strike down a rival, and punish my son for preferring Irga to you!"

The assembly roared. Eloti's eyebrows shot up to her hairline; this was the last thing on earth she'd expected. Behind her, Zeren swore sulfurously and struggled to his feet through restraining hands.

Wotheng clanged for silence. "Let the Accused answer!" he bellowed.

"Well," Eloti marveled, "this is news to me."

Her class laughed in appreciation.

"First, though I admit Losh is a handsome and clever boy, I've never had any, hmm, romantic interest in him. For one thing, he's a trifle young for me."

Pado, who'd been staring at Eloti in wide-eyed horror, now ducked her head and squirmed furiously on her bench.

"For another, I never so much as knew that Irga existed, nor knew her name or face, until she was already afflicted. I will submit to truth spell upon that." Eloti smiled sweetly out at the audience, knowing full well that there was no such thing as a "truth spell." There was only ill-wishing and well-wishing, nothing else; but let the crowd—and Yotha's wizards—believe what they liked.

"No one can truth spell a wizard!" Oralro shouted from the front of the horde. "Everyone knows that!" He glared around him defiantly, as if daring anyone to contradict him. Of course, no one did.

"For a third," Eloti continued, "I already have a lover, whom I intend to marry at spring planting."

She turned to gesture at Zeren, who got to his feet and glared daggers alternately at Losh and his mother. "That's me!" he thundered, hand visibly clenching the grip of his sword. "Does anyone want to challenge the Lady's word on that?"

No, nobody did. The throng buzzed with speculations and

comparisons. A mere boy's appeal, against that of an obvious warrior-magician—and handsome, to boot—seemed very little.

"You're going to marry Eloti?" Doshi gaped, while Yanados tugged warningly at his sleeve.

"I hadn't intended to announce it this way," Zeren admitted.

The surrounding students laughed.

"For yet a fourth," Eloti went on, "when would I have the opportunity to filch Losh's drawings—assuming I even knew they existed—and place a curse on the girl? Irga was afflicted only a little after dawn; Losh did not come to school until much later. I could not have stolen the drawings when he left class the day before, since he did not make them until much later that afternoon, at Irga's farm. Neither could I have gone secretly to Losh's house to steal the drawings—again, assuming I knew he had made them, and how could that be?—because I spent the rest of that day and all the night here at Ashkell House, in the company of the Lady Gynallea."

"True," announced Gynallea, glaring around the assemblage as if defying anyone to doubt *her*.

Nima took a half-step back, still frowning. "Who knows what your magic can do?" she grumbled. "Who knows but you might have used it to spy on Losh, see where he went, whom he met, and what he did. You could have used magic to fetch the drawings—or even curse the girl without them and make him look guilty. We've only your word for it that you can't!"

Eloti rolled her eyes, but answered patiently. "*When* could I have done this? Losh claims that he went to meet Irga after school, and stayed with her until sundown. During all that time I was quite busy discussing uses of herbs with the Lady Gynallea, as well as various other members of her household, who might also be called as witnesses. After sundown, I was at dinner with all of Ashkell household—and such dinners, as many can attest, tend to run late."

Various servitors of Ashkell House laughed agreement at that.

"Afterward, as usual, I went to the wash house with several others of Ashkell house, and thence to bed. By such time Losh was surely asleep, with his drawings safe in his schoolbag. Thus, even if I could use magic for scrying—which, I dare say, nobody in the vale can do—just when was I to spy upon Losh and discover whom he met? When, for that matter, was I to ill-wish the girl? Such things do take time, you know."

"You could have done it that night, or next morning, when no one else was awake and about," Nima insisted. "You could have scried into his schoolbag—"

"But the drawings weren't there!" Losh shouted, jumping to his feet. "I remember, I put the pictures of Irga under my pillow, so I could dream about her!"

The crowd laughed. Irga blushed prettily.

Nima glared briefly at her son. "You could have scried on his dreams, then. Or you might have scried him long before, found the girl, and waited for a good time to make your revenge. You could have done it! We've only *your* word to say you couldn't, or wouldn't!"

Eloti sighed loudly with impatience. "Why, then, when Irga was first brought to Ashkell House, did the Lady Gynallea's medicines ease this 'curse,' long before I heard anything of it?"

"Do you dare to say *I'm* a witch?" Gynallea shouted. "Or that I connived with Eloti on such a fool's venture? No, woman! That girl was poisoned, or I've never seen it."

Unnoticed, Wotheng shook his head. The crowd buzzed, enjoying the juicy fight.

"She could have set the curse to look that way," Nima grumbled, retreating. "She might have deceived you."

"Hardly," Gynallea snorted.

"You've invented a pretty tale yourself, Goodwife," said Eloti, "and with no shred of proof. From what facts we do know, 'tis far more likely that someone crept into Irga's house and poisoned the herbs she used next morning."

"Even that could have been some agent of yours!" Nima retorted.

"Who?" Eloti shot back. "Someone at Ashkell House? Ask the household if anyone stole out that night to go all the way to Irga's house, or if any were missing from the house all the night and didn't reappear until the next day."

"Someone from Deese House, more likely! Anyone there would tell tales to protect you!"

"And how would I have sent word to them, ten leagues away, that now was the time to go to Irga's house and poison her drink?"

"Magic! Magic again!"

"And would magic tell them also where to find Irga's house, which none of us ever visited? Would magic carry someone there, unseen and unheard by man or beast across all the farms in between? Woman, if I had magic like that, I wouldn't bother with such petty stuff; I'd have magicked Irga and Losh and you yourself straight to the bottom of the Midworld Sea. I certainly wouldn't waste time sitting here arguing with you."

The throng roared with laughter at that. One of the laborers who had worked on Deese House's walls commented loudly that with that sort of magic the wizards of Deese wouldn't have needed his help to restore their house—and could have saved themselves a good bit of money. Students speculated that, with that kind of power, Eloti wouldn't have had to spend so many moons teaching them; she could simply have magicked the knowledge into their heads.

"Sure as nine hells," Zeren roared above the clamor, "she could have magicked your stupid mouth shut!"

That set everyone bellowing with laughter. Wotheng rang repeatedly for order, finally gave up, and let the crowd laugh itself tired.

Nima, blushing red as a ripe apple, looked about her for help. No use: nothing could have been heard in that din anyway. At length she sat down, muttering bitterly to herself. Her husband huddled down in his robes and looked elsewhere.

As the noise dwindled, Wotheng rang again for silence. This time the crowd obeyed. "Has anyone else questions for the Accused?" he asked.

"I do!" snapped Oralro, striding forward. "Lady, if I dare use the term, I truly do resent the slanderous suggestion you have made against this goodwife here and against the House of Yotha besides. Slanderous, I say, to accuse any in our herd of most vilely and lecherously bewitching a young virgin!"

Several in the crowd snickered. Irga blushed furiously, and didn't look.

"Worse still to accuse us of any dealings with poison—and this is not the first such vile accusation! Nay, nor the first instance of harm come to the innocent through the careless witcheries of Deese House and its wizards. Was not our own stonemason crushed to death while working upon their walls?"

"His own damned fault!" yelled one of the workmen in the crowd.

Oralro went on as if he hadn't heard. "And more slanders:

when their own workmen were poisoned with bad food, did not these Deese wizards hasten to blame our brotherhood, even though the baker's carter confessed to the deed?"

"He named one of your under-priests, too!" shouted a peeved guardsman.

Oralro sailed on, blithely unheeding. "All this harm has come to the vale with the presence of these Deese wizards! Has not Yotha warned and warned his faithful herd, repeatedly, of this danger? Have we not done our best to warn others, though they, being blinded with greed for petty wonders, have not heeded us? Have we not warned the folk of the vale that these wizards of Deese are careless in both magic and morals—allowing male and female priests to sleep under the same roof—"

"Is this your question?" Eloti snapped, spots of color showing in her cheeks.

"No it isn't, and I'm not finished!" Oralro stamped a heavy foot. "We have maintained, as Yotha bids us, that the gods are troubled by such proud carelessness. We, m'lord, are troubled also by such immoral quickness to slander others for the harm done by Deese's wizards. We are also appalled, as all good folk should be, to hear from this witch's very lips her contempt for the law! Did she not boldly admit to breaching the law against image making? And did she not blatantly claim before you all that the law itself was wrong, and should be abolished? What can we expect of those who have such contempt for law itself?"

"Common sense," Eloti answered. "Next question?"

The crowd brayed with laughter.

Oralro purpled slightly, took a deep breath, and preached on. "More, she claims, as you heard, that drawn or graven images have no power—more, that objects in themselves have no power, nor even purpose. I say before you all, this is a most blasphemous lie!"

The audience rumbled to itself, wondering.

"Of course objects have purpose! Anyone who looks at them knows that. A sword, for example, has no purpose except to kill people."

"Bull turds!" Zeren bellowed, springing to his feet. "I've used *my* sword to chop wood, make fire, and stir soup!"

"A wagon," Oralro continued fiercely, "has no purpose save to draw loads."

"Or to burn for firewood, or rot and feed wood ants!" Zeren retorted.

Wotheng wearily clanged his bell, but said nothing.

"I do not say objects cannot be put to other uses than their obvious purpose," Oralro conceded, glaring daggers at Zeren. "But they rarely are. When one sees a shovel, one may safely claim that it is to be used for digging."

"Or for clanging an enemy over the head!" yelled Zeren.

"When one sees the image of a god, one may safely claim it is used for prayer and worship."

"Or for scaring money out of the gullible!"

"And when one sees an image of a living person, one may surely claim it is to be used for purposes of magic!"

"Or for kissing and sticking under one's pillow!"

Wotheng clanged the bell repeatedly, quelling both the shouting match between Oralro and Zeren and the appreciative laughter and cheers of the assembly.

"Sir Priest," he insisted, "get to your question for the Accused."

"Why, 'tis only this. Witch, does or does not the House of Deese bear ill will toward the House of Yotha?"

The crowd hushed, listening.

"Certainly," said Eloti, "and for good reason."

"Oh, indeed?" Oralro smirked. "Such as our complaints against your careless use of magic? Such as our warnings against your blatant immorality? Such as our thwarting your attempts to ill-wish our priesthood? We could say much about *those* reasons."

"Not at all," Eloti replied calmly. "We have but one reason: you attacked us first."

"You've no proof of that!" Oralro shouted, stamping again. "You've nothing but your own vile slanders! Only your word, against that poor innocent woman whose son you endangered, saying there's no harm in images! You expect folk to trust in that, do you, when all knowledge and even legend say otherwise? Do you—"

"Certainly not," Eloti snapped, rising to her feet. "I can put that to proof before all this gathering. Lord Wotheng, bid Losh come forward."

The crowd hushed in shock. Wotheng rubbed his jaw and gave her a long look. "Losh, come forward," he said at last.

"Lord Wotheng, please hand him a pen, some ink, a piece of

blank parchment, and a board upon which to brace it," said Eloti.

Wotheng raised both shaggy eyebrows, but handed over the requested items to Losh. "Hope you know what you're doing," he murmured.

"Now, Losh," said Eloti, smoothing down her dress, "I pray you, draw a picture of *me*."

The whole assembly drew its collective breath. Gynallea waved frantic signals to her husband, who ignored them. Sulun and his friends looked at each other in bewilderment. Eloti smiled prettily.

"Go on, Losh. As I've said, *things* have no power—not until people give it to them."

With shaky fingers, Losh sat down and did as he was bid.

The minutes crawled. The audience crept closer, trying to peer over Losh's shoulder at the growing image. Those who could see any of it agreed that Eloti's passing judgment was right; Losh did indeed have great skill at drawing. There, that was surely the line of Lady Eloti's skirt, real as life; and there, yes that was the very angle of her wrist. Slowly the form took shape, and then the face, smiling confidently. The crowd murmured softly in appreciation. Losh drew on, sweat beading on his forehead and trickling down his neck.

Oralro tapped his feet and jittered with impatience. Sulun and company sat quietly, sweating nearly as much as Losh. Gynallea shot puzzled glances at her husband. Wotheng alone was calm, smiling serenely, hands clasped on the table before him.

At length Losh heaved a deep sigh, set down the pen, got up, and handed the drawing to Eloti. He put the board, pen, and inkpot back on Wotheng's table and trudged off to his seat on the benches without a word. Irga took his hand again, radiating sympathy.

"Very good, Losh," said Eloti, studying the drawing. "Quite flattering, in fact. Now—" She turned to Wotheng. "Would you please ask Goodwife Nima to step forward."

The crowd buzzed like troubled bees as Nima bustled to the center of the courtyard.

Eloti calmly handed her the drawing. "Lord Wotheng," she said, "if, as certain parties have claimed, things have power in themselves which any person can use for ill purposes, then let Nima prove it. Let her turn her back on me, look only at the drawing, and curse *me* if she can."

The audience gasped in concert.

On the rightward bench, Folweel caught his breath in furious hope. Gods, if only he could signal to Oralro, if only the man would face him for a moment, they could use this chance to quietly cast their own curse. It would have to be something simple, done without tools or preparation—but then, a simple curse could more effectively be disguised as something Nima herself might do. Once the curse struck, everyone would think Nima had done it and that Oralro had been right. So perfect! But Oralro wasn't looking at him, couldn't be signalled. He'd have to do it himself, and wait for just the theatrically proper moment.

On the leftward bench, Arizun had just come to the same conclusion. "Gods, this is madness!" he whispered. "We don't know how many wizards they have, or what power. . . . Nine hells, I'll have to help her alone." He closed his eyes and began silently chanting the meditative formulas while Ziya watched him, fascinated.

None of this was lost on Eloti. She was aware of the prickling, nonphysical pressure behind her, with that characteristic tone/color of Arizun's mind. Clever of the boy to think of it so soon, and she could certainly use the protection if this ploy failed. She silently recited the formulas herself while carefully keeping that utterly confident smile on her face, keeping it turned toward Nima. Much depended now on that silly woman's character.

Nima stared for a moment at the drawing, then glowered at Eloti. If mere target and malice were sufficient to cast an effective curse, everyone in the assembly could see that she would have done it then.

Arizun softly chanted, Folweel held his breath and waited, Eloti smiled.

Nima's assurance broke. "What nonsense is this?" she shouted, her voice noticeably shrill. "How should I put a curse on a skilled sorceress? Surely she knows means to prevent me, ward off the curse, turn it back on me, gods know what. It isn't fair, it isn't the same at all."

The crowd rumbled disappointment, speculation, contempt.

"Aughhh!" bellowed one of the former work gang. "A pigeon just splattered me! It must be the curse, deflected on the innocent. Ey, witchcraft!"

"Oooeee!" One of Eloti's students took up the game, tumbling to the ground and kicking theatrically. "I've gas pains from the beer. She must have bewitched my belches downward! Magic! Magic!" In the middle of the performance he cut a loud fart. His neighbors flinched away, holding their noses. "Praise be to all the gods," the student improvised merrily. "I've been cured!"

The audience roared with laughter. Wotheng tried quelling it with his bell, but was shaking too much with ill-held guffaws to ring properly. Oralro purpled again, stamped his feet, and stuck out his petulant lip. Folweel silently cursed the lost opportunity, and bitterly hoped for another.

"It's not *fair!*" Nima shrilled in fury, her headdress slipping in disarray. "I'm no wizard! Let some real wizard do it!"

She spun on her heel, turned to the nearest of the Yotha priests—which happened to be Oralro—and thrust the parchment into his hand.

"You do it," she snapped. "You'd be a match for the likes of her."

Oralro was startled for only a moment; then a broad smile spread across his face. He glanced warily at Eloti, then set to studying the parchment.

The crowd roared, argued, railed, and stared.

Folweel sat up straighter, struggling to keep his grin of victory from showing.

Eloti kept smiling, but it wasn't easy. She concentrated on the formulas, driving her mind up the levels to the plane where magic could be released, feeling her wave front spread and link with Arizun's. She hadn't, she fleetingly admitted, expected this to come so soon.

"Halt!" Wotheng roared, startling everyone. He lurched to his feet, swinging his handbell like a club, looking as ferocious as anyone had ever seen him. "I'll have no wizards' duel in my court! No, nor in my villa, either—nor anywhere on my lands. By the gods, my land's suffered too much from wizardry already."

He glared around him, ignoring his wife's amazed look. The guards, with no signal given, snapped to attention. Everyone else stared in silence.

Wotheng smiled grimly and rang his handbell three times. "Here's my judgment on this case," he thundered. "Since this matter cannot be proved nor decided save by methods of wizardry, let it so be proved. This case shall be decided in trial by combat."

Everyone gasped at that. Folweel threw caution aside and waved frantically at Oralro. Nima turned around and around, looking dazed at the sudden change. Eloti's students cheered. Sulun's coterie looked at each other and all started talking at once.

Wotheng clanged his bell once more for silence.

"I hereby decree," he announced, "that at noon tomorrow this assemblage shall gather on the field outside the walls of Deese House, there to witness said combat. The wizards of Deese shall stand before their walls and the wizards of Yotha shall face them at not less than fifty paces. Upon given signal both shall duel with their respective skills until one or the other is defeated. Upon the victory of one or the other shall this matter be decided. So be it known and written." He clanged his bell three more times, and added, "This gathering is now adjourned."

With that, he drew his robes around him and marched back toward the doors of Ashkell House, not glancing to either side.

Gynallea gaped at his retreating back, then ran to gather up his assorted parchments and tablets and hurried after him. The two nearest guards looked at each other, shrugged, and went to pick up the table. Other guards hurried to carry in the other furniture.

"M'lord, m'lord!" Oralro was howling. "What's to keep yonder wizards from stealing a march and bewitching us, to their advantage, before combat tomorrow?"

"You have my picture, do you not?" Eloti snapped, nimbly hopping to her feet as a guard came to pick up her chair. "Keep it in surety, then. I'd advise you, nonetheless, not to try ill-wishing *me* beforetime."

"Witness!" Zeren bellowed at the guards, snagging their attention. "If any harm—*any* harm—comes to the Lady Eloti before the combat tomorrow, you'll all know that the priests of Yotha are guilty beyond doubt!"

Oralro snorted disgust, rolled up the parchment drawing, and shoved it firmly in his belt pouch. "No one shall so much as see this image beforetime," he announced, ignoring Folweel's flailing hands. "That *I* vow, by Yotha's flame."

Arizun ran to Eloti and clutched her arm. "Will you be safe until then?" he whispered.

"Once inside our walls, I will be," Eloti hissed back. "Let's get there with all haste."

The milling crowd was roaring with delight and anticipation at the coming duel, splitting into factions within factions, and already the bet makers were offering conflicting odds. The brewer pulled out his better bottles, and did a lively business. Several students formed a protective honor guard around Eloti and her friends and helped push through the throng to the gates, the wagon, and escape.

Sulun grabbed at Zeren's sleeve, utterly bewildered. "Why did he do it?" he asked, as if the brawny soldier would know. "Why did he throw us into this? I thought he was our friend."

"He planned it so," Zeren growled, glancing back toward Ashkell House in mingled fury and admiration. "That wily old wolf—he planned for this all along."

✧ CHAPTER SEVEN ✧

"Come, Brother Oralro, give me the drawing," Folweel wheedled. "You know we have much to plan, and so little time, and I need to, er, study the witch."

"I'll not," the burly Second Priest huffed. "Upon my honor and oath, I'll keep it safe and untouched until tomorrow noon."

" 'Twill be too late, then!"

"Too late for what? Do you intend some breach of honor, sir? I swore to keep the picture in surety against any such same connivance toward Yotha House."

"But there have been magical attempts already," Folweel tried. "The last just an hour ago."

"Aye, and I felt that." Oralro sneered. "That was practice work by our own under-priests, and quite poorly they did it too. Really, Brother Folweel, after all these years of instructing our novices in basics of magecraft, did you think I wouldn't know the feel of the spirit of every mage in the house?"

Folweel sighed in frustration. "Well, then *you* deal with them! Make them practice properly in strategy for tomorrow, for I've work enough to do with the tools."

"That I'd planned to do, Brother, once I finished meditation." Oralro hesitated. "If you truly need to raise extra defenses against the witch tonight, why not simply use your memory of her as focus?"

"That I could do in any case," Folweel fumed. "I was hoping for something more concrete."

"Hm, well, it would not help you," Oralro admitted. "She's within Deese House, and the place is most thoroughly warded."

"Ah?" Folweel perked up, wondering if Oralro truly had

discovered the legendary—and never proved—technique of scrying. "And how would you know that, Brother Oralro?"

"Umm . . ." The burly Second Priest looked actually embarrassed. "Because I've already tried to, er, chastise her. The attempt failed. There is effective counterspelling."

"Oh." Folweel sighed. If Oralro couldn't get through Deese House's shields, *he* certainly couldn't. "So that drawing is useless to us."

"Er, yes. And upon my honor and sworn word, I may yield it up to no man."

Easy honor, that! Folweel fumed, stamping off to see to the distillery.

Cloaked and hooded to anonymity, Gynallea stepped through the doorway of Deese's temple—and stopped to stare at what was there revealed.

The floor before her was carved with deep, narrow ditches in concentric rings, each labelled in strange letters or perhaps numbers. In their center the forge blazed, heated to eye-searing glare by a mammoth bellows. The bellows was powered by no human hand but a complex arrangement of gears, which ran from a thick leather belt, which was turned by a whirling axle set high in the wall. Above the blazing forge hung and swayed an enormous blackened bucket of unidentifiable stone, swaying like a pendant on its thick black chains, clearly just hauled up from the roaring furnace. Its controlling chains hung also from heavy gears upon an axle running across the ceiling, and the half-naked Deese wizards hauling thereon looked like toiling trolls in the flaring light. One of them—Omis?—shouted a command, and the priests ran to pull on other chains. The rest of the crowd jumped back beyond the third ditch ring, watching tensely and wiping sweat from their faces. The huge bucket swung forward, halting just above what appeared to be a block of clay with holes in the top and a complex clay funnel with many spouts leading to the holes. As Gynallea watched, fascinated, the wizard in charge shouted another order. The others pulled on the chains, and the spouted bucket tilted slowly toward the waiting funnel.

Its contents *glowed*. Creamy white and shining like the sun at summer's noon, exhaling a blast of intolerable heat, the nameless fluid poured like milk from a pitcher. It spilled, gods' milk surely, into the clay funnel and down, down the series of spouts, into the waiting holes. The holes filled to the brim, gleaming yellow, then orange and now Gynallea could see that they contained cores of clay, originally white, now dark by comparison. The last of the gleaming gods' milk filled the holes and covered the tops of the cores, and Omis shouted again. The emptied bucket, its pulled chains rattling, swung upright and away from the furnace. The filled holes in the clay block shone like suns in the shadow of the forge's walls.

"Ease off the fire," Omis commanded, pulling a lever by the wall. The gears of the bellows promptly disconnected, and the roar of air died away, leaving only the higher-toned wind sound of the flames. "Deese be praised: a good, clean pour!"

The other wizards cheered.

"Sorcery," Gynallea whispered. "No magic greater than this."

At that point one of the wizards noticed her and came forward wiping sweat and soot off his brow. It was Sulun, she saw.

"Lady Gynallea!" he marveled. "What on earth do you here? Won't it prejudice the case, you being the judge's wife come visiting us?"

"Oh, pish," snorted Gynallea. "I came secretly, and no one saw me. Besides, I've noted that Yotha's priests place little regard on the doings of women . . . hmm, save when it serves them. Shall we go someplace cooler to talk? I swear, 'tis like the worst of summer in here."

Sulun gladly led her into the side dining room. A common fire twinkled on the hearth, and the air seemed wonderfully cool. Sulun fetched cups and a jug of good ale from the sideboard. "What in all the hells was that sorcery you were performing out there?" Gynallea asked, accepting her cup. "I never saw the like."

"Metal-casting," said Sulun, pouring for them both. "Omis had set up to melt iron down to pure liquid—which, I admit, I'd thought couldn't be done. He'd intended to cast a statue of Deese for the Ashkell House shrine, but then all this business came up, and now we have to cast quickly some tubes, for, hmm, firepowder and burning-mineral displays. We need them by noon tomorrow, of course. Everyone who isn't here is off making firepowder— save for Eloti and Arizun, who need their sleep, and Zeren, of course, who's busy guarding them. I swear, I don't know when I'll rest."

"Hmm, firepowder workings," Gynallea considered. "No magic in that?"

"No, m'lady: pure chemistry and mechanics. Wotheng did warn us to put on a good show." Sulun mopped his forehead again. "I don't know how much this will frighten Yotha's wizards, but it should distract their ill-wishing enough to let it fail."

"Aye, good tactics. And take care that *you* not be distracted by their tricks. You can be sure, they'll use the Yotha fire; prepare for it."

"That we've done. Also, we'll have the advantage of standing under our own walls, which are already well-wished. I suspect Wotheng thought of that when he set the conditions of the . . . wizards' duel."

Gynallea studied her cup, fiddled with it, took a deep breath. "I must confess, friend Sulun, somewhat has been kept hidden from you."

Sulun raised an eyebrow and scratched his beard. "I know that none of you warned us sufficiently when first we came here, about the sheer power and threat of Yotha's wizards."

"Well, dear, we did want you to settle here and make us rich with your skills." Gynallea gave him something nearer her usual smile. " 'Twouldn't do to scare away potential wealth-makers by saying much about local troubles, now would it?"

Sulun laughed. "I'm happy you thought so highly of us, and I must confess I've never seen better patrons than we've found at Ashkell House."

" 'T'as been mutually rewarding." Gynallea's smile slipped away. "But we didn't warn you of the possible trouble with the neighbors, either."

Sulun rolled his cup in his hands, though it wanted no warming. "Wotheng told me he needed to appear strong if he was to become noticeably rich. Without numbers for armies, he must need to look well protected by wizardry."

"Ay, dear," Gynallea sighed. "That was another reason we tolerated Yotha for so long, besides the difficulty in ousting him."

"I see."

"Not entirely, friend Sulun, and neither do I." She set down her cup. "I confess, I don't know why he rushed both of you to this wizards' duel. Had he simply decided against Yotha on the evidence given, Yotha would have continued to dwindle away—

oh, sniping here and there, perhaps, but doomed nonetheless. This way, he may rid himself quickly of Yotha, but he also risks losing *you*. He's kept his counsel tight upon that, even with me. Have you any idea why he'd take such chances?"

"No . . ." Sulun pondered long. "All I can think is that he needs this settled fast, for some reason. Perhaps he fears Yotha's continued troublemaking, or he may have cause to worry strongly about his greedy neighbors. Perhaps he fears such continued squabbling would tempt them, make us appear weak and divided. He warned me to make our 'magic' look fearful enough to discourage such hopes. That's one thing that made us decide to cast and use those fire tubes. It's also why I made such a show of testing the bombard before all the workmen. By all means, let people carry tales outside the vale of our marvelous sorcerous powers. If it helps keep Wotheng—and us—safe, then I'll be happy to add to such."

"Bombard?" Gynallea asked, an odd faraway look in her eyes.

"That large fire tube mounted on the wall." Sulun took a long pull of his cup. "The one we used to, hah! plow the north field. The workmen took to calling it a 'storm tube,' and the name spread."

"The storm tube," Gynallea murmured, gazing off into the darkness. "Yes . . . Hmm. Friend Sulun, I think you'd best use that, too, to make a most spectacular display tomorrow. You must look as fearsome as you can . . . and I doubt not that the north field could use some more plowing."

"North field? But the duel is to take place before the east gate."

"Well, then," Gynallea said with a shrug, "move the storm tube as close to the east gate as you may. Indeed, I'd suggest setting it to plow the ground between your folk and Yotha's. *That* will distract them, you may be sure."

"Distract!" Sulun gulped. "Oh, indeed it will! Have you seen how it tears up the ground? I'd not want to risk it so close to our folk, not ever."

"You'll have a good fifty paces, at least, between you and them."

"Still too close!"

"Then set it to strike to one side, far enough to be safe. Or . . . aim it closer to Yotha's priests. Measure the ground yourself." Gynallea shrugged again and got to her feet. "But *use* it, Sulun.

Set the storm tube on the east wall and use it, where its use may best be seen. I do not doubt this is important, and may be what decides the victory."

"Well, if you truly believe I should . . ."

"I do most firmly believe it. And now I should go, lest the servants at home make too free with the wine cellar. Take care, friend wizard."

Sulun rose to show her out, and stood pondering a long time as he watched her ride away into the dark. Her advice had always been good, and he'd be foolish not to take it now, with so much at stake. But what, indeed, did Wotheng intend?"

The sun climbed through a rare, cloudless autumn day, gilding the sparse-grown ground and the vast procession on the road. Lord Wotheng and Lady Gynallea led the horde, wearing their best robes and jewelry, in a freshly painted cart garlanded with fir branches. Their guard surrounded them, sporting fine, sharp new swords and polished shields, dressed in their new winter livery of bronze red and dark forest green. Behind them, on horses or mules or in cloth-covered wagons, rode the priesthood of Yotha; they rang chimes and chanted endlessly, and the clear sun glittered on the embroidery of their red, orange, and yellow robes. Several paces behind the priests, giving them a wide berth, came what seemed to be half the population of the vale. Losh and Irga shared a borrowed horse, and chatted as merrily as if they were going to market. Nima rode a cart with her husband and their other children, and studiously ignored Losh and his lady-love. Pado, several lengths back, rode a wagon with the other women and children of her family, glaring occasionally at Losh, otherwise keeping her eyes primly lowered. The brewer and vintner talked business as they rode, side by side, on two wagons loaded with barrels of their respective wares. Behind them came Tygg the baker, whistling merrily, his assorted goods and apprentices piled into a new wagon he'd bought just the day before. Eloti's students clung together in a raucous assemblage, those on foot clinging to the stirrups of those fortunate enough to have mounts. Other factions gathered, walked or rode together awhile, fragmented, and re-formed. Here and there a gaggle of farmer's children rode in file on plow horses, and not a few on the backs of oxen. Stuffed like sausages into wagons or carts, riding any available beast, even

on foot, the horde plodded down the road to the valley before
the gates of Deese House.

"Kula," Sulun groaned, watching from the window, "it's like
All Gods' Day back in Sabis." He shivered, wondering how the
sacrificial goats had felt on those days. At least those beasts had
no idea, until perhaps the last instant, of what was to happen to
them. He cast another look around the great workshop/temple/
front room. "Are we ready?" he asked.

Zeren promptly stopped fencing with shadows on the wall,
sheathed his sword, and took his planned space in the marching
formation. Arizun and Eloti, already dropping into meditative
state, silently nodded. Omis, Doshi, and Yanados hefted their
heavy covered baskets and stepped awkwardly into line. Ziya
looked around quickly, grabbed a tinder box off the shelf, and
ran for the wall. Tamira, huddled in a corner with the two
youngest, watched them silently with wide eyes.

"Now, just as we practiced it," said Sulun, feeling absurdly like
a temple dancing master. "Wait until we hear Wotheng's
summons."

The others murmured tense agreement.

Sulun rechecked the baskets for the dozenth time, knowing
his worry was only what Zeren called "combat nerves," still fearful
that they'd left out some small tool that would prove vital in the
coming trial. *And it would be my fault,* he gnawed at himself, *if
our distractions fail and Eloti or Arizun loses concentration just
when we need it most. . . .*

But everything was in the baskets, even spare tools and
tinderboxes, everything they'd need. Sulun chewed his lip and
glanced out the door at Ziya, industriously climbing to the top of
the wall and scampering along it to where the loaded bombard
stood. With the spare elegance of an expert, she slid the oiled
cloth covering from the bombard, so smoothly that none of the
approaching crowd could have seen it done. Yes, the child was
very good at her task; she'd do as instructed. Pray Gynallea was
correct—but then, she usually was.

Gods, from the noise outside the crowd must be close, huge,
and hungry!

The procession wound up the road between the two hills,
officials somber and formal, audience gazing about them with

wonder and some trepidation. The combat was supposed to take place before the gates of Deese House, and that was a good way up the hill ahead. The two low hills to either side of this narrow valley would provide an excellent view at a safe distance, and the more cautious in the crowd peeled off right and left to settle there. Others, bolder, followed the Lord Wotheng's party and the priests of Yotha into the valley proper and up the rising road. As the wall of Deese House drew near though, more and more folk thought it wise to spread out to either side of the road and take positions on the sidelines. For the last hundred paces and more, up to the gates of Deese, Lord Wotheng and the Yotha priests proceeded alone.

At sixty paces out, Wotheng halted, turned, and gestured imperiously to the Yotha priesthood behind him. Everyone caught his meaning: wait here. Yotha's priests did so, halting where they were but continuing to chant and ring their hand chimes. Wotheng rode almost to the bronze-sheathed gates and signalled briefly to one of his men-at-arms. The guardsman lifted and dropped the iron rings that served as door knockers and handles, once, twice, three times.

"Let the challengers come forth!" Wotheng bellowed in a voice that could be heard to the near hilltops. Then he turned his cart, his guards neatly circling with him, and rode back to a point midway between Yotha's assembled priests and the still visible char-mark some ten strides before the gates. There he reined in and waited.

The bronze and oak doors swung open with barely a creak, pushed by two matched Deese priests, and the small procession marched out. In their forefront paced Eloti and Arizun, empty hands formally clasped, eyes deep and distant. After them, including the two who closed the doors behind the procession and resumed their place at the end of the double line, came no more than half a dozen priests of Deese.

The crowd compared the sizes of the two wizard armies, and muttered loudly.

"Gods, is that all they have?" Patrobe chuckled at Folweel's elbow. "And led by that woman and a boy? Oh, much cry and little wool!"

"Take care," Folweel shushed him. "We know not what level of sorcery they've attained."

The wizard priests of Deese advanced until they stood directly over the charred spot on the ground and stopped there, all together, with no signal given, neatly as a trained company of soldiers in some high king's guard.

The audience murmured, impressed. Wotheng raised a respectful eyebrow, then stood up in his cart and solemnly rang his judicial bell.

"Challenge has been given and accepted," he announced, in his trumpeting public-gathering voice that echoed so well from the hills. "Combatants shall not approach each other any closer than this, nor shall they depart their ground save in surrender. You shall employ no weapons save those of your wizardry, neither shall you harm any present save each other's combatants. You shall have this quarter of the hour to prepare your ground. Combat shall commence at next ringing of the bell, and shall end only when one or the other party is clearly defeated. On your lives and your honors, do you understand these terms?"

"Aye!" shouted the priests of Yotha, a trifle raggedly.

The priests of Deese only nodded their heads silently, in concert.

The crowd glanced at the Deese wizards with a touch of awe; such tight precision and utter silence were a bit unnerving.

Wotheng sat back down and steered his team to the sidelines, a good seventy paces to the south. The crowd carefully made way for him. There he turned his cart to face the field, and settled back to wait. His guards dutifully spread out along the edge of the assembly, forming a broad circle around the opposing teams of wizards. In the throng, the assorted vendors opened their wagons and set about peddling their goods. Gamblers scampered through the press, offering various odds.

Among the priests of Yotha, half a dozen of the under-priests put away their chimes, hurried to their cartload of supplies, and hauled out several kegs and baskets. The remaining under-priests continued to chant hypnotically and strike their chimes, but the senior priests put their chimes away and two of them—Oralro and Folweel—drew out meditation gems as well. The two remaining priests, Patrobe and Jimantam, directed the mobile under-priests in drawing large circles of fire fluid around the group and neatly arranging piles of covered baskets close to the circle's center.

Oralro glanced once around his knot of chanting under-priests, making certain they were well into the proper meditative level, feeling the growing wave front of their mage power. Yes, they were responding well and obediently, their power ready to be tapped and channeled where he chose to focus it. He'd need that much power, and a good tight focus, to punch through the blanketing defensive spell the Deese wizards had already placed on their house and land.

A remarkably tight and precise spell that, given the size of the area it covered, he could feel exactly where its near border lay, almost exactly between the two groups. How symbolic. Had Wotheng, in his obvious favoritism toward the Deese wizards chosen the ground of the duel for just that reason? Well, no matter; Oralro knew that with enough power and focus he could punch through it.

The real problem would be maintaining a second focus. Complex business for one mage; yet Folweel had skill and power sufficient to handle the second task, leaving himself free to concentrate on the first. Already he could feel the high priest's characteristic field widening, pulling in selected others from the pool of under-priests.

Oralro frowned as he noted which ones Folweel was taking: three of his strongest and best trained. Ah well, perhaps he was right; they'd need a good strong defense against the Deese wizards, who—already having a preset shield—were free to concentrate on attack. Then again, the Deese wizards were fewer in number if not in power; just one of them sufficiently distracted—or otherwise removed from the reservoir—could make a significant difference. Oralro chuckled silently as he thought of some of the "distractions" Brother Folweel had planned. Reassured, he peered into the meditation gem and concentrated on drawing his power net tighter.

The air was mild and cool, but Sulun and Vari were sweating heavily as they finished drawing the last of their three concentric rings around their base zone: the outer ring of water, the second of powdered sulfur, the inner one of firepowder. How many minutes past? How many to go? Now to set the loaded fire tubes in the holes they'd carefully dug the night before, put in the fuses, and make sure they had enough air for proper burning. A quick glance to the walls showed Ziya crouched behind the bombard, ready and waiting. He hoped that the secondary protective spells they'd set last night on both Ziya and the bombard would escape the Yotha priests' notice. What next? Oh, yes: place the buckets of water around the others, ready to use in case any of that damned fire fluid made it through the shield and hit too close to people. Now to set up the small brazier, fill it with waiting coals and pour in the lighted ones, make sure the new coals caught well and the tapers were ready to hand; it wouldn't do to be without fire when they needed it. Now to take the old bellows, make certain it was still full of water and not leaking, prop it at just the right angle to shoot the ink-dyed water into Yotha's circle—a clever idea from Omis, that—and set the handles so that a quick stamp from a hurried foot would fire it.

Fire . . . Sulun wiped his face and shivered, feeling the horrible weight of his responsibility. Eloti and the others—see, they'd joined hands now; one could almost feel the power flowing from them like heat from the forge—would do nothing but maintain shields, constantly well-wishing themselves and their ground. All the physical defense—and all the attacks—would come only from Vari and himself.

Attacks? Sulun looked around again at his preparations. *Attack is not of my nature! I'll put on a good show, startle and distract Yotha's wizards, throw enough harmless stuff into their circle to make them look foolish, make it clear they've lost. . . . But truly attack? Throw firepowder, as Zeren urged me? I don't think I can do it.*

He rubbed his back, glanced at Omis, mentally reviewed the signals they'd designed, and finally went to stand beside Vari near the brazier. The shadows were so short, there couldn't be much time left now.

There wasn't. Wotheng glanced at the small hourglass set beside him on the cart, stood up, and rang his bell again. "The hour has come," he bellowed to the suddenly hushed throng. "Let the combat begin."

On his word, the under-priests sparked their tinderboxes and lit their circle of fire fluid. The crowd roared as the flames sprang up and formed a ring of yellow-tipped blue fire around Yotha's priesthood.

Must be hot inside it, Sulun thought inanely as he lit a taper at the brazier, took it to the innermost ring, and set off the firepowder. Again the assembly howled, seeing the snapping circle of orange-red flames run, sparking fiercely, around the priesthood of Deese.

For the next few moments nothing seemed to happen, although everyone could feel the tension. Invisible waves of will, arms of power, grappled and wrestled with each other, making no headway.

Folweel, concentrating on maintaining his net against attack, waited and waited and finally wondered why no attack came. Long moments passed, and there was no pressure of any kind on even the edges of his field. What were those Deese wizards doing? He withdrew enough of his attention to focus on the enemy. They didn't seem to be doing much of anything. Oralro, however, was clearly sweating and straining with effort. So were the obedient under-priests in his power net. Aha! So the Deese wizards were concentrating all their strength on defense! Well, he had other means to get through that, other ways to attack, and even that pompous ass Wotheng couldn't properly call them ordinary weapons. He gestured briefly to Patrobe, then sank back into concentration. Best not leave the net weakened too long by his absence.

Patrobe nodded acknowledgment and signalled to his contingent. The half-dozen under-priests obediently reached into the waiting baskets and drew out thin-walled jugs sealed with trailing rags. They briefly upended the jugs and let the contents soak the rags, then righted them, lit the trailing rag ends, paused for a short prayer, and threw the jugs toward the center of Deese's circle.

Eloti's shield held well; the jugs all hit far from center, damaging nothing, and half their wick fires were smothered out on impact. Most of them broke, however, spreading sharp-smelling fire fluid on the ground. Two of them succeeded in catching fire, and the crowd gasped upon seeing the pools of Yotha's flames spring up, even in harmless patches. Sulun and Vari grabbed buckets, ran to the fires, and doused them quickly.

"No more water than we need," Vari panted in warning. "There'll be more, and we can't go back to the stream until this is over."

Sulun nodded quickly, smothered the last fire as economically as possible, and headed back to his post by the brazier.

On the way, he came across a full and intact jug. An imp of perversity nibbled. He picked up the jug, relit the rag taper, and threw it back.

The crowd whooped.

The jug landed and broke, just within Yotha's circle. The wick went out, but the contents splashed far enough to contact the sinking edge of the ringing fire, and catch. A blob of blue flame sprang up briefly, distorting the circle's shape. One of Patrobe's under-priests started toward it, then hesitated, unsure what to do without orders.

Not distraction enough, Sulun thought, hurrying to the nearest of the loaded fire tubes. He thrust his taper's flame against the end of the fuse, waited until it had caught well, then ducked aside and ran back to the brazier.

Nothing interfered with the fire tube's functioning. The powder ignited with a bang, shooting sparks and smoke out its muzzle—as well as a cloth-wrapped packet of sulfur. The cloth ignited also, and then the sulfur. The sizzling package erupted in mid-air on the downward arc of its trajectory, just outside Yotha's circle. Yotha's defenses still held good, but there was no way to completely avoid a widespread hail of burning sulfur, let alone its secondary effects. The ground in the forward third of the circle—and one unfortunate under-priest in Jimantam's unit—were pelted with fine grains of burning, stinking chemical. The under-priest yelped and danced and tore at his robes.

The watching assembly stood up and roared, not least with laughter.

Jimantam gestured furiously, and two more under-priests ran to their stricken fellow to help drag off his multipunctured robe and splash water on him. They coughed and gasped as the sulfur smoke rose around them, stinking to the heavens and obscuring sight.

Folweel heard the shouting, glanced up quickly, and saw what was happening. *Wide-area weapon!* He cursed silently. There was only so much that even the best protective well-wishing could do against anything that splattered over a wide range. Shift probabilities as he could, some of the nasty stuff was bound to hit a target. Damn!

Well, he could respond with something similar. Folweel

signalled again to Patrobe, who likewise signalled to his division of under-priests, who lit and threw more jugs.

Again, the fire jugs failed to reach their mark. Again, Vari smothered fires, Sulun found another intact jug, lit it, and threw it. This one, unfortunately, landed outside Yotha's circle. It broke and burned there, making no difference and no distraction.

More sulfur? Sulun considered. *No, save them. Wait, see what they do.*

Oralro, sweating and panting, came up from meditative level far enough to reach out and tug Folweel's sleeve. "Their shield's too strong," he whispered. "Can't get through. Join me and help!"

Folweel thought for a moment, making sure there was no pressure whatever of ill-wishing on his shields, and acquiesced. Nine hells, let Yotha protect his own and keep the Deese wizards from attacking, just a few minutes more. He tapped his entranced under-priests on the wrists and hissed to them, "Join the ill-wishing!" Then he dropped back to deeper meditative level, rejoined and refocused their mingled fields. Last, he carefully joined his power net to Oralro's field, felt them interlock, expand, engage the front of the Deese wizards' shield.

Oralro smiled for the first time, feeling that enemy shield give way. He focused tighter, took the power of the net, and pushed it hard, hard as he could. Degree by slow degree, the Deese field weakened.

Whatever Eloti and the others felt, they gave no sign. Sulun and Vari felt the change like a sudden change of wind, an almost audible *snap* of power in the air. They looked at each other, guessing what had happened.

As if in confirmation, the unlatched gates of Deese House swung open—and this time one of the hinges creaked.

The house has no defense! Sulun realized. He thought of what harm those Yotha priests could do to the building, its contents, his tools, if they chose—and a roused fury burned him like a hot coal.

He ran to the waiting bellows and fairly jumped on its upper handle.

The inky water shot out in a tight, hard stream, arching high into the air before turning downward. The top of the arch was well beyond the middle of the ground between the circles. The black rain fell in a good wide circle inside Yotha's boundary ring.

Some of it fell on the leading edge of the diminishing blue fire, and put it out. The rest drew a fat black arrow-head shape on the ground, pointing straight into the knot of hard-worked wizards. A little of it caught the priests themselves: Folweel across the chest and Oralro smack in the face.

Startled out of concentration, they yelped in dismay and brushed frantically at the murky stuff. They had no idea what it was, what it would do, and they couldn't get it off them. The force of their ill-wishing attack wavered and shrank.

Everyone in Eloti's circle felt the pressure slack away. It was temptation to shift to attack themselves, but Eloti said "No," aloud and signalled to Sulun and Vari.

"Fire tubes!" Sulun shouted, running to the nearest with a taper.

They lit and fired three in quick succession before Sulun thought to conserve what was left. Three booming, whistling packets of burning sulfur sailed through the air to land neatly inside Yotha's circle, bombarding the wizards with pepper grains of fire, smoke, and choking stink.

The crowd danced up and down, roaring with delight.

Only Wotheng, watching the combat through slitted eyes, showed no great joy. "Not enough," he muttered to himself, barely catching even Gynallea's quick ear. "Hit harder. More."

Within Yotha's circle, Folweel and Oralro fought yattering chaos. They yelled for Jimantam to bring water, beat flames out of their robes, coughed and choked in the reeking smoke and tried to rally their under-priests to concentration again. Jimantam's troop of servitors ran among them with water, sloshing it wildly at anyone who seemed to need it, which added further distraction.

Only Patrobe and two of his crew, to one side of the circle, missed the onslaught of water and sulfur. Snarling a curse and an order, he ran to the nearest basket of fire fluid jugs and began lighting and throwing as fast as he could. Many of the jugs flew wild, wasting themselves on neutral ground; many others landed within the circle and went out, but enough landed and burned to keep Sulun and Vari busy.

Up on the wall Ziya watched, teeth bared and breath hissing through them. Fire wakened old memories, hurtful and dark: fire thrown at her house, her friends, her family. . . . Fire, from the bad people. Wicked people. The enemy. She clenched her hands on the bombard's carriage, furiously wishing that Sulun would send her the signal, let her strike at the enemy.

And not just beside them.

A coal of fury lit an idea.

He hadn't told her to *leave* the bombard aimed where it was. He hadn't told her *not* to change the setting.

Well-learned details of angle, trajectory, direction played through her head as she tugged the bombard sideways, just a trifle, just enough.

Folweel stripped off his sodden outer robe, grateful that the fire chemical hadn't burned through to the skin, and frantically dropped back to meditative level as fast as he could. There: yes, thank whatever gods, Oralro was doing the same. So were the obedient under-priests. If they could raise their defensive shields again, push back the Deese wizards' attack before it got any worse . . .

But he couldn't feel any attack.

It's all on the physical plane! he realized, with a sudden jab of hope. The Deese wizards were concentrating all their mage power on defense, come what might. That was their strategy: save magic for defense only, attack with physical means only.

They didn't have enough trained wizards for both attack and defense at once.

Folweel grabbed Oralro's sleeve. "Attack!" he hissed. "Beat down their shield and attack! Put everything into that!"

Oralro nodded, snapped out the orders to the reassembled net of under-priests, and concentrated. Folweel dropped into concentration with him. They joined and tightened focus, probed—found that suspected second shield.

Folweel almost laughed as he realized what the Deese priests were doing. They'd started with a preset, passive area defense. Under that, within their drawn circle, they now held a standing, active shield. Punch through that, and they'd have nothing. He signalled to Patrobe to keep on with the distractions, and pushed harder behind Oralro's attack.

Patrobe obligingly threw more fire jugs, and his under-priests did likewise.

Under that steady barrage, Sulun and Vari were kept hopping. Enough fires sprang up to need constant attention with the diminishing water, enough to keep them too busy to use the remaining fire tubes. The best they could do was seize unbroken jugs in passing, light them, and throw them back. Hardly any landed within Yotha's circle.

"We're running out of water!" Vari gasped, smothering one fire with her empty bucket. "How much of that stuff do they have?"

"Don't know," Sulun panted, using the last of his bucket on another. *Too much*, he guessed. That, he realized was the flaw in his strategy; Yotha's priests simply had more of everything: long-range weapons, supplies, wizards, everything. Given time, they'd wear Eloti and the others down.

Gods, there: one of the jugs broke nearby, splashing the hem of Arizun's robe. Blue flames crawled up the cloth, perilously close to his leg.

Arizun didn't move, didn't notice. His concentration was total, far from immediate physical concerns.

None of the others in the mage circle noticed the fire, either.

Vari ran up to Arizun and beat out the flames with her bare hands.

Gods, we have to break their concentration! Sulun knew it was time to bring out the last reserve, the grand distraction. Once the Yotha wizards' attack was broken, and hopefully their defenses down, he could rain them with the last of the sulfur—win time to reload the tubes and rain them further, until they gave up and ran from the targeted circle. It had to be done now.

He waved up toward the walls and shouted the code phrase to Ziya, praying the child would hear it, not freeze, do as she'd vigorously sworn she would.

"Ziya!" he shouted. *"Fire ready!"*

Ziya heard. She smiled tightly, peered once more down the bombard's realigned barrel, and touched her lighted taper to the end of the fuse.

The fuse burned, sizzling, up toward the hole and the firepowder and torn metal waiting beyond it.

On the field below, Folweel felt the first flinching, the first ever-so-slight give in the Deese wizards' shield. *They're tiring!* he thought jubilantly, feeling Oralro's answering joy as he noted the change too. Just another few minutes of this and they'd have that last defense broken, no shield left between their furiously tight-focused ill-wishing and the target. It would probably strike that witch first. With this much power behind it, the attack might be enough to stop her heart right there. And yes, yes, their shield was definitely weakening.

Then something roared like thunder in the sky.

Folweel looked up just in time to see a cloud of smoke and sparks blossom high on the wall of Deese House, and realized it had come from the storm tube.

The watching crowd screamed together, seeing the earth shoot up like a monstrous fountain, stones and bodies and unidentifiable rags and pieces flying like leaves on the wind. Again voices wailed, seeing those unbelievable fragments fall back to earth amid a haze of smoke and dust. Then came a long, quavering, multiple groan as the smoke cleared, revealing the full sight of the damage in the unflinching sunlight.

In the center of Yotha's circle, where the knot of Yotha's priests had recently stood, lay a wide, shallow hole. Around it were scattered rags of stained cloth, bits of glass and stone, small clods of torn earth, unsightly pieces of flesh and bone, puddles and streaks of fire, fluid and blood. Further out lay torn and tumbled bodies, still bleeding but too obviously dead. A lone under-priest near the far edge of the circle staggered, blood-splashed and dazed, a few steps forward. He stumbled on a tattered body, stared at it, looked wildly around him, at the earth and bodies torn to rags and ruin by the flying stones—then he fled shrieking out of the charred circle and away. They could hear him howling all the way down the road.

Sulun rubbed his stunned ears until he could hear again and stared at the field before him in unthinking shock. *Hole* . . . his mind feebly registered. *Bombard. On them, not beside them . . . Oh gods, so that's what it can do!*

Vari sat down right where she was and covered her eyes; Sulun could hear her quietly cursing, and dimly marveled that she even knew such words. Omis took a half-step forward and stared stupidly at the fresh crater as if wondering how it had gotten there. Yanados swayed, grabbed at Doshi for support, and they both collapsed together. Arizun simply and quietly fainted. Eloti, eyes wide, spread her hands and staggered like a blind man. "Gone," she whispered. "What . . . ? How?"

Zeren took her by the shoulders and pulled her close. "Will of the gods," he growled, "and will of Wotheng." He turned to face the Ashkell lord's wagon and raised his sword hand in ironic salute.

Wotheng stood up in his cart and solemnly returned the gesture. Then he lifted and rang his bell. "The combat is ended," he announced, harsh-voiced. "The priests of Deese are found innocent of all charges."

"Yes," Zeren muttered, lowering his arm. "And I hope you're satisfied."

Gynallea, white to the lips, clutched her husband's arm. "Is this it?" she hissed at him. "Is this what you wanted?"

"Aye," Wotheng growled, looking abruptly older than his years. "I knew from first report what a weapon that could make; fierce enough to defend the Vale, scare off greedy neighbor lords, keep us and our descendants safe. I had to make Sulun use it, would he or no: show everyone what it could do, spread the word all over the northlands. Now, by the gods, we're safe."

"Safe! Safe? With that?"

"I confess . . ." Wotheng briefly chewed his lip. "I didn't know it would . . . do quite that."

The crowd, still moaning quietly in horror, melted back from the sight of the field. The motion grew into a current, slipped off the hills, out of the valley, off down the eastward road, safely away from Deese House and its hideous new landmark and its vast and terrible power. Slowly the crowd moved, cautiously, politely—but away.

Sulun looked about him, cold with stark comprehension. Yes, he'd won, and Yotha House was no more, and Deese House was safe. But Wotheng had used him, and now the vale folk feared him, and the souls of his family were forever stained with a darkness. He wondered what would become of Eloti's school now, of his hopes for spreading knowledge and enlightenment, of forming the core of a new civilization in Ashkell Vale. The family of Deese had won their survival, certainly, but at what cost?

And how did it happen?

He looked up at the wall, at the bombard. No, the muzzle was not pointed where he'd seen it last; now it was aimed straight at that damning hole in the field.

Beside it, straight and tall and smiling coldly in unshamed triumph, stood Ziya. She caught Sulun's eye, waved a merry salute to him, then turned and—before all the gods—began reloading the bombard.

Gods, what has she become? Sulun wondered, shivering.

Ziya finished her task, lifted her lighted taper and waved again to Sulun.

"This is not the beginning I wanted," he said, to himself as much as her. Guessing she couldn't hear him, he shook his head. "Child, can't you understand? this was a bad beginning!"

If Ziya heard, she gave no sign. She cocked her head to one side and called down from the walls, as if asking for further orders.

"Fire ready," she said.

Book Two
Wizard Spawn

✧ CHAPTER ONE ✧

The midday sun managed a brief deception, illumining the Great Hall of the ducal palace, casting illusory warmth on grey stone walls. For a moment tapestries and banners blazed out above the crowded tables. High in the sooty rafters, smoke from the great cooking fires eddied about like a man-made mist.

Members of the ducal court packed the tables set beneath the high seat, their garments a sea of color highlighted in torchlight. Grey-clad priests of Hladyr sat elbow-to-elbow with richly dressed lords of the Duchy; dark blue robes of court wizards contrasted sharply with the House artists' polychrome. Several alchemists sat together, a knot of black in the midst of the tables.

Facing them all, His Grace Duke Hajun vro Telhern sat at the center of the high table, his wife at his left, his eldest son and heir, Brovor, at this right; the other royal children, daughter Alwisa, and son Saladar, his youngest, sat to the wife's left.

Sated and drowsy from rich food and drink—to say nothing of the cups of wine he had downed—Hajun would have nodded had ducal dignity permitted.

But outside, the clouds closed, and once more the hall grew shadowed. A sudden gust of rain slatted against the windows and Hajun winced: *Shining One,* he prayed silently, *keep the winds furled. Guard my ships, Hladyr . . . keep them safe.*

He met the eyes of a grey-haired man sitting at the table closest to the high seat. "Jorrino," he said. "Attend me."

The man rose from his chair, bowed, and walked to the table to face Hajun.

"It's raining again," Hajun said unnecessarily: the sound of it on the windowpanes behind him was audible over the

399

conversation in the hall. "I'm sick to death of this weather. What are my wizards doing about it?"

Jorrino drew an uneasy breath, met Hajun's gaze squarely. "What we always do, Your Grace. Wish it off on another city."

Hajun scowled. "Dammit, wish a little harder then."

The wizard spread his hands. "My lord, I assure you, we're doing all we can."

An old, old doubt came back. "Could someone—some enemy of mine—be responsible for the storms?"

"Possibly, lord. While we aren't sure one can ill-wish the weather, we aren't sure one can't: we keep searching."

"For what do I fund you? For *aren't sure?*"

The wizard bowed distressedly, and stood in silence.

"Well?"

"There are whispers, lord,—"

"Whispers. Gold to my wizards . . . and they bring me whispers. . . ."

Jorrino gnawed at his moustaches, folded his hands, bowed. "Sabirn, Your Grace—somewhere in this city, a gathering of powerful Sabirn wizards—"

Hajun let go his breath and fell back with a wave of his hand. "Gods, if I've heard that one once—"

"My lord, they say this information *is* from a Sabirn."

Sabirn: little dark people of the alleyways and back streets of Targheiden, people good for little else than the most menial tasks. Hard to think of any of them as being wizards . . .

"And who was this Sabirn who so freely whispers these dire plots?"

"A fortune-teller—"

"Gods . . ."

"In the market. The Guard caught him stealing and put him to the question. *He* admitted to fakery, but he swore—*swore*, lord, that genuine wizards among his people have powers—"

A small, icy snake uncoiled in Hajun's stomach. "Do you believe him?"

Jorino edged closer, dropped his voice. "Lord, the Sabirn have no love for us."

Hajun started to protest, but frowned and thought on it, on the weather, the ill winds—inconceivable that Sabirn might have wizards powerful enough to bring the kingdom down . . . but they were secretive, they were ancient: wizards, legend said, long ago . . . before Targheiden stood—

Before Hajun's duchy existed . . . prosperous, powerful . . . holding a place of importance in the Ancar realms that Hajun's cousin, the king, fully recognized: the king might hold control of the plains and the trade coming from them, but it was up to Hajun to keep that trade moving in and out of the kingdom of Ancas.

And now Hajun's chief wizard echoed rumor of a Sabirn rebellion, some alliance of powerful wizards.

Hajun gnawed his lip. "I want you to keep me advised on this, Jorrino. I want to hear everything you hear, is that understood?"

The wizard bowed. "I do, Your Grace."

"And, whatever it's worth, keep wishing this weather onto someone else. For our trade's sake."

"Aye, lord." The wizard bowed again and returned to his place.

"Sabirn?" a deep voice asked.

Hajun glanced sidelong at his eldest, Brovor—like looking at himself twenty years back: the same height, blond hair, broad shoulders, blue eyes. Like himself if only, Hajun thought, Brovor could find more use for his brain and less for his physical strength. The days when lords ruled by might of arms were fading; more often now, prosperity settled on the lord who was smart enough to use diplomacy to get what he wanted. The nurturing of trade, not the conduct of war, was the new business of princes. . . .

"Speaking of Sabirn," Brovor said, leaning toward Hajun. "Did you hear about the near riot in the slough?"

"Damned nasty. Several of the Guard knocked about."

"They got the bastard who started it," Brovor said, "and he was Sabirn. Nailed his butt to the wall, from what I heard."

Hajun lifted an eyebrow. "I thought it was a crowd out of hand, a crowd chasing down a thief."

"Ah, but the thief was Sabirn." Brovor poured himself another glass of wine, took a long drink, and belched. "We ought to burn all of them. Damned demon-worshippers!"

At which Saladar stared meaningfully at the ceiling, lost in thought. "Saladar," Hajun asked sharply of his youngest. "What's your opinion?"

"Regarding the Sabirn or the riot?" Saladar's smile did not touch his eyes. "I certainly don't agree with Brovor."

402 *The Sword of Knowledge*

"And why not?" Brovor leaned on one brawny arm. "You never *were* much of a warrior, brother."

"Hush, Brovor," said the duchess. "Saladar's matched you in every feat of arms he's been set to."

"Fah!" Brovor took another gulp of his wine. "Book-reading. Scribbling."

"Saladar?" Hajun said, ignoring his eldest son's grumbling. "Why don't you agree with Brovor?"

"Slaughter the Sabirn? Who would we find to sweep the streets, then?" Saladar asked, smiling again. "Or collect the slops? I say, keep the Sabirn around. They have their uses."

Brovor made a rude noise. "*I* say kill them all. Let the commons sweep and slop. Then you won't have to worry about rumors. Or the dole." He reached for the pitcher of wine.

"Enough wine," Hajun said quietly, stopping his son's hand. "You don't want to trip over yourself when you leave the table."

Brovor's face went red. He took a deep breath, but subsided back into his chair.

"Tomorrow's your name-day feast." Hajun released his son's shoulder. "Surely you don't want to wake with a headache that will keep you from enjoying your festivities."

"No." Brovor's eyes wavered slightly. "But you won't mind, sire, if I celebrate tonight with my friends. . . ."

Hajun sighed, his eyes flicking down the tables at his eldest scion's company. Stories had filtered back to him of the parties Brovor had attended in the company of these young lords.

"I won't keep you from it," he said, as Brovor relaxed. "But in your cups, do possibly remember the ceremony at the temples starts not that long after midday. If nothing else, grant your future subjects the sight of a man fully in control of himself."

Brovor nodded, then grinned widely. "I won't disgrace you, Father, and I won't trip over my own feet. I promise."

"Let him have his night," Tajana said, a smile softening her face.

"I'll be back before the midnight bell, Father." Brovor grinned again. "Don't wait up for me."

"Ladirno, what do you think . . . about the Sabirn wizards?"
Ladirno glanced sidelong at the alchemist who had spoken.
"Do you believe it?" the other pressed him.

"I reserve my judgment." Ladirno met his colleague's eyes. The man who sat to his left was elegant as any lord in the Duke's hall, his black robes as rich, if more somber. "And you, Wellhyrn?"

Wellhyrn's lips curled. "Sabirn? Wizards with the power to bring down a kingdom. If malice could serve—"

"I wonder what our Sabirn-lover would say about this?" asked one of the younger alchemists.

Ladirno shrugged. "One has to guess what Duran's thinking. Years since he's been to court."

"Maybe there's a reason." Wellhyrn waved a languid hand. "If anyone might know what's going on with the Sabirn—"

"He hires them to go out into the country with him to gather herbs," said the other alchemist.

Another: "Maybe he's sleeping with them."

Wellhyrn snorted: "Herbs. Midwifery, next."

Ladirno said: "With his father banned from court—"

"Consorting with Sabirn. A man of the Profession should have standards—"

"What *does* he do?"

"Midwifery. He runs an apothecary." Ladirno reached for his wine-cup and drank. "He's been making his living that way for over thirty years. Lives in a garret. Looks twice his age. Deals for pennies. By now, it's probably the only thing he knows."

Wellhyrn leaned forward on the table, his arms crossed before him. His eyes glittered in the torchlight. "He'd have money, he'd have a good deal else if he weren't out to spite the Profession. He's got his father's books, the gods know what he's got. *He* deals for pennies, he hands it out free, hands physic to any beggar in the quarter. Free! Hands out his cures, *tells* them to midwives— the gods know who they poison, who knows what he hands out? Or think what would happen if he stumbled across some great alchemistic secret. Gods, he'd hand it out on the streets."

"A fool." The younger alchemist chewed on his lower lip for a moment. "And where would the Profession be, colleagues, if we all gave away our secrets?"

"Folk poisoning each other all over town. Burning the town down to melt metals. *We're* highly trained, my friends, the gods only know what this fellow is."

Ladirno said: "He doesn't experiment. As Wellhyrn said, the only thing he's interested in is medicine."

"Oh, aye . . . and look what he did with his great discovery."
Wellhyrn toyed with one of the heavy gold rings that graced his
right hand. "The fool discovers a cure for the sexual pox, and what
does he do, but come to court and tells everyone. Now *any* quack
doctor can treat the pox. Think of it! Duran could have made himself
richer than all of us combined if he'd kept the cure to himself."

"Thank the gods he's a fool." The older alchemist scratched at
his beard. "He could imperil all Targheiden if he *does* discover
something big in alchemy. There's no sense of professional ethics
in the man."

Ladirno shrugged. "Small danger. Right now he's so damned
poor he's barely making ends meet."

The light in the hall brightened as the sun slid out from behind
the clouds. Wellhyrn leaned back in his chair and crossed his
long legs out under the table.

"I'm off to the harbor," he said. I'm expecting a shipment.
Come with me, Ladirno?"

Ladirno contemplated the long walk from the upper city to
the wharfs. "Ah, why not. We've been cooped up long enough as
it is with these damned storms."

After a brief hour of sunlight, the clouds had gathered again
and, accompanied by thunder, rain fell on Targheiden in sheets.
Duran looked out the open door at the water rushing by in the
street and gave up on the notion he might have any customers
this afternoon.

Despite the open doorway, the thick clouds cast the interior
of his shop into deep shadow. Duran walked back to the counter,
reached for his flint, and struck a light. Cupping an oil-soaked
rag between his hands, he carefully lit the lamp and drew the
glass down around it.

Its feeble glow barely reached the walls of the narrow shop. A
large yellow dog rose from its place on the other side of the
counter and ambled through the shadows toward Duran, its tail
swinging side to side.

"So, Dog," Duran said, glancing out the doorway to the street,
"*now* you want to go out. Well, go then, though gods know you
won't like it much."

Dog nuzzled Duran's knee in passing, stood for a moment on
the rain-spattered threshold, then carefully ventured onto the

overflowing walk. The rain was easing somewhat, but Duran did not expect the dog to go far.

He turned away from the door and found a long splinter of wood. Lifting the glass side of the lamp, he kindled the splinter and lit the lamp that hung over the counter. *No more,* he cautioned himself, *unless customers come. Fish-oil's not getting cheaper.*

Wind gusted through the doorway, setting both lamps to flickering. Duran considered closing the door for warmth but that would reduce the light and discourage customers. He sighed quietly, and sat down on the high stool behind the counter to wait, disconsolately, for business. In the street, water overflowed the gutters, poured off roofs.

Ha. The only people who will visit me this afternoon are the drowned.

Behind him, neatly arranged on wooden shelves that ran up the wall, sat his herbs and medicines, each resting in small pottery jars. He was not rich enough to afford glass, so he had labeled each jar in small, neat printing. His more precious medicines sat in a locked cabinet toward the rear of the shop; he kept the key on its chain around his neck at all times. Certain crazies would kill a man for what rested in that locked cabinet.

He laughed to himself. From the Queen of Sciences to herb-pottery. Here he sat in a narrow shop, surrounded by herbs, poultices, and whatnots, visited by the poor folk of Old Town, for whom he was the only thing coming close to a doctor. He healed their fevers, their sores, dispensed drugs that took away pain, and even more dangerous drugs that ended unwanted pregnancies. *Those* he never admitted to having, and the women who sought him out—even the whores—knew that blackmail worked both ways.

There was his cure of the sexual pox; gods knew he saw enough business from the poor who could not afford to go elsewhere, but he occasionally treated richer folk who desperately wished to protect their identities, *and* keep the knowledge of their disease from the High Town doctors—in which cases, Duran never asked any of his clients more than the most general of questions, and they were happy to return the favor, and to pay at least what kept the shop going. Not more. There were ways and ways to guarantee a poor apothecary's silence: one preferred a modest coin—and risked no higher fees.

Oh, Father, Duran thought, settling back against an upright in the shelving. *What would you say of your son now? How far have I fallen?*

Thirty-five years in Old Town sat on a man, made him grey and grim and bent with study in dim light. Duran's blond hair had whitened, his gaunt shoulders stooped more than in his youth, and he had to hold things decidedly farther away these days to see them clearly.

Time, and time—the marks of which were deeper in Old Town than in the High City up the hill, despite that his art had kept him free from sickness and hunger: rain still caused his joints to complain. He grimaced, realized he had not had his midday meal yet, and got down from the stool.

A hunk of cheese and a fresh loaf of bread sat on the shelf under the counter. He cut a slice of that bread and the end off the cheese, wishing he had something besides water to wash the meal down . . . naturally, as if drawn back on a string, Dog appeared at the doorway, dripping rain-water, tail wagging in hopes of his share.

The rain had nearly stopped by the time most folk in Old Town closed their shops. Duran stood in the opened doorway, watching a grey steady drip off the second story overhang onto the street . . . the rush of the gutters grew quieter as the storm rumbled off to the north. Duran snorted: save for old Mother Garan, not one customer had darkened his door all afternoon, and the old woman had only bought willow tea for her headache, one of the simpler and least expensive of Duran's physics.

Dog lay curled up by the doorway, dreaming in the late afternoon, his ears twitching and his tail thumping now and again on the wooden floor—chasing rabbits in his dreams, Duran guessed, though in this part of town it might as likely be mice or the occasional young cat unaware of where Dog's territory began—Dog, just Dog, because Duran had never come up with a name that fit his companion: and Dog had never complained.

Neither had Duran repented the expense of Dog's healthy appetite. Dog's presence served as a deterrent to burglars, and gave Duran a sense of security. Though he never made much of what he kept in his locked cabinet, a large protective animal on the premises eased his mind somewhat.

Duran sighed, giving up hope of making more than his one afternoon sale, and looked at the inn that sat across the street from his shop. "The Swimming Cat" was the inn's name—a name given it generations back by its owner whose cat had fallen into a half-full rain barrel one night. Old Puss had survived the ordeal, and the innkeeper found her the following morning, clinging claws hooked to the side of the rain-barrel, water up to her neck—a stubborn talisman for a tavern always borderline on ruin.

The "Cat" was somewhat seedy now, but still reputable. As the largest inn in this section of Old Town, it catered to travelers who could not afford the better inns farther away from the harbor—excellent food for the price, a gathering place for the neighbors, as well as passers-through from the harbor.

Duran took his cloak down from behind the door, gathered up his keys, blew out the lamps, and stepped outside—Dog, lost in dreams, opened one eye, yawned, stretched, and went back to sleep. Duran locked the door, put the keys in his belt pouch, and started across the street to the inn.

"Bad rain, eh, Duran?"

The woman's voice made Duran wince and turn: it was his neighbor, the seamstress Zeldezia.

"Aye," he said. "Nearly drowned coming back from the docks."

Zeldezia leaned against her doorjamb, shoving a lock of her brown hair back over one shoulder. She was near Duran in age—not ill-favored, but one seldom saw her smile. "We been having more rain than usual, don't you think? Them as says it's witchery—"

"Aye, that we have. Perhaps it will end soon." Duran put on a stubbornly pleasant smile, nodded to her, and turned away. A conversation with Zeldezia was the last thing he wanted on a gloomy afternoon. Damned woman. Enough to curdle a man's appetite.

He stepped over the stream of water flowing down the gutter and made for the "Cat's" doorway. One benefit of the rain, even Old Town smelled better for it, washed and clean, refuse swept away in the gutters—redistributed down the block, generally. But not near the "Cat." Tutadar, the innkeeper, kept his frontage and his alley clean, holding it bad business to have his clients stepping over garbage.

He kept the inside the same—scrubbed. The inn was more

crowded than usual for this time of afternoon; doubtless the rain had kept folk indoors who would have otherwise been elsewhere. Duran paused at the doorway steps, letting his eyes adjust to the dimmer light inside.

"Greetings, Sor Duran."

He glanced down, just inside the doorway, at the man who had addressed him. The fellow sat on the floor, a walking stick leaning on the wall of the tavern behind him. He was white-haired, clad in clothes patched, but quite clean. The dark eyes that looked up at Duran were full of intelligence and wit.

"Greetings, Old Man," Duran said. "Do we have another story from you tonight?"

The old man shrugged. "Perhaps. If I feel in the mood."

Duran smiled. Old Man was always in the mood. The locals in the tavern had heard all his stories time and again, but no one seemed to grow tired of them. For a few coppers, the old fellow would spin tales that kept his audience enthralled, despite their familiarity with the stories. But Old Man truly shone when the common room was full of travelers who had not heard his tales before. It was then that Duran could swear he was hearing new stories, not those he had listened to for years.

Old Man was Sabirn. But Tutadar had even allowed him inside the inn. Despite a few nervous glances from newcomers, Old Man had become such a fixture of the neighborhood that locals hardly took account of his race.

"So." Duran dug in his belt pouch and came up with a copper . . . one of the three that Mother Garan had paid him for the willow tea. He placed the coin in Old Man's upheld hand. "For a story, then . . . *if* you're in the mood this evening."

Old Man's smile was most engaging. "For you, Sor Duran," he said. "I'll tell it for you."

Duran nodded and walked on into the common room—quiet at this hour, due to grow noisier after evening traffic had had a few cups. He saw a few of the tables occupied: Bontido, the potter, for one, who lived on the other side of the seamstress; Ithar, whose smithy neighbored the inn; a few rain-soaked, better-dressed passers-through from the harbor warming themselves . . .

"Your usual, Duran?" the innkeeper called out from across the room.

"Aye." Duran sat down at his accustomed table, shrugged his

cloak back from his shoulders, and stretched out his feet. It was then that he got a look at the two well-dressed men who sat at a table a few paces away from his.

Ladirno and Wellhyrn! What, by all the gods, were *those* two doing in "The Swimming Cat"? Duran considered ignoring the two, thought, actually, of changing his table or coming back later, but that was a coward's choice, not to mention it would draw attention from his neighbors. The pair turned their heads to stare at him: he smiled, tight-lipped, nodded a perfunctory courtesy, intended thereafter to pay his attention elsewhere, deliberately.

But: "Ah, Duran." It was Ladirno who spoke, the older of the two. With silk-lined cloaks, softly woven tunics above supple hose and neatly shod feet, the two were totally out of place among the local trade. "We've heard this is where you spend your time."

Duran nodded again, jaw set.

Ladirno's companion lifted an elegant eyebrow—Wellhyrn, the younger, the more handsome of the pair (and he knew it, Duran thought). His clothes were that much richer, gods, velvet and silk in the somber colors of the Profession, and he bore himself with an easy arrogance. "Duran," Wellhyrn said, pitching his voice loud enough to be heard by the other customers. "What a surprise—in a seedy place like this—"

"*I* like it," Duran muttered.

"Really?" Wellhyrn turned to his tablemate. "Shall we be going, Ladir? The wine's sour, the storm's delayed the ship until at least tomorrow. We can certainly do better than this uptown. . . ."

Ladirno shrugged, shoved his chair back from the table, and stood, gathering up his cloak. "And when can we expect to see you at court again, Duran? Or in the guild meetings?"

"Sometime soon," Duran promised, making an effort to sound friendly.

Wellhyrn had risen to his feet. He swept his cloak up from the back of his chair and settled it around his shoulders. "I'm sure we'll all look forward to that day. And the guild fees. But that can't be in your way, can it?—Coming, Ladir?"

Duran watched the two men cross the room and saw the clink of the coins they tossed to the innkeeper. He could have lived on such extravagance for days.

Damn, damn! He knew he should not let them bother him, but by Hladyr the Shining he could not help it. Fellow alchemists.

Ha! Ducal favorites, they spent their days at court, amusing the nobles with petty tricks . . . sleights of hand that kept gullible patrons interested in funding. Tricks of the Profession—all honorable, of course: research materials came dear, and one could hardly explain the *real* secrets. . . .

The hell. Duran took several deep breaths and settled back in his chair. He would not call the present elite of the Profession charlatans, but by his lights they came close. In his father's day—

In his father's laboratory—

Lalada, the cup girl, brought Duran his ale. He took the mug, smiled a silent thanks, and drank. The brew tasted bitter on his tongue, less the fault of the ale, he was sure, than of his mood. There was nothing wrong with what the "Cat" served, damn, there was not.

He took another drink, waiting for his supper—meat pie tonight, an extravagance: every fourth day, Duran allowed himself real meat . . . beef from the herds that grazed to the north of Targheiden—that much a one-time nobleman allowed himself, every fourth day, no oftener.

Tutadar himself brought Duran's supper to him. "Don't let them gilded donkey-butts get to you, Duran," he said, straightening and crossing his arms on his chest. "Bet them black crows never saved any kid like you did Sora Mitti's son. Think on that 'un, Duran. Them folk ain't' got nothin' on *you*."

"Thanks, Tut," Duran said, cutting open his pie and sniffing the sweet smell of beef. He glanced up, remembering the innkeeper's wife. "Is Anha's hand better tonight?"

"Aye, thanks. She wanted me to tell you that, Sor Duran. She's puttin' that salve on the cut like it'd save her, she is."

"If it flares up again, have her see me." Duran reached for his belt pouch to pay for the pie and ale, but Tutadar nudged his shoulder.

"No, no, this 'un's on Anha and me. For bein' a good neighbor." He glanced over his shoulder at the doorway. "And for not bein' snot-nosed like them two. Enjoy your meal."

Duran stared for a moment, then nodded and smiled. He set to his pie, aware now that he had it before him just how hungry he was.

✧ CHAPTER TWO ✧

Well into dark, the warmer for beef pie and ale, Duran finally quit the inn. More of his neighbors had come to the "Cat" for their dinners, and their company had lightened his mood—after-dinner talk had flowed from table to table, warm friendly talk, for it was all Old Town in the tavern this evening: the few uptowners and harbor trade who had come in had returned to their rooms, or gone off uptown and down.

Duran fumbled for his keys and felt for the lock: hard to see, though the "Cat" had torches burning by its front door so long as they lasted. The key habitually stuck in the ancient lock. Duran cursed, jiggled the key, shoved the protesting door open.

Dog stood waiting by the door, uncomplaining as usual. He leaned up against Duran's leg, inviting a quick scratch on his head, then trotted off into the deepening night, about his own necessities. Duran lit his lamp, set it down on the counter, and hung his cloak behind the door. Full of meat pie and ale, he sat down on his stool to await Dog's return, so he could lock up his shop for the night.

Then his eyes fastened on a packet that lay on the floor: someone had slipped something under his door. He stared for a moment, got down from his stool, and picked the packet up. It was made of paper—a fine grade of paper, not the coarse stuff one purchased here in Old Town. He took it back to his lamp, leaned close, and opened it.

Two silver donahri slipped out of the folded paper and dropped ringing onto the countertop.

For you, our poorest brother. May this small sum keep your body and soul together. The note was signed, with an artistic flourish: Wellhyrn.

411

Duran cursed and flung the packet down on the floor. *Damn Wellhyrn! Can't he leave me alone? He still goes out of his way to torment me. Why should he bother?*

Dog came back and stood in the doorway, his tail wagging. Duran glanced up from the paper, noting that the butcher must have left bones on his doorstep: Dog held one in his mouth. "Come on, Dog . . . in, in!" Duran shut the door behind Dog, locked it, and then contemplating the two silver coins glittering in the lamplight, thought that if he had more pride, he would have sent those donahri back to Wellhyrn with a terse note suggesting how to apply his charity. But pride had long ago found its proper place in Old Town: these two silver coins could keep him and Dog in food and drink for days upon days. Adding the coins to what he had seen Wellhyrn and Ladirno toss about at the inn, he suspected the Duke had given both men another grant to pursue their research.

I could use that. I could do more good with it.

But I don't play the game. I don't cater to the desires of the nobles at court.

Besides, the nobles dislike me. They remember . . . at least those of them old enough to remember my father.

Duran sighed heavily, swept the two silver coins up into his fist, and dropped them into his pouch. So be it. If the gods chose to gift him with this silver—though the method of that gift was less than palatable—who was he to turn it down?

Duran gave Dog a goodnight pat on the head, and, lamp in hand, walked to the back of his shop, and to the steps that led upstairs.

It is the nature of all things, Duran read, *that they belong to one class or another. There is the prime matter which is the basis for all substances found in the world. It is the interaction of form with matter that gives rise to the elements: earth, air, fire, and water. They, in turn, through various combinations, produce all the objects that surround us. Therefore, if an object has a preponderance of earth, it is solid in form. The presence of water in an object gives us the ability to produce liquids, or to melt what seems solid. Fire allows us to unlock other forms of matter through combustion. And air, the material of ideas, of the very soul, gives us the intelligence to see all these things.*

*Granting the above as undeniably true, then it is easy to see
that changes in the proportion of the elements may result in a
change of the form of prime matter. It then follows that, if this is
true, any substance may be changed into any other substance if
the right conditions can be found. . . .*

Duran sighed and set his notes aside. All this was basic, first-
year study, but it was one of his dreams to turn the language of
alchemy into something any learned person could understand.
He longed for a return to the old days, when alchemists labored
in their laboratories, dabbling less with mysticism and more with
metals he could not, in his present estate, afford. . . .

And he would be damned if he was going to go back, hat in
hand, apply to the duke and the guild, pay his fees to strut around
court, mouthing nonsense that sounded learned, blithering about
the mystical union of all things in the great aether beyond the
stars. That he left to the other alchemists, the astrologers . . . them
with their ducal grants and their rich patrons, that they kept duly
astonished or alarmed by sleights of hand and dire predictions.

Not that he discounted astrology: he believed in the
macrocosm, the wonderful world of the sun, stars, and planets
reflected in the microcosm, the tiny world where man lived. Man
grew and changed, so it was natural to believe that other things
did the same. It stood to reason that under the proper astrological
influences, certain metals might be changed to others. Even lead
might turn to gold . . . Theoretically. Not, the gods knew, that he
or anyone else had ever seen.

Time and again, when he was younger, he had gone to his
small furnace and "killed" metals, melted them down over and
over, trying to stumble across a purer form. Gold, his teachers
had taught him, should lie at the end of numerous "killings." *If*
the conditions were right. *If* the moon was in the proper quarter,
the planets in the most advantageous houses, and the wind was
blowing just right. If, if, if.

Small chance he would ever find the solution. He had received
no grants from the Old Duke, though the present Duke honored
his late father's invitation for Duran to attend court. What he
needed was access to the great furnaces, the fires hotter than he
could produce, the help of assistants nearly as knowledgeable as
he. And that, he knew, was held from him because he did not—
could not—play the game Ladirno and Wellhyrn played.

And years back, he had given up practicing all but the medical side to alchemy. Maybe one day, if the gods smiled on him, he would take the study up again.

Maybe.

He leaned forward in his chair again and shoved his notes aside. Another pile of papers rested on the desk: his writings also, but not devoted to alchemy—pages full of his small, neat handwriting, back and front, with hardly any margin to them. What he had written here concerned the Sabirn, herbs, and Old Man's stories.

He held to the notion that somewhere in their legends and the stories they told, lurked a kernel of truth . . . the learning that had once made the Sabirn a world power. So, when he took Sabirn helpers with him into the countryside to gather herbs, he always asked them to tell him stories of their people—fanciful tales, gods and heroes; some of the stories he sensed truer than others, but he did not know enough yet to separate fact from fiction. Or to know if there were deeper secrets.

One asked the sweepers of streets, the pickers of garbage, the carriers of slops—one disturbed one's neighbors with such inquiries; and aware of that disturbance, Duran tried to keep such journeys to a minimum, talked lately with Old Man, whom none of the neighbors considered a particular threat: Old Man had lived in the neighborhood so long, had become so *ordinary*. . . .

But Old Man, the consummate storyteller—his stories were of events that had taken place far in the past . . . great heroes, quests, the intervention of gods whose worshippers had died long ago, fables all, tales for children and the curious. But when Duran questioned him closely about what the Sabirn empire had *really* been, the old fellow had gone silent on him, shaken his head, refused to answer.

Duran flipped through the pages of his notes. He saw in his mind's eye the way life might have been in the Sabirn empire. Gods. If he could only journey back through time—

He rubbed his eyes. Tonight he was plagued by the "if's." He could only deal with what he had at hand, instead of what he did *not* have, or could never possess. And the alchemy he practiced had more to do with the pot bubbling away over the small flame, that filled the air with the stench of sulfur and herbs and lard—

hence the window braced slightly open: more of Anha's salve, an improvement, if his notion was right, to keep a wound supple and yet healing—

Dog barked downstairs, and barked again. Duran sat up straighter: he recognized that bark, a noise Dog made only when strangers came near.

"Damn!" Duran stood, and took up his lamp, blew out the fire beneath the lard—the front door was locked, he was sure he had locked it. He heard the sudden hammering of a fist, Dog's deep barking. "Who in Dandro's hells could be after physic at *this* hour?"

But children got sick, old folk took spells: an apothecary did have night calls, and they were generally the bad ones.

Duran opened the peephole, discovered two cloaked men on his doorstep, hoods drawn up so he could not see their faces in the lamplight. "What's the matter?" he called out. "Who is it?"

"Business," one said. The accent was uptown. "Discreet business, dammit, open."

One made the best judgment one could of such visitors. Duran carefully unlocked the door, pulled it open. Dog stood to one side, fur raised along his spine, growling deep in his throat.

"Call off your cur," one of the men said: the voice was young, cultured, and arrogant. The other said: "We won't hurt you."

Duran lifted the lamp higher, but the hoods still shadowed the faces. "Dog, . . . back off, that's a good fellow. Go on now. Go lie down."

Dog growled again, retreated to the center of the shop. Duran stepped back and gestured the two men inside. "How may I help you?" he asked, setting the lamp down on the counter.

"We hear you have the cure for the pox."

So, Duran thought, two highborn, most likely. Highborn with highborn liaisons. No wonder they had come to his shop in the dark of night, cloaked to protect their anonymity.

"Aye," he said, closing the door. "I have the cure. Which of you has the pox?"

A pause. Then the taller of the two tapped his chest.

"So," Duran said. "Please bear with me. I must ask you certain questions, and I'm afraid they'll be rather personal. Be assured, Sor . . . I mean no disrespect."

"Ask," he said gruffly.

Duran sighed quietly and lit the hanging lamp above the counter. "How are you certain you have the disease?"

"I . . . I visited a whore," the fellow said, sounding frightened and belligerent at the same time. "Two ten-days ago. Today I noticed a sore."

"Where?"

The tall man gestured briefly at his crotch.

"Is it weeping?"

"Aye. Somewhat."

"Have you visited this whore before?"

"No."

"Do you know anyone else who has?"

"No." The man folded his arms. "Listen, fellow, are you going to cure me or talk to me all night?"

Duran ducked his head, a small bow. "Please don't be upset. The questions are to help you."

The tall man's companion set a hand on the fellow's arm. "Easy, m'lord. I know this man's reputation. Trust him. He's the one who *discovered* the cure."

Lord, was it? Duran tried again to get a glimpse of the man's face, but failed.

For a long moment, the tall man stood with face downcast, then moved his shoulders slightly in an attempt to relax. "This man looks familiar," he said at last, looking up at his comrade: one could see a young squarish chin.

Duran tried to place his voice, but could not. "Perhaps you've seen me in the market."

"Hardly." The chin jutted. "*I* don't frequent such places."

"Ah, well." Duran spread his hands and omitted to mention the young man's consorting with whores. "Perhaps somewhere else, then. But that's no matter. You want to be cured of the pox, and with this disease time is of the essence. You said you visited the whore some twenty days ago. Have you noticed any swelling since then?"

The young lord nodded briefly. "Some."

"Around your groin area?"

A pause. "Aye."

"Anywhere else?"

"No.—It's only a slight swelling."

"Does your sore hurt?"

"No." The chin went squarer and squarer.

Duran thought a moment. The disease had obviously not advanced beyond its first stages, much easier then to effect a cure. "I'll treat you," he said, looking up slightly into the man's hidden face, "but you'll have to agree to return for further treatment. This is very important. You *must* return each time for a new application of the paste. Do you understand?"

"Why?" The belligerence entered the young lord's voice again. "Why can't you give me enough of this paste of yours to treat the pox myself?"

"Because it will kill you if it's misused."

"Gods! What kind of medicine is this?"

Duran kept his voice very level. "This is a particularly virulent disease. It calls for a cure equally strong. I can't agree to treat you unless you return to me for subsequent applications: omitting that, we'd as well not begin."

"He not lying, lord," the tall man's companion said. "I've heard what he says about this treatment before. Remember Khaldori . . . his doctor told him the same thing. Trust him, m'lord. We can find excuse to get back, your father won't find out."

Khaldori? Duran blinked, but kept all expression from his face. Old Lord Khaldori, Duran knew all too well from his early days at court: he had heard sniggering rumor that Lord Khaldori's son had picked up the pox not a year past.

And his visitors spoke so casually of a member of the Khaldori family.

"All right." The tall man sighed quietly. "I've no choice, and I'm told you're the discoverer of this cure. Get on with it then, man. I'll pay you."

Duran dipped his head in a small bow. "I have no doubt. But I do want to impress on you certain things: you realize you're highly contagious now, don't you?"

The young lord glanced sidelong at his companion. "So others have led me to believe." He swallowed heavily, and a note of fear entered his voice.

"And that this is extremely serious. Consequences—"

"I haven't waited too long, have I?"

"No, I don't think so. But don't be tricked by the pox. It can seem very mild at first. Untreated, it can kill you surely as any sword or spear. Not mentioning—"

"I'm ready. Do you want me to remain standing?"

"It would be easier to treat you that way." Duran walked around his counter to the shelves that ran up the wall. He pulled the stool over to one side, and climbed it. The lamplight cast his shadow against the shelves, but he knew exactly what he was hunting for.

"This won't hurt, will it?" asked the young lord.

Duran picked up his sealed jar of mercury paste and carefully descended the stool. "No," he said turning to face the tall man. "Not excessively."

The other fellow had stepped back into a darkened corner to give his companion some privacy. Duran set the jar down on the counter and slowly opened the lid, while the young man wrapped a scarf the more closely about his lower face.

"Don't worry," he said quietly, taking a thin paper wand from the shelf behind him. He dipped the end of the wand in the paste: he saw eyes beneath the hood, dark and anxious. "I've cured far worse cases than yours."

The two young lords left as heavily cloaked as they had arrived. Duran watched them go, standing in his doorway, Dog sitting vigilant at his side. The light from the torches outside "The Swimming Cat" dimly lit the two figures walking away down the street. Duran turned to go inside, then halted. Snatches of what the two men said as they walked away came to him on the breeze.

" . . . my father would kill me if . . ."

"Don't worry." This from the shorter man.

The other young noble had said something, only the last of which Duran could understand. " . . . my brother would say."

"How's Sal to know? He's not . . ."

Duran stiffened, and very slowly drew back into his shop. His pulse beat in his ears and he felt his face go hot. Sal? Saladar?

That was the Duke's youngest son.

Which would make the tall young man—

Brovor. Heir to the duke of Targheiden.

Duran's mouth went dry. He had just treated the second most important man in the Duchy for the pox. For a disease that, if left untreated, could have robbed the Duke of his chosen heir.

"Gods!" Duran shut the door, and stood leaning his forehead on it. No wonder Brovor had all but recognized him. Though it had been years since he had been at court, and the light in his shop had not been the best—Brovor had seen him many times as a child . . . a square-faced, obstinate boy, a bad temper—

A grown man with a dynastic marriage to make, a secret to protect . . .

Hladyr protect! What did he do now? The two men had taken great pains to hide their identities; but the companion had let slip one clue by mentioning the Khaldori family, a second by reference to Saladar . . . and Brovor was no fool: some small, nagging sense of recognition might set him to asking discreet questions, closer questions that might turn up a name—an association—that might make him believe his secret in danger—

Himself vulnerable to blackmail . . .

O gods! Why did I answer my door? They could have found other doctors to treat the pox, other physicians who would keep secrets. Why me?

They had paid in gold. For the silence as well as treatment. An ordinary apothecary would be overawed, have no notion what the scandal was worth, politically—but a disenfranchised nobleman, an alchemist with guild connections, a son of a disgraced father—with possible motives for political revenge, or alliance . . .

Not mentioning the chance of the heir dying if he miscalculated in his dosage—forget all hope of claiming it was the disease . . .

He would have to be careful, *very* careful, both in his treatment and in keeping his identity secret—and the chances of doing that seemed frighteningly slim. . . .

The one who discovered the cure, the companion had said.

Gods, *hope* the companion never mentioned names, *hope* the companion never understood his previous court connections, never connected Duran the Apothecary with Duran the Alchemist, Duran vro Ancahar . . .

Nothing to be done. Absolutely nothing to be done. One walked a narrow line and hoped—and did not look for much sleep this night.

A day of better trade, a quiet day, thank the gods. But it drizzled. There was a brisk trade in febrifuges, in willow tea. One could forget about ducal heirs, keep one's eyes on Old Town, put palaces and princes out of one's mind and worry about the Wirrin baby, who took colic; and Eemi, from harborside, with a knife-cut from one of her customers: Eemi feared scarring . . . Duran wanted a test for the herbs and lard. . . .

It seemed dishonest to charge, the girl being out of work and all. . . .

Dog barked downstairs, and barked again. Duran sat bolt upright in his chair where he had all but fallen asleep, his notes on his lap, another experiment bubbling away in its pot. This was Dog's most unfriendly bark, a bark more vicious than that reserved for mere visitors.

Another chorus of barks.

Duran walked across the room to a side window. The clouds had fled and a full moon rode above Targheiden now, and by its light Duran could see movement in the alleyway below. He stared through the darkness, trying to make out what was going on.

And then he saw and stepped back from the window. Someone was being beaten in the alley. Though he had heard no cries for help, the scuffling, the heavy breathing, and the muffled sounds of blows were easy enough to hear in the intervals of Dog's barking.

"Damn!"

Without thinking, Duran grabbed for his lamp and took to the stairs at a run, down the steps, across his shop as he fumbled for his keys. He snatched up his heavy walking stick, the only weapon the law allowed commoners. Hefting the staff in one hand, he unlocked the door and jerked it open wide as Dog joined him, his back bristled, a low growl rumbling up from his chest as he loped out into a street deserted at this late hour, light from the "Cat's" torches shining on damp cobblestones. Duran followed Dog, staff in hand, around the corner of his house and into the blind alleyway.

The combination of moonlight and distant torchlight showed him who his opponents were: mere boys, three of them, probably no more than fourteen years old—and running up behind the young toughs, he was upon them before they heard him coming. He lashed out with his staff—once, twice—hitting two of the boys, then jabbing up at the stomach of the third.

"Damn you!" He spun around to take a blow on his staff from

the first tough he had hit and to deliver the butt-end to an unguarded kneecap. "Don't like the odds now, do you?"

One of the boys sprinted off into the darkness: Duran heard a snarl and a yelp of pain—Dog had entered the fight, one remaining thug attempting to tear from Dog's hold, the other, lamed, sidling around Duran, his back to the wall of the building on the opposite side of the alley.

"Hey, Grandpa!" the other taunted, and Duran saw the dim glint of light on metal in that hand. "See if you can get this!"

The young tough stabbed out with his knife, but Duran had expected the move and, jumping back, brought the end of his staff around in a blow that sent his opponent staggering back against the wall. A second swipe of the staff knocked the boy's knife from his hand—at which, with Dog chasing after the second thug, the boy Duran faced spun and lurched off into the dark, decidedly the worse for wear.

Panting, Duran leaned on his long staff, his ears ringing. Damn. He had not lost his touch.

Dog gave up the chase and trotted tamely back. Quiet descended on the block. Somewhere shutters banged close again—none in this lane but his own, that cast a wan light to reflect on the walls. The victim of the toughs' attack sat leaning up against the wall of Duran's house, arms wrapped around his chest.

"Boy?" Duran said, walking closer. No response. "Are you all right?"

The boy looked up, nodded briefly, once.

Sabirn, the hair, the features were distinctive even in the dim light. A Sabirn out walking this district. *That* explained the attack.

"Can you stand?" Duran asked. The boy nodded, gathered his feet, and made an attempt. After a brief moment, he subsided. "Here." Duran held out a hand, grasped the youth under one arm, and helped him to his feet. "Got you pretty bad, didn't they?"

The Sabirn youth nodded again and stood swaying on his feet. Dog had come back from investigating the battle-site, and snuffled at the boy's shoes.

Duran looked across at the "Cat," at the end of the alleyway, but the tavern lay silent: many of its customers had gone home by now, and the travelers who were staying the night would have likely gone to bed: too late to rouse Tutadar, no sign of Old Man, who might be of some use.

"Lean on me," Duran said, taking some of the boy's weight on his left side. He took the lad toward the street, toward his front door—gods, he had left it open. But Dog trotted ahead and stood waiting on the doorstep, tail slowly wagging back and forth, evidence of property unmolested.

The Sabirn boy balked at the threshold, wobbled: Duran insisted, Duran helped the youth across the doorstep, Dog complicating matters by trying to enter the shop at the same time.

"Go on, Dog. Good boy. Lie down now." Duran nodded, let the boy lean against the counter, picked up his lamp. "Then let's take it slow." He reached out to put the other arm around the boy: the youth flinched. "Easy. *Mehciya*."

The boy looked at him, set-jawed, scared-looking in the lamplight.

"That's the limit of my Sabir. But I'm a friend. Try to help me if you can."

Slowly, taking as much of the boy's weight as he would give, Duran walked him to the rear of the shop. The steps leading upstairs were steep and narrow; he took them one at a time, pausing now and again to let the youth gather strength for the next. Finally, Duran gained the second story, and led the boy into his room, to his bed.

Another hesitation. "Easy now, take it easy." He insisted, brought the boy to the bedside, let him slide from his arm to sit on the bed. Duran set his lamp down on the table close by, looked down at the Sabirn youth. "Well, now. Let's take a look at you. . . ."

The boy flinched as Duran brushed his long black hair back from his forehead. His gaze flicked back and forth across the room, toward the window—

"Dammit, lad, I won't hurt you. Don't fight me now. *Mehciya*, understand? I'm trying to help."

The boy murmured something inaudible, but sat silent as Duran inspected the cut. That was not as bad as it looked, just bloody. Duran knelt and looked at the youth's ankle: sprained and swelling—if it was not broken. The ribs—the gods knew. The boy had no inclination to let him see.

"All right." He stood and walked across the room to a small cabinet. "I'm going to get you something that should make you feel better." He glanced over his shoulder. "For Hladyr's sake, boy . . . I'm not your enemy. Relax."

Duran always kept a few essential herbs and poultices upstairs in case he found the need for them. He came back with a splinter of kindling, lit it from the lamp, moved his current project off the stove and set on a clean pot, from the stores on the shelf, wormwood mixed in wine. He waited patiently while the mixture heated, then dipped a clean rag into the steaming solution.

"This may sting some at first," he said, "but it will take away the pain." He met the youth's eyes. *"Amegi?"*

The boy nodded, and Duran set to work on the lad's cut forehead. The boy's hands clenched on the edge of the bed.

"I'm almost done . . . There. Now. You want to let me see the ribs? Mmmn?"

The youth frowned, hesitated—then untied his belt, and set aside a small wooden flute he had kept bound at his waist. Gingerly lifting his tunic, he revealed bruises that had already darkened his thin torso.

"Huhn. Wrap in the sheet. I'll mix something stronger." He went back to his shelves and took out another jar, filled this time with white vinegar and a stronger tincture of wormwood. This, too, he heated a little, poured half into a pan he set to heat, then returned to the boy. "I'll be gentle as I can."

The youth shut his eyes and nodded. Duran generously swabbed the bruised areas of the boy's chest, side and back, then with strips of rag tied the soaked cloth against the lad's bruises.

"That should do it for now," he said as the youth lowered his tunic. "The ankle's what worries me." The water on the stove had begun to steam: Duran brought the pan back, encouraged the lad to slip off his ragged shoe and put his foot into the water.

The boy winced at the heat. Slowly, keeping his eyes closed and his jaw clamped tight, he lowered his foot into the water.

"Ahh!"

"I know," Duran said. "Hurts like Dandro's hells, doesn't it? Patience, lad. The pain will start to go away."

Dark eyes followed Duran as he went back to the stove. "Why're you doing this?" the boy asked.

Duran shrugged. "Why not?"

"I'm Sabirn."

"Aye, that you are." Duran came back to the bedside.

"You're Ancar."

"That I am. I'm also an apothecary. Sometimes a doctor."

"Nobody else'd help me." The boy's eyes were steady. "Why're you different?"

Duran cocked his head. "I'm me," he said. "And I don't like to see folks hurt. How'd you end up in that alley anyway?"

The boy frowned. He remained silent.

"Don't answer if you don't want to. Have you ever seen those three toughs before?"

"No."

"Chase you far?"

The boy nodded. "*Chochi*. My fault." He wiggled his toes in the water. "Damn stupid to get caught like that."

Duran fetched the chair from against the wall, and set it by the bedside. He lowered himself down and crossed his legs. "Have you got any family? Anyone who will worry where you are?"

The boy stared at Duran in sudden, stark suspicion.

"All right. You've scores and scores of relatives. All of them formidable. What's your name?"

After a long pause, the boy replied, "Kekoja."

Duran waited, but that was all. Kekoja. "I'm Duran," he said. "Is that ankle feeling any better?"

The youth frowned, looked at him sidelong. "Doctor, huh?"

"Of sorts. A herbalist and an apothecary. An alchemist, by profession—Mmmn, you don't trust me, do you?"

The boy kept his gaze level. "Why're you doing this?" he asked for a second time.

Why indeed? Duran asked himself the same question. He had always been kind to the Sabirn, but he had never had one of them in his house. He thought of the neighbors. . . .

And felt just the least apprehension.

"Why're you doing this?" the boy insisted to know.

"Humanity," Duran said. "Was I to leave you lying in an alley?"

"I'm Sabirn," the boy repeated as if that explained it all.

✧ CHAPTER THREE ✧

Duran woke, the morning sun just slanting through the shutter-slats. He stretched—gods, he was stiff; and ached in more places than he thought possible. He grimaced, rubbed his eyes, rolled over on the pallet, and glanced over to his bed.

The boy was still asleep; curled up in a little ball, he had kicked the rest of Duran's blankets down toward the end of the bed. Duran snorted softly. From the still air, the lack of draft from the window, there would be small need of those coverings tonight. Warm, moist air, no morning wind from the sea—it promised a muggy, nasty day.

Duran sat up, arms on knees, and stared at his sleeping charge. The boy had had his suspicions—extreme suspicions—for which Duran did not blame him. Hence the night on the floor—but only one night, damn the young fool. And what in hell could he do with the boy? Turn him out on the streets? Good as Duran knew his medicines to be, that ankle would take several days to heal, maybe need more than wormwood. Maybe need rest—else the boy would limp his way through life: and a Sabirn lad had no prospects but portage and a hand-to-mouth existence. Lame, he had no hope but beggary.

He wiped the hair back from his face and sighed, feeling all the indiscretions of last night. Maybe he *was* getting too old to be fighting in alleyways. Forty-five. He shook his head, remembering his youth, when he thought anyone who was forty-five had one foot in the grave, and the other one slipping in behind it.

But he did not *feel* old. Inside, he was still in his twenties, still at the prime of his life. He scratched his beard, raked a hand through his hair, and levered himself to his feet, by degrees.

425

He nudged the table, grabbed after the edge, for balance. Kekoja stirred, stretched his legs out, and groaned softly.

"Hladyr bless," Duran said in morning greeting. "You're better?"

Kekoja rubbed his eyes, sat up in bed, and yawned. He glanced at Duran, then eased his foot out to the side of the bed and looked at it. It was spectacularly puffed, red, and angry.

In addition to which, the boy looked decidedly uncomfortable.

"Chamber pot?" Duran asked, feeling the need for the same.

Kekoja squirmed his way to the edge of the bed and slowly lowered his feet to the floor. He winced, his eyes narrowed in pain.

Duran knelt and drew the pot out from under the bed. He held out an arm and helped the boy to his feet. "I won't look, if it makes you feel better," he said.

The boy shook off the help, turned his back, balanced gingerly against that foot. . . .

No trust of him. No.

Traffic was beginning to stir in the streets below. Duran kept his eyes fixed across the room as Kekoja performed his duty, thinking if they did not both hurry, the slop gatherers would be come and gone—*not* a pleasant prospect for an upstairs bedroom on a hot day. . . .

"Shit!"

Duran glanced around just as the boy wobbled and fell sidelong onto the bed, slid halfway to the floor.

He hauled the Sabirn lad up to his knees, trying to be careful of the ribs—helped him lie down then. The boy's eyes were slightly glazed and his face had turned decidedly pale, broken out in sweat. But he shoved the help away.

"Boy?"

Kekoja was breathing hard. He wiped his face, glassy-eyed, said, thickly, "Lost my balance."

"Lie still," Duran commanded, despite the boy's hazed objections lightly running his fingertips over the boy's skull.

"Yeow!"

Duran jerked his hand back. "You've got a lump on the back of your head the size of an egg. Where else did they hit you?"

"Don't remember." The Sabirn lad took a deep breath. "I'm dizzy."

"I'd expect. People who get lumps that size on their heads don't feel especially wonderful afterward.—Does it feel better when you lie down?"

"Not as dizzy . . ."

"Listen, son. You stay put in that bed until you can stand up and not fall all over yourself. Head wounds aren't anything to treat lightly."

Kekoja nodded slowly, eased his head back on the pillow, and looked at Duran, his eyes still glassy. Duran ignored him, used the chamber pot himself, took it toward the door.

"Stay put!" he ordered the boy.

The Sabirn lad nodded.

"I mean it. Don't try to get up. You'll do yourself lasting harm. Do you understand?"

"Aye." Faintly.

"Good." Duran started down the stairs. "Remember it.—I'll go get us something to eat."

Dog stood waiting at the doorway, excited and turning around in circles.

"Poor fellow," Duran said, opening the door and letting the dog outside. "Don't have your own convenience, do you?"

He set the chamber pot on his doorstep, stood up and stretched, with a deep breath of the morning air, paused for a glance up the street. Zeldezia had opened her shop and was now busily sweeping around her front door. Efdin, the baker, had already started his day: the sluggish air carried a scent of fresh bread. There was the rattle of chains as Ithar opened his smithy. Apprentices began to gather at the doorways of the other shops on the street, laughing and calling out to one another.

Duran thought of Kekoja waiting upstairs on the bed, with not a little worry, having the lad alone with his shelves, his medicines, his personal things—

Damn it all, anyway. Here he, who had always been courteous and kind to the Sabirn, was worried about robbery—on the part of an injured boy. *With an ankle like his, and that knot on his head, he'd be lucky if he could make it down the stairs.*

He closed the door behind him, locked it, and crossed the street to the "Cat." The door stood open, food was cooking. Old

Man had stirred out of his night-time place on the floor inside to sit on the wide doorstep, a bowl of food in his hands.

Duran nodded at Old Man in passing, and entered the common room of the inn. This early in the morning, there were no people at the tables. Tutadar stood behind the bar, going over last night's take, arranging the coins in neat rows before him.

"Morning, Duran," Tutadar said, glancing up from his work. "Want your usual today?"

"Aye. A double portion. I'll take it with me if I can."

Tutadar shot Duran a questioning look but said nothing, and walked back toward the kitchen. Duran leaned up against the bar, keeping his eyes to the street outside. Should he tell Tutadar about his unusual guest, or not? Double portions alone of his breakfast would serve as a clue that something odd was going on.

"Got company?" Tutadar asked casually, returning from the kitchen, carrying two covered metal plates. He set the plates on the bar, and filled two mugs with wine.

"Aye." Duran glanced around the common room. He and Tutadar were still alone. "Last night three toughs beat up a boy in the alleyway. I chased them off, but the boy's in a bad way. Won't be able to move for a couple of days."

Tutadar snorted something under his breath. "Damned punk kids are startin' to make life miserable. Himself the Duke better do somethin' about it. Bad for business." He met Duran's eyes. "Got any idea whose kid? Some 'prentice?"

"No." Duran risked it all. "He's Sabirn, Tut. About fourteen. Nice looking boy, smart—"

"You left that kid in your house? Alone?" Tutadar leaned forward on the bar. "I know you don't mind workin' with them Sabirn, Duran, but don't let 'em fool you. Once your back's turned, they'll take you for everythin' you got."

Duran signed for quieter voices. "This one's in no condition to do that right now. Those toughs really knocked him around. Hit him hard enough on the head, he's still dizzy. On top of that, he's got an ankle sprained bad enough to keep him from walking for at least another day or two."

"And what're *you* going to get from this, Duran? 'Sides another mouth you can't afford to feed."

"I couldn't leave him out in that alley, Tut. And I don't think you would have, either. I thought of Old Man—"

"No!" Tut said, waving his hand. "No! Old Man I don't mind, Old Man's got his place here, he's *our* Sab, all right? He's old, he knows his place, he don't make no trouble. But there ain't no kid comin' in here, no. You've got too good a heart in you, Duran. One of these days, it's going to cause you trouble."

"Tut,—keep it quiet, will you? He's just a kid."

Tutadar set the covered plates and two mugs in a well-worn basket. "Just a kid," he muttered. "Listen," he said, then, leaning forward on the bar, his eyes locked with Duran's. "You ain't helpin' yourself by keepin' company with them Sabirn. *I* know you're too damned good-hearted, but—tongues is going to wag, Duran. They already do. It's one thing, hirin' some Sab to dig herbs, port baskets and all, but there's a limit, man. There's a limit t'what folk will understan'. You get my drift? Ain't *me*, you know that . . . but you know you can't keep that kid in there much longer without *everybody* findin' out."

Duran nodded. What Tutadar said was all too true. Because of his uptown ways, because of the . . . odd smells from the apothecary shop, lights at all hours, the occasional midnight customer, his neighbors already considered him peculiar. There were apothecaries who dabbled in . . . elimination of persons unwanted; there were those who sold things . . . unapproved by the clergy and against the law, as murder was. . . .

A man who dealt with harbor trade, who treated whores, a large part of whose trade was harborside, in diseases law-abiding folk disdained to name—

"I hear what you're saying." He dug in his belt pouch and set out four coppers on the bar. "I'll bring the plates and basket back after I'm done," he promised.

"Keep your eyes on that kid," Tutadar warned, setting Duran's money aside for the first of his morning sales. His voice grew gruff. "Don't want anythin' to happen to you. You're a good neighbor."

Duran smiled sadly, lifted the basket, and went outside. Old Man was finishing his breakfast, his dark eyes roving up and down the street. Duran nodded again in passing, nothing said, and crossed over to his shop, where Dog sat waiting on the doorstep. Duran juggled the basket in one arm, took out his keys, and opened the door—

While the seamstress, Zeldezia, stood leaning on her broom,

her sharp eyes watching his every movement. Duran nodded a dour good morning to her as he went inside. Damned nosy woman. Before the hour was out, she would have told all the neighbors that Duran was eating in his house this morning, rather than at the tavern, and *probably* know exactly what he had for breakfast. . . .

The slop gatherers had already been down his side of the street: the chamber pot sat empty by the steps. Later, Duran advised himself. Breakfast first. He waited for Dog to come into the shop, shut and locked the door, and went upstairs.

Kekoja sat propped up in bed, pillows stacked between his back and the wall, silently watching Duran lay out the two plates and set out mugs of watered wine on the table beside the bed. Duran noticed a glitter in the black eyes: hunger, most likely. He wondered how long it had been since the boy had eaten a good meal.

"Fish," Duran said, removing the covers from the plates. "Fresh fish. Straight up from harbor. The 'Cat' is fastidious. Are you still dizzy?"

The youth carefully shoved himself upright on the bed, his eyes moving from the dishes to Duran's face. The scowl persisted.

"What do you want?" Kekoja asked, turning to the edge of the bed, carefully putting his swollen ankle off the side.

"What do I want what? What kind of question is that?"

"You got something in mind, or you wouldn't be doing all this."

"Eat your food," Duran said, shoving a short knife across the table to the boy. "It's going to get cold."

Kekoja hesitated, then accepted the knife and began cutting up his fish, spearing small bites of it.

"Why do I have to want something from you to feed you?" Duran asked.

"Never had any Ancar treat me decent before." Kekoja took another bite, chewed hurriedly, and shot him a scowling look. "An' if they did, they'd want something."

"Well, I don't. So take your mind off it." Duran drank and set his mug down. "Now I'm going to ask you again—seriously: do you have any family or friends who will be worrying about you?"

The boy's black eyes measured Duran with a look too mature for his apparent youth. "Hundreds of 'em."

"Hladyr's Light, boy! You'd think I was out after—"

The boy stared at him, jaw clenched.

"I'd *like* to find your kin, boy, let them know where to find you, get you *home*, for Hladyr's sake, I've no other motives. Why would I go to this trouble? There's whores harborside. So what would I be after?"

Kekoja's eyes dropped. He speared another bite of fish. "I don't know," he said, his words muffled by the food in his mouth. "Sell me, maybe."

"Nothing worth the night on the floor.—Lad, I don't bother boys. And I don't sell them, either."

Kekoja looked at Duran again. "I got a grandfather," he said at last.

"A grandfather. Where does he live?"

" 'Cross the street."

"Across the— You don't mean the old, white-haired man who sits in 'The Swimming Cat,' do you?"

A nod.

Duran leaned back in his chair and regarded the boy with renewed interest. Old Man's grandson? He had never thought of Old Man as anything but Old Man. That he had once been married and had a grandson . . .

Not here, Tut had said. . . .

"You want me to tell him you're here?" Duran asked. "He can't take you in, but, hell, wouldn't he like to know you're here?"

A brief flash of emotion passed behind the boy's black eyes. "Aye. If you'd do that . . ."

"After breakfast. And before I go, I'm taking another look at that ankle. Can you wiggle it? Wiggle the toes?"

Kekoja moved his foot carefully. Toes moved. "Hurts."

"Then we'll soak it again." Duran finished off his fish and drained his mug. "I have to run my shop," he said, leaning back in his chair as the boy ate the last of the fish. "I'll open up, heat up some compresses. Will you be all right up here?"

"Afraid I'll steal something?"

"Not really."

"Everyone else thinks so."

"I'm not everyone else," Duran said, putting his plate into the basket and following it with Kekoja's. "The sooner you realize that, the more comfortable you'll be. Besides, you try that window, lad, you'll break your neck. Hear me?"

Old Man sat on the doorstep, his face relaxed as he leaned his head back against the wall, outside, this warm morning. Duran looked all directions, saw no one he knew, hunkered down on his heels. "Greetings, Old Man."

"A good morning to you, Sor Duran." If Old Man was astonished at this behavior, he failed to show it.

"Last night three toughs beat up a boy in the alleyway next to my house. I ran them off and took him upstairs. He's got a sprained ankle, a knot on his head. . . ." Duran waited for a response, but Old Man kept silent, his gaze as placid as ever. "This lad *says* he's your grandson. Says his name is Kekoja."

Old Man's expression hardly changed. "Where is he?"

"In my upstairs. In my bed. Eating my breakfast. He's not fit to walk. I don't know where else to send him. Or how."

Old Man's black eyes strayed from Duran's face to the shop across the street. "That's who you took the food to this morning?" he asked.

Old Man missed nothing. "Aye. Where shall I take him?"

"Did he ask for me?"

"He said you were related. He didn't ask for anything."

"He's got his reasons."

"Do you want to see him?"

Old Man's black eyes scanned the street about. Came back to him. Old Man nodded faintly, reached after his stick.

Duran stood, took Old Man's walking stick from the wall, and gave it to him. Old Man rose walked beside him across the street.

Zeldezia's door opened. She shook a dusty rug into the street, stopped, mouth open. Duran cursed inwardly, fished out his keys, opened the door to his shop, and followed Old Man inside. Dog waited by the counter and ambled over to sniff Old Man over.

"Go, Dog. Lie down. You know Old Man. That's-a-boy." Duran shut the door and waved a hand at the stairway. "Upstairs."

Old Man nodded, limped to the stairs, slowly ascended them. Duran came behind, indicated the doorway, which Old Man opened.

"Grandfather!"

Kekoja sat on the edge of the bed, his foot soaking in water and salts. Old Man took another step forward, and spoke rapidly in Sabirn, of which Duran could understand only a few words, none significant to him: the boy responded with words equally swift.

"He says you helped him last night," Old Man said, turning to Duran, "that you don't want anything from him. Is this true?"

"I *don't* want anything from him." Old Man's look at him seemed too sharp, too careful. "Anybody would have done the same, if they'd heard the fight. No one in Old Town likes thugs."

Old Man squared his shoulders. "No one likes thugs, aye. But some of your neighbors, Sor Duran, like Sabirn even less. He says he ate your breakfast."

Duran shrugged.

"You fed him. Do you know what that means to us?"

More than he knew, by Old Man's stern look. Duran shook his head, embarrassed, confused.

"You're willing for him to have this food?"

"Of course I'm willing. He doesn't owe me anything."

"You are bound by that giving. He is bound. We Sabirn do not take other people's food willingly."

"I didn't know. And I don't feel that he's bound to me, if that makes any difference."

"What's done, is done," Old Man said. "Since you offered him food out of concern for him, and since you don't know our customs, I don't hold you to the rules we live by." He gestured briefly. "But the boy knows. He knows."

"Look, Old Man, debt or no debt—he's clear. He's free. Where shall I send him? Where's his father? Where's his mother?"

Old Man shrugged by way of answer.

"Where does he live?" Duran asked. "He comes from somewhere."

"He lives on the street. So do most of us Sabirn."

"He's not going to be using that ankle for the next few days. He's not going to be living on the street."

Old Man shrugged.

Duran stared.

"I'm all right," Kekoja said from his place on the bed. "I can walk."

"Be still," Old Man muttered. "Pay your debts."

The boy set his jaw. "But, I—"

"You know I can't let you stay with me. Don't argue."

The lad's face turned red, and he angrily launched into a rapid stream of Sabirn. Old Man replied in the same language, making a few cutting motions with his hands. Duran watched the exchange, wondering what in the hells he had managed to get himself mixed up in.

"My grandson," Old Man said at last, turning away from Kekoja, "has a mind of his own . . . and a sharp tongue to go with it. I'm sorry, Sor Duran, but he must stay with you. He has no choice."

"Grandfather—"

"No choice, Kekoja!"

The boy frowned, his shoulders still stiffened in anger.

"Since he's staying here," Old Man said, "I insist that you let me pay you something . . . at least for the food he eats."

Duran drew a long breath. *With what?* he wondered. Aloud he said: "Can't either of you understand that I'm trying to help? That I don't expect anything in return?"

Old Man lifted his chin.

"All right," Duran sighed. "Pay for his food, if that's what bothers you."

"You're a very strange one for an Ancar," Old Man said, leaning on his walking stick. "You always have been, as long as I've known you." He looked Duran directly in the face—which no Sabirn did. "You've given more than you understand, Sor Duran. You don't know our customs, but let me say that what I'll give you in return means much to us." He spread a hand over his heart and bowed. "My name is Dajhi."

Duran reckoned suddenly—he *knew* fewer Sabirn names than he did Sabirn words. "Dajhi," he repeated, and then, making a blind leap of logic: "Your name is safe with me. So is your grandson. Whatever his real name."

Old Man's eyes softened. "You *are* a strange one," he said. He turned to Kekoja. "You've heard. Trust this one. Do what he says. Behave yourself, *tehiji*."

The boy looked sullenly at his grandfather. "Aye."

"You have your shop to run, Sor Duran," Old Man said. "I've taken enough of your time. Take me downstairs and I'll leave you."

Duran nodded and led the way down the steps, stood by the doorway as Old Man left, thinking.

He dragged his mind back to his business. Hladyr sent him a

few more customers today. The silver Wellhyrn had given him would only last so long.

The gods—even the Shining One—seemed to have better things to do than listen to one man's prayers. All morning long Duran sat behind his counter, waiting for customers who never materialized. Mother Garan, alone, returned for another dose of willow tea, saying her head felt better. Duran charged her the usual three coppers, and sent her off with strict instructions. One worried. Like many others in Old Town, she could not afford a doctor of the kind that practiced uptown. Duran was the next best thing . . . affordable. Knowledgeable enough to worry about the old lady—to ease the pain as he could. To do as much as he could and refrain at least from doing harm.

Duran thought of Kekoja upstairs, and wondered what the Sabirn boy was doing to pass the time. He had not heard the lad leave the bed; his floor had several singing boards, and someone not knowing them would alert a listener downstairs.

"Duran," Ithar said, entering the shop. "Got me a cut that don't seem to heal."

Duran got down from his stool. "Where?"

Ithar extended one burly arm. "There. Got cut t'other day . . . well, three, four days back, and it ain't healed up like it should. Thought you might have somethin' to help me."

"I might." Duran looked at the sore: it was red and swollen. "Did you wash it good after you got burned?"

"Hells, I didn't have time. Had a man comin' to pick up his goods and I was runnin' late. I just smeared some mud on it."

"Washing's better." Duran turned around and consulted the shelves of neatly labeled jars. He pulled one out and pushed it across the counter toward Ithar. "This ought to help."

The smith eyed the jar. "How much d'you think I need?"

"Not the whole thing." Duran looked at the cut again. "Maybe a quarter jar will do."

"Just rub it on?"

"Aye. And when you're working,—keep the cut covered with a clean cloth. Does it hurt?"

"Sommat. Not as bad as when I did it . . . but it don't seem to hurt any less lately."

"Huh." Duran stooped, reached under his counter, and pulled

out a small earthen bowl and its lid. He carefully poured some of the oil from the larger jar into the bowl and set the lid in place—the tangy smell of cinnamon filled the air. "When you get back to your shop, heat some water hot as you can stand it. Soak the arm till the water cools. Then get a clean—clean! stick, drop some of this on."

"Aye. Clean stick." Ithar took the bowl. "What do I owe you, Duran?"

Duran calculated. "Five coppers should do. If you should have some oil left when you're healed, keep it clean and sealed with wax, and it should keep."

Ithar nodded, dug in his belt pouch one-handed, and set the copper coins on Duran's counter. "You ain't gettin' rich doin' this, Duran. I charge *twice* that to fix a broken anchor chain, and that don't take no mixing with foreign stuffs."

"Your customers can afford it," Duran said, pocketing the coppers. "So."

Ithar stared at Duran a moment, then grinned. "Hladyr bless," he said, then turned and left the shop.

Duran sat down on his stool and looked down at Dog. "Eight coppers so far today. We might not do badly."

Dog merely wagged his tail, turned around several times, and stretched out at the end of the counter.

Eight coppers. Duran remembered when he and other noble children spent more than that on sweetmeats at the market. He now lived on less than he could have ever conceived, and not all that badly, either—as poor went.

He caught movement out of the corner of one eye: Zeldezia stood in the doorway, holding her apron in hand.

"Better business today than yesterday," she said, coming inside. "Rain scared off all but the determined, or the desperate."

Duran's contentment vanished. "That's true. You're doing well today?"

"I should be," the seamstress said, lifting one eyebrow. "After all, I *am* the best in this area."

Duran nodded. Obnoxious as Zeldezia could be, she was justified in her pride: she was by far the most talented seamstress in this section of Old Town: people came to her from better sections of the city, knowing they could get a bargain; and went away happy, too.

But Zeldezia never was.

If she didn't spend so damned much time telling everyone how good she is, Duran thought, *someone* might *find a chance to tell her.*

"You still got that boy in there?" Zeldezia asked bluntly.

Duran started. Damned if the woman had not seen him take the Sabirn lad upstairs last night. But he should have known . . . not much went on in the neighborhood that Zeldezia could not ferret out.

"Aye."

"Got beat up bad, did he?"

Duran shrugged. "Bad enough."

Zeldezia cocked her head and looked up at Duran. "Not very talkative today, are you? Who beat him up? You recognize 'em?"

"No. Three boys. Tut calls them 'punk kids.' "

"Well, we don't need them sort here in *this* neighborhood. If they move in, we'll be no better than the Slough."

The Slough . . . the roughest part of Old Town; lair of thieves, whores, and bullies. It lay to the west, by the marshy side of the river, a breeding place for vermin—human and otherwise.

"Hladyr forbid they move in," Duran said, for once in total agreement with his neighbor.

"That boy *is* Sabirn, ain't he?" Zeldezia asked, eyeing Duran closely. "That why you brung Old Man up?"

Duran nodded, knowing he could not deny what she had seen.

"Gods, Duran! Them folk ain't no good. An' you've got one in your house? In your bed? On your *sheets*?" Zeldezia's lips thinned into a frown. "Lady bless, Duran! He'll steal you blind. He'll have all his friends comin' in. You think about your neighbors? *We* don't want no Sabirn hangin' 'round here."

"Old Man doesn't steal," Duran pointed out, trying to keep his temper.

"Old Man's different. He don't bother no one. Besides, he's a cripple and he wouldn't be able to steal nothin' without *someone* noticin'."

"If it makes you feel any better," Duran said, "the boy's Old Man's grandson."

Zeldezia lifted both eyebrows at this news. A tidbit always excited her. He instantly regretted saying that. Especially as her face settled back into its angry expression. "They're devils, them

Sabirn. Necromancers. Demon worshippers. Ain't no good come of 'em. I tell you, you're a gods-fearin' man, Duran, but you come close to damnin' your soul, havin' anything to do with 'em."

"Now, Zeldezia . . ."

"You got to think! Think what could happen to your business . . . to *my* business if folk found out you're hangin' around with Sabirn, that you got one of 'em in your house, fer Hladyr's sake! Think o' my uptown clients! What'd they think? We hobnob around with them dirty Sabs? We could lose all our customers!"

"Well, we don't have to worry, do we?" Duran interposed smoothly. "If *you* don't tell anyone, and *I* don't tell anyone, no one will know, will they?"

Zeldezia frowned the darker. "I'm tellin' you, Duran, you're makin' a mistake. You can't trust 'em. Nowhere. Nohow. They'll get you so's you like 'em, an' then they'll run off with everythin' you own. Gods, drinkin' out o' your cups and eatin' off your dishes—"

Duran got down from his stool and walked to the corner of the counter so he faced Zeldezia. "I've dealt with Sabirn for years now," he said, "and not one of them has ever been anything but polite.—Why do you hate them, Zeldezia? What have they ever done to you?"

"They're wizard-spawn!"

"There's nothing they do that the Temple wizards or the Duke's wizards don't do."

"Oh, that's what they want you to think! Them Sabirn wizards practice the dark arts." She lowered her voice. "Priest says anyone who has anything to do with 'em is in peril of his *soul!*"

"Horseshit!" Duran exclaimed, hoping the vulgarity would chase Zeldezia off. As usual, it had no effect. Vadami. Damned snot-nosed district priest. Always spreading *his* version of the Eternal Scheme of Things . . .

"Well, if *you* end up knifed in your bed one night, I won't be surprised," Zeldezia said. "An' let me tell you, Duran . . . if you know what's good for you, you'll get rid of that boy 'fore folks find out he's up there."

"Not until he's healed," Duran countered, drawing himself up to his full height. "If anyone finds out, I'll know who told them. And it won't have been me!"

Zeldezia threw back her head so she could look Duran in the

eyes, set fists on ample hips. "I can see I ain't going to change your mind. Just think on what I said, Duran. Your business an' mine could suffer for your stupidity! Folks ain't going to take medicine you mix with no Sab kid slinking 'round this shop!"

Duran clamped his jaws together, afraid of what he would say if he spoke.

"So." Zeldezia shifted her apron to her other hand, and straightened her dress. "I'm going to the Temple. The Duke's going to be there, him an' his family. It's the Heir's name-day."

Duran's heart went thump. The duke's heir, resplendent at the ceremony—

Due, soon, for his next treatment for the pox.

Zeldezia turned to go, then looked back over her shoulder. "An' while I'm at the Temple, I'll pray Hladyr that he give you some good sense!"

With that, she swept out of the shop. Duran let loose his pent-up breath and stared after her. Gods! He had told Tut about Kekoja, knowing the innkeeper would keep his mouth shut. How in hell had Zeldezia . . .

Duran glanced upstairs, hoping with any kind of luck, Kekoja had heard nothing. Damned woman. But she could be right.

Dammit all anyway. He had never flaunted his dealing with the Sabirn—the way Tut had said, one hired them—there were few people besides them he could afford to hire. Besides the stories—about which no one knew. He started pacing up and down in front of his counter. He would have to be less obvious in dealing with the Sabirn, possibly cease talking with them at all till this blew over. All of them except Old Man. Old Man was safe. . . .

People knew Old Man. They would surely take it better, if they knew the boy was Old Man's grandson.

✧ CHAPTER FOUR ✧

Storm bore down on Targheiden: Duran heard the rumble of thunder out on the sea; the sunlight faded as clouds moved over the city. He thought of the ceremony taking place in the Temple, and of how this storm would not be viewed as a particularly good omen. . . .

As for the main participant in the ceremony, the Duke's son had promised to return for another treatment this very night— punctually: Duran had stressed that. He was sure Brovor had understood. But the dates added up to today, to name-day—not easy, he feared, for Brovor to slip away from the feast held in his honor, but the young man was terrified enough of his disease that Duran hoped escape for the short time it would take to come to Old Town—

Hoped the secrecy would hold up. And that Brovor would ask no questions—nor come to any sudden recognitions.

And the Sabirn boy upstairs—

Duran looked out his open door, gnawing his lip. In one uncalculated act, his life had become more complicated than he could have ever imagined. The Duke's son, then the Sabirn lad. Gods! If his neighbors only knew *half* of what was going on in his shop, if Zeldezia—gods!—if *that* rattle-tongue looked out her shutters tonight—

The thunder grew louder. Duran looked up at what sky he could see. Dark, menacing clouds rolled in over the rooftops; a stiff wind had begun to blow, rattling the apothecary's sign over his door, setting signs to swinging on their chains all up and down the street, a worn-out basket blowing and tumbling down a street rapidly emptying of traffic.

Evil weather . . . aye, the summer had been plagued by it, folk talked in the streets and taverns about it. What was bad for trade was bad for Targheiden, merchants worried, tempers flared over insignificant things; small fortunes vanished each time a ship went down. There was only one benefit of the rain: cooler weather this summer kept disease from running rampant through the poorer sections of town.

It also kept customers from his door.

He sniffed the wind. Rain would fall very soon now, rain which—

CRASH!

Duran spun around in the doorway; Dog had risen to his feet and stood growling, glaring at the stairs.

"Oh, Hladyr bless!" Duran ran to the steps, hurried upstairs, and stopped in the doorway. Kekoja lay on the floor by one of the side windows, his eyes closed, an upturned table and the shattered remains of a porcelain washbowl scattered around him.

"By all the gods!" he cried, "what in Dandro's hells are you doing?" He rushed to Kekoja's side and knelt to touch his face. "Are you all right?"

The Sabirn looked up at Duran with an unsteady gaze. He tried to sit up, but fell back into Duran's arms.

"Dizzy," he mumbled, closing his eyes again. "Damned dizzy."

Duran sighed, glanced at what remained of his late wife's washbasin, and helped the boy to his feet.

"What were you trying to do? Climb out the window? I *told* you to stay in bed! Why did you disobey?"

The boy kept silent as Duran set him down on the bed; he rubbed his forehead and groaned softly.

"You don't want me here," Kekoja said at last, leaning back so he lay stretched out on the bed. "Thought I'd leave."

"By the window? Gods, boy! That lump on your head addled your brains. You could have *killed* yourself trying to go out the window. And who told you I—"

God. Zeldezia. Shrill voices carried.

"Nobody need to've told me. *I* know. I'm Sabirn. Nobody wants me." His eyes shimmered with tears; he angrily blinked them away. "Not even my grandfather!"

So there lay the crux of it. Duran propped the boy's head up on the pillows. "Don't talk like that. I'm sure your grandfather has a good reason for what he's doing. *Does he, or is he not as kindhearted as I think he is?* And I never said I didn't want you here." *I'd much rather you'd gone with your grandfather, though. It would have made my life a damn sight easier.* "Take a couple of deep breaths. You'll be all right."

Kekoja did as Duran instructed; after a few moments, he seemed calmer.

"Now listen to me. I don't want you out of this bed except to use the chamber pot, you hear? And until you're steadier on your feet, I want you to call me when you have to go."

"Aye."

"And stay away from the windows." Duran straightened the boy's hair gently. "Hear?"

The boy said nothing. Duran went to shut the window, pick up the pieces.

Perhaps if he found them all, he could barter Bontido the potter into fixing the basin.

No. The glaze had splintered. No hope that the basin could be reconstructed. The shards were too small.

He let the pieces fall. Another tie with the past . . . gone . . . shattered like his youth. . . .

"Can you fix it?" Kekoja asked.

Duran rose, looked down at the jagged pieces of the basin. "No. It's beyond repair."

The Sabirn lad bit his lower lip. "I'm really sorry. I didn't mean it."

"I know. It's just that . . ." Duran waved a hand full of broken porcelain. "It was my wife's, and she's been dead for . . ." His voice trailed off. He met Kekoja's dark eyes. "You stay in that bed, hear?"

"Aye," Kekoja said faintly.

Raindrops spattered against the roof, sudden gust of storm.

"I'm going back downstairs. You need anything, you call."

"I will." Kekoja stirred on the bed. "Sor Duran?—I won't break anything else. I promise."

Duran forced a smile to his lips. "See that you don't," he said, and turned toward the stairs.

The rain had slacked off to a drizzle. Duran sat on his stool, gazing out the opened door at passersby hurrying to drier destinations before the next spate. A ship must recently have made port: he had seen travelers entering "The Swimming Cat." One wondered . . . one dreamed . . . where those folk were from, what their business in Targheiden was, and where they were going.

One must have had a dream of voyages—of travel to far places—in one's golden youth, when such things were possible. . . .

But the farthest he ever went was to the country.

And, gods, that was not far enough for his troubles, not far enough for safety from a duke's son, his father's past, his own damnable stupidity—

He had made another ten coppers since his midday meal, which brought his total day's take to eighteen. It was not the most he had ever made in a day, but—considering the rain and the fact summertime brought fewer illnesses than winter—not bad. He had broken even and seen a modest profit.

But medicines did not happen by magic. Nor come out of moonfluff. Fees bought supplies. Customers did. And he was running low on both.

Ah, well.

Duran walked to the back of his shop, drew a large earthenware jug out from under a table, and lugged it back to the counter, poured white vinegar from the large jug into a smaller one, dropped wormwood leaves into the vinegar.

Now, for the next two months, those small jugs would sit high on his shelves, the wormwood steeping in the vinegar. Duran plugged the large jug, carried it back to rear of the shop—

The bang of a door down the way said, considering the direction and a familiar sound, that Zeldezia had returned from the Temple ceremony and was reopening her shop. Hladyr keep him from the woman's thoughts . . . a prayer, he knew, that would likely go unanswered. By now, she had probably told everyone she had met that her neighbor was harboring a Sabirn in his home, a wizard, no less, a practitioner of dark sorceries. . . .

He had known the risk he ran in taking Kekoja in: or at least he had *thought* he had known. His neighbors were good folk, all of them, working as did he simply to make a living in Old Town. But Tutadar's words came back to him: no! Absolutely not! Not here! Not in my tavern—

Damn. Why were people so fearful of what they did not

understand or what was different? In all his years of dealing with Sabirn, Duran had not seen one genuine wizard. The Sabirn played a good game, some of them, and had people convinced they had far more powers than was true—any alchemist uptown knew *those* tricks; and any temple wizard could do sleight of hand, conjure doves—

Or fire.

"So, Duran. How's your afternoon been?"

He winced, turned from his search after alum he *knew* he had, and faced Zeldezia in his doorway. She wore a bright blue gown, graced with some of her finest embroidery, and her hair was neatly done up in braids and coif—a handsome, an impressive woman, in her temple finery: except the sour expression on her face had not changed from several hours back.

"Not bad," he said, keeping his voice light. "I've turned a profit, and the day's not over—not *everyone* went to temple."

She looked at him, then lifted her eyes toward the room upstairs. "Still got that Sabirn kid up there?"

Duran pursed his lips and wished he could say otherwise.

"S'pose I couldn't expect you to come to your senses," Zeldezia said, shaking her head. "You're a stubborn man, Duran . . . you don't listen to good sense. You been upstairs to see what he's thieved yet?"

"I doubt he's stolen anything," Duran replied, sitting down on his stool. "He's in no condition to do much but sit and soak his ankle. Leave it alone, Zeldezia. Leave it be. The boy'll go. He's just a kid with a sprained ankle. Let him be."

"I prayed for you," she said. "I did. Them Sabirn can corrupt you, taint your soul—they got charms can confuse a man, so's he's got to do what they want—and he don't even think anymore. . . ."

Duran snorted. "Now you're sounding like Priest Vadami," he muttered.

"I told him to pray for you, too."

Duran's heart constricted. "What . . . did you tell him?"

"That you was needing prayers. That this boy's moved hisself in—"

"Zeldezia!" Duran snapped, stepping down from his stool. "Can't you stay out of my business? Who gave you the right to prattle on to Vadami about what I do?"

Zeldezia stepped back a pace. "It's *my* business too. Damned kid'll drive customers away from *all* of us!"

"And who was to know if you hadn't told? He's not going to be here much longer. He's got a sprained ankle! He's not in anybody's sight!"

"Listen to me, Duran," she said, squaring her shoulders. "You can't even see what's goin' on under your own nose. The boy's bespelled you, that's what he's done. Them Sabirn can do it, turn your mind to helpin' him, then mixin' god knows what, gettin' 'im moonwort and them whore's babies—"

"Oh, good *gods*, Zeldezia!"

"Vadami was shocked. He was real shocked."

"Did you tell him the boy was injured? Did you tell him that, or only what you wanted him to hear?"

Zeldezia's chin lifted. "I told him. Vadami says that don't make no difference. You're still comin' close to corruptin' your soul. You don't even know that kid's hurt. He can make you *think* he's hurt. An' this a 'pothecary's shop, with all these drugs and such— who knows what he can do with hands on stuff like this? He could put it in the public well—"

Duran drew a short and furious breath. "He's not putting anything anywhere, Zeldezia. He can't walk! He can't stand up! Now I have business to attend to, as do you, I should think. And from now on, I wish you'd keep your nose out of my business, and your damn mouth *shut*!"

"Go on and treat me like this, Duran, but I'll *still* pray for you. Blessed Hladyr will bring you to your senses." She spun on her heel and stalked to the door. "You lissen to yourself, Duran, swearin' at you neighbors, bad-talkin' a priest, bad-talkin' me for prayin' for you—what's that sound like, hey?"

She left.

"Oh, damn, damn, damn!" Duran slammed a fist down on the countertop. "What's she *done* to me?"

A priest. A simple district priest, Vadami might be—but he had the ears of higher placed brethren, some of whom frequented the court.

Duran leaned his head on his hand and rubbed his eyes.

Vadami sat at a small table toward the front of "The Golden Shoe," a High City tavern frequented by well-to-do merchants, an occasional petty lord or two, and lower placed dignitaries of the Duke's court. He sipped his ale, and met the eyes of his companion, another priest—his immediate superior.

Priest Sorgun returned the stare, his eyes calm as the expression on his face. Vadami had chosen the inn as a place to talk because he felt comfortable here, and it was neutral territory, where neighbors paid little attention to him and his companion: priests from the Temple often came here in the afternoon or evening.

"You wanted advice, Vadami."

"Aye." It was the ale—Vadami knew, in some distant part of his mind, that he had imbibed more than he should. It *was* the Duke's heir's name-day.

"What is it you want to talk about?"

"My feelings, Superior."

"What feelings?"

"Rebellious thoughts, Superior. Discontent. Envy. I—know that's unworthy of me."

Sorgun lifted an eyebrow. "What—kind of thoughts?"

Vadami glanced over his shoulder. Several fellow priests sat at a table toward the back of the room: ducal favorites, those priests, whose parishes incorporated the better sections of town.

"Do you see those men, Superior?" he asked, indicating the priests with a motion of his head. "I've served Hladyr from an early age. I gave up what could have been a promising career as a merchant. *I'm* no less a priest than those court favorites, and yet what do I have to show for it? *My* parish is Old Town, where donations—while sincere—are next to nothing."

"Each according to their means—"

Vadami set his mug to one side, and leaned forward, his hands gripping the edge of the table. "But why have I been allotted such a position in life, Superior? I'm smarter than any priests I know, and I love the Shining One with equal fervor. Why have I been doomed to minister to Old Town?"

"Ah, Vadami . . . not everyone gets what he wants from life. Hladyr must test some of us more than others."

"But, why me?" Vadami straightened in his chair. "Why not someone else?"

"Patience," Sorgun said quietly. "We all have to start out somewhere. You're young, Vadami, only twenty-five, you have years of ministering before you. Many chances."

"I know, Superior." Vadami lowered his head. "But there are times. . . ." His voice trailed off, and he looked up at his companion. "Patience is difficult."

"Be strong. This is but a test put before you." A faint smile touched Sorgun's face. "And, whether you believe it or not, it's a test other priests have faced."

Loud laughter rode over Sorgun's words. Vadami heard a group of men at the table next to his discussing the near riot that had taken place in the Slough the day before. Vadami made a sign of aversion, turning that fate far from his life. Gods bless! Worse than ministering to Old Town was the saving of souls in the Slough.

"A wizard," the men were saying. "A Sabirn wizard, bold as brass."

Vadami took another gulp of ale. Sabirn. Warlocks! Traffickers in the dark arts! He hated the Sabirn nearly as much as he feared them. And now, from what the seamstress Zeldezia had told him, it was not only the Slough that harbored them. . . .

It was not only the Slough where sedition and riot threatened good folk.

A dismal future. If the temple blamed him—

"You do a good work, Vadami."

Vadami's face went hot. "One tries, Superior. One desperately tries. But there are deaf ears."

"Specifically?"

"Have I ever told you about Duran?"

"The nobleman."

"Ex-noble. He's poor as his Old Town neighbors now. But—"

"Is he a problem?" Sorgun asked.

"His shop is a focus for—midnight visitors. Whores. Persons with—" Vadami felt his face go hot. "Disease."

"He's an apothecary, isn't he?"

Vadami squared his shoulders. "He deals with Sabirn. Trades with them. *Harbors* them."

Sorgun's face went very still. "Have you advised him?"

"Aye. More than once. Duran listens; then—"

"He still sees them?"

"Aye. There's this old man who begs at the tavern across the street, a hanger-on, sweeps up—"

"Sabirn, you mean?" Sorgun's gaze had grown uncomfortably direct.

Vadami chose his next words with care. "A true daughter, a woman named Zeldezia: she's very pious, very reliable, always at temple. I saw her today. She asked for intercession, for—prayers for the neighborhood. She told me Duran actually has a Sabirn boy living in his house."

"Go on."

"Zeldezia said there was some kind of attack. Duran beat off the attackers, drove them off, took the boy into his shop—" Vadami stammered, looked at the table. "Into—" he coughed. "Into his bed, by what this good woman says."

Sorgun said, "Tell me about this—resident at the tavern."

Vadami blinked, felt his face still over-warm. Sorgun's question was hardly the shocked response he expected. "Everyone calls him 'Old Man,' and he lives inside the door of the tavern. 'The Swimming Cat.' He's a storyteller. A menial. Aside from that, I don't know much about him."

"How long has he lived there?"

"Years." Vadami shrugged. "No one pays much attention to him. He's obviously harmless—but this boy—"

Sorgun nodded slowly. "Vadami . . . I want you to feel you can talk to me like this at any time, for any reason. That's what I'm here for. Isn't it?"

"Yes, Superior."

"Keep an eye on this Duran." Sorgun lifted his mug of ale. "I do want you to keep careful watch on this Old Man."

"The old man's no problem. He's been there for—"

"Just watch him. I want you to tell me if you see him talking to anyone who doesn't live in Old Town."

"Aye." Vadami drained his mug to cover his confusion. If Sorgun was concerned about Old Man, then—then, all things considered, it certainly would do him well to be equally concerned.

Ladirno flung open the windows to catch what breeze blew in from the harbor, but there was little of it: the air even in this large room was stifling in its closeness. He sat down in his chair, loosened the collar of his tunic, and stretched his feet out before him. Temple bells had just rung out, announcing the tenth hour, well into afternoon, but Wellhyrn had not appeared yet.

Making me wait, just like he does everyone. Damn! He can get to anyone with his airs . . . even me, who first championed him at court.

At times Ladirno questioned his friendship with the younger man. They both shared the same attitudes and philosophies of life, but there was a malicious streak in Wellhyrn that Ladirno did not share.

And a self-centeredness and carelessness of others' annoyance.

He yawned, drowsy in the summer afternoon heat, and shook his head. As long as he had his place in life established and felt moderately unthreatened, he was fairly content. Wellhyrn, on the other hand, was always busy trying to keep anyone else from the same step on the ladder.

Steps sounded in the hallway outside, and Ladirno looked up. Wellhyrn at last . . . he would recognize those footsteps anywhere. "Come in," he called out, before the knock.

The door opened. "I've got it!" Wellhyrn said with uncharacteristic fervor, stepping into the room. He opened his belt purse and took out a lump of something that looked vaguely, from Ladirno's viewpoint, like a rock.

Ladirno took the object Wellhyrn gave him. Weighing it in his hands, he smiled. "It looks good, very good. It should fool the Duke, or anyone uninitiated."

Wellhyrn's green eyes sparkled in the sunlight. "Damn right it should. It took me long enough to bury that lump of gold in mud and coat it. But it took the firings. Now, when we set up our furnace and insert this 'rock' of ours, a little tap of the tongs and we'll have gold to reward the Duke's patience."

"After which the Duke, of course, will reward *us*." Ladirno handed the object back to Wellhyrn. "Well, sit down. Sit down. Wine? I have a new bottle."

Wellhyrn put the "rock" back in his belt pouch, nodded, and took a chair, expecting to be waited on as usual. Ladirno smothered angry feelings: if the relationship he shared with Wellhyrn was not so profitable, he would gladly put the younger man in his place.

He got up, poured two glasses of wine, and walked to Wellhyrn's side. "It's a masterful job you did," he said, as Wellhyrn took the glass.

"Of course. After all, I *am* a master at what I do." Wellhyrn took a sip of the wine, then leaned back in the chair, a thin smile touching his too-handsome face. "I wonder what old Duran did when he found my two silver pieces?"

Ladirno shrugged, sitting down again, and drinking his wine. "Kept them, I'll bet."

A momentary expression of anger twisted Wellhyrn's face. "That's not what I meant, Ladirno," he said, swirling the wine in his glass. "I *meant* . . . I wonder what he thought."

"Hard telling." Ladirno looked carefully at his companion: Wellhyrn had something on his mind, something bothering him. "Why are you so angry at Duran all the time?" he asked casually. "He's certainly no threat to folk like you or me."

"Ah, but you don't know that, do you?" Wellhyrn sat up straight, leaned forward, one elbow on the chair-arm. "I think he very well *could* become dangerous. You know how he talks to those damned Sabirn all the time."

Ladirno lifted on eyebrow. "That's a threat?"

"Have you forgotten what we heard at court? The Sabirn plot? The wizards trying to bring down the kingdom?"

"Gods. Sabirn with wizardry. Pigs will fly."

"Use your head, man," Wellhyrn snapped. "You and I both know that once the Sabirn ruled an empire, that they enjoyed a level of life that we haven't rivaled."

"Aye . . . but that was a thousand years ago. Their empire fell, man! What good were their wizards?"

"Did *they* fall?" Wellhyrn cocked his head. "Or did they somehow preserve their secrets, their knowledge? *Do* they have wizards who remember techniques from their past? What if—" He lifted a hand to keep Ladirno silent. "—they actually *are* able to do things that we can't? What if their wizards *are* stronger than ours?" Wellhyrn leaned forward, jabbed Ladirno's arm with his finger. "More to the point, dear colleague,—what if they have alchemists among them? What if *that's* what Duran's after?"

Ladirno made a rude noise and took another drink. "Rumor. Rumor on both counts. Nothing's ever been proved that alchemy ever predated—"

"Not if the secrets went with them! I'm saying 'what if.' I'm saying what if they *do* have such secrets—or they hold out secrets, what if that's where Duran's father got his information? Duran might make himself quite, quite something, thumb his nose at the Guild—"

"Huhn."

"Listen to me. Duran's got every reason to be angry at the ducal family after what happened to his parents. He could be involved in this plot . . . an Ancar protecting Sabirn in an Ancar city. It makes sense, doesn't it?"

Ladirno contemplated his glass. Wellhyrn might be right; the rumor of Sabirn wizards seemed genuine enough—at least that the Sabirn harbored secrets. At least that few people—save Duran—ever gave them more than an angry glance.

And an alchemist outside the guild—came up with a cure for the pox—

Plot against the kingdom aside, if Wellhyrn was right, and if the Sabirn *did* possess superior alchemistic knowledge, and if Duran discovered it . . . in the face of the Guild—in spite of the Guild . . .

Ladirno scowled. His position at court, Wellhyrn's, and the other alchemists, would be worthless.

To say nothing of the subterranean power Duran might wield having allied himself with subversives, plots against his own race, his own kind—

"Ah-h-h." Wellhyrn smiled coldly. "So you *do* see it."

"I see a possibility." Ladirno gestured sharply. "But I think you're overreacting, Wellhyrn. Duran's a fool, a virtual hermit, nothing left in life besides ministering to the poor of Old Town. He's dealt with Sabirn for years now. If they had such secrets, don't you think he would have found something more important than a pox-cure?"

"Maybe he has."

"Mmmn."

"I'm simply telling you why I think we should—contain this problem. I don't mean by doing anything—criminal: gods know we don't want a confrontation: but just by doing little things, like leaving the silver in his shop. Keep him unsure of himself and his place in life. Keep him questioning why we're living so well, and he isn't. Let him make a mistake."

"You've got a mean streak in you," Ladirno said. "Do what you want to. I won't stop you. But I still think you're expending a lot of energy on a problem that isn't a problem."

"Yet."

"Yet," Ladirno admitted. "Yet."

❖   ❖   ❖

Duran counted his take for the day, came up with twenty-four coppers, and congratulated himself. Tonight he would be able to eat well, to have, yes! a second mug of ale.

Dog stood up, shook himself, and ambled outside. The late afternoon shadows had darkened the street, and Dog knew his master's routine. Duran watched the animal turn down the street, nose to the ground, reading what only other dogs could read. Dog would be back before he shut his shop down for the night and crossed the street to "The Swimming Cat" for his nightly meal.

He glanced upstairs, wondering what Kekoja was doing to pass the time. He had slipped up several times to look in on the boy, found the Sabirn lad asleep, or quietly staring off into nothing. He had shared his bread and cheese with the lad at midday, made up a new pan of hot salts, and instructed Kekoja to soak the ankle again. Kekoja had complied, saying little more than necessary.

Duran rubbed his eyes, leaned back against his shelves. What in Hladyr's name had Zeldezia told people about the boy? Her talking with Vadami—gods! The priest would certainly be paying more attention to this street after today. . . .

Duran cocked an ear—heard flute music, coming from upstairs; he remembered the small, wooden flute Kekoja kept in his belt. For a moment he let himself be carried along with the music, until the strangeness of the melody made him sit straighter on his stool.

That was no Ancar melody the boy played, or Torhyn either. There was a haunting loneliness to the song, an alienness to it. Sabirn music. Music that spoke to Duran of twilight evenings, places with no names, and gods that had died with their worshippers.

Duran felt the hair at the nape of his neck stir. He glanced out the door, afraid of who might be listening to that playing, and drew a deep breath. He could hear Zeldezia now, complaining to all the neighbors about Duran's Sabirn boy, who played music that trapped souls in darkness.

But it was only twilight the boy played . . . twilight, and a loneliness that could not be comforted.

✧ CHAPTER FIVE ✧

Two days passed. Duran glanced over his shoulder as he crossed the street, but Zeldezia's door was shut. He had exchanged nothing more than brief greetings with her since their argument that day, and he frankly found her silence a blessing. Hladyr only knew what she was saying behind his back, but at least she had quit trying to get him to throw Kekoja out on the street.

Old Man sat in his usual place by the doorway and, as Duran passed, smiled broadly. Duran smiled back, then carefully erased the expression from his face as he entered the common room. He did not know how far rumor might have spread the story of his guest, but it would not do to rub his neighbors' noses in the fact.

Tutadar looked up from what he was doing at the bar, and lifted an eyebrow as Duran stopped. "Eating here, tonight?" he asked, setting a freshly drawn mug of ale on the counter. "That's a change." A lower voice. "Kid gone yet?"

"No." Duran glanced around the common room, found it not all that busy, filled mostly with his neighbors, and kept his own voice down as he paid attention to the mug Tut offered. "A few more days should do it. His head's a lot better, and he doesn't lose his balance that often. That was a damned nasty sprain he suffered. Came close to breaking his ankle, I'd say."

"You want your usual?" Tutadar asked.

"Aye.—How's Anha's hand, by the by? Any better?"

Tutadar's face broke into a smile. "Oh, aye. Think your medicines got her back to her old self. She been yellin' at me lately just like she used to."

"Good." Duran turned and walked back to his table and sat down.

And noticed a change.

Slight, that change, but a change nonetheless in the atmosphere of the common room; though his neighbors had nodded to him as he passed by their tables, there had been none of the usual good-natured bantering back and forth with him that he was used to.

He leaned back in his chair, cursing himself for seeing shadows where there probably were none. On the other hand, if Zeldezia had been as busy telling people about Kekoja as he feared she had, then there could be a damned good reason.

The tavern girl, Lalada, came to his side carrying his plate. Duran smiled up at her as she set his dinner on his table, and felt his expression freeze: she had not returned the smile, and moved with an uncertainty he was not used to seeing in her—some days ago.

Damn Zeldezia! She *must* have been in the "Cat" the last couple of days, spreading all kinds of rumors about the Sabirn boy. Duran took up his ale, sipped at it, and pretended he noticed nothing amiss.

The smith Ithar got up, came over to his table. That was encouraging. "Mind if I join you?"

"No. Please, sit down. How's your arm doing?"

Ithar pulled out a chair and sat. He extended his arm and, even in the lamplight, Duran could see that the cut was healing normally, new pink skin.

"Feels lots better," Ithar said, letting his sleeve fall. He took a long drink from his mug. "Wanted to thank you for what you done."

"No thanks needed. You just be careful in the future to wash any cut you get, never mind the mud, and you shouldn't have any more trouble."

The smith nodded, wiped his moustache with the back of his hand, leaned forward on the table. "Want to ask you a couple questions, Duran. Man to man."

"Certainly." Duran's heart lurched. "What?"

"You got yourself a Sabirn kid in your house?"

Duran briefly shut his eyes. "Has Zeldezia been telling *everyone* in the neighborhood, or just a select few?"

"Then you ain't denyin' it?"

"No. Did she also tell you the boy had been hurt . . . badly?"

Ithar's eyes wavered a bit. "No. She didn't."

That figures, Duran thought. "It is true. He was beaten by three young toughs in the alleyway outside my house. I chased them off and I'm keeping him until he can walk again."

"Chased them punks off?" Ithar asked. "With that stick of yours? Them as been hangin' round—"

"Aye."

"You could've been hurt bad, Duran. Any of 'em could have had a knife."

"One did."

Ithar drew a long breath and took another drink of his ale. "Why didn't you call for help? We would've come a-runnin'."

"I was too busy.—Now, let me ask you a question. Did Zeldezia tell you the boy's Old Man's grandson?"

The smith shook his head.

"It seems to me that someone who's so free with other people's business could at least get the story right."

"But, Duran . . ." Ithar shook his head. "The boy *is* Sabirn."

"So's Old Man! I can't imagine you leaving an injured boy on the street just because he's Sabirn, Ithar. I truly can't."

Ithar scratched his head. "Maybe not. But I wouldn't have let him into my *house*, f' the gods' blessed sake—"

"Ithar, none of the Sabirn I've ever dealt with have stolen from me. That's the truth. None's ever done me an ill turn."

Ithar stared at Duran for a long time. "Tut always said you got too kind a heart for your own good. I agree with him."

"For Hladyr's sake, Ithar! The boy's no demon. He's just like you or me."

"Look, Duran: Old Man . . . he don't worry me. He's old and he's crippled. But a young kid now, fast on his feet—"

"Ithar." Duran reached out and set a hand on the smith's forearm. "A skinny, fourteen-year-old boy's no threat to you or anyone in the neighborhood. He's been here three days and nothing's happened. Has it? Tell me if it has."

"You're an honest man, Duran, but you got a soft spot's going to do you hurt. You took in that dog when he was starvin' and you was little better. Now, you're taking in this Sabirn kid when you *know* better, and he ain't got no uses." Ithar's brown eyes were level. "You tell me: you going to stand surety for 'im? Pay us for anything he steals? 'S only fair. . . ."

Duran leaned back in his chair. "He's not going to steal anything from you," he said, "and if he does, *I'll* be the first one to turn him in to the Guard."

"You mean that?"

"I swear to it."

"Well . . . if *you* stand for 'im . . ." Ithar drank again. "But I'll tell you for damned sure, Duran . . . makes me nervous just thinkin' 'bout one of them little, dark folk livin' this close to me. Gives me the creeps."

Duran chewed and swallowed and reached for his ale. "If you met the boy, Ithar, you'd change your mind. He's intelligent—a good lad . . . polite *and* smart. He's a kid, Ithar. Like any kid. What in hell's everybody spooked for?"

"If you say so." Ithar looked at Duran for a moment, then self-consciously grinned, reached across the table, and rested a hand on Duran's shoulder shook in comradely fashion. "You're all right, Duran . . . you really are. Twenty years I knowed you, an' you been honest. I just hope to hell what you're doin' here won't do you hurt."

"That I can't help. Zeldezia's doing the hurt."

"Feh!" Ithar waved a hand. "She talks too much. We don't believe *everything* she says. . . ."

"You believed this, didn't you? Didn't ask me?"

The smith nodded slowly. "Aye, that's so—but, dammit, ain't nobody took in a gods-cussed Sabirn. Sneaky bunch. None of us likes 'em. . . ."

Duran finished his fish and wiped his mouth on his sleeve. "Sneak is as sneak does. Some don't care who they hurt. Some don't care what the truth is."

"Zeldezia? Believe me, Duran . . . I'm going to let everyone know about it, too." His face grew serious. "But that boy give you any trouble, you tell me. Givin' you any trouble?"

"No. For one thing, Old Man's talked to him, and told him to mind his manners."

"Dandro's hells . . . you do be careful. You been lucky in the past dealin' with Sabirn. Hope your luck's still with you."

"Come over and meet the boy yourself, if it'd make you feel better. He's a kid. See for yourself. He won't bite."

The smith's eyes wavered. "Not me, Duran. You can keep that kid in your house long's you want to, by me, but don't be tryin' to get *me* to be friendly to 'im."

"All right. But don't worry, Ithar. Your tools will be where you leave them—same as always. If anything *is* missing in this neighborhood, I'd look to the gang that beat this lad. Sure won't be him taking anything. I promise."

"That's all I can ask." The smith finished off his ale, spat into the rushes on the floor, and stood. "Got to be goin'." Ithar lingered, said, on an apparent second thought: "You take care."

Duran watched Ithar return to his table and wondered if Ithar knew something.

Heads got together. By the hour Duran left "The Swimming Cat," a number of heads had gotten together, and the atmosphere in the common room of the inn had returned to near normal. A number of his neighbors still looked at him from the corners of their eyes—still, he felt sure, distrusted him, thanks to Zeldezia's spreading rumors. But Ithar, both honest and forceful, would set the neighbors right, and Duran thanked Hladyr he had known the smith as long as he had. Next to Tutadar, the smith was probably the most respected man in the neighborhood.

As (Duran smiled wryly, balancing the basket containing Kekoja's dinner in one hand, fumbling for his keys) he himself certainly was not.

He opened the door to his shop, set the food down on his counter. He was lighting the lamp when he heard Dog growl a warning.

The two young lords stood in the open doorway, cloaked as before.

"Come in," Duran said. He held on to Dog until both men had entered his shop, then ushered Dog out the door. The animal growled again, and refused to go any farther than the doorstep. "It's all right, Dog." Duran scratched Dog's ear, shut the door, faced the two men. "I have to take something upstairs. I'll be right back down."

The Duke's heir and his companion glanced around the shop. "See that you are," Brovor growled. "We don't have all night."

Arrogant young cock, Duran thought, and lit the lamp over the counter for his customers' benefit, keeping his chin down— gods, they had known each other as children, he and Brovor. And he was that much changed. . . .

He picked up the basket of food and the other lamp, and climbed the stairs, opened the door.

"Duran?"

Duran set the lamp down, giving light as the boy sat up and rubbed his eyes.

"I've got a customer," he said, opening the basket and setting Kekoja's food on the bedside table. "I'll be back. It shouldn't take me long."

Kekoja's nose wrinkled. "Fish again?"

"Beef pie tomorrow. I promise you. Eat your food, lad. I'll be right back."

"How many more times do I have to come here?" Brovor asked, from behind a fold of his cloak.

Duran paid attention to his work. "The sore's started to disappear. The swelling's gone down."

"How many times? I asked you a question."

"This will be your fourth treatment," he said. "With luck, ten more."

"Ten?" The prince's whole body jerked. "You damn quack, that's intolerable!"

"Lord." The heir's companion spoke from the corner. "It does take time."

"And if I don't come back?" Brovor asked, his voice edged with menace.

"You die," Duran said with a shrug, tossed the swab, got up, and wiped his hands. "Sooner or later, you die."

"Damn you!" Brovor took a long breath. "You—"

Someone knocked on the door.

"Who's that?" Brovor asked in a hoarse whisper, clutching his cloak about him, his hand reaching for the hilt of the short sword he wore.

"I have no idea." Duran had not heard Dog bark, so he assumed his visitor was someone Dog knew. He put the top on the jar and set the wand beside it. "It's probably a neighbor—"

"No one must know I'm here!"

"I suggest you and your friend go to the back of the shop where the shadows are deepest. I'll try to keep this brief as possible."

"Gods! I'll—"

The heir's companion took Brovor by the arm. "Come, lord. He's right. Patience. Please."

Brovor glared at the door a moment longer, then followed his friend to the rear of the shop.

Another knock.

"Just a moment," Duran called. He glanced once over his shoulder to be sure the two young lords were hidden, then opened the door halfway and stepped outside.

Vadami stood waiting in the street.

Hladyr bless! The priest! Not now! Duran resisted the urge to glance behind him as he held on to the door.

"Good evening, Duran," Vadami said. "Hladyr's blessing on you."

Dog sat a few paces away, tail dropped. He was not fond of Vadami, but he was too well mannered to growl at someone he recognized.

"Good evening, Priest," Duran said, stepped out past the priest, pulled the door shut. "Been boiling up medicines. It's a warm night. Pleasanter air out here, I assure you, Father.—What may I do for you?"

"Just a social call. How are things going here in your neighborhood? Are you and your neighbors in good health?"

Like hell, Duran thought, *a social call. Where was Vadami going with these questions, at this hour—*

With the prince in the shop. And Zeldezia's going to him about the boy—

"Everyone's doing fine, thank you. Aside from normal complaints, headaches and such, no one's been sick."

"That's good to hear. Summer can bring on bad fevers."

"True, but I haven't seen the fever so far this year. My business isn't doing all that well, but I don't mind if it means folk are healthy."

Vadami rubbed his clean-shaven jaw. "I haven't seen you at Temple in some time. . . ."

"Difficult to close my shop—folk do need medicines. I've no help."

"I saw Zeldezia there," the priest said, his voice holding mild reproof. "She manages."

"That may be true, but Zeldezia makes better money than I do. And *her* clients can wait. A sick youngster—"

"Of course, of course." Vadami dismissed the subject with a brief gesture. "But I thought you *had* help. A Sabirn."

Duran bit his lip. "A boy. A boy beaten and left in the alley. He's not help, Father, far from it. His family's poor, the boy might have died. A work of charity."

"Charity to someone who deals with the dark powers. Do you understand that? You're putting your soul in peril."

"I doubt the boy has anything to do with powers—dark or light. He's a frightened kid—"

"Duran. This boy—this boy sleeping in your house—is an agent of deception. Of temptations—"

Duran snorted. "Why? Because they're dark, short, and speak a different language? This is a fourteen-year-old—"

"They're wizards. Demon-worshippers. Dealers with the dark. They reject the worship of Hladyr."

"Were they ever invited to worship him?" Duran asked.

Vadami's face tightened. "They could come to the Temple if they wanted to . . . if they evidenced a sincere desire to change their ways. But none of them has ever done that. They've no souls. They *can't* repent."

"That's for priests to say," Duran said, making a desperate effort to avoid controversy. "They're servants in all the noble houses. I see no difference in principle. . . ."

"What's wrong with you, Duran? Of course there's a difference. They're servants. But *you* deal with them, you trade with them. . . ."

Duran spread his hands. "They're the only help I can afford—when I can afford it at all."

For a moment, Duran thought that he might have broken through the priest's narrow view of things, but Vadami's face hardened. "So you take this boy into your employ—"

"Not my employ!"

"They're already starting to bespell you, just like Zeldezia said. Duran, I'm warning you. Don't have anything to do with the Sabirn! If you do, you'll be denying Hladyr and all his works. You know the Book of the Shining One, where it says:

"*A fool is he who turns from Hladyr's face,
For darkness shall rise to engulf him,
Birds and dogs shall strip his bones,
And his name shall be taken away.*"

Duran rubbed his eyes wearily. "I received an excellent

education in my father's house. I know the words of the Book, too, like:

"Turn not away the man from your door
Though he be ragged like a thief,
It might be one of the god's come to test
The love of the Shining One's children."

Vadami frowned deeply; from the expression in his eyes, he hardly expected to be met verse with verse.

"You twist things. You twist them into that you want to believe. Beware arrogance. Most of all beware arrogance. The holy words don't apply here."

Duran worked sweating hands, searched for persuasive argument. "I'd not quarrel, Father. I assure you—I'll be in Temple."

"I fear for your soul, Duran. I truly do. You're better educated than folk hereabout: and because of that you can use the holy words—but don't misuse them. I urge you, *urge* you most strongly, don't let the Sabirn fool you. They're minions of darkness. I'm afraid for your soul, Duran, I'm afraid for all those around you."

"I'll be careful, Father."

"Surely, with all your learning, you've heard stories of their wizards? There was one named Siyuh—feared in all the northlands. They say that Siyuh and his followers could make fire leap from their hands—a pact with the Dark—"

"A thousand years ago."

"Will you wager our soul on it?" The priest shook his robes free, stepped off to the walk, and looked back at Duran. "Please, Duran . . . as you hope for Hladyr's heaven . . . have nothing more to do with the Sabirn. Don't think I'm persecuting you. I'll be offering up daily prayers for you."

"Thank you, Father."

"Hladyr save. Good evening."

The priest turned and walked away down the darkened street.

Duran stood, numb a moment. Dog came ambling out of the shadows, sat down, and nuzzled at his hand.

O Lord Hladyr, Duran thought, *Shining One, maker of all things. If you are Lord of everything . . . are you also Lord of hate?*

Behind him—muffled by the shut door, he heard a footstep.

Gods! Brovor!

Duran opened the door without letting Dog in, slipped hastily inside—

"Took your own damn time, didn't you?" Brovor walked out of the shadows. "What was that?"

"I'm sorry. It was the local priest. He's the *last* one I'd think you'd want to know you're here."

"Damn!"

"He's gone," Brovor's companion said. "Lord, let's be out of here."

"I needn't remind you," Brovor said, "of discretion."

"I am," Duran said, "discreet."

Brovor dug in his purse. Laid down a gold piece. A second.

"One," Duran said. "One is enough, lord. Discretion is part of the charge."

A moment the blue eyes stared at him above the muffling cloak—straight at him. Sweat ran on Duran's ribs.

"Who's upstairs?"

"A sick old man, lord. Quite deaf."

Brovor stared, fingering his sword-hilt. At last, he nodded briefly, motioned to his comrade, left.

Duran stared at the closed door, long after the two young lords had gone. Gods! Vadami on his doorstep, the Duke's heir hiding in his shop, the Sabirn boy upstairs! His knees were shaking, now that he was alone. Dog settled down by the counter, another one of the butcher's bones between his paws, his tail wagging slowly back and forth. Duran smiled bleakly.

"Dog, you have the answer to an easy life, don't you? When things start getting bad, go off into some corner, curl up with a good bone, and watch the world go by."

Dog wagged his tail again and gnawed at his dinner. Duran shook his head. One moment's thought, one moment's recollection on Brovor's part, and Brovor might remember him—Brovor might think he had motives—

Brovor seeking a state marriage, on which peace or war might depend—

And a Sabirn boy in the question—he wondered if Zeldezia had any idea what she might have done by telling about the Sabirn boy. He doubted it. Zeldezia more than likely never thought beyond the moment she spoke.

But who might Vadami tell—and where might it go? Duran rubbed his bearded chin. Again, he did not think he was dealing with a malicious soul; Vadami was merely . . . pious.

And if Vadami told one of his superiors, he might find himself in the temple answering questions. On the other hand, if Vadami told some of his secular friends, *they* might—

Duran squared his shoulders. No use trying to foretell the future. For his entire adult life he had walked a fine line between respectability and notoriety: an alchemist without Guild connections could hope for little else.

Best, he thought, best try to put the best face on things—do things in the open, where it regarded the boy—

Daylight on a sore—worked some cure. So might public exposure of a situation—the boy in some ordinary, harmless context—stop the speculations.

He stooped, patted dog on the head, took the lamp, and walked back to the stairs, up the steps—

To the door where Kekoja sat up in the bed and set aside a— Duran stared. A book? Gods!

The boy—reading?

He set his lamp down on his desk and faced Kekoja. The Sabirn lad stared back, his eyes dark pools in the lamplight.

"Sorry," Duran said. "That took me longer than I thought. What were you reading?"

Kekoja's eyes wavered. "Just looking at the pictures."

Duran walked over to the bedside and picked up the book. It was one of his philosophy books, a rather dry treatise by a fellow named Artoni who had written several centuries in the past. Duran lifted an eyebrow and ruffled the pages.

"There aren't any pictures in this book, Kekoja."

"Now you tell me."

Duran smiled. "Don't lie to me," he said mildly. "I don't like that. You can read, can't you?"

Kekoja flinched, then grimaced. "Aye. Some."

"That surprises me."

"S'pose so."

"Who taught you?" He thought of a lasting puzzle: the storyteller, the foreigner whose Ancari was sometimes— astonishing good. "Your grandfather?"

"Aye." The Sabirn boy shifted uneasily in bed, then looked up at Duran. "But I don't read too good, and I can't read fast. I can speak Ancari better'n I can read it."

"I think you're not telling me the whole truth, Kekoja." He took the book back to the desk and laid it down. "I think you're a damned lot smarter than you want to show."

Kekoja lifted his chin. "An' what difference'd *that* make, that I can read, or that I'm smart? Who'd care one way or the other?"

"Your grandfather obviously cares, or he wouldn't have taught you. Knowledge is never anything to be ashamed of."

"You ain't Sabirn."

Duran drew a long breath. "No, I'm not. But I think I understand what you're saying."

Kekoja's wary expression persisted. "Grandfather says you're a fair man. Even when it gets your neighbors mad."

"I guess that sums it up."

"Why?"

Why? The question Duran had asked himself over and over. Why are you doing this? Why are you courting disaster? Why, why, why?

"I'm not sure," he said, falling back on utter honesty before this boy, this street urchin he had rescued from a beating at the hands of other ragtags who looked and lived much the same. "I suppose I don't like to see injustice. I don't like to see things misunderstood." He waved a hand at the books, the shelves. "That's why I'm an alchemist that's why I operate my shop. Because I want to know what things *really* are. . . . I want to understand them. And I can't believe something's bad simply because I don't understand it."

"That could get you in trouble," Kekoja said seriously. "Understanding things."

Duran laughed quietly, folded his arms, lighter-hearted, he had no notion why. "You're damned right it could, lad. It has. But I haven't given up trying to understand things."

"You aren't afraid of us Sabirn?"

"Oh, yes, as much afraid of you as I am of my own kind. There's good and bad in all of us, whether we be Sabirn, Torhyn, or Ancar. It's simply easier to overlook our own bad traits and assign them to people who aren't like us. Have you ever been afraid of things like that?"

Kekoja nodded slowly.

"Of something new? Of something strange?"

Kekoja nodded again.

"Because it was truly frightening, or because you'd never seen anything like it before?"

"Both."

"Smart boy. Aye, we can be afraid of something we know all too well . . . or too little. Ah, lad! Now there's the thing—I suppose I'm not afraid of Sabirn because I think I know you better than most folk. I've heard all the tales spread about your people, but so far I haven't seen any of them coming true."

"They say we steal."

"And I imagine some of you do. So do some Ancar. So do some Torhyn. Some have titles." Duran shook his head. "Nothing special in that."

"They say we're wizards."

"Now *that* I would like to see," Duran said. "Most cheat. I haven't met a real one yet, though I suppose that doesn't mean there aren't any."

Kekoja cocked his head. "Grandfather was right. You *are* a strange one."

Duran laughed and drew the chair out from behind the desk so he could sit facing Kekoja. "I suppose I am."

"Why do you talk with Sabirn?"

"I'm interested in your legends, your stories. That's why your grandfather fascinates me."

"Why?"

"I save stories. I collect them like some men collect books. Somewhere in those stories is a key to the past, to what really happened."

"When?"

"Hundreds of years ago—when your people ruled their empire."

The Sabirn boy's face went very hard in the lamplight. "That was a long time ago."

"Aye. So long ago most of the facts are probably forgotten by now. But legends can hide facts, lad, beneath their fanciful surfaces. That's what I'm after. I'm like a man who sifts sand through a sieve hunting for gold."

The room grew silent. The windows stood wide open to the summer night. Duran could hear crickets, the cry of nighthawks, the barking of a faraway dog. He looked at Kekoja, but the boy seemed lost in thought.

"Grandfather knows," Kekoja said finally. "He knows the most stories of any of us."

"Maybe sometime he'll tell the ones he hasn't told."

"Maybe. You write these stories down? All of them?"

Duran nodded. "What I can remember of them after they're told."

"In these books?"

"In some. I write what your grandfather says. What the other Sabirn say, the ones I've hired to help me when I go to the country." Duran suddenly remembered what Vadami had told him about a legendary Sabirn wizard. "Have you ever heard of someone named Siyuh?"

Kekoja's eyes widened; he sat bolt upright in the bed. "Ziya!" he whispered.

"A story you know?"

"No." The boy looked down, leaned back up against the wall, and folded his arms across his chest. "I don't."

"Are you sure?"

The lad would not meet his eyes. "Nothing," Kekoja repeated.

Duran knew he had missed something there. The moment was gone; he could not recapture it.

"I'm tired," Kekoja said, turning his back on Duran and stretching out on the bed. "Let's go to sleep."

"If you want." Duran frowned at the boy, wishing he knew what had happened. One moment, Kekoja had been open and friendly; the next, he exuded all the charm of a stone.

And gave him the floor again.

✧ CHAPTER SIX ✧

A huge clap of thunder shook the house the following morning and jarred Duran out of a deep sleep. He sat up in his bedding, rubbed his shoulder, and looked around. It was dark enough outside to be night, and the rain had started to fall heavily.

"Damn." He rose to his feet, lit the lamp on the bedside table, and stretched the stiffness from his neck and back. Yawning, he walked across to an open window.

The wind had picked up and blew in off the harbor. Duran could hardly see across the narrow alleyway that divided his block from the building next door. He cursed again, drew the window shut, and hurried over to the other window. Rain blew in there, too, and Duran's sleeves were soaked by the time he got the window closed.

He walked to the window at the front of the room, shut it partially, and returned to the bed. Kekoja was sitting up now, rubbing his eyes. Duran nodded a good morning to the Sabirn boy, drew the chamber pot out from under the bed, and used it.

"You next, lad," he said, standing and pulling on his hose. He stuffed his feet into his shoes and walked away from the bed to give Kekoja some privacy.

"Slops men'll be drenched to the bone this morning," Kekoja said.

"If they come now," Duran said, looking out the window at the downpour, "they'll be drowned. Is your head better?"

"Aye. Doesn't hurt near as much."

Duran turned around. "How's your ankle?"

Kekoja set the pot down, sat down on the bed, and rubbed his foot. "Feels fine. But it felt fine yesterday, too."

Duran crossed his arms on his chest. "Walk for me. Just across the room and back."

Lightning flared, followed instantly by another crash of thunder. Kekoja flinched, stood, and made the limping trip back and forth. He waited by the bed, his dark eyes watching Duran's face.

"Looks good," Duran said. "Better than yesterday."

"Then I can go?" Kekoja asked, his face lighting up.

"Where?" Duran waved a hand to the storm outside. "You want to go outside in this?"

"Well, maybe not now. But you think I can walk good enough to let me go?"

Duran sighed softly. "Aye. But I wouldn't go anywhere until the storm lets up." He came and picked up the chamber pot. "I've got to get our breakfast and let Dog out. Are you hungry?"

"Not very." Kekoja sat back down on the edge of the bed. "You go on an' eat at the inn, if you want. Bring me back some of what you have."

"All right." Duran picked up the lamp, too, and started toward the steps. "If you're interested, you can look at any of the books I have up here." He glanced over his shoulder at the Sabirn boy. "Some even have pictures in them."

"Duran," Kekoja said, "I'm sorry I lied to you. You been good to me, and I shouldn't have done it."

"Well, don't lie again. You don't need to be afraid of me."

"I learned that." Kekoja smiled slightly. "You can tell when I'm lying anyway. You got a good eye on you. And, Duran?"

Duran paused on the first step. "Ask Grandfather if he wants to look at me walk. Even if you decide I can leave, he's the one who'll have the final word."

Duran nodded and descended the stairway to his shop. Thunder boomed again and Dog whined as Duran walked toward the front door.

"Sorry, Dog," Duran said, unlocking the door one-handed. "You stay close to the building, or you'll float away."

Dog stood on the doorstep, sniffing the rain-soaked wind, unsure whether to go out or stay inside. Duran leaned out the door, set the chamber pot on the doorstep, and ducked back. The gutters were deep underwater already, and a steady stream of rain poured down from the second story overhang.

"In or out, Dog," Duran said, reaching behind the door to get his cloak. "I can't wait forever."

Dog wagged his tail, and stepped out into the street, shook his head at the rain and trotted off around the corner. Duran pulled his cloak on, and cursed the weather, for it told him he would suffer another day with few customers. He leaned up against the doorjamb, and watched the rain fall. Quicker than he would have guessed, Dog was back, dripping with rain and anxious to be inside.

"Bad day for all of us," Duran said, stepping aside to let Dog in. Dog wagged his tail, distributing rain outside of the puddle he was dripping on the boards, sat down, and began to lick the water from his coat. "Stay here like a good boy. I'll be back."

Lifting the hood of his cloak up, Duran stepped outside, pulled the door shut, and locked it. Drawing a deep breath, he turned and ran across the street where the door to "The Swimming Cat" stood cracked. Duran entered, stood for a moment dripping in the doorway, and flipped the hood back from his face. Thunder rumbled overhead.

"Morning, Sor Duran," said Old Man from his place inside. "Bad storm again today."

"Aye. I'm drenched from crossing the street. Your grandson wanted you to watch him walk today. He said *you're* the one who'll tell him if he's well enough to leave."

"You think he is?"

"He's a lot better, aye. He's not dizzy anymore, and I think that ankle of his has healed."

Old Man's eyes sparkled in the lamplight. "I'll come," he promised, "when the rain lets up."

Duran nodded and looked up as Tutadar walked in behind the bar, taking his usual morning position. "You're brave," Tut said, looking up from his money-counting.

"No. Hungry." Duran came to lean on the bar and glanced around. "No one else in here yet?"

"Not likely till the storm lets up. You eatin' here this mornin' or takin' out?"

"Here." Thunder rattled the windows. "Hladyr grant it'll slack. I'm not anxious to go back out in that."

"Who would be?" Tutadar walked to the kitchen and bellowed something at his cook. "Can't remember havin' such bad weather at this time of summer," he said, returning to the bar and pouring Duran a glass of wine. He shoved the mug across the bar and leaned forward, his arms crossed. "Trade's gone to hell—'nother ship gone."

Duran took a drink, wiped his moustache. "Another?"

"Word is, I hear it from Efdin, the Duke's got one well overdue. The *Gull's Pride* comin' out of Padis loaded down with spice—likely straight to the bottom in that big storm last week."

Duran frowned. Efdin the baker would know news having anything to do with spices. Last week. That must have been the storm that roared into Targheiden the same day the thugs had chased Kekoja into the alleyway.

"Hladyr bless the crew. I'll bet the Duke's not pleased. The price of clove will go up now for sure."

"*Gull's Pride* ain't the only ship out of Targheiden might be in trouble. From what some of the folk stayin' here in the upstairs say, weather's been foul at sea for the last fifteen days." The door to the kitchen cracked open and the cook stuck his head out, hailed Tut. "Sit," Tut said, "I'll bring you your breakfast. Might join you myself."

Duran picked up his mug and sought his table. Lalada the serving-girl came out from the kitchen, nodded dourly his way, too early for cheer, and began setting up the mugs behind the bar for the morning crowd. Thunder rumbled again, and Duran wondered if there would be much traffic in and out of the "Cat" as long as the rain kept up.

Two men came down the stairs from their rooms and entered the common room; they paused for a moment, as if checking to see who was present, then took a table close to the bar. Travelers, Duran noted, most likely traders from Fresa by the cut of their tunics. They talked quietly to each other and gave brief orders to Lalada, who disappeared back into the kitchen.

Tutadar came back into the common room carrying two plates, and set them down on Duran's table. He returned to the bar, poured three mugs of wine, and set two of them out before the travelers.

"Your food'll be out shortly, Sori," he said with a small bow. "Get you anythin' else?"

"Not unless you have good weather in your kitchen," one of the men said.

" 'Fraid not. You come far?"

"From Fresa," the other man said. "Business with Porandi."

"Luck to you then," Tutadar replied. He turned away and joined Duran at his table.

Duran started cutting up his fish. Porandi was one of the more successful traders who had few ties to the noble houses. He wondered if any of Porandi's ships had suffered losses.

"Damned weather's bad for everyone," Tutadar said around a mouthful of fish. "Gets me by havin' few travelers in and out. Gets you by havin' fewer folk show up at your shop.—Heard you had a visit from Vadami last night."

"Aye." Duran lifted an eyebrow. "Was he here?"

"No. Efdin saw 'im when he was at bakin' last night."

"He would." Efdin again. The baker, like himself, kept night hours.

"So what'd Vadami want of you?" Tutadar asked. Then his expression changed; he glanced over his shoulder and back, lowered his voice. "Wasn't anything t'do with Zeldezia tellin' 'im about the Sabirn kid?"

Duran frowned. "He warned me." He finished his fish and lifted his mug. "I don't think I've ever done anything that's caused more of a stir than this, Tut. And all because I helped a boy in trouble."

"Ithar told me he'd talked with you, an' you'd told 'im what really happened. Don't like Zeldezia much, myself. Always got her nose stuck somewhere it don't belong." Tut leaned back in his chair, turned his head at another rumble of thunder, then looked back. "She used to be soft on you, Duran, back when she first took over that shop. Thought you was really somethin'."

Duran nearly choked on his wine. "She *what*? Me? You've got to be joking, Tut."

"Ain't." Tutadar leaned forward and lowered his voice. "I knowed you near as long's Ithar knowed you. 'Member when she bought that shop, near seventeen years back? She found out you were pure Ancar, an' thought you'd make a fine catch, her bein' a widow an' everythin'. You never paid much attention to her, and I think that took 'er down a notch or two."

"Gods," Duran murmured. "I'd sooner lie down with a spider!"

Tut laughed, his eyes twinkling in the lamplight. "Thought so. Me, too. Woman's got a tongue that'd cut stone. You should'a seen the looks she used to give you.—Ha! Maybe that's why she been so nasty to you. What she cain't have, she don't want nobody else havin' neither."

Duran shook his head and finished his drink. "Save us.—Could you get me another plate of fish and a mug of wine, Tut? The boy's probably starving by now."

"Sure." Tut waited as Duran set out four coppers for his meal and Kekoja's and swept them up in a practiced hand. "That kid healed by now?"

"Near back to normal as far as I can see."

"Good. Now, when he leaves, maybe things'll quiet down 'round here."

"Maybe." Duran watched Tut walk off toward the kitchen, and wondered.

The thunder still rolled. Ladirno sat in one of the chairs by the windows, and stared disconsolately at the downpour sheeting down the mullioned glass. Wellhyrn and he would have to wait at least another day to show the Duke their newest attempt at changing lesser metals into gold. Bad weather had always put the Duke in a foul mood; and now that Hajun had entered the shipping business, storms tended to worry him into depression.

So. Another day, then. Ladirno suspected Wellhyrn was equally disappointed at the turn of weather and the postponement of their demonstration. If there was anything Wellhyrn loved, it was being the center of attention. He probably lay buried beneath his covers in bed, cursing the bad luck—or the wizardry—that had brought another storm to Targheiden.

And since Wellhyrn would be foul company this morning, Ladirno either faced a lonely day in his rooms, or seeking company elsewhere—which meant going out in the downpour.

"Damned rain," Ladirno muttered. He left the depressing view and dressed, choosing dark colors for his hose and tunic that would not show the dampness—or the mud. He took down his cloak from a peg on the wall, blew out his lamp on the way out, and felt his way down the darkened hall.

Cheap landlord.

Ladirno's apartments were on the second floor of a building that housed a well-to-do merchant and several court functionaries. He wished he might have been able to buy the apartment on the first floor, but that place had been occupied for generations by the Farchendi, and—short of the entire family dying at once—they would never give up their rooms. All in all, Ladirno lived at a more than respectable address, only a few blocks from the palace and the Temple—and the damn skinflint Farchendi would not afford a nightlamp in the hall. . . .

The rain was falling in sheets when Ladirno opened the door onto the street. He considered where he might find company: two taverns sat within equal distance of his building, and his friends frequented both—both served good food. It was simply the direction of the wind that made up his mind; better to walk with the wind at one's back, and to hope the storm might lessen, than to face the driving rain.

Ladirno pulled the hood of his cloak up and dashed outside, ran down the street, hugging the building, protected somewhat by the wide overhangs of the upper stories. Water swept down in torrents: the cobblestones were treacherously slick, the gutters spilling well onto the walks. But Ladirno reached the doorway that led into "The Golden Shoe" with no incident, and shoved his way inside.

For a moment he stood at the entrance to the common room, dripping rainwater in puddles at his feet. His heart sank: not one acquaintance in the place: he should have guessed that the bad weather would have kept them indoors: the court functionaries would stay home later than normal given the Duke's mood in stormy weather—not for the first time, Ladirno wished he had a wife, a house of his own, and a gods-blessed cook to make his meals.

But he was well known in the "Shoe" and its ambiance was homey and warm. Sooner or later some crony would show up. Ladirno pulled the hood back from his cloak, unclasped it, and held it out to one of the serving-lads who stood close by.

"Breakfast, Sor Ladirno?" the fellow asked, holding the dripping garment at arm's length.

"No. I'm looking for company, not food. I *will* have a glass of wine. . . ."

Ladirno walked across the room: his shoes squished water between his toes as he walked.

Taking a chair at a table directly beneath a lamp, Ladirno leaned back and simply took to watching till the wine came—then he took a small book no larger than his hand from his belt pouch, opened it, and began to read.

All this, of course, was calculated to place him in the public eye. He had a reputation for being one of the ducal favorites, one of the alchemists who frequented court. Sitting as he did now beneath the lamp would show off his rich clothes, the gold chain he wore, and the fact he was always studying. Small matter that the book had nothing to do with alchemy . . . it *looked* impressive.

"Ladirno."

He glanced up: a prestigious senior colleague stood beside the table. "I didn't see you," Ladirno said, slipping his book back into his pouch. He hastily moved a chair. "Do sit down."

"I was in the back." Garvis gestured over his shoulder to the rear of the room. "I've already had my breakfast. I need to return to my laboratory."

"A few minutes won't hurt."

Garvis sat down. The waiter brought more wine; Ladirno paid twice the amount asked, letting the coins fall on the table with a flourish.

"So, Garvis," he said, turning to his companion. "What have you heard regarding the Sabirn plot?"

Garvis shrugged. "Not much more than you already know." He lowered his voice. "I'd say it's a genuine rumor though; the Duke's been set thoroughly on edge—"

"Have they found any other Sabirn who knows about the plot?"

"No. They've been staying out of sight. What with the bad weather, they know when it's best to stay hidden."

Ladirno nodded sagely, recollecting his discussion with Wellhyrn the day before—decided if *Garvis* saw some seriousness in the matter—

Mmmn. "You remember Duran, don't you?"

"That one!" Garvis drew in a breath. "Like his father. Stubborn. What's he to do with it?"

"Sabirn. He's searching for something. Sabirn alchemy."

"Sabirn alchemy! No such thing! They were sorcerers! Black sorcerers!"

Ladirno shrugged, not willing to seem—incorrect with this man.

"What have you heard?" Garvis asked.

"That he—has resentments against the court."

"The stiff-necked fool *chooses* Old Town. His father's banishment—was ameliorated and his father left him sufficient, I hear, but Duran thumbed his nose at respectability, set up this shop—to 'pursue his father's studies.' So-named studies. The fabled notes."

"Do you honestly believe his father ever kept such notes?"

"I've heard he did a lot of experimentation . . . of what sorts no one knows." Garvis leaned forward, jabbed the table with a gaunt finger. "A few of those experiments went wrong. *That's* why the Old Duke banished him."

Ladirno's eyes widened. "Dark sorcery?"

"I'll lay odds—mark me, those notes had Duran's 'discovery' of the cure for the pox. He's nothing!" Garvis exhaled a heavy, wine-laden breath. "Sabirn, is it?"

"So the rumor goes. Digging in the hills. Going off with Sabirn hired help. For days."

"Looking for herbs."

"So they say."

"Being a fool, he'd immediately give all the knowledge away."

"A *dangerous* fool," Ladirno murmured.

"Dangerous indeed," Garvis said, looking to the front of the tavern. "The rain's slacked. I've a meeting. *See* me about this."

"Absolutely."

Garvis pushed back his chair, stood, and left the common room. Ladirno sipped at his wine. He was beginning to sound like Wellhyrn, talking about shadowy plots and Duran's possible connection with them. But connections with Garvis, Garvis whose favor with the Duke was—very sure . . .

Ladirno had never considered the Sabirn more than a nuisance; he discounted tales of their powers, their abilities to foretell the future and cast curses. Certainly they must have wizards: everyone had wizards, but—

Still. There was the unseasonable, the most unreasonable weather—

The rain slacked: other patrons began to filter in, rain-soaked. Ladirno took a long drink of his wine thinking of ducal favor . . . of funds that had nothing to do with Wellhyrn's inventions—of an apartment with well-tended lamps in the hallway—

He looked up from his glass. The priest Vadami passed his table, his grey robes dark with rain.

"Vadami," he said.

This priest he knew from his connections. *This* priest dealt with Old Town—

If anyone would know the gossip—

"Join me, Father?"

The priest looked mildly puzzled, drew out a chair, and sat down.

"May I buy you a glass of wine then?" Ladirno offered. At Vadami's nod, he lifted his glass, caught the waiter's eye, and held up his other hand with one finger extended.

"Thank you, Sor Ladirno." The priest kept silent until the waiter had brought the wine to the table, taken Ladirno's coins, and left. "You're very kind."

"It's nothing."

Vadami drank deeply, wiped his mouth with the back of his hand, and sighed. "Warms the insides, doesn't it? Excellent."

"It is that." Ladirno leaned back in his chair and studied Vadami. "Your district is Old Town, isn't it? You know 'The Swimming Cat'?"

"Aye."

"Do you know a man named Duran?"

Vadami's cup hesitated on the way to his mouth. "Aye."

Ladirno swirled the wine around in his glass. "One wonders—we've fallen—out of touch. I worry about him, being poor as he is. I'd like to help him."

"*You* may worry about his being poor, Sor Ladirno, but *I* worry more about his soul."

"In what regard?"

The priest frowned, a very troubled look passing over his face.

"Ah." Ladirno's heart lurched, but he kept his face only concerned. "Is he—in some difficulty?"

"His associations. With the Sabirn."

"He's always been friendly to the Sabirn. We twit him about it—his friends do."

"Are his friends aware—he has one living in his house."

Ladirno's eyes narrowed. "Really? How odd. A man or a woman?"

"A boy." Vadami's face colored. "I've warned him. I told him I was afraid for his soul. He quoted me scripture."

"Scripture?" Gods above and below! If Duran had a Sabirn living with him—

Was Wellhyrn onto something? Could this boy be involved with the plot? What if Duran—was dealing with—some ancient knowledge?

"Overmuch learning," the priest was saying, his voice pitched to quiet complaining, "can lead a man to pride, master alchemist."

Ladirno smoothed down his moustaches, hardly hearing a word the priest said on dogma. Damn! Interesting in the extreme—

The storm had decreased from a downpour to a steady rain. Gusts of wind still blew in off the harbor, several tiles from a roof near the "Cat" lay scattered and broken on the cobblestones.

"Hladyr bless," Duran murmured, glancing up at the dark sky. He tucked the basket containing Kekoja's breakfast under one arm and quickly crossed the street, hopping across its flooded edges. He made his front door, took out his keys, and let himself into the shop.

Dog got up, stood in the doorway, and inspected the lessened storm with canine disdain. Duran set the basket down on his counter. "Make up your mind, fellow," Duran said. "Inside or out. I want to go upstairs."

Dog wagged his tail, evidently decided another foray into the puddles was not worth it, and curled up in front of the counter.

Duran closed and locked the front door, and took breakfast upstairs.

Kekoja was sitting on the edge of the bed. He had lit the lamp, opened the shutters, and sat with a book open on the table.

"Breakfast," Duran said, leaving the stairs and crossing the room to Kekoja's side. "You're probably starving by now, aren't you?"

"No." Kekoja set the book aside and dug into the fish and bread. "You see my grandfather?"

"He says he'll come over and watch you walk soon as the rain stops."

"Way it's still raining, that'll be five days from now." He sipped the watered wine. "Thought the windows'd blow in."

"I know. If it happens again when I'm gone, close the shutters on the outside. Reach out and pull them." Duran walked over to his desk, sat down, and opened his belt pouch. He took from under the desk lid a small purse where he kept the shop money and spread the coins out on his desk. Twenty-one coppers. He opened a battered notebook, unstopped his inkwell, dipped his pen.

"Doin' your accounts?" Kekoja asked from across the room.

"Aye. And I didn't do too bad yesterday. Made a profit."

Kekoja took a drink of wine. "You as kind to all your customers as you been to me?"

Duran smiled. "I try to be. My job's different than most people's. I see folk at their worst . . . when they're sick. It never hurts to be kind to people who don't feel well."

"Grandfather says you're the only thing close to a doctor this part of Old Town ever sees. You could get more'n coppers."

"Maybe so." Duran wrote down the total of yesterday's take, returned the coins in their purse to his belt pouch, and capped the ink. "But Hladyr knows how much each item I sell costs me. I have to live with myself, lad, and overcharging people makes me angry. I take just enough to make a profit some days."

"Today'll hurt you, won't it?"

"Aye."

Kekoja stood up and walked to Duran's side, winecup in hand. "I could help you," he said, "if you'd trust me with your numbers. I've got a good head for doing sums."

Duran leaned back in his chair and looked up at the Sabirn boy's face. "Who taught you numbers, Kekoja? Old Man?"

"Aye."

"Five plus six, plus twelve, minus eight, plus two equals what?"

"Seventeen."

Duran lifted an eyebrow. "You *are* fast.—But you know what I could use more than someone helping me with my books? A runner."

"A runner?" Kekoja cocked his head. "For what?"

"I'm tied down to my shop all the time it's opened. If I had someone to take medicines to people too sick to come see me, or someone who would brave weather like today to go around to people's houses and take orders—this summer, that could mean something."

He watched the Sabirn boy think that through.

"Mother Garan, for example," Duran said. "She's old and she has a lot of headaches. I give her willow tea for them and that makes her feel better. But she can't get in if it's raining like it's been today. Do you see?"

"Aye," Kekoja answered, nodding his head. His eyes met Duran's. "But you couldn't pay much, could you?"

"No." Duran smiled. "That's why I'll probably never have a runner. No one would work that cheap."

"What'd people say if you had a Sabirn runner?"

Duran looked at him steadily. "People might get used to it. People might get used to the idea you're here. People might use their heads, instead of their mouths—maybe decide this *isn't* some great secret. It's secrets people are really afraid of—"

"I'll do it," Kekoja said. "I'll be your runner."

Duran frowned, shook his head. Help the sort the boy offered—that was always out of reach for him. And even for a good reason, with the best of thought behind it—he could not, he told himself, expect a fourteen-year-old Sabirn to take on the burden of community distrust. "There's some actual physical danger, the toughs that gave you trouble, for one. And people are bound to—say things, especially at first. Besides which, I can't pay much."

"I'm a damn sight cheaper than anyone else you could find."

"I thought you wanted to be out of here."

"That don't mean I never want to see you again. I *like* you."

Duran looked at the boy, found an unexpected longing in his heart. The house had not been so quiet these last few days; there had been a bright, quick wit to deal with—there had been someone . . . waiting for him at home. . . .

Besides which—the boy in the open was no threat to the neighborhood, the boy would quickly be like his grandfather, just a Sabirn who worked for someone . . . a Sabirn who had a place and a reason to be on the streets . . . for the boy's own sake, as much as his . . .

"Let's deal," he said to Kekoja. "What I can pay you is this: if I make a profit for a day from your running my medicines, I'll give you a third of it. Does that sound fair?"

Kekoja thought for a moment. "Aye. And if you don't make a profit, we both suffer. I'll work hard."

Duran drew a deep breath. *Gods! Could this actually be happening to me?* "You know Old Town at all?"

"Aye."

"Well enough to make deliveries and pick up orders at places you've never been before?"

"You tell me how to get there an' I'll do it."

"What about those thugs? What if you run into them?"

Kekoja stiffened; Duran could see the visible effort it took the boy to relax. "I'm not afraid. Was damn stupid of me to get caught like that in the first place."

"Remember, you'll be carrying money. Not a lot of it, but money that will pay me *and* you. Do you think you can skin out of a fight?"

"If I have to, I have to." Kekoja's shoulders squared. "When I'm on the job, I work for you, Duran. When I'm off the job, you don't hold anythin' over me."

Duran nodded slowly. "That sounds like a fair exchange. But if you aren't staying here—where will you be staying?"

He hoped Kekoja would say—*I'd rather stay here.* But Kekoja glanced away. "I got places," Kekoja said. "Don't worry 'bout me, Duran. I lived on the street 'fore you found me in that alleyway."

The house would be empty again. So. One settled for half, if there was no hope of the whole. "I can't help but worry, but I won't ask you where those places are. But if I need you—if I do have to find you, what should I do?"

"Ask my grandfather. He'll know where I am."

"I'll also want to tell your grandfather what we've agreed to," Duran said. "I think he should know, don't you? I think he should agree."

"Aye."

Duran stood and faced the Sabirn boy. "Then let's strike our bargain, you and I."

Kekoja held out a hand and Duran placed both his around it.

"Hladyr witness: I promise to abide by my word, to give you a third of the profits you make for me in return for your services as my runner."

"Gods of my people witness: I promise to work hard for you."

Duran grinned widely and pressed Kekoja's hand. "Done, boy! We're in business together now."

"When you want me to start?"

"Tomorrow. This afternoon, I'll tell you where my customers live. I've got medicines to mix. You'll help me."

"Will you teach me herbs?"

"Aye, if you've a mind to learn it." Duran walked over to the bed and put Kekoja's plate and empty mug into the basket. "I've

got to open my shop. Someone might need something. Will you
be all right up here?"

Kekoja sat down on the bed and lifted a book. "I can always
look at the pictures," he said with a lopsided grin.

Duran smiled, picked up the basket, and went downstairs,
where Dog was waiting to be let out. The rain was still falling
heavily when Duran opened the door.

Duran leaned up against the opened door and stared at the
rain-hazed street.

Now that he had done it—now that he had actually *hired*
Kekoja—a chill of misgiving knotted in his gut. He *hoped* he
understood his neighbors. He most sincerely hoped that.

✧ CHAPTER SEVEN ✧

"Duran!"

Duran looked up from the alembic he was heating: Kekoja stood before the counter, soaked to the skin, a growing puddle spreading beneath him on the floor.

"I've got orders, Duran! People actually gave me orders!"

Duran set aside his book and smiled widely—so a little talk up and down the neighborhood had worked, his customers did have faith in him—

"Anyone seriously ill?"

"No."

"Good." Duran remembered the alembic, picked the head up in thick rags, poured out his decoction from the cucurbit, wrinkling his nose. "Who ordered what? You remember them all, I hope?"

"Aye." Kekoja closed his eyes and cocked his head. "Young Filland's teeth are bothering him again. Says he needs what you usually give him."

"That would be watercress," Duran said, taking a jar from the shelves behind him. "Who else?"

"Sora Mitti's son's got a toothache. She says it hurts him real bad."

"All right. What she needs is clove seeds." Duran got out another jar. "And she'd better have him to Heimid, get that seen to. Are you paying attention to what I'm giving them? You said you wanted to learn herbs."

"Aye, I'm listening. Cardilla says you know what you give her."

Another jar came off the shelves. "Hemp tea for Cardilla."

"And Mother Garan's headache's back."

482

"Poor woman." Duran shook his head. "Willow tea for headache. Any more?"

"No. That's all." Kekoja's dark eyes looked suddenly worried. "But it's a start, isn't it?"

"It certainly is. You did marvelously. You have an honest face. Now pay attention to how much I'm giving to each of these people." Duran started making heavy paper packets into which he inserted the various remedies. As he worked, he briefly named off the dosages and how to figure, while Kekoja watched every move. "You *are* a help," Duran said. "None of these folk would have come in today. They'd have suffered. Especially Mother Garan."

"Why don't you sell the old lady a big lot? She says she's got it all the time."

"Because—she only affords a bit. And I'll tell you a secret: I'd *give* it to her at cost—except she'd take too much, she'd take it all the time—and willow tea hurts the stomach if you take too much, too long: and she'd be worse off."

"She says she really hurts."

"If it doesn't clear up—if it gets worse—there are stronger things. You give them—if you have to. If there's nothing else can be done. And they'll ease the pain—but that's all they'll do."

"You mean she'll die. . . ."

"People do." He finished wrapping the last of the packets, and carefully placed them in the small waxed basket he used when gathering herbs. "Try to stay as dry as you can," he said, handing Kekoja the basket. "And take your time. Don't slip on the cobblestones."

Kekoja grinned. "If I do, I know a good 'pothecary to treat me." He drew his cloak over the basket held tight under one arm. "Don't worry, Duran. I won't get into trouble."

Duran watched the boy step back out into the rain and disappear down the street. Dog lay by the opened door, his tail thumping against the wall.

"Dog," Duran said, "if this works, I *might* see a comfortable living."

Dog whuffled once, and settled down for a nap, unconcerned whether Duran made a profit or not.

Two more days of storm and rain. The first day, Kekoja returned with twenty-five coppers off his orders; the second day, it was twenty-two. Duran immediately paid the boy his share: eight coppers—a couple of good meals at an inn like the "Cat."

Now, sitting on his stool and watching the afternoon sunlight break through the clouds, Duran congratulated himself. The deep dark secret was out on the streets—no wizard, a bright-eyed, cheerful boy: folk relaxed, he had given the boy a chance to do more than . . . gods only knew *what* Kekoja had done before Duran had rescued him from the thugs.

And, gods, if his business continued to hold—if having Kekoja's healthy legs to run for him could bring orders in from streets up and down Old Town—he had always lived so frugally and saved every copper he could; he kept his small hoard hidden beneath one of the boards in the floor upstairs. *If* he continued to make the profits he had seen in the past two days, he might—

A scratching at his door brought Duran out of his daydreaming. He looked up at the skirted shadow in his doorway.

"Afternoon, Duran," Zeldezia said, stepping into the shop. Dog lifted his head, sniffed twice, and the beat of his tail stopped. "Never seen the like of this weather."

Duran put on a polite expression and nodded. He had not seen much of Zeldezia lately, a state of affairs he considered most fortunate. He had *not* talked to her since the boy had taken to the streets, he was sure she had that on her mind, and he vowed he would not let her make him lose his temper, that he would be polite to her no matter what she said.

"Sure been strange," she said. "All them storms comin' in. More like spring."

"Aye. It certainly has," Duran replied. "I hope you're doing well."

"Pfft." Zeldezia waved a hand. "It'd take more'n rain to keep business from *my* door. Folks got to have clothes to wear." She walked over to the counter and leaned up against it. "See that Sabirn kid up and down the street. He stayin' here?"

Duran drew a deep breath. "He isn't staying here anymore, Zeldezia. I promise you."

"Then where's he livin'? He stole anything?"

"No."

"He's taking medicines to people." Zeldezia's dark eyes narrowed. "Who knows what he's pilferin'. Duran, where's your good sense? How, by all the gods, can you trust 'im?"

"I trust him. He's a good runner, *and* an honest one."

"Ha! Honesty an' Sabirn ain't even in the same *world* with each other. I bet some o' your stuff ain't ever *gettin'* to your customers. You ever checked?"

"He hasn't done anything of the kind." Duran shifted on his stool, determined not to be angry. "I know how much I charge, and he's returned with every copper of it. I know my doses, I sell exactly what's required, and it gets there."

"But how you know he's been tellin' you the truth? How you know he ain't got more orders than he tells you? That he ain't takin' money for 'em and not givin' it to you?"

"I'd find out."

Zeldezia snorted something under her breath. "You're a damned trustin' man, Duran, if you think that kid ain't stealin' from you. An' what do you think he's doin' for your reputation? It's a little uppity of a Sab, runnin' medicines! Ain't never heard the like."

"Uptown shops use Sabirn all the time," Duran said. "As for my reputation—my good customers take care of that."

"Huh. Next you'll have 'im mixin' and boilin'.—You *don't* let him, do you?"

It hit too close.. Morally he hated the lie. "Of course not." He arched an eyebrow in her direction. "And he saves people time . . . which *most* of us who work don't have in abundance." As usual, Zeldezia did not rise to his pointed remark. Duran doubted she understood him. "You know how it is. Old folk needing medicines and can't get out in the bad weather; and I can mix or I can be running up and down the streets getting soaked."

"Huhn." She straightened her skirts. "I still say you're out of your mind, Duran. An' I don't like havin' that kid runnin' in and out of your shop. Some of my uptown customers might see 'im."

"So? Your uptown customers wouldn't blink. They're used to Sabirn. And you certainly haven't been shy about telling everyone you know *I'm* responsible for the boy's presence. What's to keep you from telling your customers the same thing?"

An odd look passed across Zeldezia's face. "Do you honestly think I'm nothin' but a gossipy busybody? That I don't care what happens to you?"

"I don't know what to think," he said sternly. Gods, could Zeldezia be softening?

"Believe me. I *am* concerned."

"You certainly have a strange way of showing it. I'd far rather be left alone."

"—I'm concerned for your *soul*, Duran. . . ."

"Listen, what I do is between the Shining One and myself . . . not all the neighbors!"

"But Vadami. . . ."

"He's already talked with me," Duran said, keeping his voice even. "At your instigation, no doubt. Zeldezia, I wish you'd let it lie! Trust me to know whether my soul's mine or not!"

Zeldezia's face darkened. "I talked to him about you, aye, I did, an' I *told* you so. An' I told you what Vadami said to me." She drew a sharp breath. "I been outright and plain, everythin' I done. I care about you! But nothin' I've said, an' nothin' he's said, seems to've made any difference."

"Gods! Is that how you care? Who made you that way?"

"An' what do you mean by *that?*" she asked, drawing herself up and crossing her arms on her chest.

"Just what I said. Someone must have been damned nasty to you for you to be so bitter. And it wasn't Sabirn. I doubt you ever knew any Sabirn. Why can't you leave people alone, Zeldezia? Why can't you keep your nose out of other folk's business?" He lifted a hand. "Before you say the Sabirn lad I hired is your business, too, let me remind you he doesn't come into *your* shop. He doesn't even pause by your door. And as for you . . . you don't have to come over here and talk with me. You don't have to associate with someone who's obviously a damned soul!"

"That's not fair!" she cried. "Not fair at all. I done fair with you—"

"Even the Sabirn?"

Zeldezia's dark eyes glittered. "Them folk ain't got no souls! They sold 'em to demons and other crawlin' things of darkness in exchange for their nefarious powers!"

Hardly Zeldezia's own words. He saw Vadami in that. "And do you know that for a fact, Zeldezia?"

"Don't have to *know* it: Vadami told me so."

"If Vadami told you a country pig would be our next duke, would you believe him?"

"You be careful, Duran." Zeldezia's voice dropped to a harsh whisper. "You're comin' close to heresy. Vadami's a priest! You should have respect!"

"I won't dispute that. I talked with him that night . . . we quoted scripture. He quotes at me, I can cite him holy words that say the exact opposite of what he says."

"You a priest, too, you an' your uptown ways?" Zeldezia looked ready to be impressed. A lie tempted him; a dangerous lie, but:

"No." Duran allowed a small smile to touch his face; and he remembered Old Town *had* no sense of humor about the Temple. "But I had a fine education in my father's house. Surely you know that."

For some reason Zeldezia's face went red. "Oh, aye, Duran . . . lord it over the rest of us, you bein' Ancar and noble. Well, you're poor as us, now, ain't you? An' as for bein' Ancar . . . if I remember what the priest told me, it was Ancar destroyed the Sabirn empire and put them demons down! That's why there's the Duke, Hladyr bless 'im! Don't you snigger at prayin' an' tell *me* you know more'n Hladyr's own priest!"

Duran nodded toward Dog, who lay asleep by the doorway. "Once all dogs were wolves. They preyed on man's livestock, and man himself when they were pushed to it. Now some of them live with us, guard us, and are our friends. Just because two of Hladyr's creatures were enemies once doesn't mean dogs were demons. Or that old enemies can't change. Hladyr can change them. Maybe Hladyr has. Would you hate his creation? Because he put the Sabirn here. Would you say demons are powerful as Hladyr? I don't. So what happens is *his* doing, isn't it?"

Zeldezia snorted. "Very pretty, Duran. You're even tryin' to *sound* like a priest." She turned toward the doorway. "Mark my words, you're huntin' for trouble keepin' that boy workin for you. One of these days it's all goin' to come home to you, your jokin' an' your lookin' down your nose at folk an' you're sendin' this slinkin' Sab kid around so's poor sick folk got no choice but deal with 'im, that's the respect you got for your neighbors. I tell you, some woman alone, she's got cause t'be scared of that kid, *sure* she's gon' t' pay 'im, *sure* she ain't gon' t' tell if he ask't more money than you said—she's scared!"

"Tell me when this happened! Name me names!"

Zeldezia would not meet his eyes. She flounced toward the door. "Any decent woman! Any poor old woman or ailin' old man, for that matter! You deal with your neighbors with that Sab kid, you go right on, and when it comes home, you remember what you done, 'cause not a one of your neighbors'll come to help you!"

She walked out of the shop, nearly stepping on Dog as she did so.

Dog scrambled out of the way, looked reproachfully at Duran, then shook himself and ambled outside. Kekoja was due back any time now, and Duran felt relieved the boy had not returned to find Zeldezia in the shop.

Duran shook his head. With people like Zeldezia in the world, it was no wonder one of mankind's favorite pastimes was war.

Thunder over Targheiden as Duran locked his door and ran across the street to the inn. The rain had started falling heavily just as he left his shop and, by the time he ducked inside the "Cat's" opened doorway, his cloak was wet.

"Good evening, Sor Duran," Old Man said from his place on the floor. "Do you think this rain will ever stop?"

Duran shook his head and gave Old Man a copper. "For your story tonight, if you're in the mood to tell one."

Old Man smiled and slipped the coin into his belt pouch. "I may tell one you've never heard before," he said.

Duran paused, looking at him. But Old Man looked elsewhere.

Duran walked to his table. The mood of the customers in the "Cat" was subdued tonight, the gloom of yet another day of rain, Duran thought. Tut came, took his order, and vanished back toward the kitchen without more than a few polite words.

During which Duran found himself the object of several furtive stares. Hladyr bless!

Then he thought sourly: Zeldezia.

Damn her.

He sighed, rubbed his eyes, and glanced up as a red-nosed Lalada brought him his ale.

"You don't look like you're feeling well," he said.

"Not," she sniffed. "Got a bad humor in my head."

"Come over to the shop, and I'll give you something to make you feel better."

Lalada stared for a moment. "Only if *you* give it to me. Don't want no Sabirn handlin' it."

Duran matched the ale-girl's stare. "You'll get it from me," he promised, "and no one else."

"Then I'll stop by tomorrow. 'Fore I come to work. You be up that early?"

"I can be."

"I'll be there."

Duran watched her go back toward the bar and shook his head. Damn Zeldezia! Gain a bit and that woman's mouth undid it all again . . . He had gotten around her before. He dropped his chin on his hand and thought. . . .

Tut came up with the beef pie—beef pie more often these days, thank the boy for that: nothing wrong with fish . . . in fact, he *liked* fish . . . but gods, a body could get tired of second-choice. . . .

The door to the inn opened, a momentary rush of rain-sound, a rumble of thunder overhead.

Ladirno and Wellhyrn entered the common room.

Gods . . . not tonight.

What in hell brings them down on the harbor-route?

The two ducal favorites made quite a show of shaking the rain from their costly cloaks and slowly walking to take a table near Duran's. In a perverse way, it warmed Duran's heart that none of the "Cat's" customers paid any attention to the newcomers' fastidious settling-in.

"Duran." Ladirno nodded slightly as he took a chair close by. "I hope you're doing well."

"I am. And you?"

Ladirno smiled. "Excellently. We did an experiment for the Duke a few days back—in between the storms—and produced him gold from a stone."

"And received quite a handsome gift from His Grace for doing so, I might add," said Wellhyrn, inspecting his fingernails. He looked at Duran and lifted an eyebrow. "We've just come back from the harbor. My shipment's been delayed again by the weather.—How are you doing in this dreadful summer? How are the finances?"

Duran tried to keep his face expressionless. "I'm doing all right. Thanks for your concern."

Tut came out from the kitchen; Ladirno and Wellhyrn placed their orders in loud voices, the "Cat's" most expensive, individually-prepared selections. Duran busied himself with his pie, though neither alchemist seemed interested in talking with him again.

Pompous asses! He chewed a bit of pie, swallowed, and took a long drink of ale. He was doing far better than they thought. . . .

But he had no inclination to compare finances and he certainly had no desire for their attention. Ladirno he never minded much; the fellow was competent but all too willing to practice the tried and true without ever seeking the new. It was Wellhyrn who puzzled Duran: there was something hard and dark and twisted about the man . . . something Duran did not like or trust.

He kept his head down, eating his pie and drinking his ale, and trying not to pay attention to his colleagues' conversation. Most of it, he thought was aimed directly at him, since Wellhyrn was recounting events that Ladirno must already know . . . successes at court, admiration from fellow alchemists, and gifts of money from the Duke and other nobles.

Dammit, man! he chided himself. *If you wanted a life like theirs, you could play the game, too.*

And have them for permanent company . . .

" . . . hear about the necromancer they hanged over on the west side?" Wellhyrn was asking Ladirno, as the two of them started their dinners. "The Guard caught her practicing and took her before the priests. They say she never would admit to anything—but one knows."

"They put her to the question, of course. . . ."

"Hot irons," Wellhyrn said. "She cursed the priests when they were hanging her. Quite a show. Big crowd."

"In all this rain? Gods."

Wellhyrn laughed, a cold laugh, unnerving to hear coming from one so young. "Folk know there's something odd in this weather. You should have seen it. All these hundreds of people standing in the storm and the lightning—"

"You saw it?"

"Oh, I did."

"Huh." Ladirno gave a shiver or a shrug. "Demon-worshippers. I want no part of it."

Enough to curdle a man's appetite, Duran thought, listening to it. He finished his pie—he had no inclination to be chased out of the warm tavern in the height of the rain, and he hoped they would leave soon—turned slightly away, and leaned back in his chair, trying to give the impression he was dozing after a rich meal. He heard Wellhyrn and Ladirno rise, finally scatter coins on the table in payment for their food, and leave.

But he heard the gossip they left in their wake. He heard people mutter—*sorcery* . . .

"Duran."

He looked up: Ithar stood at his side, a mug of ale in one burly hand.

"Mind if I join you?"

Duran shook his head and gestured to a chair.

"Saw them snot-nosed rich boys tryin' to bother you," Ithar said, sitting down. "Don't you let 'em get to you, Duran. Them kind ain't worth more than fish food." His dark eyes sparkled. "An' maybe the fish'd spit 'em back."

"Sometimes it's hard to ignore them," Duran admitted. "Them and their money."

Ithar cocked his head. "Why?"

"Hladyr only knows. I can't think of anything I'd want from them."

"Fah! You just remember that them kind don't never do nothin' for anyone but themselves. They may have all the money an' importance, but they can't take it with 'em."

Duran drew a deep breath. "I think you're right, Ithar, but there are times when I'd like to punch their smirking faces in, and me, a gentleman."

"Don't waste your time. You got better things to do." Ithar crossed his arms on the tabletop. "That Sabirn boy of yours workin' out?"

He looked hopefully at Ithar. So maybe the damage was *not* that widespread. "Aye. I wish I'd thought to hire someone long ago. I never thought I had the money for it."

"An' Sabirn come cheap."

Duran nodded. "I've been doing all right lately than I've seen in years. I might be able to buy some better equipment for the shop if things keep going so well. I might want some smithing. . . ."

"Be glad of the work. But you just be careful, Duran. An' you tell that boy of yours to keep his head down an' never look like he's doin' anythin' but run for you. You understand?"

"Zeldezia's been talking again."

"It's not only that," Ithar said. "It's that hanging—"

"The boy's nothing but an orphaned kid! He's damn sure no wizard, let alone any—"

"No, no. I didn't mean it that way." Ithar lowered his voice. "We ain't seen no necromancers in years, Duran. Not in years. Now they go an' find themselves one that's probably been spellin' the weather . . . bringin' on the storms and such . . . An' maybe that's it an' now it'll stop—"

"I don't believe anyone can control the weather," Duran said. "Not even the Duke's wizards, else he wouldn't have lost so many ships at sea."

"Ah, but what if his enemies got themselves a bunch of wizards to counteract *his* wizards? Eh? What then?"

Duran closed his eyes. What had caused his father to fall from power and the friendship of the Duke? Was it wizards again?

"You just keep yourself out of trouble, Duran . . . an' keep an eye on that kid. Whatever that necromancer did, she got caught at it."

"Or, she was an easy one to blame for the bad weather," Duran suggested. "Some poor old soul—"

"Duran. Duran, lissen to me. That necromancer they hung?— She was Sabirn."

Duran left "The Swimming Cat" earlier than was normal for him, while the rain was still falling and lightning played in the heavy clouds. He ran across the street, stood in the windy space beneath his second story overhang, and cursed the key that stuck in the lock. The warm feeling of late afternoon had disappeared from his heart, leaving coldness behind . . . a coldness next to fear.

Gods above and below! If Targheiden's folk decided that Sabirn were at fault for the weather—

He shook the rain from his cloak, hung it behind the door, absent-mindedly patted Dog, who stepped outside to his nightly duties all oblivious to hazards—

He resolved to say something to Kekoja in the morning, warn the boy—gods, how did one explain such lunacy to a boy?— warn the boy to keep the lowest profile he could.

And himself? Damn. He was Ancar. His personal danger was negligible. He was no courtier, had no enemies with political reasons—he refused to be a coward, could not turn back from what he had done, from hiring Kekoja . . . honor forbade that. Pride did. He could not desert the boy—or fling him off, out of some stupid, weaseling fear—

By the time Duran had lit his lamp, Dog came back into the shop, stopping in the doorway and shaking the rainwater from his coat. He sat down, scratched at one ear, then jumped to his feet and whirled about.

"Sor Duran."

Old Man stood in the doorway beneath the overhang . . . Old Man, and Kekoja.

"Come in," Duran said, wiping his hands on his tunic. Gods hope there was no problem. He tried to tell himself it was otherwise, a personal business. Gods, who might be seeing him here, from the "Cat's" door? "Come in, you'll drown out there."

He lit the lamp hanging above the counter and turned up the wick in the other. Old Man and Kekoja came into the shop, shook the worst of the rain from their cloaks, and sat down on the floor.

"What can I do for you?" Duran asked, coming round the counter to face his guests.

Old Man's dark eyes were steady in the lamplight. "You left early tonight, Sor Duran. I've come to tell you that story I promised you."

A sense of guilt washed over Duran—for all his fears. For a woman hanged . . . For thinking—instantly—why? What will the neighbors think?

"Please." He shut the door against the rain—wondering again who might see, as if that door being shut—made it clear it was no case of Old Man being customer. But he hated cowardice. "Can I get you tea?"

"Tea, yes, thank you," Old Man said; and Duran got the pan he used for tea, lit a spill, and fired up the little apothecary's stove at the end of the counter—while Old Man settled into the only chair, while Kekoja settled cross-legged at his feet—

Like some personage with his escort.

"Thank you," Old Man said, when Duran brought the tea, and sipped it while Duran found himself a seat on the stool, his own cup in hand. . . .

"This is a story I doubt our neighbors would appreciate," Old Man said after several sips. "You've asked me several times what

things were like before our empire fell. Well, I thought I'd tell
you a story about those last days, if you want to listen."

Duran's heart beat in fear. "Of course I'll listen." He realized
in his panic what Old Man was offering—he knew what he ought
to do, and set the teacup down on the counter at his elbow. "Did
your grandson tell you I keep such stories written down? To
prevent their being lost? Do you mind?"

"No. Write anything you like."

Duran hurried behind his counter and pulled out a sheet of
coarse paper and a stick of charcoal. Seating himself on his stool,
the paper on the counter, he took up the teacup again, poised
himself anxiously to take notes.

Old Man smiled and began his story. At the first, it seemed a
mere recounting of old myths, old accounts reassuringly
familiar—agreeing with what the Temple held the world was like
a thousand years ago: the barbaric Armu had pushed eastward
across the Irdanu River into Pesedur, thrust out of their
homelands themselves by the tall, fair Ancar. Kingdom after
kingdom fell to Armu hordes and Ancari armies, all advancing
toward the west and the heart of the Empire.

Then Jarrya fell, the breadbasket of the inner world, and the
Ancar came southward into the Sabirn peninsula—toward the
capital, where authority tottered—as at sea, Sakar harbored
pirates and worse, sitting poised to do any kind of damage they
could to failing shipping . . . taking advantage of the Empire's
weakness, adding to that weakness by raiding ships, ruining
mercantile houses . . . increasing poverty and dissent—

Duran dutifully made brief notes, interested that once
Targheiden had been called Cerinde and that fabled Sakar was
now known as the Sacarres. But of greater matters, secret matters,
he heard nothing he had not been told before, albeit in pieces
and disconnected as a whole.

Then Old Man spoke of the Empire itself.

Sabis was the capital of that empire, and the center of the
once thriving trade that had made the Sabirn wealthy, drawing
substances and goods from all around the Inner Sea. Sabirn ships,
far more advanced than those of other nations, carried Sabirn
trade into all the surrounding world, bringing back wonders from
other countries—arts, slaves, furs and silk and spices. The Sabirn
had boasted banks, a class of traders with power in the imperial

court, and a beginning guild of artisans. In short the level of their civilization had rivaled what existed today—in everything but the blessings the Temple provided, the knowledge of Scriptures, the work of Hladyr's priests—

There had been other gods.

"And wizardry?" Duran asked, as Old Man paused for a moment, "You had your wizards, didn't you?"

"Ah, wizards. Aye, we had our wizards, as you have yours. Their methods didn't vary much from yours."

"No more powerful?"

"No more powerful."

Duran found himself vaguely disappointed.

"But there was other knowledge," Old Man said.

"Alchemy?" A chill went down Duran's back. His hand paused, waiting.

"Alchemists . . . who were wizards. Wizards who were alchemists. *That* gave them the power. . . ."

Duran swallowed. "Did you ever hear of any of them who could turn base metals into gold?"

Kekoja ducked his head to hide his expression, but Old Man disdained such subterfuge. He laughed quietly.

"No." His dark eyes glittered in the lamplight as he looked up at Duran. "Can you?"

"No," Duran admitted, shaking his head. "Not I. And no one I know can—" Thinking of Ladirno and Wellhyrn this evening—and their claim of gold. "—despite what they say." He could hang for what he admitted. The Guild would see to it. "They're simple tricks."

"What we *did* have in the twilight of our empire was a man named Sulun, who called himself a 'natural philosopher',—and who came close to developing a weapon to drive the invaders out of Sabir."

"A weapon—of wizardry?"

"Of natural force. Sulun and other like-minded folk survived the downfall of the Empire, and went off into the wilderness, taking all their knowledge with them." Old Man smiled slightly. "They were known as wizards, Duran . . . and some of them were. But wizardry only gave them luck. Their wits gave them what they made."

"Then they could have *saved* the Empire—"

"Aye. But when an empire is falling, even philosophers find themselves dealing with time and fools. There was no time. And there was an abundance of fools. So Sulun and his followers took with them a knowledge of medicine, of shipbuilding, of manufacturing . . . of all kinds of things. We remember. We do remember."

"But remembering—" For a moment Duran was conscious of himself as Ancar, tall, fair, blue-eyed—themselves as Sabirn, the dark, ancient folk—who might want their Empire *back*—

Or want revenge for it . . .

"Your barbaric ancestors crushed Sabis like an overripe fruit," Old Man said, and clenched an uplifted hand. Let it fall. "Say nothing, Sor Duran. You are not your ancestors. We are not ours. Sabis was ready to fall . . . hollow from the inside out. Kingdoms and empires age. They have their lifespans. They breed descendants. Your ancestors happened to be the instrument."

Duran felt the flush on his cheeks. "Nevertheless, the waste of it all—"

"Nothing is wasted—nothing lost."

He stirred on his stool. "You know the priest, Vadami? He told me there was once a great Sabirn wizard named Siyuh—Ziya? Who made fire leap from his hands. Is that a true story?"

Old Man's smile never wavered; only his eyes became hooded, shut off, remote from Duran's questions. "Perhaps that's a story I can tell you one day. But not tonight. I've talked longer than I should."

"What would *you* do," Kekoja asked suddenly, leaning against Old Man's knee, "if you knew what we knew in the days of our empire?"

"Me?" Duran blinked in the lamplight. "I've never really thought about it. I'd try to make better medicines first, I suppose. When I see people die and I can't help them . . ."

"And being an alchemist," Old Man said, "you're interested in changing base metals to gold. What would you do if you could?"

Duran studied Old Man for a long moment, trying to guess why he and Kekoja were asking such seemingly unrelated questions. "I'm not denying I'd like to have more money. Money can buy many things, Old Man, and it can help people if it's used right. But consider this: if I was interested only in making money, I'd be up in the Duke's palace with the rest of the alchemists."

Old Man frowned and ducked his head. "I must be going," Old Man said, then, reaching for his walking stick. "At my age, sleep is something I value."

Kekoja stood, drew Old Man's cloak up, and helped him to his feet. The suddenness of this departure puzzled Duran, but he left Old Man's secrets alone. He stepped down from his stool, set his paper and charcoal stick on the counter, and faced the two Sabirn. Should he tell them about the necromancer who had been hanged, and warn Kekoja to keep very quiet? No. Tomorrow. It was quite obvious Old Man and his grandson wished to leave.

"When you come to work tomorrow, remind me to tell you something," Duran said to Kekoja. "It's important, but it will keep."

"Aye."

Duran watched from his doorstep as Old Man and Kekoja walked across the street. Then, just as he started to turn away, he noticed two men standing in the shelter of the building across the alleyway. Dog joined him at the doorway, growled softly, and sniffed in the newcomers' direction.

"Old Man," one of the men called out softly. "It's us."

Brovor, returned with his companion for another treatment.

Aside from the one time Brovor had let Duran know he recognized him, no one had mentioned names again. Duran's estimation of the heir had gone up; the young lord had not missed one night of coming for his medicine, though it meant going out in the rain and visiting a section of town he otherwise might never have frequented. It must have been difficult for Brovor to get away from the palace every night. But fear was a great motivator, and if getting the pox kept Brovor away from the whores, the lad might have learned a lesson.

✧ CHAPTER EIGHT ✧

"Gods-cursed storms!" Wellhyrn snarled, flinging his sodden cloak to the floor of Ladirno's apartment. His light brown hair was plastered to his forehead where the hood of his cloak had not kept the rain out. Damp spots marked his expensive jerkin, and his hose were dark to the knee above soaked glove-leather boots. "I don't think I've ever seen the like! Has anyone told you about the river? It's flooding the lower areas of the Slough."

"Bah!" Ladirno waved a hand. "It could flood the Slough right into the sea, and the world would be a better place for it. What in the gods' names brings *you* out on a day like this?"

Wellhyrn's green eyes caught the light from the grey, rain-spattered window. "News, Ladir. News we can possibly turn to our benefit. Do you have something to drink?"

"Aye." Ladirno walked over to the sideboard, poured himself and Wellhyrn a glass of wine, then extended one of the glasses to his guest. "What is it now? Gods, you pick up more gossip than anyone I know."

"Duran," Wellhyrn said, dropping down into a chair and sipping at his wine. "I was out early this morning, before the downpour. I stopped for breakfast at the 'Shoe,' and who should drop by but your new friend, Vadami."

"Vadami? *My* friend?" Ladirno snorted. "That fellow's nobody's friend but his own. Well, what about him?"

A thin smile touched Wellhyrn's face. "Vadami, oh, so humbly asked if I'd seen you. He seems to think you're a friend of Duran's."

"Gods."

Wellhyrn chuckled. "Anyway, I didn't shatter his delusion and

498

asked him to join me. I said I might be seeing you later in the day and if he had a message, I'd be happy to pass it along."

"So?"

Wellhyrn lifted an eyebrow. "Vadami had been ministering to some poor creature in Old Town last night and was on his way back to the Temple. He happened to be walking up Smithy Street by 'The Swimming Cat,' when he noticed—of all things—that old Sabirn from the tavern—*and* that Sabirn kid—"

"—his grandson, by my sources."

Wellhyrn's handsome face was alight with malice. "Both of them at Duran's door. Him *and* this young boy. Now I ask you why. I ask you why Duran let them in and shut the door fast."

Ladirno frowned. "Puzzling."

"Isn't it?" Wellhyrn's mood changed: all humor had fled from it. "It makes me damned nervous, Ladir. What in Dandro's hells is going on in that shop, that's what I'd like to know! Why's Duran buying good ale of a sudden—eating beef like a gentleman? Did you catch that?"

"Did Vadami hear anything?"

"In a storm like the one last night? Hardly. He was afraid of being seen, and only got close enough to make sure he saw what he thought. Then he retreated to shelter at the front of 'The Swimming Cat' to watch what happened next."

Ladirno swirled the wine in his glass, watching the lamplight in it. "I'd give a lot to know what was going on in there."

"So, dear colleague, would I." Wellhyrn stretched in the chair, his movements graceful and refined. "I'm very much afraid that Duran might be involved in something."

"Such as?" Ladirno asked.

"Sabirn secrets. Such as—hidden knowledge. One wonders what he's doing—and what the Sabirn's price is."

"He's been talking to that old man for years."

Wellhyrn took a sip of wine. "Doing gods know what for years."

"Fah! *I* think there's no secret to be had. If that old man knows secrets like that, if any Sabirn does—why are they so damned poor?"

"I can know many things," Wellhyrn said softly, his voice smooth, "but if I don't have the tools to make use of what I know, I might as well not know it."

"Gods. You don't think—"

"What better cover for a wizard than to appear as an old beggar?"

"Now you *are* grasping for straws. I'd believe Duran capable of searching for Sabirn secrets—but credit him with wanting to bring down the kingdom . . . For gods' sakes, Wellhyrn . . . he's an Ancar noble!"

Wellhyrn sneered. "*Was* an Ancar noble. His father was banished—for treason."

"Treason being the old duke's whim, by what I hear, not Hajun's. And Duran's still Ancar. I can't believe any Ancar—"

"Would do what? Consort with Sabirn? Think about it. Obviously he's after something from the Sabirn. We *think* it's alchemical secrets. It could be worse. But even if it's only the one, they provide him with alchemistic secrets we can only dream of—if only to keep him on the string. And where would that leave us, and the other members of our profession?"

Ladirno stared at Wellhyrn, and rubbed his forehead, fighting down a headache.

"Now you're beginning to see it," Wellhyrn said.

Ladirno stared at the rain-washed window. "I suppose," he murmured, "we'd better brave the storm. It's time both you and I had another conversation with our little priest. I want to get to hear his story for myself."

Vadami stood in the doorway of "The Golden Shoe," abhorring the thought of going out into the rain and wind of Old Town, but if word of his loitering got back to his superiors, they would take his hours here for softness. He sighed deeply in resignation, took a long breath, opened the door, and nearly ran head-on into a dripping Ladirno accompanied by an equally sodden Wellhyrn.

"Ah, Father Vadami," Ladirno said, thrusting the hood of his cloak back and smiling. "The very person I wanted to see. What luck to find you here."

Vadami pushed his own hood back, bowed slightly, and kept a smile on his face, unsure whether he was being mocked.

"A table for three," Wellhyrn said to a serving-boy. "And your best half bottle of wine."

Feeling caught up in something he did not understand, Vadami followed the two alchemists to a table at the rear of the common room, far from the crowd near the windows. Seating himself across from the two hosts, he unclasped his cloak and let it hang over the back of the chair.

"How may I help you, Sori?" he asked, trying to read the expression on their faces, but their smiles never wavered. Hladyr bless! If only *he* could be as important as these men. If only the Shining One would bless him with the luck . . . would bring his love of the gods and his work to the attention of his superiors.

And get him out of Old Town.

"I got your message," Ladirno said conversationally, leaning back in his chair. The waiter brought a carafe of wine and three glasses to the table, left them unpoured at the wave of Ladirno's hand.

"My . . . message, yes." Vadami watched the lamplight glitter on Ladirno's gold neck chain. "About Duran—"

Ladirno tilted his head, implied invitation.

"I'm getting increasingly worried, Sori. He doesn't want to listen to me—and—considering you have some concern for him—rather than go to Temple authorities, you understand—"

"We appreciate this," Ladirno said.

"I thought maybe *you'd* be able to talk some sense into him. After all, you're his—" Cough. "—friend in the Guild—"

"You mean about his visitors last night."

Vadami nodded. "He's endangering his soul, consorting with the Sabirn. It's become extremely serious—this business on the west end—"

"We understand that," Wellhyrn said smoothly. "Necromancy is a very serious charge."

"I'm trying to rescue him. I can't make any headway with him, though gods know I've tried. He doesn't believe they're dangerous."

"What was the old man talking about?" Ladirno asked, pouring Vadami a glass of wine, then filling his and Wellhyrn's glasses. "Did you hear anything at all? Can you guess anything?"

"No." Vadami took a sip of the wine, marveling at its smoothness. "I couldn't get that close. But whatever it was—it undoubtedly had to do with the dark arts."

"You think so?"

"What *else* would a Sabirn be talking about? They're devils! What can they want but to snare the innocent? I've tried to warn him, Sor Ladirno. Duran's soul is in my care, it's my duty as a priest of Hladyr to keep him from falling into darkness."

"Could the old man have been telling Duran secrets?" Wellhyrn prompted, running a languid fingertip around the rim of his glass. "Things the Sabirn might—remember?"

"No one could know. The old man usually tells tales at the inn. But people have seen Duran writing while he talks."

The two court alchemists exchanged a brief look, one full of obvious concern. Vadami's heart warmed: these were good people. It was good to know that men so powerful still had concern for a friend in danger. Maybe, with their help, he could talk Duran into leaving the Sabirn alone.

Maybe—with their help—and a good outcome for this affair— he could find friends at court—

It was very wise of him—to have gone to them and not his superiors.

"I *am* concerned." Wellhyrn shook his handsome head. "Have you noticed this old Sabirn talking to anyone strange?"

Hladyr bless! Sorgun orders me to tell him if this old man ever talks to anyone who lives outside of Old Town. Now I get the same question from these eminent alchemists. . . .

"No. Not that I can remember. But I'm not in Old Town every hour of every day. I certainly could keep an eye on things—"

"That *would* be appreciated. But don't worry too much. We'll see if we can talk some sense into him. Meanwhile, keep up your watch. We'd like to know how he's doing." He smiled and spread his hands. "Unfortunately, we don't see much of him at court. It's probably very embarrassing for him to attend, poor as he is."

"Perhaps we ought to help him again," Ladirno suggested.

"Aye. Perhaps."

"I—" Vadami hesitated, cleared his throat. "I did—observe the shop last night—out of concern, you understand. Attempting to be sure I understood before I—approached anyone with this information—"

"Did you see him leave the premises?"

"No. But I did see—other traffic that night."

"Be more clear."

"I can't be. Two heavily cloaked men—I'm sure they were men—went into Duran's shop. They—went uptown. I followed them—as far as the palace gate."

"And?"

This was frightening. Vadami wished he had more

understanding *what* he had seen. Wellhyrn's eyes frightened him. "They went inside. The guards evidently knew them. They passed without question."

"Anything distinctive about them?"

"One very tall. Broad-shouldered. Both in black cloaks, wrapped up to here—" A measure at his nose. He swallowed heavily, wondering if he was in some danger. He searched his recollection frantically for detail. "One—the small one—had blue boots. Blue with silver piping down the side. . . ."

That got a reaction: both alchemists went very attentive and stared at him.

"Sori?" Vadami asked.

"And?"

"That's all. That's all I saw."

"Interesting." Wellhyrn reached into his belt pouch and pulled out two gold midonahri. "Take this as your donation for the day. And don't worry about Duran. We'll talk with him."

"And you'd best be off for Old Town," Ladirno said. "Just—be as discreet as you have been. This is important."

Vadami reached out and took the coins, trembling. Hladyr bless, it was more than he usually saw in a month for all of Old Town.

He pursed the coins, stood, took up his cloak. Ladirno and Wellhyrn nodded him a courtesy. "Father," Ladirno said by way of parting, as if he *were* somebody.

"The blessings of Hladyr," he murmured, signing them both. "I'll remember you in my prayers."

As the priest walked off to the door, Ladirno met Wellhyrn's eyes, said in a hushed vice, "You *know* who that was."

Wellhyrn's voice was unsteady. "What in Dandro's hells was *he* wanting with Duran?"

Ladirno's face shone pale in the lamplight. "Let's get out of here." And out on the street, in the downpour: "The duke's heir!" Ladirno hissed. "Gods, man, what's going on?"

"Knowing Brovor, Duran could have been selling him a love potion."

"Don't joke!"

"But we'd better hope it *wasn't* anything more than a love potion."

"What do you mean by that?"

Wellhyrn looked him in the eye, water streaming down a face paler than its wont. "There's another possibility. What's Duran best known for?"

"He's an herbalist—a part-time alchemist."

"Think, man! The famous cure for the pox! What if—"

"O gods above and below!" Ladirno felt his heart lurch in his chest. "You don't think he—the heir—good gods, Brovor's negotiating for Mavid's daughter—the alliance with—"

"Why else would he be visiting someone like Duran? If you were the Duke's son and had the pox, would you call in the court doctor to treat you?"

"Of course not. I'd . . ." Ladirno rubbed his eyes. "Gods! If Duran *is* treating Brovor, and he cures him—"

Wellhyrn smiled nastily. "He's either rich, or dead—when Brovor's the duke."

"Hells!" Ladirno shook his head. "But this Sabirn connection!"

"Worrisome. Damned worrisome." Wellhyrn gnawed at a hangnail and Ladirno stared helplessly at his younger companion, wishing his mind worked with the same speed as Wellhyrn's. He felt certain Wellhyrn had other things in mind, *dangerous* things—

"I think," Ladirno said, cautiously feeling his way forward, "if we mentioned that Duran's tied in with the Sabirn to the prince himself—just happen to mention it—"

Wellhyrn shot him a furious scowl. "*Why* would we just happen to mention Duran? Don't be a fool! That's a way to get both our throats cut!"

"But—"

Wellhyrn's smile dazzled. "But the Duke! His Grace has the rains to contend with, he has the *suspicion* of Sabirn necromancers—if he finds out an Ancar, the son of a pardoned traitor—is dealing with Sabirn—"

"Talk about dangerous! Good gods, Wellhyrn!"

"No, no, if we phrase this exactly right, stressing Duran's Ancar heritage, the Duke might take it personally—personally enough to take action—and uncover this conspiracy. . . ."

A cold chill ran up Ladirno's spine. "What kind of *action*, Wellhyrn. We're talking about Duran's *head!*"

"Exile. Exile's what his father got, exile's the most likely thing."

"But what about Brovor?"

"There is the other possibility, you know."

"What?"

"That the heir's in on it—the wizardry—the Sabirn—"

"God, no! Not Brovor."

"Wouldn't be the first son wanted his inheritance early. Say the Sabirn knew that impatience. Say the Sabirn found a way to Duran—who has a way to the heir . . . you know what we're talking abut here?"

"Hladyr save—"

"We just talk with His Grace, we just quietly—quietly handle all this. Tell him a non-Guild alchemist is . . . friendly with the Sabirn. With all this anxiousness about the situation—the Duke *will* be concerned, the Duke *will* move. . . ."

"Gods, this is dangerous."

"Steady. Steady. It's also profitable. For us, you understand. When you play at these levels—you take risks. Brovor's one. But one thing we know—he's not working with the Sabirn. If he's being double-crossed—he'll come to *us* to sound us out—and we can position ourselves—"

"I don't like this!"

"Easy. Easy. Let's go back in, have something to eat, calm ourselves. Gods only know how long we'll wait at the palace, and I'll be damned if I'm both hungry *and* wet."

The wind rattled the expensive glass windows of the Great Hall, and the Duke—in tedious and sparsely attended audience—winced at the noise. Another day of storms had swept down on Targheiden . . . another day of weather that could sink a ship and lose all its cargo: more complaints. A minstrel played something soothing in one corner, and the courtiers stood or sat together in small groups, their conversations low enough so that nothing could be heard.

"Damn soggy bore," Hajun muttered to his wife, who sat a few paces away with her daughter and their ladies, all of whom were busy with needlepoint. He had not been in the best of moods all day, and it was a wonder she was even speaking to him after he had snarled at her over breakfast.

His two sons sat with a group of friends their own age, other lords' sons, brought to Targheiden to learn manners of the court. They laughed, told jokes, and diced together, the weather preventing their usual summertime entertainments of hawking, arms practice, and hunting. Brover had been much out on the town lately. Granted he had not stayed out late, and had not returned drunken as he had so many times in the past—such partying worried Hajun: that was the fight at breakfast. His wife dismissed it as the last fling of a young man on the verge of state marriage and true adulthood, counseled him to ignore the late-night outings.

But there were hopeful signs. Today, for instance, Brovor and Saladar were not feuding—an unusual but welcome sight.

"Your Grace . . ."

The door to the hall had opened: his steward entered, paused, and ushered two black-clad men into the room: Ladirno and Wellhyrn. Hajun smiled in greeting, though his heart was not in it. He wanted nothing to do with their speeches or demonstrations today; but—in a slow day—they promised, perhaps, diversion. . . .

"Wellhyrn, Ladirno," he called out, stirring in his chair. "You attend me in vile weather, gentlemen. I do commend your faithfulness."

The two alchemists bowed and approached the dais, past the idle courtiers, conversations briefly paused, the eternal estimating glances following whoever walked that route. Wolves, Hajun thought, estimating the town dogs.

"Dreadful day, isn't it?" Hajun gestured Ladirno and Wellhyrn to be at ease, hardly interrupted his signing of permissions and warrants, thick on the desk.

"The river's beginning to flood the Slough," Wellhyrn said. "As I'm sure Your Grace has heard. . . ."

"Good riddance." Hajun signed another document and blotted it, guarding his sleeve. "Surely there's something *else* going on in Targheiden besides the floods."

Ladirno glanced at Wellhyrn and bowed slightly, lowered his voice. "If it please Your Grace, we've come here today for a reason."

"Aside from keeping me company while the storms rage? Laudable. I need diversion."

Neither man reacted to his sarcasm, and Hajun felt briefly cheated. Town dogs indeed.

"A matter somewhat touching the Guild," Ladirno continued, leaning a bit forward in his chair. "Something—of great delicacy—"

"So tell me, man. Don't let me die of old age before you get around to it."

This time a faint flush stole across Ladirno's face. Hajun chided himself for being snappish: Ladirno and Wellhyrn were hardly responsible for the vile weather. He smiled quickly, to pass off his words as levity.

"It involves the Sabirn, lord," Ladirno said, "and one of your court."

"Oh?" Hajun's quill stopped on its way to the inkwell. "One of my—*court?*"

Wellhyrn cleared his throat, attempted to whisper: "One of our colleagues—"

Hajun beckoned him up a step on the dais. Both advanced anxiously.

"One of our colleagues," Wellhyrn said, "a member of this court—at least—in entitlement, if not in fact."

Hajun felt his wife's eyes on him, and lowered his voice. "Who's involved?"

"Duran vro Ancahar."

Hajun let out his breath. "So. Duran's hardly one of the luminaries of this court," Hajun said. "In fact, it's been a long time since he's even darkened my door."

Ladirno nodded and gestured quickly. "That may be true, lord, but he has access here. As well as to the Guild."

"He's been known for years—to have contacts among the Sabirn," Wellhyrn said, keeping his voice as low as his companion's. "Being his colleagues, as Ladirno said, we have a professional responsibility to report—" The young man glanced around, and lowered his voice further. "—possible involvement in the dark arts."

Hajun blinked. "Duran?"

"There's perhaps reason he keeps to Old Town, that he's— ignored your late father's generous restoration of his rights. He goes off into the hills with the Sabirn. He's taken a Sabirn into his house. There are rumors—" Wellhyrn coughed. "—of moral nature. He ignores his priest—his closest associates are Sabirn."

"Why?"

"Why indeed, Your Grace," Wellhyrn said. "In this most unusual summer—in this year of disasters—why these nightly visitors, why these strange associations, why this sudden distance from his priest?"

"Which is strange," Ladirno said. "Duran's always seemed to be religious in his own way."

"Huhn." Hajun studied the two alchemists. There was something going on here, something that lurked beneath the surface of their ready concern. He had not seen that concern evidenced so obviously before. Maybe there was a great deal going on he had not paid close attention to.

"It's a matter of concern," Wellhyrn said. "Understand: we know this man. We mark changes in him. And considering his discovery, his trade in—medicines certain individuals might have reason to want in extreme secret—there's such a chance for blackmail. Understand, Your Grace, we've no proof. But we've abundant witnesses of his Sabirn contacts. This boy—a storyteller at a certain tavern—whom he entertains late, behind closed doors—an Ancar nobleman, Your Grace. In these anxious times . . ."

"Your Grace," said Ladirno, spreading his hands, "it's well known that *all* Sabirn practice the dark arts in one way or another. Their very gods . . ."

Hajun nodded. He looked up at the windows—at the perpetual, unnatural spatter of rain.

Wellhyrn said softly: "I know you've been concerned, lord, by the weather. As have we all. Uncommon. Malicious. Flooding in the Slough."

"The necromancer they hanged," Ladirno said, softer still, "Your Grace, she *was* Sabirn. But not the only Sabirn."

"All Targheiden knows you've lost ships," Wellhyrn said. "If it *were* a plot—how better to undermine the duchy? Even the kingdom itself . . ."

Hajun stared at the two men, forcing his face expressionless.

"Why would Sabirn," Wellhyrn said, "woo someone like Duran? And *why* doesn't he return to court?"

"Jorrino, Chadalen," Hajun said, beckoning the two of his court wizards in the hall. "Master Jorrino. Master Chadalen. These two gentlemen have suggested *Sabirn* agency turning the weather against me. Is there any chance of this being true?"

Chadalen was a tall fellow, his dark blond hair and blue eyes speaking of mixed Ancar heritage. He bowed slightly. "Anything is possible, Your Grace."

Jorrino, the elder of the two wizards, shook his head. "We're aware of the hanging. But whether it's so—I can't answer. We simply don't know enough about them to say for sure. It's *very* difficult to locate a wizard by his effects—unless you know his motives, Your Grace."

Hajun leaned on the armrest of his chair and propped his chin in his hand. Everyone knew the Sabirn for demon worshippers, down to the last child of them. He remembered their dark, silent faces, seen from his remote viewpoint of royal carriage or shipboard. He remembered their soft, unintelligible language, the way they seemed to drift from shadow to shadow—servants, even in the highest houses, clinging to dark, ancient gods, even those who professed to convert—one always had to doubt—

"Lord?"

He looked up: the two wizards and the alchemists were watching him, waiting for some reaction.

"*Could* the Sabirn be responsible for the bad turn in the weather?" he asked.

"It's certainly possible." Jorrino shrugged. "They operate outside the jurisdiction of the Temple. We've thought mostly of foreign enemies. But—if there *are* secrets we've not yet met, I suppose—I suppose if one truly dealt in the dark arts, which we do not, Your Grace! Being gods-fearing men—one *might* indeed gather enough power to control the weather."

Hajun frowned. Gods above! If the rumor about the Sabirn wizards was true, could they be behind the bad luck that had been plaguing his trade fleet? Was it possible they were powerful enough to ill-wish him in such a fashion *despite* his wizards—who confessed to their own impotence against forbidden, ungodly magics—

The plot . . . always the plot.

When one of those little, dark people looked at him, he had always shuddered.

"Chadalen . . . *if* the Sabirn are ill-wishing this weather on Targheiden, can you and your colleagues deflect their power?"

Chadalen looked worried. "We can only try, Your Grace. Perhaps—abandoning our concentration on *foreign* enemies, directing our attention much closer to home—may make us of more effect."

Hajun rubbed his eyes, looked again at the four men facing him: the two alchemists' faces betraying nothing of what passed in their thoughts; the two wizards, impressive in their dark robes, equally expressionless.

Damn! He felt forced into a corner, beset with maybe and might-be.

Duran was hardly a threat to Ladirno's position, or Wellhyrn's, for that matter. They had no reason for professional jealousy. Duran had bothered no one, never tried to ease his way back into favor.

But consorting with Sabirn, leaning toward use of the dark arts, *and* of possibly plotting the end of Ancar rule over Targheiden—*could* a son's bitterness over his father's exile go that far?

Hajun took a deep breath. "So be it," he said and sat up straight in his chair. "I'll bring Duran in for questioning."

✧ CHAPTER NINE ✧

The common room of "The Swimming Cat" stood almost empty; most of the customers were travelers marooned at the inn by the storm. The neighborhood folk had left a while ago, rain or no rain, to return to their shops and finish out their business day.

Duran sat at his table, taking longer than normal for his lunch. Lunch. He smiled to himself. Hiring Kekoja as his runner had given him enough of a profit that he had decided he could afford lunch. It was fish, to be sure, but it was warm, and the ale that had accompanied it tasted ever so much better than water.

Tut walked up, a mug of ale in his hands. He had finally finished setting out clean mugs behind the bar, and supervising the cleanup of the tables after his noontime customers had left. Now it was Tut's turn to sit for a while, to relax before preparing his staff for the dinner crowd.

"So," he said, sitting down at Duran's table. "That kid of yours doin' real fine for you, ain't he? I can't remember a time when you been in here for a meal other than breakfast or dinner."

Duran nodded. "Aye, Tut. I can afford a mug of ale every noon now, a hot lunch now and again. And perhaps a meat pie for dinner, who knows?"

Tut took another swallow of ale and lowered his voice. "Keep your eyes on that Zeldezia. She been goin' around talkin' 'bout you again."

"Hladyr bless! Now what?"

"She been sayin' you're comin' close to demon-worship yourself. She says even the good priest ain't been able to change your mind."

"Gods, why doesn't she stay out of my business. That boy doesn't bother her at all—he's never been around when she's come to my shop. Why can't she leave me alone?"

Tutadar dipped one fingertip in a puddle of spilled ale, and drew an idle pattern on the tabletop. " 'Cause you don't pay her no mind, Duran. She don't like people who pay her no mind. Now if you were to tell her you'd *think* 'bout what she been tellin' you, maybe she'd leave you alone."

"For a while."

"For a while," the innkeeper agreed. "But you *don't* tell her what she wants to hear, you see? You ignore her, an' go on 'bout livin' your life, fine as you please. That must be eatin' at her."

"Why can't she bother someone else?" Duran asked. "You'd think she'd grow bored with me."

A wide grin crossed Tut's face. "You're a challenge. I don't think she's ever met anyone who don't pay her no mind." He gestured briefly. "The rest of us . . . we just tell her what she wants to hear an' then go on 'bout our business. You tell her what she *don't* want to hear."

Life was an eternal compromise in Old Town. One compromised with what one bought, not having the money to afford better. Where one lived was a compromise, for the same reason. And, as Tut had said, dealing with people one met or had to deal with on a daily basis, was an eternal compromise.

Duran had learned many lessons living in Old Town, but compromising what he believed in was something he found the hardest. It galled him even more to give in on something when it made, or should have made, no difference to anyone else one way or the other.

"Maybe so," he admitted, "but, gods, Tut!"

"Hey," Tut said, "you want to shut her up, there's one way."

"What's that?"

"Sleep with 'er."

"Good *gods*, Tut!"

Tut shrugged. " 'At's what she wants."

"And then I'd have her for good and all. Thank you, no!"

"Long as you don't—she's got nothin' to do but stew an' be religious. Mostly it's that Sabirn kid. I been tellin' you that, an' I thought you understood."

"I *do* understand, but, gods, she should be able to see the lad isn't driving her business away, that no one in the neighborhood has had anything stolen. None of the *other* neighbors are put out by his working for me—"

Tutadar looked down into his ale, swirled it a few times, and slowly lifted his eyes. "It ain't exactly that way, Duran."

A cold chill ran Duran's spine. "Are you trying to tell me something?"

"Guess I am," Tutadar said softly.

"By the gods! What is it that they're upset about *now*? I thought between me, you, and Ithar, they'd calmed down."

"They had," Tut said, shaking his head, "but Zeldezia been talkin' necromancy and demon worship. An' nobody's real comfortable with that—"

"Me either, Tut, and you know it."

Tutadar met Duran's eyes. "I know it. I knowed you for years and you never been into the dark arts that *I* could see, but them Sabirn dabble in demon worship all the time."

"I'm sure they have their own forms of wizardry. So do we. You use what works in this world, and wizardry works. Up to a point." He leaned his elbows on the table. "Beyond that point, it's only conjecture. Period. I've yet to see anyone use wizardry the way it's portrayed in the sagas and poems. That's storytellers' fables. If such things really *could* work, don't you think we'd see evidence of it all around us?"

"Well, you got a point. But most folk don't have your mind, Duran. We never been educated like you. We can only believe what we hear."

"Have you *seen* any wizardry lately . . . *real* wizardry, not street-seller wizardry?"

"No. Can't say I have. But Zeldezia, she been talkin' 'bout the *dark* arts, not somethin' you'd see everyday."

"Dandro's hells! Just because some people are different from others, does that mean they're evil?"

"I s'pose not. But, I still don't like them little people 'round my inn." The innkeeper lifted a hand. "An' before you start in on remindin' me I still let Old Man stay here, you know what I think 'bout that. He's old an' crippled, an' he don't bother no one. *I'm* talkin' the young ones, the ones who don't like us any more'n we like them. Who's to say *they* ain't using the dark arts?"

"You think the boy who works for me is a demon worshipper?"

Tutadar's gaze wavered. "Maybe not him . . . he always been polite and nice to me when I seen him. But that don't mean other Sabirn ain't makin' pacts with demons. You ain't forgotten that necromancer they hung outside town, are you?"

Duran sighed. "No. I haven't forgotten. And I've warned the boy what happened, told him to be very quiet and very polite—"

"He *better* be quiet, if he knows what's good for 'em. If the neighbors suspect he been involved in anythin' smackin' of sorcery, they'll take it out on you."

"I haven't heard any complaints from my customers," Duran pointed out, flinching at another loud boom of thunder overhead. "If *they* thought the boy was a devil worshipper, they wouldn't be letting him deliver their medicines."

"Any of 'em stopped by your shop to talk since he been takin' your physics to people?"

"No. But the weather's been too bad for most people to be out. I haven't seen more than six or seven people a day in my shop lately. Why should they walk in? It's *convenient* for them to have the stuff delivered, that's why I hired the kid, Tut, *convenience!*"

"What do the folk who *have* stopped by your shop think 'bout your boy?"

"They don't seem to mind."

"Huhn. Where's the boy now?"

"I told him I was going to sit a while after my meal. I don't know where he went. But he'll be there when I get back." He sat up straighter in his chair. "In fact, I'd probably better go. Not that I expect to have all kinds of people waiting at my door, but there's—"

The door to the inn opened. Duran lifted his head and Tutadar turned in his chair.

Two men stood at the edge of the common room. Lamplight glittered on their helms and mail; their bearded faces were expressionless, their eyes shadowed.

Tutadar rose quickly and went to greet them. Duran stared. The Duke's own Guard. Two of them. In Old Town. His chest tightened. Why, in Hladyr's name, had they come to Old Town and, more specifically, "The Swimming Cat"?

He shoved his mug to one side and watched the two men brush by Tutadar and come toward his table.

"Duran Ancahar?" one of the guards asked.

"I'm Duran," Duran said, amazed his voice was steady. "May I help you gentlemen?"

"The Duke requests your presence at court," the other guard said. "Sor."

Duran's mouth went dry. He glanced at Tutadar, but Tut seemed speechless. The other customers were watching with unveiled curiosity.

"I'll come," Duran said, standing and pulling his cloak over his shoulders.

The two guards turned, walked across the common room, and waited by the doorway. Duran took a deep breath, fastened his cloak, and followed.

"Please tell the boy I've gone to the palace," he said to Tutadar. "I shouldn't be long."

Tutadar nodded, his eyes gone very wide. "Hladyr bless, Duran," he said. "I'll watch your shop."

Duran nodded, squared his shoulders, and walked toward the door where the Duke's Guard waited.

No sooner had Hajun sent two of his Guard to Old Town to bring Duran back he had regretted the decision. He glanced around the hall now, saw the two alchemists over by the edge of the room, deep in conversation with two of his courtiers. His wizards had retired to their side of the hall, and stood silent, watching everything that went on around them with hooded eyes.

Damn! he thought. *It's like a battle. One side draws up their troops over here, and the other army deploys its lines over there.* He disliked the image that had come to mind. During his reign, he had put more than a moderate effort into keeping factionalism at a minimum. The last thing he needed now was for there to be "war" between his alchemists, his wizards, and his priests.

With the chance of a wizard-war mixed in with it.

He remembered Duran, the Duran he had known as a very young child, the boy with whom his eldest son had studied, played, and learned rudimentary arms. Duran had never seemed anything but forthrightly honest, honest as his father—so much so that one had feared even then that honesty would not stand him well in the future. Politics was the air Hajun had breathed—even in those days; not that he liked it . . . Hajun had much rather return to the fabled past when a man's word was a man's word, and the fine shading of meaning did not overlay everything a man said.

But Duran's father, Hajun's friend, had been banished from court and had his title stripped from him, Hajun frankly had never understood why. The old duke had counseled his son, saying this is what a duke must do sometimes, even when he doesn't like what he's doing. . . .

By which Hajun had taken it that his friend had powerful enemies at court, and knew that placating those enemies had been more beneficial to the duchy at the time than protecting a longtime ally.

Politics stank.

And now Hajun was embroiled in his own politics, maneuverings which, in an odd way, mirrored those of his father—hoping his friend's son had not gotten himself involved in something—irredeemable.

Dabble in the dark arts himself? Gods, no. Duran was like his father, a kindred soul of sorts, a throwback into the earlier days of Ancar rule, when a man *proved* himself, rather than talked himself into power. One could admire a soul like that. One had.

And here Hajun sat, about to look down from his high seat at the son of his friend, and make decisions he might not like, or even—personally—believe in.

Thunder rumbled overhead. Hladyr keep him from making hasty judgment, from letting himself be maneuvered into something, or argued out of justice—or into it—

He glanced at his wife, found her eyes on him, and grimaced. This was not going to be an entertaining afternoon.

Somewhere, in the depths of his heart, he prayed it would not be a tragic one, either.

Duran let the guards lead the way into the ducal palace, shaking the water from his cloak as he walked. He was dressed in his work clothes, threadbare but serviceable—hardly the attire he would have chosen to attend his duke.

But if the need for his presence at court was so demanding that guards had been sent to escort him, Hajun would have to take what he got.

The guards stopped outside a heavy wooden door, one of them rapping on it with a heavy fist. Duran's knees had started to tremble. He had no idea what was going to happen to him on the other side of that door, but had a notion what it was about.

His father's shade stood to one side, ghostly against the stucco wall. *You are Ancar,* his father's voice whispering in Duran's mind. *Remember that. Whatever happens to you, remember your pride.*

The doors opened. Duran followed the guards into the hall, keeping his pace even with theirs. Let no one say Duran Ancahar had been a coward—or flinched from a meeting with his duke.

And there, over to the far side of the room: Ladirno and Wellhyrn. Duran nearly broke stride when he saw them, their presence here throwing his thoughts into disarray.

Nor was Brovor present, and Duran thanked every god he knew he did not have to cope with *that* complication while he spoke to Brovor's father.

"Your Grace," one of the guards said, saluting with his fist on the center of his chest. "Before you stands Duran Ancahar, come with no delay from Old Town to do you honor."

Duke Hajun's eyes met Duran's, his fingers moved slightly, and the two guards stepped back in unison, then turned with a smart clash of metal and each took up a position slightly to the left of the high seat.

"Come forward, Duran," Hajun said, motioning to the foot of the dais.

Duran swallowed, stepped forward, and stopped, looking up into the Duke's expressionless face.

"I apologize for bringing you here on such short notice," Hajun said, and Duran heard only sincerity behind the words. "But you've been accused of certain things that must not go unanswered."

Perhaps he was expected to reply. Duran kept silent.

The Duke cleared his throat. "What do you know of the dark arts?"

"With regard to what, Your Grace?"

"Have you ever had anything to do with use of the dark arts?"

"No, Your Grace."

"Never?"

"Never, Your Grace."

The Duke drew a deep breath. "On your honor as an Ancar, you can assure me of this?"

"Aye, Your Grace. I do. I have no such dealings. Nor know of any."

The Duke leaned back in his high seat, rested his chin on his fist in silence. Duran shifted his weight, glanced quickly from one side of the room to the other, in the direction the Duke himself was looking.

"Your Grace," Duran said softly.

"Aye?"

"Do I have the chance to know who has accused me?"

The Duke straightened in his chair. "Aye. You're Ancar. It's your right." He turned and gestured. "Ladirno. Wellhyrn. Attend me."

Duran's heart lurched. Why? Why had those two accused him of such idiocy? They knew him better than that. What in Dandro's hells did they think to prove?

The two alchemists stepped close to the high seat and bowed, neither of them meeting Duran's eyes.

"These are your accusers, Duran," the Duke said. "Would you question them?"

Duran smiled suddenly, recognizing one of the pivotal points of Ancar law. At a trial before his lord, the Ancar accused was not assumed guilty until it had been proved beyond a doubt—and as accused, he could question whoever had brought him before his lord's justice. He wondered if Wellhyrn and Ladirno—Torhyn themselves—were familiar enough with Ancar legalistic principles to know the old law, the rights of Ancar with Ancar lord. . . .

He turned toward his two colleagues of the Profession, folded his arms, and smiled at the sudden confusion on their faces.

"What gives you the right to accuse me?" he asked—not the accent of Old Town, not Duran the apothecary—not at all.

Ladirno glanced sidelong at Wellhyrn, a flush reddening his face.

"By report, Sor Duran," Wellhyrn said in his most urbane tones. "We've had reports about you that lead us to believe you're involved in the use of the dark arts—with utmost concern for your soul. . . ."

"A report. In other words, you have no *personal* proof of this. It's hearsay."

"Our source is impeccable."

"Who?"

"Your priest. Vadami."

"Vadami." Duran felt a tide of anger welling up inside: Vadami, aye, but urged on by Zeldezia, he had no doubt. He said, coldly, deliberately: "And by what right does Vadami, a Torhyn, accuse me?"

"By virtue of your continued association with the Sabirn. He's warned you, has he not, that dealing with the Sabirn is dangerous, that it puts your soul in peril? Yet you have ignored him, haven't you, and continued to deal with the Sabirn?"

Duran turned toward Duke Hajun. "My lord, what Wellhyrn says is true—up to a point. The priest Vadami *did* warn me to see less of the Sabirn."

"And did you follow his advice?" the Duke asked.

"No, Your Grace."

"Why not?"

"Because he couldn't prove to my satisfaction that the Sabirn were evil. All he could do was repeat the same, well-worn suspicions people hold concerning the Sabirn; and we do not, *not*, my lord duke, desert loyal servitors on simple hearsay."

"You've had dealings with the Sabirn for years now, haven't you?"

"Aye, Your Grace. And not once have I personally seen behavior that in the least indicated an interest in, or use of, the dark arts."

"Hladyr as your witness?"

"Hladyr as my witness, Your Grace. I will not lie, in any cause."

The Duke nodded slightly, then gestured one of the court priests forward. "Take note of this. Duran Ancahar, once Duran *vro* Ancahar, has sworn in Hladyr's name. As an Ancar, he has taken the oath against his soul."

The priest seemed only mildly interested, though Duran suspected otherwise. "It is so noted, Your Grace."

"Very well." The Duke turned back to Duran. "Your accusers also maintain that you habitually entertain the old man who frequents 'The Swimming Cat.' That you frequently take notes on this person's utterances. Tell me why."

Duran shot a glance at the two alchemists. "Someone must have nearly drowned himself to see that, Your Grace. I had no idea my humble life was interesting enough to draw an audience in a storm."

A low murmur of laughter ran through the crowd gathered to watch the proceedings. Both Wellhyrn and Ladirno frowned and drew themselves up straighter.

"As for taking notes, absolutely I do, Your Grace. For years, I've collected Sabirn legends and tales—a purely scholarly interest. They ruled a great empire. My hope is that, in some of their legends and stories, they've left behind truths that could help us in modern times."

"In what manner?" the Duke asked, a spark of genuine interest lighting his face.

"As Your Grace already knows, I deal in medicines. I dispense what help I can to poor folk in Old Town. It's been my hope to discover forgotten medicines in the Sabirn legends—medicines to ease suffering, medicines to equal what must have been in the old Empire."

For a moment, no one spoke or moved. The Duke leaned forward in his chair.

"But could we trust such medicines? The Sabirn are known to be demon worshippers, Duran. Necromancers! How can you deal with devils and do good?"

"To my observation, Your Grace, and on my honor, I have never seen, nor heard of, any Sabirn working the dark arts. The Sabirn I know are far too busy surviving, to be using the amount of time necessary to perform such draining tasks; and I would reject anything that came from such sources."

"And how do you know dark sorcery would take such a great amount of time," asked Wellhyrn, a sly look on his face, "unless you've been involved in it?"

"Would you like to inform His Grace how long it takes for an alchemist to perform some of our simpler tasks? Or is it effortless? A snap of the fingers, perhaps?"

Wellhyrn dropped his eyes. "His Grace is already aware that we work very hard to produce what we give him."

"Then if you're working with nature and find things arduous and time-consuming, doesn't it make sense than any actions taken contrary to nature would be much harder?"

No one spoke. The Duke motioned one of his wizards forward.

"Jorrino. Is what Duran said true?"

The wizard bowed slightly. "He makes an uneducated guess, Your Grace, but—naively close to the truth."

"But—" Wellhyrn said.

"Wellhyrn," the Duke said, his voice gone very cold. "You've not been asked to speak."

Wellhyrn subsided, his face gone white with shame.

"All of which is getting us nowhere," the Duke said, leaning back in his high seat. "Wellhyrn, Ladirno. You told me you *fear* Duran may be involved in the dark arts. The key words here are 'may be.' You've no proof beyond hearsay. Is this true or false?"

"To our own concern, Your Grace—" Ladirno said. Wellhyrn seemed to have lost the faculty of speech.

"The priest Vadami has spoken to Duran about consorting with the Sabirn, and Duran has—for his own reasons, reiterated here—refused to comply. This is the central substance of your accusations. True or false?"

"True, Your Grace.—But—"

"None of you has *proven* that Duran is guilty of anything more than *speaking* with the Sabirn, and that in the course of master to servant. True or false?"

"On the surface, true, Your Grace, but his writing—"

The Duke turned to his wizard and his priest. "I find no guilt in this man, either of performing the dark arts, or of lying. Do you concur?"

"We find no cause, Your Grace," the priest said. "We have ways of seeing such things. He's telling the truth as he sees it."

The wizard nodded. "I don't sense he has ever dabbled in the dark arts, Your Grace, and we wizards have ways of seeing that, too."

Duran let loose his pent-up breath, his eyes fixed on the Duke's face.

"Then hear my judgment," the Duke said. "I find Duran innocent of all charges of dealing in the dark arts. I find Ladirno and Wellhyrn guilty of bringing unfounded charges against him. As for the priest, Vadami, I suspect him of being overzealous."

The two alchemists stiffened in their finery, their faces gone pale and still.

"Duran Ancahar."

Duran stepped closer to the dais.

"I urge you to keep your dealings with the Sabirn to a minimum. They are not well-liked in Targheiden, and are—rightly or wrongly—suspect of nefarious dealings. I pass no judgment with present associations, but beware new relationships. Do you hear me?"

"I do hear you, Your Grace."

"Wellhyrn. Ladirno.—I assume you thought you had reason. But consider: bringing accusations against another citizen without adequate cause can be slander. By holy Scripture, slander is perilous to one's soul. Both of you are banned from attending court for the next ten days, during which time you may meditate on this. Do you hear me?"

"We hear you, Your Grace," Ladirno said faintly.

"Good," Hajun said. "You have my leave, gentlemen."

Duran's knees were shaking again, only this time from relief. His two colleagues bowed to the Duke, turned, and stalked off down the hall, neither of them affording Duran so much as a glance.

Duran stood his ground and caught Hajun's eyes.

"Duran?" the Duke said, lifting one eyebrow. "You have something else to say?"

"Yes, Your Grace. It's good to see that Ancar justice has not died with the past. My thanks, Your Grace."

With which he bowed deeply, and turned away.

"That gods-be-damned, no-good, lying bastard!"

Ladirno sank back in one of the chairs in his apartment and let Wellhyrn rage, pacing up and down the room, his face livid with anger.

"Do you realize what he's done to us?" Wellhyrn howled, turning to face Ladirno. "He's *disgraced* us in the Duke's eyes, that's what he's done! We've been banned from attending court for ten days, Ladir! *Ten* days!"

"He certainly has," Ladirno said acidly. "Thank the gods it's nothing worse."

"I'll see Duran Ancahar damned before he gets away with this! I'm *twenty* times the alchemist he is! If he thinks Ancar blood can ingratiate him into the Duke's favor by disgracing us, he's got horseshit for brains!"

Ladirno gazed out the window at an overcast sky, some disconnected portion of his brain marveling that all Targheiden had not begun to flood yet.

"Dammit, Ladir! Pay attention to me!" Wellhyrn stopped in front of Ladirno. "If I hadn't listened to you about taking our suspicions to the Duke—"

"Now you wait just a damned moment," Ladirno snapped,

rising. "Don't you try laying the blame on me. It was your idea!"

Wellhyrn glared.

"Thank Hladyr's mercy our banishment wasn't permanent," Ladirno said, doggedly keeping his tone mild. "The Duke's not known for his sweet temper—no more than his father was."

"How did we know we'd get ourselves involved in some kind of damned Ancar trial?" Wellhyrn raged, pacing again, periodically slamming a fist into his open hand. "And Duran . . . can you believe it? He talked his way out of *everything!*—sweet as one of the Duke's own courtiers!"

"You forget," Ladirno said, still in the same mild tone, "that Duran's father used to be the Duke's companion and, as such, he was Ancar of the Ancar. What do you *think* that name means? Ancahar. That's *aristocracy*, man—blue-blood, to the utmost."

Wellhyrn's face grew red, and Ladirno allowed himself a small smile. He had always suspected that Wellhyrn hated Duran for once having thrown aside what he would give his soul to be—an Ancar lord of the highest degree. Title aside—Torhyn were Torhyn—and Duran had been *born* a noble.

Wellhyrn seized a book from Ladirno's table and threw it against the wall. Ladirno winced, but kept silent, afraid of Wellhyrn's violence.

Wellhyrn spun around and faced Ladirno, his eyes narrowed to slits. "I'm not going to take this lying down," he snarled. "I'll get that son of a dog for this. I swear it!"

"And what are you going to do?" Ladirno asked, watching Wellhyrn pace.

"There's got to be a way we can get back at him without anyone knowing. And, by all the gods, I'll come up with one." Wellhyrn halted abruptly. "I've got it! By all that's holy! We'll set our wizards at him!"

Ladirno sighed heavily. "Would you get control of yourself, Hyrn? Stop raging and *think!* We can't afford to set our wizards at him. We have enough enemies of our own; diverting our wizards from *them* could be disastrous!"

"No more disastrous than letting Duran get away with what he's done!"

"He's done no more than defend himself," Ladirno said, "as you or I would have in like circumstances. He accused us of nothing more than inaccuracy—"

"Which could have gotten us banished for good! What's the matter with you? How can you speak in his defense."

"I'm trying to get through to you. Now . . . *sit down!*"

Ladirno had seldom used that particular tone of voice with Wellhyrn: in shock, the younger man drew a deep breath, then sat down in the matching chair.

"I don't mind hiring someone to set on Duran," Ladirno said, most reasonably, he thought. "But our resources are limited. And if ours are—his certainly are."

"Maybe you're right." Wellhyrn brightened. "He couldn't afford it. Gods, he couldn't hire a junior apprentice—and if we bought even an hour from a second-rate wizard—"

"Now you're thinking."

The old, malicious smile was back on Wellhyrn's face. "Then let's do it," he said, leaning forward in his chair. "Tomorrow morning." He laughed coldly. "We'll ill-wish that bastard. If Duran *is* treating the heir for the pox, maybe we'll get lucky and he'll fumble the treatment."

"Dammit, Hyrn! I don't care what you do to Duran, but don't even think of misfortune on the Duke's son! I won't stand for that."

"Take a joke, Ladir!"

Ladirno held Wellhyrn's gaze until Wellhyrn looked away. "Do you want to contact the wizards, or shall I?"

"You do it." Wellhyrn's eyes glittered coldly in the lamplight. "I'll think of other ways we can get to this problem of ours. And believe me, I'll think of something!"

✧ CHAPTER TEN ✧

"Duran."

Duran turned from his shelves to Kekoja, who was already spreading out the coppers he had earned on the countertop.

"Good day?" Duran asked.

"Oh, aye." The Sabirn boy grinned widely. "You hear about that warehouse fire, next block over? Boom!"

"I heard. So waterlogged it wouldn't burn, thank the gods. Rain's to *some* advantage. . . . Well!" Duran counted up the coppers and shook his head in wonder. Thirty-one coins lay on his counter.

"Best yet," Kekoja said pridefully.

"Here, lad." He gave the boy his percentage, and deposited the rest in his belt pouch. "You did a damned fine job."

"Guess so.—Had many people in here today?"

"No." He knocked into a pot, grabbed after it before it went off the edge. "Damn! I've been so clumsy today!" He gestured at the waste-bin. "Two pots, *two!* I've broken."

Kekoja lifted an eyebrow. "Not like you," he said, not smiling in response to Duran's tale.

Duran looked at him with a sudden, cold thought.

Kekoja dropped his pay into his belt pouch. "You be careful," the boy said, wiping the dark hair back from his eyes. "Don't you do anything risky for a while. Nothing with the furnace—"

"The way my luck's running? Nothing dangerous today, I promise you."

"You 'bout ready to close up?"

"Aye. Pretty soon."

"Then I'll see you in the morning.—Duran? You *do* be careful—"

Duran waved him out: Kekoja left; and with a sigh, Duran sat down on his doorstep, content to simply sit, doing nothing.

Could it be someone had hired a wizard to ill-wish him?

One could guess who.

And if so, there was little he could do about it: he could afford no protection.

Damn them. He could not understand why he should threaten them—but they must see him as such: that was the only reason he could think of for them accusing him before the Duke.

And the prospect of some wizard's ill-wishing made him shudder. All sorts of things could go wrong in his business: a mistaken dosage and possibly kill a patient. He could drop acid on himself. A firing could explode. The house could burn down: in a neighborhood so closely, ramshackle-built—the whole of Old Town could go—

Or a nosy neighbor—might look out a window at the wrong time of night—

It needed so little—

All because he had saved a boy from a bad beating and possible death.

He sighed and closed his eyes. It was pleasant to sit here like this after such a muggy, tense day—unmoving. Breaking nothing. Making no disasters. Pedestrians passed him. He paid no attention.

"Duran."

Zeldezia.

Gods, some wizard *was* after him.

He opened his eyes: she stood there with her sleeves rolled up to her elbows in the heat, fists on hips.

"I heard you was called in to see the Duke."

He nodded.

She sniffed virtuously. "If you listened to folk—"

"So." Duran leaned his head against the doorjamb, and looked up at her. "Then I suppose you know everything about it. I wouldn't bore you with the details."

Not what she hoped for. She set her jaw. "The Duke let you go."

"Of course." Duran gave her nothing satisfying, willing her to lose interest and walk away. Obviously *he* had no wizardry: she did not move.

"Ain't you going to reply to that?" Zeldezia asked.

"Why should I?" Duran kept his voice calm. "You know all about it."

"Duran. Listen to me if you won't listen to Vadami: he says if you repent an' give up seein' them Sabirn, Hladyr will still forgive you—"

"Oh? And does Vadami now have a special conduit to the Shining One? I didn't realize he had become so exalted in the past few days."

"You're mockin' at me," she said, her voice going cold. "An' at a priest o' god. That's what they done to you. One of these days, Duran, you're going to be so sorry, an' there ain't no one goin' to help you."

He looked her straight in the eye. "Are you threatening me, Zeldezia?"

"I ain't doin' no such thing. I'm just warnin' you, that's all. Hopin' you'll change your stubborn mind an' see the *right* way to live."

"It's the right way because *you* think it's so," Duran said, struggling to keep the anger from his voice. "Anyone who dares believe differently than you is a heretic."

"That ain't so! Vadami thinks the same way, too. Ever' right-thinkin' person thinks so!"

Duran felt a wave of weariness wash over him. "Then go talk with the good priest, Zeldezia, and have the courtesy to leave me alone."

"Ain't you concerned for your soul?"

"As much as anyone else. Now are you going to leave, or do I have to get up and slam the door in your face?"

Her eyes narrowed. "Don't insult me, Duran, who's tryin' t' help you—"

"Get! Leave me alone!"

She drew herself up, puffed as if she would say something else, then spun on her heel and went, hips swaying, down the street and into her shop.

Duran shrugged. There was no hope for it. He did not see how he could continue to live his life the way he pleased *and* keep Zeldezia and the priest off his back. He had received some protection in the Duke's decision, but he dared not fool himself, trusting his luck would hold: luck in his case was in serious question.

Dog came back, his tongue lolling out the side of his mouth, and walked into the shop. Duran heard him settle down in his accustomed spot by the counter. He reminded himself to pick up a bone or two from Tutadar for Dog's dinner, stirred on the doorstep, stood, and fished for his key.

Ah well. A good meal and a fresh mug of ale should lighten his mood. He drew the door closed, locked it, and crossed the street.

"The Swimming Cat" was only moderately full: it was early yet. Duran nodded to Tut and walked back to his table. The other customers watched him pass, a few nodding a greeting in his direction, but for the most part they were silent—as if he had walked in on some discussion his neighbors did not want him to hear.

Him, he thought. A man from Old Town did not make a forced visit to the Duke of Targheiden and return without comment.

Once Duran had seated himself, his neighbors began to talk again, but their conversation was muted, without its usual animation. Tut walked over, wiping his hands on his apron. "Fish tonight, Duran?"

"Aye. Breaded, if I can have it. And a mug of ale."

Tut nodded, went to the kitchen door, and shouted Duran's order to the cook. He brought a mug of ale back to Duran himself.

"Have a good day?" Tut asked, pulling out a chair and sitting down, as he would, in slack moments.

"Good enough," Duran said. Perhaps he was too apprehensive that he read more into this approach.

On the other hand, judging by the expression on Tutadar's face—

"Duke lost himself another ship today," Tut said quietly. "Word come."

"Dandro's hells."

The innkeeper shrugged. "Duke, he's lost a damned lot of goods. Folk got a lot of hard luck—lot of hard luck. People get desperate."

Duran took a swallow of ale, then leaned forward on the table. "Is this news aimed at me, Tut?"

Tutadar dropped his eyes. "S'pose it is. *I* ain't believing it, Duran, but—there's a lot of folks beginning to ask—where all this luck is comin' from. An' you can say it ain't Sabirn, but they ain't in the mood to listen. The Duke loses trade, Old Town loses business—hard times coming. Taxes'll increase to make up for the Duke's losses. We seen it before."

"They can't honestly believe any damn Sabirn has anything to do with the storms," Duran protested. Tutadar stared back. "Can they?"

"Startin' to seem that way. It ain't nature. It sure ain't any run of plain luck. Somethin's doin' it."

"Foreign enemies—"

"Sabirn are foreigners. Right among us. Here ever' day."

"Fools." Duran gripped his mug tightly. "Ignorant fools!"

"Then you're callin' me a fool, too, Duran," Tutadar said, lifting his eyes so he met Duran's gaze. "I know you ain't a demon worshipper, an' I know you wouldn't want to do anythin' that would bring bad luck down on you, but, dammit, man, you got a blind eye to them folk—an' I ain't sayin' it's you, I ain't sayin' it's that boy, but it ain't real discreet, you puttin' that kid up in ever'body's faces—you havin' him real conspicuous—you givin' him access to all sorts of shops an' places—he works for you, but who knows who else he knows, who knows who he talks to? Them folk all get together. They all talk—"

"How in all hells can you think that way, Tut? You know me. You know I'm no fool. The boy's honest; he doesn't bother people, and he's helping me make the best living I've ever seen."

"Money won't buy your life, Duran."

"Gods, what are you talking about?"

Tut murmured, tapping his head, "I *know*, up here, you ain't made no pacts with demons. But here—" He tapped his chest. "—here, I'm scared. You can't force folk, Duran. You can't force 'em overnight to change the way they been thinkin' for hundreds of years. Some say—you can't fire that kid. Some say he got a spell on you."

Duran stared, his heart chilling. "You're saying I have to fire this kid, is that it? I have to run my business the way Zeldezia's damn hate-mongering wants?"

"It ain't all Zeldezia. I'm sayin' you got yourself in big trouble, Duran, because I can't change the way folk think, and you can't change 'em either. Me and Ithar have kept tellin' everyone you ain't changed none . . . that you're the same man they've always knowed. But you *ain't* the same, deep down. You been actin' real odd. Like this kid was real important." He took a deep breath. "It ain't natural, folks to mix. I dunno what this kid prays to. I don't want to know. I got me second thoughts about Old Man—"

"Listen to me, Tut." Duran struggled to put words to his thoughts. "I can't let the boy go now. I have a debt of honor, since I've taken him on. I made a vow to him; we sealed our agreement and swore by the gods. I can't back off an agreement because I'm *scared*, Tut. For better or worse, I'm Ancar. You know what an oath is worth to me."

"You swore an oath like that to a Sabirn kid?"

"I swore. Zeldezia says my soul's at risk. My soul's at risk if I break my word, Tut! I swore to that kid and I'm not backing off because of any threats! I can't! Maybe this neighborhood better damn well understand *why* I'm not going to fire that kid!"

"You never lied to me before," Tutadar admitted, "an', far as I know, you never lied to no one. Look, why don't you tell the boy to go off for a few days? Go somewhere no one can see 'im? That ain't firin' 'im—send 'im off to the hills, have him dig you some roots or somethin'—"

Duran ran a hand through his hair. "I'll think about it . . . I really will. I understand your worry. You think that would calm it down?"

"Chance it might. An' right now, if I was you, I'd take it. If the storms keep up—"

"I know where they're coming from!"

"Zeldezia. Aye."

"The Duke heard the whole question—someone accused *me* of association with warlocks! He threw the accusations out of court—*and* threw out the accusations against the Sabirn!"

Tut shook his head. "Some'd say the Duke was makin' a big mistake about that last. Duran, Zeldezia ain't agin you. She's scared you're close to bein' damned."

"As if she was the authority!"

"Some of your neighbors been listenin' to her, Duran. Listenin' to her real serious."

"All right." Duran leaned back as Lalada brought his fish to him and set it down on the table. His appetite had vanished. "I'll send the boy off, Tut. Maybe I can do without him for a handful of days." He met the innkeeper's eyes. "Now you tell me, what's going to happen if the weather suddenly turns good? Will that convince everyone they're right about the boy being a demon worshipper?"

"It ain't going to make 'em happy, that's for sure. Now, if he come back an' the weather stays good, that's another thing."

"Or if the weather stays bad and he's nowhere to be seen." Duran spread his hands. "Damn! It's crazed, Tut, it's no damn sense!"

"Don't seem it is, does it?"

"Tut—do you believe this crap?"

"Me? I trust you, Duran, an' I speak for you, do ever'thin' I can to keep the neighbors calm. But I'm only one person, an' Ithar's only one person. We can't do more'n what we can do."

"That's all I can ask for."

Tutadar shoved his chair back from the table. "You enjoy your meal, Duran, an' think 'bout what I said. At least it'd give the neighbors time to calm down."

Duran sighed, and began cutting up his fish. "I'll talk to the boy, Tut. I promise you."

Duran left the inn—heard the low rumble of conversation start up the moment he exited the door. He had stayed no longer than necessary. No. No. Not in that atmosphere.

Wind swept debris down the cobbles, rattled shutters. He turned his head from the blast, and blinked a wisp of hair blown in his eyes, blinked again, seeing a grey-wrapped lump sitting against the wall of his shop, beside the steps.

Old Man—like sin come home to roost.

Had the neighbors driven him from the "Cat"? Duran wondered.

He fished out his key, opened the door as Old Man rose and stood beside him. "Come on in," Duran said—anxious to get him out of sight, quickly; and guilty and angry for that small, prudent cowardice. "I'll light the lamp."

He did that, turned, saw Dog had gone to stand by the doorway, his tail wagging uncertainly—held between duty and his usual foraging.

"Go, Dog," Duran said, waving a hand, "before it truly gets bad."

Dog obviously was of the same mind, for he trotted quickly off into the wind.

Duran shut the door. The air in the shop was close and still, smelling of shelves and shelves of herbs.

"Why weren't you at the 'Cat' tonight?" Duran asked.

Old Man said, "I may not be there much longer, Duran. I barely make enough to survive anymore."

Duran frowned. "No one pays you for your stories now?"

"No one but you. No one else asks to hear them."

"Ah." Duran was at a loss for words. "I—should have guessed."

Old Man smiled slightly, a mere movement of the lips. "Perhaps it's just as well. You've too much else to account for with your neighbors—to be the only one giving money to a Sabirn."

Duran leaned back against his counter. "The neighbors aren't pleased with me on many counts, so I hear."

"You've heard right. They aren't. That's why I'm here."

Duran's shoulders stiffened.

"Your neighbors," Old Man said. "Your neighbors are talking about violence."

"You're serious, aren't you?"

"I've heard them discussing it."

"Was Zeldezia the ringleader?"

"She and the priest Vadami."

Duran clenched his hands. "Before or after I was called to the ducal palace?"

"Before *and* after."

"Hladyr bless!" Duran slammed his hand on the counter.

"It was serious, Sor Duran. This weather—they seem to think—"

"I know. I heard all about it. Tut advised me to send Kekoja off somewhere for a few days. He seems to think that might calm everyone down."

"Tutadar is a good man," the Sabirn said, "and more open-minded than the rest. But even he has his blind spots. I think things have gone beyond sending Keko off and bringing him back a few days later. If you value my advice, Sor Duran, you should start thinking about leaving town, *before* your neighbors do you some harm."

Duran was trembling now, his stomach was a hard knot, and his hands shook. Leave Targheiden? Leave everything he had known for thirty-five years? An Ancar run in cowardice from the town his ancestors had built? A wave of anger swept through him. By Hladyr's light! He *was* Ancar . . . he was of a noble house! He could not evade a fight like this. . . . It was dishonorable . . . as dishonorable as negating the bargain he and Kekoja had struck.

O gods! Go off into the countryside—go back into exile. I had enough of that with my parents. Everything I know is here!

Everything I've built . . . all my work . . .

"Didn't you realize that this might happen?" Old Man asked.

"Maybe in my heart of hearts I thought it *could*," Duran said, "but I didn't . . ." He looked up at the ceiling, at the lamplight playing with the shadows across it. "It happened to my father. I never thought it would happen to me."

"You make them nervous, Sor Duran. You traffic with demon worshippers."

"Bah!" Duran began to pace up and down in front of his counter. He heard a faint whine, a scratch at the door. He stalked over and jerked it open, let Dog and a gust of wind inside. "Sorry, Dog. Curse me for a fool . . . I forgot to bring you your bones. Perhaps some cheese until morning, eh?"

He went and got that. Dog wagged his tail, took it—more grateful and more faithful than others he had helped.

"All right," he said to Old Man. "You think the neighbors are going to run me out of town. So where the hells do I go? What will I do to survive?"

"You're a doctor. Whatever you choose to call yourself, you're better than most poor folk ever see. You'll never be hungry. A traveling doctor is always welcome, no matter where he goes."

"To what end? Old on the road and starving? I'm not an active man. I've no knowledge how to survive—I want my food from the tavern, my supplies from a market, I want a bed at night—" *I want my books. I want familiar things . . . I want to die somewhere I understand. . . .*

"You want. It was no helpless man who rescued Keko from the thugs in the alleyway that night. And it's no helpless man who has the mind you have."

"What's *that* supposed to mean?"

Keko tells me. Keko tells me how you make your medicines. How you have your little jars—your little jars with the old bread, the cheese—how you cured the smith with a salve of herbs and mouldy bread—"

Duran shrugged, finding no hope in that, against the thought of exile.

"Our physicians understood moulds. In the Empire they did. *We* use such remedies. But no Sabirn told you."

"It cures cuts," Duran said glumly. "It can't cure human stupidity, Old Man, it can't cure hate!"

"You have a mind. You want proofs, you want substantiation of things. You don't think like your neighbors. You look past what seems. You *think*."

"It does me no good."

"Do you want learning? Come with us, and we'll give you what knowledge we have."

Duran stared. "Come with you where? And who is 'us'?"

Old Man leaned on his walking stick. "Not all the Sabirn you see in Targheiden have lived here all their lives. We come and we go. No one notices. You remember when I came to the 'Cat'— not all that many years ago? I suppose you, along with everyone else, thought I came from some other section of town."

"Aye."

"I didn't. I came from elsewhere . . . from beyond Targheiden."

"Why?"

"To serve as a gatherer of information. To find certain trade stuffs we need and can't easily obtain. Targheiden is, after all, a shipping capital."

"What—trade stuffs?"

"Sulfur. Niter."

"For what?"

"I'll tell you—once we're outside Targheiden."

"We."

"As I said—time I was traveling again. You've asked questions. I'll answer them. I'll tell you stories you don't imagine."

It was the storyteller's voice, that mesmerized, that stole a man's sense about what was real and not real. It was a spell in itself—a spell—that broke down the lines between possible and impossible.

"Once," Old Man said, softly, "we had a ship that sailed with no wind."

"With no wind?"

"And no sail. Think about that, Duran."

"But—"

"We digress," Old Man said: the voice became sharp, incisive—

commanding. "We were talking about your neighbors—and my advice. Will you take it? Are you willing to come with us?"

"But . . . who is this 'us'?"

"Targheiden doesn't love Sabirn." Old Man shifted, taking some of his weight from his crippled leg, and leaned back against the wall. "We've become unwelcome here—those of us that have become . . . too visible."

The Sabirn woman—hanged as a necromancer.

Duran's head spun. Thirty-five years of his life here—with his parents and on his own—in the same shop, the same small apartment upstairs. He had spent his youth here, had roots here, friends here. And . . .

He could die here.

Possibly.

After what he had heard tonight, *more* than possibly.

"But I can't take all my things with me," he protested. "I have my alchemist's tools, my books, my notes, my medicines. . . . Without those, I'm worthless!"

"We have a wagon," Old Man said. "We can get others. How much room do you need?"

Duran chewed on his lower lip. "But how in Dandro's hells can I move this stuff without the neighbors knowing?"

"We'll help you."

"Who," Duran asked again, "is 'we'?"

Old Man waved a hand. "Myself. Kekoja. Several more. We have our own possessions to take."

Duran shook his head slowly. There *had* to be some other way to approach this. He could not run—merely because his neighbors were upset.

Or could he?

Was his pride worth his life? Was it worth all he ever meant to do, all the notes, the knowledge his father had collected, that he had added to over a lifetime, the pages and pages—

"It's simple, Duran." The Sabirn's black eyes glittered in the lamplight. "We know the dark ways . . . the streets the Guard never travels. We load your belongings—we go. That's all."

Duran shuddered.

"And," Old Man said, "we aren't without wizards of our own."

"Gods . . ."

"Them, too."

"You're asking total trust from me," Duran said at last. "*Total* trust."

"You have my true name," Old Man said with quiet dignity, "You *know* what I am. That is a sacred bond."

"Are you—"

"You know," Old Man said, in that Voice, "—what I am."

"I suppose I do," Duran said, and shivered. "When do you suggest we start?"

"I don't think trouble's imminent. Not by what I've heard. And if Kekoja doesn't show up for work tomorrow . . ."

"Wait. If Kekoja doesn't come to work tomorrow, won't the neighbors think something's strange?"

"You said Tutadar suggested you send him off. I would imagine he'll tell the other folk you're going to do something like that."

"All right," he said. He lifted his chin, decision made. "I'll start gathering everything I need tonight."

"Good. You have enough baskets for your medicines, don't you?"

"I'll manage."

"And your alchemist's tools?"

"The baskets I keep things in. But my alembics, my furnace—"

"We can make you new ones."

"And where is that? Where will we be?"

Old Man's face was very serious, still in the lamplight. "A place where the mind can run free," he said.

Ladirno sat at his lately habitual table in "The Golden Shoe," contemplating the walk back to his apartments, but dreading the unpredictability of his companion and looking, still, for some decision, some sense that things might have settled. Wellhyrn sat in a chair opposite him, looking frustrated and angry. As yet, Wellhyrn had not come up with a suitable punishment for Duran—a revenge that nobody could trace back to its source. The lack of inspiration had thrown Wellhyrn into a beastly—and dangerous—mood.

Oddly enough, some small part of Ladirno took a bleak satisfaction in his companion's discomfiture—but he did not trust him.

Distant thunder rumbled and Ladirno winced. Gods-blighted storms! He, himself, chose to believe that no one controlled the weather, but he could not remember a stretch of weather like this.

Perhaps the Sabirn *were* behind the weather.

Perhaps.

A darkly cloaked man walked toward their table, and though Ladirno could see no face below the hood, he thought he recognized him. Wellhyrn lifted his head and stared, then smiled coldly, his face relaxing in dark pleasure.

"Ah, Mandani. Please join us."

Ladirno drew in his breath: Mandani, he recalled, was the name Wellhyrn had mentioned, the wizard he had set on Duran— and the wizards he dealt with, this one—this man was *not* a comfortable drinking companion.

"I have interesting news," the wizard said, still not throwing back the hood of his cloak. "I believe Duran to be protected."

"What?" Wellhyrn's face stilled to a portrait in ice.

"I had an apprentice spell him in 'The Swimming Cat' tonight. Though I was still working on him, he didn't drop a thing."

Ladirno flashed a dismayed glance at Wellhyrn. "But he has no wizard—he couldn't possibly afford a wizard!"

"I don't know."

"We have to suppose," Mandani said softly, "that someone *is* protecting him. I don't know the nature of this wizard, I don't know where he is, or what he is, but he exists."

"Are you asking for more money?" Wellhyrn's green eyes were cold in the lamplight. "Perhaps it's *you*. Maybe you're not as good as you say you are."

"Hyrn," Ladirno said, shooting his younger colleague a silencing look, his heart beating in dread of this man. "Forgive him. Things haven't gone well lately. We're—in some personal difficulty."

Mandani's expression did not change.

"Do you think you might need help?" Ladirno asked carefully.

"Assistance might be useful. Assuming his adept has none."

"I don't see how he's affording *one!*" Wellhyrn snapped.

Ladirno signed him: caution. "All right. If you think two of you can get the job done, then choose your partner. The fee for his services will be the same as your own."

"Thank you." Mandani's deep voice never varied. "We'll start immediately."

He rose and walked away.

Ladirno stared at Wellhyrn. "It seems," he said, "Duran's not innocent."

✧ CHAPTER ELEVEN ✧

Hail fell—heavy, large hail that coated the streets of Targheiden with ice-white pebbles, shattered two panes of glass in the Great Hall, killed livestock, killed an old man on the West Side.

Hajun sat and glared at the silent Hall. None of his courtiers were talking; stiff-legged, they stood with their backs to the wall, their expressionless faces telling him more than words. The priests stood in a corner, whispering among themselves—and not a wizard was to be seen.

Cowards.

A runner came into the hall—spoke briefly to the priests. Faljend, the chief priest of Hladyr, quickly left that cluster and approached the dais. "If I might talk to you, privately, Your Grace. . . ."

Hajun beckoned him closer, closer still.

"There's a certain panic, Your Grace," Faljend said in the faintest of voices. "People gathering in various places, in the markets—they're afraid—"

"So?" Hajun snapped. "Their shingles are lying in the streets—their windows battered—what's remarkable they should be afraid?"

"Gently, Your Grace. We must stand as an example—"

"How in Hladyr's name are we going to do that?" Hajun leaned forward. "The merchants are at each other's throats . . . they're ready to lash out at anything that moves. And, depending on shipping as I do, I know how they feel, dammit!"

"We priests are doing everything we can, Your Grace. We've had special prayers offered at the Temple. Common folk are praying for a change in the weather. None of this seems to have done any good."

Hajun grunted a reply.

"It's wizardry, Your Grace, it's the Sabirn!"

"I'm so damned tired of hearing everyone howl about the Sabirn I could puke! What do you suggest? That we round up every Sabirn we can get our hands on and hang them?"

"Your Grace, if something's not done soon, we could be facing riots in the streets. *Everyone's* suffering, everyone, from you, Your Grace, down to the smallest shopkeeper in Old Town. No one's immune."

Hajun rubbed his forehead, willing his headache to vanish. "So?"

"I know, Your Grace, I'm telling you nothing new. I do, however, suggest that you make a public plea for calm. Send your heralds among the people to tell them your concern. . . ."

"How am I supposed to do that in all this wind and rain? Who'll listen? Everyone's inside."

"They'll listen, Your Grace. When people become as emotional as they are now, they'll listen from their windows, to anything that tells them what they *want* to hear."

"Words! Words are nothing! The question is *doing*, priest!"

"Search out the necromancers—there's more than one, Your Grace, there must be a nest of them. And hang them, one and all!"

"If my wizards can't *stop* them, priest, how in Dandro's *hells* are we going to lay hands on them?"

"We have to try, Your Grace! We have to smoke them out, *divert* them with danger from different fronts—"

"Give me names, dammit, give me names!"

Faljend bowed deeply. "We have our spies, Your Grace, as I'm sure you know. We do know names, Sabirn who hold themselves out to be wizards and fortune-tellers. We know who they are."

"*Fortune-tellers* aren't the ones involved!" Hajun said. "You're dealing with a furtive people, you're not going to find anything!"

"Divide their attention," the High Priest said. "But first, Your Grace, first you have to have the people behind you."

Hajun scowled, smelling disaster, thinking of his ships. His hold on this city. "Huhn. All right. I'll write up a speech. My heralds will be out among the people by this afternoon." Rain spattered against the windows, thunder boomed, and Hajun gripped the armrests on his chair. "Damn them!"

✧   ✧   ✧

Vadami stood in prayer in the cavernous Temple, his eyes shut as he sent his pleas to Hladyr the Shining. He could hear other folk around him constantly praying, their muted voices added to his own.

He gazed up at the altar, hoping that the sight of it would warm his heart as it had always done. Surrounded by hundreds of burning lamps, overlaid with pounded gold, it sparkled as with captured sunlight, and towering over it was the intricate mosaic of the Shining One himself, standing above the entire world, all creation at his feet. It was a masterwork—a young man in the prime of life, golden hair blown back from a divinely beautiful face, looking down on his worshippers, compassion in his eyes. On either hand the gods and goddesses: beneath his feet, the dark regions of Dandro's hells.

A crash of thunder. Vadami flinched. Rain spattered against the costly windows.

The Sabirn were responsible for this, Vadami would stake his immortal soul on that. Dealers in darkness, they had brought this evil on the city. *Everyone* knew it now—

Except Duran.

Vadami said a brief prayer for Duran's soul, though he felt certain that soul was lost forever. Why had such a kindly man succumbed to the Sabirn and their dark ways? Why would Duran not listen to what might have saved his soul?

Duran did nothing but laugh in Vadami's face.

Duran blasphemed the Shining One.

And prayers went unanswered.

Duran was Ancar—was no Sabirn heathen, but one of their own.

That was the link the evil had. *That* was the linchpin of their plot—the seduction of one of the noble blood, the drawing-astray of an Ancar lord, the breaking of the bond between Hladyr and this city—

The Duke himself—had sent Duran away with only the mildest admonition to not seek out any new Sabirn to befriend.

Vadami lifted his head again, and stared at the image of Hladyr, terrified.

Lord of Shining Light, he prayed. *Give me a sign. Tell me what I should do about Duran.*

Nothing happened. No sign appeared. Vadami's heart felt cold and empty.

Then, of a sudden, a thought. Hladyr *has* answered. *I* know the truth. *I* know the source of the evil—at least where it lodges. . . .

In my own flock.

Remove Duran: then Targheiden and its people might be saved.

He had spent hours upon hours, seasons upon seasons, trying to save Duran's soul. Some souls, it seemed, were destined not to be saved. By anyone.

Hladyr, guide me! I don't know how to kill! I don't want to hurt any of your creatures, and so far Duran himself is surely no demon worshipper—only perilously close. What can I do? What should I do?

The image stared back, aloof, unreachable by any man's prayers.

Duran stood in the center of his bedroom and stared at the baskets he had leaned up against the outer wall. In those baskets he had carefully packed his most precious possessions: his father's notes, his alchemist's tools, his collections of various metals, his vials, beakers, a few of his small alembics. In what space remained, he had tucked in other sentimental odds and ends he could not see leaving behind.

He shook his head at the sight, and looked around at the rest of the room . . . at those things he knew he could not take with him.

There was the bed his parents had brought with them from the Ancahar estate, along with its nightstand. Next to it stood the old bookcase his wife had brought with her when they had married—the only thing of hers he had. They were among the last physical ties he had to those long-dead people he loved the most . . . the last things he could touch, knowing they had touched them, too.

He snarled a curse and turned away. He still could not believe he had agreed to leave town, no matter how desperate the reason: he could not conceive of himself living anywhere else but Targheiden—going—

Where? Old Man had never yet said.

But the danger Old Man had warned him of, what Tutadar had said, were obvious facts. Why the hells had he not been able to see this before? He had known when he had helped Kekoja that he was dealing with fire. He had known.

I suppose, he thought, *it's like everything else in life: we see terrible things; but* nothing *can happen to us.*

It had happened.

He had no choice. If he was going to live out what years he had left of life in peace, if he was going to live at all—he would have to leave the city he loved.

And to do this, he would have to place complete trust in the Sabirn, in Old Man, in Kekoja. All last night, into the small hours, he had wrapped his prized possessions in water-proofed paper: his herbs, medicines, books, and tools. Then, after stowing everything in baskets, he had lowered three of those baskets out the upstairs alley window down into the alleyway and the waiting hands of gods only knew who. He had seen Kekoja, and someone he thought was a woman.

Where the Sabirn had gone with his baskets, he had no clue.

And now, he waited for darkness to fall again, so he could deliver the rest of his possessions into those same shadowy hands.

He began to pace, up and down, past the desk on which he had written so many things. Past the bookcase, nearly empty. Past the table on which his small furnace sat. He reached and ran a hand over the top of that furnace, remembering all the years he had worked in front of it, trying time and again to unlock the secrets of nature and the gods. . . .

The enormity of it all was beginning to sink in. He would never stand in this room again. He would never see the same sights again. Never, as long as he lived, would he be able to walk across the street and spend an evening with his neighbors in the "Cat," spinning out the day's happenings, and listening to homely gossip. He would be severed from everything he had known since he was a boy.

Twice now, in his overturned life. Twice a pilgrim in the world.

It hurt, the thought of it . . . burned in his heart like a brand.

He stopped pacing, and considered the step he was taking. His standing here in his apartment, visually recording the sights and sounds of it for the future, was like being present at someone's deathbed. But it was his own death, so to speak . . . a personal death, an ending of all the things he knew.

But dying at the hands of a mob was no way for an Ancar noble to leave the world. He still had things he wanted to do, wanted to learn, wanted to see. And if the gods had decreed that he would have to do all that somewhere besides Targheiden—

There was no choice.

A crowd had gathered in the street outside Ladirno's apartment, some of them having to stand out in the rain, away from the protection of the second story overhang. Ladirno drew the hood of his cloak up over his head and pushed his way into the back of the crowd. He was taller than most, so he had some kind of view.

It was a ducal herald, on horseback. The fellow looked as miserable as the folk who had assembled to hear him. His royal green cloak was drenched and dark, his wide-brimmed hat drooped, a steady stream of rain pouring off one side. The sight was enough to amuse—except the extraordinary fact of a herald out at all, in streets littered with broken shingle, except the grim, rain-chilled pallor of the faces that nothing would cheer.

"Attention citizens!" The herald's well-trained voice boomed out in the street as thunder rumbled overhead. "I come to you with word from His Grace, Hajun vro Telhern, Duke of Targheiden. These are the Duke's words:

" 'All citizens of Targheiden: measures to bring an end to this freakish weather are being undertaken. His Grace the Duke, assures you he is confident that, by the grace of Hladyr the Shining, there will soon be an end to these storms. He urges you add your prayers to those the priests are offering. Rest assured that every wizard employed by His Grace the Duke is actively involved in turning this evil from the city.' So says His Grace, Duke Hajun vro Telhern."

A mutter ran through the crowd. The herald drew his horse's head about and rode on. Ladirno snorted under his breath. Prayers? One hoped for more than that.

And the Duke's own wizards. All the Duke's wizards trying to do what Mandani and his associate were trying—

But the Duke would not believe—not believe the source of the evil.

As if—Ladirno shuddered—the Duke himself had fallen under some spell.

The rain increased and Ladirno broke into a slow run. The sign outside the "Shoe" was just ahead; swaying in the gusty wind, it offered a haven from the storm, and a chance for much needed companionship.

The rain had driven Vadami into "The Golden Shoe" some time ago, but his cloak was still cold and dripping. He sat at a small table toward the rear of the common room, sipping on a glass of hot mulled wine: such a drink had seemed right on this dreary day.

He had spent as little time as possible in Old Town today, visiting only the critically ill—sharing the Shining One's words with any who would listen. He had dropped in at "The Swimming Cat" for a brief while, and there had found out from Bontido, the potter, that Tutadar had managed to convince Duran to send the Sabirn boy away for a handful of days.

Such news should have made him happy, but Vadami had a certain feeling that as soon as things began to settle down, Duran would have the boy back in his place as a runner, and the neighborhood would be set off again. In all the years he had spoken with Duran, Vadami had not seen any urge on the other man's part to change his ways.

Especially now. Especially considering the influences being brought to bear on him.

He flinched at the measures that might be necessary. He shrank from the bloodshed that might be necessary, to stop this, remove his heretical thoughts from Old Town.

If there is a growth on a healthy body, don't leave it there, maintained an old Temple saying, *cut* it out.

And so he would have to make sure that Duran was removed from Old Town.

He did not want to be responsible for such decisions. He never wanted to harm anyone.

Why then, had the gods saddled him with this problem? He attempted to talk to his Superior—his harried Superior curtly bade him solve his own difficulties with his own district—

I have no time, his Superior had said, awash in papers, awash in petitions from priests in every district—for charity, for dispensations—

One thought Duran might have been called to the priesthood himself: if not for Duran, and Duran's charity, countless people who lived in Old Town might have died. The man had always seemed unconcerned for his own aggrandizement in the world, choosing to help those who lived in poverty. Such a person should have been highly respected by everyone.

Should have been. Such was the Sabirn evil they could turn aside even such an exemplary life.

And make him blaspheme . . .

Memories swept over Vadami—his own schooling, the years of hard work and study spent in preparing him to become a priest.

And to have Duran stand up to him—someone who had not endured the study, the fasting, the grueling examinations—and for Duran to turn the words of the book of the Shining to his own advantage—

No! to *Sabirn* advantage—

That sophistry could not be tolerated. Priests were the only ones qualified to interpret those words. If everyone could choose a meaning for what had been written down in that Book, the cohesive structure of the Temple would be in danger.

For two reasons, therefore, Duran must be punished: his dealings with the Sabirn, and his most dangerous notion that he could interpret the Holy Words.

"Priest Vadami."

He looked up from his wineglass. The alchemist, Ladirno, stood before him, thoroughly soaked.

"May I join you, priest?"

"Aye. Please."

"Damned storm," Ladirno said, tossing his cloak back from his shoulders to let it rest on the chair. He turned to give his order to a waiter, then looked back. "What brings you here, Vadami?"

"The weather. And I needed somewhere to sit a while and think." The waiter brought Ladirno his glass of wine, took the money the alchemist handed over, and disappeared back toward the kitchen. Vadami watched Ladirno—remembering he was Duran's friend.

Was Hladyr leading him?

Was it—guided, this encounter?

"Sor Ladirno. Do you mind if a share a problem with you?"

Ladirno quirked an eyebrow.

"It's about Duran," Vadami said and, as the alchemist's face went dead sober: "He's—gone far past anything we believed. I fear—he is irretrievable."

"In what regard?"

Even now Duran had friends, people who thought him a good man. It worried Vadami, and at the same time made his heart ache to see such loyalty about to be hurt.

"It's true. I fear—he has contact with Sabirn wizards. I fear they've snared him—corrupted him beyond what any reason can deal with. He dares to argue with me. He mocks the Scriptures. He despises reason."

Ladirno shook his head sadly. "I feared so, Father. I did fear it."

"I'm sorry." There was so much respect in this man, so much learning, so much concern, so much . . . stature. "Add to that his consorting with the Sabirn. Something has to be done. I've very sorry. But—"

"Believe me, I do understand. But I fear—" Ladirno lowered his voice further, leaned across the table, whispered: "Father, the Duke himself met these charges. The Duke heard all the evidence—gave him only the slightest of reprimands. Dare I say it to you, Father—dare I say a terrible thing?"

Vadami's heart beat faster and faster.

"I fear—" Ladirno whispered. "I fear the extent of this influence. . . ."

Vadami caught his breath. Someone who understood! Truly understood.

"Dark dealings," Vadami said, "understates it. I'm very much afraid—and I don't want to say this to you who are his friend— Duran's gone, completely sucked into that darkness."

An odd look passed across Ladirno's face, quickly gone. "Hladyr bless, Father. I fear—I fear the same. If you're correct—if I am— then . . . anyone dealing with him could be led astray."

Vadami whispered, "The time has come, Ladirno, when we must move. We must keep Duran's heretical ideas from the rest of the people. We must *remove* his influence from Old Town."

"Remove . . ." Ladirno echoed, fearfully. "You don't mean . . ."

"Sor Ladirno." Vadami shook his head vehemently. "I don't want to hurt Duran. I truly don't. But he has to be *stopped,* removed from influence—before his corruption spreads. Before his blasphemous interpretations of the Shining One's words fall on fertile ground."

"What are you suggesting?"

Vadami took a sip of his wine, set the glass down, and consciously steadied both his mind and his voice. "If we were to run Duran out of Targheiden, we could solve this problem. As a weapon then, as a channel for darkness—he would be useless to them."

"Run him out of . . . ?" Ladirno rubbed his chin. "What about his friends? What about all those poor folk he's helped? Don't you think they'll prevent such a thing from happening?"

"I've taken that into consideration. Maybe if the weather was its usual fine self his friends would back him up. But no longer. More and more people are becoming convinced the Sabirn are behind the storms."

"Are you?"

"Is there another answer? They hate us. They deal in the darkest of dark arts. If they have wizards drawing directly from the demons of darkness, who's to say *what* they can do—with an Ancar to spread their poison?"

"I hear you. But, Duran . . . I can't believe *he's* wrapped up in such acts."

"He is. He's totally involved. How can he not be, seeing the Sabirn as he does? A rotten apple will spoil an entire basketful. Everyone knows that. What we have to do is remove that apple *before* it rots the others."

"Why are you telling me this?"

"For the same reason I spoke to you before about Duran. You're his friend. I need your help in getting him out of town without hurting him. I was hoping you'd have some idea on how that could be accomplished."

Ladirno sat for a long while in silence, studying his glass held in his hands. Vadami's heart went out to the alchemist, so obviously torn between friendship and a sense of what was right.

"The people are disturbed, you're correct about that," Ladirno said at last. "Did you hear the ducal heralds?"

"Aye. In Temple Square. The crowds—just stood in the rain. . . ."

"Father, the citizens of Targheiden are ready to take up stones.

Running Duran out of town could get dangerous. If anything starts—one can't say how far it would go, with what bloodshed."

Vadami nodded. "If we think this through carefully, there's a chance the folk of Old Town will just want to persuade him away. To frighten him. He's done too much good there for them to want to do him bodily harm."

"I don't know. We'll have to be *very* careful. Have you ever seen a mob in action?"

"No . . ."

"Well, let me tell you . . . you want to pick your leaders. You want to pick them extremely carefully. They should be respected enough to maintain control. They should be respectable people— his neighbors, his friends—who, however they may be frightened right now—will not want to hurt a longtime neighbor. Or stir up wider disturbance."

Vadami rubbed his forehead. "Wise words. I think I have the very person in mind who could talk to Duran's neighbors. She's a seamstress and she runs her shop right next to Duran's. She's been trying to talk him out of this fascination with the Sabirn for years—a good woman, Sor Ladirno . . . she believes in the right things."

"You think she can stir Duran's neighbors up to a point where they'll act? And keep it going? Responsibly?"

"Aye. They're already riled up. Considerably. It won't take much to convince them they'd be better off without Duran around."

Ladirno slowly shook his head, a look of sadness in his eyes. "I was hoping I'd never see such a day," he said, his voice weary. "Duran's always been . . . a little strange. Every one of his colleagues has noticed this. Some of us have even spoken to him about it."

"Hladyr will bless your intent."

"We so hoped he would listen to us, to the Duke, to the Duke's advisors. What we didn't count on was the man's flare for words, and the Duke's leniency." Ladirno smiled crookedly. "But then it's that bond between Ancar. Perhaps that's why Duran wasn't punished as he should have been."

"Perhaps. I pray so."

"If it has to be, it has to be. Duran can't go on working against— honest folk. That's for sure."

"Then you think what I'm planning is right? That it can work?"

"Aye. You have all the arguments on your side, Father. After all, *you're* the priest . . . you're the one to counsel these people—to counsel all of us. And I think it can work, if you're very careful. My advice still stands: use this seamstress. Only agitate Duran's neighbors as well—be sure to involve as many of his true friends as you can gain—that way there'll be no question of sincere purpose in this—"

A warm feeling filled Vadami's heart. He was finally taking some action. He was given a chance to save an entire section of town from practitioners of the dark arts, a chance to redeem Old Town from heresies and to preserve the Scriptures against attack—surely Hladyr had to bless that—in many ways.

That was why the god had left him in this dismal post—for Hladyr's greater glory, for his ultimate good.

"Hladyr bless, Sor Ladirno," Vadami said, signing him. "And prosper you and yours. Hladyr has used you to advise me—though you're Duran's friend—and friendship is nothing to be scoffed at—you know what is right and just; and Hladyr will reward you."

"In my own humble way, I try," Ladirno replied.

Now that he had an active plan at hand, one that the alchemist agreed was viable, Vadami could hardly sit still. He gathered up his cloak, slipped it over his shoulders, and stood.

"A thousand thanks, Sor Ladirno," he said, bowing slightly. "You'll be in my prayers. I'll always remember your advice, your patience, and your intelligent suggestions."

Ladirno looked up, his face very serious. "Father, I'm sure you're doing what's right. You're being far more gentle in your solution than any other law might be. Only be careful. Guard yourself."

Full shelves—and hundreds of empty clay pots—kept the shop looking normal. Duran stood, hands on hips, and surveyed what was left downstairs, what he could not take with him. He had delivered nearly all of his drugs, herbs, and medicines to the alley window, only leaving behind enough to do the absolutely necessary routine business from his shop.

But few customers had stopped by. With the continuing rain and wind, his lack of business was not surprising. And since Tutadar had told the neighbors the Sabirn boy was going to be gone for a few days, it should seem natural that deliveries and solicitations should stop, and that the shop would settle to a quieter routine.

One hoped—that that was the perception on the street, at least.

But, thank the gods, the last of his belongings would be smuggled out tonight, storm or no storm. When he had gone to the "Cat" for his midday meal, the looks he had received from his neighbors were not—neighborly.

That was certainly part of the strange sense of urgency that filled his mind. And part of it, he was sure, was a desire to be done with this: now that he had decided to leave Targheiden, he wanted nothing more than to do it quickly—like any parting: the longer it drew on, the more painful it began to be; and the more a man tried to settle his mind—the more the old place began to seem irrelevant and strangely disturbing to him.

Dog, too, seemed keenly aware something strange was in the wind. As Duran's books, papers, medicines, and alchemist's tools had disappeared into the baskets, Dog had walked from place to place, sniffing the emptiness left behind. More than once he had turned his head, looked at Duran in canine puzzlement, and whined softly.

He was taking Dog with him—damned sure. Dog was going to be of great comfort on the road and—wherever else . . . the only living contact Duran would have of what his neighborhood had once been like. But he could not tell Dog that; and perhaps Dog—having experienced loneliness before—could not trust in things.

Duran sighed, scanned the shelves again for forgotten details, things overlooked, things that he might still regret. There was nothing. The shelves with their false, empty containers, stood as a reminder to him of how empty his life had become.

The past was dead, the present was dying.

Only the future seemed of import.

✧ CHAPTER TWELVE ✧

"Can you believe it?" Wellhyrn fairly shouted, pacing Ladirno's rug. "That damned man has *got* to have more than one wizard backing him! There's no other way to explain it!"

Ladirno leaned back in his chair, watching Wellhyrn sputter. His young colleague had burst in not long after he had gotten home, his handsome face red with rage and his hands clenched as if he were prepared to strike out at anyone who got in his way.

"Calm, calm," Ladirno said. "Be patient."

"Patient!" Wellhyrn cried, facing him. "We're near the end of our resources. Two, *two* wizards, who don't come cheap! And from what Mandani's spy tells him—nothing's working!"

"He has his eye on Duran, then."

"Evidently he's been to that inn for his midday meal. The spy says that it was the same as yesterday. Duran seemed quiet, but not moody—showing no signs of bespelling, nothing in the world *wrong!* What in Dandro's hells are we going to do? We can't afford to put *another* wizard on him!"

"We may not have to do anything at all," Ladirno said, taking a sip of his second glass of wine. "I think the little priest might have solved our problems."

"Vadami?" Wellhyrn was incredulous. "That priest?"

"Aye. I just happened into the 'Shoe.' Ran into Vadami. He's utterly convinced Duran's damned, that he's lost his soul to darkness by dealing with the Sabirn."

"So? We tried that argument in court, and it didn't get us anywhere."

"This isn't the Duke we're dealing with, Hyrn. This is a young, ambitious priest, who's *very* pious, and *very* interested in doing something that will draw that piety to the attention of his superiors."

"What has that to do with our situation?"

"He still thinks I'm Duran's friend," Ladirno said, "and I'm not going to dissuade him of that fantasy. He told me today that he's reached the end of his patience, that Duran's beginning to corrupt the minds of Old Town." Ladirno leaned closer and lowered his voice. "He plans to run Duran out of town."

Few things ever caught Wellhyrn at a loss for words, but this did. Ladirno found satisfaction at his colleague's stunned expression.

"He's what?"

"Planning on running Duran out of town," Ladirno repeated.

"Are you certain?"

"Aye, I'm certain. Vadami's going to talk to that shrew who has her shop next to Duran's. He seems to think she's the most pious woman he knows."

"The seamstress?" Wellhyrn curled his lip. "She's nothing but a gossip and a troublemaker. She's had that reputation for years."

"That may be. But this time, all her gossiping and trouble-making will benefit us. She's the one after Duran; she'll get the entire neighborhood stirred up against him." He took another sip of wine. "Trust me, Wellhyrn. Not everything requires wide actions. We'll be rid of Duran without having to lift a finger ourselves."

"And without any suspicion coming to roost in our nest."

"Exactly.—I'm only sorry if the Duke's heir is receiving treatments for the pox from Duran, there's no chance that Duran can finish. He won't have a chance to save Brovor's life— personally. But there are other doctors. And we can discover who."

Wellhyrn smiled coldly. "That's beautiful. We couldn't have thought up anything that would have worked as well. But do you think Duran's neighbors will act? After all, he's been a well-liked man. And that woman—"

Ladirno shook his head. "He's taken the Sabirn side against them—what do you expect they'll do? What any pious folk would do—and they are that, Hyrn, they are that. They don't know statecraft from hogswill—but they do know their own pocketbooks. Trust that."

"Then our wizards *are* working."

"Perhaps. Perhaps you have someone else to thank—but let's wait a day or two. At least until we know for sure that Duran's gone. He may have some protection—protection of a sort we'd rather not deal with. It won't hurt to keep ill-wishing him."

"It's money we can ill afford," Wellhyrn pointed out.

"Let me tell you—friend. You involved us in this. *I've* found our solution. I want you to remember that."

Wellhyrn gave him a hard-jawed stare. "You—"

"The storms, friend. You want to know why our wizards aren't having any luck. Perhaps it's because Duran *is* involved up to his neck. Perhaps it's because he *does* have protections—from wizards the Duke's own wizards can't beat. Personally I don't want to *touch* this mess—but we're in it; and being in it, we'd damned well better put somebody else between us and the trouble—somebody with special protections: let the Temple fight this thing."

"A petty priest."

"A very zealous priest. Duran's human. What's human has soft spots. There are things he cares for, things he cares about—that's where we can get him. That's where this priest can get him. *We* don't have to touch the situation. Whatever black arts are behind him—they'll lose him. They'll lose the only reason they could possibly have to pay attention to *us*, do you follow me, Wellhyrn? Have you thought—if Duran is protected like this—what he could do if he turned those wizards' attention on *us?*"

Wellhyrn's eyes glinted in the lamplight. "So we use the priest, the priest uses the woman, the woman—runs that whoreson Duran right out of town. And *his* notion of who's responsible has to be his own neighbors."

"Exactly. You see—I do think of things. Slowly, but I do think."

"Gods! I'd give a lot to be there."

"Which is precisely where we're *not* going to be. We want not the slightest hint that we had anything to do with this!"

"Aye, aye. But our wizards can do a little something to speed things up."

A cold shiver ran down Ladirno's spine. "What are you thinking about?"

"Nothing that can be traced back to us. I'll make sure of that. What I have in mind will simply make the neighbors a bit more— nervous about Duran."

"You're not going to do anything illegal, are you?"

"I won't answer that. This way, you won't know."

"Dammit, Hyrn! Think things through! Just give it time, let things work the way they will—let the priest handle it!"

"Because I want this nailed down," Wellhyrn said, a cruel smile twisting his lips. "And I want to make sure this works. Damn Duran and his airs. An Ancar noble. I'm five times the man he'll *ever* be."

Ladirno met and held his colleague's eyes. "Don't let revenge get you in trouble. Don't. Stay away from this!"

"Pfft. You're getting jumpy as an old woman. I won't have anything to do with it."

"You've got a cruel mind," Ladirno said, eyeing the smile on Wellhyrn's face. "Damned cruel."

Wellhyrn leaned back in his chair, and lifted his wineglass in a graceful hand. "Oh, aye, I do. And isn't it wonderful?"

The rain had momentarily stopped; the sound of it running from the eaves down into rainbarrels was loud in the comparative silence of Old Town.

Vadami walked slowly through the cloud-covered twilight, his eyes roving around the street. He was cloaked against more than the rain: it would do him no good to be noticed right now. He walked till he saw Zeldezia's sign swaying in the wind, and made for her door with all the stealth he could manage.

Duran's door was shut, which either meant he was sequestered inside, or that he had gone across the street to the inn. Good, Vadami thought. He wanted no contact with the man tonight—just a word with the good woman.

The evening weather was warm. Zeldezia's door stood cracked open, and lamplight spilled a gold sliver onto the wet cobbles.

"Zeldezia!" he called out softly, and rapped softly at the door. "It's Father Vadami. Are you there?"

He heard footsteps, and the door opened. Zeldezia opened it wider, swept her skirts out of his way, dropped an anxious little curtsy—pleased to see him, worshipful of his office: she always was. "Father! Come in, Father, please, an' get yourself out of the weather!"

Vadami entered the small shop. As always, he could have eaten off the floor. Everything shone, from the wooden floor to the tables laden with sewing, to the good brass lamps hanging from the ceiling.

"An' what can I do for you?" Zeldezia said, offering him one of two chairs that sat by a table. "Can I get you some cakes? Some wine?"

"No, no," he said, sitting down. With a rustle of her skirts, she took the chair opposite. "I've come to you out of concern, daughter—perhaps for a little help in a situation. I need someone—brave and committed to Hladyr's commandments. I think you're that woman."

Her dark eyes glittered. "Ask, an' if I can, I'll help. How could anyone turn you down, Father?"

"It's about Duran."

Her face hardened and her mouth curved down into a deep frown. "Duran! If I hadn't owned this shop long's I have, I'd move! I don't want no dealin's with 'im, Father, I truly don't, I avoid 'im as I can—"

Vadami leaned close briefly and patted Zeldezia's hand. "I know, I know, daughter. And surely you're not the only one. I fear—I fear there's worse than we thought."

"Oh?" she sat up straighter in her chair, her hands nervously playing with the tongue of her fine leather belt. Her eyes were frightened. "What could be worse?"

"Actual practice of the dark arts."

"Next door?" Zeldezia wailed.

He kept his voice calm, tried to assure her by his steady gaze that he was doing what he thought was best. "That's what we have to stop, Zeldezia. For your sake—for the sake of everyone involved."

"You know he sent that Sab kid somewheres?" she asked. "But, mind you, that kid'll be back, an' we don't know what devilment he's off to—or who he's dealin' with! Father, we got to do somethin'."

"I know. That's why we have to break up this Sabirn nest, Zeldezia. I don't want to hurt Duran, and I don't think you do. But for the safety of all concerned, for the souls of the folk hereabout— Duran's already lost, Zeldezia, and he's spreading his corruption. He's perverted holy Scripture. He's blasphemed. All these things he done—but what his Sabirn allies have done—"

Zeldezia signed herself nervously.

"They're aiming at the Duke himself, Zeldezia. It's power they want. They're *using* Duran's Ancar blood to find and curse things they couldn't touch. He's the canker that will spread, spread through all this town—"

"What can we do?"

"Get him out of this neighborhood! Out of Targheiden!"

She sniffed quietly, gnawed her lip, twisted at the fringes of her shawl. "I been thinkin' the same thing for a long time now, Father. I been worried, oh, I been worried! But Duran's got hisself some good friends. He got Tutadar and Ithar, two of the most respectable folk in this neighborhood. Gettin' them to go along with your plan ain't going to be easy."

"Maybe there are some we can't trust. Maybe there are some we shouldn't tell. But surely there are those that will do Hladyr's work. . . ."

Zeldezia nodded vigorously. "If you bless us, Father, if you tell them yourself that the Sabirn are behind all this wickedness, if you say it—aye!" She squared her shoulders. "Some of 'em may not like me, but I got a good reputation! I make more money than a lot of 'em. I'm a respectable woman. An' with you, Father—"

Vadami nodded. "Exactly. Exactly. Go to your neighbors. For their soul's sakes."

"I will! I will, Father! Bless us!"

"Hladyr bless you," Vadami said. "You're a good woman, and a pious soul. You have to be discreet."

"Aye, aye, I know who to talk to, an' I know what words to use. I done it before an' they listened. They only got to look around 'em and lissen to the thunder. I'll do it, Father, we'll see there ain't no more sneakin' Sabs among us. . . ."

Duran walked into the "Cat," ignoring the coldness from his neighbors; Tutadar was one of the few even to acknowledge his presence. Duran sighed softly and continued to his table.

He knew Tutadar had spread the word that he was going to send Kekoja off for a few days; he had hoped that would calm things.

It seemed they had miscalculated. Badly.

Several gloomy fellows sat in a far corner of the common room, merchants, by the cut of their tunics, harbor traffic—which could not be happy. They looked to be Sacarreans, most likely, from the looks of them. Probably in town to trade their spices for grain and metals mined to the north. If that was so, they had been marooned here in Targheiden for days now, unwilling to chance passage across a storm-ridden sea.

Damn the weather. Damn all this wretched summer, its storms, its ill humors, its frustrations and its angers: in any better season no one would have faulted him hiring Kekoja to serve as his runner. The customers Kekoja had taken physics to had not complained. Several of Duran's neighbors—Ithar and Edfin the baker—had been happy to see Duran making a good profit.

That was the way life had always been in Old Town. When one of your neighbors was doing well, you wished him all the best of luck, hoping some of it would rub off on you. Good business in one trade had a habit of begetting good business in another.

But the weather had soured that. For good.

And changed everything.

He looked up as Lalada came to his table with a mug of ale. She did not meet his eyes; she merely set the mug down on the table, took his order for breaded fish, and walked away, dumb as a post. Duran watched her go, a sadness creeping into his heart. He had cured the bad humor that had afflicted her head, and she no longer sniffed and sneezed. That should have been enough to convince her she was safe in his presence. Obviously not.

Then the thought reached him that this might be the last evening he ever spent in "The Swimming Cat." Suddenly, everything took on a new importance. He stared at the old wooden tabletop, gouged here and there by knives. He heard the squeak of his chair as he changed position. Everything—the flickering lamplight, the sawdust spread on the floor, the two grey cats who slept in a far corner, the sound of muted conversation—seemed magnified. The relative calm of the common room, the friendly atmosphere that was usually present . . . all those things would dwell only in his memory.

He rubbed his eyes. He *was* growing old. He cheerfully admitted it. And, as the proverb assured him, it was far easier to teach a young dog new tricks than an old one set in his ways. A piece of his life—a major piece of his life was going away from him—or he was going from it—and he was less interested in looking to the future than in looking at what he was losing. . . .

Was that not the attribute of age? He was forty-five: that should have been still young. But it was late to be starting over. It was late to lose everything. There were not enough vital years left— to build a life on.

So what did one do? Exist. Exist was all, without a past, with only a dozen or so baskets holding his whole damn life—

And no interest in where he was after that.

Maybe it was better to stay, fight it out, die here, if that was what it came to—

Except the books—

"Duran."

He looked up. Tutadar had brought his breaded fish; the innkeeper set the plate out before Duran, then pulled out a chair to sit down facing him.

"Thanks, Tut." Duran began cutting up the fish, and lowered his voice. "I hoped the neighbors would at least be easier with the boy out of town. What's going on?"

"I don't know," Tutadar said, crossing his arms on the table. "Hail this morning. Warehouse roof collapsed, folk goin' about the Slough in boats, f'gods' sake. That's gettin' close to home, you know what I mean?" He nodded toward the front door. "Nobody been givin' Old Man a copper. Not a one. Maybe I misjudged everyone. I'm sorry. I did hope they'd look on you kinder. But folks is scared. Folks is scared an' mad an' they got nowhere to send it."

"Tut, I've lived here, I've dealt here, I've barely kept my head above water for years. I get the kid and I do—well—for the first time in my life. Is that evil? Is there any evil influence in that?"

Tut shrugged uncomfortably.

"Today I only had six customers—and them up from the harbor. Not my neighbors. I don't understand that, Tut."

Tut shrugged and never met his eyes. "Don't know. Don't know, it's what I said, folks is just nervous. I'm sorry about the kid. I am. You know it ain't me holds agin him. I don't want t' see you hurt, Duran!"

Duran stared at his friend. He hated pretending this night was like any other night. He wanted more than anything to confide in Tutadar, tell him where he was going, make some tie he could keep. . . .

But he dared not. For the first time in years, a hint of distrust had entered Duran's heart, even toward Tut. Even as he despised the feeling, he recognized prudence when he saw it.

"Well, so we keep our heads down. What happens next?"

"Hard tellin'." Tutadar looked ceilingward. "Long's the weather stays bad, I don't think you got a chance in Dandro's hells of keepin' 'em happy with you."

"Tut, I want you to listen to me carefully. If anything happens to me, I—"

"Don't you go talkin' like that, Duran!" the innkeeper interrupted. "Nothin' going to happen to you if *I* have anythin' to say 'bout it. Or Ithar, for that matter."

"Thank you, Tut. And I know you mean it. But hear me through, if for nothing else than amusement. If anything should happen to me, I want you to take care of Dog. He knows you and trusts you, and he makes a good guard. And sell what I own, down to the shop itself, and give the money to some young doctor who might want to make a few trips to Old Town."

"Duran." There was a warning in Tutadar's voice. "Don't you bring no bad luck on yourself by talkin' this way."

"All right." Duran let a smile touch his lips. "Just you and Ithar keep in mind that you've been good neighbors all these years. That I've been proud to know you."

Tutadar blinked rapidly. "That's somethin', ain't it, when an Ancar noble says he been proud to know Old Town rats like us."

"This Ancar noble's one of those rats, too, courtesy of the old duke."

Thunder rumbled loudly. Duran and Tutadar both flinched.

"I confess," Tutadar muttered, "I don't trust these storms no more. They been gettin' real nasty.—An' I know you ain't goin' to agree, an' I know you're going to hate me for sayin' it, but I still think Sabirn're involved somehow."

"I can't seem to convince you, can I?"

Tut shook his head. "Now, I *will* admit they ain't all bad. I never did mind Old Man. An' that kid who been workin' for you, he never been nothin' but polite to me. But that don't take into consideration the rest of 'em. I can't. I can't like 'em, I can't deal with 'em. . . ."

"I wish I could make you understand," Duran said. "I hope someday you'll find a reason to believe that because a man's different doesn't make him a bad fellow—just different."

"They're *too* different. They're spooky."

Duran smiled and took another sip of his ale. "Enough of this gloomy talk. I don't' want to go home with a bad taste in my mouth. I like you too much, Tut."

Thunder rumbled again. "Sounds like you're going to go home with rain on your head. 'Less you want to stay 'round here."

"I'm afraid not." Duran sighed, gulped down the rest of his ale. "I think I'll be going to bed early tonight."

"Probably not a bad idea." The innkeeper shoved his chair back from the table and stood. "You take care of yourself, hear? An' don't you go givin' me any money for your fish. The meal's on me."

The sound of a rock thrown against the shutter of his apartment woke Duran from a sound sleep. He sat up in bed, rubbed his eyes, and stood. Fully dressed, he walked through the darkness to the back window, and threw open the shutters.

It was raining again—which actually reassured him, for no one in his right mind would be out on the streets in this downpour.

"Hsst! Duran!"

Kekoja's voice. Duran could make out the Sabirn lad standing directly below the window, along with another man. Duran waved, and felt his way back across the room, while rain blew in on the gusts.

The last few small items were packed—everything in four remaining baskets. He lifted one, grunting slightly under its weight: the last of his books and writings, this one. Walking back to the opened window, he carefully balanced the basket on the sill, tying the rope about it for a sling.

"Hssst!" He saw Kekoja lift his head, hand held over his eyes to shield off the rain. "Heavy!"

Kekoja waved and Duran eased the basket out of the window, bracing himself against the wall below it with his knees and feet. Gently as he could, he lowered the basket into Kekoja's hands, then watched Kekoja untie the long rope. The other man took up the basket on his shoulder and trotted off into the darkness and falling rain.

Duran hauled up the rope, returned to his baskets, and readied the next to be lowered—a lighter one: it contained all his clothes, his blankets, and what linen he possessed. He lowered the basket out of the window, Kekoja untied it, shouldered it and with a wave, disappeared around the corner into the deserted street. It would be some time before the two Sabirn returned, so Duran dragged one of the chairs over to the window, sat down in the water-laden draft, and stared off into the darkness. Lightning flashed overhead, subdued, and the thunder that followed, a gentle rumble. Thank Hladyr. Conditions could not have been better for the task at hand. Maybe something was going right. Maybe the gods did not disapprove what he was doing.

They showed no lights: the bedroom was dark. Even so, he saw the long, narrow room in his mind's eye as if the sun were shining. It was his last night here. The last time he would sleep in his own bed. The last time he would listen to the homely creaks and groans of the building—*his* home, his shop—

A wave of sadness filled his heart. If only things had turned out differently. If only his neighbors could see that the Sabirn were little different than themselves.

If only. If only Hladyr could come down from heaven and walk among men again: it would take a miracle of the same magnitude to turn the hearts of his neighbors.

He heard the scuff of steps on wet cobble. He stood, looked out to see Kekoja and his companion returned from whatever hole they had nearby. He prepared the next basket, his alchemist's tools, mainly vials and beakers.

"Fragile!" he whispered down. "Glass!"

Kekoja received the basket: his partner took it. The last, then. Duran hauled the rope up, tied it to the last basket—and this was the hardest to see go—this contained his father's weapons, the sword, the daggers, all had been passed down from father to son for generations of Ancahar noblemen. Heirlooms of the heart—his mother's carefully wrapped jewelry: he had never sold them—no matter how desperate things became.

Maybe things would have been different if he had. With those jewels, he could have bought a far better shop and not lived so near to the edge of poverty.

Maybe.

The sword, the jewels, his father's notes—all that was irreplaceable.

"Hssst!" He saw Kekoja lift his head. "You sleep on this one, hear? Take care of it."

562 The Sword of Knowledge

Kekoja lifted his hands, received the basket—and the rope, this time.

Duran stood in the window after they had gone—realizing suddenly he was standing in a house bereft of everything he owned . . . everything that was valuable to him. All of it carried away to gods know what destination in the hands of the Sabirn. And he had to trust them. He had no choice. He was empty-handed now. They had everything.

Name-brothers, Old Man had said. Old Man had talked about trust. About friendship. But so had Tut. So had his neighbors—once.

He sighed and drew the shutters. There. It was done. He could not turn back now; he had committed himself to the most unsettling future he had ever chosen in his life.

"Oh, gods!" He rested his eyes against his hand in the dark, shook his head. Brovor. Brovor would have to seek another doctor to treat his pox. He *had* to do that. He had only a few treatments left, but it was vitally important he receive them. Brovor had to understand that—and he dared not, *dared* not send any message to him.

There was Mother Garan. Who would help her? Thunder rumbled distantly. The rain poured down outside the window, the sound of it hitting the roofs and pavement, unnatural, malevolently persistent.

At least Kekoja had gotten the baskets away. Duran thanked the gods for this one small favor.

And prayed for Brovor's good sense, and an old woman's comfort.

At this late hour, in this downpour, the few souls on the streets walked briskly to their destinations. A fool would be standing here in the rain: but Ladirno did—in the shadows of the alley across the street from Wellhyrn's rooms. He could not sleep. His instincts, his curiosity, had finally driven him out at this ungodly time of night to take up this watch—

All because of the threat Wellhyrn had made.

Ladirno had no idea what Wellhyrn proposed to do to Duran, but if it *was* against the law, he wanted to know. He had suspected Wellhyrn in the past of shady dealings he had never been able to prove—but in this, for various reasons—

This time if Wellhyrn was being a fool, he fully meant to disassociate himself—leave Wellhyrn to twist in the wind, if that was the case.

He froze, leaned closer against the wall: a man approached Wellhyrn's building, obviously taking his time and appearing slightly drunk. Ladirno glanced up at the doorway, and saw Wellhyrn step outside. Head bowed, a purposeful gait to his walk, Wellhyrn left the doorway and stepped directly into the other man's path. The two of them collided, and the drunk staggered, nearly knocked from his feet. Ladirno held his breath, hoping to hear something . . . anything.

But no words were exchanged, aside from a muffled curse or two. Wellhyrn reached out to steady the drunk and quickly dropped something into the man's hand. Ladirno drew a sharp breath. The lamps which burned at the doorway to Wellhyrn's apartments lent a fair amount of light to the street, and in this light he had seen the glint of gold.

The drunk snarled something at Wellhyrn, appeared to get his directions totally mixed up, then lurched off again, this time headed down the hill toward Old Town.

Wellhyrn glanced up and down the street, while Ladirno held his breath, plastered against the side of the building and praying his colleague would not look his way.

Some bored god must have heard his prayer, for Wellhyrn turned around and went back inside.

For a long moment, Ladirno stood shivering against the wall. What was it that Wellhyrn had paid this man for? He had seen the flash of at least one gold donahri, sufficient price for a murder in some quarters.

A sour taste filled Ladirno's mouth. Ladirno spat into the street, gathered his cloak tighter, and hurried off into the dark down the alley.

A bell rang somewhere. A distant bell, muffled and indistinct. The sound of it filtered into Duran's sleep and woke him from a dream of rain.

He sat up in bed, his heart pounding. He listened, unsure whether the bell had rung only in his mind, or in the real world.

No. There it was again—the "Cat's" bell—that only rang for theft and fire—

Duran sprang from bed, and ran toward the front window. Flinging open the shutters, he stared down into the street.

The rain had stopped. Torchlight from the "Cat" lit up the street, people running—

But not only that light—

"Fire!" someone called—Ithar, he thought. "Get buckets!"

Duran cursed aloud, lit his lamp with shaking hands, flung his clothes on, grabbed the lamp and rushed down his stairs—Dog was barking now, frantically. Duran set down the lamp, grabbed his cloak, unlocked the door with trembling fingers.

He stepped into a scene of chaotic motion. People ran here and there, searching for buckets. He could see the flames now, and his heart lurched. The fire burned up against the walls of Zeldezia's shop. Duran glanced around and found Tutadar. The innkeeper was standing in the center of the street, directing his fellow neighbors to various rain barrels, instructing them where buckets were kept.

"When did it start?" Duran yelled over the commotion.

"Don't know! But it's burnin' good!"

Duran stared at the fire. The blaze was impossible—in a puddle-filled alleyway, debris soaked and sodden—

"Dammit!" He ran to Tutadar's side. "Don't throw water on it, Tut! Call back the buckets!"

The innkeeper stared at Duran as if he were mad.

"It's an oil fire, Tut! For gods' sake, don't throw water on it! Can't you see? It's too damned wet for anything but oil to burn like that!"

Tutadar narrowed his eyes and looked back at the fire.

"Wait!" he bellowed, his voice carrying over the yelling of the neighbors. "No water! You hear me? *No water!*"

"Get mud, get dirt. Flour! Something that will smother the flames!" Duran glanced around. "Find Bontido. He's got to have something like that around his shop!"

Several of the neighbors were beating at the fire with heavy blankets now. Someone ran off with Bontido toward the potter's shop. Zeldezia stood in the street, her hands clasped, wailing in a shrill voice. A man ran back from the inn, struggling under the weight of a heavy bag of flour.

"Hurry!" Tutadar hollered. "All of it! On the fire!"

The man approached Zeldezia's shop, held the bag firmly, one hand keeping it open, and began tossing flour onto the fire. The flames fell back some, but did not die.

"Move aside!"

Duran stepped back as Bontido and two other men pushed a manure wagon full of soaked stable-dirt toward the shop. One of the men grabbed a shovel and started tossing the dirt onto the flames. Duran watched, his heart pounding raggedly. How the hells had an oil fire got started?

Who would have done such a thing to Zeldezia?

A ragged cheer went up from the neighbors as the fire guttered and slowly began to die. Duran drew a deep breath, not surprised to find his knees shaking.

A hand landed on his shoulder. He turned to face Tut. "That'n was set," Tut said grimly. "Ain't no accident."

Duran nodded, still shaking.

"Damn you, Duran!" Zeldezia's shrill voice penetrated the voices of the crowd. "This is all *your* fault! Sabirn-lover! They witched my shop, they tried to burn me in my house!"

"Gods," Tut murmured, holding tight to Duran's shoulder.

The seamstress elbowed her way through a crowd grown suddenly silent.

"You brought this here fire on me!" she raged. "You an' them damned Sabirn!"

"Calm down, Zeldezia," Ithar said, reaching out to take her arm.

She yanked away from the smith, her eyes narrowed to slits. "You think I don't know! That I can't guess! You—"

"Zeldezia, shut up!" Tut roared, leaving Duran to step between. "You shut your damned mouth! You been nothin' but trouble the past few days, an' now you're accusin' the man who had enough sense to know what that damned fire was, and how to fight it!"

Zeldezia backed up a step. "What d'you mean—he knowed what it was?"

"It ain't sorcery! It's an oil fire. If we'd poured water on it, we've made it worse. You got Duran t' thank we saw it in time!"

"He *knowed* what it was! How'd he know? Oil don't get on the side of a body's building by fallin' from the sky!"

"For the gods' sake, Zeldezia, if he'd started that damned fire, he wouldn't've tried to stop it—"

Zeldezia spat at Tut's feet. "The Sabs started that fire—probably that damn boy's skulked back t' get me, near burned the block down! An' you, Duran, you're guilty along with 'em! Ever since I started tryin' to change your ways, you been settin' 'em on me— They wanted to burn me out, that's what, they know what I know—that they been witchin' the weather, that it's them plottin' agin us—"

Duran kept silent. Anything he said at this point would only make matters worse.

Tears were running down Zeldezia's cheeks now. "You low-down scum . . . you Sabirn-lover! I *hate* you for this! An' you'll pay, Duran! You'll pay!"

She spun around, ran into her shop, and slammed the door.

For a long moment the street was silent, so silent Duran could hear the water dripping from the eaves.

"She's crazy," someone muttered. "Damned woman's crazy."

"Maybe not," somebody else said.

Tut gripped Duran's shoulder. "Duran, I think you'd best go back inside. Hear?"

Duran nodded, turned, and walked slowly to his shop. Dog stood in the lighted doorway, his tail wagging slowly now that the noise had died down.

Duran shut the door behind him, leaned up against the counter, staring off into the shadows.

Someone had deliberately started that fire.

Kekoja? Gods, no, no. Not Kekoja, not Old Man—not fire, that could have burned Zeldezia alive.

Who would do such a thing? Who in the world would do a thing like that?

A jar was out of place on the counter. It weighted a paper.

It said, in a boy's uneven letters, *The river gate. Tomorrow sundown. Fire not ours.*

✧ CHAPTER THIRTEEN ✧

It came down to waiting now—only waiting—wondering over and over again where Old Man was, why they waited at all—

Duran sat on his stool and listened to the work going on next door. Since morning, people had been over at Zeldezia's shop, removing the burned and scorched manure and flour, and washing down the wall with—the gods knew—no shortage of water.

He stayed to his shop, kept the door cracked—indecisive between the pretense of being open for business and the fear of his neighbors.

Mother Garan was the only visitor, desperate, on the edge of one of her headaches.

He gave her the whole pot of willow-tea, he held her gnarled hands and impressed on her as gravely as he could the danger of too much use.

He scared her, perhaps. She looked as if he had.

He wanted not to charge her, wanted to give her some money to go to an uptown doctor—but he knew her pride; and he feared she might spread that story.

Zeldezia had spent little time in her shop. Duran had seen her wandering up and down the street, whispering to various people, and throwing hateful looks in the direction of his door. Gods alone knew what she was telling everyone, what charges she was making.

He could not believe that Zeldezia had any enemies who would take the time *and* the risk to set a fire.

Could it have been someone after him, confusing his shop with Zeldezia's? He shuddered at the thought. Whoever had been the target—

If it had a bit more time to burn, it might have caught the second story on fire, and then gods help everyone up and down the block.

Now, seated on his stool, waiting as the day drifted on to afternoon—waiting, and not knowing—he simply hoped.

Tonight—he and Dog would take a walk. Lock the door to delay anyone finding him gone—

And just walk away.

"Have you seen the priest today?" Wellhyrn asked, swirling the wine around in his glass, his legs stretched comfortably before him. It was Ladirno's apartment. It was mid-afternoon.

"No. And neither have you, I suppose."

Wellhyrn shook his head. There was a curious expression on the younger man's face this afternoon, a look of smug, predatory satisfaction. Ladirno had heard the news from Old Town already, and it took no great wit to add things up.

"I know what you did last night," Ladirno said.

A look of surprise widened Wellhyrn's eyes.

"What—do you mean?"

"There was a fire at the seamstress's shop. A very suspicious fire."

"Bad luck, I suppose."

"Luck had nothing to do with it. You're very smart, Hyrn— but *not* smart enough, not smart enough to cover your tracks— not smart enough to know me. I'm not as stupid as you think I am."

"I never thought you stupid," Wellhyrn protested.

"You made mistakes. You said yesterday you were going to make Duran suffer. As happens—you've pushed a situation already about to move. But let me tell you, friend, there's someone knows how that fire started. Your reputation is in those hands. That's a *fool*, Wellhyrn. And I'm not a fool. I won't stand for it."

For a long moment, Wellhyrn stared at Ladirno. He blinked twice and then smiled. "You did that with remarkably few clues, Ladir. I'm amazed."

"You aren't upset. You aren't even upset."

Wellhyrn lifted a velvet shoulder. Gold chain glinted in the light.

"Fool," Ladirno said. "You're brilliant, Hyrn, in your work, but leave politics alone. In that you are most definitely a fool."

"Ladir, Ladir." Wellhyrn's voice warmed to a companionable tone. There was just the slightest hint of patronization in it. "I turn your statement around . . . do you think *me* that stupid? The fellow I hired is a lackwit—"

"Wonderful."

"I made sure he left town," Wellhyrn said, lifting an eyebrow. "I had someone follow him this morning. It'll be taken care of—"

"And where does it *stop*, Wellhyrn?"

"It stops. It will stop." The assurance was gone from Wellhyrn's face. His lips made a thin line.

"You listen to me. We may fool people out of money now and again, the Duke being no exception, but by the gods! We haven't *robbed* them of it. And we don't murder."

"Getting soft, aren't you?" Wellhyrn sneered.

Ladirno got up, walked up to Wellhyrn, reached out, and grasped Wellhyrn by the front of his tunic. "You listen to me," he hissed. "*I* made you at court. *I* took you on as my apprentice. And I can just as easily dump you right back where you came from. Of the two of us, you tell me who the Duke respects most!"

Wellhyrn reached up and removed Ladirno's hand from his tunic. His face was white.

"You keep that in mind, boy," Ladirno said, standing over him. "And don't try to get back at me in any way. By now, I know your tricks. And, if you try to take revenge, *I'll* go to the Duke with what I know. You might be surprised just how much that is."

A hint of genuine fear crossed Wellhyrn's face.

"You listen to me, and listen well. The Duke won't stand for your kind of goings-on. You may think you can deny it, but I caution you again. Do you want to face up to the Duke's wizards? *They* can get the truth out of you."

Wellhyrn shook his head slightly.

"We can go far, you and I," Ladirno said, letting warmth re-enter his voice. "But you need to learn to control your ambition. You're a damned fine alchemist. You could be one of the best. Don't ruin your chances by overstepping yourself. Or by underestimating others. Do you understand me?"

For a moment, Wellhyrn held Ladirno's gaze. Then he seemed

to shake himself from his fear: his smile came back. "Ah, well. There won't be need—once Duran's gone. Will there?"

Vadami looked at the crowd which had gathered before him. A sidelong glance at Zeldezia sent a cold chill down his spine: the woman seemed utterly changed since they had met last. Her face was stony, her eyes narrowed, and when she spoke, there was a terrible violence in her voice.

He supposed it was to be expected, having lived through the attempted burning of her shop last night.

That was what things had gotten to—the Sabirn *knew* there was movement against them—and they struck.

And they all had cause for fear.

He had tried to calm Zeldezia, he had attempted to keep her on the path of Hladyr's will—keep her from the sin of hate in what she did—

"Do you understand what we're to do?" he asked of the gathered men and women. No one answered, but he saw several nods. "And you understand that we do the will of Hladyr. What we do we do for his sake—for the sake of souls' salvation—drive away the sin of hate, drive out the demons—"

"Who else *but* the Sabirn would do something like that to me?" Zeldezia cried above his voice. "Who else but Duran, who shelters 'em?"

"Tut ain't going to like this," one man warned. "He's a friend o' Duran's."

"Aye," added another. "Him an' Duran sit together all the time at the 'Cat.' He won't go for this."

"What Tutadar thinks isn't important now," Vadami said quickly, before other members of the crowd could agree with the speaker. "What's important is saving this neighborhood! Fire and flood! And Hladyr only knows what next?"

"The Duke," a woman shouted, "he let Duran off when 'e 'ad 'im—"

"Duran witched im!" someone shouted.

"Demon worshippers!"

"Maybe if we *asked* 'im to leave," another man said, "he'd—"

"No. We don't want him coming back. And he would, once the furor dies down." Vadami drew himself up. "Forget all the good things Duran did for you in the past. He's not the same man anymore. He *hired* a Sabirn to work for him. He even had that same Sabirn *live* with him! What does that tell you?"

Suddenly, Zeldezia stepped forward. "Father Vadami ain't tellin' you all! I seen—I *seen* them Sabirn look at Duran like he's some kind of a lord of theirs. I *seen* that old man hangin' 'round his shop. I *seen* Duran talkin' to any Sabirn he can lay a hand on. He's a wizard! Ain't nobody can tell me otherwise."

"Zeldezia—"

"I heard that damned Sab boy playin' his flute! Music gave me the creeps! It was demon music, on my soul it was! I seen him look at me, that kid, with nothin' in his eyes but darkness."

The crowd murmured louder now. Vadami felt sweat break out.

"Kill that Sab-lover!" Zeldezia cried. "Ain't no pity—he never showed *me* no pity. I asked him to save his soul by givin' up seein' the Sabirn, an' look what 'e did to me!"

The crowd stirred now; their voices had grown deeper, had grown ugly.

"Ever since that Sabirn kid showed up, we ain't had nothin' but evil weather!" Her voice went shrill as she turned to the crowd. "You lost business? Your customers been stayin' away! It ain't *your* fault you been goin' hungry. Duran's done this to you, an' you know it! I say, let's go after him an' give 'im back some of what he's given us!"

"I hear you!" a few men called back. "Let's get that bastard!" others growled. "Burn 'im out!"

"Wait!" Vadami took a step toward the crowd and lifted both hands over his head. "Stop! Think what you're going to do! Don't start anything the Duke's Guard will have to deal with!"

"Duke won't care if we get ourselves a demon worshipper!" Zeldezia shouted. " 'Less he's witched, too!"

"Get 'em all!" someone cried.

The crowd surged forward, their faces distorted with anger, following Zeldezia who had started off toward Duran's neighborhood.

"No! Stop!" Vadami was pushed aside. Sweat ran freely down his face now. Gods! It was getting away from him—totally out of his hands. He gulped down a huge breath, and sprinted off after the crowd. Maybe . . . Oh, Hladyr make it so . . . he could keep them from undirected violence—

Gods above and below! What *had* he done?

✧   ✧   ✧

Duran stepped outside, turned, and locked the door behind him. Dog sat waiting close by, panting in the sultry heat. The storm still had not broken, but thunder muttered ominously in the distance.

The street was strangely deserted for this time of day. The men had stopped work at Zeldezia's shop, and he saw life at only a few of the neighboring buildings.

He shrugged. It would make it easier if he could leave without seeing any of his neighbors. He pocketed the key, aware of the uselessness of the act, took up his staff he had leaned against the wall, and started off down the street.

He had written Tut a short note, explaining he was leaving and why . . . that he did not hold anything against Tut or Ithar: they had been the truest friends, in good times as well as bad.

He reached the corner, paused, and turned around. His eyes misted slightly, and he blinked. *That was your shop,* he thought, *your home. And now it's nobody's. You're done here, Duran, through. Leave it in the hands of the gods.*

He sighed and started off down the street that ran perpendicular to his, headed east. He had a good half hour of walking before he reached the east side of town where Kekoja and Old Man would be waiting for him.

He quickened his pace, Dog running along ahead, anxious now, only for it to be over. . . .

The Great Hall was nearly empty at this hour—Duke Hajun himself had come from his dinner-table. He stared at the young guardsman who stood panting before him, having spilled out his news—

A mob—gods. . . .

Loose in Old Town?

"No idea what stirred them up?" he asked, and the Captain of the Guard, who had brought the boy—

"Sabirn, Your Grace."

"Damn.—Where are they headed?"

"South, Your Grace. Toward the harbor." The Captain licked his lips. "It's a small mob, Your Grace, and we—"

"I don't give a damn if it *is* a small mob! Get your butt moving! I want a squadron dispatched! Get it stopped!"

"Aye, Your Grace."

"Reasonable force! You hear me?"

The Captain saluted, the young officer saluted, and ran from the hall.

Hajun found himself shaking. A small mob? There was no such thing.

Duran kept to the center of the street, avoiding the standing pools of water, and quickened his pace to a fast walk. He did not want to be caught by darkness outside his own neighborhood. Strange streets always made him nervous, a good indication of how limited his world had grown.

He had not traveled this far east in a long time, but the streets and the buildings looked much like those in his own neighborhood. Dog seemed to think the walk to be a holiday of sorts. He frisked and danced down the street, his tail wagging, every once in a while barking for the sheer joy of it.

Duran calculated he had been walking close to a third of an hour now. The clouds had grown thicker and thunder rumbled incessantly. He noted people had begun to light lamps in their homes and shops, though they kept their doors and windows open in the heat.

He looked ahead and saw a slight figure waiting by the edge of a house, a shadow in the early twilight. His heart raced. A thief? He thought of his moneybelt, and tightened the grip on his staff.

Dog, however, had recognized the figure, and ran ahead, tail wagging. The person reached down and patted Dog's head, then straightened.

Kekoja!

Duran quickened his pace again. Why was Kekoja here, instead of waiting at the edge of town?

"Can you run far?" Kekoja asked with no preamble.

Duran blinked. "Why?"

"Because there's a mob after you, Sor Duran, an' it's an angry mob, an' I don't want to stay around an' see what happens."

A bolt of fear struck through Duran's heart. A mob? Who had raised it? After what had happened last night, he knew the answer even as he asked himself the question. "Let's go!" he said, and set out after Kekoja at a slow run.

Why, why, why? he asked himself in time to his running footsteps. *Why couldn't they just let me go?*

His breath came harder now, and he felt the sweat run down his sides. Dammit! He was getting too old for an all-out run like this. His heart beat raggedly. Maybe he would die of heart failure and save the mob its trouble.

He concentrated on Kekoja running before him, on the long thin legs pumping tirelessly up and down. There was more strength in that wiry body than many people could guess. *Just stay with him,* he urged himself. *Don't fall too far behind!*

The moneybelt felt like it weighed as much as a heavy stone, and bumped up and down on his waist. He was burning hot, and wished he could stop long enough to remove his cloak. Several passersby turned in amazement to watch the race, and a strange one it must have appeared to them: a large yellow dog far out in the lead, a dark-haired boy loping along, and a middle-aged man bringing up the rear. If Duran had not been running for his life, he would have found it amusing.

He heard a muted roar off to his left and chanced a hasty glance in that direction. His heart lurched. Coming down the street he and Kekoja were passing was the mob.

"Here they come!" he called out, his breath growing shorter. "I think . . . they've . . . seen us! Run! I'll make it . . . fast as I can!"

"Not far," Kekoja shouted back over his shoulder. "Three more blocks."

Three more blocks. Gods! He would die before then. He reached down inside himself to gather needed strength. *You're Ancar,* he told himself. *An Ancar doesn't tire in a race. An Ancar will die on his feet rather than give up! Keep going! Make your ancestors proud!*

He stumbled once, caught himself, and ran on. Dog had sensed his master's panic, and stretched out a dead run, ready to turn and fight if need be. Kekoja began to pull away, and Duran knew he would be left behind.

"Keep going!" Kekoja called over his shoulder. "I'll get the others ready!"

The others? Duran dimly wondered how many "others" there might be. As many as made up the mob? He doubted that.

As he very much doubted his ability to run those three blocks more.

✧   ✧   ✧

Vadami had caught up to the head of the mob before they had gone very far, but that was all he had been able to accomplish. He had tried reasoning with them, but the men and women who stalked along after Zeldezia were beyond reasoning now.

He and Zeldezia had called the men and women together in a neighborhood far to the east of Duran's, so no casual observer could guess what was going on. They had started off to the west, traveling a route that would bring them into Duran's neighborhood several streets to the north. Along the way, they had added a few more people to the mob, and Vadami estimated their numbers were now forty-five strong.

He did not understand how he had gotten into this position. He kept thinking of going off to the side and returning to the Temple. No one was listening to him. Everything was—

"There he is!"

The mob roared. Vadami could barely make out a distant figure several blocks south, down the street headed east.

"After him!" shouted the burly fellow who had been so vocal earlier. "Don't let him get away!"

"Wait," Vadami yelled in a very unpriestlike voice. "Listen to me!"

Thunder rumbled overhead and lightning lit the sky. People began to run, waving sticks, pausing to gather up loose cobbles.

Then Vadami heard another noise over the thunder, the noise of hooves. Several other people had heard the sound, too, and they broke stride as they ran to glance around.

Suddenly, the street that crossed directly in front of them was filled with horses, and on those horses sat the green-cloaked Guard of the Duke himself.

"Halt!" their commander bellowed over the thunder. "Stop where you are, in the name of His Grace, the Duke!"

The mob halted and began to mill around, some men and women looked frightened, while others seemed increasingly defiant.

"Down with the Sabirn!"

Zeldezia's screech split the heavy silence. She darted off to one side, somehow escaped the arms of a guard who leaned halfway off his horse to catch her, and pelted down the street.

Her action spurred the mob into unthinking motion. Several

men charged at the guardsmen, brandishing rocks they had picked up in their hands.

"Swords out!" The Guard commander roared.

Even over the yelling and the rumble of thunder, Vadami heard the rasp of steel on steel as the guardsmen drew their weapons.

The mob howled.

"Death to the Sabirn!" someone yelled.

The commander brought his hand down. "Engage!"

Vadami closed his eyes at the sound of the first scream. Confusion reigned: horses neighed, people cursed and screeched. A body pitched into Vadami, a horse went down— Vadami started to run, heart pounding in his chest, in the direction Zeldezia had taken, fear giving him a speed he had not known he possessed. His legs ached, and he wondered how Zeldezia could keep up the pace: others did—men passed him, with sticks in hand—

Hladyr . . . Shining One! Help me to stop this!

Only the thunder answered him, thunder and the sound of Zeldezia's exhortations.

A large wagon stood in the center of the road. There were no buildings around Duran now, only the ancient arch of the river-gate, the harbor, and the fort built there to protect it. He ran— hearing the shouts closer and closer behind him—the pelting of stones—Dog loping, panting, beside him—

"Duran!"

Kekoja was with the wagon! The sight of the boy frantically beckoning him on gave Duran new energy: he ran, his ears ringing, and small black specks beginning to dot his vision. Behind him, he heard the shrill voice of a woman crying out for death to all unbelievers—

Zeldezia. He would have recognized that crow's voice anywhere.

He stumbled, staggered, caught himself painfully, and kept running—

"Duran! Hurry!"

Kekoja's voice. A stone hit to his left—he threw himself into final effort toward that wagon—ran and ran until he lost his vision, lost his footing entirely.

Strong hands lifted him up. He hung in their grip, limp.

"Get him into the wagon," another voice said. Old Man. Old Man had made it to safety, too.

"They're on us!" Kekoja cried.

"Aye, I see them."

Duran was half-dragged, half-carried over the side of the wagon—tried to help himself as men lifted him up and then unceremoniously dumped him down on his baskets—his baskets—!

Dog landed in the middle of him—

Stones hailed about them, the shouts grew—Duran looked down the street, and his chest tightened: men running at the wagon, armed with knives and large stones. In the forefront ran Zeldezia, her dark hair come loose from its ribbons, streaming out behind her like a storm cloud.

And Vadami.

Duran closed his eyes. He had never particularly liked the priest, but he had not thought Vadami one to stoop to mob violence.

"Ready?" Old Man called.

"Aye," someone answered.

Three Sabirn men stood at the side of the wagon, long metal tubes held in their hands.

Old Man stood facing the mob, not moving, not saying a thing. Duran wanted to yell, to curse, to do anything but lie in a shivering heap in the wagon, waiting for the mob to take him.

"Now!" Old Man said.

Duran had been in situations of danger before, and knew that time could do one of two things: it could speed up so he had taken action before he knew it, or it could slow down so that each moment felt like an hour.

The thunder cracked close at hand: all of Dandro's hells seemed to explode from the tubes—smoke, and fire, and screams from the crowd. Smoke cleared on the wind—there were people on the ground—the crowd running in terror—

The men scrambled aboard, Kekoja and Old Man, too. The wagon jerked into motion, wheels rumbling on the cobbles, and Duran held on to Dog, held on to him for dear life.

He had finally seen true wizardry, he thought: he had seen it with his own eyes.

✧ EPILOGUE ✧

Not more than two leagues off from Targheiden, beneath a sky that poured cold rain, Old Man brought the wagon to a stop. Duran and Dog sat covered by a tarp in the rear among his baskets; Duran's head still spun, but his breath came evenly again.

"Will anyone follow us?" Kekoja asked Old Man.

"In this weather?" Old Man shook his head. "I doubt it. Not the mob and not the Guard. I don't think they'll dare. I only regret we had to let them see the weapons—"

"They'll call it sorcery," one said.

The other Sabirn standing alongside the wagon laughed. Duran stared at them in wonder. How casually they acted after having delivered fire from their hands—hard men, dangerous men. He shivered, held on to Dog's collar, sitting in his nest of baskets.

The rain slacked to a drizzle, and the thunder and lightning diminished. Even so, Duran agreed with Old Man: no one would come after them. No one in his right mind, at least.

"And now, Sor Duran," Old Man said, turning sideways on the wagon's seat, "we'll try to make amends to you." He glanced at the other Sabirn. "Hear me," he said, "this one is called Duran. He has my name and Kekoja's. You now have his. The only thing lacking is for you to tell him your names."

"Fenro," one of the men said.

"I'm Domano," another.

"Aladu!" called the third man from the other side of the wagon.

The woman who shared the wagon-seat with Old Man smiled in the rain, her black hair plastered to the sides of her face. "I'm Turchia," she said. Her voice was low-pitched for a woman's.

Duran remembered what he had told Dajhi, Old Man, what seemed a lifetime ago. "Your names are safe with me," he murmured, touching his heart.

He sensed the Sabirn relaxing, saw the sudden warmth in them—though he was certain Old Man had told them this Ancar was different from most.

"There's a small grove of trees down the road a ways," Aladu said. "Let's make camp there."

There were no more questions until Old Man stopped the wagon for the night. The men dragged out another tarp from the wagon and secured it to three long staffs of wood, making a tent of sorts out from the wagon. A third tarp they spread on the ground so everyone could sit in comfort.

With a minimum of fuss, Fenro had started a small fire. Duran and Dog settled: Kekoja scurried about on small errands—but among the first he brought Duran a cup of heated wine.

"My father," Kekoja called him— "my second father—"

At which Duran found his eyes stinging, and his throat tight, and the wine most welcome to hide the fact.

"Now for questions," Old Man said. White teeth flashed in the firelight as Old Man smiled. "One of mine first. Then, I promise you, I'll answer anything you want."

Duran nodded. "Ask."

"Did you have any enemies who would have been able to hire wizards against you?"

Duran started to shake his head in denial, then nodded slowly, seeing Wellhyrn's face, and Ladirno's, in his mind.

Kekoja reached out and tapped Old Man's knee. "I *told* you." Old Man smiled.

"But I was only clumsy for a day," Duran said, recalling everything he had dropped and tripped over. Suddenly, why things had returned to normal dawned on him. His skin tightened. "You knew," he said softly, his eyes holding Old Man's gaze, "and you counteracted the ill-wishes aimed at me. Who was the wizard, and how did you afford him?"

Old Man smiled.

"But, Ladirno and Wellhyrn could afford some of Targheiden's best. . . ."

"Then I'm complimented," Old Man said. "Next question. Ask."

"What you did . . . back there . . . the mob." He looked from one dark face to the next. "What in Dandro's hells was it?"

"*That* wasn't wizardry," Old Man replied, "but just as well they think it was. You're an alchemist. You've seen things explode."

"Aye—"

"Explosion in an open-ended cylinder—" Old Man opened his fingers. "Boom! A pellet flies—"

"Set that damned mob running, that's for sure," Domano said.

"I'm sorry I had to do it, though." Old Man's voice was soft. "Now life for the Sabirn of Targheiden will be even more difficult. Perhaps impossible. There'll be blood. There already has been. It may shake a throne—"

"Was it you—the weather?"

Old Man had no expression. He only sipped his wine.

"Did you?" Duran demanded to know.

"Say that times change. Kingdoms end. This one—has run its course. All the accumulated magic—all the spells against it—call it nature. Call it a run of luck. No. I didn't. Their own wizards— wished the luck on their enemies. They feared—and they hated; and they wished with all they had. And their enemies—are *in* the city: do you see? Their enemies—"

"—were themselves," Duran said, with a chill.

"There are those worth saving," Old Man said, "those that aren't so blind. When we come across a mind like yours—we make every effort to draw it to us: we make no difference of race."

"We," Duran said, and looked at the dark faces in the firelight. "Who is this—we?"

"Northeast of here. We've a place there. If this kingdom falls— we'll not be part of it. We'll wait. We've waited before. A thousand years."

Duran's head spun. The Old Empire—

"Dajhi," Duran said. "Are there—alchemists where we're going? Are there those—who can transmute metals—turn base metal into gold?"

Old Man laughed. "Once an alchemist, always an alchemist. No, Duran, I'm afraid not. That's something no one has ever been able to do."

"I wonder why?" Duran mused, staring into the flames.

"Maybe that's something *you'll* discover," Old Man said.

Silence fell, and in that silence Duran heard his pulse beating in his ears. He was not so old. He had his medicines and his alchemist's tools. He had his Sabirn friends—

A cold nose touched his hand. He put an arm around Dog's neck, and stared off to the west where Targheiden lay, hidden by the darkness and rain.

Strange: he mourned the loss of home with a real grief, but at the same time that life seemed pale and distant. Few men were ever given the chance to start their lives over.

Duran smiled, and turning his eyes east, began to dream of what he could find.

Book Three
Reap the Whirlwind

Dedication:

To my partners in crime
Nancy Asire
Leslie Fish
But most of all, to the lady
who made it *all* possible
for all three of us
C. J. Cherryh
with respect, admiration,
and a touch of impertinence

✧ CHAPTER ONE ✧

Felaras stood in the open window of her study and let the cold night wind whirl around her, tying her hair into knots and cutting through the thick red wool of her tunic. That wind was the herald of a storm crawling its way toward her; thunderheads blackening the already dark night sky, growling and rumbling. Lightning danced along the tops of the mountains to the east in blue-white arabesques; jagged streaks of fire that leapt from the clouds to lash the world's bones.

There was no real need for Felaras to endure the ice-fanged wind. The study traditionally belonging to the Head of the Order of the Sword of Knowledge had one of the few glazed windows in the Fortress. Felaras could have shut that window and still been able to see the storm. But the current Master of the Order preferred to feel the wild wind on her face this night. The wind was uncontrolled and cleansing, and she had a need to remind herself that such forces existed beyond the petty squabblings of humans. That they would continue no matter what happened here below. That they waited for some human to learn their whys and wherefores, and to tame them to human hands. And one day—one day she knew it would happen. Some day, some man or woman would call the lightning, and it would answer.

For a moment it almost seemed to Felaras that if she called in her need, it would answer her.

But—no.

Hubris, old woman. Hubris and desperation. The gods aren't listening—if they ever did.

The storm wouldn't answer her, as the superstitious believed—

but it was nice to imagine, for a few moments, that the foolish tales about the "Order of Sorcerers" were truth.

Ah, you winds—if only you would blow those damned horse-nomads right off the face of the earth—or at least back to their steppes.

She sighed, and lifted her face to the first scent of cold spring rain.

Gods above and below, I do not need this mess. An invading horde—and me *expected to magic up an army. I don't suppose they'll take this storm as a sign from their gods to turn around and go home—*

Someone pounded on the outer gate, set into the Fortress wall almost directly below her window.

I'm the only one going to hear you, sirrah. You'd best find the right way of getting our attention before you break your fist. Unless you really didn't intend to spoil the wizards' rest, just make a show of trying.

But after doubtless bruising his knuckles on the obdurate portal without getting a response, the pounder discovered the bell rope and set up a brazen clangor not even the thunder could drown.

That one of the valley-folk would dare the storm *and* the wizards' wrath could only mean one thing.

—my luck's out.

Felaras remained at the window savoring her last few moments of freedom, while Watcher novices scuttled about with torches and lanterns, and the gate below creaked open and shut again. Her hair might be mostly grey, and she might be moving a bit stiffly on winter mornings, but there was nothing wrong with her ears—she heard every stumble the messenger made on the stone staircase leading to her study, and heard how long it took him to recover and resume the climb.

Whoever he is, and judging by the weight and pacing it's either "he" or a damned big woman, he's fagged out. Must've come all the way from the other end of the Vale on his own two feet.

A light tap on her door; then the creak of the door itself. The wind streamed in as the newly opened door created a draft, plastering Felaras's clothing against her chest and legs.

"Master, a messenger from the Vale." Felaras knew *that* voice; a high, breathy soprano, female, and more often heard shaped into profanity than into such a studiously respectful phrase. That was Kasha, Felaras's own Second and strong right hand, and she was putting on the full show for the newcomer.

"Bring him in," Felaras replied, only now surrendering her last fragments of pretended peace; closing the window and turning to face the room.

It took a moment for her eyes to adjust to the lamplight; a moment while tiny Kasha opened the study door wide and the messenger shuffled uneasily into the soft yellow glow.

Farmer, and, like Kasha, almost pure Sabirn; his race was plain enough, he was smallish and dark, and Felaras read his trade in the tanned, weathered face with the oddly pale forehead where his hat-brim would shade him all through the long cycle of plant, tend, reap. Read it in the stoop of the shoulder and the hard, clever hands; the wrinkles around the eyes that spoke of years watching the sky for the treacherous turning of the weather.

And also read the fear of something worse than the wizard he was facing, for the farmers of the Vale were directly in the path of the oncoming horde.

Not a man that she knew personally. *Ah gods, one of the superstitious ones. Which means* my *people have their hands full. Worse and worse.*

He shivered; from nervousness, and from cold. He was soaked to the skin, and as he stood before her, twisting his hat into a shapeless mass, a puddle of rainwater was collecting on the polished wood at his feet.

Poor, frightened man. You may be Sabirn, but you're as legend-haunted as any of the Ancar.

"Kasha—hot wine for the Landsman—"

Kasha nodded, round face as unreadable as a brown pebble, and slipped out the door without making a sound.

High marks for the stone face, m'girl, and high for spook-silence, but a demerit for not thinking of the wine yourself.

Felaras ghosted around her desk and slid into her massive chair with no more noise than Kasha had made. She nodded and waved her hand at the heavy chair beside the farmer.

"Sit, man; a little water isn't going to harm the furnishings."

While he was gingerly seating himself she reached over to the fireplace and gave the inset crank of the hidden bellows a few turns. The flames roared up and the man jumped, and stared at her with eyes that looked to be all startled pupil.

Gods.

"Just a kind of bellows, Landsman. Built right into the chimney—like what your smith has in his forge."

Felaras cranked it again, sending the flames shooting higher.

"I thought that you needed some quick heat, from the look of you."

The farmer relaxed; a tiny, barely visible loosening of his shoulder muscles and his grip on his hat. "Aye that," he agreed slowly. "Storm in th' Vale; raced it here."

"So I see." She leaned back in her chair, rested her elbows on the carved wooden arms, and steepled her fingers just below her chin. "And raced it because of the barbarians, I presume?"

"Aye. They be just beyond th' Teeth." He leaned forward, hands once again white-knuckled from the grip on what remained of his hat. "Master, they be comin' straight for us—on'y way through's the Vale. We need yer help! We need yer wizard-fire!"

Felaras stifled a groan. "Landsman—excuse me, but what is your name, man?"

He gulped, then offered it, like a gift. "Jahvka."

"Your name is safe with me, Jahvka. I am Felaras, Master only of those who allow me to guide them; I am not *your* Master, and you need not call me so."

A bit of a lie, though not in spirit—

"Now hear me and believe me, Jahvka; the Order cannot stop these nomads."

He looked shaken and began to object in dismay. "But—the wizard-fire—the magic—"

She shook her head. "The truth, as others would doubtless have told you if they didn't have their hands full, is that we have no more magic than these barbarians. The wizard-fire isn't magic, Jahvka, it's just something like my bellows. We have twelve fire-throwers, of which six are built into the walls and can't be moved. That leaves six more. How many passes into the Vale besides the Teeth?"

His eyes went blank for a moment as he thought. "Dozen, easy. More 'f ye count goat-tracks."

"And those steppes ponies are as surefooted as goats, let me tell you." She leaned forward, gripping the arms of the chair to channel her own anxiety into something that wouldn't show. "We can't cover all the passes with the fire-throwers, and nothing less is going to stop them. They're trapped between us and the River Ardan, and there's no fording that now that the spring rains have started. I have no army, and getting one out of Ancas or Yazkirn is—not bloody likely. I've tried; they won't believe the nomads are a threat until they're trampling the borders. We are— expendable. Have you any suggestions? I am not being sarcastic, Jahvka, if you have any, I'd like to hear them, because I'm fresh out of ideas."

He swallowed, bit his lip, then looked her squarely in the eyes. "Nay. Nothin'. They been eatin' Azgun alive—"

"I know." She sighed, and sagged back into the chair. "All right—here's my only suggestion, Jahvka. You go home, and you tell your people to run; make for the hills. There's caves, you'll be sheltered and safe—" She raised her voice, though not her eyes. "Kasha, get me copies of the maps of the caves—"

Kasha had made another silent entrance; in her charred-grey tunic and breeches she was a lithe, dark-haired shadow. Jahvka started as she set the earthenware mug of hot wine on the desk in front of the farmer, made a tiny bow, then slid back out without speaking.

Now if I could only get her to give me that kind of respect when there aren't strangers about. . . .

"We'll give you complete maps of the caves; we've been stowing what we could in there against some time of need like this one for as long as we've been here. You people can take your choice; you can head either for there or come here to Fortress Pass and go through. We *can* hold this place against all comers, and it's the only way into Yazkirn for miles about. We'll keep this bunch off your tails if you want to go for sanctuary in Yazkirn or Ancas."

"But—" he gestured helplessly, hat still clutched in one hand. "The plantings—the stock—"

"What won't come willingly, easily, kill and *leave behind*. Seed can be replaced."

—I hope. Are you listening, gods?

"And stock can be bred back or bought. The land won't run away. The one thing we cannot replace is you, your families, your lives. Listen to me, man. It'll be a hungry winter, but if you take what you can and destroy what you have to, these nomads will have nowhere to go and nothing to raid. Then they'll try the pass—when we scare them off, they'll go home."

—oh you gods, I hope you're hearing me—

"Then you can come back; we'll work together to make your lands bloom again. But we cannot sow a seed that will bring forth your dead; and your wives, your children, and you yourselves will die if you don't run from these horse-warriors while you can!"

She closed her eyes for a moment and pinched the bridge of her nose, feeling a headache coming on.

Jahvka looked about ready to cry; she didn't much blame him. She was about at that point herself.

"Drink your wine," she said gruffly.

He looked at the mug as if he had forgotten it was there, then, as obediently as a child, picked it up and cautiously sipped it, his eyes never once leaving her face.

"It isn't the end of the world, Jahvka," she said quietly. "I know it seems like it is, but it's not. The Order ran farther, faster, and with less than you'll be able to save, and we survived."

He bobbed his head, but his eyes were doubtful in the lantern-glow.

"So tell me; what's your people's choice likely to be? Sanctuary or the caves?"

"What you got in them caves?" he asked bluntly. "What they like?"

"Well, let me think; fodder mostly, there's wild grass all over those hills and we set the novices out for a haying holiday every summer."

And fair bitching I used to hear about it, too. No novices to cook and clean and run errands for four whole weeks. Now maybe my lazy children will understand why I ordered it.

"The upper caves are dryer than this Fortress; there's hay up there ten years old that's still good. Some grain; not as much as I'd like, though, and no good for seed. And some things you folk have no use for, books and the like."

Oh precious blood of our Order, you books. Stay safe.

"If I were to put my people up there, I'd put the stock in the upper caves near the fodder and where they can smell the outside; they won't get so twitchy that way. The middle caves would be best for living; the lower are damp at best. There's a couple underground rivers and a lake, so you'll have good water."

Jahvka took all this in, and nodded. "The caves, then; be hard enough gettin' most of 'em out of sight of their land. Most of 'em likely to see goin' over Fortress Pass as givin' up. And my kind don't give up easy."

She inclined her head with real respect. "I take it, then, that you speak for the whole Vale?"

"Aye. I didn't want it, but I was the only Elder still in the Vale, able t' leave the people with someone else, and fit enough to run up here. Mera's on the Teeth with some of the wilder kids; she reckoned on giving them something to do that'd keep 'em out of bowshot. Other younger ones, they with their people, keepin' 'em calm. Old Thahd's with mine; he got wounded he don't want t'leave, so he's watchin' both our garths. Lenyah an' Beris are too damned old t' be runnin' about in a storm."

"No argument from me."

I trained Mera myself; she's no Watcher, but she's as canny as they come. Same for the other younger ones; and I'd bet on them getting their folks ready to march right now. They knew what my answer was going to be. Wounded—I don't like the sound of that; I'll send somebody on down to see if we can do anything. If only these farmers had horses instead of oxen—if only we had more of them trained.

"Will you have enough able-bodied folks in your two garths to run the alert through the Vale?"

He nodded emphatically. "Guess we got no choice, an' might as well go now. Most seed hasn't been put in yet; likely we can save it. 'F Mera an' the kids can hold the Teeth a bit, might even be able t' save the oxen."

Felaras sighed, and glanced out the window. The storm was almost on top of them; she could hear the low grumble of the thunder even through the thick stone walls. A moment later Kasha slipped back in the door, her hands full of waterproofed map-tubes.

"Right enough." She stood up; he nearly overset the chair in his haste to get to his feet. "Kasha, take Elder Landsman Jahvka down to the Lesser Hall and send a novice out for some food for him. Not even a barbarian horse-nomad is going to make a move in this rain, so see him fed and completely dry before you let him go back down the Pass. Tell Vider I want him to go along; the Elder says they've got some wounded. Then get Zorsha to do a supply inventory—yes, I mean *now*, I want it on my desk before

I go to bed—and have Teokane see if the Library has anything to say about these steppes riders."

Kasha bowed—a little more deeply, this time—and ushered the Elder out with one unobtrusive hand behind his left shoulder blade. She closed the door behind them, and Felaras sank back down into her chair just as the first burst of rain pattered against the glass of the window.

Damn. Damn, damn, damn.

She reached for the thin pile of reports. No one would believe her three months ago when she'd figured these nomads wouldn't turn back when they reached the River. Half the Order had figured her for crazed, sending out Watchers to try to get information on the barbarians.

Now they'd be on her back to evacuate.

Evacuate to where? The biggest sister-house, the one at Yafir, is right in their path if we fall. The other one at Parda is there on sufferance; in no way are the Yazkirn princes going to let more "wizards" in at their back door.

She skimmed through the hastily written reports one more time, hoping to pry a little more information out of the barely legible scrawls, but didn't learn anything she didn't already know. No ideas as to the size of the "horde"; their habit of having four to six ponies each made them hard to estimate.

Their course was easy enough to follow. They'd cut their way through nominally "civilized" Azgun in a straight run west with Fortress Pass right on the line through Yazkirn; didn't stop for much of anything and seemed to loot only the most portable of goods, mainly the foodstuffs and the horses.

Hm. Wonder why? Usual style is to pillage everything that isn't nailed to the floor, and round up the herds and the kids and women.

She made a mental note to herself to consider that question later, and went on with her gleaning. She chewed absently at her ragged thumbnail as lightning flashed by right outside the window and the stone walls vibrated to the thunder.

The leader was very young, by all accounts; a nomad going by the name of Jegrai. The group was not just a raiding party; their women and children were with them. But not their food herds. Or their family tents and carts. Only their horses. Their riding horses, their packhorses.

Another anomaly. Strange. Very strange.

She came to the end of the reports with nothing more than questions, no answers.

She leaned her head back against the leather of the chair cushion, closed her eyes, and tried to take the whole mess she was facing down to its component parts. *If all things were wonderful and I wasn't having to fight my own people, what would our options be?*

Well, there's running.

There was always the option to escape; over her term as Master, she'd re-opened all the old escape routes and had enforced the rule that demanded every member of the Order have his escape-pack ready and to hand in his quarters, from the novices on up.

Oh, they truly thought I was crazed. I wonder what they're thinking now?

It wouldn't be the first time the Order had fled, the gods knew, although never in living memory had the Order been forced from their strongholds. But flight was how Duran and Keko had found this Fortress in the first place, in their own flight eastward away from the persecution of the Sabirn in the city of Targheiden. Although the interior was in ruins, it overlooked a strategic pass, and the walls were still sound. Most important of all, no one seemed to be claiming it. According to Duran's diary, the old Sabirn Dahji swore it was one of the original Sabir Empire border-posts. Well, that could be; it was surely built well enough to withstand about anything, including the centuries.

Still—this time there weren't many options.

Where to run to? East puts us in their laps; south may be cut off by now. West we aren't welcome, and north—gods above, I'd sooner face this horde than the savages up there.

They could just stay where they were, of course; a fair share of the members of the Order were pretty complacent about their ability to withstand a siege. Felaras's policies of building the fortifications back up hadn't been popular with the Seekers and the Archivists, but at this point even her worst critics were probably singing her praises and telling each other that no barbarian horse-nomads were going to get past those walls, nor have the patience to wait out a siege.

So; they could sit tight and hope that Jegrai's horde never found out about them—

Huh. Not bloody likely.

—or indeed, did not have the patience to wait out a prolonged siege. Superficially, the second would seem quite likely, given Jegrai's actions so far.

So far. But what if our food runs out? We're at the end of our winter stores, and the Vale folk aren't going to be coming up the hill to trade food for made-stuff. Those nomads might get tired and go away, but they might not. They might decide that they like what they see, and settle down. Nomads don't necessarily want to remain that way. A good half the time they're wanderers because their land isn't fertile enough to support farms. I'll have to see if Teokane can dig anything up on their mythos. It would tell me a lot to know if their vision of paradise is a garden or an endless plain.

She opened her eyes long enough to make a note of that last, before closing them and settling back into thought.

The last option was her personal choice; treat with them.

Gods, will I be in for a battle over that *idea, should I try it. Half of this ragtag lot will howl loud enough to hear in Targheiden—and that brings me back full circle to our internal problems, doesn't it?*

She rubbed her tired eyes, sat back up, and blinked at the flame of the lantern on her desk. *Thank the gods I can count on most of the Watchers to stand by me, from Watcher-novices to full Swords. I think I've managed to brand the Oath into their souls.*

She looked up at the Three Oaths carved into the living rock of the Fortress wall where the Master couldn't avoid seeing them every time he raised his eyes from the desk. There was no other ornamentation on that wall, and each Oath was set in its own square, neither above nor below the others. Farthest to her left was the Oath of her chapter; when she read the Oath of the Watchers she felt the weight of all her responsibilities settling a little heavier on her shoulders.

"When the pursuit of knowledge requires the peace bought at swordpoint, I shall be the Watcher at the sentry-post; I shall be the Sword that guards the gate. Even unto death, I shall not fail those who Preserve and those who Seek."

They truly believe that Oath these days—even Zetren, mad dog that he is. Thank the gods he's older than I am. Even if he survives me he won't have time to undo what I've done.

Her eyes fell on the Oath of the Seekers next: "The gods have given man a mind that he may use it. There is nothing to bar the Flame of the mind of man. What his mind can discover, his Hand can achieve. I shall Seek, and I shall Create."

One corner of her mouth quirked up. *They should have added, "and I will blow things up on a regular basis."* Her eyes itched again. *Now there's a House with internal divisions; Flame and Hand might be two separate chapters. Thaydore will want to fling the gate open wide the moment he hears that Jegrai's horde is coming over the hill. If I hear him give me that lecture about "all men can live together in harmony" one more time—I may push him down the well and not wait for him to fall in again. How someone with a mind that keen can be such a fuzzy thinker when it comes to the real world—well, the Flame will follow him— and if somehow I can placate him, I'll have the Flame on my side. And he will support me if I try to work something out with the nomads—that's right along his "peace-and-shared-wisdom" line. But the Hands—hm. A problem. That's Halun; I can't guess where he'll jump, except that he doesn't want the real world to even guess we exist. Let me think; I might be able to convince him that we can use the nomads as a shield between us and the rest of the world. And I've got Zorsha; that should give me a direct ear in the Hand camp. If I know what's coming I may be able to head it off.*

"All knowledge is worth the preservation, all wisdom the dissemination" read the next and final Oath. "Mine the Book where it shall be recorded; mine the Book that shall preserve it. Mine the duty to bestow it wherever and whenever it is needed."

Kitri is going to side with Thaydore; which means with me, except I may have to tie her up to keep her from rushing out to the nomads with her arms full of books. And she's going to be on me again for not educating the Vale folk. Diermud, on the other hand, will be up in his room the moment he finds out about how close the barbarians are, to consult with the spirits and look for Signs and Portents. Another of my unworldly idiots. If he wasn't such a powerful wizard—

The itching behind her eyes grew unbearable; and as she reached for the bottle of saltwater she kept to relieve late-night eyestrain, her arm barely brushed the half-full earthenware mug that Jahvka had left on the desk.

It promptly fell over, cracking in half and spilling red wine everywhere..The puddle headed straight for her notes—

And she finally recognized that itch at the back of her eyes for what it was—the sign she was being ill-wished.

She snatched the notes out of the way of the wine, and angrily blocked the wish, flinging it back into the teeth of whoever had sent it.

Damn you to bottommost hell, whoever you are; I will not have internal politics jostling my arm!

The puddle slowed and stopped without harming anything. Felaras sighed and got a rag to mop up the spill and the pottery shards.

I wonder who that was, anyway? She chuckled nastily to herself. *Hope he or she got it in the teeth. Glad we've never put it about that one of the qualifications for anyone being considered for Master-candidate or Leader is that you have to be conversant with all the martial arts—including wizardry.*

A draft of high wind suddenly blew *down* the chimney, sending smoke and ash across the breadth of Halun's workroom. Halun bent over in a fit of coughing, and batted at the smuts heading straight for his book.

There was a glass beaker full of brown liquid being heated over an alcohol flame on the table. As Halun choked in the smoke and tried to clear his watering eyes, the flame beneath the beaker licked high in that wind, and the flame beneath the beaker licked high in that wind, and the beaker was suddenly under stress of heat on one side, cold on the other, that it was never made to meet.

It shattered, spilling its contents all over everything on the bench. Brown liquid splashed and hissed on the metal of the lamp.

Halun cursed, and promptly canceled his ill-wish; the draft vanished, and the smoke began dispersing.

He stood and surveyed the wreckage with his hands on his hips. There was ash spread halfway across the floor. His good blue robe was now smutched with it. The lamp-flame was out, the lamp probably ruined; at the least it would need a new wick. There were shards of glass all over the workbench, and it was pure luck he hadn't had anything *on* that bench except the lamp, the stand for the beaker, and the beaker itself. Brown liquid, full of ash, dripped down onto the floor. Thunder growled overhead, sounding almost like laughter.

He sighed, collected an armful of rags from the pile ready in the corner, and went to deal with the mess.

Thank the gods all I was doing was heating some chava. That could have been naphtha in that beaker.

But he found himself grinning sardonically, as he dirtied his robe further, down on his knees on the ashy floor. *You're a worthy opponent, Master Felaras. Forethought enough to have someone guard you, hm? Wonder who it is. Hm. Probably Diermud. He's good; better at deflection than offense, but good. As I should know, who trained with him.*

He swept the ash back into the hearth, then changed his robe when there was no more sign that his wish had been turned back on him. Last of all he picked up the bits of glass carefully. Lisan would want the shards to re-mold, especially with the barbarians out there barring the way to the best sand-pits.

Well, so much for my hot mug of chava before I go to bed—but I wonder—

He padded across the smooth wooden floor, opened the door leading into his novice's room, and poked his head around the edge of it. Jeof, a lanky blond Ancar boy of about fourteen in nondescript clothing three sizes too big for him, was still awake, curled up beside the fireplace with a book, oblivious to everything about him. Halun cleared his throat. Jeof jumped, and went crimson when he saw Halun looking in at him. Halun got a brief glimpse of bright pictures before the book vanished behind Jeof's back.

Halun raised one eyebrow. "If that's the book I think it is—no, Jeof, don't tell me. I don't officially want to know, that way I don't have to officially reprimand you. Just make sure it's back in the Library before dawn, hm? Come to think of it, the Library is on the way to the kitchens, and I'd like some hot wine if there's any left."

"Yes, Master Halun." Jeof jumped to his feet, managing to hide the illustrated *Pillow Book of the Prince of Beshem* behind him as he rose. Halun would know that particular battered cover anywhere. . . . "I'll get you some; there was a messenger from the Vale, so they'll have put more wine in the kettle for him. Likely there's plenty left."

He backed up to the door, got it open with one hand, and slid out without ever letting Halun "officially" see his erotic prize.

Halun returned to his study, chuckling. It didn't seem all that long ago that *he'd* been the one hiding the Prince's Pillow Book from *his* Master.

But Halun's Master had also been the Master of the Order.

Which was the reason why Halun was not the Master of the Order now, instead of Felaras.

The Master of the Order could never be from the same chapter of the Order as the previous Master. That was the rule laid down by Master Vahnder, who had seen the need to divide the members of the Order into the three chapters of Watchers, Seekers, and Archivists in the first place.

It was a reasonable rule, in that it kept the power from being concentrated in the hands of one chapter.

But it was an unreasonable rule when it put people like Felaras into the Master's seat in preference to someone with twice her qualifications.

And twice her sense.

Better her than Zetren. Halun shuddered at the thought. *He'd have turned us into an Order Militant and probably gotten us all killed doing so.*

He brushed the last of the scattered ash off his book and went back to his chair, to stare at the fire and brood. *Damn the woman anyway! Can't she see she's not the leader the Order needs, especially now? And if I could just get her out of the way—I am the only logical candidate for the seat, and if I'm following her, I'm no longer disqualified. I have got to think of a way—*

Before those barbarians out there leave me with nothing to lead.

Kasha pushed the study door open with her foot. "He's gone, Felaras," she said softly.

Felaras looked up from her rapt contemplation of the lamp-flame. Her high cheekbones were more prominent that usual; Kasha had suspected her of skipping meals lately, and now she was certain of it. The Master's clear hazel eyes were a bit darker than usual with brooding, and there were rings under them that told her Second she'd been skipping sleep, too.

Kasha waited in the doorway for the Master to respond, steaming jug in one hand, two clean mugs in the other.

"I hope that's more wine, girl. If it's chava, I'll never forgive you."

Kasha laughed. "Of course it's wine, I'm no fool. I know you—remember, I started as your novice. Besides, you need to get some sleep tonight, and chava would only keep you awake." She crossed to the desk and planted one of the mugs on the softly gleaming wood in front of Felaras, the other in front of the visitor's chair, and filled both without spilling a drop.

Felaras took her mug in both hands and sipped at it gingerly. Kasha took up her own mug, breathed in the cinnamon-scented steam with pleasure, then planted her rump in the visitor's chair and propped both her feet on the desk.

"Have you no respect for your Master, girl?" Felaras chuckled. "Zetren would have a litter of snakes if he saw you now."

"Zetren *is* a litter of snakes. I respect you; you know it. That's enough." Kasha dismissed Zetren with a shrug of one shoulder. "The Elder is on his way back down the Pass; Vider is with him, and he took a donkey-load of medicines; says he plans to stay with them until this mess is over."

"Good for him." Felaras rubbed her broad forehead with the heel of her right hand. "He'll do more good down there than up here, but I didn't think he had it in him to stick out an exile in the caves."

"He says he doesn't mind; says he wants to train some of the midwives the way you've been training some of the Elders." Vider's actions had surprised Kasha too; he was so quiet she'd mostly overlooked him. "Well, Zorsha is getting inventory from the cook; he's already been to the armory. Teo is ankle-deep in scrolls; he thinks he may have found something to give you an edge—if you still want to deal with these folk instead of holing up and pretending we don't exist or trying to fight them."

"So?" Felaras leaned forward eagerly; Kasha worried as the shift in light revealed more clearly the dark circles under her eyes and lines that hadn't been in her face a week ago. "What?"

Kasha snorted; Teo had been his usual obdurate self. "He says he wants to tell you himself; you know Teo—'three independent sources or it's only hearsay.'"

Felaras sighed. "I know Teo. Thank the gods for him, too. He won't go raising my hopes for no reason." She leaned back and took another sip of wine, retreating into the shadow cast by the back of the chair until all Kasha could see were her eyes glittering in the darkness. "Thank the gods for you, too. And Zorsha. You're all sensible and I can depend on you, and you know this situation may prove to be the life or the death of the Order. And if everything goes to hell either one of the lads can train himself in this seat, and you'll help. Because I surely won't have time to tell them everything they'll need to know."

Kasha shivered. "Don't say that. It sounds like you're ill-wishing yourself."

"Why not? It's true. We of all people should be able to face the truth."

They both took good long pulls at their mugs; Kasha as much to drive the night-fears away as for any other reason. It worked; she felt the wine going to her head.

Felaras brooded a while longer in silence until Kasha couldn't bear it. "Say something, Felaras. Anything."

"Like what?"

"What you're thinking."

Felaras coughed. "It's pretty selfish. I'm thinking it isn't fair. I am sixty-two damn-'em years old. I should be taking things easy, training the Terrible Twosome, enjoying a comfortable old age. I should be getting respect! What do I get? The Order playing politics under my nose, barbarians on the doorstep, and a Second who puts her feet on my desk!"

"If you really didn't like it," Kasha pointed out, "I wouldn't do it."

"I know it; and I was as snippy with Swordmaster Rodhru as you are with me," Felaras replied. "When you're snippy, I know I can trust you. Kasha, I wish I wasn't Master. And not just because I never wanted it. I wish I could pass the seat on to you. You'd make a better Master than either Teo or Zorsha."

The chair creaked as Kasha shifted uneasily. All this talk of passing on the seat—Felaras was fey tonight. It wasn't like her to be this gloom-ridden. "I wouldn't have your seat; Swordmaster I'd take under protest, but not that—"

"That's the point—you *don't* want it. The Master's seat goes to the most qualified person who wants it the least." The fire popped and Felaras took another large swallow. "That's how I got stuck with it. Ruvan frankly wasn't qualified—even he said so, when you could get his nose out of a book. Zetren wanted it too much. So did Halun, for that matter, but he was automatically out of the running. So it was me."

Kasha shivered in a bit of draft, and listened with half an ear to the fury of the storm outside the study window. "I didn't know that."

"You're not supposed to. Just like nobody outside the Watchers is supposed to know that a third of us are wizards." She coughed. "Kasha, how long have you and I been working together?"

"Since I was novice; um—twelve years, almost."

Felaras put her mug carefully on the desk and laced the fingers of her hands behind her head. "I've stayed out of your private life as much as I could—"

"I know—" Kasha began.

"Don't interrupt. I'm about to crawl into it with a vengeance. You and Zorsha and Teo have been a triad from the time you could crawl. Which one of them are you sleeping with?"

Kasha's face flamed, and she choked on her wine.

"Both?"

"*No!*" she exclaimed, trying to get herself back under control. "I mean we—you know kids, but—when it started to—I wouldn't—dammit, Felaras, you've got no right to ask that of me!"

"I know that," Felaras replied calmly. "I have a reason. You know them both better than I ever could. I need another perspective. Should I pass the seat to Teo, or to Zorsha?"

Kasha went from hot to frozen. That was the very last question she'd ever expected out of Felaras.

"You're drunk," she stammered, finally. "You're drunk, or you'd never have said that."

Felaras shook her head, gently curving grey strands just brushing the tops of her shoulders. "No, I'm not. Or not that drunk."

"Felaras—I—" She was at a total loss for words.

"Have either of them asked to be your permanent lover yet?"

"No!" She flushed hotly again. "We're . . . friends. That's all. I don't want to have to choose between them, not ever! Not for that, not for any reason!"

"You're a Watcher—"

"I know that. I'm a Watcher before I'm anything else, Felaras, and—"

"So focus and give me the answer to my question."

Kasha took a deep breath and focused down until her stomach stopped churning; stilled her mind and let whatever would come rise to the surface.

And when the thought came, it seemed an odd one, but she spoke it anyway.

"Zorsha has never had a nickname. Teo has never been Teokane to anyone except as a signature."

Felaras took her words, turned them around, and looked them over; Kasha could see it in the slightly unfocused eyes, the frown-line between her thick grey eyebrows.

"Meaning?"

Kasha followed her thought, as carefully as she would have followed a track over barren ground. "I'm not quite sure. Except that—nobody ever gave you a nickname either. Or me. Can people obey somebody they still think of as 'young Teo'? Can they trust the decisions of a man who is still bearing the diminutive he wore when he was a child?" She had to shake her head. "I'm not sure what it means; I'm not sure it means anything."

"Let me lead you down a side path, then; suppose I told you to choose, not for the Order, but for yourself. Told you that you would have to make up your mind between them. Then what?"

Kasha shoved the extreme embarrassment and the uncomfortable feelings that question caused down into a corner of herself and sat on them until they weren't getting in the way of her thinking. "If I were forced into choosing one of them as my lover, it would probably be Teo. And that would be because Zorsha would be hurt, but not as badly, nor as deeply, by my making a choice. Which is why I won't." Her mouth was dry, and she was feeling very off-balance and unsettled, and she didn't want to have to deal with it anymore. "Felaras, I don't like having to think about these things—"

"Enough of it, then. Drink your wine; you look like hell."

"Do I?" She willed her insides to stop fluttering. "I feel like hell. I've avoided just this topic ever since the three of us figured out that boys and girls were different. And that *I* wasn't a boy. Like I said, we—but when it looked like it might get into something other than a game, I started saying 'no' to that. I enjoy what we have and I don't want it ruined."

"But you've told me what I needed to know, girl. That Teo isn't as resilient as Zorsha. That other people view him—how to put this?—with a little less than the full respect the Master needs."

Kasha laughed, hearing the edge of hysteria in her voice and hoping Felaras didn't. "*You* talk about respect? With all the fights in Council—"

"They fight me; that doesn't mean they don't respect me." Felaras chuckled out of the dark depths of her chair. "Somebody out there respected my abilities enough to try and joggle my arm tonight. An ill-wishing. I sent it home with its tail between its legs."

Kasha sat bolt upright, mug sloshing. "An ill-wishing? But—"

Felaras waved her alarm aside. "Don't fret yourself. By tomorrow whoever it is will have other things to think about. We're going to have those blamed nomads at the door; that should keep *everyone's* attention, and—"

There was a tentative knock at the door. "Come," Felaras called, and Zorsha slid around the door-edge with his hands full of papers, his blond hair and brown clothing dark with either sweat or rain, grey eyes looking a bit less sleepy than usual.

"Master Felaras, you said—"

"—that I wanted that inventory on my desk tonight, thank you. Yes, I meant it."

"Well, this is everything, down to the last straw in the stable." He put the neat pile of paper exactly in front of Felaras with a half-smile of pardonable pride.

"Good man; go get yourself some of that wine and get to bed; I'm calling a full Convocation tomorrow." She shifted her gaze to Kasha. "Finish yours and get yourself off. I'll need you tomorrow, and not muddled."

Kasha downed the last swallow in her mug, and left it on Felaras's desk. Zorsha waited for her just beyond the door in the dark stairway.

She stumbled over a rough place; he caught her elbow. Roughly sensitive after her bout with Felaras, she twitched away from him. Wisely, he let her go, and let her lead the way down the uneven stone steps.

"Is it that bad?" he asked her, about halfway down. "There's a lot of rumors below, but no real facts."

He had a very pleasant, rich voice; lower than a tenor, higher than a baritone. It unsettled Kasha in a way she did not want to deal with, and she simply nodded, forgetting for a moment that he probably couldn't see her gesture in the ill-lit staircase.

"Kasha?"

"It's bad," she replied shortly.

"The messenger was from the Vale, then? The nomads are at the Teeth?"

"They're at the Teeth," Kasha got out around her clenched jaw, exerting control over herself to answer. "They'll be in the Vale in the next few days. That's why the inventory. What we have now may be all we'll have for a while."

Zorsha made a soft little sound, like a cross between a sigh and a grunt. "I rather thought that was it." As they reached the bottom of the staircase, he gave her arm a squeeze, surprising her before she could pull away. "Go get some rest. You may not get any for a while."

She turned to glare at him. But he was already gone.

✧ CHAPTER TWO ✧

Teo's eyes misted over, and he lost the sense of what he was reading.

Gods. He blinked; blinked again, but the old and fading words on the yellowed parchment page kept running together into illegibility. Teo rubbed his eyes with the back of his hand to clear them, but they wouldn't stop blurring. He glanced over to the corner of the scarred desk, at the time-candle he'd brought with him into the Library. He shook his head in mild surprise. *Half burned-down already?* It only seemed an hour ago that he'd started his search.

Is it really midnight? He sneezed and rubbed at his nose as another sneeze threatened; his eyes felt gritty and sore. He looked around, certain that the candle must have burned too fast, but he was alone; nothing but battered, empty desks and full, dusty bookshelves. His fellow Archivists and their novices had slipped away while he was deep in researches. *I guess it must be. I guess I got pretty involved.*

He closed his eyes for a moment; felt contented, rather than exalted, by his discoveries. But then, that was what being an Archivist was all about, anyway. Not the Seeker's sudden thrill of seeing something new arise out of your investigations, but rather the slow process of putting all the bits together until at last you could stand back and see the whole.

The whole—Hladyr bless, I have put together a whole indeed this time!

He opened his eyes again and contemplated the neat pile of papers before him with profound satisfaction. Each page was covered with notes in his own careful hand. He had put together a picture of the horse-nomads and their ways that had waited unnoticed in the Archives for a century—and that only Felaras had guessed (or hoped) existed. More than enough to inspire a soul-filling contentment.

An aged but still musical contralto interrupted his reverie.

"When I told you to burn midnight oil on this one, Teo, I didn't mean you to take me quite so literally."

He blinked, and came back to himself; not with a start, but slowly, carefully, as he did everything. He turned around to face the door, wondering what could have brought the Master of the Order down at this hour. Unless . . . unless things had gotten worse since this afternoon.

Master Felaras leaned against the frame of the open Library door, the only spot of color in the room full of dark wooden bookcases and leather-bound books. Her scarlet wool tunic and darker red breeches made her look like a flame in the light from the time-candle and the carefully shielded oil lamp beside the door.

No outward sign identified her as the Master of the Order. Not her age, nor her iron-grey hair—there were others in the Order who looked (or were) older. Not the sword at her side, nor her clothing; Masters wore what they pleased. Some Masters of the Order had gone robed in precious silks, and some in rags.

She certainly didn't look or act nobly born; if an air of pedigree was a prerequisite for the Master's seat, Halun, (silver-haired, blue-eyed, holding himself with all the pride of his Ancas ancestors) would have had it long ago.

Maybe it was the aura of calm authority. Maybe it was the feeling she seemed to project that she would, somehow, get things done.

Whatever it was, it was obvious that she was the Master even without the tiny badge on the shoulder of her tunic, of Sword, Flame, and Book—the badge that only the Master wore.

"Dreaming awake, lad?" Her generous mouth quirked in a smile. "Hadn't you better be doing that in bed?"

He gave himself a mental shake, and returned the smile. "I'm sorry, Master, I was woolgathering."

"I hope you were gathering more than that." She sniffed, and rubbed the side of her nose with her knuckle. "I hope you gathered me some answers. I need them; we've had bad news. The nomads are at the Teeth."

"I have what you wanted, I think," he said cautiously. "I found a whole set of Chronicles taken from some silk merchants who came through the Teeth about a hundred years ago."

"Isn't that a bit old to do us any good?" she asked doubtfully, pushing away from the door frame and walking over to lean on his desk instead.

He shook his head as she planted both palms on the desk top and looked over his shoulder. "No, not really. Things don't change much for the horse-nomads. Not that much *to* change, really. They would probably be much the same today as they were when the Sabirn Empire collapsed . . . except for one thing."

He launched into a fairly concise summary of what he'd gleaned, pausing now and again to check his notes. Felaras followed his speech with narrowed eyes, nodding now and again when something he said seemed to touch on something in her own mind.

His throat was dry and his voice cracking a bit as he built up to the really choice bit of his gleanings. ". . . so this wandering healer, whoever he was, and the merchants seemed to think he was one of us, made one really important change in their outlook. Almost in their religion. By the time the merchants came through, he'd risen in the legends of the Clans to something like a saint or a demigod."

"Which means what? That a scholar gets nearly the same treatment as a shaman?"

"Oh, better," Teo hastened to tell her, not concealing his glee, the glow of discovery making him forget his aching shoulders and burning eyes for a moment. "A man that's a scholar or a healer is sacrosanct. It's assumed that the Wind Gods have him under something like divine protection. If you molest him, you bring the gods' anger down on your whole Clan; if you shelter him, you bring their blessing. A scholar can move about among the Clans pretty much at will, and virtually unmolested. All he has to fear is outlaws."

"What if this bunch is—"

"No," he interrupted, "these aren't outlaws; they have their horsetail banner with them, so they're a real Clan."

"Gods bless." She gripped the edge of the table and closed her eyes, leaning all her weight on her hands; and suddenly Teo saw not her strength, but her bone-deep weariness.

It frightened him. They *depended* on her.

"Master Felaras?" he said, reaching out to touch the wool of her sleeve with tentative fingers. She sighed; and he saw not the Master, but an old, tired woman. One with terrible weariness behind what was no more than a facade of strength. "Master?" he faltered again in dismay.

She opened her eyes quickly, and the strength was back; real, and not an illusion. It was surely the weakness that was the illusion—

She was looking at him measuringly, and he wondered why.

"Teo," she said, slowly, "Would you . . . ?"

When she didn't finish the question, he prompted her. "Would I what? Anything you need, Master Felaras. Just tell me what to look for."

"Never mind." She favored him with another of her half-grins; back to being the Master Felaras who was as predictable and dependable as the stone of the Fortress. "Get on to bed, there's a lad. I'm calling a Full Convocation in the morning, and I want you to have a clear head for it; as one of my three pets, you'll be in for a lot of questioning, after, from your own chapter. I want you in shape to answer clearly and remember who asked what for me." When he hesitated, she jerked her head impatiently in the direction of the door. "Off with you! I'll secure the Library."

He nodded obediently, gathered up his paper and his pens, and handed her his notes on his way out the door.

But as he left the Library he thought he could feel that penetrating stare on his back—as if she was looking for something in him. It seemed that her eyes followed him all the way back to the door of the Archivists' Quarters.

The boy slept uneasily beneath his blankets of felt and horsehide, his face pale and haggard in the light from the clay-lined fire-basket, his dark hair matted with sweat. From time to time he moaned in his sleep, as the pain of his wounds and of the injury to his head passed the drugged wine he'd been given; it bit at him and made him toss his head on the hard, flat leather pillow. He shivered too; and that was a bad sign, for the round felt tent was as warm as a sunshine-gilded spring day, so that meant that the last of the mould-powder had done him no good. Yuchai was undoubtedly in the first stages of infection, and the Healer-woman

Shenshu might not be able to grow what he needed quickly enough to do him any good.

Shaman Northwind (he'd borne the name for so long that even he had difficulty recalling the time when he'd been Taichin, or sometimes Taichin Wanderer) sighed and began unpacking his medicine rattles and sacred incense from their basket. The scent of precious sandalwood rose from the packing; nothing less would call the Wind Lords' attention to their need. He'd helped clean and bind the boy's injuries; he'd well-wished him with all the strength and skill at his command. When all else failed, there was always prayer.

At least the storm has stopped, he thought. *But everything else . . . it's as though the entire world was ill-wishing us. And now Yuchai—lightning spooking his horse, sending both of them into that pit-trap—it was an omen. Wind Lords, have you deserted us too?*

Someone coughed politely outside the tent-flap; Northwind identified the cough without thinking. "My tent is always open to you, Khene Jegrai," he called softly.

The felt tent-flap was pushed aside by a strong, slender brown hand; the rest of Jegrai followed his hand in short order, and was, like the hand, strong and slender. The Khene of Running Horse Clan cast a worried look at the wounded boy, then seated himself cross-legged on the layered carpets of the tent-floor with a grace that was almost boneless.

There was something about the young man that commanded attention, demanded loyalty. Northwind sometimes thought of him as a pure flame in a fine porcelain lamp such as the Suno made and used; his spirit seemed to shine through his flesh. That spirit was powerful enough to make one forget Jegrai's patched and faded clothing, garb that was more suited to a beggar than a Khene and the son of Khenes.

"How is the boy?" That voice, as flexible and obedient to Jegrai's will as his horse, held only concern now. For once—with no one about to see him—Jegrai was not being Khene. Jegrai was being young Yuchai's adored—and anxious—cousin.

The Shaman shrugged eloquently, rippling the fringes decorating his suede leather garments. "He lives. Whether he will prosper I cannot tell you, but it is now in the hands of the Wind Lords. Both I and Shenshu have done all we can."

"The Wind Lords do not hear us," came the bitter reply.

Twenty years ago Northwind would have rebuked Jegrai for blasphemy. Ten years ago he would have delivered a lecture on the folly of man attempting to judge the will of the gods. That was in the days when Running Horse held their territory in relative peace. Before the Suno Lords chose to conquer the Clans from within, by setting Clan against Clan, turning what had been friendly contests of honor into blood-feud and death. Before Khene Sen of the Talchai turned upon them. Before their flight into this strange land where the earth rose to block the sight of the open sky. Now he only sighed.

"I do not know that either, Jegrai. It certainly seems that nothing we have done has prospered."

"Except our running," the young Khene spat. "*That* we do well enough, it seems."

Northwind looked up, and his eyes locked with Jegrai's hard, black ones. There was no doubting the power, the will behind the Khene's eyes. The tent seemed too warm of a sudden, and the Shaman was the first to drop his gaze.

"I do not know what to tell you," the Shaman said, after silence thick enough to choke upon filled the tent. "I truly do not. You know what I know; that the omens have told me that the Winds say our fate lies in the West. And truly, these people of the West cannot seem to stand before us."

"That is at least in part because we move so quickly that we outpace the rumors of our coming." Jegrai's tone was still bitter, and he played with the end of his sash, plaiting and unplaiting the faded fringe. "We are down to half the strength we had when we fled the Talchai, Shaman. At this rate . . . Tell me, should I stop this senseless, cowardly fleeing? Should I give myself over to the hands of our enemies? Will that save my people further suffering?"

To his people, the Khene was as strong, as cold, as a living blade—as fierce as a wind-driven fire. He was none of these things now; the mask was gone before his teacher and oldest companion. Northwind could not meet that burning, agonized gaze, but for that question he did have an answer.

"It was," he said slowly and carefully, "the Talchai who broke faith when your father died. It was the Talchai who allied themselves with those Suno dogs and began gathering or destroying the Outer Clans. More specifically, it was Khene Sen, who would make himself Khekhene over all the Clans. And he did so because you dared to speak the truth of him in Khaltan, the Great Council. Would you have us bind ourselves over to one who licks the spittle of dogs so that he may bear the Banner of Nine Horsetails, so that sons of dogs will call him Khekhene?" His voice strengthened. "You kept honor; Sen has destroyed his."

"What good is honor," Jegrai cried, his voice tight with anguish. "What worth is honor when it is bought with the lives of Vredai children? When the First Law of the Wind Lords is 'Cherish the children, for they are the lifeblood of the Clan' and what I have done has spilled that blood as surely as the swords of the Talchai?"

He says "Vredai children," but he means Yuchai, the Shaman thought. Then he rebuked himself. *Nay, that is less than the truth. I have never seen any but a healer or shaman take the First Law so to heart as Jegrai. Yuchai is the first youngster to be so badly hurt since the raid that near destroyed us—and Jegrai knows full well that it was because Yuchai was striving to emulate him. Jegrai would feel the same guilt over any other child suffering what Yuchai has.*

Yet another thought occurred. *And the boy lived in his shadow. He is the son Jegrai longs to have. . . .*

"What worth is freedom?" he replied softly. "I tell you, it is everything. And if we bought safety at the expense of our freedom, then the Wind Lords *would* turn their backs upon us."

"But—" Jegrai began.

The Shaman cut him off ruthlessly. "And what if you turned back and faced the wrath of Khene Sen alone? What good would that do Running Horse?"

"You would live—"

"We would die," Northwind said fiercely. "Vredai would be no more, her banner trampled, her women and children distributed to Sen's hangers-on, her men sold in the slave markets of Kalandu. You know this, Jegrai. There is not enough grazing for all the Clans since the drought, and that has continued for three years; that is what allowed the Suno to twist fear into the quarrels that began this. That is why when we fled, we fled west, where no one goes. Because there is water and grass in the West, and because Khene Sen will destroy us if he takes us."

Jegrai bowed his head, and his shoulders sagged. "And that too is my fault. If I had not stolen the Talchai shrine—if I had not thrown it into the path of those who pursued us so that their horses trampled it into the dust before they knew what had happened—"

"You called your 'council.' You asked me; you asked all of us before you did it," Northwind reminded him. "And all—myself, Ghekhen Vaichen, your mother Aravay, and Shenshu—we all agreed. Khene Sen had already trampled his Clan's honor into the dust; it were well to remind his people of that. For them to trample and destroy their own shrine was a terrible omen, and we hoped it would shake them deeply. And besides that—"

"We had thought there was no way to escape him; we thought we were doomed," Jegrai finished for him, dully.

Northwind did not like this lifelessness that had come upon his Khene. Even Jegrai's fire could not burn forever, and it seemed he was coming to the end of his will. Northwind put force behind his words in an attempt to shake him from this sickly mood. "Think, Jegrai! We all thought—you and your advisors—it was the only chance we had to distract them from the chase long enough to have a *hope* of eluding them. The Wind Lords favored us, Jegrai. They favored us then; and I—I somehow have the feeling that I *am* reading the omens aright. There is something they wish for us here. . . ." Shaman Northwind sighed. "And we have not done much to find it."

Jegrai shook his head. "Now *that* I shall take the blame for. A winter's march, a spring campaign—we have not done much but trample the land-folk beneath the hooves of our horses. And the crops."

Northwind felt the pain any of the Vredai felt at the abuse of good land. It was not through will that Running Horse Clan wandered—it was through lack of good grazing lands. Any of them would as lief gone back to the settled, pastured life of their ancestors, before the Suno drove them into the steppes.

"This land is leaderless, and I cannot see how these folks have lived all this time without a leader to rule them. It is a good land, ill-used," Jegrai continued, "but we are hurting it further—I can hear it groaning, Shaman. It is spring, and there should be, there must be, planting. But we, *we* are keeping the land-folk from that planting. We rob them, when we should be trading with them. Now they will starve, and then there will be nothing and we will starve—"

"But we are starving now," Northwind said with reluctance. "What choice have we but to live off them? And the Talchai may be yet on our track."

"I think . . . I need a council, Shaman." Jegrai finally seemed to have regained some of his resolve. "Tell the others; speak to the warriors, the scouts, then come to me at midmorning. We need, perhaps, to change direction. Perhaps the time has come to stop running."

"I shall," Northwind replied soberly, heartened again. "And I shall speak with the Wind Lords this night. If there be anything I may do to gain their aid . . ."

"So long as you gain Yuchai's healing—and an end to the deaths of my people—that is all that matters to me, Shaman." Jegrai rose, his head brushing the roof of the tent. "The rest must be, as you have told me, done or undone by our own actions. Tell the Wind Lords that when you speak to them."

"I shall," Northwind replied soberly, as Jegrai slipped back out into the cold, damp night. "Believe me, I shall."

Felaras surveyed the Convocation with what she hoped looked like calm authority. Every person in the Fortress truly a member of the Order was here, in the Great Hall. Once this had been some huge assembly room, perhaps an armory or training-room, or a dining hall, but Master Duran had caused it to be altered so that it matched his memories of the great lecture rooms in the colleges of Targheiden. It was useful to have one place within the walls where all members of the Order could gather at one time. Tier after tier of wooden benches built like three huge staircases, one on each of the three blank walls, rose to the ceiling, so that the room had taken on the look of a lopsided bowl, or half a bowl, with the lectern at the bottom of it.

It was a perishing *cold* bowl, though. No fireplace, and mostly stone. Her nose was cold, and her fingers, and she hoped her nose wouldn't start dripping. That would surely put paid to the little dignity she could muster.

The room buzzed with the sound of those assembled muttering to one another. The room was nearly full, and the folk on the benches hardly looked to be members of the same organization. There was no "uniform" for the Order, not even an approximately uniform way of dress.

That was the legacy of Duran; their diversity. They came to the Order from every class, every race, every nation. Half of those here in the Fortress had been born here—but there were plenty, like Felaras herself, who had come from far away, hot on the scent of learning. Some had come seeking a legend of magic; some, like Halun, had come on the advice of their teachers. All shared the same dream: to learn, to teach, to preserve old knowledge and seek new.

That was the *only* commonality within the Order. And the varied dress of the members reflected this.

Those of the Watchers tended to wear breeches and tunic regardless of sex, but the cut, color, and style of those garments ranged from the dark cotton gabardine garments typical of the island kingdom of Bergem that Kasha wore, to the heavy, brightly dyed, fur-trimmed wool of Albirn that she herself favored. The Archivists tended to robes, with deep pockets and wide sleeves that could also serve as pockets, but that did not even hold true throughout the chapter. And the Seekers wore anything and everything; Flame tended to knee-robes and breeches and Hand to short tunics and breeches—but there sat Halun in a rich blue robe more suited to an Archivist, and beside him was Zorsha in a dark-grey tunic that could have come from Kasha's wardrobe. And the minds and souls about her were as varied as the clothing their bodies wore. Felaras wondered how in the name of all the gods she was ever going to get this motley crew to agree on anything.

She had never enjoyed lecturing, nor holding these Convocations. She always felt like a Seeker's prize specimen of new insect under all those eyes. She'd held Full Convocations perhaps four times in her twenty-seven years as Master. This would be the fifth—and the most important.

She cleared her throat, and the dull hum of voices ceased. Silence fell over them all, a silence that seemed fragile, and prone to shatter at a breath.

"You've probably heard the rumors," she said, deciding that blunt directness would serve her better than anything else now. *Tell them the bad news, get the shock over with, and then get those fine minds moving; that's what I need to do.* "I called you all here to tell the exact truth. There's a Clan of horse-nomads out of the East that's been pounding through Azgun since fall.

Nobody's managed to hold them, or even make an effective stand against them. Now they're here; just on the other side of the Teeth. I've been warning the Yazkirn Princes and the Court of Ancas that they're coming; I wasn't believed, and I see no reason why they should suddenly send an army to rescue us. They won't lift a finger to help us; they will move only if they see a threat to themselves. As you should well know. So we're alone in this."

Near two hundred pairs of eyes were on her; brown, grey, blue—some shocked, some frightened, some thoughtful—and some, still, full of an arrogant contempt for the danger on their doorstep.

"There are, at minimum, nearly a thousand fighters. That's a guess, but probably a low one—*I'd* reckon more, and you all know what *my* chapter was. And that's assuming their women don't fight, or their youngsters, which may be a stupid thing to assume. The Vale folk are running for shelter; I sent them to the caves—"

"I thought the caves were supposed to be *our* shelter!" shouted an angry voice from the back.

"Would you rather they came here for refuge?" she replied sharply. "There's at least *room* for them in the caves! Tell me where in Hladyr's name we'd put them if they came here, why don't you?"

The tense silence fell again. This time the silence held a strong note of fear. They were beginning to see the danger. And take it to heart.

"All right, now you know the worst of it. There's no doubt in my mind that we can keep them off the Pass. The question I have is if we can—or should—try to do anything, and in that I include trying to outwait them. We've got supplies enough for about two months, but no way of getting more except from Yazkirn, and that means trading. And you all know the only coin we have to trade with."

She paused, but it seemed that there was no one else ready to make any protests yet.

"I want you all to think about this problem; we've a couple hundred of the finest minds in the world here. I want to hear if any of you have any answers *or* questions. We all know that sometimes it's the questions that make the answers. I'm including you novices in this—sometimes what seems to be a stupid question or answer turns out not to be so stupid after all. When you leave this room you'll be given duties to cover so that we can get the Fortress ready to withstand a siege. But while your hands are busy, I want your minds busy too. Whatever you come up with, put it in writing. Leave it in my study. Sign it or not, I don't care. I want your thoughts, men and women of the Order. I can't make a decision that will determine the fate of the Order without knowing those thoughts."

Once again she raked the room with her eyes.

There was very little fear there now. Some dismay, but very little fear. And a great many faces that had gone quiet and inward-focused. She began to hope.

"All right, then; see your chapter Leaders about your duties—and remember what I told you." She made a dismissing motion. "You may go."

"So." Jegrai settled himself on a thin pad of stuffed felt beside the cold fire-pot in his tent, and surveyed the faces of his four councilors. Light came through the white felt; it was shadowy within, but not at all dark. Beyond the felt walls he could hear the sounds of the camp; children playing, folk talking, normal and sane sounds that had not been heard among the Vredai tents in far too long. He hoped that what they decided here might bring those sounds back again.

He had trusted the wisdom of these four since he first took the reins of Running Horse at fifteen. Then, they had ruled him. . . .

Now he ruled them, and the change had come about so gradually that no one of them could put a finger on a particular moment and say, "That was when things changed." But the change was there. And he had thanked the Wind Lords that they had been great enough of soul to accept that change.

On his right, Shaman Northwind; a man so old he had outlived Jegrai's grandfather. He looked as fragile as one of those pampered little birds the Suno Emperor kept in gold cages. In some ways he was as frail as he seemed, but not in any fashion that had any significance to his duties. His eyes were oddly gentle, and full of good humor even at the worst of times; his face was as wrinkled as a dried berry. His silver hair, worn loose and as long as his waist, marked his calling, for no warrior would have grown such a convenient handle for an enemy to seize. His moustache and neat little beard were as silver as his hair, but not nearly so long. Today he was wearing his fringed ceremonial robes and his buffalo-skull helmet, which indicated to Jegrai that he, too, felt this council might well decide the fate of Running Horse Khenat.

To Jegrai's left sat his mother, Aravay, as she had sat at the left hand of his father. She was like an antique carving of fine ivory; nothing could be read upon her face, which was a serene, feminized version of her son's. *After all these years,* Jegrai thought in sudden wonder, *after all she has been through, suffered through, she is still beautiful.*

But she was more than beautiful; she was clever and cunning and wise. She heard everything that any woman of the Clan said; knew within a day what any of them did. She knew entanglements of kinship and honor-debt going back generations; remembered things Jegrai would have long since forgotten. She had advised his father, and he had had the sense to listen to her. Some had scoffed at Jegrai for keeping her on his council, but Jegrai had no intention of *ever* letting her go. The man who put away the gifts that Aravay had to offer simply because she was his mother was a fool who did not deserve to be called "Khene."

To the Shaman's right sat Shenshu, the chief of the Healer-women. Where Aravay was an ivory carving, Shenshu was a round little earthenware statuette; everyone's favorite aunt, the person who heard everything troubling anyone. Nor would she reveal those secrets—not directly, at least. But Jegrai could depend on her to tell him—indirectly, if need be—what he needed to know.

To Aravay's left was Vaichen, the warlord of Khenat Vredai. Dark as old leather, aged, wrinkled and weathered, and bald as a stone—but he sat straight and tall, and met his Khene's level gaze with perfect fearlessness. Injured in a fall that killed his horse this past winter, his right leg stiff and without feeling. There were those who said he had outlived his usefulness, for what good was a warlord who could not lead the charge? To which Jegrai would immediately reply, "What use is a warlord who does not know his brain from his buttocks?" So long as Ghekhen Vaichen could use that brain and speak his mind, Jegrai would see that the horsetail banner *remained* in front of his tent. . . .

"So," he said, looking from one to another of his advisors. "We are met. I would hear what the people will not tell their Khene."

Shenshu cleared her throat and began, with an apologetic side glance at the Shaman. "They are frightened, Jegrai. They say that the Wind Lords have either abandoned us, forgotten us, or can no longer hear us in this land where the earth blocks the sight of the sky. But they are also afraid of the Talchai." She ran a string of wooden beads through her fingers, as if the feel of the carved wood in her hands soothed her; they clicked softly in the pauses between her words. "They say we must not stop; that we must keep running. They think that the Wind Lords will not be able to hear the Talchai either, in this place, and that . . . you have seen, perhaps, the consequences when a rabbit is chased by a dog through camp? The rabbit, running swiftly, may overturn waterskins, may frighten the horses—but he surprises the encampment and they do nothing to *him*. But the dog, following after—ai, the women chase with sticks, the men with whips, children throw stones, and every hand is against him. So they think it may be with us, as the rabbit, and the Talchai, as the dog. We scatter these land-folk before us, but when the Talchai come they shall be aroused and they shall have regathered their wits. We must let nothing stop us but the Great Western Ocean. So say the frightened."

Jegrai nodded; in some ways that turn of thought had a great deal of merit. Surely it was true that they had, so far, met little resistance. But there was no guarantee that this fortunate state of affairs would continue. He did not know what lay beyond the mountains. At this point, none of them knew. If it was another organized empire such as the Suno ruled, they would be crushed.

He reached beside him for the skin of *khmass*, and poured each of his councilors a full wooden cup of the powerful fermented milk. He had no fear that any of them would lose his or her head to it, and he wanted them to know he truly wished to hear everything, however distasteful. And indeed, there was a slight relaxation of posture in everyone around the circle at this gesture of hospitality.

"So, the frightened would continue to flee, and hope we may still outpace the rumors of our coming." He sipped his pungent *khmass* and nodded thoughtfully. "There is merit in such a thought—but we have not yet met a people who can stand against us. And when we do, we may find ourselves trapped between the grass fire and the raging torrent."

He rolled the cup between his palms, the wood silken and warm under his fingers, and waited to hear what this observation would elicit.

"That is the more likely as we force deeper into the West," rumbled Vaichen. "The warriors have a liking for this valley beyond the Pass, what they have seen of it. They say it is a good place for defense. They are saying that we should take it, and make our stand here. Then, when the Talchai come, we should die in honor and glory, making them pay, and pay, and pay."

"And you, Ghekhen?" Jegrai looked at his warlord's hands, clenched around his wooden cup.

"To survive and prosper is a better revenge," the old man said reluctantly. "To take this valley—if we can—would be no bad thing. It is defensible—and is like the old tales of the home the Suno stole from us. But I cannot counsel making a stand; I would not care to have our banner in Khene Sen's tent, no matter how many lives it had cost him."

"Can we take this valley?" Aravay spoke softly. "I do not know that we can. You know that my care is the scouts. The young scouts have brought tales to me, of wizards on the western pass. They say that it is only because they are vowed not to meddle in the lives of lesser men that we have not been struck down before this. They say that the storm of last night that sent Yuchai's horse shying into the pit-trap is a warning not to go further. They say that the wizards of the mountain can call upon the lightning—"

"Any man can call upon the lightning," Northwind said skeptically. "The question is, will it answer him?"

"They say that the lightning has answered the wizards, and out of a cloudless sky and bright day," Aravay replied. "They captured those who had seen it with their own eyes."

"Men will say anything," interrupted Vaichen.

"But these were not men, they were children. And they had seen this less than a year ago."

Jegrai clenched his jaw, angry at the thought that his orders regarding youngsters had been disobeyed. "Children? We took children? How? What became of these children?" Jegrai asked sternly. "We are burdened enough with Vredai children, but—I gave orders that there was to be no slaughter of women and young things. Vredai has *honor*. We fight only those who will fight us—and we make no warfare on the helpless."

"The scouts surprised and scattered a party of fleeing land-folk in the pass itself," his mother answered serenely. "And two children were left behind. As you ordered, the scouts took counsel of me. Upon my advice, Obodei, who has some of their tongue, took them blindfolded through the valley pass and released them." Aravay smiled a little. "But only after telling them to tell their parents that we numbered in the tens of thousands and ate babies, and that they were fortunate that Obodei was not hungry at that moment."

The Shaman grinned, Shenshu snickered, and Vaichen shouted his laughter. Even Jegrai had to chuckle.

"Old schemer, well did your husband name you Fox-woman!" Vaichen snorted. "I think perhaps I should take the horsetail banner and have it placed before your tent!"

Aravay inclined her head to him, her eyes twinkling.

"These wizards," Jegrai prompted. "Did the children have anything else to say of them?"

"That they are very strange; more scholar and healer than wizard. They sound something like to Holy Vedani. That they keep mostly to themselves, but have been known to take a very clever child into their ranks should the child wish to become a wizard. That they have lived upon the mountaintop for time out of mind, and trade wondrous devices for food and the like, but have otherwise little to do with the folk of the valley."

Jegrai whistled between his teeth, softly. "So," he said, after turning all this over in his mind, "we have one choice: to make a stand. And another: to continue to flee. I think perhaps we have a third. We might seek allies and settle here, so that if the Talchai follow, they find us in the position of strength."

"Allies from among the wizards?" the Shaman asked, one eyebrow rising high. From his expression, Jegrai judged that he was surprised, but cautiously approved. "What of the land-folk, then?"

"I do not know; I do not think it matters for now. Eventually we must win them if we are to remain, but first we must win the wizards. It would be best to come at the wizards with at least the appearance of strength, hm? It would make an alliance to their advantage, I think."

"Aye," Vaichen said, slowly. "What say you to this: let us harry these land-folk, but gently. If they flee, pursue only so as to let them know we do pursue, but allow them to escape. Raid only to take what we need, no wanton wastage, no despoiling, no burning. Most of all, take this end of the valley and hold it, so that we have a secure camp to work from."

"Good." Jegrai nodded, and felt a rising hope. This might well work. "The warriors are weary enough to accept this, I think. Listen out there—I think the Vredai are equally tired of running and warfare. I think they would welcome the chance to rest. All of you—pass the word that we *do not* harry the wizards; we will tell the people that they are dangerous, and probably quick to anger—"

"And like to Holy Vedani," his mother interrupted. "That will hold them when naught else will. The Wind Lords would surely curse a man who caused harm to such a wizard. Fear of the Wind Lords will stay their hands where fear of magic would not."

"Very good." He put his cup down on the carpet and leaned forward. "This is what we do not want the wizards to learn; that we are fleeing the Talchai, that we are not here to conquer, but in retreat. If they rally their folk and cause them to come upon us from behind, we *surely* will be caught between fire and torrent. If the Talchai do not come upon us this summer, they surely will the next."

All four of his advisors nodded at that, faces sober. "Is there anything else?" Shenshu asked.

"I need to learn more of these wizards," he replied, chewing his lip. "Much, much more."

Though Jegrai had his own tent, he had neither wife nor sister to tend it for him. Though Aravay had her own tent, which had been his father's, she found time to tend to his. The arrangement worked well, for she could bring him the scouting reports—if they were less than urgent—with his dinner.

So she had tonight. The light from the lantern hanging from the centerpole cast a gentle glow that made her seem as ageless as a Wind Lord. She handed him the covered bowl of thin stew she had brought from her fire, and knelt beside him while he ate.

"The wizards are of a surety aiding land-folk over the pass," Aravay said softly. "So all the scouts say."

Jegrai flexed his aching shoulders and leaned back against the tentpole. He had ridden out with a raiding party, but what they had brought back with them was firewood; a singularly awkward prey to carry. "These land-folk either will or will not return; it is of no consequence. If we do settle here, our own folk will make up for those who flee. How do the folk care for this new camp?"

"They do not like the mountain at our back, but the pasturage and good water make up for it," his mother replied. "My son, you are worried. Have you learned something which troubles you?"

"Aye," he brooded for a moment, then concluded that Aravay might as well know the worst. "We can go no further. It is as I feared. Beyond the western pass lies a land that is well ruled, and strong. It is called Yazkirn, and governed by princes. They have ignored our presence because they care not overmuch for these lands; they are hard to reach and tax, and besides, contain the wizards. But—should we force our way over the pass, it would be up with us. They *would* come to the defense of their land, and crush us. If they even think we have become a threat, they will come to us, and I think we would have no chance."

The fire in the fire-pot flared, and Aravay's eyes showed her alarm, though nothing else did. "How came you to learn this?" she asked, cautiously.

"That merchant we let pass. I questioned him myself; promised him no despoiling in return for truth." Jegrai sighed. "I have some skill at reading men, I think. He told truth. We are in the cooking pot. . . ."

"Unless we can gain the favor of the wizards."

"Aye." He bit his lip, and told her what he would tell no other living soul. "They frighten me, Mother—and they fascinate me. They *can* call the lightning, for every prisoner we have taken has tales of it, tales so unlikely I think they can only be true. They have used it—imagine this, Mother—to gain metals, and to level great rock outcroppings, and to change the lay of the land about their fortress! And if they can call lightning to do that for them, it should be the work of a single thought to use it to start a fire in the grasslands where we cannot escape it."

Only once in Jegrai's memory had the Vredai been caught in a grass fire. They had lost a third of the herds, and many lives, and there were men and women among those left who still bore the ugly keloid scars from it. It had been in the first year of the drought, and the memory still gave him nightmares when storms passed overhead.

"The stories I hear say they are very wise," his mother replied thoughtfully, her hands busy with plaiting a new riding quirt. "And that they do nothing without good reason. *And* that they are no friends to the kings over the mountains."

Jegrai sat straight up. "That is something I had not heard!" he exclaimed.

His mother looked up and smiled at him. "The kings over the mountains drove them here, or so it is said," she told him serenely. "And wizard or no, I have never yet seen the man who does not thirst for revenge."

"So-ho. A reason to ally to us. Their magic—and our warriors . . ." Jegrai fell silent, considering the possibilities.

"You have ever been a Khene who respects good advice when you can get it, my son," his mother said demurely, breaking the long silence.

He roused from his thoughts and gave her a half smile. "If there are strange gods to have the blessing of, and wizards to come upon my side—it would be folly to foul my chances, no?"

"And you have never been foolish, not even as a child." Her eyes darkened with affection; then a sadness passed across her face. "The Shaman wished me to tell you that there is no change with Yuchai."

Jegrai cursed under his breath, and his food lost its savor. He started to push his bowl away, then recalled how little they had, and finished it grimly.

"My son—I speak as a mother." Aravay put her hand over his, and her eyes were soft with concern. "I cannot see how Yuchai's hurt is your doing, nor does his mother blame you for it."

"You cannot—but I can," he replied harshly. "The boy follows after me with his heart in his hand. He strives to copy all I do. He wishes so much to have my approval that he would do anything to get it. There was no need for him to have joined the scouts. He was barely within the age. I could have told him he must wait a year. But I was a scout at fourteen summers, so therefore he must do likewise—I should have forbade it. He is not the rider nor the fighter that I was at twelve, much less having the skill I had at fourteen. But I could not find it in my heart to tell him no. And this is the result of my ill-judgment. Bones broken, and flesh torn by the stakes in that pit, and a blow to the head from which he may never awake—and it is only by the grace of the Wind Lords that those people have honor enough not to poison the stakes. It is only by their grace that he is not dead already."

"Jegrai—" Aravay said, after a moment of brooding silence. "I wonder—the Holy One was a healer—and if the wizards *are* of his kind, could it be that they could help young Yuchai?"

He started, for the thought had not occurred to him. "It may be—it just may be. All the more reason to ally with them. And may the Wind Lords grant it be not too late!"

✧ CHAPTER THREE ✧

Kasha shaded her eyes from the brilliant afternoon sun with one hand while she clung to the polished wood of the Fortress flagpole with the other, and strained up on her toes as high as she dared.

"I wish you wouldn't do that," Teo complained from the window below her, his uneasiness plain in his voice. "It makes me dizzy."

She grinned down at him, perfectly comfortable on her tower-top perch. He squinted up at her; from here his blocky face and wide shoulders made him look a little like a granite statue that had never been completely finished. *Hladyr bless,* she thought impatiently, *I've got both feet planted on the pole-socket. What's to be nervous about?*

"Why should it make *you* dizzy?" she asked mockingly. "It's not *you* that's up here!"

He shivered visibly and looked away. "I can't help thinking about how Benno fell from up there."

"Benno was a thirteen-year-old fool who didn't live to see fourteen *because* he was a fool," she retorted, reveling in the brisk east wind that was playing with the short strands of her hair. "He climbed up right after a storm when the slates were slippery, and he didn't have a rope on him. I do, because I'm *not* a fool."

"We know you aren't a fool, Kasha," Zorsha replied. "You keep forgetting Teo saw him fall."

So did I, and so did you, she thought, but didn't say. *People die; it happens. You learn from it, but you try not to let it live in you forever.*

"Now that you're up there," Teo said, carefully not looking at

625

her, "can you see them?" He tugged at his neat little beard with his right hand; an unconscious gesture that showed how nervous he was.

She squinted at the eastern end of the Vale. "Maybe . . . I can see a big dust-cloud, anyway. That'll be their horse-herd." She groped for the far-glasses looped around her neck, and put them to her eyes. It wasn't easy adjusting them with only one hand, but unlike Benno, she wasn't out to prove what a great daredevil she was. The blurs of green, white, and brown finally leapt into clarity.

"Well, I sort of see them," she called down. "Too far away to make out people, but there's a bunch of white things that are probably tents. And if there's as many people as there are tents, we've been undercounting."

She swung the lenses slightly right, to see if she could make out anything under the dust-cloud. "Hladyr bless—" she said in awe, the words trailing off.

"What?" Teo asked anxiously. "Something—something wrong?"

"No, nothing like that. It's just—I've never seen so many horses before in my entire life." Even with the far-glasses they were just tiny dots—but so *many* of them!

"There must be hundreds—thousands. No wonder they move them every day; they'd eat the grass down to the ground if they stayed put for long." She let the glasses fall, and felt for her footing on the slates of the peaked roof. "I've seen enough; I'm coming down."

The window in Halun's study stood wide open to the balmy breeze, and it faced westward, down the side of the Pass opposite the Vale. It was seductively easy to believe that the danger posed by the nomads simply didn't exist. Even the sight of the novices beyond the walls (cutting back all brush that could conceal anything bigger than a rabbit) didn't break the illusion of safety.

Halun was swiftly coming to the conclusion that he had been as much a prey to that illusion as anyone else. Young Zorsha's report of the afternoon's observations had been unsettling, to say the least.

"That many?" he asked again, still surprised. "Truly that many of them?"

"That many," Zorsha replied grimly, pushing his hair out of his grey-brown eyes. "Felaras was not exaggerating the danger, I can tell you that. We haven't heard from the Watchers she sent out to try and get a closer view, but from the size of the encampment these nomads are traveling with a population the equal of a small city."

"I never said she was exaggerating, lad," Halun answered, crossing his arms on the table between them and leaning his weight on them. "I just thought she might have been misinformed, or have miscalculated. She was right; I was wrong, and I should have known better than to challenge a Master in her own specialty." He produced a rueful chuckle. "Serves me right, too. Pride begins, a stumble follows."

Zorsha half-smiled, but his deep-set eyes were still shadowed with unvoiced worry. "Kasha thinks we're in even deeper trouble than Felaras has let on. It could be; of the three of us, she talks more openly to Kasha than to Teo or me, but even I can see she hasn't been sleeping much or eating regularly."

"I don't suppose you have any notion of what her plans are, do you?"

He was faintly disappointed when his former novice shook his head. "She's still collecting opinions," Zorsha told him.

There was silence for a moment. Sunlight was beginning to shine in through the window, and it made a square of bright gold on the satiny brown wood of the floor. Halun watched dust-motes dance in the sunbeam until Zorsha spoke again.

"I can tell you about those. Since they seem to fall into categories, she's been having me tally them. About a third of the ones we've gotten so far are variations on the theme of running and hiding. About a third want us to stay where we are and pretend we're invisible. Another third are variations on negotiating with them—"

"Do we have any notion of what we're dealing with?"

"Well, Teo says they're definitely the Clan called 'Running Horse'; that's *Vredai* in their tongue." Zorsha managed the strange name with an ease Halun found enviable. He'd never been much good at speaking languages, although he'd mastered the written version of several. "He says this is a real Clan and not some outlaws, and something he uncovered in the Archives has Felaras a little more hopeful. But whether it's to give us an edge in frightening them off or in talking to them, I don't know."

"My personal choice would be to remove ourselves to one of the two sister-houses," Halun replied, "but I can see the difficulties. The only conceivable way we could get by with it would be to slip in a few at a time; otherwise the Prince of Parda or the Duke of Albirn would forbid any more of us within their borders. Failing that, we *could* pack ourselves up wholesale and try somewhere else, I suppose."

Zorsha sighed and shook his head, and his straw-gold hair tumbled back into his eyes. "I told that to Kasha," he said, raking it out of the way again. "She pointed out that more than half of our members are over forty; a third are over fifty. Can you see yourself making a trek across the mountains, when you've never been outside the Vale since you were a novice?"

Halun was forced to admit young Kasha had a point. "I suppose not. It is altogether galling, but I am afraid I must admit I couldn't make an unassisted trek to the caves, these days. And even with the help of you younger folk—Hladyr bless, but we'd have to devote four of them just to keep Diermud from following a portentous cloud-shape or mist-wisp right off the side of the mountain."

"And he's not the only one," Zorsha agreed. "Halun, at this point leaving is right out of the question. Kasha *has* been out of the Fortress this past month, out on the peaks, and she told me what a trip would be like if we tried to make it—"

"She's been out on the mountains? Why on earth would a woman—"

"She told me it's one of the duties of all the Watchers to take a kind of long-range patrol in rotation even when nothing's threatening us. She's gone out at least twice a moon since she was promoted from novice."

Halun was briefly annoyed at himself for forgetting something so basic; if he intended to take the Master's seat away from Felaras, he should at least keep in mind that the women of the Watchers were not the sheltered creatures his mother and sisters had been! It would behoove him to keep that factor ever in mind when dealing with his rival.

Zorsha was continuing. "Anyway, the point is that while it's pleasant enough here in Fortress Pass, she says that those thunderstorms we see over the mountains can literally be killers even for the young and fit. For the old, the sickly—it would be suicide."

"It would be folly to think we could hide from these nomads," Halun mused, drumming his fingers on the wood of the table. "If we know about them, they most assuredly have learned of us. And while some of my less worldly colleagues may have forgotten the fact, we are hardly self-sufficient. While our Vale land-folk are hiding in the caves, they are not out planting crops. And if they are not planting, there will be nothing to harvest. I have seldom seen foodstuffs coming to us from the west side of the Pass. . . ."

Zorsha nodded tiredly. "Exactly. That's exactly what Kasha said."

"A bright young woman, is Kasha," Halun said absently, then saw a tiny twinge, almost too insignificant to be called a reaction, pass across Zorsha's thin, bony face at the sound of her name.

Hm? Something odd there, Halun thought. *I think perhaps a change of subject is in order.*

"Zorsha, I hesitate to interfere in your personal life—but I *was* your Master when you were a novice, and I feel a certain— ah—proprietary interest in your life. Is there some trouble between you and Kasha?"

Zorsha flinched a little. "No . . . well, not precisely trouble . . ."

"Something troubling you, then?" Zorsha had been Halun's favorite among all the dozen or so novices he'd trained. The cheerful young orphan passed up from the sister-house in Albirn had quite won his solitary heart, and was the nearest he had to a son. "Would you care to talk about it?"

Zorsha sighed. "You know how long we've been friends, Halun; practically since the first moment I arrived here."

Halun nodded. "The Unholy Trinity, we called you—Zorsha, Kasha, and Teo. We never saw one of you without the other two somewhere about." He shook his head with a reminiscent chuckle. "You children!"

"We aren't children anymore," Zorsha said glumly. "And—I would like to have more from Kasha than to just be a friend. And she's not interested."

"Why?" Halun replied in amazement. "Hladyr bless, I thought every young woman wanted—well—" He coughed. "Well, a marriage and a family, anyway."

"Not Kasha, at least not from me—and the worst part of it is, I have to agree with her reasons." Zorsha looked as forlorn as a lost spaniel puppy. "She says that if she—favored me that way, Teo would be hurt. And if she favored Teo, I'd be hurt. And no matter which of us she favored, we'd never be the same kind of friends again, afterward. So she isn't going to favor either of us."

Halun was totally dumbfounded. "Hladyr bless. I didn't think there was a young person in the world capable of thinking past his cr—ahem. Past his primal urges. She could be right, you know. At least for now."

"Oh, she is." Zorsha's thin face grew longer. "That doesn't mean I have to *like* it. I know very well that if I knew she and Teo were lovers, I'd—I'd—well, I'd be angry, and pretty hurt. And it would take an awfully long time to get over that hurt. And even if I could, well—they'd always be two, and I'd be on the outside. We'd never be three again. And the same would be true if the positions were reversed for me and Teo, only worse, because Teo would be terribly hurt and try not to show it. He'd probably just sink into his books like Master Diermud and we'd never see him again except at meals. But—" He colored. "—sometimes I can't help but wish he'd fall in love with somebody else, or—have a religious conversion or—or—something—"

Halun nodded sympathetically, and put one paternal hand on the boy's—or rather, young man's—shoulder. *So my Ancas imp is grown up enough to think beyond the moment. I shall have to cease thinking of him as a boy.* "Well, never having been afflicted with your problem, I can't very well advise you. I fear I never was that attracted to anyone, inside or outside the Order. But you have my sympathy, if nothing else."

"Thank you." Zorsha smiled wanly. "At least if you'll let me wear your ears down about it, now and again—?"

"Of course."

"Well, that'll help."

"But the cost to you, young man—" Halun wagged an admonishing finger at him "—is that you are going to have to keep me informed. While I can understand Felaras not wanting every bird-brained flitter-head in the Order to go flying off on tangents because of a little bad news, I rather resent that she feels she needn't tell those of us who are levelheaded until she's ready for us to hear things."

Zorsha grinned. "Well, I kind of tend to agree with you there. No fear, Master Halun. What I know, you'll know. But right now, I'm afraid I've got brush-cutting detail, so I'd better get to it."

Halun stood up with a scraping of chair legs across the wooden floor to let him out, and thought with some little satisfaction that Felaras hardly reckoned on his having an ear in her camp.

Yes indeed, my dear rival, he thought, shutting the door behind his former pupil, *I know very well you've been getting information on the Seekers from Zorsha. But this time you have forgotten something. A window like Zorsha can let you see* out *into the Seekers—but he can also let me see in—to your plans. And I just may be able to turn those plans to uses you never imagined.*

Young Vredai riders showed off their horsemanship and high spirits, yipping and catcalling each other as they milled in an eddy of barely controlled chaos with Jegrai in the center. The raiders were all of them Jegrai's age and younger, but tough, and far from inexperienced.

The pity of it was that there weren't any inexperienced fighters over the age of fifteen in the Vredai. Not anymore.

Jegrai raised his fist high over his head, and the riders reined their mounts in with instantaneous obedience. Quiet hung in the air like the dust they'd stirred up. Now there were only the camp-sounds, the clink of harness, the occasional stamping of an impatient hoof.

Then, when he thought he'd held them long enough—

"Hai *ya!*" Jegrai shouted, bringing his fist down, and digging his heels into his own mount's sides.

The entire party swirled out of the encampment in a tangle of tails and legs and dust, with Jegrai in the lead on his tough little roan gelding.

Jegrai had taken charge of this raiding party himself with two purposes in mind. The first—well, his people required frequent reminders that their Khene was also a warrior. His father had led raiding parties—

—yai-ah, and it was a raiding party that killed him—

But that was a thought Jegrai would not dwell on for long. There had been other reasons for the failure of that raid, and none of them applied here and now. This was a different set of circumstances, and a different sort of raid.

The fact was that the Khene of Vredai had best be prepared to prove himself on a regular basis, and it had again come time for Jegrai to do just that.

The other reason for leading this raid was more personal. Jegrai was hoping, in his deepest heart, that in the excitement of the raid he might forget the spectre of Yuchai moaning in pain and delirium in the Shaman's tent. At least for a time.

But at first there was little to distract him. There was no one and nothing at the first few farms they came upon, only the fields and deserted buildings. It was a good land they rode across, and Jegrai felt a twinge of guilt at driving the land-folk from it. Rich black soil, well watered, but now going to grass and weeds; windbreaks of strange, tall evergreen trees with pungent needles. And all of it deserted, forlorn in the morning sun.

Still, that was hardly surprising; the scouts had been reporting for days that the land-folk were packing up and fleeing—westward somewhere. Some—few—had gone over that far pass guarded by the wizards.

Ah, but the rest had just disappeared, as if the ground of the western mountains ate them, their goods, their livestock. They simply vanished, leaving neither trace nor track. It was a mystery. It was one Jegrai did not care to have solved, particularly. He would just as soon not slaughter defenseless farmers; such a slaughter had no honor in it, and bought Vredai nothing but the possibly dangerous ill will of the land-folk that remained.

And it felt too much like the time the Talchai had ridden through the camp, slaying combatants and noncombatants indiscriminately. Riding down children. No, Jegrai wanted no such stain on his hands.

He shook off the dark thoughts and listened instead to the jokes and jibes of his followers. They rode in sun-gilded high spirits for most of the morning, without seeing a single thing worth stopping for. As morning turned toward noon, they penetrated deeper into the valley—much deeper than any Vredai party had ever passed before. And as they topped a rise, they found themselves riding into the yard of a dwelling-place that bore the unmistakable signs of having been abandoned mere hours ago.

Possessions had been dropped on the roadway, strewn as if kicked out of the way, and discarded by those in too much haste to bend to retrieve them; a thin tendril of smoke still curled up from the chimney of the house.

With the wariness of long habit, the raiders scattered and took cover. But when there were no sounds of life, they crept from shelter and began prowling the abandoned buildings.

They found a few animals still remaining, two nursing sows in their pens and a couple dozen half-feral goats and chickens; the former too large and too protective of their young to move from their styes with any speed, the latter too stubborn and wild to catch. The warriors made fine sport with what they found, slaughtering the pigs to take back to the camp, rounding up the goats, decorating themselves with the strange garments and utensils. One young warrior flung a bright quilt about his shoulders like a motley cape; another topped his helm with a foolish-looking cap, and a third traded his helm for some kind of metal basin. Jegrai sat his horse, aloof from it all, checking for signs of which way the land-folk had fled—until his sharp eyes caught an unmistakable sign on the soft ground of one of the empty pastures.

The print of horse-hooves!

He whooped to get the raiders' attention; they abandoned their foolishness and joined him in following the tracks all the way to the western fence.

One panel of the fence was down; had been *taken* down. "What do you make of this?" he asked Abodai, the best tracker of the lot of them.

Abodai pursed his lips, which made his moustache squirm on his upper lip as if it had a life of its own. "I would say that this was a true herd, mares, foals, and a stallion. I think perhaps the fear of the land-folk spoke to the herd, made them spooky and impossible to catch. This may be what delayed these folk so as to abandon so much. So. It may well be that the herdsman felt that to let the horses free would keep them out of our hands, no? Or it may well be that the herdsman is with them, mounted, driving them before him. And he thinks we cannot catch them."

Jegrai grinned. "Foolish herdsman!" The shiny copper, brass, and silver trinkets, the other booty they had picked out of what had been abandoned, was now cast away. The goats were left in the care of the youngest, least experienced member of the raiding party to be driven back to the Clan. He would lead a foraging party back for the pig carcasses and the rest.

But the remaining members of the raiding party would be going after the booty that truly mattered: the horses. Gold and silver were fine for ornamentation, brass and tin useful, but horses were life itself. So far they had captured only two old mares, both too old to breed, and one half-broken gelding. The young gelding had called up a fire of lust in the heart of every person of the Vredai that had seen him; nearly four hands higher than the sturdy little steppes horses, he was clean-limbed and strong and swift. Jegrai badly wanted a stallion of his kind to breed into his heard, and mares to breed to his stallions. With such tall, swift horses, they might hold even against the Talchai.

"Hai-ya!" he cried, giving his gelding his head and urging him with his legs into a gallop. *"Let us ride!"*

They pounded after the vanished herd, the excitement of the chase building as the trail grew fresher and fresher; they urged their mounts over pastures of lush grass of a thickness and luxuriance that no one of the Clans had seen since before the drought. And their building excitement was such that they hardly noted the rich pasturage except as something to cross. They raced through orchards of tall trees covered in white and pink blossom without a backward glance. All that mattered was the trail, and the quarry at the end of it.

Jegrai was the first to actually see them, so far in the distance and high up on a mountain road that they were little more than moving dots beneath a cloud of dust. He gave a whoop of victory, and the others looked up almost as one to see what he had spotted. Their fierce warcries must have been loud enough to carry up the side of the peak, for the little group of dots sped up a moment later—sure proof that they were being herded.

It was only when they were halfway up on that trail themselves that Jegrai realized with a shock of dismay just where that unseen herdsman was taking his horses.

This is the wizards' mountain! he thought with a chill, and fought down the urge to rein in his gelding there and then. *Wind Lords—he's heading right for the wizards' pass! If they see us— oh, Wind Lords—what if those are the* wizards' *horses?*

He wanted, with a desperation the like of which he had not felt except when faced with Yuchai's illness, to turn the party back around and give up the chase. But one look at the faces of the others told him that he dared do no such thing. He would lose face before them—and they would go on without him.

And when they all returned to the camp, there might well be a challenge for his rank of Khene. Probably from his half-brother, Iridai.

So he whipped his horse up to the front, and prayed to the Wind Lords that the raiders would be able to overtake the herd before they passed into the wizards' protection.

The Wind Lords were not listening.

The track turned into a trail cut into the very face of the cliff. Their quarry had vanished somewhere up ahead, but the dust of the herd's passing still hung in the air, and the nearness of their goal heated their blood still more. They pounded around a bend in the trail in a cloud of dust and sweat. . . .

Only to pull up in startlement at the sight of what lay across the place where the main road joined the trail they had been following.

They had scarcely a moment to take in the incredible size of the structure before them—larger than anything any of them had ever seen before, even Jegrai, who had been to the Suno Lords' city once as a child. They had just enough time for their hearts to stop dead and start again with the astonishment of it.

There was an eerie whistling that seemed to come from somewhere above—

And Jegrai had a fleeting impression of something large and boulderlike thudding down into the trail before them—

Then the wizards called lightning down upon them out of the clear and cloudless blue sky.

Thunder roared in their ears, flames and dirt sprang up before them; the trail itself was torn and flung into the air in front of their panicked horses, and scarcely ten horse-lengths away.

The horses screamed and fought their bits—but not for long. As one man the raiders let them have their heads, and turned tail and ran for the shelter of the cliff face they'd just come around. There they did rein their panicked, sweat-sodden beasts in, before they could break legs in their headlong flight. Afraid to move lest the lightning find them, the Vredai cowered under the cliff and looked to Jegrai to get them safely out—

—Jegrai, who had no more notion of what to do than the rest of them did.

"Felaras!"

Teo burst into the Master's study, white-faced and breathless. Kasha dropped the mug of chava she'd been drinking, and the pottery cup shattered unnoticed on the floor.

"Fe—Fe—laras—" Teo panted, clinging to the door frame. "Zetren's—on the—wall. With the—gunners—"

"*Damn!*" Felaras spat, "that mad dog will ruin everything!" She leapt out of her chair and vaulted over the desk, but Kasha beat her to the door. Kasha sprinted down the dark staircase as fast as she dared, with Felaras right behind.

Gods above—Kasha thought angrily. *—we go to all this trouble of* setting *this trap, risk young Eldon and the horse-herd—if Zetren ruins it for us—*

She hit the entrance to the hallway with enough momentum to have bowled over a dozen tall men, had there been anyone blocking her way. The stone floor was slippery; she skidded, bounced off the wall opposite the staircase, and kept going. Behind her she could hear Felaras making the transition from stairwell to hall with a little more control.

At the end of the hall was the wooden door to the outer yard that lay between the Fortress building and the wall. She hit the door at a dead run, and it slammed against the stone. The sun nearly blinded her, but she didn't stop to give her eyes time to adjust, just ran, scrubbing at her watering eyes, and trusted to memory and habit to put her feet where they should go.

She ran up the stairs to the top of the Fortress wall still half-blinded, just a little ahead of Felaras, hoping Teo's breathless warning hadn't come too late. At the top of the flight of stone steps were three of the six permanent mortars, their Watchers— and Zetren.

As she ran through the gap in the waist-high barrier on their side of the wall, she could see Zetren talking to the gunners. He was facing her, a wall in human form, and his dark eyes glittered like a half-mad bear's. He ignored Kasha's presence entirely. The bloodthirsty glee in his voice could not be concealed, and the Watchers manning the mortars on the wall did not look to Kasha's eyes to be comfortable hearing it. "When they reach the first mark," he said, "touch off the—"

"*What in hell is going on here?*"

Felaras climbed the last of the stairs two at a time, her eyes cold with anger. The Watchers had been uneasy at what lay in Zetren's eyes; they shrank desperately away from the look the Master was wearing. She hadn't worn that look often in her tenure as Master, but out of the half-dozen times she had, twice she'd killed a man with her bare hands. For good reason, admittedly; and she only hastened the sentence that would have been delivered anyway—but none of them had ever forgotten the incidents. Felaras in full wrath was not something any of them faced willingly.

Except Zetren, who feared nothing. He drew himself up to his considerable height and stared down at her.

She ignored him, going straight to the mortars. "What in hell have you got these set for?" she asked, with icy calm.

"Last notch, Master," said old Amberd, the most senior.

"Which plants our little eggs right at the mouth of the trail." She wasn't asking; she knew exactly what that setting meant, as did Kasha. "You know what my instructions were. Reset them the way I ordered."

Zetren gave an inarticulate, angry little growl.

Felaras turned and gave him a long, measuring look—

Then shrugged, and turned her back on him, plainly dismissing him as something of no importance.

Whatever he'd been expecting her to do, it wasn't that. He was left staring impotently at her back as she ordered the mortars reset by two notches so that the explosive shells would land considerably ahead of the mouth of the trail. He went red, then white; clenched his fists as if he would like to strike her. . . .

Then did the unforgivable; made one step toward Felaras's undefended back with his hands coming up.

That was why Kasha was there.

Sweating with fear—for this was the first time she'd ever done this outside of lessoning—she *ill-wished* with all her strength. And got ready to move in case it didn't work, or Zetren was protected.

Her vision narrowed, as if she was looking down a long tube, and things seemed far away and ill-defined, like in a dream. Well, that was fine; that meant she was directing the power correctly. And there was a sharp pain between her eyebrows which meant she was focusing right. . . .

She put every bit of her concentration into it; her entire universe narrowed to one thing. Zetren.

Zetren made another step.

His foot came squarely down on a piece of round shot from the loading of the mortars that *shouldn't* have been there. His foot skidded, flew up and into the air, right out from under him. He flailed, both his arms windmilling wildly for a moment, wearing an expression of such amazement that Kasha almost laughed and broke her concentration.

Then he landed on his back, hitting his head on the stone of the wall and knocking himself unconscious.

Kasha cut off her *wish*.

Sight went back to normal, although she was as tired as if she'd just gone a full ten rounds of hand-to hand with one of the senior Watchers.

She daren't show it, though; she took a deep breath, steadied her legs, and went to Zetren's side. She studied him for a moment, then knelt and pried open one eyelid.

Perfect. Out like a snuffed candle.

"He tripped over something," she said with feigned innocence, looking over her shoulder at Felaras. "I think he must have hit his head."

Felaras sighed, as if she believed her aid. "Amberd, I think the sun must have gotten to him. Get him on his feet and back to his quarters, will you?"

Amberd snorted, but obeyed. The others sighed with relief and went back to resetting the mortars.

No one seemed to have an inkling as to what had really happened at that moment—which was precisely as both Kasha and Felaras wanted it.

They got the mortars reset just in time; for a few moments later Eldon pounded up the trail driving the weary herd of horses belonging to the Order before him. They poured in through the Market Gate with a sound like distant thunder, streaming sweat that ran in muddy runnels through the dust covering their flanks, and Watchers on the gate slammed and locked it behind them. Now . . . it shouldn't be more than a few moments . . .

Kasha strained her ears and eyes both, but it wasn't until the Watchers below got the weary horses safely away into their stabling for a deserved rest that she heard it—the drumming of more hoofbeats on the herd-trail coming up the mountain.

It seemed to take forever; her heart was pounding in her ears, she clenched her hands on the stone of the parapet before her, and her breath came harsh and panting. Would they turn back? Would they sense the trap?

Then, suddenly, there they were—hauling up short at the sight of the enormous structure that guarded the Pass.

"Fire!" Felaras ordered—and the mortars spoke as one.

The trail between the Fortress and the nomads erupted with thunder and flying debris. It was much too far away to do them any harm, but it was virtually guaranteed to make the most hardheaded of horse-nomads believe in wizards with sky-fire magic.

When the dust cleared the nomads were nowhere to be seen.

The horses stood, spent, heads down, exhausted. Sweat collected on their flanks, the sweat of fear as much as of exertion; they slobbered around their bits, and their eyes still showed white around the lids. His raiders said nothing, but there was that same stark fear in their eyes, and pleading. *You are Khene,* said those eyes, white-rimmed in their sun-darkened faces. *Think of some way to get us down off this mountain alive!*

Once his heart stopped racing with fear, Jegrai felt oddly calm. He dismounted, handed his reins to Abodai (whose face was drained nearly bloodless), and walked cautiously up the trail to peer around the side of the escarpment protecting them.

There were three truly enormous holes in the trail.

Whatever these wizards had, it wasn't lightning; it was *worse* than lightning. Lightning didn't leave huge, smoking holes in the earth. Lightning didn't reduce boulders to a pile of fragments and pebbles.

He considered the Fortress, the trail, and the craters in it with a strange calm and detachment. *They could have killed us easily,* he decided after a moment. *They probably could kill us now. If they can do that—there's no reason why they couldn't reach all the way to the camp if they wanted to—*

His heart began racing at that, and he sternly told it to calm itself.

It wasn't listening. It was convinced that if the wizards cared to, they could keep them from ever getting off this damned mountain.

And the worst of it was, Jegrai's head agreed with it.

That had him in a panic, until he turned the thought around and looked at it from the other side. *They could have killed us, and probably still could. So why didn't they?*

That thought seemed to ease the tightness in his chest, the panic that squeezed the breath from his lungs.

Maybe they are *like the Holy One,* he thought in a burst of inspiration. *Maybe that was a warning? Maybe—maybe this is the chance to speak with them—*

He waited for a moment more, to see if lightning was going to strike him down, either from the wizards or the Wind Lords, at the audacious thought.

Nothing happened.

Taking that as a sign, he turned to call the others to him.

"Where in Hladyr's name is Teo?" Felaras growled under her breath, watching the spot where the nomads had hidden with far-seeing glasses. "If these flea-bitten nomads make a move, I need to know what it bloody well means!"

The Fortress sat in a kind of shallow depression split by the Pass; it was screened on the east by rocky outcroppings that rose about half as high as the Fortress walls themselves. The main road ran straight through those outcroppings, but the wilder trail the nomads had followed ran beneath them before joining the road at the point where it crossed the rocks. She could see the barest edge of a head peeking around the side of the boulder-face from time to time, then pulling back quickly. It looked like the same head each time, provided those nomads weren't all wearing identical fur hats.

So they aren't running away—gods, I would give five years off my life to know what they're thinking! Are they staying put because they're afraid I'll blow them to Yazkirn if they move? That's got to be at least part of it, but that wouldn't account for that head that keeps poking around the rocks.

The watcher was getting bolder; he put his head above the rock almost to the chin and kept it there.

"Master?" asked one of the gunners, nervously.

"Stay quiet," she warned. "Let's not startle them."

"But, Master—what if they charge?"

She took the glasses away from her eyes and turned to stare at him incredulously. "Reder, there are maybe two dozen of them. They have bows. No siege engines, no armies. And we just brought magic lightning down on their heads. Would you mind telling me just what you're worried about?"

The Watcher looked sheepish; Felaras remembered now that this man had been one of the few Watchers who had been truly spooked by the presence of the nomads in the Vale below. *Well, he'd better get over his fear of barbarians, and fast,* she thought to herself. *Because if this works he's going to see a lot of them.*

"Sorry, Master," he mumbled, shamefaced. "I guess I just wasn't thinking."

Felaras snorted, and put the glasses back up to her eyes. "The gods gave you a head, Reder, and they didn't intend it only for ornamental use. You might try using it now and again."

His fellow gunners chuckled; evidently they were a little tired of Reder's nerves. "Yes, Master Felaras," Reder said unhappily.

"Kasha, would you see what's keeping—"

"He's coming up the stairs," Kasha interrupted.

"And just in time," she growled, trying to fine-focus the lenses of the far-seeing glasses. "I think we're getting something happening over there. Teo—"

"Wait a minute, Master Felaras." She glanced over her shoulder to see that Teo had somehow pried the only other really good far-seer in the Fortress out of the hands of Diermud; this one was a single tube rather than the linked pair of tubes Felaras was using. "All right, I can see him."

The man was making his way out of the cover of the rocks; he was a bright splash of dull scarlet paint against the dun of the boulders.

"He's got—yes—he's wearing the right sort of hat to be a leader, Felaras!" Teo said excitedly. "I think he's either the Clan Chief or the warleader!"

The lonely figure just stood there in the middle of the road for a long moment, and even this far away Felaras thought she could read a bowstring-tight tension in his stance.

You do have courage, stranger, she thought wryly. *I hope you have sense as well.*

"Is he waiting to see if we take another shot at him, do you think?" she asked the young Archivist at her right elbow.

"I'd say yes—wait a moment—they're handing him something from behind the rocks—"

That "something" was long and thin, like a spear or lance, but Felaras's glasses weren't good enough to make out any details.

But Teo's tube *was*.

Felaras looked to him for enlightenment, dropping the glasses to hang around her neck.

"Well?" she asked, tightly.

And as the figure raised the stick over his head, and began walking slowly and cautiously—but with evident determination—toward the Fortress, the young man let out a long sigh and took the far-seer glass away from his eye.

"Master Felaras," he said, grinning at her so hard she thought his smile was going to meet at the back of his head. "I think you just got your wish. That's a peace-staff he's carrying. They want to talk."

✧ CHAPTER FOUR ✧

"Don't get too excited," Felaras said warningly, watching the envoy with one eye, half afraid he'd vanish if she turned her back. "Just because they want to talk, that doesn't mean we're going to come to any kind of an agreement. But they made the first move; that's hopeful."

She looked to Teokane, and reached up and tapped him on the shoulder when it was obvious that all his attention was still on the nomad. He started a little, and took the far-seer tube away from his eye.

"All right, Teo," she said as calmly as she could. Half of her wanted to run right down onto the road. The other half was looking for hidden traps. "You're the closest thing I have to an expert. How do I answer this truce-staff?"

He frowned, but not with anger; it was only because he was concentrating, Felaras knew him well enough after having him under her eye for the past two years to know that. "You either send somebody else out with a truce-staff, or you go out yourself," he said finally. "The staff is just a spear with the head wrapped. It'll be easy enough for us to make one to match it."

"Which would you do?" she asked him, sensing the answer might be important. "If you were me, would you go out yourself, or send someone?"

"Are—are you asking me for advice?" he faltered, his eyes widening with alarm. "I'm not—I mean I don't—"

She restrained herself from sighing with exasperation. "Yes, Teo, I am asking you for advice. You know more than I do about these people. You can make an informed judgment; I can't. Should I go myself, or send a proxy?"

He gulped, but finally gathered his scattered wits and answered her. "I—I think that's their leader out there. It would show that you consider us to be very much their superior to send a proxy. They put a very high value on 'face,' and while that might be a good thing in the short run, in the long run it could make for resentment."

She nodded. He hadn't answered her question, but he'd given her the information she needed to answer it herself. "All right. How do I go about showing that I'm the Master here, that I'm the equivalent of their Clan Chief?"

He shook his head. "I don't know, Felaras. Clan Chiefs usually have those foxtails on the sides of their hats, but you don't have a hat, and I don't know where we could find a pair of foxtails. . . ." He faltered, and she kept the sharp rebuke she wanted to give him behind her teeth. More and more she was coming to the conclusion that her choice between the two candidates was correct. Teo was crumbling under the first real pressures the Order had seen. Now if Zorsha responded positively under pressure . . .

Teo finally finished his statement. "I guess—I guess you'll just have to tell them and hope they believe it. They speak Trade-tongue; at least, that's what the chronicles said."

She thought about the risks for a moment, rubbing her aching head with her hand. *This could be a trick, a trap. On the other hand, if I move now, before anyone knows what's going on, I can get the Order so firmly on the road I want that my rivals—like Zetren—won't be able to fight me as effectively.* She looked out over the wall to the road, white in the bright sunlight, and the dull scarlet figure standing patiently halfway up it. *Gods, what am I worried about? I'll be within bowshot of the walls!*

Then she thought of the converse. *Gods. I'll also be within bowshot of his people.*

The sunlight seemed weak, and a chill went up her back.

Oh, hell. There's no living without taking chances. Time to trust to luck-wishing and take one.

"Kasha, go open the night-gate," she said abruptly. "I'm going out."

✧   ✧   ✧

The terrible, bloodthirsty nomad came as something of a surprise.

He's so young! Great good gods—if this is their leader, their warriors must be babes in arms.

Felaras studied the young man standing rigidly before her, every fiber of him projecting dignity and a fierce pride. Thin, dust-covered, and shabby. Frightened, but that wouldn't be evident to anyone who didn't have her long years of experience at reading the telltale signals people's bodies showed. Not inexperienced, one could bet on it, but still very young, perhaps all of twenty or so. That was a very tender age to be a Clan Chief. Quietly handsome, in an intriguingly exotic way, with his almond-shaped eyes and dusky gold complexion. Beneath that round fur hat with foxtails falling on either side of his face, he wore his straight black hair very short, which wasn't surprising in a warrior; she wore her own nearly that short for the same reason.

He was dusty, yes, but not dirty. He didn't smell of anything worse than clean sweat and horse. *Points for his people; anybody who reckons being clean is important is a leg up on civilization. Bet they don't lose many people to disease.*

She grounded the butt of her truce-staff on the road at her feet, feeling very much aware that they were both within bowshot of the opposition. "I'm Master Felaras," she said in Trade-talk. "I'm the leader of the wizards, something like a Clan Chief. You have something to say to us?"

The slight twitching of one black eyebrow was all the reaction he showed. Her words had surprised him. She couldn't tell if that indicated surprise that she was the leader and not a proxy sent out to meet him, or surprise that the leader was a woman.

"I, Jegrai am. Khene Vredai. Master for Vredai." He regarded her for a few moments, scarcely blinking. "You, killed us could have," he replied slowly and carefully, enunciating each syllable exactly.

Was that a question?

He seemed to be waiting for a reply.

"Yes," she said shortly.

"You, killed us not."

"Yes."

"Why?"

She shrugged. "Dead men cannot speak." She paused. He

waited patiently for more, his face as calm as a stone, his posture outwardly arrogant. "We want to know why you came here, why you raid our land-folk."

His turn to shrug. "Need. Food, grass. Both there, we need, we take."

"Take any more and we will grow angry," she growled. "Take more, and we will not be patient."

His eyes widened just a trifle, and he covered a flinch, but said, "Many are we. Strong in warriors are we."

Felaras snorted. "We have the lightnings to answer our call."

He remained silent.

"There may be," she said slowly, "another way."

While he pondered this, she considered him a bit more carefully. There was a charisma, a power about this young man that made you forget his relative youth and the shabby and threadbare state of his clothing. As a fighter herself, she could evaluate the implied ability in the way he moved and stood; balanced and controlled, very like a powerful predator at rest.

It's a damned pity I'm not thirty years younger, she thought wryly. *I'd see what else he can do besides fight. . . .*

"There other Clans are," he said abruptly. "There is—there is no rain in Clan country many summers. We look here, for grass. Maybe others grow hungered, maybe they come, look here."

"*We* have the lightning," she reminded him.

He took a deep breath, and braced himself. "Then why not you call lightning when Vredai on east pass? Why not call lightning when Vredai take from land-folk?" He scowled, and Felaras stifled a smile.

Very good, young man, she thought. *My bluff is called—maybe.* "Dead men," she repeated, "cannot speak." *Time to drop the hot rock in his lap.* "We seek new knowledge above all else. You come from the East, a place new to us. We do not kill what we do not understand."

"You—" There was something like wild hope in his eyes for an instant before he shuttered them. "—You seek new learning? You heal too?"

"Sometimes. When we can. So?" she said, raising one eyebrow and attempting to look as if his answer was of complete indifference to her.

"Maybe we keep other Clans out of valley?" he offered, tentatively. "Strong Vredai warriors be good to guard."

"Maybe," she answered, trying not to show her elation. "The lightning is not to be wasted on foolishness. Maybe we could have a bargain? Trade grazing for learning and use of your warriors. Such a trade would save us tedious work."

He pulled himself up higher. "You call not lightning, we raid not valley? We meet three days? Have trade-talk? Trade learning, maybe? Speak treaty?"

She nodded slowly, after pretending to think about it. "You move your Clan here—to the bottom of the road. Where we can watch you." *Which should make you think twice if you aren't serious.*

His eyes widened again and he swallowed once before he replied. It took him a moment to recover his arrogance. "We move," he agreed reluctantly, and not at all happily.

"Three days," she reminded him. "Here."

He nodded again. "Three days."

Her back itched all the way back to the gates, just waiting for an arrow to come winging out of the rocks, and it didn't stop until she was safely back inside.

She leaned against the closed gate and breathed her first easy breath in days—and, she suspected, her last.

Then her knees went to water as she realized just how easily she could have been assassinated down there; how simple it would have been for those horse-nomads to have taken her prisoner. All she'd had to go on was the assurances of Teo that this "truce-staff" of theirs was sacrosanct, and the hope that they were too frightened of her wizard's power to try anything so close to the walls of the Fortress.

Hindsight nerves. Damn, thought I was over that. Guess not. Now I'll wake up in a cold sweat for the next three nights.

So she just braced herself against the rough stone wall, felling every bump and raspy spot on the skin of her back through the cloth of her tunic; closed her eyes, and shook from hair to toenails.

All three of the "Unholy Trinity" came clattering down the stairs leading to the top of the wall within moments of the closing of the gate. She opened her eyes as they surrounded her. She expected an avalanche of questions, but they kept silent, and kept everyone else at a distance. Kasha's idea, she suspected.

When she was over her shakes, she got hold of herself and looked over that blessed barrier of protective shoulders at the double handful of curious and apprehensive Watchers and Seekers that had gathered, not even really noting the varying expressions they wore.

"Pass the word," she said briefly. "Convocation tonight at sunset. The nomads gave us a three-day truce, and they want to talk about a permanent truce and maybe an alliance. I'll tell you all everything then. Meanwhile you've all got things to do. Go do them."

The small crowd did not immediately disperse—and it was Zorsha who drew himself up to look much larger than he really was, took on an air of authority, and growled, "You heard the Master's orders. Let's see some backs!"

Felaras blinked in surprise at his sudden show of strength, but didn't have much time to think about what he'd done; Kasha gave her a gentle shove and she headed for the sanctuary of her study, where she could think.

"Here." Kasha shoved a mug of chava into her hand and pushed her down into her chair. "What happened out there?"

"Truce, at least temporary, like I said." She looked from one to another of her favorites. Kasha had perched herself on the side of the desk. Zorsha had the chair, and Teo was draped over the back of the chair above Zorsha's head. "That man I spoke with— Teo, what's a Khene?"

"Clan Chief," he said, and grinned shyly. "So I was right?" His blocky face brightened when she nodded yes.

"There's something going on with them, but damned if I know what," she continued, after a mouthful of cold, sweetened chava. "He admitted to part of what drove them here—a multi-year drought—but from what I was reading, that's just the bare beginning of the truth."

"Why?" Zorsha asked sharply. "I mean, I hope you're relying on something more than instinct. I'd like to know what. Forgive me for stating the obvious, but you can't afford to be wrong on this."

From the dumbfounded looks on Teo and Kasha's faces, they hadn't expected that speech from Zorsha any more than Felaras had.

She was startled, but pleased—because this sounded exactly like the kind of questions she used to confront *her* Master with. It was beginning to look like her choice of Zorsha as her successor was the right one. Since this mess began, Teo was faltering every time she asked him to assert himself. Zorsha was rising to the challenge of the situation, or so it was beginning to look.

"Well, I'm a good deal older than this Jegrai—he's about your age, Zorsha—and while he may be very good at hiding the fact that he's not telling the whole truth from people his own age, he hasn't had my experience in prying information out of what *isn't* said. I've been dealing with the Order and with envoys for a good few years now. And think about it—it's me who deals with the Traders, and a more closemouthed lot you're never going to find. I end up reading more off them than they ever tell me."

Teo chuckled, and even Kasha smiled, but Zorsha still looked worried.

Felaras decided to elaborate, to tell him how she was reading those she faced. "I asked him why they came. He mentioned the drought, then looked briefly away. Then he said, a little too casually, that other Clans may look westward for grazing lands. Now that's probably all true; but if they needed grazing land so badly, where's their other herds? All they've got with them are the horses. Teo? What should they have?"

He frowned in thought, and his heavy eyebrows came together to form a solid bar across his forehead. Now that it was just the four of them, he seemed to have regained his confidence. "They should have goats, sheep," he said, finally. "Or maybe—the chronicles talk about some other kind of animal, called a *yaeka*. There was a sketch, but it's hard to describe. I suppose a hairy sort of cow is the closest I could come. Something like an aurochs. Those should have been able to keep up with horse-herds, unless they were really forcing the pace."

"And all any of my scouts saw was horses," Felaras persisted. "All of the tents were very small, none of the big ones Teo's chronicles described. What does that tell you, Seeker?"

It was Zorsha's turn to wrinkle his brow in thought. "Well, my first guess would be that maybe they didn't come this direction voluntarily. They ended up leaving behind everything that slowed them down. They were driven? Maybe by a bigger Clan?"

"That would be my guess," she said, settling back into her

chair, and very pleased that a non-Watcher had deduced the same conclusion she'd come to. It was even more gratifying that her choice of successor had done so as quickly as he had. It meant that he was able to see things as a Watcher would. "Now, unless I misread him, he also made a genuine offer of alliance against the poaching of other Clans. Which would do what?"

"Confirm your guess," Zorsha replied positively, looking much less worried. "So what did you tell him?"

"That we'd have formal talks in three days—and that I wanted his whole Clan to move to the bottom of the mountain, where we could keep an eye on them."

"And he agreed?" At her nod, he raised an eyebrow. "Great good gods, he has to be thinking he's moving them within *our* striking distance. Sounds to me like he's serious."

"I think so. I also think we could do worse than have an alliance with these nomads. If nothing else, I suspect they have a fair amount they could teach us. And there's a lot more advantages— and I'd like you to see if you can come up with some on your own, because I'm going to count on your bright young minds during this Convocation tonight. Because now that you've seen what I've seen, and concluded we ought to talk with these nomads, the really hard part is going to begin." She grinned crookedly. "And that is to convince your fellows of the Order that we're right."

This was the first time she'd ever held a Convocation after sunset. If anything, it was less pleasant. By night the hall felt even more like a bowl than by day. The only strong lights were lanterns placed in a little circle around the podium. Felaras could see nothing of the others with her eyes so dazzled by the light— although they could see every move she made. And she was uncomfortably aware that, despite the babble of voices all around her, she was the focus of all eyes. When she held up her hand for silence and got it, immediately, it only confirmed her feeling.

"All right," she said into the darkness, wishing she could see the faces of those that surrounded her, instead of nothing but vague shapes that didn't even tell her what sex they were, much less their identity. "The nomads have found us. We showed them what we can do. I arranged a three-day truce with them, and got them to move down to the bottom of the mountain where we can keep a tight eye on them. You all know that—now I want to hear what you think of it."

The babble began again, and began rising toward an uncontrolled roar until she silenced them with a grimace and a wave of her hand. "Ladies and gentlemen, you aren't children in the schoolyard! Let's have some order here! Thaydore—what's your say?"

From out of the dark to her right came Thaydore's soft reply—which she could have recited with him, word for word. She knew what he would say, and so did just about everyone else in the Order. She'd called on him just so as to have a place to start, and to let the others begin choosing their own words.

"Our knowledge must be used to serve all mankind," he said, with as much force as Thaydore ever said anything. "That means East as well as West, horse-nomads as well as those who dwell in Ancas or Yazkirn. We must open our gates and our books to these folk, and teach them—"

"The Order has no place in the material world!" shrilled a female Felaras couldn't identify (though she suspected Archivist Brendis, a signs-and-portents type). "The material world must not pass—"

Someone else interrupted her, a male voice, but trembling and high; it sounded like Regas, but in the dark she couldn't be sure. "Exactly! There are some things 'all mankind' isn't ready to know! And it's our job to keep those things secret! We have no responsibility to teach anyone anything! Our purpose is to preserve and protect, not hand knowledge over to people who would only misuse it!"

Kitri flared up at that, her aged but strong, sharp voice carrying over the objections that followed that rather insular statement. "And just who's to decide when mankind is ready, hm? *You?* Great good gods, man, that makes you worse than those meaching priests back in Targheiden! Who the hell do you think you are? Hladyr's avatar?"

"A damned sight more sensible than you are, Kitri," growled one of the Seekers—and that deep bass could only belong to Jezeran. "Hladyr bless, what do you want us to do, hand out the formula for Sabirn-fire so these barbarians can burn down whole towns instead of just farmsteads? Shall we give them the knowledge of explosive powder too? Just imagine what they could do with that! What we know should be given to people worthy to have it, civilized people, people we know and can predict, the people of Ancas, of Yazkirn—not to a pack of unwashed, unlettered barbarians!"

Kitri's voice cut across the other objections—raised by those who did not happen to have been blessed with birth in either of those two lands. "People just like us, is that it?" Her voice dripped venom. "What noble, self-sacrificing sentiments! I suppose that's exactly what Duran should have thought. After all, everyone *knew* those Sabirn were worthless thieves and charlatans!" She laughed angrily. "And *of course* we all know that the gods check a person's pedigree before they assign him his eternal reward. We all know that only the worthy get the privilege of Ancas blood!"

Oh, that's *set the cat in the dovecote*, Felaras thought, doing her best to conceal her amusement. It didn't help that Jezeran was almost pure Ancas and tended to flaunt the fact. Anybody who'd ever been snubbed by him had a chance to give him a piece of their mind at this moment, and there didn't seem to be anybody who wanted to pass that chance up. *If this situation wasn't so serious, I'd be willing to let this go on all night!*

She debated whether to exert her authority and break the argument up—but Zetren beat her to it.

"Fools!" he roared, like a spring-hungry bear. Silence fell, heavy and sudden. "You're damned fools, all of you! What do we owe any of those decadent bastards back there? Have any of them come to our aid? No!"

There was a certain grumbling of agreement from those who remembered the last Convocation, and Felaras's statement that she had asked for aid and gotten none.

"We should give these barbarians what they want," Zetren continued. "Open the Pass to them, let them through! We've been quiet long enough—it's time we took our own back, by the gods! These nomads can be our tool. We can let them through to overrun everything west of the Pass, let them wear themselves to nothing against Ancas, let Ancas bleed itself white against them. Then let us follow in and pick up the pieces of both sides, and become the power we were always meant to be!"

The absolute silence that followed that made Felaras's heart stop. *My great gods—they can't really believe that, can they? Oh gods—please, they can't agree with that—*

Then the storm of objections rose, even more cacophonous than the one following Jezeran's outrageous statements, and Felaras's faith in the good sense of her fellows was restored. And her heart started again.

Finally everyone seemed to shout themselves out. Felaras waited, hoping for someone, perhaps one of her three, to say what she dared not—that they should treat with the nomads as allies. It couldn't come from her; but it was a logical notion—and, strangely enough, something similar to Zetren's far more radical idea.

"You know, friends," Zorsha said quietly into the muttering, "despite the fact that Ancas and Yazkirn both claim this area, neither one rules here."

"Aye," replied Amberd, sounding thoughtful. "If anybody rules here, it's us. Quiet-like. The Vale folk come to *us* for judgments and the like, they look to us for protection."

"So why don't we make the reality official?" Zorsha asked. "Why don't we simply declare this area to be independent of both lands?"

"Because we haven't got a bloody army to back that claim up, young fool!" Watcher Kirnal snarled.

"Don't we?" Zorsha asked mildly. "Just what is it that's going to be camping below the Pass for the next three days? As motley as it seems to be, it's still an army, and a big enough one to have *us* shaking in our boots."

The silence was profound enough that Felaras could hear every member of the Order breathing. Or rather, could hear the ones breathing who weren't already holding their breath in startlement.

And Zorsha followed up on his advantage just as neatly as Felaras would have. "Ladies, gentlemen, we can ally with this Jegrai—we can use him. Yes, we can teach him and his people, but we can also use him. Set him up as the ruler of the Vale—gods know he's already in the position of ruler, he's Chief over as many people as live in the Vale and Fortress combined! So, let *him* protect the Vale—but under guidance! Give him the throne, but let us be the power behind it! And in that way, the Order remains out of the public eye, as it should be—but we also exercise a beneficial influence, as we must if we are going to remain true to Duran's plan!"

Good lad! Felaras thought with elation, as discussion—not argument—broke out all over the halls. *He's hit them exactly in the right place! Enough altruism to make Kitri and Thaydore happy, enough self-interest to wake up our baser selves—* As the babble increased, she thought, a little wryly, *I greatly fear he's better at it than I am!*

The discussion raged while the time-candle burned down, but it was fairly well evident that the majority of the members favored Zorsha's proposal, for whatever reason.

Finally Felaras called them all to order again, when voices were growing hoarse and tempers growing thin, and bodies were crying for sleep.

"I'll call for a voice vote, since I can't bloody see to count your arms. All in favor of a treaty of alliance and a delegation to this nomad—"

The roar of "aye" shook the podium.

"Opposed?"

A thin but determined chorus of "nay"—the isolationist party was clearly outnumbered, but also obviously not shaken in their convictions.

"All right, let's get the formalities over. I'll conduct the initial treaty-making and leave a presence with this Jegrai to act as primary information-sources and go-betweens. Anyone have any objections to a delegation of—let's say, four? One Watcher, one Archivist; and two Seekers, one Hand and one Flame. Any nays?"

A little discussion, from the muttering out in the darkness; no objections.

Felaras sighed with relief. "All right; the Convocation is ended. Towerleader, Bookleader, Swordleader, meet with me after you get some sleep and some breakfast. Swordleader, you might send a scout out to the caves; tell the land-folk it looks like it's going to be safe for the next three days, and that we may have a permanent treaty with this lot after that."

"Master?" The voice was young; probably one of the novices. It shook a little. "Master, how are you going to pick who goes?"

"No novices, I promise that. Probably four folk with an equal mix of youth and experience. And we won't send anyone who doesn't want to go. If, on the other hand, you'd like to volunteer, tell your Leader. I'd rather have volunteers, if it comes to that." She looked out into the dark, hearing people already moving carefully along the benches, eager for their beds. "Any more questions? No? Then good night to all of you."

✧   ✧   ✧

Kitri was the last to arrive, and Felaras closed the door of the study after her, thinking, *Thank you, oh gods, for Leaders I can work with.*

The study was a little crowded with eight people in it, and a bit stuffy; the group included Felaras and the Trinity, of course (as her personal aides they were privy to everything and very good at being invisible when the time came), and the three chapter Leaders.

"Kasha, open the window, would you?" she asked, as the three Leaders arranged themselves around the hastily brought-in table. The desk was shoved up against the back wall, the room's two chairs on either side of it. Kasha threaded her way through the furniture to obey the request, then returned to the rear of the room for further orders.

Kitri led the Archivists; Diermud had held that position when Felaras had first taken the Master's seat, but he'd thrown it gratefully into Kitri's lap when Felaras had hinted it might be better for someone with more aptitude and inclination for worldly matters to have the Leader's badge. (Kitri's reaction had been hilarious. "Well," she'd said when Felaras handed her the badge of the open Book and the key to the Leader's study, "I appreciate the honor, but I thought we'd outlawed slavery here. . . .")

She was tall—taller than any man in the Order saving only Zetren. She was so thin that she kept a fire going in her study most of the year, for she felt the cold badly. She had large, spidery hands that could copy a text, make an inkbrush, or play a zither with equal dexterity. Her long grey hair would hang down below her knees if she let it; generally she kept it piled up on the top of her head in an untidy bird's-nest of a knot, stuck together with hairpins that she shed so constantly that one of the duties of her novices was to collect them and give them back to her at day's end. Deceptively mild hazel eyes were partially hidden by a contraption of wire and glass lenses—something Lisan of the Seekers had made to correct her failing eyesight—an invention so successful that a number of other members of the Order sported them now, and not just the older ones. She wore a long, loose tunic belted at the waist over breeches, both faded blue in color; clothing nearly identical in color and cut to every other piece in her wardrobe. One of Kitri's idiosyncrasies was that she searched until she found something she liked, and thereafter never altered it. This was a trait that endeared her to her novices, since it meant that they always knew what she would want and when she would want it.

Unlike Thaydore, sitting next to her—who never really knew exactly what he wanted when it came to his own needs. On the other hand, he would be satisfied by inexactitude in anything except his work, so it didn't matter to him if the fruit juice was warm, the soup cold, and his robe too short in the sleeves. He spoke for the Tower, the Seekers; and was himself a Flame rather than a Hand like Halun. He was nowhere near as old, nor as crazed, as he looked. His wildly untamed shock of hair had gone pure white in his twenties, and the vague, slightly demented look in his eyes was due more to preoccupation than anything else. He was supremely indifferent to his own physical surroundings, as witness his out-at-the-elbows, ink-stained robe, but he was implacable when it came to creating the best possible environment for the scholars under his authority. And there was one thing on which he and Kitri were in complete agreement—that the purpose of the Order was both discovery and education.

The one way in which they differed was on the point that Thaydore would assume without ever really thinking about it that those who wished to be educated would come to *him*. Kitri, on the other hand, was perfectly willing to load up a horse with books and go crusading for pupils.

And probably coerce them into learning whether they liked it or not, Felaras thought wryly, casting a glance over to her.

But these two would be getting exactly what they wanted out of a treaty with the Vredai. Given that, they'd let Felaras have about anything else *she* wanted.

The final chapter Leader, Ardun of the Sword, was an old friend, and had been one of Felaras's first novices when she'd reached full Watcher status. Bald as an egg, short, and bandy-legged; he was, nevertheless, a man not even Zetren would willingly go against. He was the acknowledged expert in more forms of combat than Felaras cared to think about, for not only did the Order gather recruits from every corner of the civilized world, but one of the duties of the Sword was to actively seek out and master new martial arts. Most importantly, he was one of the *calmest* people she knew. This could be an asset in any meeting where Kitri was involved.

"All right, friends," Felaras said, when everyone had been seated around the table she'd set up, after cups of chava had been handed round by her aides. This done, the Trinity had settled unobtrusively on or around the desk at the back of the room. "Do we want to talk about the treaty first, or the delegation?"

"Let's get the delegation out of the way," Kitri replied, a hairpin clattering to the tabletop as she reached for her cup. "That's the easiest. I'd like your young Teo on it for Archivist; that gives you *and* me a direct eye on the proceedings, and he asked me last night if I thought you'd let him volunteer."

"Did he, now?" Felaras looked over her shoulder, and Teo blushed. "I have no objections at all, seeing as he's the closest we have to a knowledgeable authority on these people. Thaydore, do you have anyone in mind for Seekers?"

Thaydore coughed, and looked a little embarrassed. "Well . . . yes. And I hope you won't think I'm suggesting him because he's troublesome—"

"Great good gods—you mean *Halun* volunteered?" Ardun exclaimed, eyes widening with unconcealed glee. "How amazing!"

"Well . . . yes."

"Nice balance," Felaras observed, making no effort to conceal her cheer. "Teo for youth, Halun for experience—I'd say fine, personally."

Kitri spread her hands wide. "No objections here. How about for the Flame side of the Tower?"

"I thought Eriel? I admit she's rather—uh—mystical—"

Thaydore's expression as he pronounced the last word was something between exasperation and extreme distaste. Eriel's star-charts were miracles of exactitude, for which she had Thaydore's admiration, mathematician to mathematician. The trouble lay in her attempts to calculate formulae that would enable her to contact the "spiritual entities" she was certain were guiding the stars on their appointed tracks. No amount of gazing through Lisan's finest far-seeing tubes would convince her that she was viewing anything other than a kind of festival lantern held in the hand of one of those invisible creatures.

On the other hand, if Eriel had volunteered, it would satisfy the "signs-and-portents" faction, and might give her a much-needed dose of medicinal reality.

"Ardun?" Felaras asked.

He shrugged. "Better than some—and puts a female in the mix. I can't think of anybody I'd suggest as an alternative."

"Kitri?"

"No common sense, but I'd trust Teo to keep her out of trouble."

"All right, Eriel's in. Ardun, who for the Sword?"

He grinned crookedly. "I know who I'd *like*—but she hasn't volunteered, and—" He craned his head around and grinned at Kasha, who began glowering, though she didn't seem inclined to say anything. "—don't get your hackles up, Sparrowhawk!—I was about to say that the Master needs you too much."

"That I do, and I'll not part with her. So who?"

"Remember a woman named Mai? Scouts, mostly."

"I think so; not pretty, not plain, sort of a face-shaped face. Very quiet. Very good at being a piece of the landscape."

"Or of the furniture. Aye, that's the one; she thought that talent of hers at being unnoticed might come in handy, and she's been one of the scouts out shadowing these folk. She's curious as hell about them, wants to see them up close. Sounded good to me, and I trust her."

"And as a scout she has to have a good memory," Kitri mused. "Sounds to me like a very good choice."

Thaydore nodded.

"Well, that's it, then. Halun, Teo, Mai, and Eriel. Next business: what Jegrai is likely to want and what we're willing to trade him."

"Felaras, what trouble can he give *us*?" Thaydore wanted to know. "Granted, he knows where we are now, and I'm certain he saw a great deal he'd like to have in *his* hands, but he can hardly take it by force—"

"The boy may be young," Felaras said slowly, "but he isn't dense. He's going to be thinking about the positioning of this Fortress—he's going to realize eventually that the reason we didn't hit him with the fire-throwers is because we *couldn't*—and he's also going to realize that even wizards have to eat. He could make life very unpleasant for us if he wanted to, and I'm relatively certain he'll have figured this out by the time we meet with him to talk this treaty."

Thaydore chewed on his lower lip for a moment, then nodded, slowly. "So what are we likely to have that we want to put in his hands? Idealism aside, I really would not want to put the secret of the explosives in the hands of a nomad we know nothing about. Later, perhaps—but not at this bargaining session."

"Maps," said Ardun succinctly, and two of the other three heads at the table swiveled to look at him in surprise. "My bet is that if he has maps, they're the ones he got off traders; inaccurate, not terribly detailed, not reliable—traders are *known* for putting mistakes in their maps. Certainly not reliable for a military campaign, which, if he was chased here, he may be planning on facing. And I would bet that every 'map' of the territory he's come through is in his head, not on paper. Whereas we know every gopher hole from here to Targheiden, and halfway to Azgun."

"Good. I can think of things he likely doesn't have that could be useful; springs, ballistics, western forging and smelting technique, the transverse cog." She thought back to her brief confrontation with Jegrai. "He asked if we did healing, and his face lit up for a minute when I said yes. There's things under that category I think both sides of this negotiation would like to see."

"There's a great deal he could probably offer us—" Kitri said slowly, drawing little pictures on the tabletop with her fingertip.

"Oh, agreed. I'd like to be able to stop importing all our wine, for one, and I'll bet he doesn't have a blamed Vintner's Guild keeping wine-making a secret! We've got some medicines and techniques I'm sure he would want badly if he knew about them— and I'd bet it's going to be vice versa."

"About explosives—should we even let him know it isn't magic?" Ardun asked.

"Morally I'm against *not* giving it to him," Thaydore said doubtfully, "but practically speaking—great good gods, I wouldn't put a loaded fire-thrower in the hands of a novice—"

"But keeping him from that information is perilous close to betraying our whole philosophy," Kitri snapped. "Certainly, letting him think it's magic *is* a betrayal of that philosophy!"

"Steady on, Kitri," Ardun replied calmly. "Nobody's suggesting any such thing. At least not in the long run. We're only talking short run here."

Kitri took a deep breath and subsided, nodded a reluctant agreement.

"The question may be out of our hands," Felaras said with equal reluctance. "I told you, my impression is of a very sharp young man. As he keeps the peace over the next few weeks, the land-folk may well come in and talk to him. He'll find out sooner or later that it isn't magic. I think the question is going to be how long we can hold out against his desire for it."

"As long as he doesn't *need* it . . ." Kitri said slowly.

"Good point," Felaras replied, relieved. "We can always claim our gods would be very angry at us if we gave the secret away when there was no need to use it. Good; that should stall him until we think he's ready for it. Now, think hard; we should be making some demands too—in fact, a lot of them, or he's going to reckon us for weaklings. What do we ask for?"

"You mentioned wine-making. All that herb lore and medicinal lore," Kitri responded. "I know Vider will want that."

"These people are experts in making things portable," Thaydore put in. "We may need that knowledge some day again, and it's beyond price."

"Their entire martial tradition. I *want* that, Felaras," Ardun's face was determined. "Their tactics alone—under the right circumstances, those strike-and-run maneuvers with horse-archers could be absolutely devastating! Can you imagine them up against an Ancas shield-wall? And weapons construction. The scouts say those little bows of theirs are powerful out of all proportion to their size—"

"Enough, Ardun—you're preaching to the converted," Felaras said with a laugh.

"What Zorsha said last night," Kitri began after a moment of silence. "Was that something of what you had in mind?"

"You mean about giving this boy something more than a set of specifics? Really educating him, making him into the kind of enlightened ruler we've all prayed for and never yet seen?"

Kitri nodded, and sipped at her cooling chava.

"Some. Some was his. I stand behind it all. I think it's a damned good idea, and I'd like to see us try it; I think this young man may be bright enough to think for himself, but willing to learn from us. This is going to sound like heresy, I know, but we don't have to remain bound by Duran's strictures—we can change, we can evolve. There is no reason why we couldn't become the guiding hand behind the throne—"

"That's dangerous—" Thaydore said, unexpectedly. "That's a temptation to control—I don't know, it's perilous, perilous. One could have absolute control there, and isn't that why we divided the rule among all three chapters of the Order in the first place? To avoid absolute control?"

"I haven't worked it all out yet, Thaydore," she admitted. "I truly haven't. This is something that is going to take a great deal of thought, never doubt that I hadn't realized this. The decisions we make on it are going to involve all four of us. I can't and I *won't* make decisions that will bind the whole Order all by myself."

All three of the Leaders nodded—Ardun with a wry smile, Kitri and Thaydore with relief.

"All right, then, let's deal with the immediate future," she said briskly. "Teo, get your materials out." She raised her eyebrows at them. "Let's get exactly what we want, and exactly what we're prepared to lay on the table in writing. So there won't be any questions by anyone."

Least of all, she thought wryly, *from Halun.*

✧ CHAPTER FIVE ✧

Jegrai was dazed; at his easy escape out of the hands of the wizards, at the near-miracle of a truce, at the thought that the wizards might, indeed, be of the same brotherhood as the Holy Vedani, and therefore to be trusted as he had trusted no one but his four councilors since he had become Khene.

Dead men cannot speak, the strange old woman had said. And *We seek knowledge*.

He hoped, and feared to hope. He feared and wondered if his fear was valid or foolish. He scarcely knew where he was going as he walked away from the woman, only realized after several moments that he was back among his riders and they were besieging him with questions.

He cut their babble short. "We have sworn truce for three days," he said curtly, handing the truce-staff back to Abodai and mounting his spent gelding. "After that we talk greater truce. Perhaps more; it may be that these folk are of the same brotherhood as the Holy Vedani. All that is for myself and my advisors to decide."

"And the cost to us?" Abodai asked shrewdly.

He looked over his shoulder at the tracker, the oldest man in the party. Was that a challenge?

No, he decided. It was just Abodai, who had to know the track he was set on. "No raids during truce-time," he told them, looking from one fearful face to another. "And—we move the Clan."

They clamored to know to where.

And when he told them, their faces went as white as when the wizards had thrown the lightning at them.

It took them most of the afternoon to bring their tired mounts

662

to the camp, and the wizard's mountain stood black against a bloody sunset when they finally reached that haven.

Jegrai had a great deal of time to think about what had happened during that slow progress. It occurred to him that the Vredai stood on the brink of either disaster or tremendous change. And *he* was Khene; ultimately it was up to him to lead them, whichever the outcome.

Wind Lords, he thought, cold in his gut as he looked back over his shoulder at the looming mass of the wizard's mountain. *I don't want this. I wasn't afraid of death at the hands of Khene Sen—but I fear those wizards, I fear that strong old woman and her lightning. And yet—my heart tells me they can be trusted. Fear. Trust. Which path, Wind Lords?*

But as he came to think about it, he began to wonder why the wizards hadn't used that lightning before this time. And the more he thought about it, the stranger it seemed. Until gradually a thought began to creep in—

Could it be they hadn't used it—because they *couldn't?*

Could it be that their weaponry had its limitations, even as the most powerful of bows had its range? Could that be why they had insisted on the Vredai moving to the base of their mountain?

And could it be—could it possibly be—that they had not slain the raiding party out of hand because the Vredai had something they wanted?

But what?

Information; knowledge, perhaps?

Or even, as the old woman had said, the strength of the Vredai fighters?

Could it be that these truce-talks would not be so one-sided as they first appeared?

And could Jegrai even begin to hold his own in such talks against a canny, clever old wizard-woman?

The prospect of trying to do so was nearly as frightening as his first impression of godlike powers.

When they reached the camp in the crimson sunset, Jegrai sat in his saddle and stared at the wizard's peak long after the others had dismounted and had led their mounts away. The lore of the Wind Lords said that a red sky at day's end was a portent of change; Jegrai found himself only hoping that the scarlet of the sunset did not betoken an omen of spilled blood to come.

✧   ✧   ✧

". . . so, now you know all."

Jegrai was as weary as he'd ever been in his life, but he had called this council together as soon as he reached camp. By now his raiders were spreading the news of what had occurred, for he had not forbidden it. He did not know if that had been wise, but he did know that trying to keep this a secret would be like trying to stop a plains fire in a high wind. It would have to burn itself out.

He took the cup of good spring water Aravay offered him with a nod of gratitude, and waited to hear what his advisors had to say.

"A woman—" Shenshu said doubtfully. "A *woman* is Khene to these wizards? It hardly seems likely."

"These are wizards," Vaichen reminded her. "Magic power does not depend upon strength of arm, eh, Shaman? So the strongest could be a woman. Certainly the cleverest often is!"

The Shaman only gave him a shrug of the shoulders and a wry look. "I see no reason why a woman could not be Khene to these people. Wizards need follow no laws but their own. They may not even pass the office by kin-right."

"She had the presence of Khene; I could not doubt her." Jegrai sighed tiredly. "To tell the truth, she had the presence of Khene, the strength of Ghekhen, and the shrewdness of Shaman. It comes to me that if she had bent her mind against me with full will, I would have held few secrets from her, for all that we shared only Trade-tongue."

The Shaman hissed softly, but when Jegrai looked over to him, his face in the flickering lamplight bore only a deep thoughtfulness.

"How say you, Northwind?" he asked.

"Sa-sa. I would see this woman. You say part of the truce is that we must move the Clan to the foot of their mountain?"

Jegrai nodded. "It may be that they cannot reach us with their lightning, but I do not wish to risk Vredai lives on that gamble. Shaman—warlord—I want to please these wizards. I want alliance with them! I want some of what they hold! Is that so wrong? Is it a fool's wish to think we might have it, if we are careful enough?"

"I think not," Vaichen replied, after a silence broken only by the noises of a restless and uneasy camp beyond the walls of the tent. "Some would call me coward—but I see no profit to any in opposing these wizards, and much, much good that may come of treating with them."

Shenshu nodded vigorously. "You know my feelings. There has been enough death."

Aravay looked to be deep in thought, and took a long time to answer that question. "It may be," she replied at last, "that there is a certain deception on both sides."

Jegrai bit at a ragged thumbnail. "I had thought of that," he said. "It came to me that both of us may be setting up empty tents and dragging brush behind the scouts. It came to me that although they hold the pass and live in stone walls, it would be easy to isolate them. It came to me that perhaps they cannot send lightning to strike what they cannot see. But it also came to me that their words are very like that of the Holy Vedani, and it were folly to throw away the chance at such wisdom as *that* one held. I truly wish to trust them; I wish to believe in their honor."

The Shaman nodded vigorously, and Shenshu nearly bobbed her head from her shoulders. "If this woman is indeed Khene, then it means there are other wise women among them. There are no secrets when wise women trade learning, Khene. I burn to speak with the wise women of these people, I thirst for what they can tell to me and my healers. And doubtless there is that we can teach to them; it is ever so when healer speaks to healer."

"In many ways, Khene, we have no choice," the Shaman said at last. "If we were to fling this gift of the Wind Lords back into their faces, they may *truly* turn their eyes from us."

"Is that how you read this, Shaman?" Jegrai said, hope making him tremble inside, although he would not betray such weakness even to these trusted councilors. "That this is indeed the way set for us by the Wind Lords?"

"I can see no other reason for these things, at this time, and this place," Northwind said positively.

"Very well. Then I, and you, my councilors, will meet with these wizards in three days' time. Tell the people that it is my will that we move to the new camp-place at dawn. We will know something of these people by the place they give us, I think."

And Wind Lords, Jegrai prayed, as his advisors rose from their places at his hearth and slipped from his tent, each wrapped in thought, *Wind Lords, if ever you have heeded me, let me be right in this. . . .*

✧   ✧   ✧

The Vredai murmured, the Vredai looked fearfully over their shoulders, but the Vredai obeyed their Khene. In the pale grey light of early dawn they were packing up their belongings and their tents; by the time the sun showed a bright rim over the eastern horizon, they were on the move. They ordered themselves in a compact file that filled the road and spilled over it on both sides, but there were no laggards. Vredai with a tendency to lag behind had been buried many leagues and moons ago on their backtrail.

Halfway across the valley, one of the outriders came pounding back to Jegrai and his advisors with word that there was a strange man waiting for them on the road ahead.

"What manner of man?" Jegrai asked the sweating, wide-eyed outrider.

"A young man, Khene; he speaks Trade-tongue and said he was come from the wizards to guide us." The young warrior wiped at this forehead with his sleeve, leaving a smear in the dust that covered his face. "Truly, he must be; he is a man as tall as the mountain, and his horse as tall as two mountains!"

Privately Jegrai thought that the outrider's fear had inflated the stranger, but when they came close enough to see the calm, patient figure waiting in the middle of the road, he thought better of his scout. The man *was* huge; standing, he would best Jegrai by a head, and Jegrai was reckoned the tallest of all his folk. And his horse was proportionately large. Behind him, Jegrai could hear the mutters of wonder and fear at the sight of such a prodigy. To send out a giant to guide them seemed unlikely. But to guard them—that seemed likelier.

Until Jegrai came close enough to see the man's face.

It was not a handsome face; very craggy, as rough as the side of one of these mountains about them. But it was a good face, and in many ways, a gentle face, the face of a man who knows that he is strong and tempers that strength so as not to overpower others. Brown of hair, of eyes, of skin and beard, of clothing, even—he could have been the personification of one of the Earth Spirits the Suno called upon, save that he showed none of the fierce harshness of one of those bloodthirsty godlets. His flat nose gave him a little of the look of one of them, and the shy smile on his face told Jegrai that it was very likely that he and this stranger were of an age.

"You are the Khene?" the strange man said when they were within speaking distance. His voice was deep, and held a note of diffidence. At Jegrai's nod, he continued, pronouncing his words with great care. "My name is Teokane; I am sent from Master Felaras to show you the way to a place of water and good grazing. The Master wishes also to know if your people have provisioning for the next four days."

"We will do well enough," Jegrai replied, carefully.

The young man blinked, and looked a bit doubtfully back at the thick column of Vredai behind the Khene. Jegrai's outriders gathered in a little closer, and there was some quiet loosening of blades in sheaths.

"I am sent to tell you that if there is any need, you must tell me of it," Teokane persisted. "The Master holds herself your host in this—she offers to you guest-right for the time until we speak together."

Jegrai felt as if the wizards' lightning had struck him directly, and from the dropped jaws about him, the others who had heard were no less thunderstruck.

"This is no trick?" he managed, recovering long before the rest did. "You mean by this *our* notion of guest-right?"

The young man nodded, almost desperately, and nudged his horse forward a little. "I am to offer you bread and salt, Khene Jegrai. More, I am to offer you bread, salt—" he paused significantly "—and water from the well of our home-place."

The world dropped out from underneath Jegrai's saddle for a moment. To offer bread and salt was a guarantee of safety—but to offer the water was a pledge of life for life. Not even Sen had dared to violate that bond; he had once shared Talchai's water with Jegrai's father, and had been forced to wait until the Khene was dead before moving against the Vredai.

This was more than unexpected—it was impossible. Impossible that the wizards should know this pledge of Jegrai's people. Twice impossible that they should offer it.

"You know what this means?" he croaked harshly, determined to try this young man, even though he heard the Shaman gasp in dismay at his rudeness and audacity even as he said the words.

Three times impossible, for the young man nodded. "That we are bound from harming one another if you accept the pledge,

Khene. Even if the talk comes to nothing, we shall not send the lightning against you. But you will be equally bound."

Shock on shock; and Jegrai almost chuckled as he realized the young man called Teokane was right. If he accepted the water, he bought safety for the entire Clan—but he also bound the Clan from further depredations, not only in this valley, but for however far the wizards claimed territory.

Teokane fumbled out a packet from his saddlebag; unwrapping it, he revealed a small brown loaf of bread, a little pile of salt in a separate wrapping, and a flask that presumably held the water.

"I am to offer, I am to stand for my people," Teokane said formally. "Khene Jegrai, do you accept for yours?"

"And if I do not?" he asked, startling a further gasp from the Shaman.

"Then I guide you nevertheless, and the truce holds until we talk, and thereafter as your gods and ours decree."

I like this man, Jegrai decided suddenly. *I like him. I trust him.* And, with a ferocity that surprised him in a day of surprises, *I want this man for my friend.*

He looked up into those frank brown eyes, and thought, perhaps, he detected some of the same sentiments there.

"Friend of the Vredai," he replied, feeling the muscles of his face stretch in an unaccustomed smile, "I do accept."

"It's a gamble," Teo'd said, when Felaras had finished reading the chronicle herself. "We don't know how accurate this is. We don't even know if we're facing a Clan of the same type as this one in the chronicle—"

"It's entirely possible their customs have changed," Felaras said into the silence when he left his thought unfinished.

He nodded helplessly.

"On the other hand," she continued, "everything else has held up so far—and to our benefit. If we take the gamble and it pays off, we've guaranteed not only our safety, but that of the Vale folk. What do we stand to lose besides face?"

"Felaras, with these people, loss of face could be a catastrophe."

"Teo, look at me."

He found it very hard to brave those penetrating hazel eyes, but he lifted his head and met them as squarely as he could.

"Teokane, knowing everything we have at stake here, do you

think it's worth the risk to try this bread, salt, and water ceremony on these nomads?" Her voice was level, her face without expression. Teo swallowed, and nodded.

"I do not dare to leave the Fortress; the Order would have my head for it at this point. They're livid enough about the truce-staff business. Of the three whom I trust, you are the best at reading people. On your honor as an Archivist of the Book, on your Oath to the Order, do you think you'd be able to read this young man well enough to know if this wasn't going to work before we found out the hard way?"

Oh gods—he closed his eyes, tried to shut out his fear, his feeling of uncertainty, and tried to weigh and measure himself. *It all rests on my being able to do what she does without thinking. Oh gods. I haven't her years, I haven't her experience—but—*

"Yes," he heard himself saying. "Yes. I can."

He opened his eyes; Felaras was smiling faintly, and nodding. "Well, as it happens, I think so too. Get yourself down to the kitchen; pick up whatever you need down there. I'll have your horse readied for you."

They differed in size, in language, in every way—except the ones that mattered, Teo thought a little dazedly. He *liked* this Jegrai, with the kind of liking that came all too rarely to him. It was almost as if they had been old friends for years without knowing it. They rode side by side in the warm spring sun, Teo towering over Jegrai, and neither of them much noticing the fact—except that once Jegrai remarked with a laugh that he would be pleased if Teo would always ride at his side—for shade! They chattered away at each other like adolescents, learning each other's language, Teo finding with a shock of pure delight that Jegrai was as quick at picking up a tongue as he was.

And they shared so many things; Jegrai even had a keen appreciation of the beauties of the Vale that was so like Teo's own that he found himself pointing out this twisted, blossom-covered tree, or that boulder-covered, evergreen-topped hillock, knowing that Jegrai's eyes would widen with delight the way Teo's must have the first time he'd seen it.

And the Khene's flat-footed surprise at seeing the campsite Teo and Felaras had chosen was well worth the long, dusty ride.

It was a lovely little side canyon, well shaded by clusters of trees, with grass that was knee-high even this early in the season, and watered by its own clear spring. The Order used it for grazing their horse-herd in the summer, but the herd had other pastures. There was no other place so well suited to the needs of the nomads.

And the steep sides of the canyon should reassure them that the Order was not going to attack them in the night. They would feel reassured that nothing *human* was going to scale up those walls. A few of the Watchers—a very few—could have climbed down from the greater heights above, but Jegrai wouldn't know that. And no Watcher was going to be a threat to them while Felaras was Master, anyway—not unless *they* broke truce.

"By the Wind Lords," Jegrai breathed, as the outriders gathered at the mouth of the place and gaped in awe. "She is generous, your Khene. Had I this place in my keeping, I would think twice on giving it over to strangers. With five men I could hold off every Clan on the plans." He looked skyward for a moment, then shrewdly back down at Teo. "And your wizards cannot overlook this place."

Teo shrugged, mouth twitching. *So he's already figured we can't bombard without being close to the walls, hm? Felaras will be interested to hear that, seeing as it bears out her assessment of him.*

But he pointed out, "We have shared bread, salt, and water, Khene. What have we to fear from you? What have you to fear from us? The only questions lying between us now are how far we are willing to aid each other."

"Sa-sa," Jegrai agreed. He stood up in his stirrups and waved to the people crowded behind him, even as he nudged his own horse aside so that they could pass. He shouted something in his own tongue that was answered by a weary cheer, and the dust-covered nomads began pouring through the mouth of the valley in a tired but increasingly cheerful stream.

There seemed to be no end to them, and the noise was incredible. As were the people themselves. Children that Teo thought hardly old enough to walk sat atop their own sturdy ponies and managed them as well as most Seekers or Archivists (Watchers didn't count, not to Teo's mind. They were riders equal to the adult Vredai fighters). Women held smaller children balanced on the saddle-pads before them, and frequently rode with wrapped babies in a kind of pack on their back. The chatter of the children as they passed Teo and looked up at him in fascination made him grin like a fool.

But then the noise faded to almost nothing—and Teo saw the living cost of their flight.

Gods—oh gods, I was right. They were *driven here.*

That was his first thought. His second was pure shock, a blow to the gut. He was seeing things he had only read about—and they were horrible. Men with one eye, or one arm, or half crippled. Some younger than he was. And not just men. There were young women—armed and with Kasha's dangerous grace, but with a hollow look in their eyes that said they had faced terrible things the like of which Kasha had only seen in chronicles.

We—we've been so sheltered. The only person I ever saw die was another novice, in a fall. I've never seen wounds like this, inflicted in war, in anger. He couldn't look away, somehow. *We've been so sheltered. . . .*

And near the end, a horse-litter, with a plump, middle-aged woman riding beside it. It was at this point that Jegrai's face lost all signs of pleasure—that it went shadowed, and brooding. He nudged at his horse with his heels and threaded his way through the last of the riders toward the litter; and, moved by some impulse he didn't understand, Teo went with him.

Jegrai spoke briefly with the woman as she stopped for him; Teo looked down at the litter. It held a boy—not yet a young man, and by the look of him, not likely to reach that state without some help. His face was greyish, the color of someone with a bad head injury, and his head was wrapped and padded. He was bandaged in several places, and though the bandages were clean, they were stained with blood and other fluids.

Teo's heart lurched, and he spoke on impulse. "Khene Jegrai—who?"

Jegrai touched the boy's forehead before answering. "My cousin. Yuchai. The night of the great storm he was riding guard; his horse shied and went into a pit-trap." He sighed. "He grows no worse, but he grows no better, either. He has not woken except to rave since he took the fall. He has taken an injury to his head, he burns with fever, his wounds do not heal, and we can do nothing."

"But—" the words burst from him; he couldn't have stopped

them if he tried. "My brother, why aren't you giving medicine for the fever? Why have you not seen to his head? Why do you let him lie in pain?"

The light in Jegrai's eyes was as bright and sudden as the lightning. "*You* can do all this?" he cried.

"Not I, but those of our Order can—and by the gods, by the brotherhood we swore, we will if you'll trust us with him!"

Jegrai swiveled in his saddle. He reached out like a striking snake and clasped Teo's wrist with a steel hand. "You will swear this by the bond of water?"

The hope and fear in his face were painful to see. Teo did not pull away; instead he clasped his free hand over Jegrai's. "I will swear this on my own blood," he said tightly. "Give me but long enough to ride to the top of the mountain and back, and what we can do, my brother, we *shall* do."

"A head injury, you say?" asked Boitan, carefully packing a traveling basket with herbs, clean bandages, and boiled scalpels. "Did you see it?"

"No, sir," Teo replied, packing a second basket with the traveling surgery lantern and other oddments Boitan laid out. The cool of the rock-walled infirmary was pleasant after the wild ride up the mountain. "The boy's head was bandaged—all I can tell you is that it didn't seem to be the temple. And although they had his wounds bandaged up, I would guess that they don't suture wounds, that they just use pressure bandages and hope the flesh heals. From what little I know, it looked like they'd wrapped him awfully tight, and he was leaking fluid."

"Probably a depressed skull fracture, by the symptoms," the physician muttered, packing something that gave off a pungent odor when he squeezed the packet to fit it in. "And if that's how they're dealing with wounding—*you* know that half the time pressure bandages do as much harm as good, cutting off the blood and letting the tissue rot. I'll probably have to open him up and cut out dead tissue. I hope to hell they don't have any taboos about surgery, or you and I may be decorating stakes down there. There. That's it."

"I've already gotten fresh horses ready."

"Good man. Damn good thing I'm a rider." Boitan smiled crookedly; Teo returned it. The absent Vider was *not* a rider;

rather than the fast horses Teo had called for they'd have been taking ambling old cobs—and would have probably reached the nomad camp well after midnight.

"Tell you the truth, sir," Teo replied, slinging one of Boitan's two baskets over one shoulder, and heading past the bench to the door. "If Vider had been here I would have—uh—not been able to find him. Besides, you're a better surgeon."

Boitan followed on his heels. "I'd be a happier physician if we just had some way of keeping incisions from infecting. Duran had it—but his notes are so vague, as if he expected the method to be common knowledge." Boitan sighed, and hitched his basket a little higher on his shoulder. "Given that, there's not a lot I can do—"

"It's going to work out all right, sir, I just know it is," Teo said fiercely. The surgeon gave him a strange, sideways look, then shrugged. "Sir—" he ventured again, just as they reached the door to the courtyard, "This is the one opportunity we have to show them that they can trust us to keep our word. To show them that they can trust us, period."

"Ah." Boitan paused by the closed door. "I wondered if you'd seen that."

"Yes, sir, I did. This is our testing, I think. If you do everything you can—well—I don't think we'll fail it."

Boitan smiled thinly and reached for the door-handle. "I could wish," he said, as they stepped out into the blue dusk, "that I had your faith."

It was fully dark and the stars were blossoming overhead by the time they reached the canyon; Jegrai himself was waiting for them at the entrance to the canyon, looking much gaunter than he had this afternoon by the light of the torches held by the two men standing sentry there. He led the way to a round, white tent that appeared to be made of felt; the flaps were standing open to the warm night, and the sides were tucked up a little to permit a breeze to come through at the level of the floor. Teo had expected the "floor" of the tent to be bare dirt, or flattened grass at best, but the tent was carpeted with what seemed to be several layers of thick rugs.

The boy was on a pallet near one side; the middle-aged dusky woman knelt beside him, but moved deferentially away when they entered. There was no one else in the tent, and only one lantern hung from the centerpole. Boitan took one look at the amount of light within and shook his head. "We'll have to do better than this, Teo, or I won't be able to see my own hands. Tell them to bring me some water, would you? Two buckets full, at least."

With that he began rummaging in the basket Teo had brought, bringing out a wooden frame with leather slings on it, four hollow glass globes, and an oil lamp. Teo asked for the water as Boitan began setting up the cube-shaped frame, putting the oil lamp in the middle and the four balls in their slings on all four sides of it. When the water came—within a few breaths of Teo's asking— he filled the balls with it, and lit the lamp.

There were sighs of wonder all around the tent as the water- filled balls picked up and magnified the light from the flame. Boitan nodded with satisfaction, set the lamp on its collapsible stand beside him, and pulled out a metal bowl, filling it with water. There was already a small fire in a kind of pot or brazier burning over at one side. Boitan nodded again and set the water there to heat. He dropped some herbs in it, washed his hands in one of the other buckets, and turned to his patient.

"Now, let's see about this boy."

The middle-aged woman inched forward on her knees and said something. Jegrai translated. "This is Shenshu; she is our chief healer and one of my advisors. She wishes to watch, and help if need be."

Boitan, who also spoke Trade-tongue, gave the woman a careful looking over. He lifted one eyebrow at Teo, who replied to the unspoken query softly. "Vider is also not as—ah—flexible as you are, sir."

"If laughing weren't so out of place at the moment—" He turned, bowed slightly, and gave the woman a real smile. "From what I can see you haven't done at all badly, lady," he said to her, directly, as if she could understand him. "I'll be able to use a pair of hands used to this sort of thing, if you think you can follow my pantomime. Teo, I fear, lacks the stomach to help me except in an emergency."

"Pan-to-mime?" Jegrai said, puzzled.

"Hand signals," Teo filled in hastily, and Jegrai translated in a burst of speech too quick for Teo to follow any of it. The woman Shenshu nodded, and scooted over to wedge herself between the boy's pallet and the tent wall, out of Boitan's light.

"Let's get the worst over first," Boitan said, unwrapping the boy's head and not looking up. "Explain to them, Teo. Then tell them how I'm going to open up the wounds again and cut the bad tissue out—maybe scrape bone if I have to."

Right. Explain to them that this stranger is about to cut open the head of the Khene's cousin, then mutilate the rest of his wounds. Thanks, sir. Teo took a long, deep breath, and launched into it.

At the description of how Boitan planned to raise the bit of broken skull off the brain, Jegrai looked as if he was repressing revulsion or horror; Teo couldn't read the woman. The description of cleaning out the wounds seemed to sit better; the woman exclaimed sharply once, but this time her expression was plainly one of "Why didn't *I* think of that?" There were many questions from the woman, some of which baffled Jegrai's ability at translation, for he could only shrug after failing to find the correct words.

Teo did his best to answer them. It was a tense moment, although Boitan, carefully examining the purpled, pulpy place on the boy's head, seemed to be able to ignore the tension.

Evidently his best was good enough.

"Wind Lords," Jegrai sighed, finally. "If you do this, Yuchai may die, but if you do not, he certainly will die. Shenshu says that she is satisfied you mean no harm and perhaps know what you do—"

"He's done this before, about half a dozen times that I know of," Teo said tentatively.

Jegrai shrugged. "Gods guide him, then."

At this point Teo couldn't watch. He really didn't want to stay in the tent, but Boitan needed his command of Trade-tongue. So he compromised, and hoped he could control his stomach. He turned his back on the physician, the healer, and their patient, and sat in the open tent-flap, resolutely ignoring the moans of the boy, and Boitan's murmurs.

The camp beyond was mostly dark; a few flickers of fires in carefully watched fire-pits, and the two tiny sparks of the torches at the mouth of the valley, but otherwise the camp might have been deserted. Teo looked up at the bright stars overhead and reflected that, given how weary the Vredai had looked, the quiet wasn't surprising. They were trusting the water-pledge, and taking what was probably the first unguarded rest they'd had in a very long time. For a moment he had to hold back tears of pity. All those bright-eyed children—the vacant and haunted eyes of their parents and other siblings. It wasn't fair. . . .

Boitan spoke up, interrupting his thoughts. He sounded a little more optimistic. "Well, the worst is over—the fracture wasn't bad, Teo. This boy's gods were surely looking after him."

A nasty stench wafted by, telling Teo that Boitan was now cleaning the boy's wounds out. He gagged, and held his stomach under control only because there was nothing in it at the moment but water.

There was a whisper of movement and a presence at his elbow. Teo noted the same thing Felaras had—Jegrai was as cleanly as anyone in the Order. He smelled at the moment only faintly of horse and more strongly of herbs. Some time before they'd arrived he must have taken time to bathe. *These are no barbarians, no matter what some of the others think. Nobody who keeps themselves and their camp as clean as these folk do is a barbarian.*

"I—cannot watch either," Jegrai whispered, his voice shaking. "Strange, is it not? I, who have faced battle many times, have faced death and seen it pass me to strike one at my very side, am aquiver, and I cannot bear to watch the healers at their work. I had to see what they did with Yuchai's broken head, but now—"

He made a little choking sound.

"—my stomach rebels. And my courage flees at the sight of all those little knives at work."

"Boitan is very good," Teo ventured. "He—the only thing that has ever defeated him is when—uh—rot comes back after he has cleaned wounds, or when it comes into the cuts he made."

Jegrai's head jerked around, his face registering a look of surprise. "What, you do not have the powder-of-mould?"

"The what?"

"The powder-of-mould, that we put on wounds—do so and they do not rot."

Teo kept himself from jumping up only by a powerful exertion of will. If he startled Boitan—but this was something the physician needed to know, and now.

He raised his voice and forced himself to speak calmly. "Boitan, the Khene tells me these people have something that prevents infection."

There was a long moment of silence behind him. Then Boitan spoke, though not in Trade-tongue; he was too preoccupied. "Teo, it is a very good thing that I am not Vider, or this boy would have a new wound, and I would have a deal of explaining to do. They have something that prevents infection. Do they also have the elixir of immortality? No, forget I said that; I believe you. The crippled men you described couldn't have survived without something like that. Would the woman happen to have any of this gods-given stuff here in the tent?"

Teo translated, but Jegrai did not even have to ask. "Of course!" he said in astonishment. "How not?"

"Then I trust when I am finished here, this good lady will instruct *me*, please?" said Boitan, an edge of pleading in his voice. Behind them, the woman actually chuckled.

After that, Teo and Jegrai watched the stars, and the silent camp, for what seemed to be an eternity, trying to ignore the sounds behind them when Boitan did scrape at bone. It was one of the longest nights Teo had ever spent and he was amazed when light showed in the east, and it proved to be the moon, not the sun.

At last Boitan gave a grunt of satisfaction, and the woman spoke Jegrai's name. Jegrai let out a sigh of relief as she chattered at him, and his shoulders slumped. "Never, never will I regret pledging to you, my friend," he murmured, almost to himself. "Shenshu says that Yuchai will undoubtedly live, that he looks better already. And—"

There was more than a hint of rueful self-mockery in his voice.

"—that it is 'safe to look now.' "

Teo craned his head over his shoulder as Jegrai inched back into the tent. The boy *did* look better; there was color in his face that hadn't been there before. Even as he watched, the boy's eyes opened and he spoke, dazedly. The healer Shenshu grinned and said something in a voice too soft for Teo to hear anything but a murmur. The boy didn't much seem to notice the presence of the two strangers, but Shenshu and Jegrai he recognized, and seemed comforted.

"Hah!" Boitan snatched at the bowl of stewing herbs and decanted some into a wooden cup, handing it to the woman. She took it, as he mimed drinking, and propped the boy up enough to help him sip at it. She managed to get more of it in him than on him before his eyes closed again.

"That was for fever and pain," Boitan told her as Jegrai translated. "Willow bark and poppy gum. You saw me make it up; I'll leave some with you. Give it to him whenever he wakes for the first three days, after that, be careful—the poppy gum calls up a craving for it." The woman nodded at that, and mimed frantic scrambling after the bowl. Boitan smiled, a bit grimly. "Exactly. We don't want that to happen. Be very careful with it. Now, tell me why it is that wounds rot."

The woman listened to Jegrai, frowning slightly, then began speaking—but this time slowly. "It is—she says—poison. Poison in the dirt, on hands that might have touched something rotten, on knives, on arrow-points. On the teeth of animals. It makes raw flesh rot. Powder-of-mould is the antidote."

"Mould?" Boitan's eyebrows shot up. "You mean, like bread-mould? Forgive me, lady, but that's an old wives' tale."

Jegrai translated, and Shenshu laughed. "She says, is she not an old wife? But she says also, look to our fighters, all the scars they bear. That speaks for the truth of the tale."

"Then why did this boy—"

"Ah, that I can tell you," Jegrai interrupted. "Yuchai was hurt when we had very little of the powder left, enough to keep the rot from killing him, but not enough to prevent it from coming. We did not know what to do then—boils I have seen lanced and drained, but never deep wounds. Never have I heard of this—to open a wound again and cut and cleanse—and then to sew it like a garment! It is a great wonder to me. To Shenshu, also. And the lifting of the bit of bone from the brain—I would not have had the courage."

The woman spoke.

Jegrai laughed, and reached over to stroke his cousin's forehead. The boy was sleeping peacefully, and Teo felt his heart lift to see it. "That is an even greater wonder to Shenshu also, and she begs that you will teach her—even if you are not a woman, you are wise, she says. So she will forgive you not being a woman!"

The tent filled with the wondrous sound of soft, but heartfelt, laughter.

✧ CHAPTER SIX ✧

Yuchai finally woke—really woke up, and not simply moved from a fevered dream into a dreaming fever. His dreams had been full of pain and terrible ghosts: Vampire Heads, Cat Women, Snow Demons, and Blood Stones. They had taken turns tormenting him—and even the bravest warrior could be forgiven his fear of facing such an appalling array of supernatural torturers. Once or twice he shook free of them, and opened dry and burning eyes to see familiar faces full of dismay and concern about him. It was then that he would realize, dimly, that his pain was due not to the claws of the Cat Women, or even the Blood Stones sucking his soul out of his head—it was from all the hurts he had taken when his poor horse shied into that pit.

But always he had dropped back into his fever dreams, and each time he did it was to fall into the hands of his torturers a little weaker than the last time. A little less able to break free.

Then a dream of great strangeness: it had felt like those times of almost-awakening, except that there had been only one familiar face—Shenshu's. And two strangers: a man with the pale face of a spirit, and a giant. Then a bitter-tasting drink, and finally peace, and sleep with no dreams.

He opened his eyes carefully, to find he was in his cousin Jegrai's tent. Sunlight that filtered through the walls made white felt glow warmly, but the air was cool, and smelled of grass and fresh water. And the camp-sounds were peaceful, as they had not been for more than a year.

This could not be their previous campsite, which had smelled only of horses and dust, always. And he could hear the cheerful gurgle of a spring or brook nearby, and that was not the sound of the great river they had crossed, either.

He hurt—but it wasn't like before. His head hurt, but he could think again, and the pain was localized and not nearly as bad as it had been.

He didn't want to move, much, especially not his head; but he could see what he really wanted to see without moving. His cousin, the great Khene of the Vredai, dozed beside Yuchai's bed, propped up by his saddle, and within touching distance.

Jegrai had taken charge of him. The thought startled a little croak out of his throat.

Jegrai came awake immediately, as any warrior would—but he smiled when he saw Yuchai's amazed eyes on him, a smile with no hint that the Khene considered his injured cousin to be any kind of burden on him.

Yuchai nearly wept with relief, and was immediately ashamed of such a maidenly reaction.

"There are too many in your father's tent for you to be undisturbed, and only me in mine—so I carried you off here, where you might heal in peace. So, young warrior, have you seen enough of battle to suffice you?" Jegrai said teasingly as he stretched limbs that must have been cramped, from the way he winced.

"I have seen nothing of battle, Khene," Yuchai whispered. "All I saw was a storm—"

"Wind Lords willing, that is all you will ever see, cousin," Jegrai replied, his face darkening. "Yuchai, little cousin, will you *now* content yourself with your father's path? I know you have it in you to be a Singer, and a great one."

"How can I think of the path of the Singer when half of the warriors who once followed our banner are *dead*, Khene?" Yuchai croaked. "Vredai needs fighters, not tellers of tales and keepers of lore!"

Jegrai shook his head. "We have said this before, you and I. I know all your arguments, as you know mine. Wind Lords willing, there will be no more of fighting for some time. But—all that is new in your case is that at the moment you can neither sing nor fight—though the *chagun* healer says that you will heal well enough to fight again, and Shenshu agrees with him." Jegrai picked up a bowl from the little flat table beside the fire-pot in the center of the tent, and stared moodily at its contents. "I could almost wish you crippled, little cousin. You have too fine a mind to waste . . . ah, enough. Drink this. This time it will not put you to sleep."

"This time?" Yuchai said, wonderingly. "*Chagun* healer?"

He remembered something more of that last dream. The man with his thin, pale face and gentle hands who brought both agony and soothing. The brown giant who filled the tent, nearly. He thought them visions.

"Whenever you woke I have been giving you of this to make you sleep again," Jegrai said. "It is from the healer-with-the-knife. But he said to leave off part of it, else it would make you crave for it."

"Cousin," Yuchai said wonderingly, "Where—*hai-kala*, in the name of the Wind Lords, where are we gotten to? This is not our last camp—I hear water—and the strangers you spoke of—"

"We have," Jegrai told him with a smothered twinkle in his eyes, "come to an unusual place, by the grace of the Wind Lords. Almost it could be the lands of blessed spirits. We have been granted water-pledge by wizards who hold lightning in their hands. One of them came himself from their home in the clouds to heal you with his own hands."

"That sounds like a tale to me, cousin," Yuchai said skeptically, sipping at the bitter brew of herbs Jegrai had handed him. As son of the Clan Singer he had a sure instinct for bald truth, the gilding of truth, and the warping of it.

Jegrai chuckled. "It *is* a tale. A tale a good many of the Vredai believe, but still only a tale. The 'wizards' are only men and women, I think; and though they have much wisdom, still, they can learn much of us. And if they are to be believed, this is their wish, to learn. The lightning I *have* seen, with my own eyes. Aya, it is powerful and fearful, but if men made it, other men can learn the use of it. The place in the clouds is a tall stone building up on the mountain pass on the western side of the valley."

Yuchai managed a feeble grin. "That sounds like less of a tale, though it is wonder enough."

"There is more wonder. One of the wizards did come to heal you, for no other reason than that another asked it of him, and both are good men. He gave us these herbs that kept you in a healing sleep and took your pain, and as I said, he also told us that after three days you would begin to crave them and that we should use them more sparingly. The Shaman thinks you are brave enough to do without except when you must sleep of nights, and I agree."

If Jegrai thought him brave enough to bear pain, then he would bear it until it tore him to ribbons before he complained. "I can bear it, cousin."

"I—I think I would like to ask another thing of you," Jegrai said after a moment of heavy silence, all the laughter gone from his face. "No—do not agree without thinking, and hear me out. We are under a three-day truce with the wizards. I go to speak with them before long, this very day, in the matter of—perhaps— an alliance. I think that there will be an exchange of hostages. Shenshu would go; she is wild to learn of this healing-with-knives. With her, Losha, equally wild to see new herbs and their uses, and to see the craftwork of these wizards. Shaman Demonsbane is to be the third. Shaman Northwind will be sometimes here, sometimes there if they permit; I think perhaps he and the woman-Khene of the wizards are two of the same mind. But I think that there should be a fourth to go." He paused. "Someone whose life they well know I value."

Yuchai blinked, and licked his lips. "M-me?"

"How better to hold my loyalty than to hold one who cannot escape them should I determine to betray them? And how better to prove my intentions than to offer that same person?"

Yuchai shivered. To be left alone, among wizards, trapped by a wounded body in a great hulking stone prison . . .

How better to serve his adored cousin, his Khene?

"Hear me, Yuchai—there may be something more here than being a hostage. The others speak of going to learn, so why not you also? You say you would be a warrior for the Vredai—would you wield your mind for me instead of a sword? Would you learn to cast lightning instead of shooting a bow?"

That possibility had not occurred to him.

"But I will not force you," Jegrai continued. "Though you would serve me and Vredai there as no one else could. You—little cousin, you are the only one of Vredai other than the healers and the Shamans—and your father, whom I do *not* trust, as you know— with the quickness of mind to learn these things for me. You know Trade-tongue. You are the only one at all who would do this out of love for me and for the learning. You are the only one except perhaps Shenshu and Northwind who would see things clearly, and with no baggage of omens and portents attached."

"I would?" Yuchai said, bewildered. "Why do you say these things?"

"Because, little cousin, you ask too many uncomfortable questions," Jegrai replied, grinning. "You accept too many inconvenient answers, provided they be truthful. You are, in short, too much like me. I have another reason for wanting you in the hands of the wizards, and it is an entirely selfish one. I want you entirely whole again, little cousin, as strong and limber as before, and with both Shenshu and the healer-with-knives within the fortress walls, if such a thing can be, it will be."

Yuchai did not really need to think upon the matter long. Jegrai wanted this: well, Jegrai would have it.

Although—when he thought a moment longer, the notion of all the new things to see, to learn—that alone would likely have been as much a temptation as Jegrai's need.

"I will go gladly, cousin," he said softly.

The Khene sighed. "You may come to regret your decision before the day is over," he replied, "and your father will want my head upon a stake before his tent. But I thank you, Yuchai. You buy me more than you know."

It had been Felaras's decision to make the nomads come to her choice of ground, so they met in a pavilion set up by the side of the road within sight of the Fortress. The Order had used this pavilion at harvest festivals in the Vale; it held fifty people and tables for all of them, and was more than large enough for the two delegations and the single bargaining table.

They lined up on either side of it, her group, then the nomads. She'd wondered about chairs, the table, but the nomads seemed reasonably acquainted with such furnishings. The nomad chief Jegrai—even handsomer now that he was clean and rested— had brought with him only seven other folk (and Eriel had babbled about auspicious numbers), so she had ordered the same. The four of the delegation, and Zorsha, Kasha, and Boitan.

Kasha, because Felaras was going to be luck-wishing this colloquy with all her strength, and she wanted someone ready to deflect any ill-wishes. It was a pity Kasha wasn't as expert at this as Felaras was; she could deflect, but she didn't yet have the level of fine control needed to send an ill-wish right back in the teeth of the sender. But this time, deflection should be enough.

Boitan was here, because one of those with Jegrai was the injured boy, in a horse-litter. The boy was half-asleep over on a cot that had been brought at some haste from the Fortress, and set up at the side of the pavilion. Before long he should be completely asleep, as he'd been well dosed with poppy-gum. That was on Boitan's orders, after one look at his strained, white face. And, without prompting, Boitan had silently put himself at the boy's side rather than make an unmatched number at the table.

That was a likely ally she'd overlooked. Vider was hers, but inflexible and very cautious—he'd take to new ways only if others tried them first. But Boitan—quiet, unsmiling, but always ready to try something new and different—this was the one to learn whatever the nomad healers could teach, and giving him that opportunity might well make him hers. A lot like Duran, from what Felaras could judge of that near-legend. *Boitan is definitely one to cultivate, a word of thanks and putting him in charge of dealing with the nomad healers will go a long way in that direction.*

There had been relief in all the nomads' faces when they'd seen Boitan was one of those in the Order's party, and more relief when he'd taken charge of the boy as if it were a given.

That boy—Felaras fancied she knew what was coming; it made very sound sense in many ways for the boy to become a hostage. It was no secret to anyone how much the nomad leader valued his young cousin. There was this—he would certainly get the best care of *both* worlds up here.

And there was the other aspect—he certainly wouldn't be able to escape if Jegrai turned his coat, so that made sense too. It virtually assured her of Jegrai's sworn word.

Lords of light and darkness—that says a lot of nasty things about the folk these nomads have been dealing with of late. If I were a betting woman, I would bet that the last leader he talked truce with would have demanded the boy. Not exactly used to dealing with anyone reasonable; wonder if they'd know a potential friend now if they saw him? But if the boy is anything like his cousin . . . hm. Felaras took her seat on her side of the bargaining table, keeping one part of her mind on the boy, the other on analyzing the Khene's expressions. *A sharp mind generally hungers after learning. I wonder if we could gain ourselves an in-camp advocate with the Khene's ear just by teaching him as if he was one of ours. It's certainly worth a try.*

She'd have preferred having the boy awake, so as to get the interactions between him and the Khene, but . . . no. The boy had endured the pain of the journey up the side of the mountain, but he did not have to continue to endure pain while his elders made noise at each other. She would have ordered that poppy-drink herself if Boitan hadn't anticipated her.

Let him sleep, Felaras thought. *It's not as though knowing what's in his head is going to make any real difference at this stage. We'll be turning his world inside out soon enough.*

So while the boy drowsed, oblivious, on one side of the pavilion, his elders drank wine and made diplomatic sounds at each other.

Jegrai was amazingly good at it for a "barbarian." Better than most of the folk in the Order.

Felaras was good at it, but she wished she wasn't. Polite noise, pretty compliments, all the rest of that diplomatic rot; Felaras mouthed it and loathed it even as she mouthed it. She was prepared to continue it indefinitely.

And then a glance at Khene Jegrai when his face was momentarily unguarded made her decide that enough was enough. That combination of tension and boredom was nearly identical to the emotions she was keeping hidden.

"All right," she said abruptly, putting her half-empty goblet down on the table. "You've danced your dance, I've danced mine. You want peace with us, we're willing. What are you prepared to give us for it?"

Jegrai's eyes widened a little. "That would depend on what you demanded," he said, his syntax having much improved after a three-day period spent in chattering with Teo. "I may tell you what we are prepared to offer. Hostages—and hostages willing to tell you of the lands we have traveled through, of our ways, of our fashion of healing and other crafts."

She nodded; this was exactly as she'd expected. "How many?"

"Four. The Second Shaman of Vredai, Demonsbane—"

A young man with very old eyes (sitting at the left hand of the weirdly bedecked ancient Felaras knew was the first Shaman, Northwind), nodded at her, and smiled faintly.

"—the First Healer of Vredai, Shenshu—"

Felaras had liked this one immediately, and not the least because of Boitan's descriptions of cleverness and competence. Shenshu twinkled as her name was spoken; there was no fear in her of what she was going to.

"—Losha, who studies plants and all their uses, not just of healing, and who teaches some of the other crafts, including that of weaponry—"

Another intriguingly handsome man, not so young as Jegrai and not quite so handsome, but in the same mold.

"—and—"

"And?" she prompted.

Jegrai simply looked over at the sleeping boy. "—Yuchai. I would have you to know that he is my heir until I breed those of my own body."

"Is it your wish, Khene, that this be more than an exchange of hostages?" Felaras asked carefully. "I am empowered to allow you the indefinite use of the place where you are now camped, and provisions, if you would help us to guard the Vale from wild beasts and . . . the like. But we could also offer you more than this. Would you have an exchange of something far more precious than hostages? Of knowledge? If we engage to teach those you leave with us and to learn from them, will you pledge likewise?"

Again Jegrai's eyes widened in surprise. "That—you freely offer this?"

"Freely offered," Felaras nodded. "There is nothing more important in our eyes."

He drew in a long breath. "We will so pledge."

"Then here is my *envoy*," she said, stressing the fact that she had not used the word *hostage*. "Four in exchange for four. Teo you already know. This is Halun, one of our finest artificer-scholars. Mai, wise in many things, including the arts of warfare. And Eriel, who searches for the ways by which we may understand the world. As much as you show to them, so they will teach you." She smiled at the young Khene, who was showing signs of the odd little light in his eyes that the best of the novices got when they discovered that they were going to be learning, and not just playing servant to their mentors. "I would take it well, Khene Jegrai, were you to keep Teo at your hand, yourself. There is much you could share with one another."

Jegrai and Teo exchanged a look bordering on the conspiratorial, and Teo began to grin.

"Master of the Order," Jegrai said formally, under far better control than Teo, "it is well. My people came prepared to stay."

"And mine to leave," she told him. "Let there be truce between our peoples, then."

"As long as the grass shall grow," he said, making it sound like a vow. "And, Wind Lords permitting, let this be the opening to something more than truce."

"Hladyr grant," she said fervently, and stood up from the bargaining table. She nodded briefly at Kasha and Zorsha, who made their unhurried way to the side of the pavilion, and picked up the boy Yuchai, cot and all, without waking him. She nodded again to Boitan, who gathered up the other three the way a kridee gathered her chicks, and with as little fuss.

"Do not fear, Khene Jegrai," she said, reacting to his look of worry. "We shall care for him as one born of us. Kasha, for the duration, the boy's a novice; equal shares with you and Zorsha until he proves out where his interests lie."

"Yes, Master Felaras," Kasha murmured, after casting her a single startled glance.

They headed for the pavilion entrance, following Boitan and the rest of the "hostages." She prepared to go after, but Jegrai cleared his throat urgently.

"Master Felaras, there is a favor. . . ."

"Ask."

"Shaman Northwind would come and go here—if that is permitted."

Felaras thought about that; it was obvious to a child that the old man could carry messages back and forth. Then again, they were asking openly. This wasn't exactly clandestine.

She looked out of the corner of her eye at the bizarre old man—who caught her eye, grinned, and winked.

By the gods, I like this old goat! she thought with amusement. *Why the hell not?*

"Why not?" she said aloud. "Surely your envoys will wish to send words to their families from time to time. He is welcome in our home—*if*—" she said with sudden wild inspiration "—I will be welcome from time to time in yours."

The young Khene was plainly not expecting that response.

She watched him grope for an answer, and the Shaman forestalled him by answering her smoothly.

"How not?" he said in passable Trade-tongue. "One wizard should always find a welcome in the home of another. It is plain to me that you and I have much we should speak of together; now, if we may." He gave her a long look, and continued, with emphasis, "Is it not always so when folk share . . . knowledge?"

She felt just a hint of a tickle at the back of her neck, the pleasant little sensation that meant someone was luck-wishing (not ill-wishing) her, and looked at the Shaman with wild surmise. *By the gods, he's not mouthing platitudes, and he's not making boasts! He's a real wizard—and he's got me pegged as having the power too! He must have felt the luck-wishing I was doing, and—*

She glanced at Kasha, disappearing with the boy.

As if in answer to her thought, he followed the glance, then winked again, slowly.

—by the gods, he felt Kasha's deflection shield, too! This is going to be a very interesting conversation.

"It isn't so as often as I'd like, Shaman Northwind," she replied courteously, gathering her scattered and ambulatory wits again. "Pray, come with me. If you will excuse us, Khene, I think Shaman Northwind and I indeed have a very great deal to discuss."

"Where should we put our new novice?" Zorsha asked Kasha's back with a half-grin as he balanced his end of the cot over a rough place in the road. A rough place that was a legacy of those little efforts of Felaras's at impressing the nomads. "I've never had a novice before—only a puppy. I don't suppose we'll have to housebreak him, will we?"

Sunlight on the top of Kasha's head gave her hair reddish highlights that looked very nice against the dark brown of her tunic. "I think we'd better put him somewhere he's not likely to be frightened when he wakes up. Some place as open as possible. With a window." Her voice had gone flat the way it always did when she was thinking. "Hm. You know, there's the Master's Folly."

"There is, and probably the best bet if what you want is 'open,' " Zorsha agreed. "I just hope he doesn't get just as frightened when he sees how high up he is. He's just lucky it's spring, though, or we'd have to shovel a path from his bed to the door every morning."

"Oh, it isn't *that* bad. I stayed there when the Master had pneumonia. I'll grant you it's cold and drafty in winter, but I've been in worse inns. And it should keep him from feeling like he's buried under a pile of stone."

"I'll give you that. It also puts him right next door to Felaras, which is no bad thing. . . ."

Kasha gave him a sharp look over her shoulder. "Are you thinking what I'm thinking?"

"If you're thinking that there are some folk who, for all their learning, would take a certain enjoyment in tormenting an injured and helpless barbarian boy—"

"That's what I'm thinking, all right." The expression on her face as she turned away again was of someone who had tasted something sour. "Easy on, threshold—and dragon—ahead."

As they neared the white stone wall and the dark, arched hole of the outer gate, Zorsha craned his head around a little and could see Boitan waiting for them.

"Stop a bit, children." Boitan's voice was unusually gentle; when they paused, he put his wrist against the boy's forehead, then pried up one of the boy's eyelids and smiled at what he read there. Zorsha nearly dropped his end of the cot; Boitan *never* smiled!

"No fever, no sign of permanent brain injury, and healing faster than any of *you* ever had the grace to do," the physician said with satisfaction. "The boy's a credit to his physicians. Where are you putting him? Novices usually go in the room next to their mentor, and you can hardly split him in two."

Zorsha actually had a solution to that—involving sharing a room, and presumably, a bed—but one look at Kasha's face convinced him that it would not be politic to voice that solution.

"Well, Kasha thought he might be frightened if he was too closed in, so we thought maybe we'd put him in the Master's Folly," he said instead.

Boitan considered this for a moment, then nodded. "If we did that, then Shenshu could take the room next to that; it's empty since I don't know when. That would put him between Felaras and his own healer. I'll meet you there, all right? The herbalist has the boy's things with him, so we'll bring them. It seems the Master has given me the duty of getting the adults settled in, and I thought since I don't currently have a novice I could pack that herbalist and the Shaman together in my novice's room."

Zorsha raised an eyebrow at that, and the look Boitan gave him said that the physician had also considered the possible unfriendly actions of his fellows, and had decided to deal with them before they happened.

"Fine," he replied, as the expectant silence on Boitan's part seemed to indicate that the physician was waiting for his approval. "I doubt Felaras will disagree with you. Now if you don't mind, this boy is not getting any lighter, nor the staircase shorter."

Boitan stepped gracefully out of the way, and Zorsha could see that the other three nomads had been—not concealed, not exactly, but certainly arranged so as not to be terribly visible— behind him.

There were plenty of curious gawkers on the way to the room they'd chosen for the boy. A few even looked sympathetic, and those few included Kitri and Ardun.

Which should make anybody think twice about trying anything, Zorsha thought.

Kitri even walked with them down the corridor once they told her where they were taking him. "Poor little lad. Gods, at an age where our youngsters are just thinking about their final choice of mentor, this child was out fighting wars. It doesn't bear thinking about."

"I think the Master has some notion of sparing this one that fate, Leader," Kasha said without turning her head. "She assigned both me and Zorsha as the boy's mentors, and she means it. She said to that Clan Chief of theirs that he was to be treated like one of our own, and told Zorsha and me to teach him until his real aptitudes show up."

Kitri looked like a cat who has just been presented with a particularly delicious cheese-rind. Surprised, then smug, then extremely acquisitive.

"Now, now, lady," Zorsha admonished her, laughing. "Felaras gave him to *us*. If you want any little nomads to drag into education, you'll have to go find your own!"

"Go on with you—" she objected, then smiled sheepishly. "That obvious, was I?"

"Leader, I could have predicted the expression on your face," Kasha giggled. "We know you."

Kitri chose that moment to get ahead of them and open the door to the boy's new room. "Well . . . if he shows any signs of aptitude as a pure scholar—"

"We'll let you know," Zorsha promised, and they stepped through the door and gratefully put their burden down.

The room called "the Master's Folly" had once been the large and airy bedchamber reserved for the Master's use. Then some unnamed Master had decided that it wasn't quite airy enough, or else decided that he or she wanted an unobstructed view of the northern mountains. The tales said both, and whoever had been chronicler at the time had tactfully "forgotten" to memorialize this particular piece of bad judgment. Whatever the reason was, the past Master had ordered the north wall of the chamber knocked out and made almost entirely window.

So it was done; the Hands being what they were, metal supports were crafted that took the place of the absent wall, the stone was removed piece by careful piece, and it was accomplished without fanfare or fuss, right down to heavy shutters to be closed against the worst weather. The view was virtually unobstructed, and the Fortress retained its structural integrity at that point.

The Master was pleased through spring, through summer; then came the fall.

The shutters were so heavy and so hard to get in place that when the first autumn rainstorm moved in, the entire contents of the room were soaked before those shutters could be closed.

But that was not the worst.

Winter brought the usual snow and icy cold—and the Master learned that shutters do not take the place of a solid stone wall the night of the first real blizzard.

The Master, so it was said, had to abandon the room that night. And in the morning the snow that had been driven in through the cracks and seams of the shutters had to be shoveled out.

The Master moved out of the room that very day, into the novice's room. And no Master had used it since.

Kasha was already putting the shutters aside, letting in light, a playful little breeze, and the most spectacular view obtainable short of standing on top of the walls or the roof.

"Should we get him into bed, do you think?" Zorsha asked, looking down at the boy and wishing vaguely that he could do something to make him get well faster. *Poor little fellow. I think I'm going to like him.*

Kasha shook her head. "No, I don't think we should. The bedding hasn't been changed or aired in ages, for one thing. For another, if he wakes up and finds himself in one of our beds, it might confuse or frighten him. That cot will do for now." She pulled back the coverlet on the bed, and wrinkled her nose at the musty odor. "Hladyr knows there's enough room in here for three beds and twenty cots without crowding anything."

The room did seem rather empty, with only the bed and a wardrobe and a couple of chests. They'd set the cot down against the eastern wall, between the two chests. It seemed as good a place as any to leave the boy. Kasha stood at the enormous window, looking out on the mountains.

The boy was still quite thoroughly asleep. And Zorsha was effectively alone with Kasha—as he had not been for months.

His throat tightened. *Say something, anything. Now, before the moment gets away. Teo's going out of the Fortress, and now, if ever, is going to be your chance.*

"Kasha," he said softly. "I'd like to talk about us. And Teo—"

"Don't say it," she replied tightly, staying exactly as she was. There was controlled anger in her voice, and he knew he'd made a mistake. "He's not going out of reach. He's only down at the base of the mountain. No matter what you think, nothing's changed."

"Except—" He groped for words, desperately. *As long as I've put my foot in it, I might as well put it in good. Besides, what do I have to lose? She's already pledged that she'll never break the Trinity.* "—things might change. I just want to know . . . if they do change for Teo, could—could they change for us, too?"

"Zorsha, things could change for you, too. Did that ever occur to you?" she asked sharply. "A hundred things could change. The point is that one of the two of you is going to have to make a decision, if you want a change in the relationship between the three of us. It won't be me. I won't change things. And you and Teo are too good friends to pick a fight—especially when you know both the winner and the loser would lose. You won't force me into making a choice between you. You know that, you know that very well."

He looked down at his feet. His chest felt tight, his throat choked—

—and yet, there was a little relief there too. Relief that the change wouldn't be coming; not yet, anyway. *I want Kasha—but not at the cost of losing Teo. There's changes enough right now. Maybe Teo will fall in love with a little almond-eyed archer-girl down there, and the problem will solve itself. If there's got to be a change, I'd like it to be for the Trinity to turn into a Quartet.*

"Sorry," he said to his feet. "I—never mind."

"Besides," she said briskly, turning away from the window. "You are going to have some more pressing problems on your hands when this boy wakes up. I believe you asked about housebreaking?"

If he hadn't heard the anger in her voice a moment before, he'd never have known she'd been close to the point of rage at him. Certainly the expression of wry humor she wore now wouldn't have told him.

"Housebreaking?" he said stupidly. "What on . . . oh." The back of his neck and his ears grew hot—hotter still when her wry expression broadened into one of pure, malicious enjoyment.

"Exactly," she said. "You are dealing with a young man who likely never saw a privy in his life, much less one of ours. And I think he would be most profoundly embarrassed if I tried to show him. This is assuming he's healed up enough to take the walk across the room—if he isn't, you'll have to show him how to use the chamber pot."

She was grinning fiendishly, and he had the distinct feeling that she was enjoying his embarrassment. "I can't say that I envy you—and I hope he speaks Trade-tongue."

"But—" he began, feeling no little panicked, when Boitan and the nomad healer came bustling in like they had been blown in the door by a gust of the boisterous breeze.

"Well! Here—" Boitan began, then looked at the two of them sharply. "Am I interrupting anything?"

And to think I volunteered for this, Halun mused ruefully, surveying his accommodations. He had been allotted the felt tent of a now-deceased unmarried warrior; it was scarcely the size of his laboratory storage closet. And no furniture except a pallet and a couple of low tables with folding legs.

He was very glad he'd yielded to impulse and exchanged his long robes for more utilitarian tunics and breeches. Sitting cross-legged on the tent floor in a robe would have been nearly impossible.

The Khene and Teo had shown him how to raise the sides of the tent a little to allow cool air to flow in, and had shown him the sanitary arrangements. . . .

Or lack of them. Bathing in the brook, and eliminating in slit-trenches. He shuddered. It was one thing to be living like this during the haying holidays when one was a novice, and quite another when one was on the downside of fifty.

It was a good thing he'd brought his own bedding. Granted, what they'd given him seemed clean enough, but still—furs, sheepskins tanned with the wool still on, and undyed wool blankets still oily with lanolin—it all seemed the perfect haven for fleas and other less savory things.

He'd used it all to augment the thin pallet, which was of clean cotton. Furs and sheepskins and all going *beneath* the pallet. *Sleeping on the ground. My bones are going to wonder what my head has done to them.*

He wondered if he was being a fool.

Tonight he was to meet with the father of that injured boy. Teo had said that the man's title translated as "Clan Singer" but that what he actually did seemed to be to act as a combination of Archivist and chronicler. Since the man was the only person in the entire Clan to speak Trade-tongue fluently, he was the logical choice as Halun's "guide" in this place.

No, I'm not being a fool. There's too much to learn here. I couldn't trust anyone else in the Hand to get it right except Zorsha, and he will go only where Felaras wants him to go. The writing's in the scroll there for all to read. She's made up her mind—it's very likely that Teo will not be her successor. Somehow I doubt that'll break his heart. But that's why he's down here with the Khene, instead of up there at the Fortress, learning to be Master.

Halun already had a hundred questions; the construction of the nomad's bows, for instance. He could understand the patchwork construction. These folk came from a nearly treeless plain, after all. But when he'd had one of the bows in his hands, he'd been amazed at the flawless mating of materials, and even more surprised at the strength of the tiny bow. Some of the materials had not been wood; there were bone plates, but some of the rest of the laminates hadn't been immediately identifiable.

He wanted to know what they were, how they were put together to obtain that incredible strength and toughness.

Then there had been some body armor he'd seen, like boiled-leather scale, but made of horn or similar substance. It looked tough, yet lightweight; an immense improvement over both the Yazkirn boiled-leather and the Ancas metal plate-mail.

In fact, the uses these people put leather to, and wood, replacing pottery—*which would be broken the first time they packed up and moved,* he reflected—was amazing. He'd seen leather made absolutely waterproof, virtually flame-proof, soft as fabric and as hard and tough as horn. And always the question of how they had done this nagged at him.

Their smiths, however, were not up to even the standards of the Ancas, much less the things the Order could do. Their swords and knives were mostly bronze, with a few that were obviously family heirlooms of inferior steel.

Halun supposed with a sigh that he would be expected to teach them *that.*

At least Felaras isn't fool enough to give them the secrets of explosives, he thought soberly, trying to find a way to sit comfortably on the floor of the tent. *Hladyr bless—I can just see it now—the slaughter these people would wreak if they had mortars and mines. Even walled cities wouldn't be safe. These barbarians would send the world floating into oblivion in its own blood, and the blame would be all ours.*

He opened his writing chest and took out his notes on the language, hoping to be a little more fluent by evening. There were some concepts that simply didn't translate well into Trade-tongue. But his mind kept circling in on Felaras, this near-alliance of hers, and his own ambitions.

Zorsha wasn't haring off on a tangent at the Convocation, he thought after a bit. *That was not a bad idea; allying with these barbarians, then declaring the Vale an independent entity. Knowing we had cavalry to enforce our sovereignty, not even Yazkirn or Ancas would dispute it. Gods above and below—no more taxes sent off to those crowned fools! Hm . . . we've gotten the nomads tied in closely enough with us so that we could use them—we could control not only the Vale, but the entire region.*

He took that line of reasoning one step further. *If we were to educate whoever is Khene just enough so that he depended on*

*what we could manufacture for him and came to rely on us for
our advice, but realized that without us the things he had come
to depend on would no longer be appearing—we could be the
real power behind the throne. Whoever was Master could dictate
and the Khene would obey.*

He sighed, and finally stretched himself full length on the pallet.
*Felaras would never agree to that; never. A fool, a fool, we have a
fool for our Master. The first chance we've ever seen to come back
into civilized lands with a power-base of our own, and she'll throw
that chance away because she refuses to use people.*

He ground his teeth together in frustration. *Damn it all, I
should be Master here! I know how to use these barbarian
children, and do so in such a way that they would never know
they were being used. If only Felaras would have the grace to
die, or become ill! Damned woman was always too damned
healthy. Not even pneumonia at the height of snow-season killed
her! She's maneuvered so that virtually everyone in the Order is
going to be supporting her on this alliance, so there's no way I'm
going to get her unseated. And with whoever it is protecting her,
I can't even ill-wish her.*

He'd tried, especially during the truce-talk. Nothing had
happened; the ill-wish had just bounced. Where it had gone,
Halun had no real idea, although he'd had a suspicion. Dosti,
and Dosti's novice Urval, had had a spectacularly bad day. On
every loom they tried to string, either the warp threads had
tangled, or they'd broken. The cats had gotten into the punched
cards for the pattern-looms, and had made a few holes of their
own, which meant Urval would have to repunch all those cards
again from the archived patterns. When they decided to turn
their hands to just plain weaving for the Order, it turned out
that the only yarn they had in sufficient quantities to make
anything in the way of garment-lengths was dyed in particularly
hideous, muddy shades of green, yellow, and dun. Checking
the records, they discovered that those stored skeins had been
dyed in muted, but pleasant, usable colors—but proximity to
the bleaching vats had leeched the color out of the yarn-skeins,
turning them ugly. They would all have to be redyed. And just
moments before Halun had given up his ill-wishing, Urval had
fallen into a (thankfully cool) vat of ochre dye. He now was
ochre, brightly ochre, from top to toe. He looked like a bad

case of liver disease, and it wouldn't wash off, it would have to wear off.

If only Felaras had some truly virulent enemy . . .

Then the thought occurred that made him sit straight up.

After that business on the walls—she does. I would be willing to bet my life that Zetren is so unbalanced now that he'd be child's play to tip! He never was all that well wrapped to begin with, and he holds a grudge like a badger holds its brock. I can't ill-wish her directly, but I can certainly work on Zetren. . . .

He contemplated the best way to set the mind-spell. *I'll have to aim this at Zetren rather than her—but—the worst thing Zetren could do at this point would be to start taking this thing from a grudge to an open vendetta. That would destroy him, because no matter how it came out, he'd be cast out of the Order. Yes. Yes. At the very worst, she'll be distracted and unable to give her whole attention to what's going on down here, which will give me a free hand to work. And at the best—*

He found himself smiling.

At the best—the Order will require a new Master. And with neither boy trained or seasoned enough to take it—I become the only logical candidate.

Yes, indeed.

✧ CHAPTER SEVEN ✧

Kasha leaned forward in her chair and shook her head in pure wonder. "You're *how* old?" she asked the nomad boy.

"Fourteen," Yuchai replied in nearly unaccented Trade-tongue, feeling worried. "Am I—am I learning too slowly?" He clutched his Ancas primer so hard his knuckles were white. Trade-tongue was very like the speech of Ancas, and he was making—he thought—reasonable progress in learning that language. But this business of equating sounds with marks on a page was very new to him. The idea that words could be saved, forever and ever, unchanged, had excited him so much he resented every moment not spent in learning how to decipher those marks.

"Gods above and below," Kasha laughed, her eyes crinkling at the corners. "Too slowly? Anything but that! You're learning as quickly as a very young child—and that's supposed to be impossible for a boy your age. You already speak Trade-tongue as well as I do, and you're learning Ancas as fast as I can pour it into you."

Yuchai relaxed, and sagged back into the pillows that had been piled behind him so that he could sit up. "It is that I have very little else to do except learn, *gadjeia* Kasha," he said. "And I— have pleasure in this learning. Besides, I certainly cannot practice the warrior arts from a bed."

Kasha snorted and made a sour face. "If I have my way you won't be practicing the 'warrior arts' at all, young man. You've too good a mind. I'd cripple you myself before I'd see you die by the hand of some stupid ox who happens to outweigh you by three times."

Yuchai felt a strange apprehension at her words. For so long he had wanted to be a great warrior like Jegrai—and yet the great warrior he admired would have been happier if he'd never touched a weapon. And now this fighting-woman who said the same thing; she was *very* good—he'd watched her at practice from his huge window, for besides the mountains you could look right down into the courtyard of the Sword-folk, if you stood— or in his case, sat—close to the edge. Would she do such a thing? To keep him a scholar—scholars were forbidden weapons. Was that her purpose, to see that he did not violate that law? He licked his dry lips. "That—that is similar to what Khene Jegrai tells me," he ventured. "But, forgive me, honored teacher, but Vredai needs warriors. Vredai does not need a man who is neither feeble nor crippled, yet who cannot raise a blade in his own defense—"

"Yuchai, do you really enjoy fighting?" she asked, her face gone quiet and very serious.

"I—I—the moving, like dancing, doing it well—I like that," he temporized.

"I'm not talking about that," she said, frowning. "I'm talking about *fighting*. Killing, trying not to be killed. Do you find that . . . attractive? Some do; acts on them like wine. Nothing sinful about that, nothing wrong, just the way some people are made."

"No—I—I haven't seen much of fighting, but—they always set me to guarding the Clan heart, the children, you know? The fighting got that far, once or twice. I—the closer it got, the sicker I got." He hung his head, admitting his shame, the weakness he had confessed to no one but Shaman Northwind. "When I closed, the moment before, you know, I almost couldn't hold my sword for wanting to throw up. But—Vredai *has* a Singer. They don't need another fool that can't even defend himself."

He colored as he realized that he had just slandered his own father.

"Did I say you shouldn't know how to defend yourself?" Kasha demanded. "Have you ever once heard me say anything like that? I'm no fool, Yuchai—your people are warriors by their nature. Wherever you go, there's likely to be fighting. There's no harm in knowing weaponry—every member of the Order knows bow, at least. I'm just saying you don't belong on a battlefield, except in a case of last resort."

"Everyone—in the Order—knows weaponry?" Yuchai's

thoughts went whirling as if they'd been caught in a dust-demon. "But—except for those of the Sword, are you all not as Singers? Is it not forbidden among you for Singers to touch a weapon?"

Kasha's mouth twisted as she labored to disentangle that last sentence. "No, it's not forbidden!" she exclaimed when she had the sense of it. "Great good gods, we'd have been slaughtered a dozen times over if we held that rule! If a novice from one of the other chapters wants to spend his free time learning Swordways, that's his business. We've actually had one or two Masters that could have been both Sword and either Book or Tower by earned skill-level if they'd chosen to ask for the Sword badge as well as their own."

"You—have?" He felt rather as if he'd fallen on his head again.

"I take it that it's very much forbidden among your people."

"One must choose," he replied carefully. "The Singer must never touch a weapon; the Wind Lords favor the wise, but—you know that among us the wise one is almost sacred? It is a terrible thing for a man to raise his hand against a scholar; the Wind Lords will surely curse him for it. So—for a wise one to bear a weapon, to fight with a weapon—that is taking dishonorable advantage."

It didn't take his tutor long to fathom the meaning of that. "Uh-huh," Kasha said, nodding. "Yes, I see what you mean. It's like a whole man taking on one with no legs. The opponent of a scholar in a fight has a choice between being dead and being cursed."

"Exactly so," Yuchai said with a sigh.

"Well, we don't have that particular restriction, and it doesn't look like the Wind Lords have cursed us yet." Kasha settled back in her bedside chair and put her hands behind her head. "My friend, if you want to go trade bruises with me or anyone else in Sword and you happen to have landed in Tower or Book, feel free to come to us in your spare time. We're always looking for new sparring partners, and I'll wager you could show us a few things new to us. And if you don't happen to tell the Wind Lords—" she grinned "—neither will I."

Yuchai felt his breath stick somewhere in his throat. It took him a moment to get it moving again. "I may?" he asked.

"You may. But not at the moment." Kasha pulled one hand out and wagged an admonishing finger at him. "At the moment you can barely hold up that book, and it takes Zorsha to get you to the privy."

He felt a blush crawling up his face.

"So at the moment, my friend, you'd best keep your attentions on that primer."

He gladly buried his nose in the book, hoping Kasha hadn't noticed his blushing.

"So, if the world is round, like a ball, why don't we fall off of it?" the boy asked. "And if it's spinning, why aren't we flung off of it?"

Zorsha grinned. At first he'd thought this notion of Felaras's— to teach a wild nomad boy—was going to be sheer torture for both of them.

It was turning out to be sheer pleasure. The boy drank in everything Zorsha could teach as thirsty ground drank spring rains. There was such a need in him to know—sometimes Zorsha could almost see him physically beating against the walls of his limitations of language and understanding. And every day those walls crumbled a little more; one day there would be nothing to stop him.

"Because," he said, answering the question with an example, "we *think*, Yuchai, that when something gets big enough, it attracts smaller things to it—the way this bit of amber picks up a feather after I rub it with the silk."

Zorsha took an amber bead from the box of oddments he'd brought with him, and rubbed it vigorously with a scrap of silk cloth. He put a feather on the comforter, and brought the bead close to it. The boy watched, his eyes bright with intense fascination, as the feather leapt to cling to the bead.

The boy reached out and pulled the feather away, then let it go, and watched it return to the bead.

"We think," Zorsha said, "that the force I generated in the amber and the force that holds us on the world are similar, though not the same. We call the first 'electricity' and the second 'gravity.' "

The boy's lips moved a little as he committed the words to his memory. "But—why don't you think they're the same if they both make things stick to other things?"

Zorsha chuckled, put the feather away, and rubbed the amber again, briskly. "I'll show you—hold out your finger."

Yuchai did, and Zorsha brought the amber in close enough to the boy's fingertip that a spark leapt from the bead to the outstretched finger. The boy yelped in surprise and jerked his hand back.

"Now, since we don't keep getting stung by sparks all the time, we probably aren't being held to the world by electricity," Zorsha told him, putting the amber and silk away.

Yuchai cocked his head to one side and stared over Zorsha's shoulder, out the window at the mountains. The Hand had noticed that Yuchai always stared at the mountains when he was thinking. His brow was creased—but not in puzzlement. "That . . . spark . . . that was like a tiny piece of lightning," he said after a moment, making it a statement and not a question.

"Very like," Zorsha agreed.

"Is the spark you made the same stuff as lightning—only small?"

"We think so."

"There's always a lot of lightning in the mountains," Yuchai mused. "Could . . . lightning happen because—because clouds rub against the ground, the way you rubbed the silk on the amber?"

Zorsha felt his eyes widening in surprise. *I hadn't expected that jump of reasoning! Good for him!*

"That's one idea," he agreed. "There are lots of possible explanations, and that's one of them."

"But clouds are only air and water," Yuchai said, turning puzzled eyes on his teacher. "How could they rub against the ground when there's nothing there to rub with?"

"Are you sure that air is nothing?" Zorsha countered.

"Yes!—No." The boy looked back over the mountains. "No, it can't be nothing, not when I've been in winds so strong they knocked me over, and wind is just air moving the way the Wind Lords tell it to. And when the wind blows like that, in a *khemaseen* or a *syechali*, it can pick up enough sand to strip the flesh from your bones, which means that it's holding the sand up. So air *is* something. Is—is air like water, only very, very thin?"

"We don't know," Zorsha admitted. "We used to think that all things were made of four elements—air, water, earth, and fire. Now we know they aren't: we know that what we call 'earth' is made of a great many things. We call *those* things elements now, because they are 'elementary,' which means they can't be broken down into anything smaller. We think water is made of several elements, but we can't tell what they are. We don't know about fire. Or air. Or light, like from the sun. Those might be what we call 'energies,' or we might be able to break them down into other things some day—or they may be elements."

"There's a lot you don't know," Yuchai observed, with a stare that had mischief lurking at the bottom of it.

Gods above and below—if I should have a son one day, grant me one like this!

"Oh, yes," Zorsha admitted cheerfully, "there's a great deal we don't know. That just makes a great deal for someone to find out. Maybe you. Hm?"

The boy returned his gaze to the clouds moving above the mountains.

"It might be. . . ." he whispered. "It might be me. . . ."

The Khene's tent was very crowded. Of all his advisors, only the Shaman sat beside him to hear what the most senior riders of the Clan had to say about the wizards—and the truce. Jegrai wished with one half of his mind that he had the others with him.

But the more reasoning half of his mind told him that this must be dealt with—and he alone must deal with it. Else the Clan might begin to wonder who was Khene—Jegrai, or Jegrai's advisors.

So he kept his face impassive and listened with patience that was mostly feigned to the arguments and threats of his most argumentative people.

"I tell you, we have them at our mercy!" shouted a stocky, round-faced rider with a strong and authoritative voice, a voice that almost forced one to listen to it. This was the Clan Singer, Yuchai's father, Jegrai's uncle Gortan. "These fools leave their gates open to us by day or night—there are not so many of them that a war party could not steal in under the cover of the darkness and force them to *give* us the secret of the lightning!"

"Pah! The secret of the lightning!" spat Jegrai's half-brother Iridai, a man so like Gortan that they could have been brothers, save that Iridai did not have Gortan's power to ensorcel with his voice. "That is only too likely a secret the Wind Lords would curse us for having! If they did not curse us for taking it by force from these wizards! I would remind you all, these folk are too like the Holy Vedani for my comfort. I would be away from them, before we lose ourselves to them! Jegrai, we have the water-pledge, we have the truce—send back the envoys, take back our people, and let us be away from here! Their land-folk are creeping out of hiding, and there can be none who could hold us less than honorable if we moved on to other pickings. The old ways are the best ways—"

"Iridai, my brother," Jegrai said softly, but with veiled menace, "the old ways would have let Yuchai die, or left him a cripple. The old ways would reduce us to *thieving* swords of steel instead of honorably forging our own. Is that what you want?"

Iridai gaped at him in surprise; Jegrai was quite well aware that his brother had claimed one of the first new swords with the glee of a child claiming a honeycomb.

"And uncle," he continued, turning to face Gortan before he lost his advantage, his menace no longer veiled, "would you have us break water-pledge? Would you have us less in honor than the Talchai, cursed be their name and Clan?"

Gortan shrank visibly.

"You are Clan Singer—would you record treachery such as not even Khene Sen dared in the songs of Vredai?"

"No." Gortan shook his head. "Khene, it maddens me, this waiting at their table for crumbs—and their choice of what we shall have, and what we shall not have. They treat us as children, as fools."

Jegrai chose to keep silence upon that point, for it sometimes galled him as well. *And it is well that Gortan does not know this. My friend Teo knows—but can do nothing. He is at the orders of his Khene, Master Felaras. And Master Felaras does things for reasons only she knows.*

Shaman Northwind spoke up at this point. "Gortan," he said pleasantly, "if you were to train a child to wield a sword, would you place your brother's sharp new steel blade in his hands?"

The Clan Singer snorted. "Of course not! I would give him a weighted practice blade of wood suited to his age, and . . . ah. I think I see where your words take you, Northwind. You are saying that these wizards teach us things that are like to a wooden practice blade."

"I am," the old man said, his eyes twinkling. "And it is a very humbling experience for a man of my years to find himself less in knowledge than the youngest novice in their Fortress. But a child must learn to walk ere he can run—and even I, perforce, must learn with the children before I can understand some of their mysteries." He sighed heavily. "Though it chafes at me, I have not the tools of understanding to compass much of what I have seen in their place of stone. I must wait to have those tools before I can understand what they do, and not simply mimic it."

Gortan mumbled something, still plainly unhappy.

But the Shaman continued, and his voice held a power no less persuasive than the Singer's. "We must work with these wizards of the Order, Gortan. There are many, many things they wish to learn of us, as well. You all know that I have spoken with Master Felaras at great length. I think, although I do not know, that she has some distant plan, a plan that involves both our peoples—but as allies, Gortan, as equals. And equality implies that we will have the secret of the lightnings, and certainly have it before the passing of too many seasons. I advise patience; and I shall take care to follow my own advice, hard though it may be."

Grumbling, Gortan, Iridai, and the others gathered to speak with their Khene agreed—

Or seemed to.

The tent was pitched on the edge of the camp, and with the edges raised for ventilation there was no chance anyone could overhear Halun's conversation without being seen. Halun sighed, and spread his hands helplessly. "I feared that would be the way of things when you told me of this meeting," he told Gortan. "Your Khene is a young man, and the young are easily influenced by flattery and won by promises. Master Felaras can be most persuasive when she chooses."

Persuasive. Gods above and below, how she would howl to hear me describe her as "persuasive"! Bullying yes, and outright threatening, but persuasive? Ha. But this Gortan doesn't know that, and it's not likely he'll get close enough to her to find out.

"So you think that your Khene Felaras has no intention of giving us the secret of the lightning?" Gortan asked, his usually impassive face reflecting strong emotion of some kind, though Halun was unable to tell what.

"Why should she? While she holds it, you fear to leave, for you fear she may strike you with it on your leaving—and you think that she may yet give it to you if you are patient and good, like obedient children, so you wait to see if it is yet forthcoming. As for the Master, well! While she has you at the foot of her mountain, she can use your warriors as an unspoken threat, a blade at the throats of the dukes of Ancas and the princes of Yazkirn."

"Ha!" the Singer barked in obvious satisfaction. "I wondered what her purpose was!"

"And I wonder somewhat at yours, Clan Singer," Halun replied, bending closer with a wince for his tender knees. After several weeks down here, he still wasn't used to sitting cross-legged on the ground. "Why is it that you wish the lightning so very much?"

The Singer stared at him for a moment, broodingly. "It is no secret that we have enemies," he stated.

"Indeed," Halun agreed.

"We have something of a blood-debt to pay those enemies. A *great* blood-debt. I wish to live to see the lightning pay that debt in the space of a single battle. I wish to see the Clan of Talchai without a single warrior left whole."

Halun gazed into those cold yet passionate eyes, and shuddered. This man was not mad, or even half-mad. He was terribly, terribly sane. But so single of purpose that Halun would far rather flee to the ends of the earth than stand between him and his goal.

It would be safer.

"I cannot tell you if you will live to see that come to pass, Singer Gortan," Halun said truthfully. "But my experience of Felaras . . ."

Again, he spread his hands, thinking, *And the best lie is to tell the truth.*

The stocky nomad grunted. "So you have said. I thank you, scholar. By your leave, I must go to tend my duties."

Halun bowed slightly, and the Singer backed out of the tent, courteously.

When he was gone, Halun stretched himself out on his pallet with a sigh for his aching joints.

It's working, he thought with satisfaction. *They're unhappy, and the longer Felaras holds out on explosives, the unhappier they'll get. I venture to say that once the boy is healed and on his feet, Singer Gortan will make his move. And that move will be a direct assault on the Fortress by the dissidents.*

He contemplated the roof of the tent, slowly turning a soft rose color as the sun set.

An assault doomed to failure, of course. The Sword doesn't let anything larger than a mouse past them after dark. But . . . an attack will throw a good fright into all of them. Just maybe a good enough fright to send them running to the caves. Felaras will find herself voted out of office, and her two candidates are too young—that leaves me. That is, assuming Zetren doesn't get her first.

He laughed silently. *Oh, Felaras, Felaras, you're like a hare in a field full of traps! Whichever way you step, you're going to run into one! If only you knew who your opponent was—but I have no intention of giving you that weapon. And now that I think of it, I believe it is time to give poor Zetren another little prod.*

He closed his eyes, centered his will, and concentrated, and the tent, the camp-sounds, and all else faded into unimportance. There was only his will, and his *wish.*

I like this place. I like these people, Jegrai especially, Teo thought contentedly, as he and the Khene lounged together in Jegrai's tent, in unaccustomed idleness. *It's almost like . . . like he was one of the Trinity.* "You know, Jegrai, if I didn't know better, I'd swear Eriel is right," Teo chuckled, half sprawling over the saddle he was using as a prop.

"Oh? About what?"

Gods. He's got almost no accent anymore. He could walk into Targheiden in the right clothing and no one would look at him twice. "That you're one of us, reborn into a nomad body."

The Khene's brow wrinkled in perplexity. "Your pardon?"

Teo laughed outright. "That's Eriel's latest pet persuasion. That souls continue to be reborn into new bodies when the old ones die. She claims you're one of us, reborn into a nomad body, and she uses the speed at which you've picked up our tongue as proof."

"Tcha." The young man clicked his tongue disapprovingly. "But I have learned every tongue I have encountered with speed, even the Suno; and *that,* my friend, is a language only a nation of torturers could have devised. Which tells you all you need to know of the Suno. So, how would she explain that?"

"That you've been born into all of them at one time or another, I suppose," Teo replied, taking a hearty swig of *khmass.* Halun claimed even the smell of the fermented mares' milk made him want to vomit, but Teo rather liked it. He passed the skin back to the Khene, who squirted some down his own throat.

"She claims the reason I like your food and drink is that I'm a barbarian nomad reborn into a civilized hulk," Teo continued, still highly amused. "She was a little upset when I laughed at her."

"You? Who cannot even shoot from horseback?" Jegrai howled with laughter that was so infectious Teo joined him. "When even our maidens can *stand* upon the back of a galloping mare and hit the mark?"

"I didn't say it was logical," Teo protested, holding his sides. "I just said that was what she has for her latest pet notion."

"And I am not so quick with your written word," Jegrai pointed out with rueful chagrin, once he managed to get control of himself. "And to your folk, the written word holds equal importance with the spoken. How could I have been one of you, and still be wrestling with your children's books and making little sense of them?"

"It'll come, brother, it'll come," Teo said soothingly. "When it comes, it'll likely come all at once."

"Tcha. Yuchai already outstrips me, the Shaman tells me he begins to—"

"Yuchai is also a deal younger than you, brother, and in matters of language, the younger, the better. Trust me. Besides, he has very little to do besides lie in bed and put his mind to work. You have all of a Clan to govern."

Jegrai sighed at that, and stared into the flame of the oil lamp hung on the centerpole above their heads. "I wish that I had not," he replied softly. "I wish—tcha, it is no good wishing. I am Khene; that is what I must be. But Yuchai—" His expression hardened. "—Yuchai shall have what I cannot. For all that he wishes to be my shadow, he hates fighting, he hates death—he is like my father. He is made for other things."

Jegrai's expression turned to one of near-anguish. "Teo—Teo, my brother, will your people give him those things? The learning he starves for?"

Teo was growing used to these confidences, and the way the Khene spoke freely to him. It was logical; he was an outsider, safe to confide in, not someone Jegrai had to command. But there was something more than logic behind it, and the confidences hadn't been one-sided. He'd told Jegrai about Kasha—how on the one hand he longed for something deeper than friendship, and feared the changes that would bring—and on the other shied away from the commitment implied. And Jegrai had listened with a sympathy he'd hoped for, but hadn't actually expected.

They weren't so dissimilar, his people and the Vredai.

Neither were he and Jegrai.

"Jegrai, I speak as the brother you have called me," Teo said carefully. "If this path should take him away from the Vredai, perhaps for all time, would you still wish him to follow it?"

Jegrai bowed his head and was silent for a very long time, staring now at the floor of his tent. Finally the words came; slowly, deeply thoughtful. "If he felt the calling—if *he* felt it was worth the sacrifice—how could I deny him?" The Khene raised his head and looked straight into Teo's eyes, and Teo could not help but see the pain there, and the longing.

If he could trade places with his cousin, he'd do it in an eyeblink. Gods. I can't give him everything he wants—but by all the gods— I'll give him what I can.

"Felaras pledged he'd be taught as one of our own, Jegrai. She meant it. Knowledge, learning—they're close to being sacred things for us. She doesn't make pledges like that lightly."

Jegrai let out the breath he'd been holding in a hiss, and nodded. His hand fell on the skin of *khmass*, and he looked at it as if he was surprised to find it there.

"You know, we have a saying. 'In drink, there is sometimes truth.' Do you feel up to more truth, Teo? Or shall we speak of the weather, or of horses?" He drank, then held out the skin, and his hand was steady.

Teo took it, took a long pull himself, and ignored the little chill that went down his neck. "Truth. If you really want to hear it." He passed the skin back.

"Northwind thinks that your Master has a plan that involves all of us—as allies. What do you say to that?"

"That your Shaman is a very wise man. And a very perceptive one."

"And my brother says as much by what he does not say as by

the words he chooses," Jegrai replied sardonically, drinking and returning the *khmass*.

Teo shrugged, drank, and handed it back.

"So. And what if we, too, have plans—involving all of us as allies? Hm?" Jegrai demanded. "How would your Master reply to that?"

"It would depend, I think, on what the plans were, and in which direction those plans turned," Teo said as cautiously as he could, while Jegrai drank with one eye on him. "There are things we—the Order—had rather not do. And if that was your direction, well, there would be trouble. I should not tell you this, but . . . my brother, this is not to go beyond your ears. The Master does not rule unopposed. She can be replaced by another if it is the will of the majority of the Order. And Felaras is not altogether the most popular of Masters." He took back the *khmass*, feeling the need for it.

Jegrai's eyes went wide with surprise, then narrow with speculation. Finally he nodded as he accepted back the skin. "Let me say that Khenes have met with challenge also—and . . . 'accidents.' There are those who do not favor the path I have chosen for Vredai. And this is not to go beyond *your* ears. We walk a narrow bridge, I think, both of us. I shall have to think upon this." He shook the bag of *khmass*; it was as flat as a child's chest. "I think we have had enough of truth *and* drink for one night, hm?"

Teo stifled a yawn and nodded. "As it is, I'm going to wish to die in the morning. I am not entirely certain that I will remember my body finding my bed!"

But as he walked back to his tent in the cool night air, Teo knew he had spoken something less than the truth about being weary. Certainly his body longed for rest, and he was assuredly feeling the impact of the liquor, but his mind buzzed with unwelcome thoughts that kept him thinking even as he crawled into his bed.

Those uncomfortable speculations kept him staring up into the darkness long after he should have been asleep.

So. Jegrai has plans, too. That shouldn't have surprised me. And if those plans involve getting rid of whoever or whatever it was that chased him and his Clan west—I'm all for helping him. But what if that isn't the direction he's looking? What if he's figuring on cutting himself new territory? Like in Ancas? Or Yazkirn? What the hell *should I do if I find that out? Should I tell Felaras? Do I tell her my suspicions now?*

The night-sounds of the nomad camp soothed him, and reminded him of how little he had in common with those to the west and south of the Pass. And how little good the folk of those nations had done for the Order. And how much harm.

What's the rest of the world ever done besides give us grief, cast us out of our homes and livelihoods, even murder us in our beds?

The horses stirred restlessly on their picket, and a voice lifted in soft—but alien—song to soothe them.

These people—what did he really see of them past their surface? They had no written tradition at all; a reverence for learning, yes, but they had remained unchanged for hundreds of years, while the Order *spawned* change. *Gods. How can we side with illiterate barbarians with the intent of taking down civilized nations?*

Teo turned on his side; he could see the watchfire that flickered in front of the Khene's tent through the gauze of the insect-screen covering the entrance to his own. *Jegrai won't be illiterate for long—if he has his way, we'll be teaching every member of Vredai who wants to learn. He favors us the way nobody in those so-called civilized lands ever has. And he's a good man.*

But the Order had to look beyond the present.

What if the next Khene is a despot? Gods, where should my loyalties lie?

Halun lay unsleeping, staring at a single star, one that seemed to have been caught in the smoke-hole of his tent. There had been another meeting tonight, this one with not only Gortan, but the Khene's own brother, Iridai, and a handful of disgruntled nomads whom the Shaman had passed over in favor of the young man now calling himself Demonsbane. On a hunch, Halun had tested them, and found they had considerable raw, if untrained, power in the wizardry of ill-wishing.

That had not been the only surprise of the evening. Gortan had made him a proposition: a strange and very seductive proposition.

Help us, the nomad had urged. *Help us to raise discontent with Jegrai. You say you wish to teach us many things, but may be forbidden to teach them by your Khene. So; help us to be rid of Jegrai, then we will go from here, and you may come with us, you will be the right hand of the Khene, who will heed you in all things. You will teach us what you will, and we will honor you above even the Khene.*

He cradled the back of his head on his arms and tried to think things through logically. He had, by the gods, *not* expected that particular offer.

And in many ways it was a sweeter plum than the Master's seat. As Master, he would have to cajole, bully, and placate his fellows even as Felaras did now. He would be honored—when it suited them. He would be obeyed—if it suited them. He would rule only by consent.

But with the nomads he would be . . .

He would be a power in his own right. So, they were warriors by nature, well, that thought didn't cause him any misgivings. In fact there was a great deal he could accomplish, given a free hand with them. Granted, he knew nothing of warfare—but he knew weapons. He could make this loose aggregation of fighters into a terrible power.

With the tools they already have, we could make explosives, mortars, small cannon. Those are all portable enough to carry on horseback. Mortar-fire to demoralize and scatter the enemy— then the nomads charge with those wicked little bows of theirs. Most armies would think demons had hit them.

The star moved out of sight, but another was taking its place.

If Jegrai were to be deposed by his own folk, that would frighten the breeches off of most of my colleagues. Having the nomads turn up armed with explosives would drive them right underground. It wouldn't matter if Felaras was Master or not; she'd be overruled. That would put them right where they belong: in hiding. Safe, as this policy of Felaras's can never make them. And I—I would be—

A shiver ran over his skin. *I would be isolated from my own kind. Likely enough I'd never see them again.*

The star glittering down at him looked very, very lonely.

There was one candle burning at his bedside, but dimly. The view out the great window was as beautiful and alien as only the mountains could be to a boy used to the flat of the steppes. Yuchai stared at the cold jewels that were stars, suspended above the black bulk of the mountains, and tried not to cry. He was healing— quickly, according to both Boitan and Shenshu—but there were times when his injuries still gave him a lot of pain, and the pain was worse at night.

Worse than the pain, though, was the loneliness. Somewhere down there—and not even in the direction his window faced— were his people. His cousin, his father; his former playmates, those who weren't dead. They might as well have been up in the sky with those stars for all that he could reach them.

What if something happens? he thought, for the hundredth time. *What if they leave me here? What if the Talchai come? They'd have to abandon me here, I can't even walk, much less ride.*

Kasha was wonderful, and Zorsha was nearly as high in Yuchai's regard as his cousin—but they weren't Clan. Their tongue was alien, and it either did not have words he longed to say, or he hadn't yet learned them. Their concerns, their way of life, the very food they ate was alien.

And Shenshu, Losha, Demonsbane—they're so excited, so involved in learning new things—they hardly ever have time to just talk. I'm just a child, anyway, to them. I'm not really very important, and I don't have much to talk about. They've got more things to worry about than me. More important things.

He sniffled, and scrubbed his sleeve across his eyes. The whole day had been like this; loneliness had made a lump in his throat that had made it hard to eat and drink, and the peculiar round-eyed faces of his new friends had given no comfort. The feeling would pass, it always did—but for now, he ached, he ached so. . . .

There was a tap at his door; someone had seen that he still had a candle lit, no doubt. He scrubbed at his face again, hastily, and whispered a "Come" that didn't quaver *too* noticeably.

"Still awake?" someone called softly. Then that someone eased around the edge of the door, and Yuchai saw that his visitor was Zorsha, carrying a pair of baskets.

"Thought you might be."

Before Yuchai could say anything, Zorsha came right over to the bed and sat down on the foot of it.

"I saw you had a candle," he said softly, "and—you know,

Yuchai, I wasn't born here, like most of the rest were. I'm from a good bit further west. I never knew my mother; lost my father when I was younger than you. One of the sister-houses took me in, decided I had a few wits, sent me on here. I loved it, I really did—but it wasn't home, you know? There were times when the food would just stick in my throat, it just didn't taste right. Seemed to me like you were having a little touch of that today yourself."

He cocked his head sideways, inquiringly, and his silky, strange gold hair fell over one shoulder and into his eye before he flicked it back with an impatient jerk of his head.

Yuchai nodded, unable to speak around the lump of unhappiness in his throat.

"Thought so; said as much to that Demonsbane lad. Did you know he's one damn fine cook?" Zorsha grinned. "Says it's because Shamans aren't supposed to have to depend on *anybody*. We— ah—went on down to the kitchen and did a little experimenting down there when the cooking crew cleared out. Losha had some of your spices in his kit. Anyway, Demonsbane says to try these."

Zorsha flicked the cloth off the top of the first basket, and Yuchai smelled home—the flat, tough bread that seemed to take days to chew, the savory, highly spiced, chopped mutton to fill it, and a chunk of raw honeycomb.

He started to stutter out his thanks, and found that he couldn't. Because Zorsha had snagged one of the rounds of bread, filled it with meat as neatly as if he were nomad-born, rolled it, and stuffed it into his mouth as soon as he opened it.

"Eat," he said, grinning. "You haven't done more than pick at your food for two days. And if you pine away on me, Boitan will *murder* me."

He ate, finding himself ravenous, devouring the food as shamelessly as a beggar at a feast. It wasn't until the last of the crumbs were gone, and he was sucking his fingers clean of the faintest hint of honey, that Zorsha replaced the first basket with the second.

"When I got half sick for home, it was old Ardun who brought me Ancas honeycakes and fried pies. And he brought me something else. 'You know,' he said, 'in Ancas they got gold hair like yours, the Yazkirn got noses you could split wood with, and us that were Sabirn are like little brown weeds—but no matter where I been, somehow a puppy is still a puppy, and boys and puppies seem to belong together.' "

With that, Zorsha upended the basket and tilted a warm, sleepy ball of soft golden-brown fur into Yuchai's lap. A round, fuzzy head, all floppy ears and eyes, lifted from enormous paws to yawn at him.

Yuchai froze, hardly able to believe his eyes. The Vredai *had* had dogs—just like they'd had flocks and herds. All were gone, lost in the flight west.

Yuchai had lost his own hound, Jumper, in the first flight. Jumper had been out minding Yuchai's little flock of sheep when the Talchai had attacked. Yuchai hoped he'd been driven off, and not killed, but he would never really know what happened to him. Jumper's loss would have broken his heart had there not been so much else to mourn.

Boy and puppy looked into each other's surprised eyes. It was the puppy who made the first move. He sniffed Yuchai's nose with great care, found him good, and sealed the decision with a wet, warm, pink tongue—which incidentally disposed of any remaining stickiness from the honey. Yuchai threw his arms around the puppy's neck, speechless with happiness.

"I'd have brought him sooner," Zorsha said apologetically, as Yuchai hugged, and the pup squirmed and licked, "but I was housebreaking him. If Boitan came in and stepped in puppy-mess, he'd murder *both* of us! Well?"

Yuchai could only stare and try to get something out as tears started to spill out of his eyes, and the pup cleaned them off his cheeks with proprietary pleasure.

Zorsha seemed to understand.

"You see if you can get some sleep, all right?" he said softly. "I'll come around in the morning and take him out for his walk. You can tell me what you're going to call him then."

He gathered up the baskets and left, giving Yuchai a last wink as he picked up the candle to take with him on his way out the door. The puppy took the extinguishing of the light as the signal to resume his interrupted dreams; he flopped down beside Yuchai with a weary, contented sigh. Yuchai gathered him close, and the pup snuggled into the circle of his arms, pressing his warm little body up against Yuchai's side. And like any young thing, he was asleep within a few breaths.

Yuchai stroked the silky little head and long, floppy ears, not knowing how Zorsha had known of his unhappiness, and unsure how to properly thank him for the curing of it. *I'd like to call you "Zorsha,"* he told the pup silently, *but then you'd get confused.* He almost laughed. *And Zorsha might not realize I mean it as thanks.*

He thought over the proper name for a long time. *How about "Lajas"—that's "Seeker."* He thought about it a moment longer, and nodded with satisfaction. *I think, yes. It's perfect. And Zorsha will know what I mean, won't he, Lajas?* He settled a little farther under the comforter, and the pup snuggled closer, laying his head just under Yuchai's chin. Yuchai continued to stroke the soft fur, and never quite noticed when he finally fell asleep.

✧ CHAPTER EIGHT ✧

I beg you to consider, my lords, what a friendly prince means to us here on the border. And what it could mean to have him consent to stay.

Felaras chewed the end of her stylus and considered the last phrase. Was there enough veiled threat in there? Too much? *Damned diplomatic jockeying around—*

Felaras raised her head from the palimpsest sharply as the triple-tap that identified Kasha as the knocker at her study door broke into her concentration.

Damn it, now what?

Kasha did not wait for an invitation to enter. The door was already half open anyway.

"Master Felaras, Jegrai and Northwind are here to see you," she said, opening the door completely and leaning through it. "They don't look happy. Ardun says there was some activity down in the Vredai camp earlier, and about twenty riders left and haven't come back. He says they had lots of spare horses with them, and what looked like all their gear."

"Lovely," Felaras muttered, rubbing her right eye. There was a headache starting there, springing into life the moment she'd heard what sounded like bad news. *It's all this tension. The gods must hate me, I guess.* "I suppose that grumbling in the ranks Teo and Mai told me about has come to more than grumbling. And they want me to do something about it."

Kasha shrugged, and kept her face expressionless.

"What do I look like, anyway?" Felaras demanded in sudden irritation, wishing she could consign the last half-year to oblivion. *Damn Jegrai and all his crew!*

717

"Do they think I'm Ruwan Dyr, the Goddess of Peace? It's not enough to be Master and juggle all the personalities of the quirkiest lot this side of Targheiden, but now I'm supposed to work miracles for a lot of nomads too?"

Her Second wisely kept her silence.

Felaras got herself calmed down, and warded off the headache with a relaxation exercise. *This isn't Jegrai's fault. He didn't ask to come here. If he had his druthers, they'd all be down on the steppes right now.* "All right, bring them up," she sighed, wishing she'd gotten more than a couple hours of sleep. "We'll see if it's what I think it is, and if we can actually do anything about it."

Kasha closed the door of the study only to reopen it a few moments later for Khene Jegrai and Shaman Northwind. They entered and walked quietly forward to stand before Felaras's desk. Kasha stayed beside the door, but raised one eyebrow, asking Felaras in their own private code if she needed to stick around for this meeting. Felaras shook her head very slightly, and Kasha closed the door and took up her post as door-guard outside on the landing to make certain that there would be no unauthorized ears prying into the Master's affairs.

Although the Shaman was wearing his "inscrutable sage" mask, Felaras could see that Kasha was right. There was a tightness around his eyes and in the set of his shoulders that told her wordlessly that he was deeply worried. Jegrai was relatively easier to read than the Shaman, though she doubted that there were more than half a dozen folk in the Fortress who'd have been able to get past that deadpan "betting face" he had assumed. But she could see that the muscles of his neck and arms were tight enough to make him move a little stiffly, and that his eyes were narrowed in what, for him, was muted anger. Neither of them took the seats she offered them with a nod of her head.

Bad sign. They either are mad at us, or they think we're going to be mad at them.

"Master Felaras," the Shaman began, not at all diffidently, but with a haughty, stone-faced air of *we're equals, and I'm telling you this only because I think you need to know.* "There has been some trouble with our people, which we fear may cause some difficulty—"

"Pardon, Northwind," Jegrai interrupted, his voice flat and expressionless. "But Master Felaras deserves plain speaking in this." He turned to Felaras, and folded his arms across his chest. "I will give you the whole of it. There has been a revolt among the Vredai, and some two hands of warriors have broken off and ridden out. They say they will not ride with Vredai while I am Khene—and that they will not ride with Vredai *at all* as long as Vredai subsists on the charity of outsiders. In other words, they expect the next Khene to break water-pledge with you, and violate our treaty."

"Charity?" Felaras said curiously. "Hladyr bless, what charity?"

"The food you granted us, the new herds, the very valley," Northwind replied, ticking the items off on his fingers. "And yes, I know that the valley is ours by the treaty, the food was part of what was granted to us to seal the water-pledge, and the herd-beasts payment for those who have begun riding patrol with your Watchers about the Vale. These who have ridden out, however, are all young hotheads who would, I fear, far rather take than earn."

Oh, so. The ones who've gotten a taste for raiding don't like giving it up. I guess I should be thankful there's only "two hands" worth of them.

"Earning takes too long," Felaras pointed out with dry humor. "And costs in terms of real work; boring, routine work. Not exciting stuff like fighting and raiding."

"Aye," Jegrai agreed, "and they have forgotten that while Vredai have always been warriors, we were warriors only to defend the herds. And the herds came first, before raids and counting coups. I heard much about the glory of war before they stormed out of my tent; enough to make me wish to take a stick to their thick heads, one and all. I should think they had seen enough of that kind of 'glory' to last a lifetime."

Northwind interrupted him. "Na, Khene, I did not once hear prating of the glory of facing the Talchai. The only 'glory' *I* heard of was the 'glory' of running down land-folk and taking the spoils."

Jegrai snorted a disgusted agreement. "Tending sheep brings no glory—and riding patrol offers no chance of fortune."

Felaras's already high estimation of Jegrai rose more. It wasn't often that a man as young as the Khene who came from a culture that had faced and adopted violence could see the benefits of peace.

"So they're going to go back to raiding my land-folk, just as we've got *them* settled back on their farms and at least tentatively convinced that you folk are going to guard them, not hurt them—"

"Exactly so," the Shaman agreed wearily. "And I could wish they had chosen some other time and place."

"How many of these dissidents have families of their own?"

"None," Jegrai replied positively.

"Huh. That has both good and bad points," Felaras replied, propping both elbows on the desk and resting her chin in both hands. Jegrai frowned and shifted his weight a little, distracting her.

"Gentlemen, I am not going to pounce on you and turn you into frogs," she said impatiently. "You've proven yourselves my allies twice over by coming to me directly with this. Now, will you *please* sit down? We have some planning to do, and I'm tired of craning my neck up to look at you!"

Jegrai and Northwind exchanged looks—Jegrai's a bit startled, the Shaman's one of "I told you so" satisfaction—and they seated themselves across from her with a scraping of wood on the hardwood floor.

"All right; they don't have families, so we can't use blood-ties to lure them back. Or maybe I should ask first if you want them back."

"No," Jegrai said quickly. "Once traitor, what's to stop them from turning traitor again? Besides, to avoid the curse of having broken water-pledge, they have declared that they are no longer of Vredai. If they are not of us, why would we wish them back? And if we took them back, are they not oathbreakers? I should have to execute them. I had rather just eliminate them; either drive them back into the east or kill them in a raid-attempt."

"Good point. All right—are your people still using those red-and-black armbands we made up to identify them as allies of the Order?"

"Oh, yes," the Shaman replied with a tight smile. "Not the least because they are bright and handsome. The young riders are fond of ornament, and we lost most such things some time ago. And I think I see your next question—the rebels tore their armbands off and left them at Jegrai's feet ere they rode out, saying they had had enough of collars and leashes."

"Well, that means we won't have to change colors, at least," Felaras replied. "Seeing as your people like ornament, gentlemen,

I'll see to it that the riders still with you get all they could desire. Headbands, scarves for their helms, ribbons for their lances, tassels for their bridles—anything you can think of, I'll have made up. Are you seeing where I'm heading?"

"Aye." Jegrai smiled a little. "Since your folk won't know one rider from another, you are intending that they should think my rebels have come from outside."

"That's it. Now . . ." she pulled a map of the Vale out of her desk and unfolded it on the desk top, clearing room for it by sweeping the papers she'd been working on to the side. "If you were whoever they'll pick to lead them, where would *you* go to hole up and make a base? And then, where would you start to raid?"

So. It's to be us.

Kasha's mare pricked her ears forward and brought her head up, and pawed the floor of the barn restlessly. Kasha put her hand over the mare's soft nose and forced it down before she could whicker a greeting to the horses she scented approaching and give them away.

Damn trouble with fighting a skirmish in spring, Kasha thought with annoyance. *Damn horses are in season, and damn nomads only geld about half their stallions. Hope they don't scent us. They shouldn't, we're downwind of them, but you never know.*

She was the only Sword among the nomad ambushers hiding in this barn, but she looked just as wild as any of them. Besides her normal dark clothing and armor, she was bedecked with a gypsy-motley of identifying ribbons. The rest of the nomads had even more; given choices of ornaments, most took everything. Red-and-black streamers and ribbons fluttered from the tips of lances and javelins and even from the pommels of swords. Red-and-black braided bands encircled upper arms and helms, and held hair off of nomad foreheads. Red-and-black tassels hung from reins and bridles, and some of the warriors sported several red-and-black scarves tied jauntily around their necks and around their legs just above the knee. The three young women in this party had even braided their hair with red-and-black cords before coiling it around their heads. They looked like they were decked out for a festival. But there would be no mistaking where the allegiance of this party lay.

There were a half-dozen of these ambush parties hiding at this end of the Vale, now that they knew where the dissidents had holed up. Between them, Felaras and Jegrai had identified that many likely targets—mostly flocks—among the Vale folk back on their lands near the rebel base. There had already been two raids by the rebels; one had succeeded, and one, by sheerest luck, had been foiled by a party returning from riding border-guard.

The rebels hadn't done much damage—yet. Mostly they'd ridden a destructive swath through a field of young oats, and stolen a handful of sheep. But both Felaras and Jegrai feared that was subject to change at any moment. The next raid could include fire, rapine, and murder—

Probably *would*, as they grew more sure of themselves.

And if that happened, no amount of red-and-black trimmings would convince the Vale folk that *any* nomad was trustworthy.

The lookout on the barn roof slithered down on the rope leading through the hatch to the second floor. Kasha tensed and turned to see what the leader of the party would signal. Though she had long since graduated to the rank of "serjant" in the Sword, this time *she* was not the leader of the party. That honor had fallen to one of Jegrai's older trackers, a hard-faced man called Abodai. Each ambush party had at least one Sword with it; and not one single Sword had been appointed as leader.

This was a calculated risk. The Watchers were going to prove themselves to Jegrai's folk—as fighters, but also as true allies, and not order-givers.

Abodai, watching through a crack in the door, jerked his fist, thumb up, in a silent order to mount. As neatly as if they had trained together, the ambushers swung into their saddles. Abodai did the same, then backed his horse a few paces.

Silence, except for the stamping of a hoof, the twittering of birds in the hayloft. Sunlight streaked through the cracks in the barn walls, the beams almost solid with dancing dust-motes. Hay-scent and dust-scent mingled with the salt smell of horse-sweat and the tang of the herbs the riders used to wash with. Kasha suppressed a sneeze.

Then—thunder of hooves in the distance, growing nearer by the moment. Abodai pulled one of his javelins from the quiver at his back; those with bows took that as a signal to nock arrows, those armed only with swords drew them.

Nearer—nearer—

War cries, and the splintering sound that meant somebody's mount had split the top rail of the fence.

Then, with a war cry of his own, Abodai spurred his horse forward, shouldering open the unbarred barn door. His horse was the only one clever enough and well-trained enough—and with enough innate trust in his rider—to do that little trick. Kasha spared half a second to envy him, and another to wonder if he'd let her put her mare to his beast when this was over—and then she was through, clattering past him in the boiling mass of flying ribbons and hooves and dust that slammed right into the path of the oncoming raiding party.

Horseshit! Torches—

They'd made this stand just in time. Given a free hand, the rebels would have burned this farm to the ground.

Even as she saw the four riders with torches, the distance-fighters cut them down; the torch-bearing rebel nearest Kasha fell out of his saddle with a javelin in his throat, to kick out his life in the dust as his horse galloped on. The black and red ribbons decorating the javelin fluttered with incongruous gaiety as he quivered and jerked.

But there was no time to stop and watch—the horses were crashing into the midst of the raiding party. The charge took them out of bow range, and it was hand-to-hand work. Kasha picked her target and spurred her mare at him; a man a little older than Jegrai, with an unkempt, straggly moustache. He saw her coming and snarled, pivoting his own horse to meet her.

Her blow bounced and slid off his shield, a smallish round-shield of brass-studded leather. She deflected his return with her own shield. Then cheated.

Felaras had warned Jegrai before this began that the Swords fought with any and all weapons, by any and all means. For a Watcher confronted by an enemy, there was no such things as "fair" or "foul;" there was only "win" or "lose." If they had not fought this way, there likely would have been no Order—but that was not yet for a stranger's ears.

And Jegrai had agreed to having the Swords along, knowing that they would resort to tactics his people would consider completely dishonorable.

Kasha deflected another of her man's strikes, ducked under a third—and swatted his horse with the flat of her blade as hard as she could.

Startled, it half-reared before he could control it, exposing the rebel's stomach as he threw his arms out and fought for balance. Her vicious backhand blow nearly cut him in half. She felt the soft shock up her arm, then ducked behind her shield; blood sprayed her as he toppled from his horse's back.

No time to think. She turned on the one behind him, feeling the fighting-drunk she'd described to Yuchai take her and spread her mouth open in a savage grin of blood-lust.

He was already busy—*when did I get turned to face the barn?* She took this one from behind as he struggled with one of the Vredai women. The nomad had lost her helm, her sword had splintered, and she was desperately trying to protect her head behind the inadequate cover of her target-shield. Kasha was not about to thrust and have her own blade lodge in the corpse, though the fighter's unguarded back presented a tempting target. Instead she shouldered her mount into his as he beat down the woman's guard, and split his head just below the line of his helm. Cutting into bone this time—it was like hitting wood, and the impact quivered up her arm. The blade lodged for just an instant before she pulled it free.

She snatched his sword in her shield-hand as it fell from his fingers, urged her mare past the horse now standing puzzled and spent, and pressed the nomad's blade into the Vredai woman's hand.

Then instinct made her turn with shield up, and she was forced to defend herself from a furious attack.

He was taller than she, stronger, and just as well trained. All she could do was to use her shield to try to keep him off.

She didn't entirely succeed in that either; before too long her ears were ringing from one too many solid hits on her helm, her left arm going numb from wrist to shoulder, and her right arm burning from wrist to elbow with the pain of a long, shallow gash. He'd managed to cut the strap of her vambrace, which now was lying somewhere under the dust churned up by the hooves of the milling horses.

He was giving her no openings, and no chance to back out.

Never go head-to-head with a man your equal, she could hear

Ardun saying sardonically in the back of her mind. *Better reach and more muscle will kill you, girl.*

Time to cheat again.

There was one glaring weakness in the strategy of these nomads—they lived by their horses, so it was unthinkable to make a horse your target. Alive, it was a trophy, and a possession that was nearly part of your family. Dead, it was just so much meat. So the horse was off-limits.

Guess again. Sorry, horse.

She maneuvered her mare in front of his, got in reach of its throat, and slashed open the great vein of her opponent's mount.

Its knees buckled as blood fountained over her and everyone else nearby, and it collapsed almost immediately.

The fighter screamed a curse at her as he kicked free of the falling horse. He staggered, caught his balance, and prepared to attack her with berserker fury glaring at her out of his bloodshot eyes.

Then fury was replaced by shock.

He fell with a javelin pinning him to his dead, twitching mount, a javelin rammed through his body at close range.

She looked up in surprise to meet Abodai's feral grin, white teeth gleaming in brown face, and then they each turned away to take on a new opponent.

They had begun this outnumbered almost three to one. Now the odds were even after a few moments of combat. They'd lost two: the rebels had lost at least a dozen, probably more. There was no way of telling for certain how many had fallen, not with the riderless horses dashing around in panic, adding to the confusion.

Only now were the remaining survivors realizing that this was a fight to the death, no holds barred.

Once again, this was something the strategists had counted on.

For Jegrai had finally told Felaras the bones of the story of how Vredai had been driven into the West. And what that meant to the people who had suffered the physical and mental torments of that drive.

They may try to wound, rather than kill, unless they know they face strangers, Jegrai had said of the rebels, soberly. *There are so few of us compared to the Talchai, and of us all, only I had acquaintances in that Clan. We are more used to saving each other than killing—and only I of my Clan have faced those who were once my friends over the sword-edge.*

This reluctance to kill—won't that hold for your people, too? Felaras had asked him soberly.

Not after I finish speaking to them, had been the grim reply. *We have been betrayed twice now within my memory. We are not growing to like betrayal, let me tell you.*

Evidently Jegrai had been right.

Each of the surviving ambushers had a single opponent now, and the combat had turned from chaos into individual fights.

Sweat trickled down the back of Kasha's neck, and dust caked her lips. Her mouth was dry as the dust her mare's hooves threw into the air, and her right arm throbbed.

And none of this mattered. The intoxication of fighting had hold of her again, an exalted state where time stretched and she was focused in on herself and out on her foe. Nothing mattered but him, and she could see clearly every little detail of what he looked like and what he did, as if she was living a little bit faster than he was. This man was her size, her weight; a perfect opponent in every way.

His image branded itself in her memory. If she lived to be a hundred, she'd be able to describe this man so that an artist could paint him accurately; that was the effect of the battle-fever. He had dark skin, no facial hair; two braids that had probably been tucked up under his helm but which now were hanging free on either side of his head. Sweat was running into his eyes, and there were splashes of blood across one cheek. She wondered if it was his, but decided not. He had a gash across one leg, but like the one running up her arm, it looked to be shallow.

They circled their horses warily about each other, taking the measure of one another. She saw him frown uneasily, as her mouth was tugged again into that hideous grin by the rush of battle-lust.

It is lust. Gods, don't let Zorsha come near me until I get a chance to clean up and cool down. Or my good intentions will go right out the window with our clothing.

The man apparently decided that he didn't like the odds, and abruptly wheeled his horse in a tight little circle and spurred him at the fence.

Sorry, horse. Time to cheat again.

There was one lone difference between them, other than sex. Her mare topped his scrubby little gelding by three hands, and outweighed it proportionally. Over a long run that might have given him an advantage; all that weight could slow her horse down.

But out of the starting blocks the advantage was all hers—the more especially since her mare was a lot fresher than his beast. She spurred the mare after him; they had him in less time than it took to breathe. And she used the other advantage of her bigger horse: she rammed the gelding with her mare's shoulder; literally bowled him over and rode them both down.

As the gelding went over she heard bones snap, and heard it scream in agony—heard him scream too, as he went down trapped under the weight of his horse, and as her mare stepped on him at least once. And then he gurgled and wailed behind her as the gelding began to thrash in pain.

That was no way to leave even an enemy.

She wheeled the mare around, and saw the gelding spasming wildly in the dust, saw the nomad clawing at it in mindless agony with one arm flopping useless and the leg he had free still lying over the horse's barrel like a thing of wood. Two paces closer and she could smell him—and knew his back was broken.

That was no way to leave *anyone*.

She dismounted, walked over, and dealt with it.

And when she looked around, after cleaning her knife on the dead gelding's hide, she saw the others in the ambush party staring at her with a mixture of approval and fear, as if they were wondering if she was now going to perform some kind of trophy-taking on the body. And she saw that the only ones left standing were wearing red and black.

It was over.

"You look like you took the first layer of skin off," Ardun observed, filling the mugs before him with wine—Kasha's full, his half full. He pushed the mug across the little table between them, then sat back in his chair, cradling his own mug in both hands.

"I feel like I have," she said, taking her wine and gulping down half of it. "I thought I'd never get the smell of blood out of my nose."

He nodded; candles on the table between them softened his age-lines and made him look younger; about her age. "Took me that way too. I'd come out of a fight and scrub for an hour or more—then I'd go find Felaras and she'd get me drunk and I'd bawl like a baby."

"Just like you do for me," Kasha observed.

Ardun shrugged, and a breeze from the open window behind him made the candle-flames flicker. "When you get battle-fever the way we do, you need somebody steady around you after—somebody who gets drunk on death like you do, who can tell you that you aren't an animal for feeling that way." He gave her a long look over the top of his mug. "And somebody who won't let you rape him."

She laughed shakily, and ran her fingers through her damp hair. "You got that right. First time it happened, if you hadn't been around, I'd have taken Teo right there in the courtyard. Poor Teo. He was only worried for me, and glad to see me back alive. He thought I was angry with him. He never knew how close he came to being raped in public. Gods, that makes me feel like some kind of savage. An animal; a brute beast."

Ardun shook his head at her. "You know what it is—your body figuring out you just escaped dying, and trying to force you into procreation before you go put it in harm's way again. Your body thinks your duty to the world is to leave a copy of yourself if you go out in glory. So do you listen to your body or your mind?"

"My mind, of course. That *is* why I'm here in your room and not in Zorsha's."

"And here I thought it was because you wanted my company." Kasha laughed shakily.

"And I'll tell you again, because you need to hear it; no, you aren't an animal because you get drunk on killing, or because you're ready to jump anything male in sight when it's over. The fever is just your body again—trying to keep itself from getting killed, it makes you drunk so that you don't think, you just react. You're not an animal, because when it's all over, you agonize over your reactions. Zetren doesn't—he *is* an animal, a rabid one. And if it weren't that he's useful to the Order, I'd have contrived an accident for him a long time ago."

Kasha nodded soberly; Ardun was far more than the Sword Leader—he was a past master at every assassination technique the Order had ever encountered. Some he taught everyone. Some he taught privately. Kasha had gotten some of that private tutelage, as had others. One of those others, and she had no idea who, would be Ardun's successor. That wouldn't be known until he died, and they opened his papers to see who he had left a certain little set of "tools" to. And whoever became his successor would secretly choose and train another.

So if tiny, wizened Ardun decided that Zetren needed disposing of—it would be done. And only Ardun would know that it had been no accident. Because if he ever did eliminate Zetren, it would be in a way that would leave nothing suspicious.

"You're not drinking," Ardun pointed out, breaking into her thoughts. "You're supposed to be getting drunk."

"I daren't get too drunk," she admitted. "Just enough to believe I'm all right. I've got guard on Felaras and the boy tonight, and I'm getting uneasy feelings. . . ."

She paused long enough to empty her mug and hold it out to him for refilling.

"Ill-wishing?" he asked.

"I think. But getting at the Master indirectly. There's just too damned much going on, and it's all muddled. Like there's a half-dozen plots going on that are not quite lurching into each other."

"Could be. It's like that last siege, when Kyle was Master. I remember the same feeling. Like there's something behind the door that hasn't made up its mind to try breaking in, but you can hear it breathing."

"Ardun—did the fever take you during siege-fighting too?" she asked, curious, and with the wine making her bolder than she might otherwise have been. The siege—the last in the history of the Order—had been long before her time. Felaras had been no more than one of Kyle's possible successors, and Ardun had only just been promoted to full Sword status.

He shook his head. "It wasn't that kind of fighting. Mostly I didn't even see the results of what I did. I was one of the ones chosen to sneak out the escape tunnels, infiltrate the army, and doctor the food supplies. What I did didn't even have any effect until the next afternoon."

"Aconite in the spiced meat?" she guessed.

He nodded, his face gone inward-looking as he called up past memories. "And ground glass in the salt, ergot in the flour, jimson

weed in the fodder. Then Kyle up on the tower right after they'd
eaten at noon, calling down death and madness on the besiegers.
It was pretty damned impressive, let me tell you; he timed it to a
hair. Between the ones dropping over dead and the ones taken
by fits—and then even the *horses* going wild—your common
soldier was pretty impressed with our direct line to heaven. Then
we let loose with the mortars, which we hadn't used yet. We
didn't hit much but the command tent; it was the only thing we
could range on, but having the commander's quarters go under
heavenly retribution was damned disheartening for them. That's
why the Yazkirn, at least, don't condemn us as heretics, and haven't
disturbed the sister-house we have down there. They figure we're
under some kind of divine protection—by their theology, the
powers of darkness can't strike at high noon."

Some of that Kasha had already known, but some was new.
This was the first time she'd ever found Ardun willing to talk
about it, and Felaras didn't even want to hear about the subject,
much less talk about it. "Weren't you risking them getting those
doctored supplies at morning meal?"

He shook his head. "No, that was what made it work so well.
You can set a clock by the Yazkirn army cooks. Oat-and-barley
porridge for breakfast, because they've cooked it the night before
in big kettles. Stuffed rolls at noon, because they can be handed
out to those on patrol. Two each, one spiced meat, one root-
vegetable, and the men are known to trade, so some would have
gotten a double-dose of aconite and some nothing but the ergot
in the flour or the glass in the salt, and some nothing at all,
depending on whether the barrels we doctored were close to
being empty. We didn't doctor anything that wasn't already open."

Kasha nodded, stowing all that away for future reference. It
was all written down in the chronicles, of course, but it was always
useful to have certain things at hand, in memory.

"So to answer your question, no—the killing didn't give me
the fever. The actual sally out to do the dirty work did. And I've
gotten the same fever just sneaking out to look over a bandit
camp, with no likelihood of combat. It's the going into danger
that does it, girl, not the killing."

"Oh my head knows that," she admitted, pulling on her wine,
and feeling a little "cleaner" than she had when she'd ridden in.
"But you have to tell my gut every time."

"Ah, well, I know that." He gave her a crooked grin.

"So what do you think of Yuchai?" she asked him, feeling comforted enough to change the subject. "I was a little surprised to see you sparring with him."

"His moves are different enough that I didn't want to chance him getting hurt, especially with him only just out of bed," Ardun replied. "Put him with the novices and he *would* get hurt, sure's stars. I like the boy, Kasha, I like him a lot. If his people are anything like him—damn if we don't have more in common with them than any Ancas tightass. That boy is bright, he's quick—and in no way is he ever going to be in Sword. He gets in over my dead body."

She let out her breath in a long hiss. "You have no idea how happy I am to hear that. Why?"

"He thinks too much, and at the wrong time. You think too much, and so do I, but it's after everything is over and done with. *He* thinks about it when it's happening. So long as he's planning on going into one of the other two chapters, I'll tutor him all he wants—but you can tell him from me I don't want him thinking he's coming into Sword, because I won't permit it. If I have to hamstring him to convince him, I will. So help me."

"Good—you're going to make all of us happy, I think, right down to Jegrai. The boy's his heir until he breeds one, you know. Teo says he loves him like a younger brother. Maybe more, because there isn't a great deal of love between himself and his real brother."

"Aye, I can see where there wouldn't be," Ardun replied, looking a great deal happier about the situation. "If that's the way Jegrai feels about it, and you, and me, then we should be able to convince Yuchai. Unless he really wants it?"

"Thank the gods, no," she told him. "No, fighting makes him sick—combat, that is. He likes the physical exercise, so long as it's for points and touches, but I'd be willing to bet he likes dancing as much. Told me earlier that points and touches is the way fighting *used* to be between the Clans until some outsiders began stirring things up."

"Interesting. Accounts for their accepting Jegrai as Khene. So—what is it with Yuchai being so keen on fighting even though he hates it?"

"He's determined that he won't be the only able-bodied person in the Clan that can't defend himself. Given their past and their intra-Clan loyalty, I'm not surprised at that."

"Agreed. About the boy: do you have any idea how much of a thinker he really is? And how far ahead he plans things?"

Kasha shook her head. "My part's been mostly confined to teaching him Ancas and Sabirn and teaching him to read. Zorsha's been the one involved in lessons that didn't involve just memorization."

"Let me give you a notion." He put his mug down on the table with a soft thud, and leaned forward, half-resting on the tabletop. "You know that pup of his follows him everywhere, and I know that breed—golden gaze-hounds are protective bastards even as pups. I was going to lock the pup in the ward-room until his lesson was over, figuring it'd come for me the way Zorsha's did—" He chuckled reminiscently. "You know, I *still* have the tooth-scars on my ankle? There I was, dancing around on one leg with the pup holding on like grim death, my ankle bleeding like fury, and Zorsha screaming at me not to hurt his dog. I wasn't minded to repeat the experience. So I asked the boy to put the dog in the room and explained why—told him I'd rather listen to howls than have my ankle perforated."

"And he said what?" She waved the pitcher of wine away when he offered it; her head was buzzing enough, and she didn't need the guilt-numbing effect anymore.

"That he'd already thought of that. He gave the dog a command in his tongue, and told me to go ahead and start a drill. Well, I did, though let me tell you, I was not at my best, watching that pup out of the side of my eye."

"Nothing happened?"

"Not a damn thing, though the pup looked fit to burst every time I touched the boy. So then, when I laid him on his butt, he went over and made a fuss over the dog, then asked me to pair him for a minute with somebody I wasn't ever likely to again. Said he wanted to show me something. I set him up with Davy. They went at it for a couple passes, then he yelled something, and damn if that pup didn't come flying across the yard like an arrow—and before Davy or I can even blink, the pup's got his sword-hand wrist in his teeth, growling like he's going to chew it off."

"He didn't hurt Davy, did he?" Kasha asked in alarm.

"Not a bit, though I wouldn't have reckoned what would have happened if Davy'd tried to fight him. Pup just held on without even bruising the skin. So the boy gives the dog another command and it lets go, though it keeps a mighty suspicious eye on young Davy all the rest of that session. Turns out the boy had another dog when he started learning sword-work that pulled exactly the same stunt Zorsha's did. So he taught this one while he was laid up that everything was all right unless he yelled for help. See what I mean by thinking ahead?"

"Uh," Kasha grunted, nodding thoughtfully. "Uh-*huh*. So, what do you see him as? Book?"

"Not a chance; the boy's too inquisitive. Tower, I'd say, and Hand for preference. He's always asking questions, and they all run on *how* does this work, not *why*. Showed me why those swords of theirs are curved, and single-edged, and it makes damned good sense for horseback fighting. Going to have some made up for us and start training you good riders with them."

"So that the blade doesn't lodge and pull out of your hand?" Kasha hazarded.

He nodded.

She grinned. "Uh-huh, I wondered about that. Tell you what else would be nice; a bit of a lanyard on the pommel-nut. Lose your blade on the ground and you have a chance to get it back. Lose it on horseback, and you might as well forget it. But loop a lanyard around your wrist, and if it gets knocked out of your hand, you've still *got* it."

"Good thought. What do you think of their soft stirrups?"

"Not much," she said, "And some of the lot I rode with are modifying theirs to match mine. Too damned easy to get your foot caught in the thing, even if it does mean you need a heeled boot to use our kind. I don't fancy being dragged, and I can't see any advantage in the soft stirrups."

"Fine. Anything else?"

"We ought to show them our soft iron javelins. If they're really going to be with us, they won't have any problem with getting metal, and the way the soft javelins foul a shield is even more useful in a horseback fight than a ground battle. I mean, figure how much is your horse going to like getting his ears whacked with a stick every time you move your shield, hey? And I don't know how Abodai trained that stallion of his to do some of his tricks, but somebody ought to see if it's the horse or the training. You already know about those laminated bows—"

"Aye, with lust in my heart. We're working on it, but not just anybody can make a bow. That Losha up here can, but it's a long process. Seems it involves wood, horn, sinew of all damn things, all laminated into the bow, and somehow bone plaques get into it too. We've got one about half made, but with that much work I don't wonder that they won't sell or trade them. Might as well ask a farmer to sell his house. Or his wife!"

"Sounds like. But the range on those things—"

"Makes them worth every damn hour you put on them. Well, feeling more like a member of the human race again?"

"Feeling more like the human race won't reject me, anyway. And it's about time for me to take my watch."

She got up, did an internal assessment of the wine on her judgment and reflexes, and decided it wasn't too bad. But just as a check, she dropped her wrist-knife down into her hand, and pivoted on her heel to place it in the target she knew was behind her.

Ardun peered at it as she went to pull it out. "In the black?"

She shook her head. "No, a hair out."

"Don't aim for the eye then, until the wine wears off. Throat's a better target."

"Yes, Father," she replied with mock humility. "Anything you say, Father."

"Watch your tone, girl; I can still take you any time I want."

"Don't I just know it." She walked back over to his side of the table and kissed his forehead. "Throat it is. And thanks for getting me out of my depression again."

He hugged her waist. "Any time, baby-girl. You do me proud, I hope you know that. I'd like to see you with the badge some day."

"Hm, well that'll depend on who happens to be Master—which is Zorsha at this point, which could be touchy."

"Seven hells, girl, I told you to think ahead, I *didn't* tell you to map out the future!"

"Yes, sir." She bowed. He made a fist and tapped her cheek. She covered the hand with her own for a moment. "I'll bet Yuchai will still be awake; your permission, I'll tell him what you said about him being in Sword—and that you think he belongs in Hand."

"Do that. It would make me feel better."

"Suspect it will make him feel better too. And me. And Zorsha. Thanks again, Father."

He waved a hand at her. "Off with you. Or I'll dock your pay for being late."

She laughed and ducked out the door, heading for the Master's quarters with a lightened step.

✧ CHAPTER NINE ✧

Don't shout. Whatever you do, don't shout. Tent walls do not muffle voices. "Why didn't you stop them?" Halun demanded, on the verge of hissing with anger, standing nearly nose to nose with Jegrai's brother. He clenched his hands into tight fists in an attempt to keep his impotent rage under control. "Why didn't you do something?"

"How was I to stop them?" Iridai growled, teeth clenched, arms crossed tightly over his burly, leather-armored chest as if to keep his own anger pent. "I was the one who roused them up in the first place! What was I to do when they ceased listening to me—betray them to Jegrai? They declared themselves and rode out before I would ever have been able to do even *that!*"

Halun's anger passed as quickly as it had flared, and he forced himself to relax, closing his eyes as much from a wave of pure weariness as anything else. *Watch yourself; if you make an enemy of this man, you'll destroy everything. Damned barbarians. Say something to placate him, or you'll strangle your hopes with your own two hands.* "I'm sorry, Iridai; I shouldn't have said that. All of us misjudged this time, I think. It certainly wasn't your fault that those young hotheads were even more hotheaded than we thought. You couldn't have predicted that. Forgive me for accusing you. I had no right."

"Ai, that is something less than truth, wise one," Iridai admitted, his own anger quenched by Halun's capitulation and apology. "I knew how wild they were—and with my talk of honor and dishonor I drove them to their deaths as surely as though it were my hand that held the blade." This was Iridai's tent; it was as martial and spare of comfort as the nomad himself. There were none of the piles of cushions to sit on that could be found elsewhere; one sat on the bare carpet. Iridai went from standing to sitting in a single graceful motion that maddened Halun because of his inability to imitate it.

Halun folded himself slowly and carefully down onto what seemed to be a marginally softer spot. He longed briefly, but sharply, for his chairs, his restful bed, his long, comfortable robes. He couldn't even be easy in his clothing. These breeches and long tunics did not feel right, binding up in unexpected places. "You're being far too hard on yourself—"

"Am I?" Iridai snorted, tossing his braids over his shoulders with his right hand. "You heard all my lofty speeches to them about returning to the old ways—did you not see them, one and all, discarding those new swords at Jegrai's feet along with their armbands? And who was to blame for that?"

Halun saw signs that told him Iridai was about to fall into a melancholy from which it might take days to wake him. *Damned fool, this is* no *time to go into a brood!* "And who was to blame for them *staying* in the Vale?" he demanded harshly. "They could have gone away from here—there was no one stopping them. Jegrai made no moves to hunt them down until *they* started the trouble. East might be closed, but there is north, south—even west; they could have been over the pass and gone long before Jegrai alerted the Order that they were rebels. No one would have pursued them, not Jegrai, certainly not Felaras. But no—instead those lazy fools made their camp in the single most obvious place in the Vale, and proceeded to raid the very folk Jegrai had sworn to protect. They weren't just asking to be wiped out, they were opening their arms to destruction and embracing it!" *Just like the fool primitives they are, no matter how much they boast about valuing knowledge!*

Iridai raised his head at that, narrowed his eyes, and nodded his round head thoughtfully.

"We are, perhaps, well rid of them," Halun continued, deliberately choosing the most callous phrases he could. "Clearly they could not keep secrets; I think we may thank the gods that none of them were taken alive to betray us—although I must admit that Jegrai's ruthlessness took me somewhat by surprise. I did not expect him to be quite so thorough. I am sorry that Vredai has lost so many fine warriors—but it seems clear to me that they were warriors that were unable to think, or to plan. If Vredai is to prosper, its warriors must learn to use their wits as well as their hands."

"Truly spoken," Iridai agreed, though with some reluctance in his voice. "It is not a truth I care to hear, but it is nonetheless truth. As for Jegrai—once again I have underestimated him. I have mistaken his cleaving to the old ways for weakness. I shall not repeat that mistake."

At least you have that much sense, my uneasy ally. "Our concerns now are for the living, Iridai, and not the dead. How has this affected the others, those who are disaffected, but not yet rebellious?"

"I—I do not know," Iridai admitted. "I could guess, but . . ."

Halun shook his head. "Speculation is useless to us. We must *know,* and know exactly. Else we act as foolishly as those foolish boys."

"That is again truth. And a truth I will act on." Iridai stood, his dark face now showing considerably more resolution than he had demonstrated when he'd risen to greet Halun.

"Good," Halun responded, getting slowly and painfully to his feet. *Oh, gods, will I ever see a chair again? Is power worth my aching knees? Ah, stupid question.* "Let us each go to those he knows best—you to the warriors, myself to Gortan and those who have been passed over when the Shaman made his yearly choices. And we will see."

"Aye," Iridai replied, his eyes beginning to show some life again. "We will see—and then, we will act."

"But if the world is a ball, and it is turning," Jegrai objected, sorely perplexed, "why aren't we flung off of it?"

Jegrai, clad resplendently in a new sleeveless tunic of scarlet and breeches of soft black cotton—more of the handiwork of the Order's looms and his mother's hands—was theoretically holding court. What this actually meant was that he was sprawled in the one chair that had survived the Vredai flight into the west, under the shade of the tree beside his tent. Teo, looking like a servitor in his comfortably shabby brown clothing, lounged in the grass beside him, doing his best to explain Jegrai's questions about the book he was currently devouring. As Teo had predicted, the Khene was beginning to fathom the mysteries of the written word, and had graduated to the level of the beginning science texts the novices read.

While Jegrai sat "in court," any of the Vredai with a grievance, real or imagined, could approach him to have it dealt with. In actuality, few of them did. The Khene was scrupulously fair—and notoriously impartial. So much so that those whose claims were a little shaky, or who might have some dealings they preferred to remain something less than public, had a very strong reason to settle their grievances in some court other than the Khene's.

So Jegrai had ample leisure to cross-examine Teo during these afternoon sessions, and took full advantage of the fact. He had little enough leisure at any other time. The Khene of Vredai was no less a worker than any of his people.

"Well?" he demanded.

Teo's brow was creased with thought. "I'm trying to come up with an example that makes sense, Jegrai," he began, when a stir at the edge of the camp caught the Khene's eye, and he motioned to his friend to hold his peace for a moment.

"Trouble?" Teo asked, sitting up straighter.

"Maybe. . . ." Jegrai squinted against the bright sunlight and the ever-present dust kicked up within the camp. The commotion resolved itself into three adults heading straight for him, followed by a horde of children, followed in turn by half the women of the camp. One of the adults was the young warrior Agroda, dressed in his finest—pale leather tunic and breeches, and so festooned with red-and-black bands and ribbons that he looked like a walking festival all by himself. But the other two—

One was a young woman of the Vale folk, with hair like a skein of spun sunlight; and the other, gold locks going to silver, looked to be her father.

Jegrai's heart sank to his boot-heels—

Until they came close enough for him to see their expressions. The young woman, dressed in a finely embroidered divided skirt, an equally elaborately embellished vest, and a delicately embroidered shirt that was so transparent it would have been obscene had the vest not been laced tightly over it, had the demure look of a cat that has just eaten the family dinner and knows the dog will get the blame. The older man, in a handsome set of riding leathers and an equally intricately embroidered shirt, was attempting to look sober, perhaps stern—and failing utterly. Every time he schooled his mouth to sobriety, he would glance at the girl or the Vredai, and a smile would begin to escape again. And Agroda was wearing the most fatuously foolish grin Jegrai had ever seen on a human face in his entire life.

The odd little party came to a halt the proper distance from Jegrai's chair. Agroda made one step forward, put right hand to left shoulder, and made the slight nod that was the formal salutation of Vredai to Khene.

"Speak," Jegrai responded, trying to keep his face still and impassive, but hoping wildly that this was what he thought it was.

"May we speak in Trade-tongue, oh Khene?" came the reply. "This good man of the Vale is also a warrior; he speaks but little of our tongue, and it were ill-courtesy to discuss what concerns him so closely in a language not his own."

I notice he doesn't mention the daughter, Jegrai thought, valiantly keeping his face straight. *Which means she probably knows our tongue as well as friend Teo. And I would not care to speculate on where or how she learned our speech.*

"Gladly," he replied. "It is only courtesy. And the warrior and his—daughter?—are welcome here. Is this a call for judgment, Agroda?"

"Of a kind," the young man replied, casting such a fond look on the young girl that Jegrai nearly choked on a laugh. "I would have my Khene to meet Venn Elkin, and his eldest daughter Briya. He was once a man of the sword in the service of the Princes of Yazkirn; now he and his daughter are both breeders and trainers of fine horses."

Oh-ho! Jegrai sat up a tiny bit straighter. *So there is more to this than a lovesick lad!*

The older man stepped forward and nodded; Jegrai returned the nod. The older man cleared his throat self-consciously. "I had occasion to meet your warrior, Khene Jegrai, under something less than ideal circumstances."

Elkin's command of Trade-tongue was excellent, as might have been expected in a horsebreeder, who probably dealt with traders on a regular basis. "Oh, so?" Jegrai replied blandly. "Was he trying to steal one of your stallions?"

The girl giggled, and the corners of her father's mouth twitched.

"No, Khene—I fear he was trying to slip his mare into my breeding herd."

Jegrai gave Agroda a long look; the young man shrugged. "It was ordered that there be no stealing and no raiding," he said unrepentantly. "How else was one to get a tall-horse foal?"

"I was far less angry than in admiration, Khene," the horsebreeder hastened to say, laugh-wrinkles crinkling at the corners of his dark blue eyes. "And I will tell you that I had been looking to *your* beasts with a certain speculation. They are small, aye, and something less than beautiful, but they have a quickness and a stamina that are admirable qualities. I had thought of coming to some accommodation, but only idly, when your warrior forestalled me."

"And he kindly did not take his whip to my back!" Agroda laughed.

The horsebreeder coughed. "I—ah—detained him—"

"He ran me down into the corner of his field on his tall-horse stallion." Agroda hung his head mournfully. "I, mindful of my Khene's orders against raising hand or weapon against the Vale folk, I ran like a rabbit. But the horse was faster."

Elkin was doing his best to ignore the interruptions, but the laugh-wrinkles were growing deeper. "We spoke—"

Agroda raised his head, and sobered a little. "Fairly, Khene, he was in his rights to demand a judgment, but he wished to speak seriously of crossbreeding."

"When I finally got him to hold still long enough to *speak* to him!" Elkin chuckled richly. "Aye, and glad I was to know Trade-tongue. We left the mare to the attentions of my stallion; on his return to redeem her he sought me out and we spoke again."

"I thought, 'This is a most wise man.' I wished to have more speech of him."

"On this occasion, I spoke of a horse-colt I could not seem to gentle—"

"—and I offered to see what I could do if he would breed another of my mares to his stallion."

"Khene, if it were not that I have wizards in the mountains above me, I would have thought your warrior a wizard!" Elkin's face glowed with enthusiasm. "I had resigned myself to gelding this one, which would have been a sad loss—but in less time than I ever would have dreamed, he had it gentled and broken to saddle and halter!"

"Na, Venn." Agroda blushed. "It was only that the colt has too tender a mouth, I *told* you so. You frightened and hurt him with the bit—never meaning to—and he smelled pain on you thereafter. Me, I do not smell like you, I do not look nor sound like you, and I put on him a halter with nothing to hurt his silly mouth. He lost his fear very quickly—and quicker still when you gave him of sweet-root. Now when he smells you he thinks of long gallops and more sweet-root! So long as he neck-reins and answers to the knee, you need never subject him to a bit, and he will go gladly for you—"

"Your warrior is too modest," Elkin said mock sternly. "He saw at once what I never thought of."

"So this is where you have been spending your time, Agroda?" Jegrai asked. "With this good man? We missed you at practice and the hunt, but I think your time was better used than ours, now! But surely not all your days were spent in gentling one colt?"

"Ah . . . well . . ." Agroda blushed even redder.

"My daughter sought out his advice on my recommendation. She has charge of halter-breaking the young foals, and gentling some of the lighter horses to saddle," Elkin replied, that grin tugging at the corners of his mouth and trying to escape again. "I have no sons, you see. . . ."

"Ah." Jegrai nodded. "But a good daughter is worth any number of bad sons."

"In truth. I have never noted the lack of sons, except . . ." Venn contrived to look mournful. "A man knows, Khene—he would feel happier going to his rest, knowing that there was a strong fighter to protect his little filly foals, his sweet little mares—"

"*Father!*" the girl protested, blushing fit to match Agroda.

"I speak only of horses, do I not? But also—knowing that there will be others to carry on his work—grandchildren, Khene, a man would like to see his *grandchildren*—and the traders are not so like to try to cheat a man, a strong, tall man, a man with a sword at his side—eh?"

"Indeed, I have often seen it to be the case," Jegrai replied as neutrally as he could. "Although I must say that any trader who chose to bargain with my own mother Aravay would be lucky to come out with a whole skin."

The girl gave her father an "I told you so" glare.

"Well, the long and the short of it is, Khene, it seems that my daughter has halter-broke a stranger young colt that ever I had seen before—"

"*Father!*"

"—and your warrior and my girl here seem to have conceived a liking for each other."

They both blushed, and the grin escaped from Venn Elkin's control.

"I'm all for the match—but the young man says he must ask permission of his Khene."

"Well that he has. I'm sure you are aware that there will be problems," Jegrai replied. He leaned forward in his chair, and fixed the horsebreeder and his daughter with as serious a stare as he could manage. "Our gods are not yours, our way of life is not yours, nor our language."

"But I'll learn—" both Agroda and Briya burst out simultaneously.

Jegrai nodded. "That is what I wished to hear," he said, sitting back a little and crossing his legs. "Look, the both of you young ones—this will be no easy thing. You do not go to a wedding as you go to a light love. You must both be willing to change at least some things. Near every moment of your lives will be one of compromise. Yours, too, good sir," he said, looking over to Elkin, who also nodded. "You realize that by having one of my people in your household, you will be bringing change into *your* life, I trust?"

"I'd like to think I'm not too old to change, a bit," the horsebreeder said quietly. "Hladyr bless, if I can learn to train a colt to neck and knee, I expect I can learn to like meat spiced to burning and a son-in-law who spends half his nights sleeping out under stars! Aye, and a daughter out there with him!"

Jegrai exchanged a wry look with him—and was relieved by it. The man was under no illusions about what had been going on these warm starlit nights. And evidently hadn't been worried about it, so long as it wasn't rape. That took one burden off Jegrai's mind, assuming that all Vale folk were of the same customs as the horsebreeder. Clan women slept where they wished until they wed, though if one were bearing it were wise to have a name-father for the child. Teo had hinted that the Vale folk were something similarly minded, but Jegrai had wondered, and worried.

Even the Vredai had not always been so cavalier about beddings and bearings, despite the old teachings of "cherish the children." But they had changed. They *had* to change. Too many children had died for the Vredai to put overmuch stock in who fathered whom. Now a child was precious of itself, and welcome no matter its origins.

"One other thing," Jegrai said, still quite seriously. "Agroda's loyalties and duties lie chiefly with me and Vredai. If I call him to war, he must obey me. Can you abide this, Briya? I will have no broken hearts that I can prevent; I would incur no resentments because of prior vows. But we have had to fight in the past, and though I do not care to think of it at this moment, we are like to do so in the future. And we will need every hand that can raise a sword to do so."

"If I were a flatlander down in Ancas, my husband could be hauled off to some fool war whenever his duke felt like a bit of excitement," Briya said in a high, breathy voice, raising her chin proudly. "At least I know who my Agroda be fighting for, and what, and that you won't be doing it as a game, like. I can abide it. Tell you truth, Khene, m'Da taught me staff 'n bow. Need came to it, I might be right there with him."

"And your children—should they choose Clan life over life in walls, could you abide that as well? For you must pledge to offer them that choice."

"Agroda told me. I won't pledge to like it—but I've not tried it either." She smiled, and Jegrai saw why Agroda looked ready to fall over his own feet whenever he gazed at her. She was utterly enchanting when she smiled, like a beam of sunlight given woman-form. "So by the time they come of age to choose, it may be me that's running about in tents, and them thinking their mam is a fool and a wild thing."

"Well spoken, lady." Jegrai gave her the bow of full respect he'd have given his mother. "I believe you have all thought this out, and I see no reason why this should not be the first of many matings between Clan and Vale." He looked out over the fertile little valley they were calling home—and realized, as he truly *saw* the "settled" look to the encampment, that the Vredai were, indeed, coming to think of it as their home, and not just another stopping-place. There were a full dozen of the great, anchored tents they called *eyerts* under construction, and they were not being anchored to wagons, but being given foundation-walls of stone from the river. Jegrai himself had never seen such a thing; only the Shaman had memories of such settlements.

They want to remain, to make a place of permanence. They'll fight for this place, he thought somberly. *They'll fight anyone and anything that tries to drive them from it.* That *was why the rebels didn't simply ride off. This place was home, and they didn't want to leave.*

"I do think," he said, half to himself, "I do truly think we are here to stay."

"Did you mean that?" Teo asked quietly, much later, after the evening meal, in the relative privacy of Jegrai's tent. "That you're here to stay?"

"If I had not meant it," Jegrai said, face very somber, "I would not have said it. This place has come to be home to us; I can see it every time I look about the camp. Indeed, it looks less like a 'camp' with each sunrise. You cannot tell me it has escaped your eyes, Teo."

Teo shrugged. It hadn't escaped his notice; the temporary jury-rigs of a people on the move were vanishing all over the camp. "Well, I thought things were getting to look awfully settled. Making that stone-lined pool for washing, for one; and there's talk of a steam-tent—and those big *eyerts*—and I overheard one of the old women talking about a kind of wooden *eyert,* and there were an awful lot of people listening to her with speculative looks in their eyes."

"Have you, in your tales of your gods, a place of afterlife, of reward?" Jegrai asked, an odd sort of longing in his eyes.

Teo nodded. "I think everyone does."

"I know not what your tales speak of—but ours speak of a place much like this valley you have given us. Much good grazing, sheltered from the storm yet open to the winds, shaded by trees, sweet water in abundance—how could anyone wish to leave paradise?" Jegrai sighed and rested his chin on his tucked-up knees, his arms wrapped about his legs. "And I ask myself: how long will we be allowed to keep this paradise?"

"But—" Teo protested, "Felaras won't—"

"It is not Felaras I fear, my friend, my very *good* friend. It is . . . what we left behind us." Jegrai's face took on a kind of grim determination. "Listen to me—some of this we have told your Master, but I wish you to hear all of it. I think it is time, and more than time, for all the truth to lie between us. I tell you: once the Vredai were twice, three times the number we are now—"

"But—"

Jegrai motioned him to silence with a wave of his hand, then changed his position to that of sitting cross-legged on his cushion, looking for all the world like Gortan about to relate a tale. "Hear me: farther than any of your breed has ever been, off to the east so far that few even of my folk have ever seen it, there is a vast, bitter salt sea."

"We've heard of it," Teo agreed.

"So. On the shores of that sea there dwelt a people who called themselves the *Suno*. In their tongue—in their tongue that means 'Masters'; and not as your good Felaras means it. Their mastery is that of man over dog, for that is how they see all not born to their ranks. Indeed, their word for 'outlander' *means* 'dog.' "

"Not auspicious."

Jegrai nodded. "So. They became great, they spread themselves upon the land—and then they encountered the steppes and the *Vreja-a-traiden*. That is my people, the riders of the steppes— that is our name for ourselves, and it means *only* that. They could not endure us. Yet they could not conquer us, for we had no cities to destroy. They could not enslave us, for we killed our masters if we got weapon in hand, or killed ourselves rather than face enslavement. So instead they sought to destroy us from within, first by seducing some of us with pleasures, then by setting those they had seduced against other Clans. Always they spread the poison of praise among the sweetmeats, saying that this one or that one should be Khekhene by right, that all other should bow to him. Many were those who heard and many who heeded, save only my father, who heard, and saw the blade of the knife beneath the platter of sugared dainties. And who saw that the old ways of raiding and counter-raiding, of counting coup, were being replaced by blood shed in anger, and blood-feud called."

Teo raised one eyebrow. "Jegrai, my friend, my *good* friend, you see very clearly for one so young."

Jegrai grimaced, and shook his head. "I can see very clearly when the truth is shoved into my nose, my friend Teo. It was Northwind and my father who saw this—it was Northwind who foresaw this even before there was proof, and whether it was a vision from the Wind Lords or simply that he saw the Suno luring the eastern Clans to them, saw how rage was replacing reason among them, I do not know nor care."

"I take it that Northwind and your father tried to turn the tide that was running against them?"

"Aye. It was my father who tried to keep this from happening, with words of warning and water-pledges with as many Khenes as would give them. And all for nothing."

Jegrai's eyes went dark and brooding, and full of such sorrow that Teo felt his own throat close in sympathy.

"Vredai was the one game-piece, the single straw, the one support that kept the whole from falling into chaos. While the Khene of Vredai was pledged friend to all the other Khenes, the Suno plans came to nothing. But my father was the keypiece to Vredai's place as peacemaker. And with him gone—"

"Surely he saw his danger," Teo protested, "if he was as farseeing as you say."

"Oh, ay," Jegrai answered bitterly. "But the Khene must prove he is warrior from time to time; my father no less than any other. He led the warriors on a common, ordinary raid, a raid for cattle against the Suno—a bit of defiance, if you will. And in the old way—lightly armed and armored. But the Suno were warned and many and well armed, and my father died."

Jegrai's eyes closed for a moment, and to Teo's profound amazement, when he opened them again, Teo could see his lashes were wet. The sight killed the words he was going to speak on his tongue. He had never suspected Jegrai of that depth of emotion.

But Jegrai's voice showed no more emotion than before.

"My father had not been able to gain water-pledges Clan to Clan, as Master Felaras and I swore, the kind that would have bound all others against raising their hands to us. He could only get pledges Khene to Khene. And when he died, all such pledges died with him."

"And you?" Teo asked, finally able to speak. "Why didn't you lead the Vredai out of harm's way when he died?"

Jegrai shook his head, and looked down at his hands. "I was only sixteen summers, Teo—there was much dissension over whether I was fit to be Khene. By the time all were satisfied, Khene Sen and the Talchai were ready, backed by the Suno, who had told him that to be Khekhene he must destroy the voice of rebellion—the voice of Vredai. And I made the poor decision to speak out against Sen and his ambitions in the Khaltan, the great meeting of all the Clans. He—Sen—saw what I was, but also what I might become. The voice, not only of Vredai, but of the *Vreja-a-traiden.*"

His voice grew cold with anger as he looked back up and focused his eyes on some distant point beyond Teo's shoulder. "They fell upon us, not warband upon warband, but warband upon the encampment itself. That was where and when we lost the most of our folk—that one raid. It was a slaughter such as had never been in all the long history of Vredai. Once, in the dark time of long ago when men were little better than beasts, there were Clan feuds of that kind, but sensible folk soon saw the folly of such things. But Khene Sen declared such a blood-feud on some trivial cause, and the other Khenes either upheld him or said nothing out of fear."

Jegrai's eyes closed in silent agony for a moment. "It was murder; there is no other word for it. With my own eyes I watched Sen trample children under the hooves of his horse. Oh, Wind Lords, my people . . . my people . . ."

Teo had never seen such emotional pain on anyone's face before, and finally had to look away.

Jegrai swallowed his grief, quieted his face, and continued. "I think the Suno counseled him in this. I think they reckoned that it would destroy the soul of my Clan, and leave me shattered and unable to lead."

"They should have known better," Teo said quietly. "That kind of atrocity only rouses people."

"Truth, it did no such thing as frighten us." Jegrai's face hardened. "Not the Vredai. We, who would not abide slavery under Suno hands, we who would not lick their feet and grovel as Sen did—how should *we* be made to fear? Never! Not though we perished to the last infant! I ordered the folk to pack what they could and scatter the herds. I ordered Northwind and Aravay to lead them into the West. Then I, and a handful of my best, young, and unwedded warriors went to work a delaying action on Talchai. We stole the Clan-altar, the shrine to the Wind Lords and the luck of the Clan—and when they pursued, we dropped it in their path, so that the hooves of their own horses shattered it and trampled their luck into the dust."

Jegrai's expression was at once proud and bleak. "We did not expect to survive that action, friend Teo. We expected to die at any point in that raid. Our aim was to buy time for what was left of Vredai with our blood. Yet—somehow—we lived."

He shook his head a little. "I still do not know why. But Sen and the Talchai could not—dared not—allow us to escape. Not after a handful of us effectively defeated them. This we knew. When we met with the rest of Vredai, we fled westward, hoping to perhaps to outrun them, or to simply find some place to make a stand. We did not expect to find paradise—less did we expect to find friends."

He raised his head a little higher and stared soberly into Teo's eyes. "Have I miscalled you, Teo? Or have I called you aright? Are you of the Order desirous of real friendship, of brotherhood with us?"

Teo found it very hard to speak. "I—we—Jegrai, we want to be your friends, truly we do—but what are you asking of your friends?"

A faded smile flickered at the corners of Jegrai's mouth. "I find I have lost the will to die, Teo. More than this, I find that I should like very much to—to be the strong warrior-lord your Order thought me when we first arrived. I come to this land of yours, and I find that, reduced as Vredai is, we are still an army compared to the armed strength here. If I stretched out my arm, and if I did not need to think about Talchai behind us, I could have such power, here."

Teo's breath caught in his throat; Jegrai looked at his paralyzed expression, and laughed dryly.

"Teo, Teo, I do not want to be anyone's master, Teo. I would very much like to be Khene of many people, of much land—but not at the cost of making war, and not out of conquest. I do not want slaves, victims—only friends, allies. I have a talent for leading; I wish to use it for more than just leading the Vredai. Is that foolishness, or vainglory?"

"N-no. I don't think so," Teo said doubtfully. "I wouldn't want a position like that, but . . . I'd rather you than the Yazkirn princes I've seen."

Jegrai nodded slowly. "That is rather what I had hoped. But—there are the Talchai. I do not think they will come this year, but come they will, and this time numbered enough to crush Vredai into the dust and destroy the very name of Running Horse for all time—"

Teo found it impossible to look away from his eyes. Like black fire . . .

"—unless I have the help of the Order. Your help in full, Teo. This means the sky-fire, and any other trick you have hidden away. Nothing less will serve. Because when the Talchai come, they shall come in the thousands, and they shall come with the intent of burning all before them. But they shall come at us in ignorance, expecting a handful of frightened, defeated, exhausted refugees—and they shall come *knowing* they do not have the Wind Lords with them, for their luck, their Clan-soul, is gone. If they are met even once with your lightning—it is *they* who shall crumble."

"Then what?" Teo whispered.

"Then . . . I should like to call what is left of the Clans together. They would make me Khekhene; I think there is no doubt of that. With my warriors and your sky-fire, we could drive the Suno into their walls, and make them fear to set foot beyond them ever again. It might even be we could destroy them, but I do not wish to waste lives—their own poisons will destroy them."

"And?"

Jegrai lowered his voice. "And when they are no more a threat, Teo, I pledge you now, on the life I gave to the Wind Lords, that I will turn my attentions to the enemies of *your* people. So that none will ever dare to raise hands against one wearing the Order's badges ever again."

Teo tried to get his mouth to work, but it was several long moments before he could get any sound to come out. "I—I can't speak for the Order, Jegrai. I can't even speak for the Master. I can't guess what she'd say—but you want me to ask her for you, don't you?"

Jegrai nodded. "I have assumed from the first that you were her eyes and ears here. And I knew that she knew. I think you are more than just her creature, now—I think you have come to know us. I hope you have come to appreciate us."

"I'd—prefer to think I'm your friend," Teo said softly. "And yes, I do appreciate you. There's an awful lot about your people I admire, Jegrai. Not the least of which is your sense of honor. There's not a lot of that around."

The young Khene smiled a little. "That is a good thing to hear. Will you be *my* advocate, then, to your Master?"

"Yes," Teo heard himself saying. "Yes, my friend, I will."

Felaras had had the suspicion from the moment that Kasha brought word Teo was coming up the mountain that she was going to need something stronger to sustain her than chava.

One look at Teo's face convinced her.

"Teo, sit down before you fall down," she ordered, pushing him into the chair beside her desk. She turned to her Second. "Kasha," she said, rubbing the back of her neck and feeling the muscles already starting to go tense, "I know it isn't even noon yet, but—"

"Wine," Kasha replied. "I'll get it for you, I think you're going to need it. And I'll get Zorsha. I think you're going to need him, too."

The wine and Zorsha arrived at the same moment, and with every word Teo recited, Felaras felt more and more in need of both. Even the good news, the wedding of one of the Vale folk and the young Vredai warrior and Jegrai's wholehearted support of it, did little to leaven the feeling that she'd just had a mountain dropped on her shoulders.

"—I told him—no, I promised him—I'd be his advocate, Master Felaras," Teo said nervously. "I—I don't know, everything he told me seemed so reasonable last night, and I've never caught him in any kind of untruth. I want to believe him. But—supporting him militarily in a coup of his own, something that's not in our plan? I—I just don't know, I'm absolutely out of my depth."

Felaras sighed, and had a long sip of her wine. "Teo, you're the student of history. Are there any parallels?"

"Maybe," he replied, voice and face strained. "If you can believe Ancas folktales, oral tradition from peoples who hadn't a notion of literacy for the first couple hundred years of their ascendancy. The folktales say the leader of the Ancas was like Jegrai; charismatic, and with a long view. That was the one who supposedly overran the Sabirn empire. But he didn't have the incredible hunger for learning that Jegrai has, nor the respect for those who have it."

"Kasha?"

"Mai says she'd follow him into hell," Kasha replied positively. "Hladyr bless, I've been down there and fought with his people, and I can tell you I'd do the same! All he needs is an edge, just the tiniest edge, and he'll *have* his enemies. We could give him that edge. And you know what he'll give us." She straightened and looked directly into Felaras's eyes. "I'll tell you what my father would tell you; the Swords like Jegrai. The Watchers would back him without a single second thought."

"Zorsha?"

"No such unity in Tower, Felaras," Zorsha said with regret. "But even though I may not be a student of history, I can tell you with Jegrai you're sitting on a dragon. You can ride it, and it will likely take you places you've never dreamed. But if you try to get off, it may crush you without even knowing it did so."

Out of the corner of her eye Felaras saw Teo bristle.

"Jegrai wouldn't—"

"Jegrai damned well would," Zorsha replied calmly. "His first, last, and holiest priority is his people. If he had to cut you down to save them, Teo, he'd do it. He'd give you the best funeral you ever saw, after, but he'd still do it."

"But—"

"You heard it out of his own mouth, Teo," Kasha agreed. "He was perfectly willing to sacrifice himself for them, and at what age? Seventeen, eighteen? At twenty his people have been in flight for years and he's suffered with every one of them; he'll buy them peace and safety with whatever coin it takes. His blood, yours, or mine."

"But the fact is, he won't roll over us unless we stand in his way—which, I trust, we're too wise to do," Zorsha continued, as Teo subsided into the chair, red-faced and abashed. "And what he's offering—Felaras, it's tempting. If I were in the Master's seat, I'd take it. We're not just one man anymore; we're not Duran. We're an ongoing organization, and we'll live beyond the span of any one man. We have the potential, not only to advise and aid a potentially very strong leader, *but all those who succeed him.* Have you thought what that could mean to the Order in particular—and the world in general? We could help to foster hundreds, maybe a thousand years of peace and learning, if we can stay uncorrupted by power. And I think that because of our organization we can."

Felaras nodded, slowly—and in her own mind eliminated Teo from the "competition" for the Master's seat altogether. Though Teo had had all night to consider what Jegrai had told him, his only thoughts had been personal, and confused. Zorsha had cut straight to the heart of the matter, and seen the long-view possibilities, positive and negative.

And being Felaras, she could not be less than honest with the three so close to her.

"Teo—what would you say if I told you I don't think you've got it in you to sit in my place?" she asked quietly.

Kasha and Zorsha went very quiet, and froze in their chairs.

Teo's face was suffused with only relief. "I'd thank the gods, Master. Honestly." Then he started a little, and his eyes widened. "Do you *mean* that? You're pulling me out?"

She nodded slowly.

He closed his eyes and sagged against the back of the chair. "Oh, gods. Master Felaras, you will never know how happy you've made me. Every time I thought about having to make decisions— oh, gods, I just got so knotted up inside I wanted to puke." He opened his eyes again, and there was no shadow of falsehood in them. "Zorsha, you can have it all, with my blessing! Gods, I can just be me again. . . ."

Zorsha looked stunned.

"It had to come some time, and soon," Felaras told him. "There can only be one successor in the end. You're it, lad. I'm not sure whether to give you congratulations or condolences."

Zorsha shook himself a little, and managed to smile weakly at her. "From all I've seen, both. Well. Thank you . . . I think."

Felaras laughed. "Lad, just now you sounded so like me you could have been my echo! All right—Teo's brought us Jegrai's offer. You've all given your opinions and they match mine. We're in for a leg; we might just as well go in for the whole lamb."

Zorsha nodded. "What's first?"

"Those Talchai that Jegrai thinks are on his heels. Kasha, I want you to consult with your father about what it would take to truly crush an army of three or four thousand at the Teeth. That includes more fire-throwers than we currently have—both mortars and hand-cannon. Zorsha, I want figures on how long it would take to make those fire-throwers and the ammunition for them. Teo, get back down there and tell Jegrai he's got a bargain."

She looked about at her aides, her successor, and felt a kind of perverse thrill of excitement.

"All right, don't just stand there, people," she said, feeling an upwelling of energy. "Let's *move!*"

✧ CHAPTER TEN ✧

The workroom was swept clean, and there was only one source of flame: a tiny candle sheltered by a glass chimney. Zorsha took no chances when working with explosives; no Seeker would, nor would any of those of the Watchers whose duties included handling such things.

"*This* is what makes the lightnings?" Yuchai asked, regarding the little pile of black powder in the palm of his outstretched hand with doubt and puzzlement.

"Only that," Zorsha agreed. "Doesn't look like much, does it?"

"Not really." Yuchai poured it carefully back into the little leather sack Zorsha held open, and dusted his hands off on a bit of cloth. "It looks like dirt. Or ashes."

Zorsha grinned, a little tightly. "Trust me, it isn't dirt, and it's every bit as dangerous as real lightning. Listen, Yuchai, Felaras gave me open-ended permission to show you whatever you wanted to know in the meeting I had with her last night—and that 'everything' includes the fire-throwers. You told me a while ago that Jegrai wanted you to learn about them. Well, now Felaras figures he should know. But we're dealing with perilous stuff here—there've been Seekers and Watchers both blown to little bits just because some tiny thing went wrong. Still want to go on? It isn't just the explosives that are dangerous—even knowing about how they work could put your life in danger, outside these walls. There've been members of the Order tortured to death over this stuff."

He hefted the little bag of black powder. Yuchai bit his lip, but shook his head stubbornly. "I want to know. Even if Jegrai hadn't asked me to learn about it, I'd have wanted to know. You told me it wasn't magic. That meant it was something anybody could learn. If anybody could, I wanted to."

"I'm going to start by showing you a few things. First, I'm going to light a little bit of this stuff in the open." Zorsha poured a tiny pile of the explosive powder on a metal plate, set the plate on the workbench, and carefully uncovered the candle. With equal care he touched the candle to the pile. Yuchai watched in fascination as it sparked, and then went up in a *poof* of smoke, consumed in a bare instant of time.

"Now, this little paper tube has about the same amount of the powder packed into it." Zorsha took one of the tiny firecrackers used at festivals out of a metal-lined drawer in his workbench. "There's also a little bit of the powder wound into the paper fuse—that's the twist of paper sticking out of the end. Now watch."

He put the cracker on the plate, lit the fuse, and stood back. The fuse was a short one; he'd barely gotten out of the way when the cracker exploded. Yuchai jumped nearly a foot into the air.

"Now . . . logic, Yuchai. What was the difference between the firecracker and the pile of gunpowder?"

The boy's brows knitted for a moment.

"Think hard."

Yuchai shook his head, defeated.

"In the firecracker the force of burning was confined. It had nowhere to go, so it broke its container."

Yuchai's eyes lit. "Like putting a lid on a boiling pot?"

Zorsha chuckled with delight. "*Damn* good!" Impulsively he hugged Yuchai's thin shoulders, and the boy's whole face lit up. "Now watch this."

He took another firecracker and this time put a small metal measuring cup over it, leaving only the fuse sticking out. He lit the fuse.

This time Yuchai was prepared for the noise and didn't jump, but his mouth formed a soundless "oh" when the metal measure was thrown into the air and off the table.

"Now, what was the difference there?"

"The—force was more confined?"

"Partially. It was also confined so that it could only go in one direction. Obviously, the force was too small to move the table, so it could only move the cup."

"You use the—confined force—to throw things?" Yuchai hazarded. "Like a catapult, only farther and faster?"

"In part; look here." He rummaged through his document-drawer and pulled out a drawing of one of the hand-cannon. "Now, this is a drawing of a fire-thrower—a small one. You pack the explosive powder down in here, see? Then you add paper, you stuff it in so that it blocks all the cracks, so that the force can't escape around the edges of whatever you're going to use as shot. Then you put in the shot, then more paper. The shot is usually a round metal ball, very heavy."

Yuchai crowded up under his arm, studying the drawing with an intensity that allowed no distractions.

"Look here—here's the hole that the fuse goes in; you light that, and when the powder explodes, the ball is propelled out."

"But Jegrai said that the ground before him exploded—like lightning had struck there. No matter how hard a metal ball hit, it wouldn't do that."

"That's the fire-throwers we have on the walls—another kind." He pulled out a second drawing. "We call this one a mortar; it doesn't send things as far, because we don't use as heavy a charge, and we let a little more of the force escape by not using wadding. What it does fire is something like a very large firecracker, but one made of cast iron; which, as I showed you, is brittle enough to shatter if struck hard enough. When you light the fuse on the mortar, you also light the fuse on the canister, which is timed so that it goes off when it hits the ground. Mortars are a lot more dangerous to the handlers than the cannon, because the act of firing them can set off the charge in the shell."

"The fire gets through the shell?"

"No. It isn't just fire that can set off the gunpowder."

Zorsha put a firecracker unobtrusively on the bench, and pulled out a hammer.

"Impact can do it too."

He brought the hammer down squarely on the firecracker—and Yuchai jumped back, wide-eyed, at the crack of the explosion.

"You see? Hard enough impact sets it off."

The boy stared at the blackened place on the bench for a moment, while Zorsha rubbed his tingling fingers. It was an effective demonstration of how dangerous gunpowder could be—but a little hard on the hand.

"Zorsha, I am probably a fool—and I am not very learned," Yuchai said, shyly, but with those intense eyes focused on Zorsha's face. "But—I have a question. Two questions?"

"Go ahead."

"In battle, even *our* arrows often bounce off armor. The Suno laugh at arrow-fall when they are in full armoring; not even our bows can pierce metal. But—could—could a man not make an arrowhead, hollow, with the powder inside? And when it struck the armor or the shield, would it not explode?"

"Hladyr bless," Zorsha breathed. "I never thought of that. Even if it did very little damage it would certainly frighten whoever it hit white! And if it hit a rider—"

"The horse would bolt," Yuchai said simply. "No horse would abide that without being trained to it. A few archers could scatter an entire force of heavy cavalry, could they not?"

"They could—gods above and below, they certainly could. And your other question?"

"You told me of the Sabirn-fire, the fire that water only spreads? And you told me that you could not use it very often because it was so dangerous?"

"So dangerous we've seldom even used it with catapults. All it would take would be for the jars to break open a little, and the fire would be all over the catapult and crew."

"But cast iron is tougher than pottery, and still breaks. Why do you not put it in the hollow canisters of the mortars? You could throw it far beyond the lines of your allies. You could destroy the siege engines you told me of before they were even put into play. You would not even need to hit anything exactly, only near it, because the fire would splash and spread. You could take whole groups of fighters that way. Am I not right?"

"Yuchai—" Zorsha looked aghast at the boy. "Yuchai, that is a terrible thought."

The boy hugged his arms to his chest, as if to ward off a sudden chill, and his face took on a strange, masklike appearance. "If you made these shells, you could hurl such things at the Talchai when they came—you could burn them, burn them up. They couldn't stand against you, no matter how many warriors they had."

Zorsha took the boy's thin shoulders in his hands and shook him. "Yuchai, you can't mean that—you've never seen the fire; I have—it's a terrible thing, a weapon of absolute desperation."

"The *Talchai* are terrible!" the boy cried, his voice spiraling up and cracking. "The *Talchai* are—are—"

The boy's voice abruptly went flat and dead; his eyes stared at the stone wall of Zorsha's workroom, but plainly did not see it. His young face held more pain than Zorsha had ever imagined in his life.

The young Hand stared at what he had thought was just an extraordinarily bright boy. The "boy's" face was transformed, aged, and so bleak Zorsha would not have known him. He looked a hundred years old, and sick to death. And when he began to whisper in a harsh, strained voice, Zorsha thought, aghast, *No puppy is going to heal this.*

"If I saw them drowning, I would call for rain! If I saw them burning, I would throw oil upon them! I *hate* them, I *hate* them, and I want to see them die, terribly, horribly, I'd set demons on them if I could!"

He started to laugh, in that same suppressed way he'd spoken—but it was hopeless, hysterical laughter. It tore at the heart, and the boy began to tremble all over, then to shake.

Zorsha couldn't bear it. He seized the boy and held him close, face against his chest. For one moment there was nothing but silence.

Then the boy made a choking sound, and seized him with all the desperation of a drowning child.

Zorsha hugged him tighter, and Yuchai clung to him and began to speak again; slowly at first, brokenly—but then the words began pouring from him in a kind of deadly monotone, a flood of appalling words.

Words that blanched Zorsha and made him tremble; words telling of atrocities committed on the Vredai that exceeded Zorsha's wildest nightmares.

This was not imagined, or something the boy had embroidered with his own fantasy; no one could have imagined a massacre like the one Yuchai was describing, a hellish kind of festival of blood and death. Zorsha could hardly begin to take it in. Every incident the boy recited was worse than the one before—and Zorsha began to realize with soul-chilling horror that the boy had witnessed all this rapine and slaughter in *a single afternoon.*

For Yuchai was reciting the tale of the raid by the Talchai on the Vredai camp—a raid that had been staged when most of the weapon-bearers were out of camp on hunts or guarding the herds. There had only been the sick, women with young children, the elderly, and the children themselves. Of which Yuchai had been one. One small boy who escaped the fate of his playmates only because he had been hidden in a thicket of bushes as part of a game.

Gods, what was he? Ten? Eleven? Old enough to remember everything clearly—oh, gods, what can I do? What can I say?

It was the voice that was the worst—that dull, monotonous recitation of horrors. That, and the way the boy clutched at him, seeking a shelter from his own memories.

"Yuchai . . ." Zorsha couldn't think what to do to comfort him. *Could* there be comfort? "Yuchai—Yuchai, stop it! Listen to me!" Zorsha's own face was wet with tears as he shook the boy's shoulders and got him to look up at him. "Listen, Yuchai, listen to me—it won't happen again! Not ever! I pledge you on my life, *I* won't let it happen!"

The boy stared at him blankly for a moment—then burst into tears.

Zorsha just held him, rocking back and forth a little, weeping with him. It was all he *could* do.

Gods, gods—who made him hold all this inside? Who left this to fester? Or—gods, are they all *like this? Every survivor down in that camp?*

Appalling sobs shook the child, tearing themselves up out of his throat and racking his thin body.

In that moment Zorsha learned how to hate.

The study was very dark; very quiet. Felaras listened to Zorsha's tight-voiced recitation with growing nausea. She had no doubt that he was retelling the tale exactly as the boy had told it to him; he was white as salt, and just barely under control. She had never seen him so angry—she rather doubted anyone had. Zorsha the calm, the easygoing, the half-asleep—Zorsha had just been awakened to something he'd never anticipated.

When Zorsha finished, she steepled her fingers just below the level of her eyes and looked at him as searchingly as she had ever measured anyone.

His face was as tightly controlled as his voice had been—but just beneath that tight control there still was a terrible and implacable anger. Merely speaking had not purged him of it; if anything, it had intensified it. She was finding herself very glad that she was not the object of it.

"And your analysis?" she said, finally.

"I was trained to always demand both sides of a story, Felaras. Frankly, I don't care to hear the other side of this one. I really don't want to know what could bring men to act like that—like rabid beasts. All I want to do is destroy the beasts and the thing that made them that way. Which, to my analysis, is the Talchai and the Suno."

"That's not a rational way of looking at something—"

"I don't *want* to be rational!" he hissed. "You weren't with the boy down there; I was. You didn't look into that dead little face— into those hopeless eyes. This was a fourteen-year-old boy, Felaras! A child that age *couldn't* make something like this up!"

"I never suggested that he had," she said, overcome by a profound weariness for a moment. *Why me? Why is it me who must face this? Deal with this? Somehow rectify this?* "Is he all right?"

"I think so. As all right as he'll ever be. When he ran out of strength to cry, I carried him back to his room; Kasha got Boitan and Boitan gave him something that made him sleep. Boitan said he thinks this actually did the boy some good—'catharsis,' he called it." Zorsha shook his head, and only now did Felaras see that his eyes were red from weeping of his own. "I stayed with him until he was under. Kasha's with him now, and his dog." He clenched his hands on the arms of the chair; a white-knuckled grip that would have cracked weaker wood. "Felaras, the weapons the boy suggested are inhumane—and I want to construct them. I want to *use* them. I want to drive home the lesson that what the Talchai did will be paid for. I want them to think that every god above and every demon below has turned its hand against them. I want to make retribution so terrible that no one will ever contemplate atrocity like that against anyone again. And I want the Talchai, above all else, to know the reason why this is falling on them."

She parted her hands and looked at them with surprise; they were shaking. She'd thought her control was better than that— but the story had gotten past her defenses enough to make her tremble with the effort of holding in her own reaction. "Do me this favor, Zorsha. First, sleep on it. Second, speak with Jegrai and Northwind. *Then* decide. If you still want to construct these things—I'll back you. Reasonable?"

He nodded curtly.

"I'm going to ask a very personal question, and remember, it's because I've made you my successor and I have to know your strengths and your weaknesses. Why *this* boy? You haven't—" Her face flamed with embarrassment, and she looked away.

He read the embarrassment correctly, and snorted. "No, Felaras, I'm not a pederast. Gods help him, that would be the last thing Yuchai would need! No, set your mind at ease on that subject; I still want Kasha, quite healthily, let me tell you. It's because—I look at Yuchai, and I see myself all over again. He's enough like me inside to be my own son—more like me, probably, than a son would be. I've come to love him for his brave little soul and his bright mind as surely as if he'd been born my son." His face hardened. "And they hurt him. Hurt him in a way no physician can deal with. I think that no matter what Boitan says, the only thing that's going to truly let him heal and let him put his mind on something besides revenge is to *get* revenge. Or at least the promise of it."

Felaras nodded, slowly. "That makes a peculiar kind of sense." She cleared her throat a little. "I shouldn't admit this, but I agree with you. On everything. Just follow through on those promises, all right? Let's at least give this the appearance of rational thinking."

The chair legs scraped harshly on the floor as he pushed away from the desk and stood up. "I'd like to stay with him in case he has nightmares. Boitan thought he might."

"Fine, go ahead," she replied absently, still trying to make some kind of sense out of the catalog of horrors Zorsha had recited so tonelessly. "Send Kasha back here, would you?"

She stared at the flame of the single candle on her desk, letting it mesmerize her, trying to see some reason, any reason, behind what seemed so unreasonable. The things the Order, as a group and as individuals, had endured in the past—those things were actually understandable. Fear of the unknown, hatred for the foreign, greed, the desire for power—all normal human motivations. But this—

Even at third hand, it chilled her. Jegrai hadn't gone into the personal details of what had happened to his Clan. If he had, she might well have given him his bargain months before. But then again, she might have suspected an *adult* of fabricating at least part of the story—

Poor Yuchai. She couldn't begin to imagine what it had been like to live through it.

A shadow passed between her eyes and the candle flame, and she started.

Kasha was sitting on the edge of her desk, and had just waved her hand in front of Felaras's eyes to get her attention.

"I had a word with Shenshu and Demonsbane," she said quietly. "They've been figuring the boy for a breakdown for a while. Seems his father is one of those stone-faced, iron-willed types who finds any show of emotion something less than honorable. They're relieved, both that it came, and that Yuchai had an acceptable father-substitute with him to get him through the worst of it. They couldn't speak too highly of Zorsha, both for his handling of the situation and for his compassion. Right now, so far as Shenshu's concerned, Zorsha hung the moon."

Felaras shook her head. "That's not what's bothering me. It's *why*. How could human beings do that to other human beings?"

Kasha sighed. "I can only tell you what they told me. First, that this Khene Sen is just as charismatic and persuasive as Jegrai—and he's twelve years older. He had a lot of time to get his people brought around to his way of thinking. Second, that Sen's mother was Suno; an alliance marriage. Now think about what Teo told us: the Suno consider all other races to be inferior. Fit only to serve, to enslave."

Felaras nodded, seeing the pieces falling into place, seeing the pattern start to emerge.

"Put those two things together, add what the Suno have probably been telling Khene Sen, about how superior, how great a leader he is, and about how much they can give him—and then produce Jegrai. Charismatic, brilliant—and young. Young enough to beat Sen just by outliving him. And you get?"

Felaras sucked in a breath. "A very frightened man; a man who sees the possibility of being cornered staring him in the face. A man who sees the way to exterminate that threat now if he just acts quickly enough."

Kasha nodded. "That was basically what Demonsbane figured. 'Exterminate' is a good word-choice—remembering that Sen is half-Suno."

"Uh-huh; I can see that, especially if he's been doing his best to ignore the nomad half of his breeding. He wouldn't let his people see it as anything other than exterminating a dangerous predator—no worse than killing, oh, a plague of rats. But why not just use assassination?"

Kasha shrugged. "Damned if I know. Maybe because if Sen had pulled *that* little trick, he'd have lost everybody but his own Clan. The other Clans would have reckoned that if Sen would use a dishonorable tactic like assassination on Jegrai, he'd be perfectly willing to use it on anybody. Remember, even Sen pays at least lip-service to honor."

"So he makes it look honorable—at least to his own folk—to take Jegrai out by getting rid of the entire Clan?"

"Exactly. And by the time he got finished speaking to his fighters, they'd be ready to exterminate with enthusiasm. Remember, I've been there when Jegrai primed us to go hunting the rebels; I know what that kind of speaker can do. Frankly, we are just damned lucky Jegrai is rational, reasonable, and willing to listen to anybody's side."

"But why haven't we seen other children as emotionally scarred as Yuchai?" That was the last piece that wouldn't drop into place.

Kasha looked sick. "Felaras—we haven't seen any, because there *aren't* any. Haven't you noticed? Yuchai is the only young adolescent. Fourteen and over—now eighteen and over—were out with the herds. Younger than ten—some managed to hide and didn't see the actual slaughter. But all the rest, including Yuchai's peer group, were out in the open and cut down. That poor boy is the only child that saw what happened and was old enough to remember it clearly."

"Oh, gods—"

"Felaras, if anyone can purge him of this, it'll be his own people and ours working together. He's in the best possible hands." She smiled, a kind of rueful, self-deprecating smile. "I never knew Zorsha had this in him, frankly. One of the things that always annoyed me a bit was the way he seemed to drift through emotional encounters without ever getting pulled into the current. *Teo* has always cared passionately for things, and showed it. Zorsha always seemed . . . half asleep. I guess I was wrong about him."

"Looks like you might have been, a bit. But if you were, so was I." Felaras stretched out her fingers, and winced as the knuckles popped. "Kasha, you have just done me a world of good. I didn't know what to make of this story. It sounded like these Talchai were all mad, or drugged, or—or bespelled."

"Oh no doubt there was some of that last, too. Demonsbane thinks Sen has a whole stable of very powerful wizards. With enough folk luck-wishing him while he was speaking, he could likely get anybody to believe anything."

"That, I can deal with. That, I can defend against. Furthermore—" she paused as a thought struck her. "You know, it would do no harm to spread a couple of these stories of Yuchai's about the Order. Let our people get some notion of what's out there. We won't frighten the timid ones any more than they already are, and we might give the complacent ones some food for reflection. I think that most of them can add two and two— and realize that even if we'd had nothing to do with Jegrai, mad dogs like the Talchai seem to be would *still* tear our throats out in passing."

"Done," Kasha nodded. "I'll get Father and Boitan on it, and Kitri. Now, as your duly appointed watchdog, I say you should hie yourself off to bed before you fall over at your desk. You're beginning to sound a little drunk, and that's nothing more than fatigue."

Felaras stood up slowly, and wanted to groan—every joint ached. "Rain coming," she observed. "Before too long, by the way my knees feel."

As if to substantiate her observation, a very distant murmur of thunder mumbled at the open window, and there was a barely visible flicker of light that showed against the edge of the mountains beyond.

"Then you need to get to bed," Kasha said sternly.

"I need to make my rounds, first," she replied just as stubbornly. "Then I'd like to look in on the boy, I think. Have a word with one of the other nomads myself, first."

Kasha shrugged, and spread her hands in defeat. "All right, have it your way. You will anyway. I'll tell you what, I'll put everything to rights, and then catch up with you. I'm not exactly ready to embrace the god of slumber myself just yet. Too many things to think about."

"And most of them grim." Felaras moved around her desk, and paused in the door. "Thanks . . ."

"Oh, get. You're so tired you'd make more of a mess than you'd clean up, putting things back in the wrong places," Kasha mocked. "And then tomorrow morning it would be 'Kasha, I can't find this, Kasha, have you seen that, Kasha, where did I put my stylus—' "

"Enough, enough!" Felaras ducked her head and winced. "I yield, I yield! I'll see you in a bit."

"*Don't* let anyone trap you into a night-long discussion."

Felaras let the door close on that last admonition, and headed stiffly down the corridor.

Gods. I'm getting old. I feel it more every time it rains. She sighed, and rubbed the knuckles of her writing hand. *I should complain—there's a child in the room next to mine with a soul in ragged little shreds. There's a young man down at the bottom of the mountain with the lives of his people literally in his hands. My successor has just learned the hard way how vile men can be. And I'm fretting because my bones ache when it rains.*

The Fortress could well have been deserted; the lamps along the corridor were turned to their lowest, and there was nothing to break the silence except her own footsteps. Being so high up on the Pass was a mixed blessing in summer—the air cooled down rapidly at night, but that same cold gave nearly everyone over the age of forty stiff joints overnight.

Still, the cool of the corridor was a blessed relief from the blazing sun that had baked its way even into Felaras's study. This was the time of year when the Master's Folly was not so foolish after all—if you were young enough not to have to worry about aching bones when there was dew on your bed come the dawn.

Selfish, selfish, thinking about myself, my aching bones. Or— is it? Maybe not. No, I'm not fretting because my bones ache— I'm fretting because that aching is the sign that my time is getting shorter. I'm getting old—my joints are going, but how long does my mind have? Or the rest of me? Will I have enough time to give Zorsha the training he needs? Did I wait too long before picking one of the lads? Gods, I wish you'd give me some notion of how much time I've got left.

As if answering her unspoken prayer, thunder boomed almost

directly overhead, so close that she could feel the stone of the Fortress vibrating with it under her feet.

She sniffed, and took the turning that led to the old dead-ended corridor lined with workrooms on both sides. *Telling me that's hubris, gods? Or just warning me that however long I have, it's not going to seem like enough time?*

This time there was a pause before the thunder pealed again, and she almost smiled at the realization that she had been on the verge of looking to the thunder to answer her.

The corridor was properly deserted at this hour—but it was part of the rounds. If there was anyone working here this late, Felaras wanted to be aware of the fact. *Gods, I'm as bad as Diermud. Next thing you know, I'll be talking to quartz crystals—and listening for answers. If fancies begin, can senility be far behind?*

Something impinged on, then disrupted her thoughts. A current of air, a shadow that didn't belong—whatever it was that alerted her allowed reflex to save her life.

She only knew that she sensed—*wrong*—and dropped to the floor and shoulder-rolled without a thought for aching joints and fragile bones.

And a stone came hissing past the place where her head had been to smack into the stone of the wall and clatter to the floor.

She was on her feet again with her back to the wall and her eyes scanning the corridor in two heartbeats. And cursing the carelessness that had left her belt-knife on her desk, where she'd used it to slit open some letters.

A blot of shadow separated from the rest and moved toward her, bulking huge against the wall. Blocky, looking like it should be clumsy—and moving like a hunting lion. Only one person within these walls looked and moved like that, or carried himself with his shoulders so high and tense.

"Zetren," she whispered.

He moved into the light. "Witch," he snarled, as thunder crashed again overhead. "Bitch-queen, think you're going to *be* a queen, don't you? Think this pretty boy barbarian's going to set you up as Mother-Goddess and then conquer the world for you, do you? Reckon you can use the rest of us as a staircase to a throne—"

"Zetren," she said, honestly bewildered, feeling the wall behind her for support. "What in hell are you talking about?"

He ignored her—really, it didn't even seem as if he'd heard her. "Going to make us all your little fetch-and-carrys, like you did with those three lackeys of yours, aren't you? Figure you've got us all outsmarted—"

"Zetren—"

"I was too smart for you, bitch. I saw where you were going, even if nobody else believed me. I had you figured. And you can ill-wish me all you want, but this time it isn't going to stop me—"

He lunged for her, and she dodged and spun herself out of his way with real, cold fear closing around her throat. This corridor was deserted; there were no eager young Hands down here *this* night. Zetren was stronger than she was—faster; she couldn't possibly outrun him, even if she could get past him into the clear corridor.

She couldn't outlast him, either.

And she didn't dare take him on hand-to-hand; *he* hadn't been spending the last few years pushing papers around, he was in better shape than she was. He'd make pulp out of her.

"Zetren, what in hell do you think you're doing?" she gasped, sidestepping a deadly blow aimed at her neck, throwing herself away from him, and coming up against the stone wall with force that would leave her bruised. "You hurt me, and—"

"Not going to *hurt* you, bitch," he snarled, the red madness of the bear brought to bay in his eyes. "Going to *kill* you—"

He lashed out again; this time she managed to get in a quick side-kick of her own to his midsection and get out of grabbing distance, further down toward the dead end, before he could react. He *oofed* under the impact, but recovered quickly and pivoted into a counterattack faster than she would have believed possible.

"Going to *kill* you," he growled again, as thunder shook the walls, destroying her hope of anyone hearing a call for help. "Drop you down your own damn staircase. Senile old bitch trips and falls—no one'll think anything about it."

She didn't even waste a breath pointing out that bruises from blows and bruises from falling look a great deal different. Zetren wouldn't listen—and anyway, what would it matter to her at that point? She'd be dead, and beyond being concerned—

He kicked, and she squirmed aside, but his foot brushed her hip and made her spin into the wall. He followed up on the kick with unnatural speed, and she only avoided his clutching hands because he'd come in to strangle rather than to strike.

He's really going to kill me—oh, gods— For the first time in years she panicked—and though it was going to do no good at all, cried out her fear.

Thunder crashed again, drowning her voice, and Zetren grinned.

"How's it feel to be the helpless one, bitch?" he laughed. "How's it feel to—"

He was enjoying this too much, and not paying attention to her. She was too good a fighter to let *that* pass. This time *she* lunged for *his* throat, fingers stiffened—

And connected, but at the last minute her traitor knee gave way under her, and turned what would have been at the least a disabling blow into one that simply hurt. And she fell in a half-crouching position, unbalanced and terribly vulnerable.

He half roared, half choked, and reacted to the blow, kicking out at her with the power of a catapult.

This time he connected squarely with her ribs before she could scramble out of the way, and sent her crashing into the wall, her impact only partially under control. A tearing pain in her knee as she hit sent her dropping to the floor in agony, and she looked up a moment later to see him advancing slowly on her through a blur of tears of pain.

Oh, gods—not like—dammit, I'm not done *yet!*

Thunder, drowning everything; her desperate "No!" and his laugh; she could only see his mouth working, couldn't hear him at all. He reached for her—and before he could touch her, suddenly stiffened.

His eyes nearly popped out of his head, and his mouth worked again, but this time the shape was all wrong for a laugh—and as she shrank back against the stone, he collapsed like a deflated bladder, coming down in a heap with one hand brushing her foot.

She stared, unable to believe in her deliverance, while nearly constant thunder reverberated overhead.

It wasn't sound that alerted her again—it was movement, movement down at the open end of the corridor.

Kasha walked slowly through the light and shadow patterns made by the tiny lamps on the wall toward her, stalking the length of the corridor, something swinging from her hand.

A sling.

About then Felaras's nose told her that Zetren was no longer among the living.

For a moment more she sat in a kind of paralysis, both of mind and body, as the thunderstorm passed on and the nearly continuous shocks of the thunder faded into the distance.

Kasha prodded the body with her toe, then rolled it out of the way and wordlessly reached out her hand toward her superior. Felaras took it, climbing painfully to her feet. Her knee burned like somebody'd set it on fire.

"Found the sling back where he'd dropped it. How badly did he hurt you?" Kasha asked, tightly.

Felaras tried putting weight on the leg—it felt like bloody hell, but she could hobble on it. "Knee," she gasped, around tears of pain. "Sprained or torn muscle, I think. Still works, so it isn't broken. And I'm bruised some. That's all."

"You're just damned lucky I was coming after you," her aid said angrily, then, "Oh, gods, Felaras, what am I saying? Why should you have to guard your back against your own people? We aren't assassins!"

"Kash—" she got out as she gritted her teeth against pain that was threatening to make her pass out. "—orders. Me to room. Boitan to me. Zorsha too. *Now.*"

It happened so quickly she was tempted to believe in a magic other than ill-wishings.

"All right," she said, as Boitan's pain medication began to make the room blur and slip sideways a little. "Have we all got our stories straight?"

Zorsha nodded. "Zetren fell off the wall during the storm. Nobody knows what he was doing up there; it wasn't his watch, and that part of the wall is bad when it's raining. You slipped on the stairs when the thunder startled you, and wrecked your knee. Right now we only know about you, we don't know about Zetren. Ardun is going to 'find' him a little bit after dawn."

"Good. Simple enough to be believed." She started to nod off, and caught herself with a jerk.

"Felaras, why the subterfuge?" Boitan asked.

"Kash—"

"Zetren said something to her about 'ill-wishing.' Boitan, this is to be dead-secret; Felaras and I are both wizards, and we've been detecting somebody trying to work against her since early spring."

Boitan sucked in his breath in surprise, bit his lip, and nodded.

"Now since that predates the Vredai, it has to be somebody in the Vale or the Order."

"It seems likely," Zorsha interjected, "at least to me, that this 'enemy' found that his wishes weren't working—"

Felaras nodded tiredly. "Defense 'shield.' Have to train you in that, boy. Master has to have it."

Zorsha started, and she grinned weakly. "One of prime requisites for being candidate is wizard-power. Didn't know you had it, hm?"

"No—" he replied, looking stunned.

"Felaras thinks that when this wizard found himself blocked, he must have turned his attentions to someone with a known grudge against her, but with less protection. Zetren, basically."

"Had it too, not's good's I am, good enough to know someone stronger was on him, not good enough to deflect it," she explained, her words beginning to slur despite her efforts at control. " 'F he'd made it to Master, he'd've had t' get a Second like Kash t' handle that."

"So, unbalanced as we know he was, the ill-wishing took him right over the edge?" Boitan breathed. "And with Zetren, there's only one direction that would lead. . . ."

"Got it," Felaras replied, catching herself again and forcing herself aware. "Good 'sassination try. Couldn't know Kash's been playin' shadow since we felt ill-wishing start."

"But why the subterfuge?" Boitan asked.

"Rule one of the Watchers," Zorsha said. "Keep the enemy confused. As long as we stick to this story, he'll never know how close he came to his goal. That might drive him out of cover, where we can do something about him. But damn if I like the idea of there being a traitor in our ranks."

"Wait a minute—how do you know—"

"What else could it be?" Zorsha said simply. "Who else would have known to target Zetren? Who else would have known of the long-standing grudge he held? To outsiders we've been very careful to present a united front."

" 'Xactly," Felaras said. "Kash I trust. Zorsh too. Nothin' for either of them t'gain. Ardun's fine, an' you, Boitan. Same logic. Could be *anyone* else. So . . . keep 'em confused an' see what . . . crawls . . . out."

She yawned, and fought her eyes open again, to see Boitan looking stern.

"Everybody out," he said. "Zorsha, you stay with the boy, and that will put you within shouting distance if there is trouble tonight. Kasha, you set up in the anteroom. There won't be anybody climbing in the window, not unless they're half-spider. And *you*—"

He glared at Felaras. She tried to glare back, without success. "Stop fighting the drug and get some rest!"

"But . . . I . . ." she protested, and then made the fatal error of relaxing just a little. She slid into sleep, fighting it every inch of the way.

✧ CHAPTER ELEVEN ✧

Darkness came early to the Pass, and to the little valley the Vredai occupied below it. Although the sky to the west was still bright red, the valley was dark enough that Halun occasionally stumbled over rocks and animal-dug hummocks in the grass. He had been sorry to give up holding his meetings with the others within the camp itself, but after the defection of those young hotheads it had just become too much of a risk. The little cul-de-sac side canyon that Iridai had found was a perfect meeting place; no one could overhear or overlook them, and with one man standing guard at the entrance, no one could get near enough to the meeting to even see who was taking part in it.

Gortan and Iridai had learned from the mistakes of the youngsters; the guard they'd posted didn't look like he was guarding anything at all. He was sitting on a horse-blanket under the stone outcropping that half hid the entrance. He had a torch beside him, and was playing a solitaire game of stones by the light of it. As Halun passed him, he looked up, grunted once, and went back to his game. And if Halun had not been someone known to him, there would have been no strongarm techniques—just a friendly skin of *khmass* and an invitation to make up a two-game. And since "stones" was a fairly boring game, it was unlikely that the intruder would stop for more than a drink or two.

There were dozens of folks scattered up and down the length of the valley this warm summer night. Some had minor hand-tasks that still needed work, and some weren't yet ready to sleep, and it was too hot to stay in the tents with any kind of flame going. Others were doing things that required a little more privacy than the closely crowded tents allowed, especially with their sides up. This guard wasn't doing anything out of the ordinary, to be out here alone.

The gathering itself had only a single source of light: a pocket-sized fire in the middle of the circle of nomads. As Halun approached, the dark faces looked up sharply, eyes flashing with reflected firelight. Then, silently, they made a place for him in the circle. He tossed the cushion he'd been carrying under one arm into the vacated spot, and eased himself down onto it, ignoring the stares. At least there didn't seem to be any derision there; while no else had brought a cushion to sit on, his age and silver hair were at least giving him a reason to do so himself.

Silence then, until the last of the group—Iridai—arrived. Halun found the silence somewhat unnerving. Crickets singing with all their might out in the grass beyond the firelight only punctuated the silence; they did not break it. Nor did the crackle of the fire. There was a tension tonight that there had not been during previous meetings. Halun fidgeted inside, but gave no outward sign of his restlessness. If they wanted to play this kind of stone-faced game, he would play it too, and outplay all of them.

Finally Iridai arrived, and dropped down into his place in the circle.

Gortan cleared his throat. "We are ready," he said simply.

Halun inhaled sharply, and got a lungful of resinous smoke; he suppressed his need to cough with an effort that left him struggling to breathe for a few moments.

"We, too, are ready," Iridai replied. "The tide of condemnation of the rebels has turned, and now folk wonder openly why Jegrai had them slain out of hand. There is restlessness among the young warriors, those who have not gone courting Vale-folk women, and they wonder how one can achieve wealth, fame, and prowess when one cannot raid nor fight. The games and hunting begin to be not enough. My chosen ones are ready to lead them into opposing Jegrai and setting up a new Khene."

Gortan nodded, and all eyes turned to Halun. He felt them more than saw them, like the pressure of a warm breeze on his skin.

"We need to manufacture an incident," he said, laying out before them the plan he had made. "We need Jegrai to make some kind of very obvious mistake—yes, and Felaras, too."

Gortan nodded. "And then we use those mistakes to rouse anger?"

"Exactly. I had one such incident in the brewing, but I lost the man to a fall the night of the storm."

"That would be the man Zetren? The one who fell from the wall?" Iridai asked shrewdly, evidently hoping to impress Halun with his intelligence network.

Halun was not impressed, mostly because half of the Vredai spying on the Fortress were Halun's already, and the rest soon would be. "Exactly. I don't know what he was doing out there in the middle of a storm, but it appears to have been a genuine accident."

"Are you certain, wise one?" Gortan asked dubiously, leaning forward a little.

"Reasonably certain. Felaras has nothing at all to gain by hiding the fact if he did make a failed attempt on her—Zetren was not well liked, and she would likely get a great deal of sympathy from it." Halun wasn't near as certain as he sounded, but he had to give these barbarians some assurances. "As I am certain you have learned, Felaras actually slipped and fell at the beginning of the storm—she was evidently in her bed and drugged against the pain of her injury when Zetren went out on the walls. I cannot see how she could have had anything to do with his death."

He shrugged then, dismissing the whole thing. "The man was half-crazed, and was quite devoted to the defense of the Order. My guess would be that he decided some of you were likely to try something under cover of the storm, and climbed up to watch for attackers. That section of the wall does face on the area from which an attack could be expected."

Gortan nodded his acceptance of the story. "Well then—how do we 'manufacture' this incident?"

"There are among you a handful who have been passed over when the Shaman, Northwind, made his selection of those he would train." Halun looked at the swarthy faces in the flickering firelight, and noted the expressions of discontent on several of them. "I have tested you, and found those of you with wizard-power. I have been instructing you in its use. Now we will use it; all together, and together we will be a force truly to be reckoned with. Half of us will concentrate on Felaras, and half on Jegrai. I have no doubt that we will meet with success."

Gortan nodded, his expression one of smug self-satisfaction. "And we will be waiting for the mistake that must come?"

"Indeed," Halun replied, "We will be waiting."

The Pass was cooler than the valley—and Felaras could just barely hobble from her bed to her study, anyway. So Northwind and Jegrai were up here tonight, with detailed maps spread on the desk top, and herself and Ardun standing for the Order on her side of the desk.

She would have preferred Zorsha, but the lad was in the throes of creation—and with this particular creation, she'd as soon have him finished with it in the shortest possible time. It was something of a symbol to him; a symbol of his promise to Yuchai. Nothing was going to keep him from working on those canisters of that vile fire-stuff until the project was complete and ready to turn over to the munitions specialists for manufacture. He said he was on the verge of finding the way to seal the stuff in without setting it afire in the process, or making the canister so fragile it would break open in the act of being fired. If he was close to a breakthrough, best to let him be. Best to have that stuff out of the Fortress workrooms and back into the munitions sheds. As it was, he wasn't using his own workroom, or even one of the bigger, common workrooms. He had taken over an older workroom, the lower floor of part of the oldest part of the Fortress; one of the original stone towers in the north corner of the wall, small and cramped and drafty, and not much used by anyone for anything but storage these days. But Zorsha had not liked the notion of working with the fire where anyone else might be endangered, and Felaras had agreed with him. So the rubbish that had been put away there had been cleaned out, and Zorsha had moved his own instruments and tools in.

"So, you think the Talchai will come in through this way?" Ardun said, interrupting Felaras's thoughts. He traced a line on the map with his index finger, a line that did not follow the course of any of the roads across Azgun, but rather moved along the line of a fairly prominent ridge.

Kasha made a little movement and caught Felaras's eye. She made a subtle hand-sign: *Somebody's ill-wishing again.*

Felaras lowered her barriers. *Strong. Damn. And this is not time for us to be distracted. Not only that, but we daren't take the time to do a proper deflection and send it back into their laps.*

She caught the Shaman's eye and repeated the sign Kasha had made. He tightened his mouth, closed his eyes for a moment, then opened them and gave a little nod in Jegrai's direction.

Wonderful. They're targeting the Khene, too.

She clasped her hands together; the Shaman considered, then nodded. In a heartbeat she could feel his shield meshing with hers—and his had the "feel" of more than one person.

Of course; he has Demonsbane, and whatever other shamans-in-training there are down at the camp, and probably all the Healer-women too—

Together they tightened a dome of protection over the Khene and Felaras herself that not even a sending that strong could breach. It would only bounce—and gods help whomever it hit.

Jegrai nodded, oblivious to the magic going on over his head. "I tell you my reasoning: first, there are many towns along this way, not too large, not too small, suitable for raiding. Like us, they will take what they need from those along their path. Second, they will be uncomfortable with the hills towering above them; we had some time to grow used to this, but Sen will be pushing them, they will be an army rather than a Clan with children, the old, and the ill to slow them, so they likely will not learn to ignore the hills about them. So they will move to the highest point in the land, not thinking that this will make them very visible. Being visible has never been a factor in our kind of battle; on the steppes one can see for many days' travel in all directions—one can see the approaching army long before it reaches one."

Ardun considered the route. "You know, if we wanted to move into Azgun, we could ambush them at dozens of places along their path, and weaken them considerably at very little cost to ourselves."

Felaras shook her head. "No good; our diplomatic relationship with the lords has never been all that healthy, and bringing an army of our own will only make it worse. Especially an army of yet more nomads. No, much as I'd like to, sending in ambushers is out of the question. Now, working on their *minds*—that's something else altogether."

Northwind looked up at her, his sharp eyes catching hers across the map. "How so, their minds?"

"Oh, well, an elaboration of the 'great wizards' show we put on for you," she said wishing her knee wasn't aching so persistently. "Consider: you people don't fight at night, correct?"

"Correct," Jegrai replied, plainly wondering what she was getting at. They didn't fight at night because fighting on horseback when the horses couldn't see was worse than stupid, it was courting suicide.

But fighting wasn't what she had in mind. "So, figure the Talchai are all bedded down for the night—not asleep yet, but settled in. Suddenly the skies fill with thunder and fire, and weirdly colored lightning, and when it passes, their attention is directed to the ridge beneath where the lightnings were. Because up on the ridge directly above the camp there's a flash of light. When they can see again, there are half-a-dozen Vredai riders with the Running Horse banner—and they're all *glowing*. What would they think?"

"That ghosts had come to haunt them," Northwind replied positively.

"Then the skies open up again, and there's another flash of light, and the riders are gone. Say this gets repeated, at irregular intervals." She grinned. "Like overcast nights, or nights with no moon, but I'd bet they don't make the connection."

"Sen would probably be able to convince them that these were demons, which would make them certain that they were in the right, but that would not keep them from being terrified," Northwind observed shrewdly. "We have too many tales where the demons are the ones who win. You can do all this?"

She shrugged. *I need to take a pain-potion, and I need to stay awake. Gods, what a choice. Guess I'll stay awake.* "It's fairly easy, actually. We already have the fireworks, we use them at festivals. The phosphor is easy enough to get. Slimy stuff, but glows very nicely after dark. Getting the riders in place without being seen is not any kind of a problem—cover them with blankets and move them in while the sky is lighting up, reverse the process when you're ready. We could even supply some fairly weird noises, but I personally think that silence would be more effective."

Jegrai grinned ferally. "This will destroy their will," he said positively, "and Sen will be able to do nothing. So; where do we actually meet them?"

"Well, now, that depends on you, Khene," Felaras said slowly.

"It depends on whether or not you want them to have the option of escape."

"How so?"

Felaras looked over to Ardun, who cleared his throat to get their attention. "Well, we can meet them either on the other side of the river, or just below the Teeth. If we hold them on the Azgun side, there's a good chance that once we get Sen—that is the plan, isn't it? Take out their Khene?"

"Yes," Jegrai replied. "Without him they will have no will to fight."

"All right, then; once we do that, they'll likely turn tail and run rather than surrender. After what they did to you folks, they aren't going to be expecting any kind of mercy out of you. But if we hold them at the Teeth, the river will be behind them and they won't have that option."

"Which means that they will fight like any cornered thing," Northwind observed. "This could be very bad for us, for we could sustain many losses. Yet—"

"Yet there is no small number of you who feel like Yuchai," Ardun replied dryly. "You want them destroyed, root and branch."

"Jegrai, I'm going to ask you to do something that would be hard even for one of my people, trained as they are in logical thinking," Felaras said wearily. "Certainly it's beyond Zorsha at the moment, and you and he are of an age—but I think you can do this. Look at the situation logically, and analyze it. Think of it as a problem in tactics, and not as if your heart were involved in it."

Jegrai did not look happy—but he did look thoughtful, which was a good sign.

"What is it you really want to do here?" Ardun asked. "Define your goals. Do you just want Vredai safe? Do you want Vredai safe and Talchai so demoralized they'll be out of the politics of the steppes for your lifetime? Do you want that, *and* to follow up on the gap they're going to leave behind? Or do you have another goal altogether?"

"If I were to have all my wishes?" Jegrai asked, face puzzled, and a little confused.

"Exactly; Khene Jegrai, assume that you know that the Wind Lords themselves have just luck-wished you. What do you plan to do with all that good fortune?"

He studied the map; if gazes had held power, he'd have burned holes in the paper.

"It is not the Talchai," he said slowly, each word falling like a stone into the silence. "It is not even Sen who is the root of our troubles. It is the Suno. They began it. Until they meddled, it was a rare thing for one of the people to spill so much as a drop of a brother's blood."

Northwind nodded, but said nothing.

"If Sen were gone—if we were to let loose upon the warriors your fire-throwers, or even that terrible Sabirn-fire of which you have spoken, the Talchai would run, if they could. If they ran, they would carry back to the steppes the word that Vredai has the powers of gods—or demons, it truly does not matter which. They would hide themselves, lick their wounds, I think—and I hope reflect on how none of this would have occurred had they not given ear to their Khene and his dishonorable plans to war against the helpless."

"Fine, to a point," Northwind said. "And Vredai is then safe. But there are those who would miss their half-breed warhound, eh?"

"The Suno." Jegrai took his eyes off the map and looked over at his advisor. "Which means—" He paused, and shook his head. "I do not know what it means. I cannot say what they will do."

"I can think of things they might," Northwind said, leaning his weight on his arms so that the desk creaked a little. "They might look to the Clans for another half-breed wardog, or even breed another themselves. They might try to simply corrupt another Khene. Certainly they will *not* act upon this themselves, sending an army out to find Vredai. But that does not mean they will leave the Clans in peace. They will do no such thing. We are too much of a threat to them."

"All wishes granted, Jegrai," Felaras prompted. "Think in the long term."

"I should like—to unite the Clans, as Sen tried," he said, eyes shining as he looked into his own dreams and picked out the best of what lay there. "But in honor, under true alliance and pledges to be trusted. And allowing those who would not come to go their own path. Then—I should like to take this war the Suno began upon us back to their own hearth."

"I think you've just answered the question about where we

meet them," Ardun said, standing up with a sigh and stretching his back. They could all hear his back pop, so quiet was the study.

"Huh. Indeed. On the other side of the river, and let as many escape as we may, once Sen is no more." Jegrai looked across to Felaras, doubt shadowing his face. "Can we do this, Master? Even your folk and mine together?"

"We can try," she shrugged. "It's no more foolish a plan that Khene Sen's, and one with a great deal more concern for the well-being of everyone involved. My only question is, can you persuade your people to the first step?"

"Letting the Talchai go? I think so," he replied. "I must point out to them that to serve them as they served us is no less without honor—and to send them back with their tails tucked in will show every Clan on the steppes that Vredai will not be trifled with." He quirked one corner of his mouth in a half-smile. "Between maintaining honor, and being able to send the Talchai running in fear, I think I can persuade them to the task."

Felaras was considering what to say next, when the room shook with a roar that was not thunder.

"What in—" Ardun shouted, startled.

Felaras knew there was only thing that could be—and given the ill-wishing going on and how close he was to *her*—

"Gods!" She threw her cane aside and ran, limping, for the door, urgency overriding pain. "Oh, *gods! Zorsha!*"

The calm of the warm night splintered.

Halun had just reached the side of his tent when the roar of the explosion at the top of the mountain destroyed the peace of the night. He jumped a foot, and grabbed a rope tent-support for balance as his eyes went immediately to the crack between the peaks where the invisible Fortress sat beside the road through the Pass. A tower of yellow-gold flame rose from there, reaching upward like a demon's arm in the silence that followed the explosion for one breath—two—

Then it collapsed back down, leaving only an ugly red blotch reflecting against the rocks of the peak above the Fortress to show that the fire still burned.

Halun's heart lurched into his throat and stayed there, and he clutched the tent-rope so hard it cut into his palm.

Gods—did I do—oh, gods, I must have!

He turned and ran back the way he had come, only thinking *I have to get back up there!* He reached the stabling area and stumbled for the picketed line of horses, arriving in time to see Teo and Mai tearing off up the road to the Pass on their own beasts. One of the Vredai—*Thank the gods*—had already anticipated him; incredible as it seemed, his horse was saddled and bridled and waiting with a young herder-girl holding the reins. He scrambled into the saddle somehow—she handed him the reins—and then he, too, spurred off into the smoke-tainted dark, following the others.

"Not *water*, you fools," Felaras shouted at the top of her lungs, limping toward the scene of the disaster. "*Sand!* That's Sabirn-fire!"

The fire crews were black blots against the red and yellow of the flames; unidentifiable. Those carrying buckets of water literally dropped them. Someone, bless his or her quick mind, ran like a thin shadow up to where the sand barrels were kept on the top of the wall against siege fires, and began rolling them right off the edge of the walkway to crash and break open at the feet of the fire-fighters. The fire crew stooped and scrambled after their dropped containers; the empty buckets were refilled with sand, and the fire-fighting continued with scarcely a pause.

Felaras clutched at Jegrai's shoulder, scarcely aware that she was doing so, and moaned. The little tower was wrecked; reduced to a heap of tumbled stones. The fire-fighters were getting the pockets of flame under control but—somewhere under that pile of rubble was Zorsha.

Or what—oh, gods—is left of him.

"Zorsha!" screamed a young voice behind them, and Yuchai darted out of the door in the wall and past them, heading straight for the wreckage.

Jegrai slid out from under Felaras's hand and sprinted like a champion foot-racer, reaching the boy before he even got close to the carnage, and tackling him.

They went down in a tangled heap of long limbs on the packed dirt of the courtyard; Yuchai tried to squirm away, but Jegrai kept a tight hold on him, shouting at him in their own tongue. All at once the boy capitulated, collapsing in Jegrai's arms and breaking into terrified sobbing.

The Khene got slowly to his feet and drew the boy up after him, holding him closely, then leading him back past Felaras.

"We can do nothing," he said as he passed her. "I will get the boy back to his bed; we will wait for word."

She nodded absently; the fire crew was doing a good job of smothering the blaze and even the thick smoke was being dispersed. Now most of the light in the back courtyard was coming from the torches and lanterns, not the fire itself.

Kasha came to take Jegrai's place as her support; her body was rigid beneath Felaras's hand, and she trembled. For that matter, Felaras herself was shaking from head to toe.

Oh gods, we should have thought of Zorsha—we should have thought and brought him under the protection too. But I was sure I'd taught him enough to deflect properly—and surely he realized that he'd have to keep a shield up when working with the fire!

Ardun strode past to take charge of the rescue crew—who were mostly Watchers, anyway. "Get those damned stones moved!" he was shouting. "No not those, *those!* No, no, you fool! Don't touch that support, you'll just start another fall of stone! Get the blocks *off* it first!"

There was nothing they could do but stand and watch—and hope.

Two horses galloped into the back court, followed by a third. The very first rider was Teo, easily identifiable because of his size; he flung himself out of the saddle, peeled off his tunic, and threw himself into the work crew all in one movement. His powerful young body made an immediate difference; he was able to get into places only big enough for a single man, and lift things from there that only a couple of the others would have been able to tackle. Tiny Mai was the second rider, had to be. The asexual shadow leapt from the horse and went straight to the bucket crew, taking the place of someone larger who was thus freed to join the rescuers.

Halun was the third rider, pulling his horse up beside Felaras and sliding off untidily.

"Who—" he panted.

"Zorsha," Felaras choked out. "He—he was working with Sabirn-fire."

Halun moaned and made as if to join one of the two crews. Kasha caught his sleeve and held him back.

"Not you, old man," she said in a dead, calm voice. "You're too old and out of shape. You'll only get in the way, or get yourself hurt."

As if to underscore her statement, Teo uncovered a pocket of the smoldering fire, which blazed up in his face. He jumped back in time to avoid more than a touch of the flames, and stood out of the way while a fire crew dealt with it.

When the flames were out he went right back in before the blocks of stone even had a chance to cool.

Boitan joined them, his arms and Shenshu's laden with supplies. "Is it only Zorsha?" he asked quietly.

"So far as I know," Felaras replied around her fear, ignoring Halun's groan. "He wouldn't let anyone else work with him; said it was too dangerous."

"What was he doing in there?" Halun demanded wildly; Felaras glanced over and saw that his face was contorted with fear, grief, and something she couldn't properly identify. "Felaras, what in hell did you set him to? What insanity possessed you to put him on Sabirn-fire?"

"Set him to?" Kasha choked. "Great good gods, Halun, she couldn't have stopped him if she'd tried! *You've* been living down there with those folk, haven't you even heard *one* story about what happened to them when the Talchai took their camp?"

Halun shook his head dumbly.

Kasha stared at him in profoundest amazement. "Zorsha got it all in the face from young Yuchai—and since then, all he's been interested in is a way to decimate the Talchai as badly as they did Jegrai's folk. That's why the Sabirn-fire, he was trying to work out a way to seal it into mortar-canisters—"

She was interrupted by a hoarse shout from Teo. "Here! I found him! He's under here!"

They surged forward in a body. Of them all, only Felaras had seen victims of Sabirn-fire; that had been long, long ago, when she was a bare novice.

She was dreading what Teo was likely to uncover.

Teo tore huge blocks from the pile by himself, flinging them to the side with frenzied strength. His face was contorted, and tears made runnels through the crust of ashes on his cheeks; his chest was smeared with ash and shining with sweat, and he looked like something out of the lowest hells.

In moments he had the little coffin-shaped area in which Zorsha was lying cleared of rubble. Felaras only got the barest glimpse of something dark and twisted—and it was moaning.

"*Move*, dammit!" Boitan snarled, shoving his way between the rescuers; Shenshu and Kasha behind him, carrying a board from the wreckage. "Here—gently—roll him over onto this—"

The moans spiraled up into harsh screams, and Felaras looked away. Into Halun's eyes. And she recognized what she saw there.

Guilt. Terrible, soul-searing guilt. But why?

She had no time to wonder about that, for the rescuers had gotten Zorsha out of the tumble of stone and down onto the courtyard, laying him practically at her feet. She went to her knees beside him, as someone brought Boitan a lantern in response to a snarled demand for light.

It was as bad as she'd feared.

He'd taken the raw fire-blast right in his face; his eyes were—gone. Just a charred swath where they had been. From head to waist, he looked like nothing so much as badly charred meat; his tunic had burned right away, and bits of it flaked off every time he moved. His hands didn't bear thinking about. There was bone showing.

She looked at Boitan, who caught her eye, and shook his head slowly.

Oh, gods—Her throat closed; she couldn't breathe. All she wanted to do was howl in agony.

A harsh whisper caught her attention, forced her to look back down at the thing at her feet that had been the handsomest lad in the Order.

"—aras—" the lips whispered again.

"I'm here," she said, leaning down, but not touching him. "I'm here, lad. So's Halun."

"—alun? Ah—" What was left of his face spasmed in pain, as Halun joined her, kneeling beside her, looking as if he wanted to gather the boy to his breast.

The mouth moved again. Gasping half-words through pain that must have been unbearable. "—alun.—elp—elaras. Got to. Help—elaras. Boy. Jegrai.—redai. Swear!" The charred travesties of hands pawed at the front of Halun's tunic. "Swear! Swear!"

Halun was sobbing as Felaras had never seen him weep in her life. "I promise. Oh, gods, Zorsha, I swear it, I swear—"

The lips almost seemed to smile. "I—love—you—all," he said, clearly, and carefully. Then, just as clearly, but cracking with anguish, "Help—me—go."

Boitan caught her eyes again; his face was wet, but the hands holding the long, thin mercy-blade were steady.

She looked briefly down—and as if he had sensed her eyes on him, Zorsha whispered. One word. "Please."

She choked, and nodded. Boitan moved so quickly she almost didn't see it happen. Zorsha surely was in such pain he never felt the keen-edged blade slip between his ribs and find his heart.

He just sighed once—then—he was gone.

Halun flung himself across the body and broke into hysterical, punishing sobs of grief.

Felaras unashamedly did the same.

The potion Boitan had given her had numbed her physical pain, and had put some distance between her and her sorrow. But the grief was still there, a constant that filled her throat with tears and would not let her sleep. She gave up tossing on her bed after too many hours of staring at the ceiling, and lit a candle to stare at instead.

Now the candle was guttering out, and birds were hailing the dawn just outside the window. And the air still stank of ashes and burning.

Kasha and Teo . . . gods. She watched out her window at the bloody sunrise, not really seeing it. Boitan had kept pouring drugs into them until he'd knocked them out. They'd been out of their young minds with grief. Kasha had gone catatonic, and Teo had begun tearing out his own hair in clumps.

She wasn't sure which had been worse; Kasha's dead eyes, or Teo's near-madness.

Boitan said it was hysteria; that they'd be mourning more normally when they woke up. She damned well hoped so; she'd only lost one damned fine lad and her successor and . . . someone who had begun to be a treasured friend. *They'd* lost a third of themselves.

She remembered only too well how that felt.

She'd dreaded telling Yuchai, but Jegrai had broken the news to the boy—with a gentle lie. So far as Yuchai was concerned, Zorsha had been working on something for Felaras, not the

Sabirn-fire. The child had enough to bear without that on his conscience.

The candle gave a last flare, and went out.

She wasn't sure what had happened to Halun; things had been very confused after Boitan had peeled her off the body.

The thought could have been a summons; someone tapped briefly at her door, and then opened it and slipped inside like a ghost.

Halun. He *looked* like a ghost.

"I thought you'd still be awake," he croaked, voice ruined from weeping. He'd cleaned himself up, but there were black circles all around his bloodshot eyes, and he was as pale as bleached parchment. "Felaras, I have to talk to you."

She pulled herself up into a sitting position and waved at the bedside chair, wearily. "So talk."

He did not take the offered seat, although he moved closer to the bed. "It was my fault—" he began.

She cut him off, angrily. "Dammit, Halun, do I have to hear that from *you*, too? I've heard it from everybody else—"

He interrupted. "Felaras, you don't understand!" he cried tightly, his face twisted with grief. "I caused what happened! I was the one ill-wishing you."

Not what she had expected to hear. She froze, her backbone turned to a column of ice. It took her a moment to recover enough to gasp out an answer. "*You?* But . . . why?"

"Ambition," he said, angrily, brokenly. "Stupid, selfish ambition. You had the chair. I wanted it. I convinced myself I only wanted it for the good of the Order, but I lied to myself, I wanted it because I wanted the power. I corrupted myself and persuaded myself I was doing the right thing—I was trying to undermine you at first, and then you and Jegrai. I was trying to get you to make the mistakes that would let us depose you both." He paused for breath, and twisted his hands together so hard the knuckles cracked. "You were protected; so I trained some with the power, and went after you tonight in concert with them. Only I added a little codicil. You probably don't understand—"

"Only too well, you bastard," she snarled. "I was the one protecting myself."

He goggled at her a moment. "I—I—" He got control of himself just enough to take up where he'd left off. "I set the wish so that if you were shielded and it bounced off you, it wouldn't go randomly—I set it to strike whoever was the one nearest you—"

"You damned fool!" She surged up out of bed and seized him by the throat. Her abused knee shot fire up her leg, pain that she ignored. "You gods-bedamned fool! What have you been doing down there? Sleeping? I just made Zorsha my official successor! Who in the hell *else* would it take?"

Halun paled down to near-transparent and shut his eyes, not struggling in her hands at all. "I didn't know . . ." he whispered. "I've been so busy with all those stupid little plots that I didn't know . . . I thought it would get Kasha, Teo—"

"I ought to break your damned neck with my own two hands!"

He opened his eyes again and looked directly into hers. His eyes were full of such pain that they nearly burned her soul. There was hell in those eyes, and self-condemnation that was worse than anything she could do to him. "I wish you would," he whispered miserably. "He was—my son in everything but the flesh."

She looked at her hands, clenched white-knuckled in the fabric of his robe, and back up into his face. It hadn't changed.

She shoved him away with such force that he staggered and came close to falling over backward. "What the hell am I going to do with you?" she asked, sagging back onto her bed, sick to the bones, and weary past all belief.

"I don't know," he replied, in profound desolation. "Just . . . I gave him my word to help you. Tell me how, and I will."

She considered him for a moment, as he stood there, waiting. *For what? Gods. Help me, he says. How in—*

Then she knew, and rang the bell beside her bed for a novice. "Is there anyone else in the Order working with you?" she asked harshly, as she waited for the youngster to put in an appearance.

He shook his head. "No. Not even Zetren. All my co-conspirators are down in the valley."

The novice arrived, slipping in the still-open door; a thin, dark girl-child of about fourteen. Memory put name to her; Daisa, another of Ardun's endless brood of daughters, and older than she looked, about to get full Sword status. Another Kasha-in-the-making, for which she was grateful. *It'll be a long time before I can see a blond lad without crying. . . .*

"Get me Thaydore and Kitri," she said, "And Boitan, if he's still awake."

The child vanished. "Get me pen and paper out of that drawer over there," she said, pointing to the little writing-desk in the corner of her room.

Halun did so, as docile to her orders as the novice. She pulled the lap desk out from under the bed and set it up.

Then she glared at him; still in a rage, but no longer a white-hot one—and a rage that was fast being cooled by his very real guilt and sorrow.

"Sit down," she ordered. "You're going to be here a while."

He took the chair, obediently.

"Now," she said, pen poised. "Let's have all this from the beginning."

✧ CHAPTER TWELVE ✧

Halun lit his lamp and hung it from the centerpole of his tent, and wished with all his heart that this farce was over.

The Khene's brother had come to Halun's tent as soon as he had returned from the Fortress; more than a week after he'd gone pounding wildly back up the road. Iridai brought word that the meeting they'd scheduled before all this happened was assembled and waiting for him.

Gods be thanked, this will be the last.

Behind him, Iridai put one hand lightly on Halun's shoulder. "I . . . my condolences, wise one," he said, awkward now that the message had been delivered. "I understand that the young man was once your pupil."

Halun shuddered, but did not remove the man's hand. *I have to act the same; thank the gods they all think it's just that I'm mourning Zorsha.* "Thank you," he said, stumbling over the simple words. *These men are acting out of belief that Jegrai is wrong. I acted out of lust for power. They aren't barbarians. I'm the savage.* "Yes, he was—something more than just a pupil, in fact, he was an orphan when he came to us. I was something of a father to him. . . ."

He let his voice trail off, and felt the muscles of his throat tensing with the effort of holding back tears.

Not that tears would matter to these people—they would understand and give him room to weep. Except for Gortan, who was like a block of stone, they were mostly as open about expressing sorrow as they were about expressing joy. *Oh, Zorsha, I needed to be brought to my senses—but I would that I could have paid a less dear coin than your life.*

He still looked like something dragged through hell, and he knew it; too many sleepless nights, no few of them spent contemplating the amazing number of poisons in his workroom. But suicide would not have served to fulfill his promise to Zorsha. And he had a great deal to make up for.

Felaras had been amazingly decent about the whole thing; she could, so easily, have made every word, every hour painful for him, and yet she had done no such thing.

Not that she hadn't been tempted; she'd told him that herself, with that disconcerting frankness of hers, the day they'd buried the boy. But she'd also told him, "There's been too damned much pain already and damned if I'm going to add to it!"

A remarkable woman. And he'd been blinded to how remarkable she was by his own ambition. Now it was too late; too late for anything except a tentative alliance. Never a friendship. And never anything deeper.

What a fool I've been.

If it hadn't been for the boy . . .

For he'd finally met young Yuchai, who until then had been nothing more than a name and a huddled form under a blanket.

He'd been waiting outside Felaras's door for her summons, when he'd heard a strangled sob from the Master's Folly. Thinking it might be Kasha or Teo, he'd looked in, figuring on finding out which it was and fetching the other. Mourning alone was a lot harder than mourning with someone—as he now knew only too well. And he couldn't think who else would have been quartered next to Felaras besides those two.

But it hadn't been either of them; it had been a young boy, crying painfully into the fur of a pale-gold dog—

A golden gaze-hound like the one Zorsha had owned as a novice . . .

Perhaps it was the sight of the dog that drew him, but without knowing why, he found himself standing by the boy's side. The boy had raised his tear-streaked face, and he'd seen the shape, the bone structure of it, so like Jegrai's; and knew then who it was, and why he wept. So he'd held out his hand. "I'm Halun," he'd said, swallowing down a lump in his throat. "I was his friend too—"

And before he could blink, he had his arms full of crying child, and then Halun found himself weeping with him, and somehow when they both got under control again, they were friends.

He'd picked up Yuchai's education where Zorsha had left off, more out of a sense of duty than any real expectations. That was when he had discovered how absolutely brilliant the boy was, and duty became pleasure—the lone pleasure in all those bleak days.

Gods willing, by tonight this whole messy business will be dealt with, and I can go back to that pleasure. Zorsha, I pledge you, that boy will have everything you'd have given him!

He looked at Iridai out of the corner of his eye, and wondered how that stolid warrior was going to take the shattering of his plans and his own disgrace before the entire Clan.

No bloodshed, Jegrai had said. *There's been enough blood shed already.* Felaras had agreed with him. Halun hoped this would work as well as they thought it would. . . .

"Where are we meeting?" Halun asked dully, half-turning, and watching the lamp flame over Iridai's shoulder instead of the man's face.

"Gortan's tent. It seems safe enough. If friends do *not* gather from time to time at the tents, it begins to look odd. And besides, Jegrai is up at the Wizard's Place."

Halun reached for the lamp again; he should have been feeling anticipation, but he felt nothing but weariness. "Now?"

Iridai nodded, and Halun put out the lamp, then ducked out the tent entrance, following him into the night. He glanced up at the sky; it was not overcast, but it was moonless.

It was going to be a perfect evening for Felaras's plan.

He followed along behind Iridai, stumbling now and again over a rock in the path. *Soon. It will all be over soon.*

His soundless litany might have been a conjuration: no sooner had they cleared all but the last circle of tents, where Gortan's tent had been pitched, than the sky above them opened up with an incredible display of—

Fireworks. Festival fireworks. But to the Vredai, it surely seemed like a visitation from the gods.

Every color possible bloomed up there, it seemed, accompanied by thunderous explosions that were close enough to hurt the ears. Not surprisingly, every person in the camp was out of his tent and gaping up at the sky within heartbeats—

some with stark fear on their faces, some with less readable emotions, and the children with mingled surprise and innocent delight.

The guards at the entrance to the valley ran back to the tents, weapons at the ready, although from the despair on their faces Halun reckoned they'd already counted on those weapons as being impotent.

The stage was set.

The last of the fireworks bloomed and died, a spectacular burst of clusters of red that told Halun to ready himself.

There was a heartbeat of silence, then—

Horns blared from somewhere above them; horns like nothing the Vredai had ever heard, deep and menacing and incredibly loud. Not surprising; these were horns that had been sent to the Order by a wandering Seeker long ago, sent from some mountainous region to the north. They were as tall as a man, and used to warn of (or perhaps trigger, he'd said) avalanches of snow. Two of the most agile Watchers in the Fortress had scaled with ropes and crampons down the mountainside just after dusk with these things strapped to their backs, to set themselves up on the supposedly unclimbable cliffs above the valley.

There was a flash of fire and sulfurous smoke at the valley entrance—and a glowing figure rode through the smoke cloud, seeming to come *out* of the smoke cloud.

It was Felaras, but a transformed Felaras. The Vredai for the most part had never seen Felaras; those who had had certainly never seen her like this, with her hair streaming free beneath an ancient, dragon-crested Ancas helm, and her body encased from head to toe in burnished chain and plate. What was more, she burned with a bluish light of her own, as did the pale horse she rode—and the horse's hooves made no noise at all on the hard ground. It seemed to flow toward them, a ghost-horse ridden by a stern and angry spirit.

The Vredai behind Halun moaned with fear; Halun heard one or two mutters of "Wind-rider!" and "Lord's Messenger!"—and Iridai sank to his knees.

"Vredai, who were betrayed, you harbor traitors among you," Felaras boomed, using the voice that could be heard from one end of a noisy practice ground to another. And she wasn't speaking Trade-tongue, either; this speech had been carefully written out for her by Teo, transcribing Northwind's words into Ancas phonemes. "Treason is a disease; the Talchai touched you, and you are infected, you are sick with it. The Wind Lords brought you here to safe haven, but you brought a blight with you, in your hearts."

The Vredai muttered, the groaning of branches in the wind. Halun stifled a cough as a gust of wind carried spent smoke into his face. It burned on his tongue for a moment.

"And your sickness has its counterpart on the Wizards' Mountain," she continued, face as masklike as marble. "Vredai, will you hear the names of your traitors and deal with them?"

Far sooner than Halun would have expected, he heard a woman behind him shout "Aye!" Then there was a chorus of shouts of affirmation until Felaras raised her hand, and a heavy, anticipatory silence fell.

"Clan singer Gortan," she began, each word having a sound of doom about it. "Iridai kan Luchen . . ."

She told off the entire roll of the conspirators, from the greatest to least, all names Halun had given them. Beside him, Iridai trembled and moaned. At the end of the list the hidden horns brayed again.

Felaras waited a moment while the list of names sunk in. "These would have betrayed your Khene, who brought you to this place under the guidance of the Wind Lords," she said, "even as he and you were betrayed by the Talchai. Now I ask you, in the name of the compassionate Wind Lords: what will you do with them, these traitors to Jegrai and to your safety?"

From the angry shouts behind them, executing the traitors seemed to be one of the more popular notions. Once again, Felaras raised her hand to gain utter silence.

"Has there not been enough Vredai blood shed?" she asked, in a much quieter voice. "Treason is a sickness; it can be cured. Treason is a rot; rot can be mended. Take these men to you, people of Vredai. Watch them, but forgive them. To deal them death earns you nothing but more pain. Shed no blood of the Clans that you cannot avoid, people of Vredai. Rather, turn the fires of your anger upon the authors of the root treason. The spreaders of the sickness. The Suno. Consider how you should deal with them—and know that *they* merit none of your compassion."

Iridai was huddled in a knot on the ground, sobbing.

Felaras's voice strengthened again. "And there is another among you who is not of your blood, who merits none of your compassion, who fostered treason as a way to his own power and not because he felt that the Khene was faulty in judgment. Halun, Hand of the Seekers, of the chapter of the Tower, stand forth!"

Halun stepped forward until he was just within twenty paces of Felaras. He heard a slight rustle of the grass to his left as he took up his appointed position—and that was the only sign he noticed of Kasha getting into place and Mai passing him to plant her next surprise.

"See, people of Vredai—learn the reward given to those who betray for their own gain!"

Behind him, a flash of heat and light reflected off the metal surfaces of Felaras's armor and shining weirdly red off her eyes and the eyes of her horse told him that another flash-pot had been set off—and Kasha, so hellishly made up and garbed he would not have recognized her, leapt up out of the grass that concealed her and seized him with a howl of wild laughter. There were strange, moaning sounds coming from above, now; sounds he knew were being made by the toys they called "bull-roarers" being whirled around and around the heads of the concealed horn-blowers.

He put up a convincing show of struggle, as a third flash-pot went up at the entrance to the valley, and another glowing horse and rider—this time shining an evil green—galloped through it. They swooped down on Kasha and her "victim" and scooped both of them up.

Actually, Kasha leapt up behind Jegrai—who was about the only rider capable of pulling off this trick—while he hauled Halun up before him.

Jegrai's horse wheeled and headed back the way they had come, and Halun closed his eyes. Facedown across a saddle-bow was uncomfortable. Watching the grass whirl by while breathing powder smoke was making him ill.

"Remember, Vredai!" Felaras called. "Remember!"

She made her horse rear and pivot on its hind legs, before following Jegrai and his poor overburdened mount back through the valley mouth as a fourth flash-pot went up behind them.

Once on the other side, all four of them dismounted as invisible hands took the reins of the horses. Invisible, because the owners were garbed head to foot in black, and their faces were smeared with soot. The glowing horses were swathed in blankets and the glowing riders in cloaks. And the entire contingent—except for Mai, who would be quietly collecting the spent flash-pots she'd set off—mounted up again and headed for the nearest farm with a well to wash off the phosphor.

Mai joined them in the lantern-lit barn before they were quite finished. "They're very impressed, Jegrai," she said quietly, dumping her four pots, still stinking of sulfur and brimstone, with the rest of the gear. "I don't think you'll be having any trouble with them for a while."

"Maybe," he said, pausing for a moment to look closely at the Master, with his hands full of towel and his hair dripping down his back. "But—Felaras, what of the time when we pull this same trick on the Talchai? They are bound to realize that they were deceived."

"Thought about that already, lad," she said, while Halun silently helped her out of her greaves. He unbuckled the straps and lifted them away, and she groaned and flexed her ankle. "Gods, I'd forgotten how damned heavy this crap was. Kasha, love, get the cloth off my horse's feet, will you? You won't be a part of that trickery, Jegrai—or at least your people won't. I'll have the Watchers do it, tricked out in Vredai gear. Some of your people will know, or guess, what we did, and some will learn how and why—but I'd rather it was the next generation down the line."

Jegrai nodded, and began toweling off his hair.

"I think you're likely to have more respect than you know what to do with when you ride in, Khene," Mai said with a hint of amusement. "They're convinced that Felaras is a Holy Messenger from the Wind Lords, and equally convinced that a pair of *kizhiin* carried Halun off to unending torture. Last I saw, Iridai and Gortan were in the process of giving away all their worldly goods, beating their breasts and praising the compassion of the Wind Lords for sparing them."

Jegrai snorted. "Give them a few days, and they'll be back to telling me I'm a fool to my face," he said, with just a hint of amusement in his voice. "But at least I don't think I need to be watching behind my back for plots for a while."

"I doubt you'll ever need to again, Jegrai," Felaras replied.

Halun nodded, and handed her a wet towel. "What they heard back there was the Messenger of the Wind Lords all but telling them that you are their special darling. There were no few of your people who'd have been willing to follow you through hell before this. Now all of them will be."

The surprised expression on Jegrai's face was rather funny. "Me?" he squawked. "God-touched?"

Halun nodded again. "Yes, Khene."

"Think about that, son," Felaras said urgently. "Think about that *hard*."

"Indeed," Halun said, with a sorrow too profound for release. "Think about that. I was told I was all but god-touched; you people have given scholars that cachet. I was listened to as if I knew all wisdom. I was offered power—and it turned my head—and because of my own ambition and pride and self-deception an innocent boy *died*, died horribly. Think very hard about that, and decide what you want to do about it."

Out of the corner of his eye he caught Felaras staring at him with a very thoughtful expression, and when he finished—

She put one hand on his shoulder.

Just that—but he knew then, without her saying a word, that out of some well of compassion of her own, those words of his had given her the strength to forgive him.

Even though he would never forgive himself.

"Khene," she said into the silence, "it's time you went back to your people, and me to mine. Our work is still only half finished."

"In truth," Jegrai agreed, and tossed his towel back to Mai, who caught it with a grin. He pulled on his tunic, and then turned to where his horse was standing—all the phosphor washed off him, now—and jumped into the saddle without bothering to use the stirrups.

"I expect a full report in the morning, lad," Felaras called.

He grinned over his shoulder at her; then, with a wave of his hand, sent his horse out the barn door at a brisk canter.

"Yes," Felaras said, looking disconcertingly into Halun's eyes, "our work is only half finished."

✧　　✧　　✧

"All right, all *right*," Felaras shouted, her head beginning to ring from all the echoing voices around her. "Get settled, damn you!"

The din in the Hall died down, and complete silence took its place.

Felaras took a long, slow look around the Hall—this time she could see her audience; she'd need to, so she'd insisted that every one of them bring a candle or a lamp. Row after row of faces, each lit from below by a yellow flame—it was, in a strange way, beautiful. The Hall glowed with light, as it never had before—

And likely, as it never would again.

"You all know what's been happening," she said gruffly, taking her seat in the chair she'd had brought to replace the lectern. After all of this evening's work, her leg was aching like a demon was gnawing at the knee, and damned if she was going to stand! She settled herself carefully, but pain still stabbed up her leg and made her catch her breath for a moment. "You all know by now what Halun did."

There was a rising murmur—rather unpleasantly like a growl. Halun, seated on the lowest tier of benches and directly across from her, flinched.

"Shut *up!*" she snarled, surprising both herself and her audience, who subsided into silence. "Don't you think he's going to pay for that every day of his life? He *trained* Zorsha! Think about that!"

A moment more of silence, then a muted sigh as his fellow scholars took in the misery on Halun's face, and saw that she was right.

"Whether we like it or not, he forced something on us that we should have faced a long time ago," she continued, more quietly now. "And that's our future. We have no choice; we're out in the world, now. The temptation to use our knowledge for mundane power is a great one, and it isn't going to become less. Then there's the question—how can we really devote ourselves to truly seek knowledge for the sake of knowledge when we have an eager Khekhene peering over our shoulders."

A murmur of surprise at that.

"Oh, yes, the three Chapter Leaders and I decided that Halun—and Zorsha—were right. We'd be damned fools to let this opportunity pass. Jegrai is enlightened, eager to learn—we can serve at his right hand, guiding him. More than that, we can be the ones to train—and select—his successors."

Felaras smiled in wry satisfaction at the buzz that last statement provoked.

"You heard me correctly. Jegrai has agreed, as part of our bargain to help him against the Talchai, and ultimately the Suno, that it will be the Order who selects his heir—male, female, first, last, or baseborn. And it will be the Order who has charge of educating all his children, in wedlock and bastard. There will be no discontented halflings if he has any say about it."

There were nods of approval and interest all about her. She smiled thinly, shifted her weight a little, and winced as her knee protested the move.

"*But*—" She held up an admonishing hand. "There lies temptation. There lies possible corruption, seduction by power, and ultimately, the end of what we know as the Order. Once again, Halun was right. We need to be in hiding in order to do our work freely and without either temptation or coercion. So now you're asking, 'how can we be both?' I'll tell you."

She took a deep breath, steeling herself. *Oh, gods, I don't want to do this—and I don't have a choice.*

"I'm splitting the Order."

She'd expected an uproar—and indeed there was one, but it died down within heartbeats. She looked about her with some surprise, then continued as she'd planned.

"About spring of last year some of the Watchers I sent out to keep track of Jegrai's Clan came back here with a report of another Fortress like this one, south and east of us, in Azgun. Roughly a week hard riding away. This one was smaller, maybe half the size of our Fortress. Thing is, it's no wonder we hadn't seen it before; it was so cleverly built into the side of the mountain that if Aned hadn't stumbled on it, he'd never have known it was there. I hadn't considered fleeing to it when the Vredai first showed up at the Teeth largely because to get to it we'd have had to get past them. The building is in good shape, the Watchers tell me—a little work, and it will be livable. Two years at most and it will be about as comfortable as this place. And nobody except Ardun, a handful of Watchers, and I know where it is. That's where some of you will be going."

"Which, Felaras?" asked a novice, in a high, unsteady voice. "Which of us are going?"

Good gods, she thought in wonder. *They've accepted it.*

They've accepted it without a fight. By the gods, Halun was right.

"Let me first tell you what the plan is that we've worked out," she temporized, giving them a little more time to adjust to what she'd already laid in their laps. "There will be two Masters—the Outer Master, and the Inner. And the Master of the Inner Order will always have the power to overrule any decision of the Outer Master. The Chapter Leaders will all be of the Inner Order. Members of the Order will be allowed one—*one*—transfer in their lifetime; in either direction, but once the choice is made, children, you are stuck with it. Seekers, there will be very little, if any, research in the Outer Order, and most of the real breakthroughs will be the secrets of the Inner until they decide to dispense them. Archivists, there will be a very great demand for you; we have three duplicates of the Library in storage; one goes with the Inner Order, one stays at the Outer Fortress, and one goes with Jegrai. You will be the keepers of those volumes and the teachers of Jegrai's people. So . . . in the Outer Order there will be a great deal of temporal power, and very little chance for advancement or research. In the Inner, the opposite. And only the Watchers and the Master of the Outer Order will know where the Inner Fortress is located. Ever."

She scanned their faces, and saw thoughtfulness, anticipation—and no fear whatsoever.

"Watchers, yours will be the hardest job; to maintain communication between the two halves of the Order, to make certain that the Inner Fortress remains hidden—and, if need be, to make certain that no member *or Master* of the Outer Order *ever* betrays his or her trust."

She looked about her, and saw with pride the way the members of her own chapter took that.

Thank the gods. I made the right decision. They'll keep us safe.

"So, children, you've heard what I have to say. I want you to take a moment to think about which way you want to go. But first of all—Halun, come up here beside me."

Halun rose from his seat on the benches and walked, slowly and stiffly, toward her. His long silver hair was limp and neglected-looking, he had the appearance of someone only recently recovered from a long illness—and he acted at this moment like he was walking to his own execution.

And when I'm done here he might wish I'd had his damned head whacked off.

"Ladies and Gentlemen of the Order of the Sword of Knowledge—I make Halun the Master of the Inner Order."

Gasps and weak protests, which she overran with her practice-ground voice.

"Can any of you think of anyone less likely to abuse his power?" she asked harshly. "After what he's done? When all of you are going to be watching him like hawks for the least little misstep? Remember, the old rules will still hold—the Convocation can unseat any Master with a two-thirds vote. If he turns out to be untrustworthy, take him down."

She cast a look over to Halun, who looked utterly stunned.

"As I'm certain you have deduced, I will be the first Master of the Outer Order. And again, the old rules still hold. My successor will have to be one *not* of my chapter. So now, while the rest of you think about who you want to serve under, and whether you're fit for a long trek and an uncomfortable couple of years, I am going to ask those of you who knew what I was going to do what their choices will be."

She looked over at Teo, who still wore his grief like a cloak. "Teokane, Outer or Inner?"

He looked up at her. "Outer, Felaras," he said simply—and a little sadly. "Jegrai needs me. And you do, too."

"Then I make Teokane my chosen successor," she said. "Not the least because the things he has faced have made him a different person from the Teo we knew. Teokane, step to my right. Halun, to my left."

Obedient to her will, they did so.

"Yuchai . . ." The boy looked up at her in astonishment, surprise replacing mourning. "I've had words with your Khene, lad, and he's released you to this choice. And he said—may I quote— you'd be a damned fool to swing a sword when you can send your mind out to the stars. Outer or Inner?"

"I—Inner, Master Felaras," the boy said, hesitating only for a moment. "Jegrai has all the strength you can give him now, he doesn't need me. And Zorsha—" a catch in his throat, then his voice strengthened. "Zorsha wanted me to stay."

"Kasha, Outer or Inner?"

The girl took a long breath, and looked her squarely in the

eyes. "Forgive me, Felaras—Inner. Yuchai needs me, and I need him. Any of my sisters could be trained as your Second."

Kasha turned and looked up behind her at the tiers of seats. "Take Daisa, she's ready for her full status, she's as good or better than I was, at everything. And she's as disrespectful as I am. . . ."

Felaras nodded; after the way Yuchai and Kasha had been huddled together this past week, she'd more than half expected that decision.

"Ardun? Do you back Kasha's suggestion?"

"I agree, Felaras. What's more, I'll make her full Watcher, as of this instant."

"Daisa?"

"I'd—" the girl gulped, and seemed unable to reply—but got up and took her stand at Felaras's right, letting her actions speak for her.

Felaras nodded again.

But what she didn't expect was Halun's reaction.

"Then I name Kasha *my* successor," he said, as soon as Daisa had taken her place. "All of you to witness. It is only because she was of the same chapter as Felaras that she was passed over before. She is fully worthy to sit the Master's seat."

Kasha stared at him for a long, long moment, then seemed to come to a decision of her own. "It isn't usual," she said, "but it isn't unheard of for the successor to name *her* successor. I name Yuchai as mine. I can't think of anyone else more likely to live up to—" She choked, and brought her hand over her eyes to hide her tears "—his teachers—"

"So witnessed," Felaras said, softly but clearly, swallowing down tears of her own. *Not now, old girl. Later. Not now.*

Kasha and Yuchai took their places beside Halun, who put his arms around them both, so that they supported each other.

"Ardun?"

"Inner, please, Felaras," he said, looking at her pleadingly.

"Inner it is. And I'm glad of it. You're the best Sword Leader we've had in decades. Kitri?"

"Outer! This is the chance I've prayed for all my life!" The—now former—Book Leader's face was alight with a fierce joy.

"Name your replacement."

"Jesen."

"Jesen, do you agree to go Inner?"

Jesen, a tolerably young man, but one who lived and breathed books, nodded. He moved across the row of benches to Felaras's left, and Kitri to her right.

"Thaydore."

"Inner, Felaras."

"Boitan?"

"Outer."

"Mai?"

"Outer, Felaras."

So it went on, name after name, from the Leaders to the youngest novice, each of them making his choice and moving to the right or left of the Master's seat.

Finally it was over. Felaras looked over her people, and sighed. It had gone as she had not dared dream. Most of the Tower would be Inner—*none* of the Flame had chosen the Outer Order, and only about half of the Hand, mostly those who were far more technically oriented than investigative. *Bridge constructors,* she thought with hope. *Healers, and toolmakers. Surveyors and teachers. Those who will build the future I can't even imagine.* More than two thirds of the Book had chosen Outer, along with their former Leader, and all of them had that same glow of anticipation in their eyes. Jegrai's people would have good teachers. And the Sword had split roughly in half—

She looked to her right, to Teo. *Poor lad—he's lost one best friend, and now he's losing the other. He's lost all chance of real advancement—Kasha will be able to overrule* any *decision he makes—*

Teo seemed to feel her regard, and turned to look into her eyes. To her astonishment, he reached out for her hand, and squeezed it briefly. "It's fine, Felaras," he said softly, though his voice shook a little. "I'm going where I'm needed. Really *needed.* Isn't that the important thing?"

She glanced at her other side; Halun, Kasha, and Yuchai. They looked nothing alike—Halun tall, and Ancas to the cheekbones, Kasha tiny and pure Sabirn, lanky, exotic Yuchai. But they stood like three generations of a *family.* Supporting each other. And she somehow had the feeling that this was no passing thing— that this was a bond that would continue through all their lives.

No worry there.

She looked out over the last Full Convocation this Hall would ever see—and still saw no fear. Only determination, and an impatience, now that the decisions had been made, to get on with it.

My children. By the gods, how proud I am of you!

Then, wryly, *And so much for a peaceful old age! Starting all over again. Training a new Second. Well—at least I got to keep the Fortress that doesn't need repairing. I don't envy Halun those winter and spring storms.*

"All right, people," she said into the waiting silence. "I'll want you on the road five days from now. Take whatever you think you'll need, we'll replace it somehow. Make your farewells—if you can't stand it, change your minds, but I don't think many of you will. May the gods go with you all."

She filled her eyes with them, one last time.

"The Convocation is dismissed."